THE CONFEDERATED WORLDS

THE CONFEDERATED WORLDS

TAKE THE SHILLING
OPERATION IAGO
A BODYGUARD OF LIES

Raymund Eich

CV-2 Books • Houston

Second CV-2 Books trade paperback edition: June 2014

10 9 8 7 6 5 4 3

TAKE THE SHILLING

1

The Recruiters

Tomas' nape prickled in anticipation. Every pair of eyes in the room would stare at him if he raised his hand. It would be so much easier to lie low. Madame Martin gave the room a final passing gaze, then moved the paper toward the corner of her desk—

He raised his hand. Someone near him murmured, and Madame Martin looked up as Tomas said, "I want to meet the recruiters."

She took a moment to reply. "You, Tomas? You aren't the type of young man to want an early dismissal from class."

His mouth felt dry. How could she think he wanted to shirk school? "I want to meet the recruiters."

A row in front of Tomas, one boy muttered to another. All the students aged about ten standard and up turned in their seats. His desire to speak to a military recruiter defied their stereotypes of him, and their guarded expressions and shared whispers showed how much they disliked his defiance. Even Véronique, who'd shared a few dances and even kissed his cheek at the last Harvest Fête, widened her eyes. Her hand rose defensively to the closed collar of her dark green jumpsuit. Tomas felt a trickle of relief at being in his final year at the *lycée* and having no one sit behind him.

"Quiet," Madame Martin told the other students. "You're disrupting the first years' work on addition." She cast Tomas an arch eye. Would she ask him if his mother knew? Instead, the quirked her eyebrows for a moment, then said, "You're old enough to make this choice." She picked up her pen and wrote his name on the paper with trim motions.

A few minutes later, the *lycée*'s secretary came in. She bowed to Madame Martin and took the paper. On her way out of the room, her gaze fell to the list and she hesitated with her hand in air near the classroom door's handle.

The same boy snickered and Tomas bent his head to his physics and current-affairs papers. The younger boy tried to catch his gaze but soon gave up. Tomas' face cooled.

He spent a few minutes skimming over a description of optical fibers. He gave a little more attention to a diagram of an array of fibers wicking light around a solid wall, but still set those papers aside as soon as he could. He turned to a current affairs paper about the Space Force's victory over a Unity relief mission near one of the artificial wormholes in the New Liberty system, but a movement outside the window soon distracted him.

The secretary swung open the wrought-iron gate, crossed the street to leave the *lycée*'s property, and took her phone from her handbag. She cradled the phone between her neck and shoulder and pulled out a paper. Calling the recruiters with the names of students from the *lycée* who would meet them later in the day, Tomas guessed. But when she lowered the phone, call complete, she kept it out, swiping across the touchscreen to place another call. Her eyes danced with excitement and she covered the mouthpiece with her free hand. *You won't believe what happened,* he imagined her saying to the other party. *The étranger twelfth year, Neumann, signed up to meet the military recruiters today!*

Soon everyone in town would know. Before long, word would reach his mother.

He forced his attention back on the printout, spending the rest of the time until fourteen o'clock rereading the article about the Space Force victory. Tomas imagined the SF men, strapped into their gee fluid pods, lifting their strong arms against the acceleration generated by their fusion drives, pressing buttons, turning dials, flying their ship into battle. The colonels and generals commanding the ships and task forces inspired their men and outsmarted the enemy emerging from the artificial wormhole inbound from Nueva Andalucia.

Soon the SF would take the war into Unity space on multiple fronts and score a victory so great the enemy would capitulate. Within a few months, he could be there, part of the Confederated Worlds' triumph.

He reread again, skimming the paragraph about the Ground Force's continued mission to clear the remnants of Unity infantry from the surface of New Liberty. Wasn't it unnecessary? Couldn't the SF destroy the enemy infantry from orbit?

At fourteen o'clock, Madame Martin looked up from the civics lesson for the middle years. "Guillaume, Tomas, you are excused to visit the recruiters."

"Thank you, Madame," Tomas said. The other boy had already risen and started through the arrayed desks for the door. Tomas followed him into the hallway. The door at the far end already started closing on the view of green-black foliage and Guillaume's untucked shirt and rumpled trousers.

Outside, the indigo sky was cloudless. In the southeast, two-thirds of the way to zenith, Soleil-de-France's fat red disk hung above the engineered maples and elms lining the *rue des Lycées*. In six hours, the hazy blue bulk of the gas giant Napoléon would eclipse the red sun.

Tomas went out through the wrought-iron gate and turned east to walk down the *rue des Lycées* to the *Place des Citoyens*. The street in front of him was empty.

Puzzled, he stopped, turned. Guillaume scurried in the opposite direction, away from the recruiters. "You're going the wrong way," Tomas said.

Guillaume kept walking.

"*Place des Citoyens* is this way."

Shoulders hunched, the other boy stopped. He looked over his shoulder with a scowl. "Just 'cause you're a goody-goody doesn't mean I am. I got out of school early, I'm going fishing at the river.

Who cares about those recruiters?"

I'm not a goody-goody crossed Tomas' mind. The thought of the river, swimming to midstream with deep strong strokes, warmly bubbled up from his subconscious.

He sighed and rejected the thought. *I promised Madame Martin I'd see the recruiters. It would be wrong to not go.* Then another thought came to him. "Madame Martin can look down *rue des Lycées.* If she doesn't see you head that way, she'll know you're playing hooky. Follow me, then split off at *boulevard Hyperborée.*"

Guillaume grunted, then trudged toward Tomas. "Didn't think of that." The two boys walked down the street. Other than the churr of tires from passing automobiles and the harsh calls of grackles and crows, they started in silence. Tomas expected the other boy to want to talk. To forestall Guillaume, he looked to the eastern sky. Sometimes ships could be glimpsed on the transit between their colony on Joséphine and the artificial wormhole to the al-Aqsa system. Not today.

From the corner of his eye, Tomas glanced at Guillaume to see if he too watched the sky. The other boy instead kept his gaze on the asphalt skin of the living street. To the sounds of the town, from time to time Guillaume added the skitter of sloughed aggregate as he kicked small, tarry pebbles to the curb.

Guillaume finally spoke at the corner of *boulevard Hyperborée.* "Go talk to those recruiters if you want, but I still don't care about them." He headed south on the boulevard, toward the river. Tomas shrugged and kept going.

Rue des Lycées soon jogged to the left and climbed uphill. Eight hundred meters ahead, the Ecogenesis Ministry's local heatwick stood like a giant mushroom on the hilltop overlooking the town. The heatwick loomed over the granite-tile roofs festooned with solar panels of the town's wealthier houses on the upper slopes of the hill. The largest building in sight was the *Lycée Superieur,* two stories tall, fronted with diorite columns. The personal automobiles, coupes and sport sedans, belonging to the LS' upper year students formed a line at the sidewalk in front of the building. None of those smug rich kids would meet the recruiters. Tomas breathed a little easier when he remembered he could avoid the LS by taking a side street, *rue Saint-Girard*, to get to the *Place des Citoyens*.

He turned and halted at the sight of a familiar face. Etien wasn't a friend, exactly, but Tomas felt closer to him than any other teenager in town. Son of a government scientist from the capital, eccentrically dressed, he too didn't belong in this small town. "You aren't home-schooling today?" Tomas asked.

Etien lifted his kepi by the visor, then placed it back on his head at a jaunty angle. "I was going to accompany my dad on a survey of magma flows in his sector, leaving at eight o'clock, but his or-nithopter's diagnostics flashed red before we took off. It's grounded until Ecogenesis gets a maintenance crew out here from Couron-nement. My schedule's been open all day."

"Your mother didn't give you schoolwork to make up for it?"

"It's the will of Odin, she says in situations like this." An odd woman, from Midgard, Etien's mother wore dresses instead of jump-suits, drank beer instead of wine, and homeschooled her only child. Etien laughed. "I've been ambling since this morning. Despite your fears, my friend, my wanderings have even been educational; I just studied anatomy with the widow DuBois." He laughed again.

Tomas noticed a red smear on the side of Etien's jaw. Lipstick. He ducked his face, cheeks suddenly hot. Envy filled his crotch, but it was soon doused by fear that Etien would ask him about his amorous adventures, of which there had been none.

"Speaking of school, Tomas, what takes you away from Madame Martin's gimlet eye?"

The change of topic gave him a moment of relief. "I'm meeting the military recruiters."

The relief evaporated. Tomas expected Etien to put on a look of mockery, or at best, disbelief, but instead, Etien took it in stride. "I heard they were coming today. Both Space Force and Ground Force."

"I want to meet the SF recruiter," Tomas said.

"I believe you. Yet I'm sure GF serves some useful purpose, else the Confederated Worlds would have disbanded it." Etien shook his chronometer out of the sleeve of his Nehru jacket, then looked at the face on the inside of his left wrist. "You have fifteen minutes. I'll walk with you." He started down the street and Tomas hurriedly caught up.

Once abreast of Etien, Tomas studied the other's face. "You aren't going to ask why I'm meeting them?"

"I hadn't planned to. Enlisting to escape this vile ville would be reason enough. Whatever your reasons, clearly they are good. Otherwise, you wouldn't meet them."

As they neared the St. Girard church, the houses and their lawns on both sides of the street grew smaller, behind shorter, plainer fences of extruded mycocrete instead of wrought iron and quarried stone. At this hour, the street was quiet, with children at school and parents working in skilled trades in the industrial quarter down by the river.

The quiet soon gave way to a churring sound rising in volume, coming up the street behind them. Tomas glanced up as the car sped past: a red teardrop, two doors, with badges on the trunk lid from car designers throughout the Confederated Worlds. Even without the *Lycée Superieur* parking sticker in the back window, Tomas identified it as Lucien LaSalle's car. Probably on his way to lacrosse practice, or to help his father dun tenants for rent. Lucien had been born lucky and made sure everyone knew it.

Four hundred meters ahead, Lucien turned right on *boulevard Hortense*, away from the *Place des Citoyens*. Yet even after he left their sight, Tomas' gaze remained on the intersection as he talked to Etien. "Aren't you going to ask what my mother thinks of me meeting the recruiters?"

Etien frowned. "I hadn't planned to, but if you want me to—"

"No."

"Are you certain, my friend? You brought it up—"

"I'm certain."

"Fair enough." They approached the corner, passing through shadows cast by flying buttresses of the St. Girard church. "I'll take my leave, friend." Etien flourished his kepi. "I wish you a productive meeting with the recruiters." Etien moved to replace the hat on his head, but hesitated. "Since I hate receiving advice," he said, "I'm loathe to give it."

Would any other townsman than Etien hesitate before telling him what to do? Tomas said, "I'm listening."

"You might consider whether you're meeting the recruiters because you want to, or because your mother doesn't want you to. That's all. Take care." He flourished his kepi again, then seated it on his head and walked away down the boulevard.

Tomas turned the other direction and quickened his steps. *Boulevard Hortense* bore more traffic, from private cars and for-hire jitneys to bicyclists and pedestrians. Cafés and the showrooms of hand-crafters lined the street, on the ground floors of buildings with walk-up flats and mansard roofs. The people sipping espresso at sidewalk tables, the shopkeepers plying custom furniture and clothing from their front windows, all glanced at him and then looked away. *Étranger*, foreigner. Observer. Preacher's kid. Not poor enough for social protection, but close enough. Not one of us. He hurried on, along the boulevard, across the lanes of the traffic circle at the boulevard's end, to reach *Place des Citoyens*.

Grass covered most of the plaza, except for the straight walkways leading to a small paved area in the center, in front of a statue of the symbolic empty throne, awaiting a legitimate heir of Bonaparte to take his seat. A dozen locals, ten boys and two girls, milled around the paved area. Two military personnel waited at the front side of the paved area, furthest from the statue. A woman, whose large dark eyes and faint unibrow looked al-Aqsan, wore a gray Ground Forces dress uniform with some chevrons on the jacket sleeve. Some enlisted rank. Next to her stood a male Space Forces lieutenant, his beard and turban suggesting he was from Navi Ambarsar, his dress uniform as deep blue as Joséphine's sky.

The SF lieutenant extended his hand. "Welcome to our presentation on military careers. The chief recruiting officers will be speaking in a few minutes." He lifted a tablet computer. "Your name, please?"

"Neumann. Tomas Neumann."

"Noy-man…" The lieutenant swiped his fingers up and down the touchscreen. "I don't see any Noyman on the list."

Tomas wanted to protest, but his mouth felt like a seized-up engine. *I'm on the list don't let your dangerous machine exclude me don't make me face my mother for nothing—*

"Lieutenant," said the Ground Forces enlisted woman, "if I may, look under n-e-u. You aren't native to Joséphine, Mr. Neumann?"

Tomas nodded. The motion freed his voice. "I was born on Sankt-Benedikts-Welt. We moved here when I was young, after my father died."

"There you are," said the lieutenant, "sorry." Someone came up the walkway behind Tomas. "Welcome to our presentation…" he said, stepping past Tomas.

"Thank you, lieutenant," the new arrival said. Tomas knew that smooth baritone voice. It belonged to a past builder of playground coalitions that excluded Tomas, a present-day charmer of girls whom Tomas fancied. "It's L-a-capital-s-a-l-l-e, Lucien."

"You're on the list. The chief recruiting officers will speak in a few minutes."

"Excellent. Pardon me, lieutenant, corporal?"

Tomas glanced over his shoulder. The SF lieutenant looked vaguely embarrassed and the GF enlisted woman stifled a frown when she noticed Tomas looking. He counted four chevrons on her sleeve and vowed to look up what rank that number signified after the meeting ended.

He avoided making eye contact with Lucien, but the other's smooth, hooded-eye gaze passed over him, then lurched back. "Tomas? I wasn't expecting to see you here, but what a pleasant surprise."

"I'm surprised too. Didn't I see you turn the other direction on *boulevard Hortense*?"

Lucien lifted a cardboard coffee cup. "My favorite café is a few blocks south of the Saint Girard church."

Tomas leaned back, wary of the other's motives in talking. "I hadn't expected you to be considering a military career."

A glint came to Lucien's gray-blue eyes. "Time and place came together. We LaSalles are well-known here on Joséphine, but I don't want to be just a member of the planetary legislature. I could gain a much higher office in the Confederated Worlds government, I'm sure, but I need some name recognition among the masses, plus contacts with the brokers of power. Service in wartime is a great first step to getting both. My father has a friend in Couronnement who can introduce me to an admissions officer at officer candidates school."

Lucien angled his head. *Now comes the mockery*, Tomas thought.

"You're interested in the Space Force?" Lucien asked.

Tomas replayed his words, looking for subtext in the other's tone but finding none. "I am."

"I knew it. It's the branch I'm looking at, too. By far, the more important one. I'm glad to know you could be serving under me. The physics you're learning is obsolete, but you're good at math, and they can slot technical skills into you easily enough." Lucien glanced at the dozen locals already waiting and lowered his voice. "I'd much rather have you than those hicks. Public schoolies, all of them, slotting in trade skills as if that's enough. You can't build a palace on a foundation of sand and you can't make a tech sergeant out of a cretin. Those ones are only good for the mudbugs."

Lucien glanced up, then slapped Tomas on the shoulder. "The recruiters are preparing to speak." He slipped forward, the local boys recognizing him and making way. Tomas drifted unnoticed to the rear of the crowd.

A riser had been placed in front of the statue of the Imperial throne. The two chief recruiting officers stood at the back of the riser, talking to each other in low voices, each with a tablet in hand. Both shook their tablets. After reviewing the results, the GF recruiter stepped back, and the SF recruiter smiled and strode to the front of the riser.

"As always, the Space Force is the first on the scene. Greetings, young women and men of Portage-du-Nord. I'm Major Bäckström." The SF recruiter looked to be from Österbotter, with steel-blue eyes and a fuzz of blond hair at the sides of his head, under his dress cap. He spoke Joséphine French with a precise, upper-middle-class accent. A Cross of Valor, second class, decorated his chest. "This is my first visit to your town, but judging from your display of patriotism, it won't be my last."

The major continued. "I'm certain you've heard about the vast opportunities an enlistment in the Space Force would open for you." He surveyed the crowd with an easy, confident manner. "I'm here to tell you they're all true."

The major spent the next minutes talking about benefits of service in the SF. Travel, technical skills applicable to numerous civilian careers, pride in defending the travel routes binding the Confederated Worlds together, respect and admiration from civilians in their ports of call. As he strode the riser, the rays of Soleil-de-France would sometimes glint in the Cross of Valor and dazzle the locals' eyes.

"There's danger, of course, given we're in wartime. But the risk is less than in—" He angled his head and motioned with his eyes toward the GF recruiter, "—other branches, and, the better you perform your task, the lower the risk. No other branch can say that. And no other branch will have as great a say as we will in bringing about a victory over the Unity. Does anyone have any questions?"

"I saw the news story about how you kept your men firing their gun in the first battle at New Liberty," said one of the local boys. "What's it like to be a hero?"

"I only did my duty to my ship and my service in spite of the damage we suffered. If you want to call that heroism, I can't stop you. Other questions?"

Lucien said, "Does the SF favor officers who graduated from the Space Force Academy over those who emerge through officer candidates school?"

The major paused, checked his tablet. "I assure you, Mr. LaSalle, whether you come to have a single brass bar or a flock of eagles on your epaulets, your rank is the only thing your men and your fellow officers will see. No other questions? Thank you for your attention. Let me turn the stage over to my colleague."

Lucien slipped back through the crowd as the recruiters changed places. "Why bother listening?" Lucien murmured to Tomas.

"It would be rude to slip away."

"Pff." Lucien shrugged. "It's your time to waste." He passed the lower-ranked military personnel at the back of the paved area on his way to his parked car.

The GF recruiter, a stocky man, had a captain's bars on his shoulders and a set of plain ribbons on the front of his dress gray jacket. "Hello, I'm Captain Schreiber. Before we start, I'd like to thank Lieutenant Singh and Staff Sergeant Bath-al-Uzzá for their efforts in organizing our meeting with you today. I also should thank Major Bäckström for his service as well."

Continuing in passable *joséphinais*, Capt. Schreiber said, "The major drew a lot of distinctions between what his branch can offer you from what the Ground Forces can. Even though he oversold some things—that travel he spoke of is in a windowless can from one space station to another—he got one thing right. The Ground Forces get their hands and their uniforms dirty. Even if you don't carry a rifle as part of your duty assignment—most GF soldiers don't—combat support personnel still face hardship and risk.

"That said," Capt. Schreiber added, "GF personnel can benefit in ways spacemen can't. The bonds you can form with your squadmates are stronger than any other, except the ones with your families. You can see the wide variety of human worlds and human beings, up close and personal. And though there's less glamour, the wisest civilians will commend your service, because they know the truth. All other combat arms, from the Space Force to the Intelligence Bureau to the Foreign Affairs Ministry, exist for only one purpose: to put the Ground Forces infantryman in sole possession of the battlefield."

Capt. Schreiber went on, his manner gruffly affable, and Tomas found himself warming to him and his branch. The captain's honesty refreshed Tomas, and made him wonder. What else had the SF major obfuscated or downright lied about?

After a public question-and-answer period at the end of his presentation, Capt. Schreiber said, "If you want to talk more informally with the major or me, we'll be around for a few minutes."

With that, the meeting broke up. Tomas stood in the same place for a moment. Most of the locals drifted away, but one figure strode effortlessly against the current: Lucien, returning for more face time. He went directly to Maj. Bäckström without a glance to either side.

Tomas swallowed once, his Adam's apple feeling thick, and walked to join SSgt. Bath-al-Uzzá and two local boys around Capt. Schreiber.

Soleil-de-France now hung a few hours away from Napoléon. A storm in the gas giant flashed lightning in its gibbous dark face as Tomas reached the group around the captain.

"But wasn't the major right?" one of the local boys asked. "GF is a lot more dangerous than SF, yeah?"

"If you look at total casualty rates, that's adding up killed, wounded, and taken prisoner, sure. But you can't be taken prisoner in a space battle, and you're a hell of a lot more likely to end up killed in a ship than you are wounded. Here, let me show you all something." Capt. Schreiber lifted his tablet, swiped the touchscreen, then turned it to them.

Tomas glimpsed a photo of a long black shape occluding background stars on the touchscreen, then shut his eyes and turned his head. *The photograph was the first step toward Earth's virtual fugue*, his mother had said a thousand times. *We may only look at what is, not what was, somewhere else, some time ago.*

"From this side, the ship looks intact," came Capt. Schreiber's voice. "Even from the other side, the only damage looks minor. Let me zoom in. See? Not much, right? Now, here are some photos the SF recovery team snapped from the interior, far from the hull puncture." A fingertip sounded on the touchscreen.

"Ugh," said the boy who'd asked the question.

"I don't feel good," said the other, voice queasy.

"There's lots of ways to die on the ground," Capt. Schreiber said. "But for your eyes to bulge and your lungs to hemorrhage, you have to be in space." He held a pause, then said, "We've excluded Mr. Neumann enough. Didn't know you were an Observer. I'll warn you next time."

Tomas opened his eyes. The tablet dangled in the captain's hand; the touchscreen showed plain text. "Thank you, sir."

Capt. Schreiber nodded in acknowledgement, then continued speaking to the group. "In Ground Force, you're a damn sight more likely to get wounded and live. Sergeant, you were in medical corps, weren't you?"

A faraway look passed over SSgt. Bath-al-Uzzá's face. "I was," she said quietly.

"I'll give you the honor of quoting medical corps' motto."

"'If they come to us alive, they'll stay that way.'" She blinked and turned away for a moment.

Capt. Schreiber held his gaze on the other boys in turn, then Tomas. "I can attest to the truth of that motto." His thick hands unbuttoned his gray jacket with surprising quickness. He handed the jacket to the staff sergeant, then opened the links at the cuffs of his white starched shirt. This close, his hands were visibly different: the left had thicker nails and larger veins than the right.

He pushed his sleeves back to his elbows. His right arm was fresher-looking all the way to the elbow, skin more pink, hair less gray. "There are civilian young ladies present across the way," he said with a nod at the cluster around Major Bäckström, "so modesty bars me from baring my chest, but you could see the beginning of my regrown arm right here." He gently chopped his right shoulder with the side of his left hand.

Tomas digested his words in a few moments of silence. "But still, a lot of Ground Force die," the second local boy said.

Capt. Schreiber gave him a firm look. "That's true. And? You think you're guaranteed to live a thousand years if you sit this war out? The more men we have who are unwilling to risk their lives, the more likely we are to lose this war. If the Unity wins, do you trust them to keep you alive? If you want guarantees, go listen to the major blow smoke." His expression changed to take in the entire group. "More questions?"

The first boy spoke. "The major made it seem like SF guys get—" He jolted his gaze to SSgt. Bath-al-Uzzá and blinked a few times. "—I mean, more, respect—"

"Spacemen get more *vulve*? Pardon my language, sergeant."

"I've heard worse, sir." SSgt. Bath-al-Uzzá sounded mildly amused.

Capt. Schreiber returned his attention to the boy. "I don't know if that's true. Now it may be that some dumb girls see Shirley Foxtrot in casual blues and give it up more easily, but I hear you can get all the *vulve* you want on Sol b." Earth, whose billions slept in virtual reality chambers while the real universe unfolded around them.

Was the captain an Observer? Or at least sympathetic to Observer precepts? Tomas wondered if his long-dead father had been as honest, as challenging, as worthy of respect as this man.

What the local boys might think now struck Tomas as irrelevant; his nervousness at school a few hours earlier now seemed unreal. "What about Observer doctrine?" he asked. "Can a man serve in the GF without being forced to see previously-recorded video or hear previously-recorded audio?"

Capt. Schreiber thought a moment. "He can. I have to tell you, some duties are impossible to reconcile. Others can be done, but you'd be in for a tough road persuading your commander you can hack it without all this." He lifted and waggled his tablet. "Live video and audio are okay for you?"

"They are."

"Then there will be duties to fit you." After a look around the group, Capt. Schreiber asked, "Nothing further? That's fine. GF isn't asking for a decision today. You have to earn your *baccalauréat* or your skilled trades aptitude cert before you can enlist. Let me print out or beam you my contact information. You can call or mail me anytime with any questions, or your decision yes or no."

He pointed at the far side of the *Place des Citoyens*, where a line of public hire jitneys stood at the curb opposite the mouth of *boulevard Hortense*. "For now, your ride home is on us."

A few minutes later, Tomas sat in the back of the jitney, heading north of town. He held the captain's business card between thumb and forefinger, flexing it. He paid no attention to the driver's route. They could be driving past the *Lycée Superieur* for all he knew, or cared.

A few minutes later, sweat broke on Tomas' forehead and the jitney's air conditioning blew louder from the vents. He neared the heatwick atop the hill on the north side of town. As they passed a hundred meters from it, a space between rows of black-green maples gave a glimpse of the heatwick's base, dirt piled up around it, graffiti staining the black ceramic. The heatwick blocked a wide swath of the eastern sky, as if the gas giant Napoléon had darkened and fallen to the world's surface.

Almost at the top of the hill, Tomas glanced over his shoulder. Portage-du-Nord covered the slope falling toward the Friedland River, three kilometers distant, with low roofs and clumps of elms and maples. He'd seen the town every day coming to school, but today, Portage-du-Nord seemed like a flattened stain on the terraformed landscape, insignificant under the indigo sky. Soleil-de-France shown amid the sparkle of a dozen bright stars, stars where he could serve, not as a cog in Lucien LaSalle's machine, but as a man with men like Capt. Schreiber.

He crested the hill and the town slipped from sight. The boulevard narrowed to two lanes. Its median tapered, then gave way to a yellow center stripe. The road now continued in a straight line as it rose and fell with the jumbled landscape. Cuts in ridgelines showed strata of primordial lava and compressed ash, splotched with moss and lichen and tufted with a few tenacious plants.

After half a dozen kilometers, the car climbed the tallest ridge since the Portage-du-Nord heatwick. Off to the right, the Observer parsonage showed as a small artificial block, in contrast to the natural lines of the ridge meeting the sky and the curves of the Observing pews. The driver slowed and pulled off onto the extra-wide shoulder approaching the driveway to the parsonage. "Take you to the house?" he asked Tomas.

"I'll walk. Thank you." The car stopped and Tomas climbed out. This far between heatwicks, the cool air made him shiver. He unlocked the gate across the driveway and went in, zipping his jacket after his first two steps.

His mother was supposed to be gone all day, Observing a funeral in Bois d'Orme, but as he paced up the driveway, he didn't relax until he noticed her car missing from the carport next to the parsonage. Relief hit him. He had a few more hours to work out what to tell her.

His relief faded when he came closer to the fence around the parsonage, carport, and lawn. The yellow flag on the gate post, next to his mailbox, had been raised. He trudged to a stop. Reluctantly, he lifted the mailbox lid and pulled out his mother's message to him.

We're doing a snap Observation of today's eclipse of Soleil. Clean the pews. Love Mother.

He frowned at the note for a moment, then slid it into the recycling bin and stalked down the path that led around the parsonage to the Observing pews. He kicked a pebble across the parallel yellow lines of the parking lot. Even though she was twenty kilometers away, he couldn't escape her commands.

Tomas yanked the microfiber mop from the custodial dugout behind the pews, then let the dugout lid clang shut. The pews formed a semicircular amphitheater facing downslope. The main entryway was at back center, flanked by two diorite pillars bearing black and white *taijitu* symbols. He waved the mophead at the *taijitus* and entered. He glanced downslope, where a lectern bearing another *taijitu*, the receding line of sparingly-traveled road, and the distant heatwick over Portage-du-Nord were the only artificial constructs visible under Napoléon's looming bulk. The Observing pews gave a great vantage point, but a snap Observation? No one would hear about it in time to plan their attendance. Mother would be lucky to have three people make the drive from Portage-du-Nord or Bois d'Orme.

He lazily swept the mophead over the granite pews in the outermost ring of the semicircle. Dust could linger in the corners, who cared, why bother digging for it. But as he went on, habit kicked in, goaded by guilt. Cleaning the pews had been his chore since they'd moved to Joséphine. He couldn't help it. He pushed the mophead deep into the corners of the first pew in the second ring, then sighed out a breath and went back to the outermost ring to redo them.

Don't be such a coward. You'd rather give her what she wants then tell her it doesn't matter. Yet despite the thoughts passing through his mind, he persisted in sweeping the pews according to his mother's expectations.

About halfway through, another thought hit him. Even if cleaning the pews didn't matter, even if he left town the day after receiving his *baccalauréat* and headed straight to Capt. Schreiber's office in Couronnement, this was the duty assigned to him, and he owed it to himself to do it as best he could. The critical thoughts fell away after that and he found himself entering a rhythm, sweeping quickly and efficiently. He lost track of time. Surprise widened his eyes when he realized he'd reached the innermost ring of pews.

He sat for a moment in the right front pew, next to the central aisle. Joséphine's tidal lock to its primary meant the bottom limb of Napoléon always just grazed the top of the lectern as seen by his vantage point. The gas giant's face was dark and already it obscured a curved sliver of Soleil-de-France.

"You better be done cleaning if you're sitting around," came his mother's voice from the top of the amphitheater. A low wall behind the lectern reflected her voice as well, pummeling him from both sides. In addition to her brusque tone, she spoke in Sankt-Benedikts-Sprach, the language she normally used when she wanted to keep her words to Tomas unintelligible to locals.

Tomas lurched out of his seat and the end of the mop handle spun in a wide circle before he settled it. He winced that he jumped even when she gave no command and lifted his chin when he faced her. "I cleaned everything."

She came closer. Though ten centimeters shorter than Tomas, he still felt small in her presence. Her brown eyes were usually narrowed in a scowl, but now the expression was more intense than usual, with her lips pressed tightly together. "Even the tops of the *taijitus*?" She lifted her hand and pointed her forefinger at him. She wore a white glove, and her fingertip bore dust.

"Sorry, I must have missed there."

"We have to be attentive to detail. The local people will probably never meet other Observer ministers. If we don't show them the Observer way as perfectly as we can, they'll end up in virtual fugue and whose fault would that be?"

His heart thudded and he forced himself to look into her eyes. "I need to talk to you about something, mother."

She leaned back. "I don't have much time. I need to rehearse the homily for the Observation of the eclipse."

"It's important, mother." Tomas swallowed. "I want you to hear it from me and not from anyone else."

Alarm crinkled her brow. "What is it? Did you get one of those girls pregnant?"

"After I finish the *lycée*, I'm going to enlist in the Ground Force."

Her expression clouded. "No you aren't."

"I'm eighteen standard. When I have a school leave-taking cert—"

"You will go to the seminary on Pénglàishān. You have a gift for Observing. You have to practice and perfect that gift for the people of the Confederated Worlds, to save them from virtual fugue." Her tone buffeted him with her certainty.

He clutched the mop handle. "I don't know if I have a gift."

"You have a gift. I've never lied to you, have I? Becoming an Observer minister is the best thing you can do."

A cold breeze flowed down the slope toward them. It lifted the ends of his mother's brown hair from her shoulders, but she stood still and her face showed no sign of distraction.

"I could always go to seminary after finishing my enlistment—"

"Enlistment?" She stepped closer and looked at him as if he suffered some grave illness. "You would throw your pearls before swine if you joined the Ground Force! All they want is boys with empty heads to give more room for their slotted skills and knowledge. Empty heads they can fill with lies of glory and sacrifice. Empty heads no one will miss when they're splattered across some foreign planet!"

Tomas flinched, then remembered Capt. Schreiber's comment to the second local boy. "There's risk in serving, but there's also risk in doing the same old thing."

His mother's head reared back and her eyes widened in passing. She groped for words. "This is your life we're talking about. You're eighteen standard. You think you're immortal and infallible. You aren't. You know you aren't. The local boys will clutch their napoleon medallions and their crucifixes around their necks, thinking divine favor will keep them alive when bullets fly around them. But you know those gimcracks make no difference. The emergence of each moment from the one before will cut down the pious and the impious alike—"

"If the GF medical corps finds a wounded man still alive, they'll keep him alive."

"And the people on both Earth and Heinlein's World count themselves kings of infinite space," she said in an incontrovertible tone. "People say all sorts of things, but saying doesn't make it true."

"They can rebuild arms and legs—"

"Can they rebuild heads? And I don't just mean you might get your head shot off. Do you know what war does to the men who fight?"

Tomas brought the mop handle, still clutched tightly, in front of his body. "They see bad things."

"Worse. They do bad things. They kill people. They destroy things. They harm the innocent. Most of the *joséphinais* who'll enlist will turn to drink or drugs to dull the pain of their memories." Her voice softened. "But you're an Observer. You see everything as it is. Drink and drugs are barred to you." She peered at him, and her tone grew cold. "Unless you renounce Observing, after all it has done for you."

He grasped the mop handle with both hand. "I can both serve in the Ground Force and be an Observer. Captain Schreiber said so."

"He lied. His only goal is to press the shilling on enough boys to meet his quota to his superiors. Soon as you would take it, he'd forget you. He'd love to get an Observer to enlist. The military wants to destroy us—"

"What? No!" She hadn't met the captain; she wouldn't say these things if she had. And she'd never denounced the military before.

"They want to revoke the limits we Observers call on our peers to follow, so they can misuse computers and time-shift recorded data to better make war. You think that's all? Do you believe you'll have any say in what they will slot into your brain? They'll make you watch and listen to recordings. They'll make you use computers for purposes other than reading text. You'll have no choice."

"I will too have a choice. Captain Schreiber told me." Anger overwhelmed meekness. He pushed the mop away. The wooden handle clattered against the nearest pew. "He's the only man I've ever met who's treated me with respect."

The corners of her mouth turned down, and her eyes looked as cold as the handful of stars at the indigo zenith. Voice dispassionate, she said, "You're just like your father."

Shame flooded him when she did that, as it always had when she'd said those words in that tone before. But now, he felt something else. The captain's demeanor was a lifeline as he thrashed to keep himself from drowning. "He was a man and I am his son. Maybe I should be like him."

"You should be a fool? Throwing his pearls to swine and getting trampled to death in the process? He had immature daydreams, just like you, and he didn't know what he was getting into, just like you. And he died for it, just as you are likely to if you enlist. You want to be a soldier? You want to come home in a plastic bag? Or with a mind forever broken by the shame and guilt your actions would earn you? Then in your last lucid moments, when you'll know your life or your sanity are ebbing away to never return, see how much it comforts you to know you're your father's son."

Her words stung him, but in a moment, his timidity fell away. *You know nothing about being a man*, Tomas thought, but then his anger faded. "Thank you for telling me what you think I should do. But I will enlist."

Her mouth opened without speaking, expressing disbelief. She blinked and her eyes glistened, and muscles momentarily worked in her throat. "Don't make me cry."

"You don't have to. I'm not dead yet."

She drew in a breath and peered down her nose, gaze suddenly hard. Arms folded over her chest, she said, "You're close enough. You're no longer an Observer. Get out of my pews."

2

Taking the Shilling

Five months later, Tomas stood in a line of recruits in the middle of the GF's main intake base, a space station in orbit high above Challenger, capital of the Confederated Worlds. From the exhaustion of weeks of travel getting here from Joséphine, the jet lag going from the standard day on board ship to the nineteen-hour Challenger day on the station, the heavy weight in the station's outer rings, and the bewildering mix of delay and hurry making up the intake process so far, the conversation going on behind him seemed unreal.

"Man, why'd they have to cut my hair?" asked a smooth-faced Österbotterman in school-slotted Confed. He rubbed his palm over the blond fuzz on his scalp.

"It's SOP," said an al-Aqsan. He must have been on the same ship as Tomas, but Tomas had first seen him at the start of intake a few hours earlier.

"But he's got all his." The Österbotterman nodded up the line, where a Navi Ambarsari waited. "A beard, and he's got hair under that headwrap, doesn't he?"

A Challengerite with a chummy manner leaned in. "I think it's called a turban." He caught Tomas' gaze and rolled his eyes without the Österbotterman noticing. The whites of his eyes contrasted with the massed green uniforms of the recruits lining the corridor behind him.

"Whatever it's called, it isn't fair."

"He gets a religious exemption from the grooming regs," the al-Aqsan said.

"Religious exemption? I checked 'Evangelical Lutheran' on the religious preference page and they still buzz-cut me."

Tomas remembered the intake form. He'd hesitated at the religious preference page for several seconds, before the intake sergeant on the other side of the table cleared his throat. Tomas' finger had hovered over *None*, spite toward his mother building up in his chest, before he shook his head and pressed *Observer*.

"They're stripping away our civilian lives," the al-Aqsan said. "Same reason we're wearing unadorned green with no rank insignia. We all start out as soldiers with nothing."

"Except our 2d barcodes." The Challengerite tapped his fingers against a dense black pattern on the left side of his chest.

"They had to cut your hair," said another Challengerite, a short fellow with dark brown hair and a bulbous nose, to the Österbotterman. "It's so they can drill the skill implanters into your brain."

The Österbotterman's eyes widened in passing, then a surly look formed around his mouth. "That's crap. They would've shaved the Ambarsari too."

The chummy Challengerite exaggeratedly shook his head. "For him, they'll have to use the penile catheter. That's why the girls got routed a different way for this part."

"In school they used medicine and video goggles," the Österbotterman said, disagreement in his voice but fear in his eyes. He looked around. "Hey, Saint Benny, isn't it like that here?"

Tomas couldn't remember if he'd only told the intake sergeants his birthworld, or if he'd also mentioned it to some other recruit. How had it gotten out? "I don't know," he replied. He winced at his poor fluency in Confed. Madame Martin didn't use any skill-slotting to teach her students.

"They've got to use more than grade school tech," the short Challengerite said. "This isn't about learning languages and arithmetic. It's got to take high powered stuff to make us soldiers."

A sergeant surprised Tomas, coming from the front of the line. His green fatigues showed a camouflage pattern with bright red bands around the arms and at the collar. "Listen to you lot. You don't even have your pubes yet." He brushed the back of his hand over Tomas' upper arm, where the solid green fabric lacked chevrons. "You know as little about skill-slotting as you do about pussy. At least you're going to find out about one of those today. To the chambers, now!"

The line moved forward in bursts. Eventually it led Tomas around the corner to another sergeant. He waved a plastic wand over the barcode on Tomas' chest. "Keep going."

Tomas went over a pleated plastic strip in the floor to a narrower, lower-ceilinged part of the corridor sloping upward. A wider, level space opened out past the top of the slope. Tomas climbed, the al-Aqsan and the Österbotterman behind him, when the sergeant paused the line. A wall hid the two Challengerites from view.

"Glad to be rid of them," the Österbotterman muttered. "From the capital and they think they're better than us—whoa!" All three of them reached for handrails. "Something happen to the station?"

Tomas remembered Capt. Schreiber's words about horrible death in space, yet he kept calm. The far end of their part of the corridor slewed over a thickness of alloy and nanotube fiber on its way to another wide, level space. "The station is okay. The corridor is moving from one destination level to another."

Another sergeant waited for them in the wide, level space. The light came dimly from ceiling bulbs and cast long shadows down his face. "One to a chamber." The sergeant jutted his hand toward six open doors on the far wall. "Lock it behind you, strip down, and climb in."

"Into what?" the al-Aqsan said.

"You'll see. Move it, prepubes!"

The doors seemed narrow, the spaces within dim. The air carried a sick-sweet smell. The scared speculation of a few minutes ago suddenly seemed plausible. "Have you seen anything like this?" Tomas said to the al-Aqsan.

"No—"

"The chambers, prepubes! And strip means *strip*! Bare-assed, on the double!"

Tomas went in and locked the windowless door. In the tiny room, he had to turn sideways to fit between the side wall and a table bearing a plastic box, over two meters long, about one wide, and sixty centimeters high. The box had an opened lid. The interior looked to be coarse black plastic with grilles and nozzles jutting into it from the box walls.

It's not a coffin, they won't kill their recruits. Though if there's a chance we'll die it would be easy to bury us.

Tomas shook his head to push the thought away. He would survive this. But another thought jolted him. The Österbotterman had talked about video and audio in skill-slotting. Those feeds had to be recorded. Didn't the recruiters know he was an Observer? The third sergeant hadn't scanned his barcode! A mistake, he'd go out and tell the sergeant—

He rattled the handle. Locked. Of course, he'd just locked it. Tomas took a breath, then reached for the unlock dial.

The dial refused to turn.

He tried again and again, putting more muscle into it each time, fear burning his chest. He had to get out. He lifted his fist to pound the door when a thought held him back. If he didn't go through with their skill-slotting, what would they do? Discharge him.

What would his mother say?

He opened his fist and turned to the coffin. He looked for video displays and audio loudspeakers in the interior. He knew what they looked like—his mother had let him watch live transmissions of public pronouncements, like the President's address upon the declaration of war on the Unity—and the coffin held none. The GF probably had better tech than a public school on a sparsely-settled planet and didn't need video and audio.

Or else most Observers weren't as fanatically against unreal images and sound as his mother.

Tomas stripped. He hung his plain green shirt and trousers on a hook on the door, then followed them with his underwear. Suddenly, the urge to piss struck him, but he glanced around and failed to see any bedpan or slot in the wall. *Climb in.* The GF had planned for this too. He could probably piss in the coffin if he had to.

He climbed and noticed another door, on the wall opposite the one he'd entered. He sat down in the coffin. The plastic felt warmer and softer under his ass than he'd expected. He stretched out. The plastic's soft warmth soon lost its luster. The room was cold. His *biroute* shrank and his scrotum pulled his balls toward his abdomen.

The second door then opened. Three figures entered in green fatigues with white trim at the cuffs and collar and red crosses on white circular fields just above the elbows. Even before he heard their first words, Tomas realized they were women. His cheeks grew hot. He pressed his legs together and cupped his hands over his genitals.

One woman, her blond hair tinged with gray and captain's bars on her collar, said, "The corporals need your arms."

"Arms? But—"

"We've seen more penises than a midwife. Arms, recruit. For the IVs."

"I need to—" He sought a polite word to use around women. "Urinate."

"You can wait ten minutes?" the captain said. "The urge will go away."

He wanted to appear in control. "I can wait." Tomas breathed shallowly, then pulled his hands from his crotch and rotated his arms to expose the veins inside his elbows. The corporals, one of them, from her dark skin tone, clearly native to Zion-against-Babylon or Garvey's World, pulled equipment from shoulder bags, plugged tubing into nozzles in the coffin's interior wall, and prepared his arms. Tourniquets squeezed his upper arms and evaporating iodine solution made his skin tingle. The needles stung when the corporals inserted them and then stopped hurting. Skintape, clicking plastic, swipes and taps on tablet touchscreens. More skintape followed, applied to sensor discs across his chest, abdomen, arms, legs.

While the corporals worked, the captain did too. "This is the TMI helmet," she said. With one hand she guided Tomas to lift his head, then pulled the helmet down. It fit snugly from occipital bump to eyebrows. She cinched a strap snugly under his chin.

"You really had to cut our hair for this," he said.

The captain ignored his words. "This goes over your mouth and nose." She held up a curved, lumpy piece of clear plastic. The lobate edge glistened with a bright blue gel. She pulled out a strap and nodded to bid Tomas lift his head. He did. She slid the mask over the TMI helmet, then guided it toward his lower face.

"Why not put on the mask before the helmet?" he asked.

She connected one end of a tube to the mask and the other to the coffin wall. Gas hissed as she moved the mask to his mouth and nose. The bright blue goop sucked itself onto his face. "Recruits are more likely to freak out from the mask than anything else." She plugged cables from the helmet into ports in the coffin interior and made a few motions on a tablet.

"Farewell, recruit." The lid swiftly lowered toward Tomas, then sealed him with thuds. Darkness. No getting out now. His breathing became ragged and he wanted to push on the lid. Not scared, just testing the situation... He resisted the urge. If the GF monitored his actions in here, he wouldn't show panic. And even if the GF wasn't watching, he watched himself. He remembered Capt. Schreiber. The captain had gone through this. Tens of thousands of other men had gone through this. If his mother thought him less a man than the all those other men, he'd prove her wrong. He might be afraid but he would stay calm.

The darkness was so deep his vision couldn't adapt. Eyes open or closed, the view was the same darkness. Tomas paid attention to his other senses. Pumps sounded in several spots in the coffin wall or nearby. Shouldn't something be happening? Did some defect delay the start? *Let's get this over with....*

His thoughts seemed stretched out. The touch of the coffin liner disappeared and a warm feeling spread up his flanks, his armpits, into his ears. Water? He thrashed his head, heard a few splashes. The feeling soon covered his eyes and all his skin.

He couldn't tell if he lay on the coffin bottom or floated in the water. Beats sounded, alternating ears, in a quick rhythm that set up a resonance filling his awareness. He couldn't tell if they came from hardware in the coffin interior or in his own head, induced by the TMI helmet. The need to piss had faded. He couldn't tell if his brain had heightened its control over his body or if his bladder had emptied into the fluid surrounding him. He couldn't find any of the answers, and it was no longer important to ask the questions.

Thoughts slowed and broke apart like crystals crumbling to powder. *What's happening? Did Capt. Schreiber get more recruits from Portage—any port in a storm—port—starboard—star—star....* His mind lost the ability to make words. Only sensory impressions remained: Soleil-de-France near eclipse. Véronique's shy smile before she pecked his cheek behind the bleachers at the Harvest Fête. Dead men in Space Force blue jumpsuits, lungs prolapsed out mouths frozen in screams. His mother's cold look. Beneath a waving oak under a golden sun, a man with brown hair and a narrow jaw, known with a sudden certainty to be the father he'd never seen....

A strip of light ran vertically through his field of vision, ends beyond the reach of his eyes. The strip widened, widened. Solid off-white in the distance, a triangle of yellow-white glow expanding as the strip widened. Faces, too, two pale, one dark.

Tomas blinked and started, pushing his weight into the coffin bottom for a moment before relaxing.

"Welcome, private," the captain said.

"Thank you, ma'am, corporal, corporal." The corporals touched styluses with glowing red tips to the skintape over his body. The skintape shriveled with a tingle over his skin. He was still naked, but unashamed. Not only had they seen more penises than a midwife, but he now knew women received recruit intake skills implantation duty after medical service in a field battalion. They'd seen more blood, torn limbs, and open wounds than even an armored grenadier or airmobile hussar.

"Doing our jobs, private," said the corporal from Garvey's World.

"Your fatigues are where you left them," the captain said. "Take five minutes to dress, then head out the front door."

"Yes, ma'am."

The skills implantation team left the room. Tomas climbed out of the coffin. Except for the taupe smears of hemostop over the IV needles' puncture sites in his elbows, his body looked no different. Yet he felt different. He stood taller, but there was more. New capabilities lurked in his muscle memory, ready to come out when needed.

He found his clothes on their hook. Underwear on, trousers on, tunic... He paused when he saw a sleeve. A single chevron pointed toward the shoulder seam. Private. He stepped into his boots and pressed the button inside at the top of the heel to tighten them, then reached for the door handle. It opened easily.

Where the mouth of the sloping corridor had been, a temporary wall stood, mounted in upper and lower tracks. In the wide, level space, four privates stood in a rank with their backs to Tomas, and as he stepped forward to join them, he realized they were his companions up the ramp.

The same sergeant waited, but this time, with three officers: two captains and a lieutenant colonel. Tomas came to attention and saluted.

"At ease," the lieutenant colonel said.

Tomas stole glances at the other privates. The Österbotterman stood two places to the right. He looked wiser than he had sounded waiting in line a few—

Minutes? hours? days? ago. How long had they been in the skills implantation chambers?

To his left, the final door opened. The al-Aqsan joined the rank of privates, saluted, was ordered to ease.

"Men, I'm Lieutenant Colonel Gallegos, commander of 1st Recruit Intake Battalion. Over the past two days, we have given you the skills to be soldiers. I know you can already sense some of the changes in yourself. There are even more you'll discover in the coming weeks, when you are assigned to a specialty, receive further skills implantation in that specialty, and get your first active duty assignment."

Lt. Col. Gallegos went on. "But there's more to being a soldier than what's in here." He tapped his temple with his forefinger. "Part of being a soldier is knowing you are part of a team, where all your teammates, whatever their rank, their world of origin, their religious beliefs, have certain things in common. Here's one of them."

Slender fingers undid the top three buttons of his fatigues, then pulled out a polished gray medallion about three centimeters in diameter and a half-centimeter thick. Tomas recognized it immediately. "This is the Multi-Purpose Individual Data Acquisition Processing and Communication Device. Charged up by the motion of your body, it is a friend-or-foe beacon, a medical telemetry device, a short range communicator, and a dog tag. We call it the shilling."

Lt. Col. Gallegos shifted his weight. "One reason we call it a shilling is its shape, like a medallion or an ancient coin. But the other reason is a custom going back to ancient England. You see, even now, you can back out. Maybe you sense the changes we made in you are ones you don't want. Fine. The skills implantation team can take those soldiering skills out of you as easily as they put them in. A little bit of paperwork, you're discharged honorably, the end. But if you take the shilling, you're a soldier till your enlistment expires."

Blunt, truthful. Just like Capt. Schreiber. Maybe just like the brown-haired man with the narrow jaw. Was that really what his father had looked like?

"Take a minute. Think about it. If you take it, you've declared, to GF as a whole, to the men before you, to your fellow privates on either side, your commitment to serve. And most of all, you've declared it to yourself. If you make this commitment, there's no backing out." Lt. Col. Gallegos let his words reverberate in their thoughts for a time, then he, flanked by the captains and the sergeant, stepped forward to each man in turn. The al-Aqsan said yes, as did the next man.

When they reached Tomas, Lt. Col. Gallegos said, "Do you take the shill—?"

"Yes, sir!" His heart pounded.

"You're certain? 'Marry in haste, repent at leisure,' ever hear that one?"

"Sir?"

"Enthusiasm is good, but flightiness isn't. Do you understand what this means? For five years, Neumann, we will own you. Are you ready for that?"

Tomas drew in a breath and stood as tall as he could. He spoke in unaccented Confed. "I am ready to take the shilling, sir."

The lieutenant colonel nodded. "Welcome to our ranks, Neumann." One of the captains handed Gallegos a chain with a shilling on it. The lieutenant colonel lowered the chain over Tomas' head. The shilling thumped gently on Tomas' chest.

The officers moved to the next private. Tomas laid the shilling in his palm and unbuttoned the top buttons of his tunic with his free hand. Regulations about proper care and safekeeping of the shilling passed just below consciousness, like a school of fish near an ocean's surface, and so too did protocols about supplemental charging and field reboots. Those thoughts faded as the polished gray metal filled his gaze. It had been proper and good, to receive the gift of new life in a womb from a woman; but even better and more fitting, to receive the gift of comradeship from a man.

The next days blurred by. Physical training in the morning, then breakfast, tests, lunch, more PT, more tests, dinner and a lecture on the GF's proper place in the Confederated Worlds' politics and society, yet more tests, thirty minutes of relaxation, then lights out. The shorter day carried a shorter sleep cycle, and Tomas went through the five minutes between reveille and the fall in for the march to the PT ground in a mix of exhaustion and epinephrine-boosted alertness.

PT was the longest length of time he got outside the barracks buildings, mess hall, and testing facilities, and under the transparent shielding roofing the station's rotating ring. Tomas couldn't remember ever seeing ground cover as green as the grass. If Tomas lucked into the timing, he would do crunches or weighted getups when Challenger, Epsilon Eridani d, was high overhead, just above or below the opposite side of the station's ring. He didn't dawdle when flat on his back between repetitions of any exercise, but he paid as much attention to the planet as he could. Clouds and deep blue oceans on dayside, the glow of a thousand cities on nightside. A hundred million people lived down there. The number boggled his mind. Half the population of the Confederated Worlds. Most of the privates hoped for a week of liberty on Challenger after finishing prelim training, but Tomas didn't. A week would barely get them up and down the space elevator to McAuliffe City. The glimpses Tomas took from here were enough.

The tests ranged from stylus-on-tablet to hands-on. Literally, in one case: a sergeant lifted a lid on a box full of parts and gave him thirty minutes to assemble a metals extractor. He worked the full time and still had a dozen pieces left over. Apparently he failed; the al-Aqsan talked a few days later about taking a second, comparable test while blindfolded.

Within a week, some of the privates received duty assignments and left the barracks, leaving only empty lockers and crisply-made beds for their fellows to find on returning before meals or at the relaxation time. Before long, it was Tomas' turn.

A sergeant stopped him on his way out of the mess hall after lunch. "Neumann, follow me."

They wound down walkways set in narrow lawns between buildings. Shadows cast by EpEri slid over their path. A turn and a glance over Tomas' shoulder showed the PT ground far up the ring behind him. At a double door, they entered a gray mycocrete building near one end of the facility.

The sergeant led him to a room with windows viewing an interior courtyard, then withdrew. A lieutenant and two enlisted stood near a major seated at a desk. The major brought a narrow-eyed gaze up from a tablet. Tomas saluted.

"At ease, Neumann. We've reviewed your aptitudes, and we are offering you a position in intelligence analysis."

In the ensuing silence, Tomas frowned. "Sir, permission to speak?"

"Yes?"

"I'm not ordered to it?"

"Normally we would, but there are some notes on your file...."

You're an Observer?"

"Yes."

"And you don't look at images? Did our recruiting officer on Joséphine get that right?"

Tomas spoke quickly. "I avoid prerecorded photography and audiography. I may see and hear live transmissions of real events."

"Do you make a distinction between prerecorded real events and fiction?"

"Prerecorded events are fiction, sir."

The major leaned back in his chair. "Hell of a strict Observer you are, son." His gaze slowly cycled between Tomas and his tablet. "This is a tough situation. Intel can certainly use you, and you can use it. It's your best aptitude. But the task it needs you for is analysis. That means looking at prerecorded pictures, video, and audio. After intel, your next best aptitude is the armored grenadiers, so if you turn intel down, that's where you'll go."

"I'll gladly serve wherever I'm assigned."

The major had a sour look. "You ever break a bone? Get cut by a knife? Injured in a car accident?"

"No."

"Ever shoot a rifle? Go hunting? Get into a fight against someone armed?"

Tomas remembered Capt. Schreiber's words. All other arms serve the infantryman. He stood taller and put more emphasis in his voice. "No."

The major took off his cap and brushed brown hair back from his forehead. "Son, I'm not trying to burst your bubble. I think you could sack up and do infantry. But any infantry duty gives you a risk of death every day. Armored grenadiers aren't immune because they ride a battle wagon into the combat zone. Intel? You'd be in a secure area on New Lib or whatever planet we next liberate from the Unity. Clean beds, three hot meals a day, Daughters of Astarte on base, no one shooting at you."

"I didn't enlist for comfort, sir."

"You enlisted to grow as a man? Here's a chance to learn and practice skills related to the best aptitude you have."

Tomas said, "At the price of my spiritual beliefs, sir?"

"Spiritual beliefs change and evolve and... hell, I'm not selling you on it. Yeah, son, it doesn't fit with how you interpret being an Observer. Now the damn Unity would say to hell with that and force you into intel. We aren't like that. Being a soldier involves making tough choices, and we'll give you practice at that. Your best aptitude or your spiritual beliefs? Which will it be?"

There were other ways to be an Observer than the one his mother had drilled into him? The thought echoed in a mental space suddenly much larger. He could both follow his talents and conform to the spirit of being an Observer.

"Neumann, we need a decision now."

Whose spirit, though? How many Observers on Earth and Heinlein's World had, in all sincerity, acquiesced to photographs, recorded television, recorded music, virtual reality, and every other form of reality-denial leading to virtual fugue? The major was right, the Confederated Worlds were better than the Unity. The Confederated Worlds didn't force doctrines on its civilians or its soldiers.

So who was the major to tell Tomas the proper way to be an Observer?

"Neumann?"

Tomas snapped his heels together. "Thank you for allowing me the choice, sir. I will join the armored grenadiers."

3

In Transit

"Get on board!" the SF captain shouted in the holding area. He raised his voice over the rumble of the airlock door opening. "Come on, mudbugs, we aren't going to hold up ten thousand tons for your sorry asses!"

"Space Force hospitality never changes, does it?" shouted back a GF soldier in the middle of the crowd in the holding area.

"You want to be in a hurry dirtside, not up here!" called a woman.

"Yeah, I hear a Unity soldier was spotted within a thousand klicks of the spaceport!" yelled a man.

The SF captain looked annoyed, but no one had impugned his dignity as an officer. "Shut your pieholes, sweaties, and board the shuttle!"

Tomas stood up and hoisted his sack to his shoulders. Two months of being shipped around like talking luggage by the SF came to a close today when he landed on New Liberty and got a unit assignment. He moved with the other GF personnel, their travel slow, their chatter echoing off the holding area's nanotube alloy walls. Nervous energy rocked Tomas' weight from side to side every time the crowd halted.

At the airlock's open door, a GF lieutenant, a turbaned and

bearded Ambarsari, swiped a scanner over the shilling hidden under each soldier's tunic. The SF captain looked bored as he swiped the touchscreen of his tablet. "The canned spam got to send a captain to do a lieutenant's job," muttered a GF private near Tomas in line.

"They do give us space supremacy," replied a captain with an airmobile hussar badge, an ornithopter above and to the right of a diagonal stripe, on his sleeve.

"If they're not too hung over to operate the lasers." The SF captain glanced up and the private blanked his face.

Through the airlock, they entered a pressurized tube the height and width of a narrow hallway, on the floor of the transport ship's docking bay. Two hundred meters square and fifty high, the docking bay was large enough to show the curvature of the transport ship's outer hull. A seam ran down the middle of the floor, where joined the two docking bay doors, now closed. A stalactite field of girders, flexible piping, and articulating arms jutted from the ceiling. Clangs of metal and throbs of fluid ran through the docking bay doors and up from the soldiers' feet.

The pressurized tube bent upward; the flat floor became a staircase. The clanging and throbbing faded. Banks of floodlights cast smeared shadows over the GF personnel in the pressurized tube. Between the lights, the press of people, and the shallow viewing angle through the tube's thick plastic wall, Tomas barely glimpsed the shuttle before he entered its airlock. He only noted a cylinder, wider than tall.

Inside the shuttle, GF sergeants stood throughout the corridors, guiding the new arrivals to a large round chamber in the shuttle's center. The floor was a black mesh and large blue sacks, roughly the size and shape of sleeping bags, hung on guide wires between the ceiling and floor. The sacks were arrayed in rows and columns like trees in an orchard, and each had two openings, a small hole about a meter and a half off the floor and a large slit running most of the way from the small hole to the floor. The sacks made Tomas think of a ruptured cocoon—

"Kali's yani," muttered a mustachioed soldier from Satyayuga.

An SF lieutenant, green-eyed and scowling, stalked between the sacks. "Pick a gee-sack. Clip your ruck on the back and get in. Stick your face out the hole, then zip up from the inside. Gee-fluid will fill up to your neck. You'll feel it pump when we're in free fall, and if we need to pull gees; this will help your heart and lungs, so don't panic. We've got better things to do than clean up mudbug puke."

The sacks hung so closely together his sleeves brushed clipped-on rucks and someone climbing into one jostled him as he passed. Tomas found an empty one and climbed in. As soon as he closed the zipper, fluid squished in, cold jets hitting his legs and torso. A far cry from the skills implantation couch back at Challenger.

Some soldier nearby called, "You want my hands in the sack? What if there's a rupture? How can I put on the emergency oxygen?"

"Sonofabitch." Tomas judged by the SF lieutenant's voice his scowl had deepened. "There's no emergency oxygen. If there's a rupture, the lack of hull integrity will tear the shuttle apart when we hit atmosphere. I'd rather pass out before getting ripped apart, how about you?"

The sounds of milling soldiers grew quieter. An SF sergeant stopped in front of Tomas, tugging on tubes connected to the back of the sack in front, checking a display on his tablets before moving on. Viscous gee-fluid sloshed around him. The gee-fluid felt warmer than at first, and the view of the backs of other sacks was monotonous. Someone nearby snored. Tomas' nervous energy faded. He almost shut his eyes—

A shudder ran through the ship, rocking him in the gee-sack. On the back of the sack in front, a video display lit up. In the corner, a clock showed current time in 24-hour standard, just past ten-hundred. Live? Girders and moving arms filled the display. One piece, in the center, remained fixed, while the rest slowly shrank and slid toward the center of the view and more filled in from the edges. The docking bay's ceiling?

Nanotube alloy walls came into view from the display's edges. Tomas put it together: an articulating arm held the shuttle by the nose and pushed it out of the docking bay. After a time, the dock doors and the transport's hull appeared on the edges of the display.

The shuttle was clear of the transport ship.

Without warning, Tomas' stomach rose and his feet lost contact with the sack bottom. The video display showed the transport's hull scrolling up the screen, and then the scrolling sped up as a low mechanical sound came from somewhere in the ship. Tomas felt queasy and shut his eyes.

He wasn't alone. "Christ, warn a fella!" yelled a sickly voice from amid the sacks. The SF personnel made no reply. Tomas decided he would reopen his eyes, and keep them open as long as he could.

The transport ship scrolled off the display, leaving a view of the stars over New Liberty. Suddenly, a deep, loud rumbling filled the ship and Tomas felt heavy. The entry burn had started.

A countdown timer appeared in a lower corner of the display. 9:52, 9:51, 9:50.... The view of the stars remained unchanging. *Switching to simulated stern view* appeared, and below it the numeral 3.

"Simulated?" A wave of anxiety flowed through Tomas' torso. "Why simulated?"

2...

"You can't see a damn thing through the drive exhaust," came a male voice through a speaker somewhere in his sack.

1...

"It's a rare GF who even wonders why," the voice added.

Tomas shut his eyes. GF personnel around him talked.

"So that's what New Liberty looks like."

"Who cares? It's all green and gray on base."

"Some of us fight for a living, pogey."

"Why no lights nightside?"

"NL's too close to its primary," came the hussar captain's voice. "Tidal lock. Permanent dayside, permanent nightside. See that greenish-black band crossed by lakes and rivers just sunward of the terminator? The only place NLers live."

"Like Nuova Toscana," someone said.

Tomas had read up on New Liberty during transport from Challenger. Sounded like he missed nothing by refusing to watch the screen.

"Band? Like a landing strip?"

"Landing strip? That's how the local girls wear their snatch hair?"

"Like you'll ever know."

The shuttle kept rumbling, and the soldiers swayed in the gee-sacks.

"Where's the cities?"

Tomas spoke up. "Two million people on the whole planet."

"Two million? Don't lie to me. That's too small for the planetary gene pool."

"Not even close," someone said. "Learn some biology. Maybe history too while you're at it."

"Goodbye, McAuliffe City," came a wistful voice.

"Screw you, smarty pants."

"Small gene pool? That means they're all inbred?"

"Woohoo! Retarded girls are too dumb to guard their landing strips!"

"Damn, isn't it getting big?"

"It better," a woman said. "We're landing on it."

"How fast are we going!?"

"Slower every second, mudbug!" called the SF voice who'd spoken to Tomas.

The soldiers grew quieter for a short time, but soon their chatter returned. Tomas gathered the shuttle approached the landing cradle of the main GF base, just outside Reagantown, capital of New Liberty, population forty thousand, all of whom had welcomed the Confederated Worlds' forces not just as liberators, but as long-lost cousins.

The apparent gravity generated by the entry burn intensified. Waves sloshed through gee-fluid, pounding Tomas like a clumsy masseur, pushing in his stomach as he exhaled, ebbing as he inhaled. "Here we go!" someone shouted.

The shuttle's rumbling cut off and Tomas instantly felt lighter. He took a few breaths. In front of him, sacks twisted as GF personnel craned their necks to see how close they were to leaving the ship. Tomas kept still. So far, his military career had consisted mostly of travel, as much spam-in-a-can as the SF personnel around them.

The major's words at the time of choosing his duty assignment back at Challenger came back to Tomas. He might look back with longing on this time of doing nothing.

Tomas set aside the thought. A pump sounded nearby, pulling gee-fluid out of the sack. SF personnel moved among the sacks, checking their tablets, then unzipping soldiers from the outside.

"GF personnel, this way," yelled a GF sergeant somewhere behind and to the right of Tomas.

An SF sergeant let Tomas out of the sack. Walking felt easy, despite the surges in apparent gravity during the entry burn and the dregs of gee-fluid dripping from his clothes to the mesh floor. New Liberty's local gravity was about point-seven gee and the air was enriched in oxygen compared to Joséphine. He knew these facts in his head, but his first step outside the shuttle's hatch, onto a pedestrian bridge extended from the lip of the landing cradle to the shuttle, put the knowledge into his body.

The white ceramic parabolic dish that made up the primary capture system of the landing cradle poured heat up his body. Dregs of gee-fluid turned to powder and drifted from his clothes.

Tomas glanced to his left. New Liberty's star, locally called Constitution, was a red dwarf, dimmer and fatter than Soleil-de-France as seen from Joséphine. Dim, but bright enough to make him squint if he looked directly at it. Low in the sky, it cast long shadows across the landing cradles, driveways, and dark green fields of the spaceport. The planet's tidal lock meant the star would never appear to move. It was permanently late afternoon on New Liberty.

The sky was a deeper indigo than Joséphine's. High thin clouds streamed away from the sun. In passing they veiled bright stars.

A GF sergeant with a scanner waited at the other end of the pedestrian bridge. Just a sergeant—Tomas wouldn't see any SF personnel until he left the planet. After the scan, the right side of Tomas' shilling throbbed against his chest. He turned that direction, toward a large building nearby. He pulled out his tablet. On a map, a yellow line led through the building to a small auditorium inside.

He started off down a walkway. Scattered across the grassy field between him and the boundary of the spaceport, antimissile lasers were parked behind berms and under camouflage netting. Outside the door to the large building, he glanced back. The shuttle passengers had strung out along the walkway. In the distance, the shuttle had two pedestrian bridges connected to it. Two? The second reached higher on the shuttle than the one Tomas had taken, mating with a hatch on the opposite side of the ship. A few people walked in clusters down the second bridge, voices too distant to hear.

"What's that?" Tomas asked.

A corporal in the airmobile hussars, with a trimmed reddish-blond beard and weary eyes, trudged past. He glanced up, then said with a Midgard accent, "The bifrost bridge, virgin. Allows the orificers to descend from heaven."

"But a captain rode with us...." Tomas said. The door swung shut behind the Midgarder. It was an honest question. The Midgarder didn't have to be rude. Maybe the airmobile hussars had a chip on their shoulder. No matter. Tomas would join his fellow armored grenadiers soon.

Tomas went in and soon found the auditorium. Eight rows of twelve seats descended to a stage. Behind the stage, a large video display, mostly black, showed in large print the text *Infantry Replacement Sitrep*. Broad stripes of Confederated Worlds red, white, and blue ran up the windowless walls. Less than a dozen soldiers waited, scattered around the room, not talking to each other. Tomas looked for armored grenadier patches on his fellow soldiers' sleeves. He saw half a dozen, but no one met his gaze. Still, they were his comrades, so he sat near one on the second row back from the stage.

A few more soldiers came in, and then a door to the stage opened for a major, followed by a couple of aides, an enlisted man and woman. The soldiers in the auditorium stood and saluted.

"At ease. Good morning, I'm Maj. Mueller." He had a round, ruddy face and he sounded bored. "I'm going to brief you on the situation here, then give you your unit assignments."

The major cleared his throat. "At this time, our operational posture is the pursuit of remnants of Unity infantry formations in order to deny them an opportunity to reorganize and contest our dominance of NL." Thanks to his skills implantations, Tomas was able to translate the jargon into plain Confed. *Keep them on the run till they give up.* "Here's a map."

The display flickered, showed an image. Though no map was ever live, a map was a pictorial representation of data, not a photograph purporting to be reality. Tomas studied the map as the major spoke. "At present, intel has confirmed elements of five Uni regiments have pulled back to a mountainous region, the New Rockies Plateau, about six thousand klicks sunleft from here."

Instead of directions relative to planetary magnetic poles or the local or galactic ecliptics, and as people did on other tidally locked worlds, the GF referred to two of New Liberty's four cardinal directions as *light*, toward the local sun and *dark*, away from it. If the local sun was to one's left, one faced *sunleft*; if to one's right, one faced *sunright*.

"The New Rockies Plateau is roughly eight hundred klicks by a thousand. About two thirds of it lies darkward of the terminator and bears glaciation at higher elevations. The glaciation spawns a number of rivers winding through the plateau. The lightward third is heavily forested. The terrain favors the defense."

The major tapped his tablet. Five red icons, replete with alphanumeric codes, appeared on the plateau, amid smears of red crawling down valleys and fading the further the smears got from the icons. "All the Uni regiments are understrength as a result of sustained combat over the last standard year, so each is smaller than one of our brigades. Locations are approximate based on last best intel and models of Uni movement potentialities. Questions?"

"Sir, aren't they recruiting locals to replace lost manpower?" asked a fusilier.

"They can't," said the grenadier near Tomas. He had a faint accent Tomas placed to the continent of Endeavour on Challenger. "The locals are descended from Challengerites who came out here three hundred years ago to terraform. They're loyal to the Confederated Worlds. No one would join the Unity forces."

The major said, "To answer the original question, no. One disadvantage of the Uni forces' current disposition is the exceedingly sparse settlement of the plateau. There are no more than ten thousand civilians residing there, most of them in three towns." Another tap on the tablet and the three towns lit up on the map. All were on the light side, within a hundred kilometers of the flatter land around the plateau, on some of the few paved roads into and through the region. "So there's a small manpower pool the Uni forces could draw from. Plus, our civilian interface officers have repeatedly emphasized to the NLers this isn't their fight. If they stay out of it, we leave them alone. The vast majority of them heed that message."

"Sir?" asked the same grenadier. "They welcomed us as liberators. *Confederated Worlds Today* has always been clear about that."

The major looked pained, and his next words came carefully. "I don't know what the civilian news organs on Challenger base their reports on. All I can say is that the people of NL are generally neutral."

The grenadier's brows still furrowed. Tomas understood his puzzlement. Every news story about New Liberty's civilians—the people whom the war was described as liberating from Unity oppression—painted a picture of joy at the Confederated Worlds' presence on planet and in the system. Those were lies?

Tomas thought further. What if Unity forces from Nouveau-Normandie had occupied Joséphine at the start of the war? Would Guillaume or any of Madame Martin's other students joined them? Etien the ambler? Lucien LaSalle might have. Not out of cultural loyalty with other descendants of ancient France, though; only if the Unity showed itself as the stronger horse. "Most people want to live quiet lives," he whispered to his fellow grenadier. "Better the devil they know than the angel they don't."

The grenadier's puzzlement turned to a surly narrowing of his eyes. "Shit, what do you know, smartypants?" He looked away.

Tomas' face fell and anxiety knotted his gut. I'm on your side I'm one of you don't you see that—

"No one is at liberty for side conversations!" The major said. "You have something to say...." A glance at his tablet, then, "Neumann? Say it to us all!"

Tomas labored for words. "Sir, I was trying to inform a fellow armored grenadier—"

"What about the grenadiers on the far side of the room? And the hussars, fusiliers, engineers, and scouts? Do none of them matter? Speak!"

He swallowed. "People would rather be governed by the devil they know than the angel they don't. Sir!"

"Hmph." The major cocked his head. "You're wiser than you look."

Relief flowed through Tomas' limbs as the major said, "Let's move on to your unit assignments." He lifted his tablet, swiped. "Bannister. Third Scout Squadron. Beltran…" Tomas' heart quickened as the major moved down the alphabet, Jäger, McPherson, "…Neumann, 2nd Battalion, 21st Armored Grenadier Brigade. The Blackjacks, good unit. Quiñones…."

The major soon finished the list. "That's it. The sergeants here will guide you to your transport. Godspeed, men."

Thirty minutes later, Tomas trudged to an ornithopter waiting on a tarmac behind the building. A Bluejay, the smallest noncombat transport thopter in the GF's hangars, squatted on four legs. Heat poured from the reactor in the thopter's tail. Tomas winced and swung wider. A cool darkly breeze felt pleasant as he reached the boarding ramp in the middle of the fuselage under the wing. At the top of the ramp, his shilling throbbed from a scanner mounted in the doorframe.

Inside, the plastic mesh seats were laid out in banks on the sides of the cabin, eight facing the ramp and six on the other wall. About half had occupants, mostly toward the front. The Midgard hussar slouched down, rucksack under his seat and garrison cap down over his eyes. Tomas had to sit next to someone. Maybe he could connect with the Midgarder this time, during the next hours in the air.

The Midgarder stirred and lifted the front of his cap a few centimeters. "Virgin, word of advice." His tone was off-hand, but kind enough.

"Yeah?"

"Never pass up a chance to take a nap." He dropped the cap back over his eyes and settled deeper into the plastic mesh.

They waited for a time. "Come on, let's get going," said one of the men from the briefing. The scout, Bannister, Tomas remembered.

"Zip it, virgin," said a private in the engineers.

"I don't want to sit here all day. Do you?"

The engineer rolled his eyes. "We're replacing dead men. I'm in no hurry getting there."

Bannister looked abashed and grew silent. Eventually the copilot, a warrant officer, sidled through the narrow opening between the cockpit and the cabin. He looked at each of the men in turn as his finger tapped the air. At the end, he made a sour face. "Yeah, seven," he said over his shoulder, raising his voice above the whine of the reactor.

The pilot's voice, muffled by distance, obstacles, and extraneous sounds, said, "Damn it."

"You knew the shillings were counted right."

"I know. Where's that damn lieutenant?"

Motion on the boarding ramp caught the copilot's attention. "Officer up!" he said.

Tomas and the other men stood and saluted. The Midgarder rose rapidly from his nap, and the pilot too emerged from the cockpit with a salute.

"At ease." The lieutenant wore gray-green camouflage fatigues. The name *Tower* showed on his breast pocket and an armored grenadier patch, on his sleeve. His name poorly fit his presence; he was shorter than the Challenger average, and lacked the stockiness of most heavy world natives. As if to make up for a soft chin, his gray-blue gaze scowled across the cabin. "Mr.... Pilot, where's the officer seating?"

"Bluejay's too small a bird, sir."

"We don't deserve a bigger one for this flight?"

"Transport assigned our bird to this run today, sir."

"I see." He turned to the man in the most forward seat on the side opposite the boarding ramp. "Private, I'll take your seat."

"Sir?"

The lieutenant raised his voice. "Do I have to quote the manual?"

"Sir, of course not. Permission to remove my stow?"

"Permission? You mean to tell me you were thinking you'd leave your ruck under my seat?"

The man put on an innocent look. "Sir, I only sought clarity of the order."

The lieutenant kept his piercing gaze for a moment. "Is it clear?"

"Yes, sir." The man knelt at his seat, slid out his rucksack, and moved to the rear of the cabin. As he passed Tomas and the Midgarder, he whispered "Paper tiger" through gritted teeth.

Tomas frowned.

Amid the rustle of the men returning to their seats, the Midgarder murmured, "Graduate of the Ground Force Academy."

"I never heard that term for GFA grads."

"I know, newb. The skills imps only gave you knowledge the orificers want you to have. Remember that."

"I will," Tomas said, but how would he know what skills he really needed?

The pilot's voice came over the intercom. "We're lifting in fifteen seconds."

"Thanks, chief," called one of the experienced enlisted men. The ramp swung up. Tomas double-checked his seat belt. In preparation for launch, the wings beat, sending big chuffs of air downward and bouncing the thopter's suspension. The cabin sank for a moment, then the thopter sprung on its legs and sped up its wingbeats.

Tomas expected the Midgarder to already be asleep, but the other gazed at the live view from external cameras, displayed on video screens above the heads of the men on the opposite side of the cabin. Maybe he would talk more if given the chance. "Why does a paper tiger act so lordly?"

"All new louies have a touch of it."

"But Academy grads worse? They think a piece of paper makes them better than us?" His last sentence froze Tomas' thoughts. Part of the status of Joséphine's *lycées* lay in granting *baccalauréats* instead of the skilled trades diplomas granted by the public schools. He'd bought into that mindset. Maybe his mother had pushed it on him, but he'd relayed it out, expressing disdain for the public schoolies. Maybe some of the dislike he'd received from the locals in Portage had been in response.

"No." The Midgarder glanced at Lt. Tower. "They fear their lack of experience makes them inferior."

The thopter climbed higher. The display showed a view of the GF base, the spaceport, and Reagantown beyond. The thopter darted, sickening Tomas' stomach for yet another time this day, and the view abruptly gave way to a rolling plain, dark green made darker in spots by the permanent shadows of the terrain's relief. By the time fresh questions came to Tomas, the Midgarder's garrison cap was back down over his eyes.

"Squad," said Sergeant Johnson, "Welcome Private Neumann."

Tomas stood at the sergeant's side at the entrance to the shelter, a low structure of reinforced mycocrete bermed with a dried slurry of plowed soil and polymer. Blocks of armored, transparent plastic formed the shelter's windows. A shaft of sunlight from Constitution caught dust motes and compounded the late-afternoon feeling dragging down Tomas' eyelids and fogging his mind. Twenty-two hours on planet, sleeping fitfully as the thopter hopped from base to base near the main routes from sunright onto the plateau. Hard to believe it was oh-eight-hundred.

Sixteen pulldown cots lined the walls in the front and middle of the shelter. Half the cots were pulled down, where men sat with tablets and earbuds. Most glanced up from their music, videos, and letters, but after giving Tomas their once-overs and terse greetings, most turned back to their activities.

Sergeant Johnson led Tomas in. "Pick a spare cot." Tomas found one in the middle of the room. A blank video display on the bottom of the cot had a slot next to it. Tomas fished out his shilling and slotted it. His name appeared on the display. He stowed his rucksack in a locker mounted on the wall to the left. A display in the locker wall also showed his name, at eye level for a man of average height.

To the back of the room stood a door to the toilets and showers, a kitchenette, and a long table. Four men sat around one end of the table, hunched over tablets, engaged in some game. One, with pale blond hair and a narrow nose, looked up. "Where's the other spare part?"

"Voloshenko, we got one replacement. We make do." Sergeant Johnson raised his voice. "Idrin, make sure you get yourselves to the oh-nine-thirty inspection on time. We have a new platoon commander and we be turning out smarter than B squad." He left.

Maybe the disinterest would fade with the sergeant gone. *They want to meet me without any superiors present.* Yet most still ignored him. He grabbed the handle of the pulldown bed for a place to sit while getting ready for the coming inspection. The bed was lighter than he expected; the swingout leg clanged on the floor.

Men at the table chuckled. "Keep it down," said one, with black hair and sunken eyes.

Tomas ducked his head. He tapped the inside of his left wrist to call up a chronometer. The visually active fabric showed the time, and another tap gave a countdown till the inspection. Less than ninety minutes. He glanced around. Might as well get ready, even though everyone else remained leisurely. He rummaged in the locker for shoeshine, a rag, and a spray bottle of water, then sat and took off his boots.

Voloshenko and the black-haired man rose from the table. As they stepped closer, Tomas noticed the name *Alvarez* on his breast pocket. "Just what we need," Alvarez said. "Another virgin." He gave the name on the locker a cold squint. "Your name's New-man? Right as shit."

"It's pronounced *Noy-mun.*"

As if Tomas hadn't spoken, Voloshenko said, "New-man wastes time on chickenshit."

"New-man wants to make us look bad," Alvarez said. "Suck up to the new louie. Were you the teacher's pet back in school, New-man?

The rest of the men took an interest now. Tomas couldn't muster a reply. He blinked a few times and realized he held his breath.

"Where you from?" Voloshenko asked.

Tomas relaxed a bit. "Joséphine—"

"Double shit," Alvarez said. "Josies are useless fuckups."

"I just went through skills implant—"

"Oh? Skills implantation? Why didn't you say so?" Alvarez's sarcastic tone filled the room. Everyone looked up now. "Goddammit, you think jacking off makes you less of a virgin?"

"What do you care?" Tomas said.

"About your ass, New-man? Not a goddam thing. You're going to be dead in a week and I'm not going to care. But if you take someone better than you with you to hell, then I'm going to care. Good men die when virgins fuck up. So stay the hell away from me."

Tomas wanted to reply, yet Alvarez's ire drove words away from his vocal cords. Before he could rally himself, a new arrival, a corporal, distracted him. He had a stout chest and a fair firmness to his features.

His voice sounded deep and profound. "Are you part of the solution or part of the problem?"

Alvarez looked sullen. "Just kicking the tires on the new spare part, Marchbanks."

"Jumping on a virgin for bullshining his boots? Maybe he knows something you don't."

"Like hell," Alvarez said.

Marchbanks went on. "I've been gathering scuttlebutt on the new platoon commander, Lieutenant—"

"—Tower?" Tomas said.

Some of the men in the background blinked, leaned forward. Alvarez narrowed his eyes. "What do you know about him?" Marchbanks asked.

"We took the same Bluejay here from the spaceport. Paper tiger. Orificer. Bifrost bridge." Tomas slowed his words. "He ordered a soldier to the back of the bus and called the Bluejay pilot 'mister' instead of 'chief.'"

The men in the background grumbled. One or two swore under their breath. Soon most of them, including Voloshenko and Alvarez, reached for their shoeshine kits, or called up the diagnostics apps on their tablets to check their fatigues for dead pixels.

Marchbanks stepped away for a moment, then returned to Tomas' cot with a shoeshine kit. "Here, let me show you the quick way."

"Sure. Thanks."

Marchbanks sat, pulled off his boots, dipped a rag in polish. "Nobody wants to get close to the new guy. Every man here has seen someone they like die and wants to armor himself against that much loss ever happening again."

"And new guys die a lot."

"The skills imps give you skills you need, but they can't teach you to work in a team. That's the second most important thing to do out here. Work as a team. No, wet the rag, not the boot."

Tomas sprayed the rag, applied it to the boot. His heart pounded. Finally, he found the camaraderie he'd been looking for. "So what's the most important thing?"

"Keep your head down. No, not while bullshining. 'Hero' is a four-letter word for 'dead man.' I want all my men to tell their grandchildren what a good old sonofabitch I was. Remember, no one wins a war by dying for his country. You win a war by making the other bastard die for his."

Tomas glanced at Alvarez, who sat near the front of the shelter with buds in his ears and a comm cable between his tablet and the breast pocket of his fatigues. "What about him?"

Marchbanks glanced along the line of Tomas' gaze. "Both things I'm talking about set him off. Alvarez disliked the Josie from the start. No offense."

"About? Josie?" Not much. That's what men did, right? Break each other's balls? "No. Plus, I was born on Sankt-Benedikts-Welt."

Marchbanks smiled. "We're practically neighbors, then. I'm from Scotia." He dropped the smile. "So the Josie wasn't just a virgin, but you know how sometimes men start off on the wrong foot? Same with the Josie and Alvarez."

Marchbanks finished brushing his polish. His boots bore a dull coating. How would he get a shine out of that? He wetted a rag and gently rubbed each boot, talking to Tomas without looking at his handiwork. "I don't know why, but his first mission, the Josie went cowboy. I should've kept him in my fireteam. Dammit. Anyway, Josie ended up in a Uni foxhole against a machine gun crew. Killed two of them, silenced the machine gun. But multiple wounds himself, and for nothing, because our platoon sergeant took a round from a sniper, and our former platoon commander's vehicle hit a landmine."

"So the platoon retreated."

"First they tried to get the Josie to the ambulances."

Tomas nodded. "Never leave a man behind."

"Yes, and there's a counterintel benefit, too; someone badly wounded may be in too much pain to pop his memory disrupters. Unis have transcranial magnetic receivers, like the skills imps' TMI helmets in reverse. Read a prisoner's thoughts, we can do it too. Anyway, Alvarez's buddy goes out to recover the Josie, but then he takes a bullet to the head. His shilling broadcasts a medical emergency over the squad's channel, but he doesn't say a word. Very bad sign. Soon telemetry says both he and the Josie are dead."

"Alvarez blames the Josie." Dead men, the experience of combat, what could a virgin say? "Maybe there's a way to persuade—"

"Don't force it," Marchbanks said. "Alvarez will either warm up to you or he won't."

Tomas took a few breaths. He wanted these men to be on his side. At least Marchbanks was. "Your boots look sharp."

"Yours aren't bad, either. Now, Neumann, what are the two most important things?"

"Work as a team. Keep your head down."

"Exactly," Marchbanks said. "Stick with me and you'll do fine."

4

New Boston Road

Seventy-two hours after crossing the line of departure, Tomas' experience of war was mostly limited to the cramped crew compartment of a Badger, the GF's primary armored fighting vehicle. Jammed shoulder-to-shoulder in the back, waste heat from the Badger's on-board fusion reactor parched their throats and made their feet swollen. The tracked Badger rode the asphalt like a boat on a rough lake, banging heads against the nanotube alloy side walls and bouncing butts on the plastic mesh seats.

At least there was live video. Displays on the inside of the rear door showed the views from the front of the Badger's body and from its turret. More displays on the side walls showed live views to those sides, overlaid with cursors showing the aim point of semiautomatic rifles mounted on the outside of the Badger. A computer somewhere processed visible light and infrared to yield composite images. The displays didn't show the plain truth, speaking strictly, but after a few hours of riding with eyes shut, Tomas told himself *the video is live, and you can't Observe anything if you're dead.*

There was little to observe. The road headed roughly sunleft and darkward, winding through valleys between eroded, forested hills on the way to New Boston, still a hundred klicks away. The valleys lay in shadow. Ahead of their vehicle, a platoon of Graywolfs, the

GF's main battle tank, showed dark, boxy shapes, heat vents glowing in infrared. Grass engineered for permanent shade, low wide stalks of greenish-black, descended from the road's shoulders down drainage ditches, then climbed up the ditches to the forests on the higher elevations of the slopes.

Though unoccupied now, the terrain showed signs of human presence. Elevated conduits and standpipes fed water to the pines on the slopes. About every three hundred meters along both sides of the road, GF obs wheels stood on poles two meters high. The turret camera showed occasional glints of sunlight from more obs wheels amid the trees on the hilltops.

They came to a point where the valley narrowed and the hills steepened. "Great place for an ambush," Obermeyer said, behind Tomas and to the left.

"You always say that." Cohen, next to Obermeyer, sounded annoyed.

"You're from Shambhala, aren't you supposed to be detached from wanting people to change?"

Despite the banter, Alvarez snored.

Lt. Tower's voice came from above them in the turret, followed a moment later by his voice in their earbuds. "Scouts swept this whole area and mounted obs wheels per the book. No Uni ambuscades."

Next to Tomas on the left, Marchbanks arched his eyebrow. *Nothing more dangerous than a junior officer who read the manual*, he'd said outside the Badger on one of their breaks.

From Tomas' right, Sharma said, "Who's got the honeypot? Neumann?"

The honeypot was the MIUCS, mounted infantryman urine collection system. An ungainly contraption one stuck his *biroute* in to piss. Tomas had only used it the first time when the alternative was wetting his pants. "Not me."

"You assume the virgin's got a nervous bladder?" Marchbanks said. "It's mounted on the sterilizer rack."

"I don't care where it is, just hand it to me."

"You got to piss again?" said Obermeyer. "You've got the nervous bladder."

"I'm trying to stay hydrated." Sharma sounded bluffly confident. "I'll perform better—"

"Not if that water goes straight out your schlong."

Behind Tomas came the sound of the piss tube unreeling. Sharma reached behind Tomas for the funnel, pulled it to his crotch, unzipped—

"Platoon full halt," Lt. Tower said. The Badger stopped, pressing them into their seats, then lurching them back to the sound of a piss stream hitting the floor. Without the clack of the tracks, the compartment was mostly silent.

"Damn," Sharma said.

"What's going on?" Alvarez sounded groggy.

Delacroix, the Badger's gunner, up in the turret with the lieutenant, spoke. "Graywolf on point detected metallic debris buried in the road." The forward display showed the tanks stopped on the road. Their turrets slewed to left or right, ready to fire if some Unis had sneaked past the obs wheels. Their heat vents still glowed.

"Standard defensive position," Lt. Tower said. The turret swung to face the hill on the left.

"I'll bet ten confeds it's another dummy mine," Cohen said. The column had paused several times so far when the sensors in the lead tanks picked up potential landmines. All the ones so far had been crude hunks of metal and plastic, lacking explosives, but requiring a halt to make sure.

"Not even the virgin will take that bet," Obermeyer said. His voice sounded friendly and he nudged Tomas' shoulder with his fist. Sharma fumbled for the piss funnel.

"Graywolf platoon commander reports further analysis finds no explosives," Delacroix said. "Company commander authorizes continued advance."

"Platoon, get ready for travel." Lt. Tower sounded irritated at the delay. *No officer got promoted for standing still* was another nugget of wisdom from Marchbanks.

On the display, the tanks ahead of them began to swing their turrets forward and start moving—

"Missiles!" shouted Delacroix. Tomas lunged forward, eyes

wide. "From our three and nine! Targeting the Graywolfs ahead, rear and flank! Attempting laser takedown."

In the floor of the Badger's main body, capacitors hummed and sharp cracking sounds marked fire from the anti-missile laser. A difficult shot by eye, even with his augmented reality display. "Missed!"

"Time to dismount!" Marchbanks shouted. The men around Tomas called out in agreement. An armor-piercing missile could destroy a Badger more easily than a Graywolf, generating jets of molten alloy killing or maiming men in the interior.

"Remain mounted while we break contact," Lt. Tower said. "B squad Badgers, suppress by fire—"

Flashes erupted on the display, followed a fraction of a second later by the roar of explosions outside the Badger and through the company's radio net. When the flashes faded, one of the tanks showed a dull bruise of heat escaping through jagged metal, while flame gouted from another Graywolf.

"Sir, I and I recommend dismounting." Sgt. Johnson's voice came deep and calm over the platoon's radio net from his Badger, next in line behind Tomas'. "We face an ambush by anti-armor weapons."

"This is a break contact situation," Lt. Tower said. "Not an ambush. Can't be. Scouts set obs wheels by the book."

Marchbanks gave firm looks around the Badger's rear compartment, then stood up, hunching slightly under the vehicle's low ceiling. He put on his helmet, picked up his rifle from a rack along the side, and made a get-up gesture with his hand. He then pressed the cuff of his suit sleeve. A pattern flickered through the plain green and his suit, boots, and helmet went into full chameleon mode, wrapping light a hundred-eighty degrees around his body. He was only visible as tricks of shading and movement. Another quick motion and Marchbanks' rifle vanished into chameleon mode.

Marchbanks' confident motions pulled skills out of Tomas' brain and into his muscles. Secure helmet, set suit to chameleon mode, prep rifle... "Did I get it?"

Through the cameras mounted in his helmet, Tomas looked

down at his barely-visible body. Video, yes, but live, and the only way he'd be able to see on the battlefield.

Marchbanks nodded. "You got it."

"Missiles, second wave!" shouted Delacroix. "Four hundred meters to our six. Targeting Supply Platoon, front and flank."

Sgt. Johnson's voice filled their platoon net. "They be trying to pocket us, sir. Looks an anti-armor ambush. Sir?"

Lt. Tower made no response over the radio net. Over the mechanical sounds of the Badger, a whisper floated down from the turret. "It's platoon break contact break contact oh Christ isn't it?"

"Sir, I recommend we lay smoke," Delacroix said.

More explosions, this time from behind them. Had those Badgers, and the mol fabs in their refitted rear compartments, survived? If not, had the men in those Badgers gotten out in time?

When would the Unis target his vehicle? Tomas wondered. He twisted his head to the side displays, looking for the glimmer of a missile launch. Both hills were dark.

Marchbanks touched Tomas' shoulder with one hand and, with the other, pressed his shilling through his suit to silence his radio pickup. He hissed past Cohen and Alvarez to the driver's compartment. "MacInnis, get the door ready."

"I'll press the button when I get the order," MacInnis replied.

"Sir," said Sgt. Johnson over the platoon net, "I and I suggest Badgers orient to provide fire support to our flanks and we dismount." Still no reply from Lt. Tower. Even the whispering had stopped.

A gruff voice burst in. Capt. Marcinkus, company commander. "Badger Two, what in the damn hell is going on? We're taking fire from both flanks. Base the vehicles to provide fire support and dismount your boots!"

"Yes sir!" Lt. Tower's voice wavered. "B squad, aim right, Johnson, your squad left. Prepare to dismount. Oh, yes, smoke."

A smoke canister *thwoomed* out of the tube. Delacroix said, "Sir, I suggest covering terrain."

MacInnis spoke over the vehicle's channel. "We can hull down in the roadside ditches and fire over and across the road."

Tomas visualized it. The maneuver would turn the Badger's

thicker top armor to the enemy up the slopes, protecting the vehicle.

"Do it," Lt. Tower said.

"Do what, sir?" Sgt. Johnson hadn't heard MacInnis' suggestion.

"Badgers go hull down in the roadside ditches. Provide supporting fire across the road." Lt. Tower found more of his voice. "Let's move!"

As their Badger slewed backward, Tomas reached for a ceiling strap and missed. Cohen and Obermeyer jammed their hands against his shoulder to steady him. The tracks clattered on the living pavement, then made softer, wetter sounds when they hit grass.

The Badger tilted backward down the side of the ditch. Tomas said, "Whoa!" and leaned away from the doors with the rest of the men to compensate. He suddenly felt his cheeks grow warm. Had anyone else spoken? What would they think—

"My first was a hell of a ride, too," Marchbanks said.

The Badger slowed, stopped. "Dismounts, now!" Lt. Tower said. "Up the ditch, cross the road, then get to cover facing upslope."

"Sir," said Sgt. Johnson over the platoon net, "We can cross-support. B squad's Badgers face up the hill we can run straight up—"

"Stick with your squad's Badgers!" Lt. Tower shouted. "Dismount now!"

In front of Tomas, the displays cut out. The armored alloy door dropped open, hydraulics catching it a dozen centimeters above the ground.

I might be virgin, but I won't let my squadmates down.

Tomas sprinted out. Two steps on the open door, then a turn to the right. Loping steps up the side of the ditch to the road. Smoke teared his eyes and scratched his throat. Even with night vision, he could barely see through the smoke's thick roils. He could only hear, not see, Marchbanks and Sharma alongside him. His breath huffed through his open mouth.

Tension skewered him when he reached the road. Even with the smoke, Uni night vision or lidar might be able to pick up his silhouette, naked atop the living asphalt. *Go go go.* He glanced down and chopped his steps to clear the ruts of the Graywolfs and his Badger.

A sound boomed nearby. Tomas felt it in his chest and through his boots. His Badger had fired its main gun up the slope at the launch point of one of the missiles. Despite the plugs over Tomas' earbuds tuned to the unit's net, his ears rang. He took another step, another, then realized Marchbanks shouted for him. "Neumann, Sharma needs help!"

Panting, he turned. A vague human shape sat on the road, another crouching nearby. His helmet augmented the sight with Sharma and Marchbanks' names. *Sharma hit I never heard the Uni fire....* He went to the two men. The smoke was thin enough to see Sharma, pain on his face, and Marchbanks next to him.

"How bad?"

"Rolled my ankle," Sharma said. "Road's damn-all rutted."

The second wave of infantrymen, Obermeyer, Cohen, and Alvarez, hesitated. "Minor wound," Marchbanks said. "Get going, we'll need covering fire! Can you move?"

Sharma nodded. "I'll stick with you guys."

"Neumann, help me get him off the road. Other arm." Tomas went to Sharma's right side, lifted the man's arm across his shoulders, and put his left arm behind the man's back. Marchbanks took Sharma's other side. "Let's go."

They took a couple of careful steps when a flash and a shrill roar came from up the slope. "Missile!" Marchbanks shouted. "Cover, now!" He lurched forward and to the side, angling away from the front of their Badger. Tomas dug the fingers of his left hand into Sharma's suit and ran wildly over the gouged road. He stumbled but kept his balance until the edge of the road, then the three of them jumped onto the drainage ditch's bank.

The missile's scream grew in volume, until a flash and an even louder explosion came from the front of the Badger. Reactive armor—a layer of explosive on the outside of the vehicle, designed to destroy an incoming missile in the milliseconds before the missile's warhead penetrated the vehicle's armor. Fragments of the missile casing and the reactive armor would wound or kill a man too close, regardless of the body armor lining his suit and helmet.

"Anyone hurt?" Marchbanks said.

"I'm okay," Sharma said.

"We reached cover in time, right?" asked Tomas.

Marchbanks spoke grimly. "Enough alloy flying rapidly enough, no cover in the worlds will help you." He glanced up at the road. "Sharma, can you put weight on your ankle?"

"Enough," he grunted.

"Get to the tree line, lads. Let's go!"

They separated a few meters from each other, then crouched and trotted forward. The tall blackish-green grass scraped at Tomas' faceplate. Five meters into the woods, he dropped prone behind a fallen pine and aimed his automatic rifle over it, peering upslope. The smoke had thinned out enough to show a blur of pine trunks and undergrowth, dark and cool, seemingly empty.

More Uni missiles fired, this time from the valley's far slope. Tomas knew the sound now. The Badger's guns roared in response, booms echoing off the hills, and their machine guns chattered as well. In front of Tomas, shells detonated halfway up the slope, midway between the line of obs wheels along the roadside and the other line on the hilltop. Dirt rained down through the pine canopies and broken trunks collapsed. Tomas breathed easier for a moment. All four of his platoon's Badgers were still in the fight. In the lulls between the firing of the heavy guns, the automatic rifles of the other squad's infantrymen banged out rounds on the far side of the valley.

Where were the Unis in front of his squad? Tomas wondered. The Badgers' lidar units didn't pick up any, but between the smoke and the woods, lidar's effectiveness at picking up enemy infantrymen would be low. His own eyes were the best enemy detectors he had.

How good was chameleon mode on the Unis' suits?

"My team, call in," Marchbanks said through Tomas' earbuds.

"Here," Tomas said. Sharma, Obermeyer, Cohen, and Alvarez called in as well. All safe. Tightness in Tomas' chest relaxed.

Sgt. Johnson's voice came over the squad net. "Idrin, we will move uphill, squad in line, bounding overwatch. Marchbanks, your team bounds first."

"Roger." Over his team's net, Marchbanks added, "When I say

go, go, low and quick. When I say stop, go to ground at the next tree." Back on the squad net, he said, "Team ready."

Their squad's Badgers fired their guns. "Go!"

Tomas set out, crouching. His gaze stayed mostly on the ground, looking for rocks and roots to step over, fearing trip wires and booby traps. An occasional glance up oriented him. Shells exploded over the same positions halfway up the slope, concussing the air, pounding the ground. How could anything be so loud? The vehicles' thirteen millimeter machine guns chuffed, firing at the Uni missile launchers. The squad's other team, led by Sgt. Johnson, aimed their automatic rifles and grenade launchers up the slope, but the Unis were quiet; Johnson's team held its fire.

"Stop!" said Marchbanks. Tomas dropped behind a pine's gnarled root and aimed his rifle upslope. What to aim at? Still no Unis in sight. High above, at the ridge line, an obs wheel glinted with Constitution's rays. How had it failed to notice the Unis on the slope below it? Behind him, automatic rifles and Badgers' main guns kept chattering, roaring. "Provide covering fire on my order."

More missiles launched from upslope, from fifty meters to sun-left, toward the front of the column. Moments later, more launched from a hundred meters to sunright. The missiles' exhaust sent bands of bright light and tree-trunk shadows racing through the forest. Explosions sounded behind and sunright from Tomas. The other squad's Badgers, in the ditch on his side of the road. Hopefully their top armor held.

"Ready now!" Marchbanks called over the team's net. Tomas aimed toward the gap in the trees torn by their Badger's main guns. His finger touched the trigger and he jerked it away, tapping the nail on the trigger guard. He wasn't going to be the virgin who shot his wad too early. Fire discipline separated soldiers from amateurs. He swept the muzzle ten degrees to each side. "Johnson's team has reached cover," Marchbanks said. "Prepare to bound. Just like be-fore."

Lt. Tower burst in over the platoon net. "Johnson, what the hell are you doing?"

"Climbing the nine o'clock hill, sir. Squad in line, about twenty meters in."

"I see that from your goddam shillings. You have to move faster! Use your power bursts!"

"Sir, standard procedure is to save power bursts for when we need them."

Tower sounded livid. "We need them now! We have one damaged Badger! Knock out those missile launchers!"

"We be moving under bounding overwatch—"

"You've taken no small arms fire!" Tower shouted. "All they have is missile teams. They're only gunning for our vehicles."

"Unis may have small arms and good fire discipline, sir." The sergeant's voice was imperturbed.

"'Sir?' Are you mocking me? You think I'm a freshly hatched tiger cub who doesn't know his asshole from his elbow? Doesn't know how to lead?" Lt. Tower hesitated, and the tone of his next words showed he sensed how much weakness he'd shown the squad. "Get up that hill." The lieutenant dropped out of the net.

"Marchbanks, your team's next bound," Sgt. Johnson said as if Lt. Tower hadn't spoken. "Ready?"

"Speak up if you aren't, lads," Marchbanks said over the team's net. Then, to the sergeant, "Ready."

Each five second bound seemed to last forever. Dread spurted through Tomas every moment he left cover. It subsided slightly in the lulls when they covered Johnson's team, but not much. The Unis above them hadn't fired at their squad. Hadn't they? Over the din of the Badgers' heavy guns, the clack of surviving Graywolfs falling back from the point, and the roar of Uni missiles, would he be able to hear the chatter of Uni rifles targeting him? Would he only know the Unis fired at them when he was hit? Or not know, his brain splattered over the pine trunks before he could know what had happened—

Stop. Breathe. You have enough microphones on your side to pick up any small arms fire coming your way from upslope. Breathe more. Apply your skills. Cover, bound, repeat.

They were within fifty meters of the hilltop. The obs wheel glinted in the sunlight above them, canted at an angle by stray fire.

Tomas peered behind the last intact tree trunk. Ahead of him, Badger shells had torn pines apart like a giant snapping toothpicks, and beyond that, craters swallowed the dim light. "Final bound," Sgt. Johnson said. "Marchbanks, ready?"

"I'll go forward with Alvarez and Obermeyer to the shell craters. Neumann, Cohen, Sharma cover us. Ready? Go, lads!" The moving men bounded forward, crouched shapes in the infrared, names shown by the augmented reality display on the inside of Tomas' helmet. He kept his rifle aimed up hill. No Uni motion or fire, still.

"Rest of my lads, forward!"

The dread mounted, making Tomas' feet curl and his legs feel leaden. He slipped past torn trunks, crashed through falling branches. Even at a crouch he was exposed to every Uni soldier on the planet—

He jumped into a crater with Marchbanks. His foot touched something hard and jagged. *Land mine why aren't I dead?* and he lurched backward against the crater wall. His limbs shook and his breath came rapid and shallow.

"Lad, you with me?"

"Something in here."

"Irrigation pipe."

Marchbanks' tone of voice grounded Tomas. "Where are the Unis?" he asked.

"Buggered off when the guns opened up."

"Marchbanks, Sergeant!" Sharma's voice over the squad net. "Found a tunnel mouth in a crater. Maybe a service tunnel for their irrigation system."

"Throw a grenade in to keep them honest," Sgt. Johnson said. "Idrin, buddy up. One looks for tunnels and the other provides security."

More gunfire and explosions from the valley and the far slope echoed around their squad. Sharma's grenade gave a muffled blast inside the tunnel he'd found. Soon a man in Johnson's team found another tunnel, and another grenade went in. Tomas looked over the crater, poking cautiously with his bayonet. The blade struck something solid under five centimeters of torn soil and he jerked the rifle back.

"Clean it off," Marchbanks said. Tomas reached under his arm to a pocket and pulled out a small packet of nanotubes and memory plastic. A press of his finger transformed the packet into a spade. "Careful."

A few scrapes with the side of the spade revealed the jagged edge of a torn mycocrete casing. More scrapes sent dirt sliding down a meter-wide hole running about forty-five degrees into the hill. Dimly seen straight lines crossing the tunnel suggested steps.

"We found one," Marchbanks said over the squad's net. Aloud to Tomas, he said, "How the paper tiger's trusted obs wheels missed the Unis." Marchbanks reached into a pocket for a grenade and tossed it in. "The Unis are probably long gone, but it's easier to have Supply fab us more grenades than Medical graft us new skulls." The grenade detonated and the tunnel soon returned to silence.

The sounds of battle raged in the valley below. Tomas and Marchbanks crouched in their shell crater, watching for Unis. The damaged woods around them held only their squad.

"Is there something more we should be doing?" Tomas asked. He hadn't even slid his rifle's fire selector toggle off safety.

"We're staying alive, lad. There's nothing more we can do for the vehicle crews or the other squad."

Tomas swiveled his neck, barely keeping his eyes above the rim of the shell crater, looking up and down the hillside for Unis. Still none. A glance skyward showed three wheeling Kestrels, thopters loaded for ground attack. Constitution's rays lit up their wings. "Why aren't we getting close support from the air?"

"Takes time for battalion HQ to decide where to send them. Eyes on the ground, lad."

"Right." Tomas settled deeper against the crater wall. Still no Unis. The roar of guns continued, deep percussive blasts, until distant, deeper booms sounded from far to darkward.

"Arty incoming!" Johnson shouted into the squad net. "Down down down!"

"Ours or theirs?" Tomas said out loud.

"Nae matter!" Marchbanks lunged toward the bottom of the

crater, then looked up. "Deep as you can, lad!" He grabbed Tomas by the arm, yanked him to the crater bottom. Marchbanks curled up, half over him. His jabbing knees and elbows drove Tomas to curl tighter—

The first Uni shell was louder than anything else Tomas had heard so far. The blast buffeted them and dirt showered down in thick fast clumps. He heard nothing but a ringing in his ears. Nothing, not even his own breaths.

The Uni shelling continued. Tomas felt their detonations through the ground, a giant's steps, poised to crush them underfoot. Tomas shrank in on himself, wishing he could be somewhere else, anywhere else. His rifle was useless against the distant guns and the hail of shrapnel. He could only cower and hope. Capt. Schreiber had said nothing about this. He was aware of Marchbanks' weight covering him, grateful he exposed himself to give Tomas a little more protection.

His hearing returned. The shelling seemed quieter. The crackle of splintering trees came from somewhere. "Unis be walking the shells toward our vehicles," Sgt. Johnson said.

Marchbanks shifted his weight. "They weren't after us?" Tomas asked, shouting to hear himself over the din of receding shelling.

"The Unis probably don't even know we're here, lad." Marchbanks winced as he spoke.

Sgt. Johnson said, "Marchbanks, casualties?"

A pause; Tomas assumed Marchbanks checked his team's medical status through his helmet display. "One very minor flesh wound, upper arm. We got lucky."

"I've got one dead, one severely wounded. Patch your man's flesh wound. I'm calling the platoon medic and an ambulance from company."

"Roger." Marchbanks winced again. "Help me with my first aid kit."

In his display, Tomas looked at his team's status icons for the pulsing red that meant a wounded man, when he realized what Marchbanks had said. "You?" he asked. Guilt gripped him. Marchbanks had taken that wound for him. "Absolutely."

Tomas fumbled with the hemostop, one ear out for more Uni shelling. More distant, deep thumps sounded. Tomas glanced up in alarm—

"That's battalion...light artillery company," Marchbanks said. "Counterbattery fire against the Unis."

Slightly more relieved, Tomas realized the ground attack thopters had disappeared. "Where are the Kestrels?"

Marchbanks popped a painkiller into his mouth and looked to lightward, past the canted obs wheel. "Heading for the other side of the valley. Hang on, this will get loud."

Tomas smeared hemostop on his fingertip and stuck it into the hole torn in Marchbanks' sleeve by the shrapnel. By feel, he smeared the hemostop over Marchbanks' wound as bombs shrieked down the sky. Detonations sounded from midslope on the far hill, louder than the din of the Badgers's guns, but much quieter than the Uni shelling. Or else his hearing had been wrecked. "I've heard worse."

Marchbanks chuckled. "You're one of us, Neumann. And thanks for dressing my wound."

Guilt returned. "You took it for me. I don't deserve any thanks."

"No, lad. I didn't take it for you." The sound of firing subsided. Marchbanks glanced across the valley. "I took it for me. Remember, I'm counting on you to tell your grandchildren what a good old sonofabitch I was."

5

Daughter of Astarte

The Bluejay gave a final beat of its wings, then settled on its landing feet. Around the cabin, men rose from their seats with smiles and cheery voices. No helmets, no rifles, no packs. A day's liberty, hundreds of kilometers from the nearest Uni forces.

"Chief, hold the door a moment!" Sgt. Johnson shouted to the cockpit. He gave a stern look to the men. "Set your countdown timers for twenty-three hours forty-five minutes. You will be back here then. If I and I have to hunt for you on base, or Jah help you, in the town, you'll be preferring combat against the Unis to I righteous anger! Be I and I clear?"

"Yes, sergeant!"

His look relented slightly. "You handled yourselves well in the ambush on the New Boston road, and you've been working hard in training since then. Go enjoy yourselves, idrin. You've earned it."

The ramp dropped. Obermeyer ran down and leaped to the tarmac. He looked back with a grin. "What are you fools wasting time for? The day is young!"

Cohen and Sharma trotted after him, followed by some men from Johnson's team. Tomas and Marchbanks followed. Tomas felt lighter, and not solely because he'd dropped twenty kilos of kit back at the battalion's forward base. He could be himself here. For a day, his implanted skills would go unused.

On the tarmac, warm and resilient underfoot, Tomas looked around. A cool darkly breeze stirred the Confederated Worlds' flag, the stars and rays, atop a tall flagpole next to a shorter one flying the Blackjacks' banner. Parallel fences topped with coils of razor wire stood at the airfield's edge, a rolling plain dense with dark green grasses beyond them. A solitary guard patrolled between the fences. The greater part of the base was behind them. "Where to?" he asked Marchbanks.

Alvarez had descended the ramp after them. "Too bad, boys, there's no such thing as Sons of Astarte. Wait, you've got each other."

"Toss off." Marchbanks watched Alvarez round the Bluejay's tail, then said to Tomas, "There are the Daughters of Astarte, of course."

"Of course," Tomas said. He hated the nervousness in his voice. Marchbanks must have heard it.

Marchbanks led them around the Bluejay. Puzzlement gave way to a kindly expression. "You've never hired a slattern before. No matter, it's just business, like getting slop at the chow hall. Is it against Observer precepts?"

"No," Tomas said, but his voice wavered. His mother would disapprove, and he imagined the man with brown hair and narrow jaw would too. Yet he had another reason for hesitating. "You call the new guys 'virgins' for a reason."

Marchbanks' mouth gaped, then he chuckled. "Lad, that's a good one." He peered at Tomas. "You're serious."

"Yeah." Tomas' cheeks felt warm.

"You're worried you won't know what you're doing? You needn't. They're professional ladies. They'll flatter a client to keep him returning."

Fear of failure hadn't inspired his embarrassment. "It's okay....?" Tomas didn't know what he wanted to ask.

"Okay that silly Josie lasses missed their chance to part their legs for so fine a lad as you?" Marchbanks waved the matter away. "We'll visit the Daughters, that's for aye, but we've some matters to take care of first."

Marchbanks led Tomas between airfield control and the maintenance hangars. The view opened up. The base stretched away to a bluff, at the bottom of which could be glimpsed a few roofs of the nearby town, Springfield, and a river in the distance. Most of the base's buildings were laid out to form a long quadrangle. A road ringed the quadrangle, surrounding a field where soldiers in gray fitness attire played pickup games of cricket, football, and ultimate flying disc. Jeeps plied the road, along with trucks and walking soldiers.

"This way," Marchbanks said, turning darkward. "Follow your nose."

Something did smell good. Bacon and eggs? "Is that—?"

"Yeah, lad. Forget the so-called food shat out of those field extruders. This is the real thing. They've got racks of incubators growing pork bellies, chicken breasts, and steaks. Get this, there's a farmer near Springfield who sells honest-to-God eggs! Squeezed out the twats of real live chickens! Vegetables, fruit, orange juice, coffee.... We've a busy day ahead of us and have to gird our strength."

The mess hall had more of those delicious smells, plus picture windows giving a view of the playing fields and the shadowed faces of buildings across the quadrangle, silhouetted by Constitution. Metal and ceramic clanked under warming lamps, where chubby soldiers, male and female, clad in plain, rear-area green crewed their stations.

The serving line was short. Most of the soldiers ahead of them had the jagged vee-shape of St. Martin's cloak on their sleeves. Supply and Support Corps. Tomas sniffed out a breath. We risk our lives and lose men while they eat three real meals a day.

Marchbanks leaned toward him. "Their service is important," he murmured, "even though not as much as ours. Remember SSC's motto. 'The spearhead needs the shaft behind it.'"

Chastened, Tomas said, "I hadn't thought of that." He mused a bit further. "How'd you guess what I was thinking?"

"I thought it too, my first time off the line."

They reached the serving stations, took trays. Despite a breakfast of extruded rations before boarding the Bluejay at oh-five-thirty, Tomas ordered widely. Bacon, a mix of scrambled eggs and diced peppers called *migas*, melon cubes, a chocolate croissant. The servers aimed scanning wands at his shilling to register payment. The first few times, he glanced at the inside of his wrist, where his account balance shrank a little with each debit. Not much; he soon quit paying attention.

Drinks were available at the end of the line. Water, milk, plain coffee? A sign promising espressos and cappuccinos caught his eye. He gave it a skewed look. Joséphine had little to offer the Confederated Worlds, but at least it knew coffee. "Espresso." He received the cup with low expectations.

"Taking coffee liqueur in that?" Marchbanks asked.

"No."

"Ah, too early in the day for you." To the server, he said, "Your tallest draft stout." The server pulled the handle and soon set a liter glass on Marchbanks' tray.

Round tables, each seating eight, filled the space between the serving lines and the picture windows. Half the tables were empty, and the rest, sparsely occupied. Marchbanks started toward a table at the windows when two SSC men hailed them. "Care for some company?" they asked.

"We'd love it, lads." Marchbanks changed course and Tomas grudgingly followed. Even if the spearhead needed the shaft, he didn't need to talk to the SSC men.

He expected the conversation to cover standard stuff, *where are you from* and the like. But the first thing an SSC man asked was, "You're 2nd Battalion?"

"Aye. Foxtrot Company."

They winced in sympathy. The other SSC man said, "Bloody hell, I heard you drove into the worst of it."

"Our squad got away easily," Marchbanks said.

"Your rides, too?"

"Unis scratched the paint on our Badger."

The first SSC man shook his head. "There was a lot of mangled metal on that road, I heard. We were running the fabs as hot as we could to get Graywolfs and Badgers to you guys. Sounds like you didn't get one of ours, but have you heard any complaints from the guys in the new rides?"

Tomas put his fork down. He felt embarrassed at being rude earlier. "They're doing well in training, I hear."

"Glad to hear that. But let the guys in them know we had trouble scraping up titanium for some of the alloys. Local soil's depleted in it and the demand tapped our supply. We skimped a little on the rear armor. The drive sprockets in the tracks won't be as durable, especially off-road."

"We'll let them know," Marchbanks said. He lifted his beer mug.

Tomas frowned. "You didn't write that up?"

"What? Mate, of course we did."

Marchbanks firmly set down his beer, the motion and sound drawing Tomas's attention. "That information has to cross a lot of tablets before it reaches the crews driving those vehicles."

"Oh." Tomas felt more embarrassment.

"Don't sweat it, mate," said one of the SSC men. To the other, he said, "Time for us to clock in. Stay safe, mates."

After they left, Marchbanks finished his beer. Dregs of foam slumped down the inside of the glass. "I'm getting another. You've had a full meal, does that make it late enough to buy you one?"

"No, thanks," Tomas said. "I don't drink."

"I thought you were joking before, but now I know you have to be. Every soldier drinks."

Tomas shook his head. He didn't want to disappoint Marchbanks, but he had to speak the truth. "I've been taught alcohol distorts our ability to see things as they are."

Marchbanks' expression grew distant. He stared out the window for a moment, somewhere beyond the sporting soldiers and the buildings across the quadrangle. "Some things you don't want to see as they are." His face grew more lively. "Like an ugly face on a shapely lass. No drink? Your loss, Neumann." He left the table.

How big a blunder had Tomas made by declining Marchbanks' offer? *Mother would disapprove everything I've done since I enlisted. Why not add to it?*

Before he could change his mind, Marchbanks returned to the table, accompanied by Delacroix and MacInnis carrying heaping trays. Their food steamed and, once seated, they dug into it with vibrant eyes. After a few bites, they started to talk.

"Heard anything about Lt. Tower?" Delacroix asked.

"Me?" Marchbanks stifled a grin. "What makes you think I'd know anything?"

"You've got your ear to the ground," MacInnis said. He sipped coffee and kept his gaze over the cup's rim on Marchbanks' face.

"I saw him fly off for here yesterday, same as you did. I'd guess Brigade is reviewing his performance."

Delacroix sniffed out a breath in a chuckle. "I hope they axe him."

MacInnis looked sympathetic. "I heard him over the Badger's net, but you were stuck in the turret with him."

Tomas cleared his throat. "Was he that bad?"

"You're not a virgin anymore." Delacroix sounded peeved.

"I heard him same as MacInnis did. He was bad. Couldn't map the situation onto the categories in the textbook and needed the sergeant to tell him what to do. But how bad was he?"

"Bad enough," Delacroix said. "Why are you taking his side?"

"I'm not."

"You're trying to see good in everyone," MacInnis said. "I can't fault you for that. Yet it's not like he's a virgin rifleman. If a virgin rifleman fouls up, he ends up dead. If a virgin louie fouls up, we can all end up dead."

"We didn't."

"We weren't the target of the ambush," Marchbanks said. "The tanks and supply Badgers were. Though you make a good point, lad; he did listen to Sgt. Johnson."

"Do you think he can learn?"

Marchbanks paused, shrugged. MacInnis gave no answer. "I hope we don't find out," Delacroix said.

After a few more minutes, Marchbanks said, "We've enjoyed it, lads, but we do see enough of your faces in the squad shelter."

"Off to the Daughters?" MacInnis asked with a smirk.

"In due time, aye."

MacInnis raised his eyebrow at Tomas. "Your first, Neumann?"

Tomas blinked, tongue-tied. Marchbanks filled the gap. "When else would he've had a chance to visit the Daughters?"

"Neumann doesn't seem the type to hack the system," MacInnis said, "but he might have been the one man to find an exploit to visit them before joining us."

"Would that I had," Tomas said.

"You haven't heard their pagan claptrap, then."

Delacroix laughed. "You don't want to listen to them, Mac, but you have no qualms about taking what they offer? You know the word 'hypocrisy?'"

"They're priestess-whores of some false goddess. Better to slot it in them than some Presbyterian girl forced by circumstance into selling herself."

"I'll make sure Neumann ignores the pagan claptrap," Marchbanks said. "Later, lads."

Marchbanks and Tomas recycled their trays and soon were outside. Marchbanks led the way across the playing fields, passing between the cricketers and the footballers. "Thanks for distracting MacInnis," Tomas said.

"Distracting? It was the answer he expected. No matter, you're secret's safe, at least until we get you rid of your condition. Oh, nice cross into the box."

Tomas looked up. A footballer leaped up to the ball and headed it toward the far corner of the goal. The keeper backpedaled, then lunged too late. "Looks like he wasn't sure whether to play the pass or the shot."

"Better to follow the wrong course of action in time, then choose the right one too late," Marchbanks said.

They soon reached the road on the far side of the playing fields. "Where are we going?" asked Tomas.

Across the road, Marchbanks turned onto a sidewalk. A sign in front of a nearby building read *Brigade Headquarters*. "MacInnis has it off. It's not my ear, and it's not to the ground." Marchbanks led them away from the sidewalk, down a narrow lawn of dark green tinged by the rays of Constitution. He slowed his steps near a rear window and whistled a few bars of some Scotian-sounding tune.

Around the back of the building, he bade Tomas wait at the foot of a stoop. A few moments later, a door swung open and a woman, insignia and nameplate identifying her as Cpl. Metzger, came out. She had a turned-up nose and squinty eyes, and a squared-off cut of hair falling to her neck. "Les, good to see you. And your friend."

Marchbanks introduced Tomas to her, then said, "Has Brigade made our paper tiger cry yet?"

"Damn near. They're playing audio and video from the Badger's turret. He's a little red-faced ball, but he's kept his composure."

"Are we stuck with him?"

"It's looking that way. Sorry to have to tell you."

"My gut was expecting it. He got less than half of B squad killed. Not bad for his first time in the saddle." Marchbanks put on a leer. "Speaking of which, when are you off-duty?"

She set her fist to her hip. "After your appointment with the Daughters, I wager. You're going to lead this young man into sin?"

"I can't lead Neumann anywhere he doesn't want to go."

Cpl. Metzger shook her head. "If you can swear off whoring, maybe there could be something between us. I need to get back in before Brigade notices I stepped out."

"Always a pleasure, Corporal. I wish in more ways than one."

She *hmmph*'d and went back into the building. Marchbanks set his hand on Tomas' shoulder. "Time to get away before Lt. Tower has a chance to notice we were here."

Tomas followed, frowning. "You and Cpl. Metzger—?"

Marchbanks chuckled. "Lad, remember what I said about lasses with ugly faces? I haven't had enough beer to goggle my eyes for her. But she enjoys the game."

"Game?"

"I let her think I want to get in her pants, so she gets to show off her virtue in refusing me. And I find out what's happening in headquarters. Everyone wins."

Excitement and trepidation filled Tomas' chest. "Is it time to visit the Daughters?"

"Almost, lad. Let's get cleaned up first."

Part of Tomas felt glad to delay the visit for a little while. But another part of him bade him ask, "Would they turn us away if we didn't?"

"It's not for their sake. It's for ours. We'll feel more like men at liberty once we scrub off the field."

A hundred-fifty meters toward the front gate stood the base's fitness center. Marchbanks led the way past glass-walled rooms filled with kettlebells and free weights. Racquetballs ponged down a side corridor. Toward the back of the building, a clerk handed out towels and a toiletries kit.

Tomas took his kit into the locker room. At an open sink, he smeared depilatory over his face, softened the calluses on his hands, then cleaned his teeth. By the end, his gums throbbed and yellowish gunk glommed on the tonguescraper. He hadn't flossed since his last day in the transport delivering him to New Liberty. Amazing how dental hygiene could feel like such a luxury.

A sign in the showers showed a strict time limit. Ten minutes. He chuckled. After the spartan conditions up at battalion, a ten minute shower seemed indulgently long. Tomas soaped, rinsed, and almost stepped out halfway through his allotted time before remembering Marchbanks' words. He stayed under the showerhead, hot water streaming down his face, until the timer cut off the flow.

After meeting Marchbanks outside the locker room, Tomas followed him up the sidewalk, past Brigade headquarters, back toward the airfield. Their destination was a building like any other, two stories of mycocrete painted in a dazzle pattern of greens and grays. It lacked a sign in front, and maroon shutters covered every window. The only other indication it had a purpose other than military came at the front door. Mounted high on the inside of the jamb, a statuette of a nude, pregnant woman, breasts and belly swollen, head back, eyes closed, face contorted, showed a dilated *vulve* between lifted, parted knees.

"False advertising." Marchbanks shook his head. "You'll neither move their world nor get them with child."

They entered a vestibule, barely big enough for both of them. The shuttered window next to the front door, facing darkward, suffused the room with a dim glow, augmented by a small candle floating in a round globe filled one-third with water. A closed door at the far side presumably led deeper into the building. Tomas remembered the skills implantation chamber at the intake station. The few months since then seemed like half his lifetime.

Next to the door leading into the building, a tablet hung on the wall, alongside a wand like those wielded by the mess hall servers. The tablet showed abstract artwork, swirls of maroon, pink, and lavender. The artwork dissolved to show text. *Welcome to the Daughters of Astarte. Your donation will help us minister to the spiritual needs of people throughout the Confederated Worlds.*

"Donation?" Tomas asked.

"Saying that lets them pretend they aren't slatterns," Marchbanks said. "They even act shocked if you bring it up in the salon, or the private chambers."

"How much should I donate?"

"They say it doesn't matter. But it only stands to reason, the more you give, the more you can get them to do." Marchbanks moved closer, shoulder-to-shoulder. "If it's your first time, donate as much as you can."

Tomas checked the inside cuff of his left sleeve. "I've got about sixty confeds, but we still have meals and—"

"I'll take care of the rest of your food and drink while we're on liberty, lad. This time. Donate all you have."

"All?"

"After today, it may be... months before you get another chance to spend money."

Carried along by Marchbanks' words, Tomas went to the tablet, tapped the screen. In response to prompts, he worked his shilling out of his shirt and waved it at the wand. A glance at his cuff showed his account balance stood at a few cents.

"My turn." Marchbanks worked the tablet and wand like an old hand. Once he finished, the inner door opened.

Slow acoustic guitar music and a faint spicy scent greeted them. Maroon curtains hung from the ceiling, marking out sitting areas.

The curtains and the dim light of candles and shuttered windows made the room look smaller than it was. Men's low voices murmured. Somewhere, a woman gave a high clear laugh.

"What next?" Tomas asked. Maybe it would be over with soon. Was that what he really wanted?

"We find seats and wait. Remember, they want to believe they aren't slatterns." Marchbanks led the way to an ell formed by two loveseats, each one backed by a maroon curtain. Tomas looked around. More high laughter. A woman in a simple yellow dress, her knees and elbows exposed, led a grinning soldier by the hand toward the back of the room.

"Les!" A woman came around the curtain behind Marchbanks. She had wide, innocent eyes and a pointed chin. Long silver spirals dangled from hooks in her earlobes. "I thought that was you!"

"Gloria, this is my friend Tomas. It's his first visit."

"Really?" She angled her head and playfully peered at him. He relaxed even more when she looked up, face bright. "Persephone might be just the lady looking for your companionship." She touched the spiral hanging from her right ear and muttered too quietly to be overheard. She then sat with Marchbanks, drawing her knees up on his loveseat and resting the back of her hand on his thigh.

Despite her body language, Gloria kept Tomas in her conversation with Marchbanks for a few minutes, until another woman sauntered up. Lean limbs, large teeth, curly blond hair; Tomas remembered a time he went swimming with Etien and they happened upon Véronique and her friends at the river bank. He'd dived deeply into the cold water and swum to the middle of the river to hide the erection distending his trunks. He shook his head to clear the thought, then stood. "Are you Persephone?" His heart thudded hard enough to rock his torso. Uncertain, he extended his hand.

"Hi. Tomas?" He nodded and she shook his hand like it was the most natural greeting in the world. She raised up on the balls of her feet and kissed his cheek. "Let's sit, and tell me about yourself."

As he did, his nervousness began to fade. Marchbanks and the other men had talked up the Daughters as something mysterious and powerful, yet Persephone was only a young woman, talking and listening in an idle conversation about his homeworld and places he'd seen.

At one point, Tomas mentioned his Observer upbringing. Behind his shoulder, Marchbanks gave a pained grunt and Tomas realized he'd made a mistake. Yet Persephone kept her smile and asked him more. She hiked one knee to the loveseat and kept her gaze on him, hands in her lap sinking into the thin fabric of her dress, playing absently with a bracelet of smoothed, polished stones around her left wrist. He couldn't phrase how, but he knew he was being tested, and he was passing.

"Care to go someplace more private?" she asked.

Disapproval burst from the mental model of his mother residing in the upper parts of his subconscious. He took a breath and slowly exhaled. He was a man, with a man's needs, and his mother would never know how he satisfied them. "I'd like that."

Faintly smiling, she took his hand and stood. He rose and followed her. A step later, Marchbanks roared with laughter. "Aye, lad!" Gloria playfully canted her eye at him.

Tomas' cheeks grew hot as he returned his attention to the back and side of Persephone's neck. "Sorry."

"About? Your friend?"

Nerves afflicted him again. "It's my first time."

She lifted a curtain across a doorway, waited till he came through, then dropped it. They were alone in a hallway with red, floral-print wallpaper and an open, wide staircase along one wall. "Gloria told me—"

"No. I mean, yes, my first time visiting you, but also, I'm a virgin."

A troubled look flickered over her face. "Let's not talk about the war and what it might do to you—"

"No...." Tomas grasped at more words, but none came to him.

"Oh." She paused at the foot of the stairs and gave him a look that seemed wiser than her years. "May I tell you a secret? Most men are, the first time they visit us. You're one of the few to admit it." She put her arm around his waist. "Upstairs."

Her room was small, a double bed with half a meter of open floor along the sides and foot. At the head, against the wall, stood a plain wooden slab, five iron rings across the top and a niche containing another statuette of the goddess high in the center. More red, floral-print wallpaper. A chandelier held a half-dozen floating candles.

Tomas returned his attention to Persephone as she lifted her dress over her head. The candles gently shadowed the lithe curves of her body. He had the firmest erection he ever remembered, throbbing, aching against his pants. She lunged at him, put her arms around him, covered his face in kisses. Her voice came hot, breathy, indistinct in his ears.

He fumbled at the front of his pants, but she took his hand away. "I'm ready," she whispered, "but for other girls you'll meet, you need to start someplace like here—" she guided his hand to her breast.

Would he ever meet another woman? He put the thought aside and observed his hand's motions.

After a time, she said, "—then here." She pulled his hand lower, over her belly, through the thatch of her pubes. He gasped as the outer petals of her vulve parted and his fingers slickened on her *l'eau venusianne*, water of Venus. Her hand on the back of his fingers guided him into a slow, rhythmic motion.

"While still working your hand, your mouth here." She turned her chest slightly toward him, jiggling her nipple.

He moved closer, hesitated. "But, nursing—"

"The goddess has given us a great gift," Persephone said. "A woman's body can unite with both a man's and her child's."

He darted his tongue out of his mouth to flick her nipple. She moved closer, pushing her breast at his mouth. She moaned a little and moved her belly to him. "Next, to the bed."

She stretched out and smiled as he climbed next to her. The sheets smelled fresh and felt warm. Now must be the time. His hand went to the front of his pants. "Still not yet." She guided his hand to her *vulve*. "A finger, inside. Two if she's a big girl or well excited. Stroke the cat's tongue."

Cat's tongue? Realization dawned on him when he found a

raspy area on the front wall. He ran his finger over it.

"More firm. Once a woman's charged up enough she can handle it." Tomas increased the pressure and speed of his motion. "Yes. And now...." She laid her hand on the side of his head and guided him further, further. She wanted her *vulve* licked? He hesitated a moment, then lowered his face to her outer petals, his finger still working inside her. Her *l'eau venusianne* tanged on his tongue. She moaned again, louder, and lifted the small of her back off the bed. "Now let's get those pants off you," she said, panting.

They both worked at the snaps and buttons of his uniform, flung his shedded garments to the floor. She laid back and parted her legs for his knees. With a soft grip, he guided his throbbing *biroute* toward her *vulve*. "A little lower," Persephone said. "That's it...."

Nothing had prepared him for the feel of her moist inner folds around his *biroute*. All the times he'd masturbated couldn't capture the intensity of the experience. He knew he should work his hips, and did, slowly. His arousal pressed for release, and too fast or too deep a motion would burst the dam. But he could no longer help himself. As he moved, she rocked her hips to meet him. He could tell she wanted to go faster and he did, deeper and he did. His shilling slid between them as he thrusted into her.

He'd heard older boys on Joséphine talk about silently counting numbers to delay their orgasm, so he tried that, lapsing into Sankt-Benedikts-Sprach, *ein zwo drei...* and then her breath caught and the muscles around her *vulve* fluttered, pulsing against his *biroute*, and he couldn't help himself. His ejaculate spurted into her and he sagged onto her, his face against the side of her head, his breath ragged in her ear.

She shifted languidly next to him.

Now what? Though the boys in Portage, and his squadmates, talked volumes about their sexual exploits, none had ever spoken of what they said and did after the act.

Tomas propped his head on his shoulder and looked at Persephone. She gazed contentedly at the ceiling. She looked lovely. A sudden intuition told him he would never see her again.

Persephone turned her face to him and studied him. "The goddess has blessed me to bring my path across yours. You truly are unique, Tomas."

Pride swelled in his chest. "How so?"

"Some boys, and especially those whom I am blessed to initiate into the arts of love, turn lovestruck in the afterglow. It saddens me because I can't return their love. My commitment to the goddess forbids it—"

"I understand."

Persephone reached toward him and brushed her fingers through his chest hair. A vulnerable look flashed across her eyes. "Most others act as if they've bested me at a game. They've popped their corks and now are done with me."

She seemed complacent. Tomas crinkled his brow. She deserved better. "Doesn't that bother you?"

After a high tinkling laugh, she said, "The male pops his cork and pours out his tiny bit of acorn soup. It flows through me into the ocean of the goddess. Deep down he knows the truth, and hates and fears it. As well he should. She ebbs and flows unchanged long after his manhood softens." Gently, she trailed her fingers over his flaccid *biroute*. Her face grew sad. "Long after he lies in his grave."

Persephone shook her head and looked slightly alarmed at her most recent words. "Again, Tomas, the goddess has blessed me." She leaned toward him and kissed him. He read from her tone and her motions that she wanted him to say farewell.

"She's blessed me too." In formal *joséphinais*, he said, *"Adieu,"* and reached for his clothes.

Later that afternoon, in a lounge on the other side of the base, Tomas had a few minutes alone. After a hesitation, he pulled out his tablet and swiped his way through the apps and menus. *Compose letter, select addressee.*

Annike Neumann, Portage-du-Nord, Joséphine

Mother, you were worried I couldn't remain true to our precepts. You can be glad that I have. I have seen combat as it truly is and I remain intact, both in body and in mind. He thought back to his final conversation with Persephone and his biroute stirred in his pants. And in the rest of the soldier's life, *I see things as they are, and am a better man for it.*

He saved the most important question for last. *During skills implantation, I recovered a memory of a man with brown hair and a narrow jaw. Was that my father?*

6

Friendly Fire

"Lad, I'd love to be twixt Gloria's thighs right now."

Tomas kept his gaze over the lip of their foxhole, watching the lightward horizon for movement. "Instead of waiting for the Unis to blunder into us? I'd rather be slotting your slattern, too."

Marchbanks caught his breath, then chuckled. "You're talking like a man, now. Yours must have truly done you right. What was her name? Penelope?"

"Persephone." He fell silent. Was that motion in the distance? Fuzzy warm spots danced on the display inside his helmet. Vehicles.

"You see them too," Marchbanks murmured, voice serious. "I make a company, in column."

Tomas studied the fuzzy warm spots, looking for the shapes of Uni fighting vehicles silhouetted in the infrared by their waste heat. Yet what else could be crossing this dark plain of near-black grass, the nearest NL town a hundred klicks away? "I concur. I'll call it in." Tomas groped in the dark for the handset. Wire had been buried back to Lt. Tower's position to remove the need for radio calls. Even if the Unis picked up no content, they could still learn from radio traffic the GF was in the vicinity.

Time to pay them back for the New Boston road. An enlisted man at platoon headquarters picked up and Tomas whispered their sighting.

"Good eyes," came the reply. "Now hang up."

The lead Uni fighting vehicles were five thousand meters from Tomas' foxhole, racing darkward on a dirt road at sixty kilometers an hour. Thirty klicks to darkward, the GF partially surrounded a Uni regiment on three sides. When the breeze gusted, the cold wind carried the rumble of distant artillery. The oncoming Unis were elements of the 2nd Nueva Andaluciano Regiment on their way to relieve their pocketed comrades. Somehow the GF had scored an intelligence coup, exploiting a gap between Uni forces to place Tomas' battalion in a blocking position, dug in and hull down parallel to the dirt road, without Uni intel noticing.

"The Badgers and Graywolfs will throw most of the steel at them," Marchbanks said. "We just keep our heads down and wait for any Uni rifles to dismount." He fell silent and Tomas did as well.

A faint hum built up, slightly louder than the moans of the cold darkwardly wind. The lead Uni vehicles had closed to within a thousand meters of their foxhole. Between their infrared signature and refracted light from sunward, Tomas identified their outlines: Marlborough tanks, followed by DeGaulle infantry carriers. The vehicles rumbled closer, bobbing like boats on a choppy lake.

Tomas hunkered, his head against the wall of the foxhole. The rumble of the vehicles came through the ground. His first encounter with Uni tanks.

Sixty tons of metal and carbon nanotubes, what if they found his foxhole, drove over it, crushed it? His skills told him the engineers followed standard procedure when they'd excavated it; the foxhole would resist being collapsed by a vehicle... yet his subconscious knew only fear of the fast, massive machines. He wanted to melt into the rocky ground when the Marlboroughs passed a hundred meters from him. The rumble of their tracks filled his head and body, as if the sound bypassed his ears and went straight to his brain.

"Come on, lads, give it to them," Marchbanks said. Badger and Graywolf gunners, he had to mean. Thoughts of *fire discipline* popped in Tomas' mind, like firecrackers on a sunny day. He knew the plan—let the Unis stretch out in front of their positions—but his legs and arms still tightened uselessly, wanting to take some action, do anything to distract the primate part of his mind from the fear of the massive, rumbling vehicles.

Tomas forced himself to step forward and peer out of the foxhole as a platoon of four DeGaulles passed. Dust settled out of the air, obscuring vision and piling on their foxhole's chameleon fabric cover, as more vehicles went by. A headquarters team came into position in front of Tomas and Marchbanks. Two DeGaulles, belonging to the Uni commander and his staff, were interspersed among eight supply vehicles. The latter, called Bismarcks, lacked turrets and had false guns aiming forward. The difference could fool a distant viewer, but from across the hundred meters of dark grass, Tomas saw it plainly.

Light flashed behind Tomas, throwing transient shadows on the front wall of the foxhole. A moment later guns' thunder and missiles' roar reached his ears. Their Badgers and Graywolfs had fired from behind their foxhole at the Uni column.

Explosions erupted on the road to their left and right. Some Uni vehicles swerved off the road, and others slewed on jammed or torn tracks. Blue-white lines jumped through the dust from Uni anti-missile lasers aiming wildly at the incoming fire. A few Uni machine guns chattered, and Tomas' skills identified the sharp bark of a Marlborough's gun, then another, soon drowned out by another fusillade from the Badgers and Graywolfs.

In front of Tomas, the Bismarcks around the Uni headquarters team milled in confusion. Supply drivers would be poorly trained for combat. The two DeGaulle fighting vehicles, though, looked to be driven by men with combat skills. They turned their heavier forward armor toward the GF line and fired their guns at the Badgers. One's machine gun ripped out rounds, smacking dirt within a dozen meters of their foxhole. Tomas shrank back, stupid instinct, too late to matter. The large caliber rounds could easily smash through their helmets and the body armor lining their suits.

"They've spotted us," Tomas said. His throat sounded dry.

"Stay calm. They can't hit us in our hole, lad. They'll need dismounted rifles to roust us."

Can't? Did he really believe that? But his comment about Uni riflemen reminded Tomas the best sensors to pick them up would be their own eyes. "You see any?"

Marchbanks peeked over the edge of the foxhole, ducked back down. "Nay."

Shells shrieked overhead on flat trajectories. More explosions sounded from ahead and behind. The GF vehicles were hull down, with just the muzzles of their guns poking over swells of terrain. Most would survive, unlike the Unis taken unawares.

He and Marchbanks were like flies, liable only to be swatted, powerless to make any difference.

"Your turn to look, lad. Only stay up a fraction of a second."

Tomas nodded. He glanced at the Uni headquarters team, then ducked back down, eyes closed as he made sense of what he'd seen. "Lot of smoke. Less motion in it."

Marchbanks took a quick look. "Aye, that's a good eye. Looks like the Bismarcks have buggered off and the DeGaulles will soon follow. Call it in."

Tomas fingered his shilling through his uniform. The need for radio silence had evaporated. He called Sgt. Johnson over the squad net and reported what he'd seen.

More GF guns fired, answered by a few Uni vehicles. Somewhere ahead, a DeGaulle fired its main gun. Soon after, a shell from a Graywolf shrieked into the smoke. The smoke muffled the shell's explosion, but Tomas could tell the Graywolf gunner had hit something.

The rest of the Unis followed their headquarters team's example. Smoke covered the road in thick billows, smearing light and infrared, muffling sound. Uni guns fell silent and the rumble of vehicles faded.

"They're all buggering off," Marchbanks said.

Tomas waited, taking longer and longer glances of the quiet road. The smoke remained strong in pockets, but wispy breaks gave glimpses of silent, immobile Uni vehicles. The holes pierced in their armor seemed tiny; blue-white flame licked at a few, but not even all. That couldn't be enough to kill a vehicle, could it? Then he remembered the photo on Capt. Schreiber's tablet he'd avoided seeing. Space Force and Ground Force had more in common than he thought.

"We be reconnoitering the kill zone," Sgt. Johnson said. "Teams by bounds. Don't go more than fifty meters past the road; that be the near boundary for our arty to mop up their retreat. Marchbanks, your team has first bound."

"Scope out some cover, then out of your holes, lads." Marchbanks covered his microphone with his hand. "See that thick tuft of grass at thirty meters?"

"Not much cover."

"Take it. I'll get another." He uncovered his microphone. "Ready?"

Tomas crawled out of the back of the foxhole, turned around, and started into a crouching run. The field between them and the road seemed impossibly broad. The near-black grasses blurred as he ran. He lurched headfirst to the ground behind the grass tuft and a memory of Persephone's bed stirred at the lower edge of his consciousness. He aimed his rifle into the smoke and caught his breath.

His next bound brought him to a Bismarck with a thrown track and a twelve-centimeter hole in the side armor. The smell of charred plastic warred with those of scorched reactor coolant and cooked meat. His team gathered around. "Who'll open the hatch?" Marchbanks asked.

Men looked to one another, faces showing unwillingness.

"It's a Bismarck. No ammo on board."

Still, no one else volunteered. Tomas lifted his chin. Finally he could do something, instead of letting the war happen around him. "I'll do it."

Marchbanks looked hesitant for a moment, then shrugged. "You'd see it later if not today. Steel your stomach, lad."

Tomas frowned. He could handle the sight of dead men. He'd avoided Capt. Schreiber's photo for being a photo, not for its contents. Squaring his shoulders, he reached for a rung of the Bismarck's side ladder—

And jerked his hand back amid chuckles from Obermeyer and Alvarez. Tomas winced at the burn in his hands. "Warn a fellow next time."

"You mean the skills imps didn't?" Alvarez chortled coldly as Tomas pulled on thermal gloves from a pocket. He climbed, fuming at Alvarez. He wasn't a virgin anymore; he was part of the team. Despite the gloves and his boots, he felt heat coming through the ladder. Atop the false turret, he danced, unable to keep his feet on the hot armor too long.

He wrapped his gloved fingers around the outer handle of the hatch and lifted. Lighter than he expected, the hatch swung rapidly and he staggered back. The stench of the wrecked vehicle grew far worse, and hot air carried charred, ashen fragments out of the interior.

Tomas mounted his flashlight to his rifle's barrel and looked in the hatchway. Melted plastic and torn metal looked ashen gray in his flashlight's beam. *Did the crew escape?* and then he noticed shriveled, burnt mannequin parts littering the interior.

He looked closer while sweat poured down his face. Torn, blackened arms clutched the driver's controls. In the commander's cupola, teeth showed amid the crisped, split skin of the man's face. Even if they were enemy, they were men just like him. Tomas' vision swam and his stomach sickened. He inhaled the hot, stinking air and somehow kept himself from vomiting. This was the world he had entered. He could try to blinder himself by focusing on details, like a white gleam of bone in one of the driver's arms——he took in the entire cabin. He wouldn't shut out his senses and think coolly about *make the other bastard die for his country.* He observed the scene as it truly was.

"I count two dead," he said to his team outside.

"Only two?" Marchbanks said. "They usually have a third crewman in the back, the fab technician."

"Can't see that far." He shut his eyes against another wave of nausea. Seeing it as it was didn't make the cabin less sickening.

"Come on down, lad. Someone pop the rear door."

Tomas climbed off the Bismarck in two jumps and sucked in cooler, cleaner air. Obermeyer grunted, tugging at the rear door hatch with gloved hands, while Alvarez sidled closer to Tomas.

"Makes you hungry for *chicharones*, doesn't it?"

"*Chicharones?*"

"Fried pork rinds." Alvarez grinned, his eyes boggling.

"Och, you're a sick bastard," Marchbanks said. "Leave the lad alone."

Tomas peered at Alvarez. Sickness? Or a defense mechanism, to keep from thinking about the reality of the dead men inside the vehicle? If that's what Alvarez wanted, he could reply in kind. Tomas sniffed and managed not to wince at the stench. "Reminds me more of a Josie delicacy." He turned off his flashlight. "Calf's brain."

After a moment, Alvarez grunted in amusement. "I can almost believe you, Josie."

"Got it," Obermeyer said. The rear hatch fell to the ground. Backscatter from Obermeyer's flashlight shadowed his face. His cough sounded like he fought nausea. "Third crewman is dead."

Marchbanks nodded. "I'll report to Sgt. Johnson." He murmured into his microphone, then said, "Sharma, Cohen, you look in the next one. Obermeyer, Neumann, security."

A distant whistle of artillery sounded overhead, followed by the faint flash of explosions, then moments later, their sound. An attack on retreating Uni vehicles a few kilometers away.

The team next searched a DeGaulle five meters beyond the road, its gun pointing in the direction of the GF tanks behind Tomas' foxhole. A Graywolf gunner had scored a lucky hit, catching a chink in the vehicle's front armor. "Looks like their commander's ride," Obermeyer said.

"Be nice if we decapitated their unit," said Marchbanks.

Tomas rushed around the rear of the vehicle, rifle raised. The hatch was down, bending the grass. A few dim lights glowed in the DeGaulle's dark interior. "Someone might have gotten out," he said.

He looked in the direction the Unis had retreated while Cohen and Alvarez went into the rear compartment. Their flashlight beams danced in the corner of Tomas' eye. There was nothing to see in front of him, and when the two men tramped back down the ramp, he listened with most of his attention.

"Driver never knew what hit him, but he's the only one in there," said Cohen.

Alvarez' voice lacked the coarse tone he'd used to talk about pork rinds. "At least one man's bleeding." A flashlight beam swept back and forth on the ground in Tomas' field of vision. At its furthest, the light penetrated a few meters into the thick grass.

"And someone left his memory disrupter behind when he evacuated." Tomas stole a glance over his shoulder to see what Cohen talked about. A black bag, almost fully covered by Cohen's clutching fingers. Cohen shook the bag for emphasis and plastic rattled within.

Marchbanks reported their finding to Sgt. Johnson, then returned his attention to the team. "Alright, lads, next—wait."

The sergeant spoke over their net. "You might have found a hot situation. The Uni commander might be wounded and have himself a head full of knowledge of their plans. Track down that wounded man."

Marchbanks let out a heavy breath. "We might be chasing a phantom, sergeant."

"We can only find out by hunting. Get to it."

Marchbanks shook his head. "Obermeyer, Sharma, follow that blood spoor. Everyone else, security, fan out. We stop at the arty boundary."

They went. The grass swatted Tomas' legs. More artillery fire flashed and rumbled a few klicks away. He returned his gaze to the uneven ground, looking for Unis. He'd heard the talk from the more experienced men. Times like this, men died from complacency, missing an enemy playing possum, blundering through a trip wire, too visible to a sniper—

"Nothing," Sharma said.

Obermeyer added, "We're at our boundary."

"A quick breather, lads, then we get back to scoping out the wreckage." Marchbanks looked in the direction of the distant artillery fire, then grunted.

Motion in the fading smoke, coming from the road to sunright of their position. Tomas' shilling identified Sgt. Johnson in an overlay in his helmet display. "What are you stopping for, Marchbanks?"

"We've reached our limit, sergeant."

"We've reached a line on a map. If I and I talk to Lt. Tower, he'll talk to the captain, and we'll get back word to cross that line."

"It's free fire for the arty beyond it."

Johnson scowled, pointed. "Arty be chasing the Unis five klicks away."

"Did they drop mines twenty meters from here? Have some Unis from these abandoned vehicles formed a fireteam lurking in the grass? We don't know what's out there. We've fulfilled our mission, sergeant."

Sgt. Johnson shook his head. "Now be the time to edit the mission. The longer we wait, the greater the chance our intel opportunity will slip away. I and I need someone to go after them. You won't be doing it, Marchbanks?" The sergeant looked to the men before Marchbanks could answer. "Who will?"

"I'll go," Tomas said.

Marchbanks spoke with a vehement edge. "Lad, the sergeant didn't make it an order—"

"I'll go."

Marchbanks gave him a flat stare for a moment, then shrugged. "Alright, lad. We'll wait here."

"Keep your head on straight," the sergeant said. "You smell something off, get back to your team."

"Yes, sergeant." Tomas glanced at Marchbanks. Why did he resist the sergeant's decision? Tomas put the thought aside. Distraction could kill as readily as complacency. He lifted his rifle and started forward.

Bent grass showed the wounded man's path from the DeGaulle. Tomas walked slowly, peering for motion or the blocky shapes of artillery-delivered mines in the tall grass, pausing every few steps to listen for movement or breath. The only sound came from gnats buzzing past his ears and the rustle of grass blades in the cool wind from darkward. He checked around him, but even as his eyes adjusted to the landscape lit by starlight, he saw nothing. Step step pause. Nothing. Where was the trail? There? His fingers touched something wet and dark in the starlight. Step step step pause—

Pained, labored breathing, coming fast and shallow. Tomas crouched and listened to narrow its location. There, behind a swell in the ground. Tomas inhaled to calm himself. Unis can understand Confed, he knew from skills implantation. Rifle to shoulder, go.

Tomas snapped on his flashlight and ran a few steps forward. "Don't move! Surrender!"

"*Sí*," said a pained voice. "*Me entrego.*"

Disappointment nibbled at Tomas the instant he saw the wounded Uni. He'd expected some exotic figure, tweaked by genetic engineering for a bizarre homeworld, or normally shaped but dripping of the evils he'd committed in his occupation of New Liberty. The only thing to make the man in front of him look foreign was a different array of insignia and unit patches on his suit. His faceplate was up to show a thin mustache, just long enough to wax and curl up the tips. Double bars at his collar, a captain. Excitement surged in Tomas. He'd captured the Uni company commander! Marchbanks would praise him for that.

The wounded Uni captain squinted and weakly raised a hand, dropping it, unable to lift it to his brown eyes. He pressed his other hand to his belly. He grimaced. "*Soy idiota, olvidando… mi poción de Leteo.*" He groaned and pressed harder at his belly.

Tomas' excitement faded. He needed to get his prize back to their lines in one piece, but more than that daunted him. The Uni captain was another man, hurt. Don't let him end up like the two scorched men in the supply vehicle. Tomas fingered his shilling. "I've found a Uni captain. He's wounded, maybe badly. I'll get him back if I can."

"Roger," Marchbanks said flatly, then dropped from the call.

Tomas looked at the Uni captain. "Can you walk?"

He gritted his teeth. "*Demasiado dolor.*"

Tomas had no grasp of Andalucian. "Do you speak Confed? *Plappern Sie Sankt-Benedikts-Sprach? Parles-tu la joséphinais?*"

The Uni captain shook his head. "*Entiendo los tres. Hable solamente Andalucían. No puedo ir.*" He shook his head again. "*Demasiado dolor.*"

Sounded like the Uni captain couldn't walk. "I'll drag you."

"*Soy una tía.*" The Uni captain grunted again, louder and more pained. He nodded and said, "*Arrástreme*" through gritted teeth.

Tomas stepped closer and crouched next to him. First, ensure the prisoner is disarmed. He took the Uni captain's pistol from its holster. Without looking away from the Uni, Tomas unzipped a pocket over the small of his back, and stuffed the pistol into it. The zipper closed most of the way, but left two centimeters of the butt exposed.

He then patted the Uni captain down for knives and hidden pistols. None. Along the way he swatted the Uni's hand away from his abdomen, and glimpsed the wound in scanted beams of the flashlight. Torn fabric, ends drenched with blood. More groans when Tomas pressed his fingers near the wound. A faint stink of shit.

Tomas sat near the Uni's right shoulder and hooked his left elbow under the man's armpit. Time to drag. He turned his shoulders to his right, rifle wavering. Slow progress, scooching on his rump half a meter at a time. The Uni groaned with each motion. Sweat beaded on the wounded man's pallid face. *"¿Veré nunca mi sol dorado?"*

Mercy and pity struck Tomas. *I should have called for help while I had a free hand.*

A few more scooches and he realized he had to call now, better late than never. Tomas let go of the Uni captain and reached for his shilling. He froze halfway.

Three meters to the right of his line of travel, a Uni with a rifle lay prone in thick grass. He too looked surprised; his rifle pointed to the side.

Tomas aimed his rifle as best he could one-handed as the Uni aimed his. Both looked over their barrels at each other, but neither moved. *Pull the trigger Tomas how hard would it be what's wrong with you—* Next to Tomas, the wounded captain cried out.

The Uni's rifle wavered. *"¿Capitán?"*

"Me rasguñan. Soy un preso de este Contrapelo."

"¿Rasguñado?" The Uni rifleman's tone revealed worry. *"¿Cómo gravemente?"*

Heart pounding, Tomas said, "No talking."

The Uni ignored him. *"Capitán, vino volverle a nuestra unidad."*

Another groan from the captain. *"Madre de dios, el dolor. No puedo ir."*

"No talking!"

"*Contrapelo. Contrapelo!*" Tomas realized the Uni rifleman spoke to him, and part of him wondered what *contrapelo* meant. "*¿Usted lo conseguirá a un médico aprisa?*"

Did *médico* mean *medic*? Tomas guessed what the Uni rifleman asked. "Our medic will treat him."

The Uni rifleman let out a long breath. "*Vaya con dios, mi capitán.*" Grass rustled. Tomas peered into the grass but caught no sign of him.

Tomas remembered why he'd stopped. He touched his shilling and said, "I need assistance returning wounded Uni captain to squad."

Johnson replied a few seconds later. "Roger. I be sending two men from my team."

Tomas dragged the Uni captain a few more times before he heard rustling from the direction of the road. His shilling overlaid onto his helmet display the names of two of Johnson's men. "Good job," one said.

"You two carry him," the other said. "I'll provide security."

Tomas reached for the Uni captain's legs. He would give the Uni rifleman a break. "All the other enemy are long gone." He and the first of Johnson's men picked up the Uni captain. He grunted and groaned as they carried him across the thick grass.

A minute later they crossed over the dirt road and soon reached an ambulance, a modified Badger stripped of armament and bearing the red cross of the medical service. They set the Uni captain down on a thin stretcher in the back of the vehicle. In a single harsh light, beads of cold sweat stood on the Uni's face. A shiver gripped him and he groaned again.

"We've got him from here," said the medic, a bearded, turbaned Ambarsari.

"Will he make it?" Tomas asked.

"He will if you let us do our job, private," the Ambarsari said. An al-Aqsan woman bustled over from a rack mounted on the front wall of the space and the two of them turned their attention to the Uni's wound. "Watch for septic shock," the medic said to the al-Aqsan woman. "If his symbiotic bacteria sense it's time to jump ship…"

Tomas left the ambulance and followed an overlay on his helmet display to his squad. He passed a human remains team pulling Uni dead from the wrecked Bismarcks and DeGaulles. They wore face shields and surgical masks, and scrunched their faces as they laid the dead into body bags. A dozen body bags already lay in a row along the roadside. A GF chaplain signed crosses over them and muttered something Tomas didn't catch.

A few more steps took him by a supply team tearing down one of the destroyed Bismarcks. Diamond blades keened and alloy hissed and popped under cutting lasers. Two men with thick gloves flung cut slabs of alloy into a truck bed.

When Tomas neared his squad, Johnson and Marchbanks stepped forward. Their helmets were up, exposing their faces, and Tomas realized he'd never opened his. He did so as Johnson spoke.

"Well done, Neumann. We should get some good intel from your captive. I and I'll talk to the lieutenant. There ought to be commendation coming your way." He angled his head, clearly listening to something in his earbuds, then hurried off to the main body of the squad.

"A commendation," Tomas said to Marchbanks. The latter looked unmoved. Tomas went on, more urgently. "The sergeant thinks I did well. You have to agree I did well."

"No, lad. I don't." Marchbanks scowled. "You got lucky. A commendation means you did something stupid and someone lived to tell the tale. You want your biggest legacy to be a medal in a display case on your mother's mantel, so she can cry every day she sees it the rest of her life?"

"I—" Tomas couldn't imagine his mother crying, not even over his corpse. And he thought back to his encounter with the Uni rifleman. "You're right."

"If we have a line on the map, don't cross it if you don't have to…. you agreed pretty quickly."

Tomas nodded, then saw Johnson about to speak to the squad. "In a minute."

Johnson spoke. "Idrin, we have new orders. We will remount

and accompany the 1st Graywolf platoon in a sweep around the right flank of the arty kill zone. If Jah be willing, we just be along for the ride. Back to our Badgers!"

The men trooped toward their vehicles. Marchbanks and Tomas were ahead of the group. "What happened out there?" Marchbanks asked quietly.

"I met a Uni rifleman." He nodded at one of their comrades. "Closer to me than Cohen over there."

"Christ! We heard no rifle fire. You bayoneted him? Christ, sometimes you have to, but that's nasty work—"

"He was trying to recover his captain, I guess. We stumbled on each other. Aimed our rifles but neither of us fired."

"Why not?"

"It didn't seem appropriate."

Marchbanks kicked at a tuft of grass. "Christ, you were incredibly lucky. Maybe some Unis are rum lads, but you can't bloody assume that. And even if they are rum lads, they're strangers to us and us to them. None of them are going to tell their grandsons what a fine sonofabitch old Marchbanks was."

"I know," Tomas said. "Maybe he did it to save his captain's life."

"Don't try to learn their motives," Marchbanks said. "Wait, where is he?"

"He wanted to make it home and I let him go."

Marchbanks shook his head bemusedly. "Lad, I know God looks out for fools and drunks.... I'm wary of saying he looks out for you."

Wary? Why would Marchbanks think he disrespected his deity? "I don't observe the gods of others, but I observe how others act out their beliefs in their gods. If you think your god protected me...."

Marchbanks' face grew solemn. "He didn't. I'm telling you, you were lucky. Once. For the love of Christ, don't let it go to your head. Whether your luck was God protecting you out of love, or some evil pagan god of war sparing you out of cruel sport, or just blind chance, is no matter. All I know is that good luck is one of the worst things that can happen to a man in his first few times in the field."

Tomas squinted at Marchbanks. "One of the *worst*?"

"Cause he'll come to believe his skills, or worse, his fate, will keep him alive through everything. There's no guarantee of survival in this for anyone. All you can do is enhance your odds of making it out of here. Remember the rules."

They approached their Badger, still hull down in a pit dug by the engineer platoon. Lt. Tower had the hatch open and talked down to Sgt. Johnson on foot, while Delacroix and MacInnis, in the back, carted fresh ammunition from one of supply platoon's vehicles. "Work with the team," Tomas said, "and keep your head down."

Keeping your head down is a lot easier when you have encouragement. Tomas sat with his back to a boulder, chest heaving and heart thudding, while Uni bullets thudded around him. Ten meters away, Marchbanks was a hazy figure in the dim light. Without his helmet display tuning the video, Tomas wouldn't be able to see him. Marchbanks crouched behind another boulder and craned his torso, apparently to scope routes uphill. Another burst of Uni fire pinged nearby and Marchbanks dropped prone.

"I don't see a way up," Marchbanks told the team. "Lads, do any of you?"

Tomas rolled onto his stomach and peered around the boulder. He was near the upper limit of the boulder field; the next hundred fifty meters of shaded hillside were bare of rocks, and bore stumps cut a hand's-breadth above the ground. The Uni defenders had stripped the hillside to deny the GF cover. His shilling overlaid the impact points of the squad's rifle fire, telemetered by their rounds, as well as probability contour maps of the source of incoming Uni fire. Two Uni machine guns nested up there, along with riflemen in foxholes and a pair of grenade launchers. A grenade had already wounded Cohen and delayed the squad's climb through the boulder field while they evacuated him.

Tomas gave the bare hillside another glance. No swells or folds of terrain to give a man enough cover. "I don't." The others echoed his words.

Marchbanks widened his connection to the squad's net. "Sergeant, we don't see any safe way up."

"Neither does my team. Hang tight, Marchbanks. I'll see what we can do."

A lull fell over their part of the battlefield. Occasionally, a Uni rifleman or grenadier would fire to keep their squad pinned down in the boulder field, and from time to time, Tomas or one of his comrades would answer.

Meanwhile, the bulk of the battalion probed apparent weak spots in the Uni defenses about a kilometer to sunright. The roar of ordnance echoed off the hills. Tomas' company had been assigned to keep the enemy occupied in their sector, on the sunleft side of the dirt road leading back to the ambush site. Being a sideshow meant expecting no support from battalion's artillery battery or the air wing's Kestrels on station high above.

"Squad," Johnson said, "they be giving us some orbital assets. A fire mission liaison be coming up soon."

Soon stretched out for fifteen minutes. The roar from the main probe to the sunright mounted in volume while they waited for the fire mission liaison. The sergeant and Marchbanks gave no word of his arrival, just directions for Tomas and the rest of the team to provide covering fire for the liaison's entry into the boulder field. A few minutes later, Tomas heard gravel crunching behind him. A glance over his shoulder showed a man in full chameleonskin coming his way. He dropped next to Tomas and peered over the top of the boulder at the Uni defenses.

"What can I do?" Tomas asked.

"It's all me, soldier." The fire mission liaison reached into a pocket for a tablet and a small wand. He played the wand in the direction of a Uni machine gun nest, then checked numbers on his tablet. The screen showed a few alphanumerics in a deep red.

More Uni fired came downslope. A grenade rocketed over Tomas' head, and shrapnel clattered off rock.

The fire mission liaison touched his shilling. "FML two-one golf to *Boyd* FCO, do you read?" His face looked attentive in the dim light from Constitution's rays refracted through the sky behind the hilltop. "Prepare to receive coordinates." His hand neared his shilling, then paused as he squinted at his tablet. "Target one, coordinates, meters neg fife oh eight seven niner two, degrees two eight niner point four eight fife fife six. Read back."

Sgt. Johnson's voice over the squad net took Tomas' attention away from the fire mission liaison. "The main attack is stalling out sunright of the road. Prepare to advance by teams under cover of orbital fire mission."

Tomas peeked around the base of the boulder at the Uni machine gun nest. A few rounds barked out. Would they know what hit them?

"Fire for effect," the fire mission liaison.

A light flashed and a boom punched Tomas and pounded his ears, a shockwave of air heated in the beam. The sound climbed toward the orbiting ship, like a rocket launching, and echoed off the hill. Electricity crackled through the air and the hair on Tomas' nape rose. He peeked at the Uni machine gun nest, expecting to see electric arcs, molten soil, vaporized men. Screams muffled by the ringing in his ears came from somewhere. How much pain could the Unis be in for him to hear them at their distance?

A chill crawled over Tomas' skin. The screams came over the squad's net.

"FML two-one golf to *Boyd* FCO, hold fire! We have friendly casualties! Goddammit, you stupid sonofabitch, we have friendly casualties!"

Tomas looked to his left. A dust cloud swirled about forty meters away. Members of the sergeant's team held that position. His shilling overlaid location and medical diagnostics on his helmet display. A yellow man-shaped icon throbbed, showing Bar-Ruda, an al-Aqsan, had been badly wounded. A dull red icon lay nearby, immobile. Voloshenko's shilling reported no vital signs.

"You need more than imped skills to do your job," Tomas muttered to the fire mission liaison.

The man set his mouth in a grim line. "Shirley Foxtrot fucked up at fire control. I gave him the right coordinates. I'll swear on all the saints I gave him the right coordinates. Now shut up and let me put photons on the damn Unis."

"Bar-Ruda and Voloshenko are down!" Sgt. Johnson shouted over the squad net. "Who's closest?"

Tomas checked his shilling. "I am."

"Go to them, Neumann. We'll cover you."

Tomas crouched and ran behind boulders. His rifle's stock banged against his shoulder with each step. His squadmates fired their weapons uphill. The Unis made no response. They had a Marchbanks too, didn't they, telling his comrades to keep their heads down? The misplaced orbital fire had warned them to take cover before the fire mission liaison and the *Boyd*'s FCO corrected their error. A few meters of soil could protect a man against a pillar of laser fire from the SF's ships.

Meters of soil Bar-Ruda and Voloshenko had lacked.

Tomas took cover behind a low boulder five meters from the crater gouged by the orbital laser. The air smelled hot and dirty. Bar-Ruda's screams hit Tomas with wrenching agony both live and through the squad net. "The medics are on their way," he called aloud, useless words. Bar-Ruda kept screaming as Tomas ran the last steps.

Bar-Ruda lay limp against a boulder near the edge of the the crater. Dirt covered him. The chameleonskin outer lining of his suit and helmet had failed in spots, leaving gray patches, and blood soaked the front of his suit. Tomas lifted Bar-Ruda's helmet. More blood flowed from his nose, mouth, and ears. Bubbles of blood burst when he opened his mouth to speak. Tomas realized his screams were harsh, guttural words, maybe some al-Aqsan prayer.

"The medics are on their way," Tomas said again. Bar-Ruda didn't seem to hear. "I'll give you painkiller." Tomas reached for his emergency medicine kit. When in doubt, numb their pain. He pulled the emergency kit from its pocket and reached for Bar-Ruda's sleeve. Fabric tore. The laser had turned dirt into shrapnel, shredding his clothes. Probably his skin, too.

Tomas pushed the sleeve up Bar-Ruda's arm. A dirty film of oozing blood covered his skin. Tomas took Bar-Ruda's hand in one of his and snapped a self-tightening tourniquet around his upper arm.

Bar-Ruda clenched Tomas' hand, painfully tight, pressing blood and soil against Tomas' skin. He screamed again, clearly a prayer. Tomas curled his feet inside his boots in powerless sympathy. *At least I can make him more comfortable.* He aimed the needle of the painkiller syringe toward a vein engorged by the tourniquet, then drove it in.

Bar-Ruda screamed twice more. Tomas shut his eyes hoping to soften the agony he heard. He could only bear so much. The painkiller soon took hold; the screams changed to a groan, then a whimper. Bar-Ruda's grip on Tomas' hand remained strong.

Tomas glanced toward the rear and checked the display on his helmet display. "The medics will be here soon." The helmet display showed them as icons picking their way through the boulder field.

Bar-Ruda whimpered in al-Aqsan.

Another look around showed Voloshenko's icon a dozen meters away, with several boulders intervening. "What happened to Voloshenko?"

Bar-Ruda took a shallow breath and gasped. He looked a little more aware of his surroundings, and spoke a few words of Confed. "Don't know. SF beam knocked me back. Can barely breathe. Can't move legs."

The same medics from the dirt road, the Ambarsari and the al-Aqsan woman, crept up. She muttered something guttural and Bar-Ruda replied in the same language. The Ambarsari reached for Bar-Ruda's collar and yanked, tearing a strip of fabric away. Bar-Ruda's chest and his shilling were reddish-brown with dirt and blood.

"Private, get him naked. I have to hemostop the whole front of his body."

Tomas nodded. Bar-Ruda's suit came off in strips over his chest and arms. His pants were stubborn; the Ambarsari cut them with a reciprocating, diamond-bladed knife. Tomas pulled the cut pants off Bar-Ruda. Blood oozed from the man's *biroute*.

"Blast overpressure. Ruptures blood vessels," the Ambarsari said. "He's bleeding in his lungs."

The al-Aqsan woman knelt and fed a clear plastic tube into Bar-Ruda's mouth. Both medics acted with precise motions. Their faces were intent and focused, but Tomas saw anguish lurking around their eyes. How many men had died in front of them?

"I'll retrieve the other," Tomas said.

"We've already triaged him based on his shilling output," the al-Aqsan woman said, voice cold. "He's lost. We can only save your man here."

"I know Voloshenko is probably dead. I won't leave him if we can help it."

She worked the tube at Bar-Ruda's mouth and her body wavered. "You stupid men and your stupid honor."

Tomas slipped away. As he rounded the next boulder, another flash of light, another hammer of air roared nearby, fading as it climbed into the sky. *Hey Shirley, am I the victim of your next error?* but being able to think those words meant he wasn't. A glance up-hill showed a bright red overlay in his helmet display marking an orbital laser impact on a Uni machine gun nest.

Behind another boulder, the icon representing Voloshenko stretched across Tomas' helmet display. Voloshenko's body wasn't there. Tomas pressed his shilling in the right spot and the overlay vanished for a moment to reveal unannotated video from his helmet-mounted cameras. Where the icon's heart would have been lay a shilling, scuffed and bloody, but otherwise intact enough to feed data into the squad net.

Where was Voloshenko? Was the shilling's report of zero vital signs an artifact of it losing contact with his body? Was he alive some-where? Tomas glanced around the nearest boulders as hope buoyed his chest.

Something lay closer to the impact site. Hope fell, leaving hol-lowness. Tomas crept closer. It didn't look like a human body, at first. The blast had badly mangled Voloshenko. His throat had been torn open and his head lolled back. His face had been ripped up from under his chin to his nose. A fly landed and scampered along the wound.

The blast had turned his shilling into a weapon, gouging his face as it flew over his head.

Tomas went closer. One of Voloshenko's eyes remained intact, staring lifelessly at the blue-black sky. Tomas sat down and moved his hand numbly to his shilling. He hadn't liked Voloshenko, but no man deserved this. "Voloshenko is dead. Separated from his shilling, at my position."

"Roger," said Sgt. Johnson. "Mark it for the human remains team."

Tomas had seen dead bodies before, but he suddenly realized the Unis didn't count. The corpses in the Uni supply vehicles had been men, yes, but strangers. Whatever his opinion of Voloshenko, Tomas knew him. Had known him. "Sergeant, I request permission to wait with him."

"No, sergeant," came Alvarez's voice. "He was my friend. Let me wait with him for human remains."

"We can both wait," Tomas said.

Another laser strike pounded the hillside above them, this one at the second Uni machine gun nest. After the echoes subsided, Marchbanks spoke. "Sorry, lads. We have orders coming through."

"That's right, idrin," Johnson said. "Link up with your teams. We be going uphill."

7

New Boston

"That's it?" Tomas said when he saw the view from the Badger's front camera after their vehicle crested the pass.

"Aye, lad. New Boston."

"We've been fighting for a couple of months to get there?"

Alvarez echoed the sentiment. "If that's what we're trying to liberate, why not let the Unis keep it?"

"Quiet back there," Lt. Tower said over the Badger's net. "All the people of New Liberty are sympathetic to the Confederated Worlds and desirous of liberation from Unity oppression."

Marchbanks and Tomas shared a disbelieving look. Yet it didn't matter whether the lieutenant believed the propaganda or lied for their sake. They knew enough to publicly acquiesce in an officer's words.

The town of New Boston had a few thousand residents, according to the GF's wiki on the planet and its settlements. Smaller even than Portage. Squat mycocrete houses surrounded a central district of taller, handbuilt buildings, a college campus, and a public square. The only charming thing about the town was its location, on a sunlit slope of a foothill of the range of hills the GF had just fought across. Tomas hadn't seen direct sunlight in weeks. He might lament the permanent late afternoon the next chance he had to sleep, but for now, he welcomed it.

The slanted rays drove his memories of dead men a little further away.

Their platoon's four Badgers followed the dirt road down from the pass into the valley where New Boston lay. The dirt road tee-ended at an asphalt road, down which, hundreds of klicks and three months ago, the Unis had ambushed them. The GF had paid the Unis back with interest since then. Tomas briefly wondered why he failed to exult over that latter fact, then let it go when their Badger turned onto the asphalt road.

Hills to sunward dappled the asphalt with uneven shadows. Further to sunward, fully shadowed at the valley bottom, a stream ran down a winding gully roughly parallel to the road. The Badger bobbed and dipped with the terrain underneath, and Tomas dozed for a few minutes.

He woke when the Badger lurched to a stop. "On alert," Lt. Tower said. "Intel says the Unis are long gone, but I wouldn't trust them with my life."

Tomas and the other infantrymen rose and slung their rifles over their shoulders without speaking. They set their suits to camouflage mode, showing mottled patterns of urban colors. They knew to enter medium alert among non-friendly civilians; they didn't need the paper tiger to tell them what to do. The ramp dropped and they tramped from their vehicle.

Their platoon's Badgers had taken up a defensive position around the center of the public square. Each of the four vehicles covered a different cardinal direction with its main gun and machine gun. Yet the defensive posture was incomplete: vehicle commanders and gunners stood in open top hatchways. Other than vehicle crews and two dozen dismounted infantrymen, no one occupied the square.

If the Unis occupied Portage, I would've stayed indoors too.

Except for intersecting streets, buildings fronted the square. In the middle of one side, lit by Constitution's rays, a mural covered a six-meter-high wall. It showed a human shape, probably male, dressed in a puffy white vacuum suit with a gold reflective face shield on its helmet. The man stood on a gray, pitted, lifeless plain, under a black sky, next to a rigid sheet on a pole. The sheet looked a little like the Confederated Worlds flag, except the white stars stood on a rectangular, not circular, blue field, in the upper left, not the center, and the red and white bands ran horizontally instead of radiating outward.

The man in the vacuum suit was not alone. The bust of another man floated in ghostly outline in the black sky behind the suited one. The ghostly figure featured narrow eyes and wavy hair in front of a nimbus of light. He gazed with serene confidence on the man in the vacuum suit.

"Is that a saint?" Obermeyer asked.

"He's a president," Tomas said. "Don't you read any briefings about the NLs?"

"I don't have to. I've got you for that." Obermeyer laughed.

"Fine. I won't answer your question." Tomas took a couple of steps away and stretched his arms overhead. A clock tower a few hundred meters away, in the direction of the college, sounded the local hour.

Obermeyer paced over. "What do you mean, you won't answer? You said he's a president. That means he isn't a saint."

"Can't the NLs think he's both?"

Obermeyer frowned, then shook his head. "On Challenger we respect the ancient presidents, but we don't worship them."

Tomas said nothing. Marchbanks squinted at the mural. "Obermeyer, d'you think we're on Challenger?"

Before Obermeyer could reply, Lt. Tower's voice echoed around the square. "Johnson, I will take Marchbanks' team into the city hall and meet the civilian authorities."

"Yes, sir. Look lively, idrin," the sergeant said. The team fell into two columns behind the lieutenant and he led them across the square.

The city hall had basalt-block walls, laser-polished to a sheen. The busts of more presidents, four of them, were carved in relief above the lintel. One bearded, another with a mustache plus rings over each eye. It looked vaguely familiar to Tomas from some ancient history class at the *lycée*.

Inside the building, a reception area greeted them. Empty chairs, blue with frayed piping and worn wooden slats on the arms. A desk bore a dark tablet. Tomas and the other soldiers swiveled their heads, looking for booby traps and hiding places. A hallway ran deeper into the building and a sign pointed arrows that direction. It took Lt. Tower a few seconds to decide the captions of the arrows read *Council Chamber* and *Mayor's Office*.

Down the hallway, they passed glass-walled offices. Lozenges of light ran along the floor, shading joints between beige tiles. Tomas peered to each side, seeing no one in visual or infrared.

The glass walls gave way to gypsum board. Tomas' heart sped up and he craned his head more. The gypsum board blocked his sight, but if a Uni lurked with a rifle, its rounds would pierce the gypsum board as if it were paper.

Lt. Tower held up his hand outside the council chamber's closed door, then raised two fingers and waved them forward. Marchbanks tapped Obermeyer and Cohen's shoulders. They nodded and padded into place. Obermeyer kicked the door open and Cohen led the way in.

"We yield up the town of New Boston," said a weary male voice from the far end of the room.

Tomas followed the rest of his team in. The council chamber reminded him a little of the briefing room at the spaceport near Reagantown. Straight rows of seats faced the town council's curved table. Yet here, instead of the seats sloping down toward the front, the floor was flat except for a dais on which the town council sat, elevated forty centimeters above the common citizens Tomas imagined coming into this room.

Behind the council table sat five people, four men and a woman. The weary-sounding man sat in the center. Purple bags puffed under his eyes and his brown hair, tinged with gray, lay disheveled on his head. All the seated council members looked exhausted. The only local in the room who showed any vigor was a tall, gaunt-cheeked man in a red turtleneck and faded blue jeans. He stood behind the weary-sounding man. He leaned forward and his hooded gaze swept over the GF men before settling on Lt. Tower.

The weary-sounding man spoke again. "I'm Mayor Schmidt. Seated here are the other four members of the New Boston City Council." He named the woman and the other three men. "Also here is Chancellor James of New Boston College."

Lt. Tower gave his name, rank, and referred to their brigade by its formal title. "As you may know, Unity infantry forces have vacated the area. In our pursuit of them, the Confederated Worlds Ground Force has taken possession of New Boston. My unit will be here for a few days to facilitate reconstitution of New Boston's political life into the provisional planetary government."

Mayor Schmidt swallowed. "We will be glad to work with you in bringing New Boston into the provisional planetary government." Behind him, Chancellor James sniffed out a breath and stretched his neck. The mayor nervously glanced in the Chancellor's direction before speaking to the lieutenant. "Please tell us what you require us to do."

"First, we will shut down the municipal fab for a few days."

"Our people won't be able to eat?" one of the seated men said. Mayor Schmidt jutted a hand toward him, palm down, and made a strangled hissing sound through his teeth.

"A team will review the fab's control system to ensure it cannot be used to fab material of military relevance."

Chancellor James leaned forward. "The Constitution is not a homicide pact," he said in a voice of settled finality.

Lt. Tower squinted at him. "Try again, in plain Confed."

Mayor Schmidt quickly said, "The Chancellor means to say the municipal fab lacks the ability to produce weapons. Planetary law."

"'Material of military relevance' includes more than weapons. Body armor, chameleonskin, armor plating for vehicles, components of target acquisition systems, and more. We'll print a full list. And no townsfolk will starve. The Ground Force will provide basic minimum rations to all civilians if the review lasts more than three days."

Lt. Tower went on. "Second, for the next forty-eight hours, residents may surrender firearms to us under a no-questions-asked policy. We'll set up a collection point in or near the square and publish and broadcast more detailed rules for the surrender."

"What happens after forty-eight hours?" Mayor Schmidt asked. A bead of sweat ran down his temple.

"After that time, possession of a firearm by a non-uniformed person will be taken as proof of irregular combatant status. Such a person has no right to prisoner-of-war status or other protections for regular combatants under interpolity law. We'll shoot him on sight."

Mayor Schmidt swallowed. "I'll tell our citizens. But don't take it as a sign of hostility if our citizens only surrender a few old hunting rifles. We don't own many firearms to surrender."

"That's because the people of New Liberty are smart enough, and loyal enough to the time-honored American spirit, to know the Constitution is a living document," the Chancellor said. "There's no need for a militia here, so the Second Amendment no longer applies. We're not the rednecks our ancestors left behind on Challenger." He gave icy stares to the infantrymen. Obermeyer, the only Challengerite among the team, scowled back.

Mayor Schmidt worked his mouth in agitation. "Lieutenant, all we mean is there aren't many firearms in town."

"That should make it simple to surrender them. Third, all offices of the town government are hereby vacated, pending a new election to be held as soon as possible. We will identify all townspeople who held positions of political authority under the Unity. Such people will be barred from holding any elected or appointed position in any town, regional, or planetary government for a period of five standard years. To be clear, that means all five of you council members."

They all looked crestfallen, but a few of them showed relief. Mayor Schmidt spoke in a measured tone. "We thank the Confederated Worlds for giving us the chance to retire to private life."

Chancellor James stood and stared at Lt. Tower. "Your logic is defective, lieutenant. The mayor and the members of the town council were elected by the people of this town. They were not given their authority by the Unity—"

"Would you be quiet?" Mayor Schmidt harshly whispered over

his shoulder.

"The will of the people of New Boston would be thwarted—"

Mayor Schmidt spun his chair around and stood, grabbing the Chancellor's shoulder. "The will of the people of New Boston is that you. Shut. Up."

"The mayor has a good point, Mr. James," Lt. Tower said. "Hate the Confederated Worlds as much as you want, but we're in charge here. All of you, go home, and await further communications from us about the municipal fab and the surrender of weapons."

"I have the college to lead," Chancellor James said. "It would shirk my duties to go home."

"All of you, clear the building." Lt. Tower's voice carried some heat. "Team, we'll follow them out."

Chancellor James went up the hallway first and gave a last, dismissive look at the mayor and council members behind him. The politicians trudged toward the reception area. "Can I clear my office?" one of them asked.

"No," Lt. Tower said. "We're locking the building until a civil affairs team arrives in a few days. Take it up with them."

The team trooped outside. Lt. Tower assigned some men to provide security, then gathered Johnson and the other sergeants to discuss how to take the surrender of firearms. "The rest of you, eat some breakfast."

Tomas looked around for Marchbanks. He angled his head toward their Badger, then led the way around it to the outside of the square. Cohen and Alvarez followed. They sat against the road wheels of the Badger's track and Delacroix tossed down their rations. The ghostly president watched them as they pressed their rations' heating buttons and peeled back the lids to let the smells of bacon and scrambled eggs escape.

"You aren't eating?" Marchbanks asked Alvarez.

He shook his head. "My rations will keep unheated for a week, right? If the town fab's down more than three days, you know the minimum ration we'll give the locals won't be much. If a local girl needs food, I'll make her a fair exchange."

"You're a master of seduction," Tomas said with dry sarcasm.

He forked scrambled eggs into his mouth. "Let me take notes."

Vehicles rolled into the square on the same road they'd taken. Tomas and the others craned their necks. Supply vehicles, trucks and refitted Badgers with St. Martin's cloaks on their front bumpers. The men slumped back against their Badger's wheels.

"Alvarez, lad, stay away from the local lassies. I've a bad feeling about this town." Marchbanks nodded at the ghostly president.

"The head of the college is attached to his desire for Unity control," Cohen said.

"He mightn't be the only one."

Tomas kept eating. He hadn't realized how hungry he was, and how enjoyable it could be to sit in open air with a hot meal and an expectation no one would shoot at you. Even the firm alloy of the road wheel digging into his back gave him a trickle of joy.

Sgt. Johnson strode around the Badger. "You be studying the local artwork? Up, idrin. We've set up the firearms surrender drop for the locals and you've drawn the first watch."

One of the supply trucks had parked between two of the platoon's Badgers. The truck's bed faced the outside of the square. The tailgate was down and the chameleon cloth rear flap had been rolled up. "Simple," Sgt. Johnson said. "See those lines?" He pointed to sprayed paint on the asphalt. The lines defined three sides of a rectangle, about the size and shape of a football goal box. The supply truck's bed was the goal. "Have them stop behind the line, lower the weapons to the pavement, and back away. Then pick them up and toss them into the truck. Supply will melt them down after that. The lieutenant be broadcasting the drop procedures right now. We should see locals soon."

The day wore on. Tomas repeatedly checked his chronometer, trying to gauge the passing time. No one came. Maybe the mayor had told the truth, and no one had firearms to surrender—

Wait. Footsteps. Dozens of them, coming toward the square from the direction of the college. Students and professors were heavily armed? Tomas shrugged. So long as they refused to back Chancellor James' bullheadedness, he didn't care.

A cool gust from darkward swept around Tomas as the crowd

entered the square. Chancellor James strode front and center. He kept his disdainful look, a look now shared by the dozens of professors and students, male and female, accompanying him. They were unarmed. Each carried only one rectangular object in their hands. The Chancellor and those nearest him reached the line and stopped.

The crowd from the college carried books.

Marchbanks took a step forward. "This drop point is for the surrender of firearms only."

"We wanted to comply with the spirit of the Confederated Worlds' order." Chancellor James stretched himself taller. "We will surrender the most dangerous weapon we possess." He tossed the book he carried toward Marchbanks' feet. Marchbanks danced away as it flopped on the asphalt. It slid and made a last quarter-turn before stopping. Tomas glanced down. *The Constitution of the United States of America 1789-2209.*

"We surrender the truth!" Chancellor James said. "The highest truth ever known by humankind! Revealed to Jefferson, Lincoln, FDR, and JFK in the sacred halls of Harvard University! Published by them on the front page of the *New York Times*!"

He turned away from the soldiers and addressed the crowd accompanying him. "A truth spurned by the Challengerites! They cling to a few of its words taken out of context to justify their tyranny, yet deny the spirit of the revelation to the presidents! They—" He jabbed a finger toward the soldiers. "—are our enemies! My fellow scholars and seekers of truth! Surrender your most dangerous weapons!"

Near the Chancellor, the crowd acted with vigor. Books spun through the air, landing near the soldier's feet. Not just copies of the Constitution, but heavier books as well, ancient history, commentaries on ancient law, and others. A few books slid past the soldiers and under the truck. One hardbound book flew into Obermeyer's shin. He hopped in place and cursed.

"They are cowards!" the Chancellor shouted. "They deny the truth yet know to cower from it!

The crowd cycled so people further back could fling their books as well. As they came up, many cast appraising looks at the soldiers' slung rifles and the Badger gunners looking out of the hatches next to their main guns. The Chancellor continually exhorted the crowd. "Cowards, I say! They will not harm a one of you!" The appraising looks faded, to be replaced with glazes of certainty as more books flew at the soldiers' feet.

When the crowd stopped flinging books, the Chancellor surveyed the people, then turned around. He sat down on the asphalt, crossed his legs like a yogi, and gave the soldiers a contemptuous look. A wave of sitting radiated out from him.

Someone in the crowd began to sing. Other voices joined in. Words about a banner, and stars? "Hey!" Obermeyer shouted. Veins stood on his neck. "That's the Challenger planetary anthem!"

"It's ours from time immemorial," Chancellor James said. "We have more right to it than do you false patriots from Challenger!"

Motion came from around the front of the truck. Lt. Tower sputtered to a stop near the soldiers. His mouth opened and his head swiveled from right to left to take in the crowd. "What's going on?"

"Civil disobedience," Marchbanks said.

Lt. Tower kept looking around. His face bore plain indecision.

Sgt. Johnson sidled closer. "We might alert Capt. Marcinkus—"

"No." Lt. Tower shook his head like a reptile shedding an old skin. He gave the chancellor a cold look. "We can resolve this on our own." He raised his voice. "Mr. James! Get your people out of the square right now!" His words echoed off the dark windows and locked doors of the buildings ringing the square.

"We have complied and will continue to comply with your broadcast rules for the surrender of weapons," the chancellor said. On the front rank, a few places to his left, a man with salt-and-pepper hair and a tweed jacket eyed Lt. Tower and, with deliberation, spat across the spray-painted line.

"You want to play it this way? I'll give you one last chance to think better of it."

Chancellor James lifted an eyebrow and said nothing.

Lt. Tower blinked a couple of times, then leaned forward with an intent expression. "You're sowing the wind." He lifted his tablet and swiped and tapped the touchscreen. Tomas glanced over and caught a glimpse of a broadcasting application's control panel. "To the residents of New Boston. Effective starting in five minutes, at eleven o'clock local time, a state of curfew is imposed on the town. All persons lacking prior approval from the GF local commander must remain indoors. Violation of the curfew is grounds for immediate arrest. Any resistance to arrest will be construed as an act of war by an irregular combatant. The curfew will remain in effect until further notice. Signed, Lt. Miles Tower, CWGF."

Glimmers of understanding lit some of the faces in the crowd. Wavering looks appeared, but glances at the Chancellor dispelled them. The crowd remained seated as the time grew closer to eleven o'clock.

"Come on, you lot, move," Marchbanks muttered.

Lt. Tower paced behind the line of soldiers and talked to himself. "Don't make us do this, Chancellor," he whispered on one pass behind Tomas. On the next, his quiet voice sounded far more bellicose. "We will tear you and your people apart and you are to blame."

The protestors will leave in time, Tomas thought. They aren't soldiers.

From a few blocks away, the college's clock tower struck eleven. The bells pealed slowly, echoing around the square. Tomas' heart pounded and he worked his dry mouth. He counted the chimes while watching the crowd for any movement. No one stirred, even when the last echoes of the eleventh chime faded from hearing.

Chancellor James gave the lieutenant an insolent look. "We appear to be in violation of the curfew."

Lt. Tower thrust his hands behind his back and walked two steps past Tomas. His right hand clutched his left wrist. The fingers of his left hand trembled, yet he kept his voice stern. "Which of your presidents said, never throw shit at an armed man?"

"Are we under arrest?"

The lieutenant turned around to face the soldiers. He brought his hands to the front of his body as he turned. "Warning shots." He paced out of the line of fire.

"You heard the lieutenant, lads," Marchbanks said. "Aim above the buildings behind this lot."

Tomas brought his rifle to his shoulder with the muzzle pointing toward the sky, then put his eye to the sight. A distant cloud scudded to darkward high in the indigo sky. A few murmurs passed through the crowd, but Tomas' peripheral vision showed everyone remained seated. *We mean this. We'll show you how much we mean this.*

"Fire!" Marchbanks said. A three-round burst rattled from each rifle. In Tomas' helmet display, telemetry streaks sliced shallow arcs over the buildings and down the sky.

His teammates lowered their rifles. Tomas did the same. His impped skills slid the fire selector toggle to safety. The chancellor and those nearest him kept their positions, and unreal calm stayed on their faces. At least some people further away showed fear. A few at the fringes of the crowd slipped away, shoulders hunched away from the mass of their fellows. Tomas suddenly realized the ones leaving now would never again oppose the GF occupation of their town, of their planet.

"Hold fast!" the chancellor shouted. A few people on the edges sat back down with guilty expressions. "From time to time, the tree of liberty must be watered with the blood of patriots. Regret that we have only one life to give for our planet!"

Lt. Tower moved between Marchbanks and Obermeyer. "Your last chance, Mr. James. Evacuate now or the blood of all these people will be on your hands!" His voice had a plaintive hint to it.

"On my hands?" Chancellor James replied. "I won't be the one to give the order. I won't be one pulling the trigger."

A sullen look formed on Lt. Tower's face. "Fire on the crowd. Not James, though." He unsnapped the flap of his holster, pulled out his pistol. He sighted down it onto the chancellor's chest. "Leave him for me."

More people fled the rear and sides of the crowd. Doubt and fear filled faces near the chancellor. Yet he himself gave the lieutenant the same contemptuous look he'd harbored all morning.

"Goddammit, you sons of bitches," Lt. Tower shouted at Tomas' team, "I gave an order!"

A few of the men raised their rifles. "It's his order," Marchbanks said. His voice sounded dull.

"They're irregular combatants," Sgt. Johnson said. "It's irie."

No, it wasn't alright, but Tomas' rifle wedged its stock against his shoulder and pointed its muzzle on the crowd. Don't lie to yourself it didn't move on its own, don't blame the skills imps either, you moved it to firing position, observe what you're doing you're going to shoot unarmed civilians... Panic clawed at the inside of Tomas' chest. He didn't set his eye to the sight this time. Maybe he would miss.

His fingertip found the fire selector toggle. It was still set on safety. He could leave it there. Lt. Tower might notice the lack of telemetry from rounds from his rifle, if he ever reviewed the data, but he wouldn't, why would he? The men around him who would fire would be enough to send the surviving members of the crowd fleeing from the square. Tomas moved his finger to the trigger and set his eye to the sight. A young man, about Tomas' age, sat there. His close-set eyes were wide and his narrow chest heaved with breaths.

I grant you life, Tomas thought.

Lt. Tower fired his pistol.

Chancellor James slumped back with pain and disbelief on his face. A woman screamed and bodies rustled at the back of the crowd. The young man in Tomas' sights showed a face contorted with fear and hate.

One of the soldiers fired his rifle, then another followed suit. Protesters fell. More people, male and female, screamed. The middle and back of the crowd broke apart, people turning and running for the square's exits. More rifle fire felled some of those fleeing. The runners sped up; one tripped over a fallen protester and sprawled face down on the pavement; another knocked over a woman with blood pouring down her arm.

More fire from some of the soldiers. Tomas returned his attention to the young man he'd spared. Where was he? There, crawling on his backside, face showing agony, one hand pressed against his belly.

Other than the dead or dying, the square soon emptied. Lt. Tower went forward, kicking the pile of thrown books aside. He stopped first at Chancellor James. The latter's wounds had stripped him of his contempt. Only pain and fear showed on his face, in the moments before the lieutenant shot him between the eyes.

Lt. Tower turned to the soldiers. "Irregular combatants forfeit prisoner-of-war protections, including the right to expect medical treatment. Come on, you sons of bitches." Tomas gaped. It seemed like a giant's cold hand grasped his legs. Icy fear froze him in place. No other soldiers moved either.

The lieutenant's pistol hand shook. "Fine. Goddammit. I'll administer the mercy shots myself." He took two steps and killed the gutshot young man. A coil of sympathy and despair knotted tighter in Tomas' gut.

When all the protesters were dead, the lieutenant looked across the square without seeming to recognize what he saw. After a time, he blinked and scowled. "You son of a bitch. You made these people throw their lives away for nothing."

He spoke to the dead chancellor? Tomas followed Lt. Tower's gaze to the president on the mural, staring down from his nimbus at the man in the vacuum suit.

"There's a three-day pass for the man to destroy his image," Lt. Tower said.

"Hell yeah," Obermeyer said. He trotted over.

"Wait!" shouted Alvarez, hurrying after.

With a scowl, Obermeyer backed him up. "This cockbiter is mine." To the image, he shouted, "You think all us Challengerites are rednecks?" He lifted his rifle and fired a burst at the president's image, then another, another. Soon he shattered the image in a haze of mycocrete dust.

When the last echoes of Obermeyer's fire faded away, an uneasy silence fell. Tomas kept his gaze on the pile of books near his feet, occasionally straying up for a hurried glimpse at one of the dead protestors. What kind of Observer did only that? He lifted his gaze and studied the bodies. It might be the cleanest way to die: a bullet destroying the brain before its hundred billion neurons had time to generate the experience of pain and death. Had Mother said that? He couldn't remember.

He stepped closer to the dead chancellor. Perhaps the cleanest way to die, but the survivors gazing on the remains could only see the jagged entry wound, the cracked skull around the exit, and the smear of gray and reddish-brown of brain tissue and drying blood. The chancellor's brown eyes stared into the sky. Tomas wavered on his feet, and his stomach clenched around the bacon and scrambled eggs, yet somehow he kept them down.

"You don't have to look, lad." Marchbanks had stolen up on him.

Tomas turned to Marchbanks and noticed the other's gaze shied away from the chancellor's corpse. Had Marchbanks fired on the protesters? Had he shot the young man in the gut? Or had he done as Tomas had and kept his rifle's safety on? A wave of acceptance flowed down Tomas' skin. Whatever Marchbanks had done had been the right thing for him to do. He would accept Marchbanks even if he had shot the young man Tomas had spared. Sympathy for his teammate filled the muscles of Tomas' face.

In response, a glimmer of hope showed on Marchbanks' features, only to vanish inward and be replaced by a gruff, avuncular expression. Tomas ached as his sympathy surrendered to sadness. Whatever Marchbanks had done, he felt he could not speak of it.

Not even to me? But then Tomas realized he could say nothing either. Admitting he hadn't fired would lead his peers who had to scorn him. *I got my hands dirty*, he imagined them saying. *Are you better than me to keep yours clean?* He knew too that those who had fired feared Tomas and any others who had refused would think of them, not as soldiers, but as monsters. Each one of them stood alone, feeling unable to share the truth with anyone.

"We each do what we feel we need to," Tomas said, and he hoped his tone would somehow communicate what he really meant.

Lt. Tower sat down. Sweat beaded his face, now pale, and his breaths came quickly and shallowly. Sgt. Johnson drew closer and hesitated. "Sir."

"What, sergeant?"

"Your orders?"

"Orders?" Lt. Tower's gaze passed over the dead protestors without showing any recognition of seeing them. "We've done enough."

Sgt. Johnson stayed near the lieutenant and wetted his lips with his tongue.

"Goddammit, sergeant, do you see any irregular combatants? They all fled."

"Many did flee, absolutely. Yet some may have simply retreated to regroup and continue operations against us."

Lt. Tower shook his head. "We won, sergeant."

"I and I strongly suggest we aggressively patrol the town to enforce the curfew. No local will be loving us any time soon. At this point, I and I submit we be committed to making them fear us."

Lt. Tower huffed a few more breaths. His head slumped into his hands. "You do it, sergeant. I'll remain with B squad here in the square. Work out with B squad's sergeant when they will relieve you...." He cocked his head and raised his hand to his ear, pressing in on his earbud. "The captain's almost here with company's supply platoon. Two kilometers sunright of town, near the intersection with the dirt road, and moving fast." He staggered to his feet and brushed the front of his suit with his hands.

A couple of minutes later, the clack of Badger tracks sounded from the streets between the road and the square. The first vehicle pulled through the gap between two Badgers already parked there. Its tracks flung nuggets of asphalt at unarmed, refitted supply Badgers behind it. They stopped in the center of the square, surrounded by the platoon's four Badgers, and a few moments later, footsteps pounded toward Lt. Tower and the men near him.

Capt. Marcinkus had wavy gray hair. His helmet faceplate was up to show a face weathered and tanned like old leather. He glanced at the dead protesters. "What happened, lieutenant?"

Lt. Tower kept his hands at his sides—standard skill, don't salute in a combat zone, apparently even Academy graduates learned that—and stood attentively. "Our standard private weapons surrender drop point was attacked by a number of irregular combatants."

The captain looked at the soldiers nearby, then stopped at the sight of Marchbanks' rank insignia. "Were you involved, corporal?"

"Yes, sir."

"The lieutenant accurately reported what happened?"

"Absolutely."

Capt. Marcinkus coughed. "The GF has encountered irregular combatants here on New Liberty before, and it will encounter more after today." He looked thoughtfully at the unarmed corpses and the heaps of books on the pavement. "We'll have to call in a human remains team from battalion. They'll be here in probably two hours. But before that." He touched his shilling. "Lt. Sigurdsdottir?"

Lt. Sigurdsdottir soon came up from the supply vehicles. She was a sturdy woman with a guileless face. "Yes, sir."

"I have some suggestions for your report on supply platoon's activities today."

"I'm listening, captain."

"By about oh-twelve-thirty, supply platoon will have stripped irregular combatant KIAs of all weapons and…." He frowned and nudged a pile of books with his foot.

"Sir," Marchbanks said, "may I suggest, 'other implements of irregular warfare?'"

"A good suggestion, corporal. Anyway, in addition to these implements of war, lieutenant, a firearm from every irregular combatant KIA will have been tossed in the recycle hopper by oh-twelve-thirty. Your report will state that?"

She looked from one to another unarmed dead protestor, then nodded slightly to Capt. Marcinkus. "It will."

"I'm glad I can rely on you, Lt. Sigurdsdottir." The captain turned his attention back to Lt. Tower. "Before we discuss future operations here in the town, I have to send away one of your men."

"Sure." Tower gave no recognition of the order's oddness.

Capt. Marcinkus looked around and raised his voice. "I need a Private Neumann."

Tomas snapped his heels together and stood taller. "Here, sir."

The captain squinted at him. "I understand you got a close look at Shirley Foxtrot's fire control—" He cleared his throat, glanced at Lt. Sigurdsdottir. "—foul-up on the dark side of the mountains?"

"Yes, captain."

"The canned spam want to cover their mistake by blaming our

fire mission liaison. Anyway, you've been summoned by the brass to a hearing on the matter in Reagantown. You'll catch the next vehicle driving to battalion headquarters, then fly the rest of the way. Lt. Sigurdsdottir, get him on the next outbound vehicle."

"Yes, captain." She gave Tomas a firm look. "Grab your pack and wait with my team."

"Yes, Ma'am." Tomas looked around, unclear what had just happened. *Reagantown? A hearing?*

Marchbanks stepped closer and nudged him with his elbow. "Your luck is holding, lad."

"Luck?"

"You get two days traveling back and forth, plus as long as the hearing might take. That gets you at least one night in a soft cot at the spaceport."

Tomas saw the downside of his summons. "I don't want to get involved in a hearing. Brass? What—"

Marchbanks put on a wry smile. "Och, lad, you've nothing to fret. Both our brass and Shirley Foxtrot's have their minds made up about what happened, and who's at fault. Whatever they decide will come out of a back room you'll never see. Just keep your head down and say 'I don't recall' until they dismiss you."

"But…." Tomas' gaze wandered to the dead protesters, then shied away. His earlier thoughts came back to him. He wanted to let Marchbanks know he accepted him. "I'd rather be here, part of the team."

Marchbanks swallowed once, then put on another smile. "Sorry, lad, you're stuck basking in our envy." He bumped Tomas' shoulder with his fist. "Now get going. Just promise me one thing."

"I'll say 'I don't recall.'"

"Oh, that too." He grinned, but the expression failed to reach all the way into the muscles of his face. "More important than the hearing: say hello to the Daughters at the spaceport for me."

8

Reagantown

Tomas checked the shine on his shoes and the buttons of his gray dress uniform for the tenth time when the door creaked outward. A military policeman stepped into the doorway. "Come with me, private."

He rose from a worn leather chair and in two steps left the room. The MP led him down a hallway. The soles of their dress shoes clacked on the tile floor. The two men turned a corner and a closed door waited at the hallway's end.

"The tribunal is seated on your right," the MP said. "Salute, give your name, rank—"

"I know what to do."

The MP showed surprise. "The skills imps have updated what they implant. Good. In you go." He opened the door and Tomas stepped through.

In front of a Confederated Worlds flag, and flags of the two branches flanking it on shorter staffs, five people sat at a long wooden table with thick square legs. SF dress blue outnumbered GF dress gray by three to two, although the highest-ranked officer was a GF colonel seated at the center, clearly presiding over the lieutenant colonels and majors of both branches sitting to his sides. Tomas reported to the tribunal. Flesh shifted against seats elsewhere in the room and the colonel raised a grizzled gray eyebrow in that direction before speaking to Tomas. "Take a seat in the witness box, private." He pointed to the far side of the room.

As Tomas went to it, he glanced around. Plain beige gypsumboard walls above a dark wooden wainscot. Two tables to his left. Behind one sat the fire mission liaison and a GF captain with a bookish demeanor. Behind the next—

Lucien LaSalle. He looked to be struggling to keep a solemn expression on his face, but a ghost of a smile touched the corners of his mouth when his gaze met Tomas'. Tomas knew that expression from years in Portage: a blind self-assurance that his peers from his town would fall into place and support him. Tomas kept his face impassive and entered the box.

Another MP, a pale, black-haired woman, approached Tomas. "Raise your right hand. Do you swear to tell the truth, the whole truth, and nothing but the truth, in full view of the officers and enlisted personnel in this room, any god or gods you may worship, and your own conscience?"

"Yes."

The MP went to the side of the room. The colonel leaned forward and cleared his throat. "Captain, your witness." He checked his chronometer. "You have thirty minutes."

"Thank you, colonel." The GF captain stood and came out from behind his table. "Private Neumann, before we discuss the incident that took place on 27th April 3011, I will ask you some formal questions to ensure the record is clear. Have you met any member of the tribunal before?"

Tomas swept his gaze across the tribunal's faces. "No."

"Have you met me or my SF counterpart before?" He gestured at a SF major with thick-lidded eyes and an imperious air, seated next to Lucien at the second table.

"No."

"Have you met Corporal Scobee before, and if so, under what circumstances?" The captain gestured at the fire mission liaison.

"Yes. On 27th April, before and during the incident."

"Finally, have you met Lieutenant LaSalle before?"

Near the tribunal's table, a transcriptionist tapped and swiped her tablet with solid strokes of her fingers. Tomas waited for the sound of her data entry to die down. "Yes."

The captain double-took. "You have? Under what circumstances?"

"We grew up together in Portage-du-Nord, on Joséphine."

The captain looked at Tomas with a gimlet eye. "Now, I must ask you a very important question. Despite knowing Lt. LaSalle, can you impartially and truthfully answer the questions I will soon ask you about the incident, and Lt. LaSalle's counsel will ask you after that? May I remind you, you swore an oath to tell the truth, so if you cannot answer our questions about the incident truthfully, you're obliged to tell us that now."

"Objection, leading the witness," Lucien's counsel said.

The captain bowed his head. "Let me rephrase. Private Neumann, despite growing up with Lt. LaSalle, can you impartially and truthfully answer questions about the incident of 27th April?"

Behind his table, Lucien watched Tomas with a glimmer of co-conspiracy. Of course you'll say you can, Tomas imagined him thinking, but I know you'll look out for your own.

Smug self-absorbed Josie. Your ancestor's name is on the founder's monument in Couronnement and you think that compels every *joséphinais* to lie for you? There's a man dead and another in the healing vat because someone fouled up, and those men have something you never will: a GF shilling.

Tomas would lie the other way. He would spin his answers to pin the blame for the incident onto LaSalle. See if you can win election to the Chamber of the People after serving out the war under a cloud.

But before he could answer the GF captain's question, another presence welled up inside the part of Tomas' mind where his models of other people dwelled. Not Marchbanks, not even his mother. Instead, a brown-haired man with disappointment turning down the corners of his mouth. His father. Tomas imagined him saying a man was better off serving a higher truth than lying for a petty gain.

Tomas drew in a breath and sat straighter. "I can and I will."

Lucien kept a hint of a smirk on his face. *He still thinks I'll lie for him.* Tomas no longer felt anger; now, instead, he felt pity.

The GF captain walked back to his table and picked up a tablet. "Very well, private. Now let's talk about the incident of 27th April. You already stated you met Cpl. Scobee that date?"

"Yes."

"That meeting was during action between your company and elements of the 2nd Nueva Andaluciano Regiment of the Unity Army?"

"I only knew at the time they were Unity Army. It was my understanding from my platoon lieutenant and squad sergeant they were from that regiment."

"Thank you for your precision." The next few questions rehearsed the situation in the hour before the misplaced laser fire. Tomas answered as best he could recall.

"After rangefinding the Unity machine gun emplacement, did Cpl. Scobee make radio contact with a fire control officer on the CWSFS *Boyd*?"

"Yes."

"How do you know that?"

"I was within a couple of meters of him. I could hear his side of the conversation."

"When he made radio contact, did he relay a set of coordinates to the fire control officer on the *Boyd*?"

Tomas thought for a moment. "He gave a series of numbers."

"A series of numbers." The captain lifted his tablet. "Was that series of numbers 'meters neg fife oh eight fife niner two, degrees two eight niner point four eight fife fife six?'"

Tomas squinted, trying to remember. This wasn't one of Madame Martin's quizzes, he realized. There was no right answer, only the truth. "I don't recall."

"Did the FCO on the *Boyd* read back that series of numbers to Cpl. Scobee?"

"I don't recall."

"Was there any further conversation between Cpl. Scobee and the FCO on the *Boyd* before the beam inflicted friendly casualties?"

"I don't recall."

The captain arched an eyebrow. "You don't recall either of those? You were under cover behind the same boulder as Cpl. Scobee, yes?"

Tomas' nape felt sweaty. "After Cpl. Scobee gave the series of numbers to the *Boyd*'s FCO, there was a lot of chatter on the squad net. I had to pay attention to my squad."

"Very well. What was Cpl. Scobee's demeanor after the beam inflicted friendly casualties?"

Tomas thought. "He was very angry. He called the *Boyd*'s FCO to hold fire."

"Thank you, private." To the tribunal, the GF captain said, "Nothing further for this witness."

The colonel took notes on his tablet, then looked at Lucien's table. "Major?"

"Thank you, colonel." The major slid back his chair and gave Cpl. Scobee and the GF captain a haughty look. Tomas pressed his lips together in disapproval, and steeled himself to face the same disdain from the major; but the major turned a congenial expression to him.

"Private, thank you for taking the time to talk to us today. First, I'd like to make sure I understand your account of the incident...." The major spent the next few minutes rehearsing Tomas' answers to the captain's questions. Tomas puzzled about the repetition, until Marchbanks' parting advice came back to him. They would talk, he would answer, and soon it would be over.

"You said Cpl. Scobee acted angrily after the beam struck the coordinates he communicated to Lt. LaSalle?"

"Objection," the captain said. "The question implies it's settled that the error arose on Cpl. Scobee's part."

The major studied the tribunal for a moment, then raised his hand. "Colonel, allow me to rephrase the question. Private Neumann, you said Cpl. Scobee acted angrily after the beam struck?"

"Yes."

"How else did he act after the beam struck?"

Tomas thought back. "He said something like, 'I swear I gave him the right coordinates.'"

Lucien perked up as the major went on. "In other words, he acted defensive? Guilt-ridden? Remorseful?"

Tomas assayed his memory as accurately as he could. "He recognized the situation as a grave one."

The major's affable demeanor flickered for a moment, but returned before he spoke. "Would that recognition suggest to you that Cpl. Scobee knew he had erred?"

A motion at the table drew his gaze. Lucien tightly closed his mouth and made a small churning motion with the fingers of his left hand. Come on, help me out, Tomas read in the gestures. Yet he had sworn an oath. "No," Tomas said.

"To be clear, are you saying you're certain Cpl. Scobee believed he was blameless?"

"I don't know what his thoughts were either way."

"All you can say is, Cpl. Scobee said, 'I swear I gave him the right coordinates?'"

"Yes."

"Alright. I have one last question." The major went to his table and picked up a tablet. "You previously said you don't recall if Cpl. Scobee gave to Lt. LaSalle the coordinates—" He read the numbers from the tablet. "Has anything in the past few minutes happened to jog your recollection?"

"No."

"Anything at all?" the major asked. Lucien made the same churning motion with his left hand, as small as before but faster.

The captain spoke from the other table. "Objection, asked and answered."

The colonel's voice rumbled. "Sustained. Make your point, major."

"Let the record show the witness offered no testimony supporting the corporal's claim to have read to Lt. LaSalle the coordinates generated by the rangefinder app on the corporal's tablet. No further questions at this time."

The colonel made more notes. Head still down, he said, "Do either of you want to keep Private Neumann on base until this hearing is closed?"

The major and Lucien shared a look, then the major spoke to

the tribunal while Lucien looked properly reticent. "We reserve the right to reask certain questions to which the witness answered he could not recall during this session."

To the captain, the colonel said, "Any objection?"

"None," the captain said. "Though I would remind everyone present that any willful meeting with Private Neumann, whether to discuss the subject of this hearing or not, would be a violation of the witness tampering statute of the Confederated Worlds Code of Military Justice."

The major slapped his hand on his table and turned a withering glare on the captain. "Are you impugning the ethical standing of a Space Force officer and a member of the Confederated bar?"

The captain stared back, face calm. "If you would never do such a thing, major, then no, I am not."

"Keep the trash talk on the playground," the colonel said. "Private, we may summon you to return here with as little as thirty minutes' notice between oh-eight-hundred and seventeen-hundred over the next three days. So don't lose both your shilling and your tablet in a craps game or at the Daughters. Dismissed."

Three days with nothing to do? Tomas left the hearing room in pleased bewilderment. He returned to his tiny room in the base's temp quarters. He pulled the bed down and sat at the foot of it, his knees almost brushing the wall. Marchbanks would doubly envy him. He sent Marchbanks a text message, then shucked his dress uniform for a garrison cap and plain gray-green fatigues, and set off.

The base at Reagantown had amenities far beyond those at brigade headquarters. Rock climbing walls, a fifty-meter swimming pool, a billiard room with two dozen tables, and a chess club with open games every half hour, plus seven restaurants each devoted to a particular planet's cuisine.... yet even as he drifted through these diversions, something nagged at Tomas. Marchbanks didn't reply to his message after three hours, which was part of what nagged him. Was the squad in a real fight, against irregular combatants armed with more than just books and an urge for martyrdom? Had Marchbanks been hurt? Or worse? Yet more bothered Tomas, and he couldn't articulate what.

It was in that troubled mood that Tomas made a chance encounter in the mostly unoccupied billiard room. As he walked in, an armored grenadier private near the door played a solitaire game, poorly. "*Scheisse.*" The cue thunked against other balls in a side pocket. He rapped his knuckles on his temple. "*Halt das Spielball aum Tisch.*"

Tomas stopped. "*Kommen Sie aus Sankt-Benedikts-Welt?*" Do you come from Sankt-Benedikts-Welt?

"Yeah," the other soldier replied in Sankt-Benedikts-Sprach. "You too? Where on Sankt-Benedikts? I can't place your accent."

"I mostly grew up on Joséphine. We went there when I was very young. I don't remember Sankt-Benedikts-Welt at all." A thought quickened his heart. "Maybe a few things from there. An oak tree, and Sankt-Benedikts-Stern casting a golden light."

The other frowned. "Golden sounds off. I'd call it orange."

Tomas' mood fell even further. "Maybe I'm misremembering. I was very young."

A shrug. "We all see the worlds through our filters." Tomas prickled—he was an Observer, he saw the worlds as they were. He eased when he realized the other's statement about filters was a filter of his own.

The other gestured at the constellation of balls on the green felt. "Care for a game?"

The next day, in the early afternoon, Tomas found himself near a restaurant named Maison DuBois when he realized he hadn't yet had lunch. Constitution's slanted rays through the front windows and the glass door lit up an interior of honey-brown carved wood. Curious, he stepped in. A chime rang at the top of the door. From a stool behind the counter roused the proprietor, a rotund civilian with a trimmed mustache and swept-up hair. "*Bonjour,*" the proprietor said, hello.

"*Bonjour, Monsieur DuBois,*" Tomas replied. "*Es-tu de Nouvelle-Québec ou Joséphine?*"

The proprietor smiled. "I'm from Joséphine," he replied, "just like you."

"How could you tell?"

"Nouvelle-Québeckers still use *'vous'* when talking to strangers."

Tomas bowed his head. "Of course."

"So where on Joséphine are you from, Private—" The proprietor squinted at the nameplate on the front of Tomas' fatigues, then shrank back, looking faintly puzzled. "Neumann?" He pronounced it *New-maw*, with a ghost of an *n* at the end.

"My family moved to Joséphine when I was very young. We settled in Portage-du-Nord." The proprietor's eyes widened at the words. "You know Portage?" Tomas asked.

The proprietor coughed and slapped his chest with his palm. "Portage? I'm from, ah, near there."

"Where? I didn't travel much as a kid, but I've been to Bois d'Orme half a dozen times."

The proprietor's arms spread in regret and his face relaxed. "I'm from the other direction. Sainte-Therese-la-Petite-Fleur."

Tomas dimly recalled that town from his bus ride to Couronnement upon his enlistment. "What led you to leave? Your pardon if I'm prying."

The proprietor waved off any need for Tomas to be pardoned. "There were things I had to do as a man that I couldn't do back home."

"I understand completely," Tomas said. He'd probably reminded the proprietor more than enough of Joséphine. He studied the chalkboards on the wall behind and above the counter. "What do you recommend?"

The proprietor relaxed further. "*Soupe à l'oignon* and a *croque-provençal*. With my compliments." Tomas nodded and the proprietor tapped on a tablet. Dishes clanked and hot water hissed in a room behind him. Yet despite giving Tomas a free lunch, the proprietor seemed diffident, especially considering the restaurant was otherwise empty. Or was that Tomas' own down mood coloring his perception? In either event, Tomas gulped down the soup and grilled sandwich, and only paused to beam a few Confed dimes to the restaurant's tip box before leaving.

Perhaps the Daughters would liven his mood? Their salon here was far more ornate than the one at brigade headquarters. Lace curtains covered dormer windows in the mansard roof. The foyer was five times larger, and next to the donation tablet, a life-sized statue of the goddess rested on a plinth. Her dilated *vulve* was at eye level and aimed at the front door.

The excess carried through the salon, and after a Daughter took his hand, upstairs. The carpets felt like maroon sponges under his feet; atomizers puffed floral scents every few meters in the hallway; the bed changed firmness at the Daughter's voiced commands. She activated some downtempo electronic music—he raised his hand. "Please don't play that. I'm an Observer. I avoid recorded images and sounds."

The Daughter angled her hips and put on a faux-naïve look. "I didn't know. Music, off." She snapped her fingers.

She stripped, stripped him, pulled him to the bed. Her long blond hair had dark brown roots, and her breasts felt oddly firm. "You work so hard out there, defending us from the Unity," she said breathily in his ear. "Lie back and let me do the work."

He did. She flung her leg over his and mounted his *biroute*. Her hips bucked and she worked her hand through her hair, eyes heavily lidded, a constant flow of moans from her mouth. Artifice. The act meant nothing to her, Tomas realized. He accepted that, but her pretense of arousal and surrender annoyed him. He lay with his hands on her hips as she bucked faster and faster. Finally she drew out his orgasm.

He said a few polite words and left. His down mood dogged him through the rest of the day and into his bed.

He found himself on the square in New Boston. The young man was in his sights again. Tomas' heart thudded and his finger slid the fire selector to safety.

"Och, lad, I'm stained with blood," Marchbanks said from his side. "Don't you want to be part of the team, by staining yourself too?"

Tomas turned to Marchbanks, but it wasn't Marchbanks. A brown-haired man with a narrow jaw stood there. "Father?"

"Over here," came from the young man's place. There sat the brown-haired man. *How could he be in both places?* and then Tomas woke up to rain tinkling the window.

He stayed in his room that morning and wrote another letter to his mother.

I trust my previous message reached you. All is well. I continue to combine service in the Ground Force with the maintenance of your standard of behavior for an Observer. The censors would probably take out the next lines. *Our campaign against the Unity Army here on New Liberty goes well. We should have them mopped up shortly and be available to press the war against the Unity on another front.*

He watched raindrops creep down the window. A far cry from the sunny day in his memory, under the oak with his father. *As I mentioned last time, I have memories of a man I assume was my father. I remember a sunny day on some world other than Joséphine. I have assumed it was Sankt-Benedikts-Welt, but I met a Benedikter the other day who described Sankt-Benedikts-Stern in a way that makes me think my memory is not of our homeworld after all. Before Joséphine, and while my father was alive, did we stay on some other planet?*

Tomas pondered more things to say, then shook his head and jabbed the *send* button. She would respond, or more likely not, and nothing could make her reply. He watched a transport shuttle make its landing burn toward the spaceport. The rain smeared his view of the shuttle's fusion exhaust.

His tablet chimed with a request for a video call. It came from the tribunal's clerk. Tomas sat upright and pressed *answer*.

"Private Neumann? The tribunal has no further questions for you."

"You mean they reached a decision?"

The clerk shook his head. "I can't tell you that. However, it does appreciate your testimony. I'll send you orders to return to your unit."

The clerk ended the call, and moments later, the orders arrived on Tomas' tablet. Report to the airfield, departure at oh-ten-twenty—Tomas quickly packed and hustled through the drizzle to the airfield. No one lingered outside, but at several places along his route, knots of personnel stood in doorways or under awnings, conversing with guarded faces.

Had something happened? He reached the airfield and found the Bluejay due to take him back to the Blackjacks' headquarters. Two other men had already boarded, a scout and an engineer. Their faces showed a heated discussion.

"It makes no difference," the engineer said. "The NLers won't answer the guerrillas' call."

"I don't know if the enemy story is accurate or not," the scout responded. "But I know if the Unity were occupying Nuevo Nuevo León, and there were reports, true or false, they desecrated a shrine to the Virgin of Guadalupe, tens of thousands of locals would take up arms against them."

"What happened?" Tomas asked.

"You haven't heard?" the scout said. "It's on the home page of *Stars and Rays*," the armed forces news site.

"I've been enjoying some liberty. Haven't bothered reading it."

"Liberty's going to end for all of us in a hurry." The scout checked Tomas' armored grenadier insignia and the Blackjacks' patch on his sleeves. "For you most of all."

"You're overreacting," the engineer said.

Tomas pulled his tablet out, then stowed his pack. After strapping in, he called up *Stars and Rays*. The headline read *Pro-Unity NL Leaders Call For Civilian Volunteer Militia*.

He read more as the Bluejay lifted off. A group calling itself the Provisional Free Government of New Liberty had issued a communiqué. Citizens could not rely on the Unity Army to protect them from the Confederated Worlds forces. Among its evidence, the communiqué pointed to a massacre and desecration at New Boston.

Tomas sat straighter and followed links to a page with photos. His first response turned his head away, but he set aside his hesitation. You could see a photo of something you'd already seen in real life, couldn't you? Not a violation of Observer precepts.

And what he would see couldn't be worse than his memory.

He opened his eyes. It showed dead protesters—he could make out the young man he'd spared, and Chancellor James as well. He thought about the angle of view. Perhaps with a zoom lens from a high building on the college campus? Taken in the few hours between the killing of the irregular combatants and cleanup by the human remains team. An extreme zoom showed a grainy image of a woman's face, her forehead caved in by Lt. Tower's mercy shot. The communiqué alleged *unarmed civilians were executed in cold blood.*

A cold feeling washed down Tomas' body. One zoom lens. The cold feeling heightened. Sgt. Johnson had been right. Pressing the fleeing protesters would have killed or broken the resistance of all of them. Instead, the platoon had dithered, giving one survivor time and space to make a world of trouble.

Images of our presidents were desecrated as well. The next photo showed the president, his face crumbled to powder, looking down on the man in the vacuum suit in the mural Obermeyer had vandalized.

Tomas returned to the main story about the communiqué. The Provisionals called upon New Liberty's citizens to form militia units to resist the Confederated Worlds.

Tomas mused for a moment. Even if the scout were right about the number of volunteers, the NLers only had a few hunting rifles and other hand weapons, and the only skills to use them they would have acquired the hard way, through long practice, one mind at a time. So he saw where the engineer had come from in the argument. Perhaps the scout worried because he was most lightly armed and most likely to blunder into those few rifles. Even with only a hunting rifle and poor training, an NLer could still kill a soldier.

He read on, and his minor concern grew like a malignant cyst. The Provisionals had set up stations to broadcast fab blueprints for heavy weapons, including copies of the Unity Army's fighting vehicles. They also broadcast instructions for implanting soldiering skills using the general purpose civilian implantation machines found in most schools. More than hunting rifles and poor training would oppose the GF.

Tomas set the tablet down and watched the passing landscape through the video displays mounted above the seats in the Bluejay's cabin. If the Provisionals got just one percent of the locals to join the militia, that meant twenty thousand people. The surviving Unity Army regiments had less than that. The Blackjacks' work wouldn't be over anytime soon.

He blinked and images from his dream fleeted across his mind's eye. There was one bright side. If the NL volunteers carried rifles, there would be no question whether they were innocent civilians or irregular combatants.

9

Strategic Redeployment

"Why the hell are we running?" Obermeyer said over the squad net. "We had the Unis by the scrotes, and now we let them go?"

"Can't say I particularly want to grab a Uni's testicles," Alvarez said, "but I don't care what floats your boat."

"Fuck you."

"Save the chatter for after we've been relieved," Sgt. Johnson said. "Right now, we be on watch."

Tomas lay behind a long, low dirt mound tufted with soybean plants and squinted against Constitution's bright disc in front of him. The Blackjacks had already traveled five hundred kilometers to sunright from New Boston as part of a 'strategic redeployment' ordered by the GF commanders on planet. They had hundreds of klicks further to go. A few kilometers sunright of a small town, their company had pulled to the side of the main road for a night of sleep and vehicle maintenance.

The low sun cast long shadows of a forest of maples and elms toward them across the soybean field. Tomas' team occupied a slight elevation, maybe five meters higher than a meandering creek dividing the soybean field from the forest. Distant birds chirped and a breeze rustled soybean leaves in their rows.

Two hundred meters to darkward, the platoon's Badgers backed up Tomas and his mates with heavy machine guns and lidar surveillance. Mechanics shouted and revved power tools as they did simple maintenance in place.

Long days of travel weighed down Tomas's eyelids. He squeezed shut his eyes and shimmied his head to stay awake. Just a few hours. Probably nothing will happen—

A distant blip on the creek's far bank, at Tomas' eleven o'clock, flickered on his helmet display, then vanished.

Tomas squinted, then reached for his shilling to call up more information on the blip. A lidar unit on one of their Badgers had registered a walking human with 40% confidence for less than a second.

"Anyone else see that blip?" he asked over the squad net.

"What blip?" said Obermeyer.

"I and I saw it." Johnson paused. "I and I'll call the mechanics to check out the lidar units."

"There's obviously no one there," Sharma said. "Chameleonskin doesn't block lidar."

Tomas peered forward over the sights of his rifle. Sound and motion pulled his attention up to the flapping wings of a passel of birds rising from the forest and wheeling in the sky above.

He spoke in the squad net. "Spooked birds at my one o'clock, three hundred meters."

"Birds?" Obermeyer asked. "We're not here to watch the wildlife."

"Shut up and listen," Marchbanks said.

Tomas peered at the forest, looking for motion. Maybe Obermeyer would hassle him for jumping at shadows, but in the Badger's rear compartment there had been a lot of quiet speculation about the New Liberty militia, *mike* from the phonetic alphabet word for the *m* of *militia*. He would take no chances.

"Nothing," Obermeyer said after a time.

"I told you, Neumann," Sharma said, "if mike's in the forest, he has fab blueprints for chameleonskin. The lidar would pick him up."

"Keep your eyes open, lads." Marchbanks' tone silenced the chatter. "If mike's there in chameleonskin, you might see side-angle distortions."

Tomas kept watching the edge of the forest. The low sun made him squint. Would he be able to see any distortions against Constitution's glare?

He squinted again. A hundred meters away, a couple of soybean plants rustled with a passing breeze. But how had the breeze left the other plants in that row, and in the rows nearby, unruffled?

"What if they aren't in chameleonskin?" Tomas said into the squad net.

"We'd see them, Josie." Alvarez spoke with annoyance.

The low sun seemed to blur for a moment. Was that a man's shape passing in front of it?

Tomas' cheeks grew clammy as he remembered the physics printout he'd skimmed in the hours before he'd met Capt. Schreiber. "Not plain fabric. Not even camouflage. Fiber optic wrap?"

Cohen shouted, "Motion at a row of soybeans, my twelve o'clock, twenty meters!"

"The sun's in your eyes," Obermeyer said. "There's nothing—"

Small arms fire barked at a spot down the line. From Obermeyer's position. And Tomas knew the sound: the Unity's standard issue rifle. A red icon throbbed dully at the side of Tomas' helmet display, coming from Obermeyer's position.

"They're wrapped up head to toe in optical fiber!" Tomas shouted. He slid the fire selector toggle and fired a burst at the direction of the movement he'd seen. He swept the muzzle across twenty degrees of arc, firing more bursts. Cohen fired as well. "It's wrapping light, including lidar, around their bodies!"

Another lidar blip, and more Unity rifle fire sounded, roughly parallel with Tomas. Mike was already in the line!

Tomas rolled over with a panicked expectation a rifle muzzle was aimed at his head. No one there. He forced himself to draw a breath. Without sunlight in his eyes, he'd be able to see the distortions resulting from the placement of optical fibers around a mike's body. Tomas returned to his belly and crawled three meters to his right to confuse any mike who might have been watching his position.

There: a wave of distortion shifted into position behind a row of soybeans. A thin distorted line with a dark round tip emerged from between plants and aimed at Tomas' former position—

Tomas fired two bursts at the man behind the wrapped rifle. "They have a bead on our initial positions!" he shouted into the squad net. "Move!"

He scrambled a few more meters down the row of soybeans. Dust wormed in between his collar and his helmet and he fought down a cough. More rifles fired up and down the squad's line and he felt faint relief they were all GF issue. From his new position, he glimpsed the mike who'd targeted him. The rifle, dimly visible as a line of distortion, lay slanted down the front of the dirt mound the mike had used for cover. Most of the mike's body remained shrouded by fiber optic wrap, except for jagged tears at the shoulder and head. Blood soaked the soil under him.

Tomas' helmet display needlessly showed telemetry from where his rounds had struck flesh.

Tomas caught his breath for a moment. Another dull red icon had appeared in his helmet display. Sharma. Dammit. But telemetered hits showed four mikes had already been killed or wounded. Mike's plan had failed. Time for him to turn tail and run off with hopes the GF couldn't track him.

But if mike was in retreat, why was he singing? The same song the protesters had sung came from a voice thirty or forty meters from Tomas. He aimed his rifle and fired in that direction. Someone else fired at the singer too. Neither Tomas nor his squadmate hit through the soft cover of soybeans and chameleon cloth; the singer kept on. His voice added a mocking lilt.

From the other side came more voices, but these did not sing. "Remember New Boston!" someone shouted, and echoes of "New Boston!" and "Martyrs for the Constitution!" came from nearby. A glance showed distorted figures running over the uneven terrain of the soybean field at Marchbanks.

Tomas fired at the running men, three bursts. One of their rifles swung wildly but remained in hand, and telemetry showed one of his rounds had been stopped by a body armor layer under the mike's fiber optic layer Tomas reached for a fresh magazine and his shaking hands jammed it into his rifle.

Bursts of fire came from Marchbanks. The mikes' rifles tumbled to the ground, and Tomas' helmet display reported all three had been hit.

"You okay?" he called to Marchbanks over the squad net.

"Those crazy mikes. What in the bloody hell were they think—"

From the edge of the soybean field came a shrieking sound. A missile streaked by, roaring in Tomas' ears and making him duck. Two more missiles followed. Tomas glanced back. The missiles pitched up. Their new flight path took them over the line of Badgers behind them toward fighting vehicles undergoing refit and crew rest. Sgt. Johnson shouted an alarm into the platoon net as the missiles pitched down and banked for the thinner rear armor of the vehicles. Explosions erupted from a Badger and a Graywolf.

"Sir, we need intel on mike," Sgt. Johnson called to Lt. Tower. "I and I suggest call a bird to give us some visuals and infrared."

Lt. Tower sounded like a dull knife. "Roger. Making the call."

"Keep your eyes open, lads," Marchbanks said. "Sergeant, the Badgers ought to pepper the field with their thirteens. It will get mike on his belly. If he's wrapping light around him, we'll see through him to the ground and getting something better to shoot at."

"Good call," the sergeant said. "Idrin, on your bellies too. We don't want mike to see what a thirteen can do from your example."

Tomas squirmed into the soil. The machine guns on the Badgers rattled out rounds. He slid the fire selector to single shot to save ammunition, and peered into the soybean field for distortions or shadows. He fired at phantoms and tricks of light. His telemetry showed no hits.

Overhead, an aircraft's wings beat. Eight distant icons of enemy appeared in his helmet display at the edge of the soybean field. Four or five more mikes had already crossed the creek and were slipping into the woods. The Badgers banged out more rounds. One of the mikes at the edge of the field tumbled and the rest scrambled across the creek.

"We're holding here, men," Lt. Tower said. "Dismounts from

the other platoon will passage our lines and conduct pursuit operations."

A few minutes later, the pursuit force went forward. Tomas' squad's net carried echoes of words spoken to the pursuers. "Godspeed." "Go get 'em." Muffled replies followed. Tomas held out his hand and shook a pursuer's. "Stay safe."

"You too."

What could go wrong back here? Before Tomas could think of anything more to say, the other man had taken a couple of steps and become a vague ripple of chameleonskin against the backdrop of the forest.

Sgt. Johnson ordered the squad to search the field for dead mikes. Tomas and the others went forward in silence, broken by the thrash of boots kicking soybean plants, and comments on finding the dead. "Hey songbird, you cockbiter," Alvarez said. "I got you for Obermeyer."

Tomas found the man he'd killed. Faceplate shattered, shoulder torn, he levered him up with the muzzle of his rifle and flipped him onto his back. Flies buzzed at the disturbance. Tomas knelt and studied what he could see of the dead man through the faceplate. Man? How young was he? The skin around his undamaged eye was pale and smooth, as if he'd spent all his brief life indoors.

I don't blame you for doing what you think you had to. Tomas felt mild pity. A wave of numb regret soon washed the pity away. A shame he and this dead mike could only meet this way. *Better you than me* soon followed. Tomas sought more words to define his thoughts, but Marchbanks' voice over the squad net distracted him.

"You whoreson. Were these your sons? You threw your own sons into battle? May God damn you to hell and the devil make you his catamite."

Tomas gave the dead mike a final glance, then went to Marchbanks. Marchbanks was his teammate, not a stranger, and alive, not dead. Moral circles can only stretch so far. He stepped over soybean plants and stopped alongside Marchbanks.

He silenced his shilling. "You alright?"

Marchbanks nodded his chin at the three dead mikes near him.

"Such a damned stupid waste."

Their helmets had been pulled off. Pain and surprise were frozen on their slack faces. One looked familiar. Had he been one of the sullen faces watching the company's passage through the small town up the road? They all looked young to Tomas. "Maybe a high school—"

"Father or teacher, he's still a whoreson." Marchbanks jabbed his rifle's muzzle at one of the dead mikes. He pressed down, lolling the dead man's head, then pulled his rifle back. A dull, distant look formed on his face.

Cohen came up. "Are you alright, Marchbanks?"

"Bloody hell, why's everyone asking me that?" A breath sloughed from Marchbanks. After a moment, he fingered his shilling to drop his microphone out of the squad net, then gestured with his chin at the dead mikes. "Christ, lads, this is nae good."

"We got them," Cohen said.

"Two million locals? Military tech out of every fab and fighting skills out of every schoolhouse? How can we fight that?"

Tomas' breath caught. He'd never heard Marchbanks sound so pessimistic.

Cohen sounded confident. "We get rid of bacteria, don't we? It's the same."

"Nae the same. Getting rid of mike is impossible," Marchbanks said, voice flat.

Tomas lifted his head. He saw the insight they had missed. "I don't know about that, but Cohen, you're wrong about one thing. We don't get rid of bacteria at all. We're inundated with them all the time. But they almost never infect us. It's in their best interest not to. Remember what the sergeant tried to get the paper tiger to do in New Boston?"

Cohen said, "Hmm," then walked on.

Alone with Marchbanks, Tomas wanted to speak more. "You understand what I'm saying?"

"If we kill enough hotheads the rest will lie low. But how many of us will they get before then? Two of us right here, against a dozen of them. All they need do is whittle us down till the politicians on

Challenger cut their losses." Distant rifle fire came from the forest. Marchbanks glanced up. The line of his shoulders showed a little more vigor. "Och, I'm thinking about things above my pay grade. We're here, and the only way out is to go straight ahead."

Tomas gave a tight smile and clapped his hand on Marchbanks' shoulder. "I'm looking out for you."

"Thanks, lad. Tell you one thing I could use your eyes for. I know it's against regs for him to carry it, but does Alvarez have his usual flask of rotgut? I could really use a nip."

After the armored bulldozer stopped moving in front of the pillbox, Marchbanks shouted at the pillbox's rear entrance. "Do you yield, mike? We'll bury you alive if you don't!"

Prone behind a fallen tree, Tomas sighted down his rifle at the rear entrance. Thick walls cast deep shadows over the entrance. His finger rested outside the trigger guard. They would give the mikes a chance to surrender.

From inside the pillbox, a mike yelled back, "You'll label us irregular combatants and gun us down on the spot!"

"Haven't you heard our broadcasts? We extend lawful combatant protections to you now, mike!"

Muffled talk leaked out the rear entrance. "You said before you would respect our laws and customs! Tell that to President Kennedy!"

"Why won't they just surrender?" Marchbanks muttered into the squad's net. The gain from his microphone dropped, and he shouted his next words over the pillbox to the engineer driving the bulldozer. "Cpl. Komatsu, keep pushing soil into their firing slits!"

The bulldozer went back into motion on the other side of the pillbox. The blade scraped more soil, pushing the top of the pile higher than the pillbox's roof. Dirt clots tumbled down onto the concrete surface.

"We yield!" the mike shouted. "We yield!"

"Leave your weapons inside, take off your helmets, and set your chameleonskin on orange," Marchbanks said. Mike had switched away from fiber optic wraps for the lighter and more versatile chameleonskin. "Come out, hands up, single file, five meters apart. Form a circle five meters across in front of me and sit facing outward. Keep your hands up all the time."

The mike called, "We have two wounded. They can't walk on their own."

"One unwounded man can help each wounded one. Still, hands up or in front of your body, even the wounded. And move slowly."

The first mike came out, one arm around a wounded comrade, the other raised. Blood spotted the wounded mike's orange chameleonskin as he shuffled forward on his good leg. Both mikes looked exhausted. "Will you bring us a medic?" the unwounded one asked.

"Get yourselves on the ground first," Marchbanks said. "Keep your hands in sight."

The unwounded mike helped the other sit down. The wounded man grunted when his leg touched. The first mike sat down two meters to his comrade's left. Tomas glimpsed quiet resignation on his face.

Marchbanks murmured through the team net to Tomas, "Escort a medic here."

Tomas didn't move or speak.

"Did you hear me, lad?"

"Leaving a man alone is against procedure—"

"You have to adapt what the skills imps taught you to the circumstances. Get going. I can watch this lot." Marchbanks rose to a seated position and slid down the side of the boulder. He went to the wounded man and patted him for weapons.

Tomas came from behind his fallen tree and held his rifle loosely in both hands. More prisoners exited the pillbox and trudged toward the circle. Their shaved heads bowed, fatigue plain on their faces, they moved into position without questioning. Certainly Marchbanks could handle it, but procedure was there for a reason. "Are you sure—"

"I'll be fine, lad. These ones are beaten." Marchbanks moved to the wounded man's comrade to the left.

Tomas kept going. Heaped soil covered the front face of the pillbox. The heaps bore the scrape marks of the bulldozer's blade. Gouges in the forest floor left by its tracks marked the path downslope, toward the main road where a destroyed Badger still burned.

"We need a medic for at least two wounded prisoners," he said to Sgt. Johnson.

"We'll get you one. Come on down to the road. Where be Marchbanks?"

"Guarding prisoners taken from the pillbox."

Sgt. Johnson hmphed. "He can handle it, but get back there quick. I and I'll send a medic your way now."

Tomas slung his rifle over his shoulder and kept going. The slope had a gentle grade, but the bulldozer's tracks made footing uneasy and the branches of trees toppled on its ascent to the pillbox scratched as he brushed past.

From the direction of the company's headquarters and supply platoons, a medic came his way. The red cross on her sleeve stood out in the forest of browns and blackish-greens.

As they more closely approached, his eyes widened in surprise. He'd expected the al-Aqsan, but this woman was taller and more buxom. Her skin was fair and blond ends showed under the rim of her helmet. His surprise kept him from checking her nameplate.

"Come with me," Tomas said. They started upslope. Her long sturdy legs kept pace with him. "You're new...?"

"I landed three days ago."

"And you're from?" He spoke idly, watching the forest beyond the pillbox for any mikes.

"Sankt-Benedikts-Welt. You?"

"Born there, but grew up on Joséphine." He wondered why he felt no excitement at meeting another Benedikter, then shoved the thought aside.

She stumbled on a track left by the bulldozer. He grabbed her hand and his arm tightened to keep her upright. "You okay?"

The medic put weight on her foot. "I should be fine." She glanced at her hand, still grasped by his. "Thanks."

He let go. He realized she was the first woman, other than a

Daughter, he'd touched while on planet. "They're just around the pillbox. I only know of two wounded but there might be more."

They rounded the corner. Marchbanks crouched behind the last prisoner in the circle. With a bored look on his face, his hands ran down the prisoner's flanks.

Behind him, one of the prisoners turned to face into the circle. The prisoner put his left hand on the ground and raised his weight off his backside. In his right hand, something glinted.

"Hey!" Tomas yelled. He lifted his arm to point at the prisoner behind Marchbanks. Marchbanks gave Tomas a puzzled look.

The prisoner sprinted across the circle and lunged for Marchbanks. His left hand reached around Marchbanks' head to grab the top front of the helmet, while the prisoner's right hand moved toward Marchbanks' neck. That close, the gap between his helmet and would be apparent. Another glint in the dappled light, from what Tomas knew with dread intuition was a knife, and both Marchbanks and the prisoner fell.

"Hey!" Tomas pulled his rifle off his shoulder as he ran toward the circle. The prisoner rolled to the balls of his feet and brandished his knife. No glint now; blood slickened the blade. A feral expression contorted his face.

Still running, Tomas fired a burst into the prisoner's chest. The mike stumbled backward. His eyes were wide with confusion and he froze in place. Tomas stopped and fired another burst at his face. His rounds tore open the back of the prisoner's skull and he tumbled backward, crushed head smacking the ground near one of his seated comrades. His limbs jerked and his body lay still.

Gurgling sounded near Tomas' feet. Marchbanks had his hand at his neck, and his eyes bugged in fear. Blood gushed from his neck in pulses.

The medic ran up. Tears welled in her eyes. "*Gott im Himmel.*" She reached for her medical kit. Her hands shook so much she took a few seconds to unsnap the flap before kneeling next to Marchbanks.

One of the prisoners cried out, a high wavering sound. His hand fluttered like a wavering bird to his shoulder. Blood and brain tissue from his comrade stained his suit. He pulled his hand back in front of his face and his expression showed horror. He turned to Tomas, and the horror turned to fear.

A cold feeling froze Tomas' face into an affectless mask. Inside, his heart pounded, and parts of his subconscious never before heard voiced themselves in words for the first time. *Yes, fear me, and die anyway—*

He fired a burst, destroying the prisoner's face, collapsing his body into the dirt. The next prisoner in the circle showed the same fear. Inside, Tomas exulted, like some ancient gladiator thumping his fists on his chest; but his face remained expressionless. A squeeze of his finger and he killed the third man.

The other prisoners reacted now. One stood and ran for the woods. His bright orange suit contrasted starkly against the browns and dark greens of the forest. Two bursts into the back of his ribcage. He tumbled and groaned once before falling still and silent.

The fifth prisoner had fallen to his knees and raised his arms high. "It's not our fault. I didn't know he had a knife."

Cold steel encased Tomas' emotions. He angled his head toward the mike who'd slashed Marchbanks' throat. "We thought he was unarmed too." Another burst through the face. Five down.

How many more? Too few. Two wounded men. The one with the thigh wound had a trace of hope in his expression, but the line of his mouth showed he knew he would die. Tomas shot him in the head.

The last one lay limply, his eyes rolled back and shivers gripping his body. The medic knelt next to him, her bloody hands working at torn cloth over his torso. "What are you doing?"

Tomas killed the wounded mike. "You can't help him anymore. Take care of our own."

"It's too late," she said. Her voice bore a gravity he could not resist. Tomas blinked and looked down at her. He expected to see fear. Even his mother would fear him if she'd seen what he'd just done. Yet the only emotion he saw was disgust.

He leaned back and finally took a half-step away from her to keep his balance. His handiwork lay all around him, drawing his gaze. Dead prisoners. Marchbanks' body lay motionless among them, his eyes vacantly staring at the canopies of oaks and maples overhead.

Tomas' breath came fast and ragged. *No, it's justified, I did this all for you.*

Can seven dead mikes bring me back, lad? he heard in his mind's ear. Tomas continued to breathe shallowly. Spots swam in his vision and he sat down. His head dropped between his knees and his heartbeats roared in his ears.

Barely-heard footsteps. "Neumann, what happened?" Johnson asked.

Tomas kept his head down. "He had a knife. I don't know how Marchbanks could have missed it. He had a knife. Slit Marchbanks' throat."

"If one did, they all might. It be irie—"

Tomas laughed and cried at the same time. "None of them had a clue what their man planned! None of them knew what was going on, until I gunned him down. Then they all waited for me to shoot them."

"Sounds like they wanted you to kill them," Johnson said.

Incredulous, Tomas looked up. Tears in his eyes refracted his view of the sergeant. His voice crackled. "How can you say that? Who could want to die? Who? Who? Who." Tomas' head slumped and he cried. Tears dripped down his cheeks and sobs came out of his mouth. He reached for his shilling and cut off his microphone. His shame burned intensely solely from the medic's disgusted look. It would explode if his squadmates heard him cry.

"I and I don't know the facts," Sgt. Johnson said. "What I and I see, some prisoners surrender under false pretenses, rise against the personnel guarding them, kill one, but be neutralized by the survivor."

Tomas pushed down his tears, grateful for a chance to be angry. "Shit! You're talking like I deserve a fucking medal!"

Johnson's voice sounded firm. "We need you, Neumann. We be alone on a planet of fanatics who want us dead. The only people we can rely on be our idrin. You got to pull yourself together. Feel whatever you want when we ride the transport home. Here and now, the only thing you can do is act."

Other men—-Cohen, Alvarez, a few others—walked up from around the pillbox. They hesitated, then hurried forward when they saw Marchbanks' corpse. "What happened?" Cohen asked.

Tomas looked away. He stared through the forest without seeing it. "I did what I had to do."

"About time," Alvarez said.

Tomas rankled at his tone. A glare formed on his face, but by the time he turned his head to look at Alvarez, the glare had faded. "Do something for me. Toss me your flask."

10

Sunright Decatur

The company's new base was near a town called Sunright Decatur, twelve hundred kilometers from Reagantown. A river spawned from the glaciers on the planet's dark side flowed past, and the wind from that direction always seemed to blow cold. Even facing Constitution made no difference; the chill stealing over Tomas' back seeped deeper into his body than the sun's low rays could expel.

In addition to operations against mike units seen in the vicinity by obs wheels, scouts, or the SF, at least one squad patrolled Sunright Decatur twice every day. Dismounted teams headed and tailed a column, with the squad's two Badgers in the middle. Their path varied, but they always stopped at the municipal fab and the town hall.

A detachment from the company's supply platoon accompanied them to or from the municipal fab and worked there between patrols, feeding the town and monitoring arriving civilian trucks for any broken military material a mike sympathizer might try to recycle.

The mayor was a woman with wrinkled eyes and dirty blond hair showing gray streaks. She had a warm alto voice Tomas heard once in a while, if she met them at the town hall's front door. The squad leader would speak privately in her office while the squad waited on the street outside. Their helmets were off, clipped to their belts, and their suits were set to a gray and brick-red urban camouflage pattern.

Despite these tokens of trust they extended the locals, pedestrians mostly turned onto side streets to avoid the GF soldiers. A few boys, released from school by the GF's ban on skill implantation units, mingled around, gazing awestruck at the idling Badgers and daring each other with whispers and nudged elbows to talk to the soldiers. Mothers and older sisters would call with nervous voices for their boys to come home. Sometimes the soldiers would see one of the women in a doorway or around a corner of a house, holding a boy behind her with one hand while the other clutched the collar of her blouse.

"Look at them, worried for their virtue," Alvarez said. "Like they could stop me from taking what they've got."

Tomas wanted to stay silent, but maybe some response would mollify Alvarez into shutting up. "I'll stick with the Daughters."

"You might have a long wait for liberty to see them."

"Daughters won't jam a knitting needle through your ear during the act."

That shut up Alvarez. Cohen caught Tomas' gaze and gave a curt, appreciative nod. Tomas made no response. He wished he could be alone.

"Where are the men of the town?" Lundergard asked. He was a tall, gangly Österbotterman. Not technically a virgin—a mike had shot in their direction during a seek-and-destroy mission in the woods sunleft of town a week before.

"In a mike unit up in the hills," Ryan said. Ryan was a virgin, and he took the squad's stories about mike with dread seriousness.

Cohen looked at the front door of the town hall. "Look lively. The sergeant."

Sgt. Johnson came up to them. "Form up, idrin. We'll walk further than usual back to base."

The squad headed into an industrial quarter, with Tomas' team on point. The cooling towers of the municipal fab dominated the skyline. Along the streets stood single-story mycocrete buildings. Intersections with side streets showed open loading docks and carried the sounds of woodworkers' saws and sculptors' arc welders to the squad. Some workmen looked up with guarded expressions, while others kept to their jobs. Tomas wanted to put his helmet on and set all his chameleonskin to full camouflage. He had no fear of the locals; he just wanted to go unseen.

"Hold a minute," Sgt. Johnson said through the squad net from his position at the tail of the column. A green arrow popped into Tomas' helmet display, pointing around a corner. "Cohen, your team follows the green arrow. My team, stay with I and I and follow the blue arrow." Tomas craned his neck. A blue arrow pointed down an alley in the same direction as the other. "Badgers remain here. The third building be a metalworker's shop. We meet inside it in forty seconds. We expect the occupants be unarmed. Go!"

Cohen led Tomas' team around the corner. As their boots pounded down the street, the green arrow yawed to the right. It pointed at a small metal door in a tan mycocrete wall. A prop held the door open and a barely pubescent boy sat on a red plastic chair outside the doorway. His eyes widened and he scampered in the doorway. He kicked the prop aside as he went.

"We've been made," Cohen said.

"Faster, idrin!"

The team ran. Ryan yanked open the door while Cohen led the others in. "Hands up! Freeze! Don't move!" they shouted, and swept their muzzles across the interior space. Across the workshop, members of Sgt. Johnson's team stood on ground level outside a loading dock, elbows and rifles on the shop floor. Metalworking equipment occupied the half of the shop furthest from the door. A closed-off loft stood above them.

Four boys, the youngest being the lookout and the oldest appearing about twenty standard, shuffled together into the center of the space with their hands up. "Check them for weapons," Sgt. Johnson said.

"I'm on it," Tomas said. "Cover me," he told Alvarez. He patted the boys down while Alvarez held his rifle at the ready. Tomas was thorough, pulling out pockets and ordering the boys to kick off their work boots. *You won't get me like you got Marchbanks.* "Clear, sergeant."

Behind Sgt. Johnson, some men of the squad checked a forging press and a turret lathe, while others pried lids off crates. To the local boys, Johnson said, "Who be in charge?"

They looked nervously among themselves. The oldest one took a half-step forward. "Me."

"Not you. Where be your father?"

The oldest boy lifted his chin. "I'm in charge here."

Behind him, one of the younger boys glanced at the loft above the tools, then started guiltily and stared at the floor. Sgt. Johnson stepped back and looked up and down the shop. "Check there," he said to one of his team as he pointed to the loft.

"On it." A few of them looked around and one found a pulldown ladder. Two men started up the ladder while a third aimed his rifle at the top.

"What are you here for?" the oldest boy said.

Alvarez snorted. "You got a big mouth for a little mike."

Tomas waved his fingers and Alvarez, looking chastened, shuffled back a step.

"Son," Sgt. Johnson said, "we not be stupid." He nodded to one of his team, who handed him a thin metal object about sixty centimeters long. Generally cylindrical, about forty centimeters of it were unadorned except for a raised, notched flange. A rectangular blocky portion made up the rest. The barrel of a standard issue Unity rifle. "You'd best tell us what you know."

"They know nothing!" called a pudgy man climbing down the ladder. Two rifles were aimed at him. He jumped off and hustled over. "My sons, my nephew, his friend. They're just boys."

"You be building rifle parts for mike."

"Sir, no, I mean, yes." His face was red and his breath labored. "But they forced me. The militia. I didn't choose it. They threatened me late in the night. Kicked in my front door and rounded us up at gunpoint. 'You have a metalworking shop and a lovely family. Which one will serve us?' What could I do, sir? Please, sir, what could I do?"

One of Johnson's team came up. "Just barrels. No other parts."

"Call supply. Get someone here who can check the equipment's programming. Maybe they fab different parts in batches."

"No, sir, I swear it. On all the presidents and the constitution itself I swear it. Just barrels. I don't know where the militia—mike—makes any other parts, or where they take these when they pick them up."

Sgt. Johnson sloughed out a breath. "You tell a nice story. It might even be true. We will corroborate it. All five of you will come back to base for scans of your mental activity."

The metalworker nodded. "Of course, sir, of course. We will prove this wasn't our idea. We just want to ply our craft in peace."

The oldest boy spoke. The family resemblance was plain. "Is that some code?" he asked Johnson. "Are you going to take us into a field and shoot us?"

His father hissed. Sgt. Johnson gave the boy a cold look. "Depends. Be you innocent civilians or irregular combatants?" He then looked to men of the squad. "Tie their hands and put them in the back of a Badger for the return trip. The other Badger will carry every rifle barrel we can fit inside over to the municipal fab. Toss the office for any paper or tablets that might tell us something about this operation."

A few minutes later the squad set out. Tomas' team now brought up the rear, behind their Badger carrying the metalworker and his sons. "We should've just shot them right there," Alvarez said. "Right, Neumann?"

"No."

"Oh, yeah, you're right. We should shoot the whole goddam town. You want to kill them all, don't you?"

Tomas kicked a pebble down the pavement. "Just the ones who deserve it." His voice sounded cool, but when he blinked, images of the prisoner on his knees, the medic's look of disgust, appeared to him. *A killing machine or a remorseful man. Which me is real and which false?*

Half an hour later, the other team trooped out of the municipal fab after tossing eighty rifle barrels into the recycling hopper. "Finally we can head back to base," Alvarez said.

"Idrin, we have one more stop on the way out of town."

Lundergard groaned. "My feet already hurt."

Cohen chuckled. "Detach yourself from your desire to lounge on your bunk the rest of the day. We have our orders."

They went through a residential quarter, under live oaks with green-black canopies canted like satellite dishes to catch Constitution's light. Behind fences of black alloy, the mycocrete houses were painted to look like stucco. The soldiers' shadows stretched up the driveways. The garages, ordered kept open by the GF command, held cars, a few pickup trucks, a trailer holding a boat.

After an intersection, the view opened up. A block held a long brick building in the center of a wide lawn. *Sunright Decatur High School*, read permanent letters on the bezel of an LED sign. The LEDs were dark. A breeze pulled seeds off dandelion heads along the edge of the sidewalk.

Near the school's front entrance, a circular driveway curved around a lawn where a GF obs wheel stood. The Badgers parked back-to-back on the driveway and Johnson led the men to the half-glassed doors. Rain-borne dust speckled the windows and the tops of the locks holding the door handles. Men waved their shillings at the locks. "This one checks," said a soldier, and the other locks checked as well. The doors had remained locked since their last visit.

"We look around even so." Johnson handled his shilling through his uniform. "Three go in and the rest check the perimeter. You have a preference, speak."

"I'll go in," Tomas said. It would be darker in there, and distant from most of the squad. Cohen and Bar-Ruda also volunteered.

Inside, the only light came from the windows. Electrical power had long since been cut. Dust lay like gray snow on the sill of a window at the principal's office and the frame of a trophy case. The building was laid out like a capital E, with the main entrance in the lower left corner. "I'll take the far wing," Tomas said, the wing furthest from the sun.

The distance from the rest of the squad was not complete. Their chatter entered Tomas' ears and data from them popped onto his helmet display. Couldn't he be alone, even for a moment? "A grate over a crawlspace entrance is loose," Ryan said.

"Good eyes," Johnson said. "Put a lock on it."

Tomas kept walking and rounded the corner. Shaded by the other wings, this hallway was the darkest of the three. Classrooms and rooms with low-power implant stations opened off the hallway. Dusted coated the vents of the lockers. Tomas carried his rifle loosely in his arms. How long ago had the mikes behind the pillbox been schoolboys in a place like this?

A noise came from one of the implant station rooms. He froze and lifted his rifle higher. Maybe nothing, perhaps the building settled or a rat sought food. Hopefully all it was. He padded closer to the open door, then ran three steps in, swinging up his rifle as he went.

In the dim light seeping around the lowered blinds, the whites of the boy's eyes grabbed Tomas' attention. The boy stood behind a table bearing an implant station. The arm holding the station's TMI helmet was up, exposing the helmet's inner lining.

The boy's chest heaved. He lifted his hands from a metal plate bearing squat cylinders, a solar panel, and insulated wires leading below the table to the electronics driving the implant station. He might have been sixteen standard.

"What are you doing here?" Tomas asked.

Eyes wide with fright, the boy said, "I wanted to use an implant station."

"You know that's forbidden." Tomas' face hardened. "I could shoot you as an irregular combatant right here."

The boy's hands wavered. "I'm not doing anything wrong. I just want to learn."

Tomas lowered his rifle. "What do you want to learn?"

"Confederated Worlds languages."

"Confed and NL are mutually intelligible—"

"No, no. Languages from your homeworlds." He put on a declamatory face. "*Il mio nome è Theodore. Parlate Nuovo-Toscano?*"

Tomas shook his head in a wide, slow motion.

"What then is your language—"

"Every GF soldier or Confederated Worlds civilian you'll ever meet on New Liberty can speak Confed," Tomas said. Theodore's mask of naïve idealism began to crumble. "You're risking your life for something that doesn't matter. Shut down the implant station and lie low until we're gone. We're locking the crawlspace grate you used to get in, so you'll have to find another way out. Do what I'm telling you or you'll end up dead."

Theodore gulped and nodded. Tomas left the room and headed toward the front door. He glanced back a few times, but the boy had no knife and no urge to slit his throat. Tomas relaxed just enough to feel how tense his shoulders still were. *There's been enough killing on this planet. Let's make peace where we can.* He trudged onward.

Cohen and Bar-Ruda waited near the trophy case. "Nothing," Cohen said. "You, Neumann?"

"Nothing either. Let's get out of here."

The next weeks passed in a routine. The company ran missions into the woods and hills to sunleft of the town. Most of their activities involved checking obs wheels and dismantling irrigation systems to wither away shrubs and thin out the forests. Mike generally lay low, but sometimes emerged from his bunkers to snipe at dismounted infantry. Makeshift landmines damaged vehicles from time to time. *Hikes with a risk of gunshot*, Cohen called these missions. Sniper attacks and other mike activity were met with fire from the vehicles and Kestrels on station above.

Patrols in Sunright Decatur were generally quiet. Tomas never saw Theodore. He never saw the metalworker or his sons again, but he heard scuttlebutt from another patrol. They found the metalworker dead on his residential street, gunshot residue on his lips and brain mixed with bone and blood on the pavement under his head. A paper note pinned to his shirt said the militia had executed him for treason.

A few days later, Tomas' squad was due to patrol. He was one of the last to fall in, arriving at the assembly point a few minutes before departure hour. As he approached, Sgt. Johnson stepped up. "Neumann, a word."

Tomas checked his chronometer. "I'm timely arriving, sergeant."

"Did I and I say you weren't? We need a few men for a special task today and I and I know you can handle it."

They were going to gun down unarmed civilians. The intuition rocked Tomas on his feet. "What's the task?"

"Can't get into it yet. It requires fire discipline and keen observation. Can I and I rely on you, Neumann?"

"Yes."

"I and I'll tell you when you're needed. Prepare to head out."

In the assembly area, only one of the squad's Badgers waited with the dismounted men. The men's suits were set to urban camouflage. Tomas found his team and noticed Cohen wasn't there. "I'm team leader today," Alvarez said.

"You? Where's Cohen?"

"What, you jealous? I must be leadership material."

Tomas shrugged. The situation would come clear eventually. Sgt. Johnson acted as if nothing was amiss; the squad rolled out the base's main gate at the usual hour.

The patrol started out as usual, but after dropping a supply team at the municipal fab, the sergeant beckoned Tomas and two others behind a corner of the fab's main fence. "Helmets on, and full chameleonskin head-to-toe," he told them.

Tomas put on his helmet and pressed the controls at his wrist. He looked down and barely saw his legs. It relieved him to be almost invisible. Any looks of disgust aimed his way would pass right through him.

A ping sounded in Tomas' helmet. "Here be your destination coordinates," Sgt. Johnson said. "You go parallel with the patrol, but stay at least a block away from us and move as stealthily as you can. Each one of you will have responsibility for one external door of a building. Attempt to take the person of interest prisoner, but protect yourselves foremost."

A green arrow appeared in Tomas' helmet display, along with yellowish ones pointing to his squadmates' destinations. On the far side of the street parallel to the squad's main path to the town hall, they hugged the front walls of workshops. A car turned the corner and they froze until it passed. Further on, they walked sideways to present the smallest visible angle to a woodworker taking a break, drinking water on a loading dock.

Near the town hall, their paths diverged. Tomas followed the green arrow to a two-story building a couple of blocks behind the town hall. In a corner of the building's front, a door had been propped open. The arrow led him inside.

A narrow entryway gave two routes deeper into the building: to his right, into a glass-doored clerical space where two young women worked with rigid backs turned to the door; and up a stairwell. The arrow pointed up. The treads were solidly built, and made no sound as he climbed.

The second story lacked internal dividers. The one large room had bare carpet and a dusty smell. Low in the corners hung spiderwebs bearing flies bound up in silk. A pair of French doors overlooked the street, opened to the breeze and the town's few sounds. A closer look showed no balcony past the doorsill; Tomas could stand in the doorway and jump easily down with a power assist from his suit. The room was dark enough that passersby would be less able than usual to see distortions in the chameleonskin.

Across the street stood another two-story building. An LED sign next to the front door read *Office Space for Rent; Entire Building Available*. Tomas' helmet display projected a red target onto the front door. Behind the building, weeds tufted an empty lot. Beyond the empty lot, across another street, the town hall's brick fence rose two meters above the sidewalk. Above the rear fence, someone sat in a corner office upstairs. Dirty blond hair streaked with gray spilled down her back. The mayor. Her motionless body language suggested she worked intently on the papers on her desk.

More icons appeared on his helmet display, telling him the bulk of the squad had arrived in front of the town hall.

"Ready yourselves, idrin," Sgt. Johnson said to Tomas and the others.

A few seconds later, motion came from the mayor's office; the sergeant walked in.

A rifle cracked the neighborhood's silence. Not GF or Uni standard issue. It came from the building for rent between Tomas and the town hall. In the mayor's office window, cracks radiated from a bullet hole. The mayor herself was slumped forward and blood stained her paperwork. Tomas couldn't see Sgt. Johnson, but his icon in Tomas' helmet display glowed green.

You knew it was coming and ducked but why let the mayor die— Tomas shook his head to clear his thoughts. The red target remained on his view of the building for rent. "Three meter fall," he said to his helmet, and jumped. Smart fibers in the legs of his suit cushioned his landing on the pavement below. He crossed the street and crouched on one knee, then aimed his rifle at the door.

"He went out the door on my side!" one of the other men said. "Neumann, he's heading for the corner near you!"

Tomas crouched and padded toward the corner. His helmet display projected icons on his view of the building's front wall, one for his squadmate, one for the shooter. The shooter would round the corner in moments—

He cross-checked him with his rifle, swinging the stock with his right hand into the shooter's chest. The shooter tumbled to the sidewalk and Tomas brought his rifle back to firing position. His squadmates pounded to the scene, rifles drawn, shouting at the shooter to remain still. Tomas didn't speak.

The shooter was Theodore. He'd lost the naïve expression from the encounter in the school. Now he gave each of the soldiers a defiant look. "You fuckers got me. But at least I shot that bitch in the head. Patriots outnumber traitors, so it's a good exchange, my life for hers."

One of Tomas' comrades sniffed out a breath. "Not a good exchange for you, mikey."

"The constitution is bigger than my life," Theodore said. Idealism glazed his voice and he stared at each of them in turn. Tomas quailed when their gazes met, but Theodore couldn't see his face through the chameleonskin on his helmet's faceplate.

More footsteps sounded, along with the whirr of tires from a Badger's road harness on the pavement. "Good work, idrin."

"Thanks, sergeant," said one of them. Tomas nodded.

The Badger's brakes squeaked and the ramp clanged open. Cohen came out, accompanied by a woman with hair tucked under a camouflage helmet. It took Tomas a moment to identify her from her crow's feet and the lines of her face. The mayor? "Sergeant, thank you for agreeing to my plan," she said. Her voice confirmed her identity.

Theodore's defiant look vanished. "I shot you in the head."

"The GF personnel and I set up a dummy. A wig on a basketball stuffed with sacks of ketchup and toothpaste."

A glimmer of defeat on Theodore's face gave way to continued defiance. "You fucking whore. Which one of these do you spread your legs for? Or do you not bother selling yourself to sweaties and noncoms, and save your illusory virtue for officers?"

She looked coolly at him. "Teddy, that's no way to talk to your aunt."

Aunt? What could lead someone to try killing his own aunt?

Theodore said to her, "You forfeited any respect I should give you when you committed treason."

She set her fists on her hips. "I keep this town alive, Teddy. All you would do is bring down on it the Confederated Worlds' wrath." To Sgt. Johnson, she said, "What do you do with irregular combatants?" Her tone made clear she already knew the answer.

"Summary execution." He looked around. "I and I think the side wall around the corner should do."

"What?" Theodore said. His eyes showed whites. "You take prisoners—"

"We take mikes in uniform prisoner on a battlefield. You be in civilian clothes and tried assassinating an official of the local government."

Theodore's eyelids fluttered. "You have to interrogate me first. A brain scan would give you intelligence on mike activity. I can cooperate, tell you what I know—"

The mayor's hazel eyes bored into Theodore. "How do you think we knew what you planned?"

Theodore looked pale and a grimace froze on his parted lips.

"You could have stopped me and didn't. You'd rather shoot me? What's my mother going to say?"

"Sunright Decatur can only survive this war if the townsfolk know I hold their best interests above my own. If my sister will hate me for that, that's just another of my own interests I have to set aside for the good of the town." To the sergeant, she said, "I'm done with him."

"Tie his hands behind his back, idrin. Who has a blindfold?"

The other soldiers got Theodore to his feet and shoved him face-first at the building's front wall. Tomas tied his hands together and cinched the rope tight. He gave the knot a final tug and Theodore grunted in response.

A pain in Tomas' mouth caught his attention. He'd been biting his lower lip. After a shake of his head, he grabbed Theodore's arm and frog-marched him around the corner.

The building presented a gray wall to the alley. Tomas and the other soldiers stopped four meters from the front corner and the same distance from the small door in the back Theodore had fled from after the shooting. Cohen carried a length of bandage Tomas recognized as being scavenged from a medkit in the Badger. He folded it in half lengthwise, then again. When he moved closer to Theodore, the boy bucked his head to keep Cohen from blindfolding him.

One of the other soldiers punched the boy in the stomach. Theodore bent over in pain and moaned as Cohen tied the blindfold over his eyes. "Face death like a man," the other soldier said.

Theodore slumped to his knees. His moans of pain became sobs. "Form up, idrin," Sgt. Johnson said.

Tomas, Cohen, and the other two soldiers formed a line across the alley.

"Any last words?" Sgt. Johnson asked Theodore.

Tomas' heart slammed and his stomach felt ill. Theodore would say he met a soldier in the school, who let him violate the ban on skills implantation and gain the skills to shoot the mayor. The sergeant would investigate. A court-martial would sentence Tomas to five standard years in a terraforming battalion on one of the raw worlds near the Progressive Republic. If they did he would deserve it—

Theodore stopped crying and stood tall. His voice wavered a little as he said, "'I regret I have but one life to lose for my country.'"

After his words echoed away, Sgt. Johnson said, "Ready."

Tomas lifted his rifle and slid the toggle to single-shot before he could think about it. The skills imps had prepared him to be part of a firing squad.

"Aim."

A cold, remorseless feeling filled Tomas as he sighted on the middle of Theodore's chest. Memories of the prior mercies he had shown to this boy and the student in New Boston mocked him. He had been a fool. He would never again show pity to anyone. Not even himself.

"Fire!"

11

The Hemp Field

Between a swell in the rolling plain eight hundred meters to sunleft of their foxhole, and a pair of distant forested hills tinged red-orange by Constitution's light, the prevailing wind from darkward carried a faint plume of dust across the sky. From sunleft came the low rumble of many tracked vehicles. Enemy vehicles, moving slowly down a gravel road that was mike's axis of advance.

Tomas and Ryan stood in their foxhole just behind the crest of a low contour parallel to the road. Tomas watched the swell to sunleft, looking for shimmers of active chameleonskin when the first vehicles would top the swell.

"I've never faced tanks before," Ryan said.

"Don't worry about them. They'll be too busy trying to return fire against the Graywolfs." Two hundred meters to their sunright, the gravel road curved to the left around a low hill. A tank platoon, four Graywolfs, waited hull-down on that hill, along with his platoon's four Badgers. "You just cover me against mike dismounts while I fire the grenade launcher at their tanks." The launcher leaned against the side wall of the foxhole. Two racks of four grenades each hung from hooks hammered into the stony soil next to it.

"Dismounts? Maybe we'll catch them in their DeGaulles." Ryan's voice switched from fearful to hopeful in five seconds.

"No such luck. You can tell they're moving slowly, can't you?"

Ryan looked at the dust cloud, but Tomas could read from his face he didn't grasp it. "Oh, yeah."

"Their infantry is on foot, looking for obs equipment, landmines, and ambushes." The foolhardy mikes had already been killed in places like the soybean field. The ones they faced today had learned how to fight like professionals. He angled his head toward Ryan. "You clear on what you need to do?"

"Yeah. Dismounts. Cover—"

Ryan shut his mouth when Tomas called for silence with a chop of his hand. The clack of tracks on the dirt road grew louder, and the first mike vehicle appeared at the top of the swell. The active chameleonskin obscured the vehicle's outline, but nothing could mask the sound of the tracks on gravel or the sight of dust rising from the tracks. The rumble of the drive wheels made it as a Marlborough, a tank.

The Marlborough came at walking speed down the gravel road. Tomas' helmet display projected a line of hostile infantryman icons rustling through waist-high hemp in the fields on both sides of the road. The software assembling the projections required some minimum probability that a shimmer of light and motion through the crop was actually a mike, and the icons flickered into and out of existence depending on sight angles and the position of the enemy's arms and legs.

"Shouldn't you get the grenade launcher ready?" Ryan whispered.

"Lamp's still red." Just as in the foxhole he'd shared with Marchbanks, the engineers had run wires to an intercom and a tablet in their foxhole. The tablet mounted on the wall of the foxhole now showed a traffic light. Red meant hold fire; yellow would mean prepare the grenade launcher; green would mean fire grenades at the mike vehicles.

"You didn't even look."

"Don't need to. The Graywolf platoon commander's in charge of this mission, remember? He's no paper tiger. He knows there's only one tank over the swell and he wants to wait for more."

A few minutes later, Ryan murmured, "How many more does he want?"

Twelve vehicles, a mix of Marlboroughs and DeGaulles, had topped the swell, as well as two more lines of dismounted infantry. The lead tank was about two hundred meters up the road from their foxhole. A glance to sunleft showed a strong dust cloud still rising from out of sight. Mike had at least a company moving against them, maybe two. *We might be outnumbered four to one.* The ambush couldn't stop mike's advance, just harass it and hope Shirley Foxtrot could put photons on it. There were fewer ships in orbit now, thanks to mounting tensions with the Progressive Republic. This ambush had low priority for any orbital fire mission by those ships remaining.

"As many as we can get. Now shut up." His helmet display projected a parabolic microphone onto a half-ellipsoid smear held by someone in the second line of mikes. "If they catch us talking, the mission is dead."

Ryan hunkered against the front wall of the foxhole. Tomas peered out the gap between the lip of the foxhole and the edge of a sheet of chameleonskin stretched over their heads. The column of mike vehicles crept forward, drawing even with, then passing, their hiding place. In the distance, more topped the swell in the ground and the dust cloud in their rear remained as dense as before. *Two companies, at least.*

On the touchscreen of the tablet, the traffic signal switched from red to yellow. Tomas tapped Ryan's shoulder and pointed. Ryan nodded and hefted his rifle, while Tomas lifted the grenade launcher to his shoulder.

Guns boomed from the low hill to their right. Moments later, reactive armor on the front slopes of the mike tanks, and shells penetrating that armor, thundered. Large strips of chameleonskin on the lead tank lost their images and showed only the 'skin's gray base material. Smoke poured out of a hole in the turret.

A few Marlboroughs near the head of the column fired back. Rounds missed, pounding the hillside below the GF vehicles or sailing over them. The mike vehicles further back in the column remained silent, their vision presumably obscured by dust, smoke, and their comrades ahead of them.

The Graywolfs and Badgers kept firing, and soon another mike tank at the column's head poured smoke into the air. Ryan lifted his rifle toward the lip of the foxhole—

Tomas jabbed his fist at Ryan's shoulder to get his attention, then shook his head. *Not yet*, he mouthed.

It took mike a few more minutes to respond to the fire from the Graywolfs and Badgers. Marlboroughs and DeGaulles back in the column veered off the gravel road and flattened the hemp fields on both sides. The mike vehicles traveled in bounds, two firing at the top of the hill for every two advancing, until they formed a line whose ends curved in toward the hill. A tank stood within forty meters of Tomas and Ryan with its thinner flank armor facing them.

Now, Tomas mouthed, as the traffic light on the tablet's touchscreen turned green. He calmly sighted on the seam in the chameleonskin between the tank's main body and the turret. An easy squeeze of the trigger and the grenade roared out of the tube, kicking his shoulder. He didn't see the rocket fire a few meters away, but heat washed his face in the instant before the grenade impacted.

The explosion thundered to their foxhole. "God damn!" shouted Ryan.

"Keep your eye on their dismounts and cover me." Tomas popped the next grenade out of its rack. The supply of eight grenades represented wishful thinking and the fecundity of molecular fabrication. He'd be lucky to fire three before mike reacted and forced them to withdraw. He mounted the second grenade on the launcher and sighted on the next tank, at seventy meters. Ryan fired bursts at infantrymen Tomas had no eyes for as he aimed and launched the grenade. Another hit.

Tomas popped out the next grenade. Uni standard rifles chattered nearby. He mounted the grenade and nodded at Ryan. The other showed fear but his hands efficiently pushed the next magazine into his rifle. Ryan swallowed and rose up to fire out of the foxhole.

The smoke from the damaged tanks drifted their way on the prevailing wind. Tomas grimaced. It would add to the increasing distance to make the next hit even tougher. Uni rifles fired their way, but not close. Tomas peered into the smoke and glimpsed his target. He launched the third grenade. The sound of its impact was lost in the cacophony of gunfire, but telemetry showed it had struck alloy. Tomas reached for the next grenade.

"Isn't it time to fall back?" Ryan said. "The sergeant said three grenades."

"He said expect three, but use your judgment. I'm using my judgment."

Uni rifle fire rattled nearby. A buzzing sound passed overhead. A fifty-centimeter rip in the chameleonskin showed a sliver of deep blue sky.

"They're on to our position!" Ryan said.

Tomas mounted the grenade on the launcher. His gaze was on the cloud of smoke in front of them. "Go if you want."

Confusion stooped Ryan's shoulders for a moment. He crawled up the sloping rear wall of the foxhole.

More rifle fire struck the dirt around Tomas or flew overhead. In a lull, Tomas stepped up and sighted another mike vehicle in the smoke, a DeGaulle with tracks visible from the front. His helmet display estimated it aimed its armament in his direction. He'd drawn their attention. *Come on, try to get me,* Tomas thought in a one-sided conversation with the DeGaulle. *I'm not afraid to die.* He fired a grenade and his arm twitched as he pressed the trigger. Reactive armor roared, blowing out a chunk of chameleon skin on the front of the DeGaulle. The vehicle kept coming.

"Neumann!" shouted Cohen through his earpiece. "Get back here on the quick!"

Tomas hunkered down and reached for the next grenade. The mike riflemen held their fire. He stepped up to launch another grenade at the DeGaulle, but didn't aim, just pointed in the vehicle's direction. He squeezed the trigger as a burst of large caliber rounds from the DeGaulle's machine gun shredded the rest of the chameleonskin cover and smacked the ground just in front of the foxhole, flinging dirt at the cameras on his faceplate.

He sagged against the wall of the foxhole and gasped for breath. They'd found him. He'd waited too long to leave the foxhole. *I don't wanna die I don't wanna die I wanna die wanna die got to get out of here...* He picked up his rifle and activated a self-destruct timer on the grenade rack, then hurriedly crawled out the back.

He slithered between rows of hemp sloping away from the foxhole, barely out of sight of the DeGaulle. Rifles fired from a few dozen meters to sunleft, splintering hemp fibers thirty centimeters above his head.

Tomas fired back, wild bursts chewing through the plants obscuring the enemy from vision. He crawled away from his firing position before they could triangulate on him. He heard them calling to one another. "Loop around to cut him off! There's only one Confed left!"

Punctuating their cries, the grenades remaining in the foxhole exploded. Dirt flew and fragments of metal snicked the foliage around him.

Got to get back to the platoon. Tomas crawled that direction as spotty fire rattled above him. He listened for the rustle of movement to the sides. His helmet display showed a low probability of mikes that far forward on his flanks. Software won't lose its life if it's wrong. He fired bursts wildly to his right until the clip sprung out of the rifle's stock. He crawled forward on his knees and right elbow while reaching for the next clip in his pack. As he groped, he realized he pulled out the final clip he carried.

He couldn't hold them at bay for much longer. He could surrender... but what would the militia do after they captured a member of the Blackjack platoon that killed irregular combatants in New Boston? A show trial, an execution.

Maybe that would be for the best—

Tomas shook his head. He had to get to the platoon before he ran out of ammunition. Still on his belly, he fired one more burst at the mikes he thought were on his flank, then rose to a crouch. "Power burst, speed!" he said to his helmet, then ran a zigzag pattern through the rows of hemp.

His feet loped across the field as the flexing fibers in his suit assisted his legs. Rifle fire smacked the plants around him as the power bar in his helmet display shrank and changed to yellow. Was he pulling away from the mikes? Their rifle fire sounded more distant—

A pain lanced through his right arm and he lost his grip on his rifle. He couldn't move his arm. His sleeve was tattered, and torn skin showed the white of nicked bone for a moment before blood poured out the wound. The pain made him want to vomit, but he kept his lunch down. He squeezed his left hand around his upper arm, thumb in his armpit, and kept running. The power bar shrank further, into the warning zone, and turned red.

Tracks ground and creaked nearby. Tomas glanced over his shoulder. The DeGaulle had crested the contour line and its weapons were aimed right at him. He crouched lower and changed his zigzag pattern just before the DeGaulle fired its machine gun.

Pain bloomed in his left thigh. His left foot struck the ground and black spots swam in his vision. He stumbled and rolled through hemp stalks, landing on his back. Wound indicators lit up his helmet display and the pain in his arm and leg made him whimper. A few shreds of muscle held his knee and lower leg to his body. Torn white heads of bone showed and ebbing pulses of blood gushed from his leg. He moved his good hand to the inside of his left thigh and pressed to slow the loss of blood. He felt cold and his breaths came quick and shallow. Agony, agony. Maybe it would be better to die.

Shells arced over him on flat trajectories, detonating thirty meters away. Reactive armor roared on the front slope of the DeGaulle. Rifles fired nearby, and Tomas recognized the sound of GF standard issue. *They're coming for me. No, don't, I don't deserve rescue, this is my recompense for all the lives I've taken….*

A head obscured by chameleonskin appeared above him. *You got me, mike.* The thought softened the harshest edge of his pain.

"Tourniquets first, leg then arm," said a familiar voice. Cohen. "Then we get blood substitute into him."

"Right." Ryan's voice sounded thin and high. His hands moved over Tomas' thigh. "Oh, god, he's so cold."

"Nein," Tomas said. *"Deine Hände sind zu heiss...."* Ryan's hands were hot, didn't he know that?

"Keep going," Cohen said, voice firm. "He's in shock. If we don't stop the bleeding soon he'll die before we can get him to the medics."

Why didn't they understand him? Right, they spoke New Tuscan. Or was that someone else? Tomas wondered who but his train of thought kept derailing. A man with a narrow jaw watched with fearful alarm. *W'aus kommst du, mein Vater?* Tomas thought as his mind slid down a dark hole away from the men tending him.

12

Peters-Stein Technique

Tomas stared at a trapezoid of light on a white surface in front of and above him. Flanking the white surface, cypresses outside a window swayed in a breeze.

Thoughts snapped into place. The hemp field. The ambush. He'd survived.

He flexed his arm, his leg. He lay in a bed and his limbs slid between crisp sheets. Tomas grabbed the near end of the top sheet with his right arm and flung the sheet toward his feet. His arm twinged and he lost his grip. The upper meter of the sheet tumbled into a rippled heap at his waist, exposing the hospital gown covering his chest.

With his left hand, he pushed the gown's right sleeve up to his armpit. A baby-pink band of hairless flesh ringed his upper arm. He turned his elbow and winced at the discomfort of motion. His right biceps was concave, shrunken under the pink band of skin.

Tomas kicked with his right foot and soon had the sheet down to his ankles. He lifted his left leg half a meter above the bed and held it trembling in air for a few seconds before he had to drop it. From the middle of his thigh down, pink skin covered thin and wobbly muscles.

He was whole and would have time to heal.

Shame gripped him.

He'd put Ryan and Cohen's lives at risk. He'd gambled with the GF's tenuous hold on the planet by pitying a mike assassin. He'd killed innocent men behind the pillbox. He didn't deserve to live....

He looked around. A hospital ward, ten beds jutting out from each of opposite walls. A few sleeping men. He sensed this room was part of a large building. A hospital would have general anesthetics, scalpels, a high roof one might access. If he didn't deserve to live, he could take his own life.

A wave of gooseflesh rippled down his sides. He couldn't kill himself. He feared death too much. The realization flooded him with more shame. Tears rolled from the corners of his eyes.

Footsteps padded nearby. He opened his eyes to see a nurse. She wore her hair pulled back under her bonnet, a severe look not dispelled by the warmth in her brown eyes. "Glad to see you're awake, Private Neumann."

He didn't want to see warmth, from her or anyone. "How long?"

"You were in the cocoon four weeks while they rebuilt your arm and leg. They moved you here last night."

Four weeks. He could have forgotten much in that time, but instead, all his memories remained fresh. Tears welled up in his eyes again.

Her eyes crinkled in sympathy. "Are you in pain?"

"Pain? No. A few aches when I move."

"That's normal. Your new muscles are less developed than your original ones, and your brain hasn't learned how to control them. You have a couple of weeks of rehab before you'll be physically cleared to return to your unit."

He wanted to get back as soon as he could. Make it up to Ryan and Cohen. Face down mike. He widened his hands and glared at her. "You've got to be kidding. Two weeks?"

Unperturbed, she said, "You have to pass a fitness test before they'll clear you for front line duty. Two weeks is usually how long it takes after a man with new limbs comes out of the cocoon."

"Sorry. I know it's not your fault." He kicked the sheet all the way off his feet and slid his legs toward the side. "Let's get started."

The nurse pressed her hand onto his chest to stop his movement. "The therapist will come for you. Two two-hour sessions every day. The rest of the time you can sleep, relax, play games... talk...."

The few other awake men in the ward seemed little interested in speaking. Her emphasis on her last word raised his defenses. "Talk? About?"

Her face turned into a sympathetic mask. "I've only seen the hospital and nearby parts of the base. I haven't even gone into Reagantown. I don't know what it's like out there. I'd be happy to listen to you if you want to tell me what you've seen, what you've done—"

"There's nothing to talk about."

She smiled sweetly. "If you change your mi—"

"I won't. There's nothing to talk about."

"Thank you for telling me your boundaries. I respect them."

He ground his next words through his teeth. "Don't patronize me."

"Patronize? Never. I respect you." She touched her warm fingers to the back of his right hand, then left. She hesitated near the door of the room to pull out a tablet and swipe in a note before exiting.

The physical therapist came a few minutes later with a workout clothes and a powered wheelchair. He led Tomas to a fitness room where sweating men in hospital gowns lifted four-kilogram weights and walked between waist-high rails while holding on with both hands. "Go light and don't push it," the therapist said. He worked chewing gum with circular motions of his lower jaw. "You want to exhaust the new muscles without damaging them. You want to do the same with your mind too. The muscle memory's still there, but it's got to learn how to cross the nerve junctions to your new muscles. That's enough biceps curls."

"No." Tomas kept going, even though his arm wobbled. He had to get back, to his unit, to combat. Even though he didn't want to die, back in combat, fate would take that decision from him.

At the top of a biceps curl, the therapist gripped his wrist and pried the weight from his hand. "You're done with these, Private."

"I want to get out of here."

The therapist's jaws mashed his gum, then stopped. "I'm going to get you out of here as quickly as possible. I won't let you malinger by overworking and setting back your progress. Now grab a weight in each hand and try some squats."

After the therapy session, Tomas wheeled back to the ward for a meal of chicken breast and protein smoothie, then fell asleep.

He woke when a captain with a white armband bent over a bed on the opposite side of the ward, talking to a soldier whose face was hidden behind a tablet he held upright on his chest. The captain gave a parting word of encouragement that the soldier ignored, then stretched to his full height. The sides of the captain's garrison cap touched fringes of gray hair, and when he faced Tomas, the sunlight striking his face from the window next to Tomas' bed washed out his wrinkles.

The new angle showed Tomas the rest of the captain's armband. It bore a *taijitu*.

The captain met Tomas' gaze, glanced at a tablet in his hand. His eyes widened and he hastily came to Tomas. He fumbled the tablet into a slot on his belt and extended his hand. "Greetings, Private Neumann." At least he pronounced his name correctly.

"Captain…" Tomas gave the officer's hand a minimal shake and checked his nameplate. "Lindemann."

"As you might guess—" The captain tapped the *taijitu* on his armband. "—I'm an Observer chaplain, posted here to minister to the spiritual needs of our wounded and our medical staff. I see you're an Observer too."

Tomas frowned. How could the captain tell? The intake forms at the station in Challenger orbit, he realized with a sinking feeling. He should have left the checkbox blank. "That doesn't make me special."

"No. I minister to all our wounded, regardless of their spiritual community. But I'm particularly trained to minister to your spiritual needs. Mind if I sit?"

Tomas shrugged. Capt. Lindemann took a chair next to the bed. His face looked as if he was uncertain what to say. "It's uncommon to meet an Observer serving in a combat position."

"Tell my mother."

"Your mother...." Wheels of thought churned behind Capt. Lindemann's eyes. "You grew up on Joséphine? 'Neumann' doesn't sound like a *joséphinais* name."

"I was born on Sankt-Benedikts-Welt, but my parents left when I was very young."

"*Wirklich? Ich komme daraus auch.*"

Tomas' desire for solitude doubled. He put on a false frown. "Is that Sankt-Benedikts-Sprach? I don't speak it."

Capt. Lindemann went on in Confed. "I'm from there too. Actually, there's a chance I knew your parents."

Tomas felt a pang of desire to hear about his father, but not if it meant exposing his thoughts to this stranger. He scratched his right hand on the sheet and said nothing.

"The Observer community on Sankt-Benedikts-Welt is relatively small, and Neumann is an uncommon surname. I knew a couple named Neumann, who had a son who would be about twenty standard today."

"I don't remember you," Tomas said.

"You were too young. I wouldn't expect it even if that had been your family I knew. The wife had a real shine of dedication to our precepts. She glowed with a passion to share our message with the worlds." Capt. Lindemann thought further. "Her husband did too. He had wild brown hair and his face looked triangular, very pointed to the chin. Do those people sound like your parents?"

A ridge of pressure tightened across Tomas' eyebrows. "My father died when I was young. I don't know what he looked like."

"You haven't seen a photograph?"

Tomas scowled. "We're Observers—"

Capt. Lindemann angled his head. "I wouldn't judge anyone, not even an Observer, for keeping a photograph of a loved one." His sage tone thinned out, letting a wistful note come through. "It sounds as if your mother is very dedicated to our precepts."

The captain must have some attachment to his mother, if he could remember her after fifteen standard years. "She lives near the town of Portage-du-Nord, if you want to go to Joséphine on your next off-planet leave."

Startled eyes, a cough. Capt. Lindemann leaned back and his chair creaked. After a time, he said, "She was probably not the wife of the couple I knew. The settled galaxy is small, but not that small. No matter. You're still an Observer and I'm here to minister to your needs."

"My only need is to get back to my unit as soon as possible."

Capt. Lindemann's demeanor switched to one of solemn inquiry. "Why?"

"I have work I need to finish."

"What sort of work? Why do you need to finish it?"

"There's a war on. We have to fight off mike. I'm not going to leave my comrades to do it alone."

"Did something happen out there? You can tell me about it."

Tomas' face blanked. "Nothing happened."

Capt. Lindemann drew a breath and turned to the window. "Combat is the most harrowing experience anyone can go through. It raises strong emotions—fear, sorrow, pity, guilt—and keeps them at a high intensity for a long time." He turned back to Tomas with a waiting expression.

Stilted words. As if he knew anything about strong emotions. "You read that in a book, captain?"

"I got that from the skills imps. It's not accurate? It doesn't tell the whole story? Maybe you can tell me more."

"You wouldn't understand."

Capt. Lindemann sighed. "Maybe I wouldn't. But let me tell you something. This ward does more than rehab body parts. That's the easy bit. We also need to make sure you're psychologically ready to return to combat."

"That's what skills imps are for."

"We've tried that. It doesn't work. From what you've told me, I conclude you need to talk to someone before you go back to the front."

Tomas shifted his weight. A wince tightened around his eyes.

"You don't have to talk to me." Capt. Lindemann emphasized his words with open, conciliatory palms. "I sense your reticence. There are plenty of chaplains and psychological staff who are not

Observers or not from Sankt-Benedikts-Welt. I don't care who you go to, but talk to someone about what you've experienced."

"Maybe. I mean sure, I'll think about it."

With folded arms, the captain gave Tomas a cool look. "I'm the senior Observer chaplain on site. I have the power to veto an Observer's return to his unit until he's psychologically fit. I know you want to return to your unit. But you will have to participate in a spiritual consultation first." He stood and let out a breath. "And I'm sorry to hear your father's dead. We've slowed aging so much and cured so many diseases that news of every death is shocking."

As soon as Capt. Lindemann left, Tomas tried to go back to sleep, but instead he could only enter a restless nap where indistinct impressions of his squadmates and his foes drifted past. After a time, he gave up and grabbed his tablet with his left hand. A few awkward swipes got him to the hospital's spiritual and psychological services.

He skimmed until he found an entry. *Warrant Officer L. Younger, Peters-Stein Technique, no spiritual tradition required*, just a four-hour block of time on one of four afternoons a week. Not an Observation; from his name, the warrant officer wasn't from Sankt-Benedikts-Welt; and a long stretch of time away from the monotony of his bed, the same quadrilaterals of sunlight on the far wall, the backs of tablets and sleeping faces of his fellow inmates, appealed to him.

Tomas pressed the *Make Appointment* button. A notification popped up in response. *We will coordinate with your physical therapist for a time when you are ready for potentially strenuous activity.*

Strenuous activity? Maybe he wouldn't have to talk to anyone. Relaxed, he set the tablet on his nightstand and soon fell asleep.

He spent a week diligently following the therapist's instructions and eating his protein-rich meals. His new limbs felt and looked stronger every day. When the therapist mentioned he could be discharged a few days ahead of schedule, he felt a faint relief. The sooner he returned to his unit, the sooner fate would do with him what it would. By dedicating himself to the rehab regimen, a crust formed over his shame and guilt. No one would ever see his emotions. He would go to the warrant officer's consultation room, do the jumping jacks or whatever else the Peters-Stein Technique entailed, and get the stamp of approval for his return ticket to the front.

Even bad news broadcast by *Stars and Rays* failed to blunt his focus. Late in his first week of rehab, the Progressive Republic declared war on the Confederated Worlds. The rumor mill soon speculated about the number of ships the Space Force would withdraw to bolster the new second front. Tomas ignored the speculations. He would return to the fight against mike and the Uni remnants soon enough, and whether or not Shirley Foxtrot could engage in space supremacy missions would not change his destiny.

Except for restless, sweaty sleeps, punctuated by vague dreams that left his mouth tasting like cotton, the week of rehab passed easily.

One noontime, after a productive session in the fitness room, he waited for his lunch. And waited. Orderlies finally brought in food for the other soldiers, but when they reached his bed, one apologized to Tomas and gave his partner a recriminating look. "You forgot his lunch."

"I didn't load the cart—"

"You didn't count trays, either. Do I have to do everything?"

The second orderly looked sheepish. "Private, sorry, we'll get on the kitchen right away to get your lunch cooking."

"Good," Tomas said. "Because I am hungry."

Yet still he waited, while plates and utensils clanked around him and his stomach growled. How had the kitchen fouled up so badly?

His tablet chimed. Tomas picked it up, expecting a message from the kitchen. The man on the other end introduced himself as a corporal in the hospital's spiritual and psychological services department. "Chief Younger will see you in thirty minutes."

"I haven't had lunch yet."

"You won't need it. Get here as soon as you can."

He was hungry, and though the endorphin buzz of strength training dulled the sensation, he still fumed after the corporal ended the call. *Making me skip lunch....* His irritation stoked up when he realized Chief Younger had planned the whole event. *He'll bribe me with the promise of food if I tell him what he wants to hear. A piston* of anger worked in his chest as he followed a map on his tablet to the chief's consultation room.

He entered a small office on the hospital's sunward side. Light spilled around a shade drawn low over a single window. Stacks of paper on an extruded foam desk, two chairs with worn padding on thin metal arms. A faint clean smell of soap. A door in the far wall had a tablet mounted in the gypsum board next to it. *Welcome, Private Neumann. Palm scan required for entry.*

He pressed his palm on the tablet. A magnetic lock released and the door thudded free of the jamb. Tomas went in.

The room was much larger than the office. Thick curtains, featuring an outer layer of gray chameleonskin, covered the walls. An oval of can lights in the ceiling shone down around a smaller oval of a half-dozen chairs. On the longer sides of the oval sat four people, two men and two women, in civilian trousers and short-sleeved shirts, skimming and swiping tablets with intent expressions.

At the nearest short side of the oval sat the only GF member present. Tall and with feminine curves under her gray fatigues, her blond hair curled from under a garrison cap. Her head was bowed over a tablet; she gave one last authoritative swipe and dropped it into a pocket between the right-hand legs of her chair. She stood, extended her hand, and as she turned toward him said, "Private Neumann, I'm Warrant Officer Younger...."

Tomas froze. He wanted to flee. All the shame and guilt he had masked with physical therapy and fatalistic surrender flooded him, like the surge of some vast storm. Only the fact that he had go through this to return to combat kept him in the room.

She was the medic from the pillbox.

She recovered first. "Welcome, Private."

Her face was impassive, yet her eyes showed she paid him the fullest attention she could. Skin crawled on his back. "Am I?" His voice sounded thin.

"All are welcome here. I will say to you what I say to everyone: as you followed the path that led you here, you made the best choices you knew how to make. You are perfect as you are. If you're willing to change something that troubles you, we can help you. If nothing troubles you, or if something does and you are unwilling to change it, then we celebrate your perfection."

"Why are you mocking me? Perfect as I am? You know what I've done."

Some of the civilians shared puzzled looks behind her.

"Yes," Chief Younger said. "We've met before. Yes, I know one thing you've done. Does that thing trouble you?"

"What do you think?"

"I think you should have a seat." She gestured at the empty chair across the oval from hers. The chair was firm plastic and lacked cushions. The civilians watched him with intent faces. "So does something trouble you?"

As she spoke, a bright can light came on over his seat. A boom of electronic equipment the size of a launcher grenade hung from the ceiling next to it, angled at his head. He squinted and lowered his gaze. "Why are we playing this game?"

"Game?" Her calm expression hardened. "If you want to play games, this isn't the place. You can head back to the ward and I'll get to my paperwork."

"You're going to force me to talk about it? I don't have a choice. I need you to sign off on my psych evaluation."

Her face remained aloof. "If you want a signature, you can find someone else. A lot of my peers would sign off on you right now. Does something trouble you or not?"

His stomach growled and he felt light-headed. Tomas couldn't resist her firm voice. "Yes."

"What?"

The foot on his new leg started tapping the floor. Its rhythm worked up his body, rocking his upper torso back and forth. "Don't make me say it."

"Tell her about it," murmured a male civilian on his right.

"Keep quiet," muttered a female civilian on his left. "Tell her nothing."

"—tell her, tell her all—"

"—don't say a word—"

"—reveal everything—"

"—keep it in you and never let it out—"

Tomas wanted to turn his head from one to the other, but couldn't decide which. He stared at Chief Younger as the civilians kept muttering. His mouth opened but he couldn't speak.

"I won't make you say it," Chief Younger said, "but if you can't say it, I don't know how to help you with it."

"Please…" The tapping and rocking sped slightly and grew in amplitude. He shut his eyes against the bright light overhead.

"—say it all—"

"—you can never tell a soul—"

"Private, if you don't want to do this, that's fine." Chief Younger's voice sounded dispassionate. "Like I said, I have paperwork—"

"I killed them!" He kept tapping his foot and rocking his torso. "They had surrendered! I killed the one who slashed Marchbanks' throat, but then I killed them all!"

After the curtains surrounding the room swallowed the echoes of his words, their chameleonskin turned a deep glacial blue, except for a patch behind Chief Younger. Spiral arms of red and white swirled behind her head. Over a slow, thudding rhythm Tomas felt as much as heard, she asked, "What makes that a problem?"

His body froze. His mind followed the path of her words and ran headlong into their absurdity. "How can it not be a problem?"

"Some men can kill without remorse."

His tapping and rocking started back up again. "You think I'm like that?"

Her voice stayed dispassionate. "I don't know. Are you?"

"No!"

"Then what's the problem?"

"If only I could go back—"

"And stop yourself from killing them? Do you know of a time travel wormhole? I don't. What's the problem?"

Dammed emotions burst out of his subconscious. They clogged his throat with mucus and congealed around his voice. "I don't want to live! I don't want to die! I'm frozen in shame and guilt and anger and I can't get out!"

"Do you want to change that?"

"Yes!" The flooding emotions overwhelmed the tap of his foot. Both his legs flexed back and forth, lifting the front of his chair off the floor. His head thrashed forward and backward in counterrhythm to his legs. When his eyes were open, the red and white spiral arms swirled faster, an accretion disc around the vast gravity of her eyes. The slow thudding struck up a resonance in his mind that stretched out his consciousness too thin to remain. He was only a sea of emotions.

"Go!" shouted someone. From another, "You can do this!" Tomas heard only encouragement. "More, more." Chief Younger's was the strongest, most encouraging voice of all. "Turn it up!"

His legs flexed faster and higher. The chair's plastic back creaked when the rigid plastic flexed behind his back. When his head thrashed forward, his fists smacked his thighs. He grunted, long and loud, a bellowing animal. Around him, the voices kept up their encouragement.

"Freeze that feeling!" shouted Chief Younger. Tomas dropped his head and hands to his lap and stopped moving. His thoughts swirled, like sediments in a glass too turbulent to settle. Her voice turned clear and compassionate. "What's the earliest you remember feeling the same feeling you have right now?"

Sensations bubbled up. Memories never recalled before. Off in the distance, far from consciousness, rang the intuition these memories were true. "I'm four. We're leaving Sankt-Benedikts-Welt. I don't want to go."

"Tell us more."

Sadness lumped in his throat. A rustic interior of honey-colored wood; oaks outside, branches bare, and a dusting of snow on the ground; blocks of fabbed wood in the fireplace; the brown-haired man with the narrow jaw. Tomas spoke Sankt-Benedikts-Sprach without noticing. "I'm telling my father I don't want to go. I don't know where we're going but it's far away. He's talking but it's all big words and he's pretending to listen to me but I can tell he's pretending and nothing I say matters and I keep crying and screaming and my mother tells me to be quiet and accept his decision just like she's doing and then he gets angry at her don't you really want this I gave you every chance to protest and she says I'm doing this for your sake and isn't that good enough and I'm crying and screaming more why can't we stay...."

Chief Younger replied in the same language. "Was it like this, Tomas?"

He lifted his face. Chief Younger seemed a million miles away yet still the center of his attention. Behind her, the chameleonskin showed the mottled gray of an overcast afternoon all around the room. "Almost. We were indoors. Warm brown paneling." The chameleonskin changed colors. "A little warmer. Sankt-Benedikts-Stern is over there." He pointed to his ten o'clock. "And the fireplace—" His pointing hand moved to his eight-thirty. Colors bloomed in the appropriate spots on the walls.

"And your parents?"

One of the male civilians, with black hair and soft eyes, stood in front of Tomas, on his left side. On his right, one of the women, blonde and hunched, stood with her hands folded in front of her torso. Tomas stuck out his forefinger and middle finger and rolled his wrist back and forth. The civilians switched places. "And my mother looked stronger. She's steel, always steel. I don't know he could have hammered her into the shape he wanted." The woman lifted her shoulders and a rigid look filled her face. "Yes."

"And you?"

The other male civilian was short, stocky, red-haired, freckled. He looked nothing like Tomas, except his face showed so well the confusion and frustration Tomas had felt that distant day, felt that present moment. Tomas' speech fell away and tears filled his eyes. He managed to nod.

"Was it like this?"

The three civilians acted out the scene, in precise, impped Sankt-Benedikts-Sprach. The fourth, the other woman, waited behind Tomas' shoulder and murmured clipped, jargony Confed into a lapel microphone in response to his mutters and his body language.

He felt as if he watched his childhood self from a distance, crying and screaming. *Why must we go? I want to stay!* His father's expression pretended to be attentive, but all he did was use big words about duty and purpose to bulldoze his younger self's resistance, without success.

Then his mother spoke. The woman's portrayal sounded through him like a hammer on a Badger's hull. Like a magnet, it pulled out and aligned memories of his mother's commands to him over their years alone on Joséphine. *Be quiet. We're doing what your father wants.* Her tone showed she didn't want it either, and then his parents argued. The heat of their argument mounted and soon led into harsh words, plus threats and bluffs of irrevocable rupture between them.

The actor portraying Tomas trembled, eyes red as some mutant raccoon's. Tomas pitied the boy he had been, a boy still inside himself somewhere. Tears rolled out of his eyes. He grieved, and the grief swelled. It wasn't just for the past him. For the current him, for Marchbanks, for all the other dead, whether GF, mike, or Uni.

"Was it like this, Tomas?" Chief Younger's voice rang sweetly through the room.

"Yes." His voice sounded clear despite the emotions burning behind his face.

"Did you learn that day to shut down and hide what you're feeling?"

"Yes."

"Would you like to learn a different way to handle situations like this?"

His train of thought, still unsettled, stumbled again on the absurdity. "There can't be a different way."

"There is."

"What?"

Her eyes remained attentive on him. "May we show you?"

Tomas shrugged, nodded.

"I didn't catch that."

He met her gaze and loudly said, "Yes. Show me."

The civilians began from the start of the scene. His father spoke past Tomas' childhood self in big words and the redheaded actor's face showed the seed of a tantrum. But instead of screaming and crying, he said, "Father, may I tell you what I'm feeling?"

His father blinked a few times. "What? Of course."

"I feel confused and frustrated." His hand broke character, beckoning Tomas closer.

"Confused? Frustrated? You don't need to feel those things. We're moving and it's for the best."

Tomas hesitated as he moved forward. He knew the actor had the truth of his father. He ached to be so close to his father, yet so rebuffed by him. He wanted to bury his confusion and frustration and hope they would go away, but Tomas' childhood self stood resolute. "Thank you for telling me what you think I should feel. I feel confused and frustrated. What do you feel?"

His father's usual mild expression grew a little colder. "I feel you should accept that we're moving."

"I hear that's what you're thinking." The redheaded actor beckoned more and Tomas realized he wanted the two of them to speak together. Intuitions crystallized in Tomas' mind while shivers thrilled his skin. "What are—" Tomas joined his voice to the actor's. "—you feeling?"

His father's shoulders slumped. "Feeling? I'm frustrated. Not with you, with me. I explained why we're moving but I guess not clearly enough. We're Observers. You know what that means? We have a special calling to see clearly. Not just with our eyes, but with our minds. Our hearts. We have to see clearly so everyone else, on every human world, can learn to see clearly too. The people here on Sankt-Benedikts-Welt don't need us as much as the people on Nueva Andalucia."

Nueva Andalucia? A Unity world? What crazy script did this actor read? But those questions came from a distant corner of his mind, where the questioning judgmental part of him had been chained for the moment.

His father went on. "I think you'll like Nueva Andalucia. I'm not making that up to deny what you're feeling. I know you, son. I know what you like. The sun over Nueva Andalucia is a lot like Sankt-

Benedikts-Stern, maybe a bit more yellow. The people are friendly—
"

"Are they?" his mother asked. Her arms were folded protectively across her chest and she peered at his father. "There's no Observer presence there now. Why? Will we be the first to ever land?"

"Mother," the redheaded actor said. He said the word with an open final tone, which hooked Tomas.

More intuitions slid into new positions in his mind. He looked at the woman and saw his mother in the glint of the can lights in her cheekbones. Even if he projected a resemblance that wasn't there, perceiving the resemblance made Tomas' heart pound. Still, he knew what he had to say. "Mother, tell me what you're feeling."

She stepped back from his father, but kept her arms defensively across herself. "It doesn't matter what I'm feeling. We're leaving for Nueva Andalucia tomorrow."

Chief Younger cut through the tableau. "Don't let her avoid your question."

"Thank you for telling me what you're thinking. What are you feeling?"

"Feeling? About Nueva Andalucia? I can't say it. It would frighten you."

Across the room, Chief Younger opened her mouth to speak. Before she could, Tomas nodded for her sake and kept his gaze on his mother. "Thank you for thinking of me. Please tell me what you're feeling."

His mother looked alarmed. "Isn't it clear what I'm feeling about Nueva Andalucia?"

"I can only know for certain if you tell me. Please tell me what you're feeling." A joyous, potent feeling welled up his neck and into his head.

His mother's face froze and her voice came softly. "I'm afraid."

"There's nothing to be afraid of," his father said. The annoyance in his tone was plain.

"What are you feeling, father?"

His father looked between the two of them for a time, tension mounting in his face all the while, before speaking. "I'm even more frustrated." He turned to Tomas' mother. His hands suddenly rose to his cheeks. His face slumped against his fingers and his tension yielded to sadness. "I've done a horrible job explaining this to you, too, dear. Nueva Andalucia is a civilized place. Settled by ancient Europeans, just like Sankt-Benedikts—"

"I'm still worried," she said. "The ancient Europeans committed plenty of atrocities against one another. I know you think I'm over-reacting."

Chief Younger said, "Tomas...."

"Tell her what you're feeling, father. Please."

"I feel impelled to do this. Excited we could establish our tradi-tion on Nueva Andalucia. Surprised you are so worried. How long have you worried? I should have noticed—"

Tomas knew what to say. "Thank you for telling us how you judge your own behavior, father. Please tell her what you're feel-ing."

"—I'm sad I never noticed how worried you are." His father drew a breath and opened his shoulders to her reply.

Tomas had never imagined his mother could say her next words. "I'm embarrassed. I know in my head they aren't going to lynch us. If they were that primitive, they couldn't have survived a sublight settlement trip or terraformed their planet. Yet I worry for legitimate reasons—"

"Tell him what you're feeling, mother." He'd had enough prac-tice now for the thought behind the words to flow more vigorously, just as the physical therapy over the past week (somewhere, out there, a vast distance from this moment) made the movements of his new limbs stronger and more assured.

"I'm worried. A new language, new customs. What if we say something foolish, or offend the wrong person? I'm worried we'll fail. I'm worried we'll come back here in shame and everyone will know we failed."

His father went to her and put his arms around her. "How can we fail if we have each other?"

In the next quiet moments, Tomas dimly noticed the redheaded actor had backed away a while before. The thudding rhythm had been going on the whole time. Yet these notices soon drained away to whatever part of his mind held his judgment and his questions. His parents, channeled somehow by these actors, held each other close and looked lovingly into each other's eyes. Sharing feelings was all it took? He wished he'd known that—and he laughed.

"Tell me what you're feeling," Chief Younger said.

"Longing. It's like a warm belonging in my chest, on the cusp of deflating. This could have been my family, instead of—" He waved as if he shooed a fly, to indicate the prior scene. "Sorrow. I can't change what I did when I was a child. No time-travel wormholes. I feel resolved. I can't change my family's past, but I can change my future." He let his feelings come and go. "I feel alive."

The chameleonskin abruptly switched to an angry red all around the room. "What about—" Chief Younger's voice caught. Her eyes glistened in the can lights. "—the problem that troubled you when you came here?"

"I killed men who deserved to live. I can't change that, as much as I want to. That hurts. All I can do is act differently if I ever again enter a situation like that." Another intuition struck him. "And though I chose to kill them, they chose to die. The mike with the knife could have struck when Marchbanks was totally alone with them. He waited to be seen by me. The mike who begged for his life, he surrendered to his fate. He wanted to die."

Tomas' torso rocked with another intuition. "Marchbanks wanted to die too. He had the skills to disarm the mike with the knife. He didn't." *Why? Does 'why' even matter? If he sought to die, he got what he wanted.*

"And I wanted all this too. I wanted to kill them." He swallowed at one thorny thought. "I wanted Marchbanks to die? What did I want to hide from him so much that part of me wanted him dead?"

Chief Younger said, "I don't know the answer, Tomas."

"And I wanted to be smothered in shame and guilt for killing them. And I wanted you to see me kill them, so I could feel feared and hated. By my mother, but she wasn't there, so I made do with you. I regret treating you like an object instead of your own person."

The chameleonskin around the room slowly transformed from

red to blue. She gave him another look of pure attention. "Thank you for telling me what you feel. What comes up when I ask about your return to combat?"

Could he face Unis and mikes? Could he stand at the side of his squadmates? "I feel a mild regret we're at war. It's pulling down the muscles of my right cheek."

"I can see it from here."

He let out a breath. "We've all chosen to be soldiers. Me, my comrades, the Unis, the mikes. We've all chosen to risk death and try to kill each other. That's painful to contemplate, but it would be more painful to quit. I don't mean it would be painful to break rocks in a terraforming battalion. I need my squadmates to know I'll stick with them no matter what."

"Thank you for telling me those things," she said. "Is there anything else you'd like to tell us?"

His consciousness was moving back into the full volume of his mind. It stumbled over memories of the experience as it went. Questions about the Peters-Stein Technique occurred to him, but he let them go unasked. Hypnosis, skillful observing, acting, it didn't matter. Just its results mattered.

There was one question, though…. He turned to the actor who'd played his father. "Where did you get Nueva Andalucia? Do you have some records on my family that I don't know about? I have no memory of ever living on a Unity world."

The man set down a cup of water and swept his hands through his black hair. "I don't know why I said Nueva Andalucia. We're hypnotized a little when we're playing our roles, kind of like you are. It just came to me and made sense. I can't say that's what happened—"

"My only memory of my father is from a world with a golden sun. I used to think it was from Sankt-Benedikts-Welt, but your description of Nueva Andalucia fits better." The blue chameleonskin ringing the room seemed to glow. His head felt clear and his body, full of energy. He could return to his unit, not to surrender to his fate, but to work with it to become the kind of man he'd imagined Captain Schreiber and Marchbanks to be. "Thank you, all of you."

Chief Younger crossed the oval toward him. He rose and waited as she worked with her tablet. His new knee ached, a glorious ache, an ache of effort and well-earned rest. A moment later, his tablet pinged, and he reached down for it. A message from her.

"That's the official psych consultation document. Private Neumann, I approve your return to your unit." Her voice sounded calm and professional, but her next word came with audible feeling. She rested her hand on his forearm and said, "Godspeed."

13

Grant River Bridge

"I'm gone for six weeks and you lot can't hold the line?" Tomas dropped his pack on the ground next to his team's Badger.

Cohen set down his ration kit and stood up. His face had fresh lines and it took him a moment to grin. He hugged Tomas, slapping his hands on Tomas' back. "Good to see you. Looks like they glued your leg back on good as new."

"I'm glad to be back. I missed all of you. Even Alvarez."

"Fuck you." Alvarez grinned around a forkful of mashed potatoes.

"You had a safe flight up from R-town?"

Tomas backed out of the hug. "Mike had a few flyboys up, but my Bluejay pilot knows what he's doing." He spoke to Cohen more seriously. "Can I tell you something?

"Of course."

"In the hospital, I felt lonely a lot. Our team has been through a lot together and I felt bitter wondering why no one wrote me. But then I remembered I never wrote you when you were in the hospital, before New Boston. I can imagine you felt some of the same things then. I want to apologize for not writing you when you were laid up."

Cohen looked sheepish. "That was a long time ago."

"Sure, but my experience reminded me of it. If you ever want to talk—"

"I know how tough it is to send messages from up here," Cohen said. "I didn't expect any when I was recovering."

"I hear you. But I know now, when I was up here, writing you in the hospital would have reminded me the same could happen to me, and I wanted to hide from that. I don't want to hide anymore." Tomas clapped his hand on Cohen's upper arm, then surveyed the other men sitting alongside the Badger. Constitution lit their stubbled, dirty faces. They chewed lamb kabobs and roasted eggplant quickly, taut muscles bulging over their jaws. Haunted looks hovered behind their eyes. "Lundergard."

The Midgarder barely raised his left hand, then returned his attention to his meal.

Two new guys sat at the end of the row. New, but in less than six weeks, they'd seen enough to have the same hard-bitten look as the team's old hands. Cohen introduced them as Iommarino and Monroe. Iommarino wore a crucifix pendant outside his suit. Facets of the pendant flung reflections over his messkit when he moved. Tomas remembered the medal on the chest of the SF recruiting officer in Portage, then laid the thought aside. He'd known Iommarino for five seconds, which was long enough to know he was Tomas' teammate. Any comparison with a canned spam orificer would only make the SF recruiting officer look worse.

"We heard a lot about you," Monroe said.

Tomas shook their hands. "Some of it might even be true." He looked around. "Where's Ryan?" His tone fell at the end. He already knew.

"Mike got him," Cohen said.

A cold feeling washed down his torso. "I hope not on the day you guys came for me."

"Two weeks later. One of the new mike units. I hear there's twenty mike regiments now."

Tomas puffed out his cheeks and sagged against the side of the Badger. "Twenty? They outnumber us three to one?"

"They got bold when the Progressive Republic declared war."

Iommarino spoke as if he knew everything going on in mike territory and the PR capital.

If we can't control things, we want to believe we can at least predict what will happen. "The hospital buzzed about the SF withdrawals of ships to bolster the PR front."

"We don't need Shirley Foxtrot anyway," Alvarez said. His voice hinted at anger and fear.

"She'd just put photons in the wrong spot again," Tomas said with a tone of agreement he didn't truly share. His earlier complacency about SF redeployment had been a mistake. The less help the team got from orbit, the worse their chances in combat. He lied for the sake of the new men on the team. A shared glance with Cohen showed each of them the other knew the truth.

Chatter came over their earbuds. "Saddle up, fifteen minutes," said Capt. Marcinkus.

Cohen reached for a cold ration pack. "You need to eat?" he asked Tomas.

Tomas waved away the offer. "Ate on the truck coming in from battalion headquarters." That, and he'd written a letter to his mother, asking if his family had ever lived on Nueva Andalucia. He didn't expect an answer and set the thought aside. "I'm going to hang my pack and find the platoon commander. It's still—?"

A glum nod.

Tomas hung his pack on one of the hooks mounted on the outside of the Badger. He trooped around it, looking for Lt. Tower. The lieutenant and Sgt. Johnson stood twenty meters away, in the shade behind another of the platoon's vehicles. They looked up as Tomas approached.

He snapped his heels to attention. "Private Neumann reporting, sir."

"At ease." Tower's face showed his martinet side had come out today. "Ready to get back on your bike, Neumann?"

"Yes, sir."

"The war's changed while you were sipping protein shakes and visiting the Daughters. There's a shitload of mikes out there now. But it makes it easy to know who are enemies are. Anyone we see.

You listening?"

"Yes, sir." Tomas wanted to share a glance with Sgt. Johnson, but kept his attention on the lieutenant until Tower looked away.

"He's yours, sergeant. Get ready to roll out." Tower walked away.

Finally Tomas gave the sergeant the glance. Johnson shook his head in a broad arc. "He didn't say we kill everyone. We only fight mike. We still be on New Liberty to liberate its people from the Unity."

"That's what I read in *Stars and Rays*," Tomas said carefully.

"You'll see it here too. We still fight clean." Sgt. Johnson glanced around. "I and I know Lt. Tower be a poor platoon commander. I and I tell the company sergeant major at every chance. But we have the lieutenant until Capt. Marcinkus comes down the bifrost bridge and plucks him away."

"Where are we rolling to?" Tomas asked.

"When you be flying here from Reagantown, did you see all those rivers flowing darkward to sunward? We be heading for the far side of the Grant River, about a hundred-eighty klicks back. It be a wide deep river across the whole habitable zone."

Tomas pictured the map in his mind's eye. "The whole brigade's retreating."

Sgt. Johnson raised his eyebrow. "Retreating?"

"Sergeant, can't us soldiers call it what it is? If the louie were here I'd say 'redeploying.'"

"We be falling back. Not just us Blackjacks. Every brigade to sun-left of Reagantown. Now get in the Badger. Our platoon be right behind the Graywolfs at the point of the company's column."

MacInnis leaned and twisted backward to shake his hand when he boarded their Badger. Delacroix shouted greetings down from the turret. Tomas took Sharma's old spot in the back of the Badger, as well as his old assignment, grenadier. He and Monroe rubbed shoulders as the vehicle lurched forward. Whenever Tomas glanced to his left, the reflection of the video screens shone on Monroe's cheeks. Still young enough to need to see everything.

Skirmishes had taken place along the road: every few klicks, the cold, broken hulls of reconnaissance vehicles slumped along the roadside. Wrecked mike vehicles, speedier and lighter refits of the DeGaulle model, outnumbered demolished Weasels by about two to one; but mike had more fab cores on his side to crank out replacements.

Also common along the roadside were the toppled poles of obs wheels. The cameras, microphones, and related hardware in the cases had been either smashed or carried off. Dozens of meters away from the toppled poles, craters and scorch marks showed where the SF had put photons on the ground, following some indication of toppling telemetered by the poles. "Shirley Foxtrot must have gotten some mikes," Monroe said.

"And mike cleaned up all his dead?" Iommarino replied.

Tomas pointed at one of the toppled poles. About a meter and a half above the base, roughly hand height on a standing man, a dent marked the side of the pole. He'd seen the same dent on other fallen poles. "Looks like mike hitched a vehicle to them and pulled them out of the ground."

"Observation posts mean nothing if we can't put rifle fire on a mike trying to clear them," Cohen said. "Same with obstacles. Remember that."

They continued onward. The high gray cloud grew thicker, blacker. Either the atmosphere's dominant convection current played with mike's aerosols, or mike had more smudge pots to sunward of this location. The low rays of Constitution, slanting under the dark cloud, from time to time glinted off the wings of mike's aircraft.

In the turret, Lt. Tower said something indistinct. Delacroix replied, over the vehicle's net, "Yes, sir, full stop." The Badger's motor grew quieter and the clatter of the tracks stopped.

"What's going on?" Iommarino said.

Tomas put his hand on his rifle and grenade launcher, standing on the rack just inside the rear ramp. "We're probably getting out soon."

The lieutenant gave orders through the squad net. "Johnson, your squad has a recon mission. Drop the ramp," he added in an aside to MacInnis.

The ramp dropped. Tomas and his teammates picked up their weapons and went out. Behind their Badger, the one carrying Johnson's team had also stopped. The sergeant and his men rounded their vehicle and joined them.

"Twelve hundred meters to sunright, the road enters a valley," Lt. Tower said. At the mouth of the valley, the road fell out of sight amid the upper branches of a stand of pines on a hidden downward slope. A caution sign rippled with heat shimmer just before the road started its descent. To either side of the valley, wooded hills rose, forming a line vanishing into the distance. "We need to know if the enemy are in the valley. There are no obs wheels remaining on station anywhere nearby. Go on foot and take a look. You have forty-five minutes. No radio beyond squad net. Get going."

They set out in two columns on opposite sides of the road, each about forty meters from the living asphalt. Tomas' team was on the darkward side. After crossing the swell behind which the vehicles waited, the ground sloped slightly downward to the valley mouth. The column wound past low, brown shrubs. A trickling sound came from a gully to his left. Cool water would be a huge relief.... Even with all the infrared ports open on the back of his suit, the warm day already drenched him. He blinked away sweat and winced when it hit his eye.

They reached the mouth of the valley without incident. Cohen waved at them to get down and spread out. Tomas went prone behind a shrub and took a look.

To his left, the gully opened up into a jumble of rocks and muddy pools, tumbling toward a stream on the valley floor. The road took a sharp turn and descended into the valley at an angle through the pines covering the slope. The war had touched the woods; downhill from a pair of toppled obs wheel poles, SF fire had shattered a score of trees and stripped a hundred more of branches.

The road and the streambed met again about two klicks ahead, in a town of several hundred houses. Tomas' helmet display named it Shermanville. The largest structures were the municipal fab, two churches, and a school. Buildings crowded the road and a single bridge crossed the streambed. The ambush on the New Boston road had been in terrain far more spacious than the streets of this town. A mike with a grenade launcher could lurk within a few meters of a passing Graywolf or Badger. For that matter, a mike could emerge from hiding with a bucket of paint to blind the vehicle's cameras, or with a crowbar to wreck a drive wheel.

Going around Shermanville would be a poor option as well. Such a route would run between the wooded hills on one side and the town on the other. Flank and top armor would be exposed to grenades and missiles from mike teams concealed in the woods.

If mike was here at all. Tomas peered at Shermanville, zooming in with his helmet display. The town lay still. No cars traveled the streets, no pedestrians followed the sidewalks, no children played in the parks. Had mike ordered them to stay indoors? Or did the people cower in basements of their own accord in view of rumors of the GF movement nearby?

He couldn't tell by looking.

His helmet display showed they had three minutes before they needed to form up for the return to the platoon's vehicles. Tomas shifted to try scratching an itch on his sweaty back with the pack tucked inside his suit. As he moved, something metallic half-buried under a black sage shrub caught his eye.

"Found something," he said into the squad net. He crawled forward to take a closer look. As he guessed, a GF observation wheel. It hadn't fallen here when mike had toppled the elevated ones closer to the road. One of their scouts had placed it here. The front cameras were free of dirt. A glance toward the town showed the obs wheel had an unobstructed view. He announced his discovery to the squad.

"We can't upload it by radio," Sgt. Johnson said. "Louie's orders."

Tomas' heart thudded. Someone had to see what was stored on the obs wheel. He could call one of his squadmates, but how much of their remaining time would it take for someone to come over? More important, could he look his mates in the eye afterward?

A contrary thought came to mind. *If you were going to watch prere-*

corded video, you could have joined intel from the start, and saved yourself a lot of blood and pain.

A final realization settled his mind. He wouldn't trade his experiences as an infantryman for all the easy duty in the Confederated Worlds.

He flipped open the obs wheel's access port. Thanks to impped skills, he knew what to expect. A retracted reel held a data cable having a male connector with a trapezoidal cross section. The external control panel in the chest of his suit had a mating female connector. His hand reached for the flap in the chameleonskin covering the external control panel. He remembered his mother's words, at the pews when he told her he would enlist. *They'll make you watch recordings....*

No, mother. I choose to watch this recording. I'm doing something more important than saving my teammates from virtual fugue. I'm giving them a better chance to stay alive. Tomas opened the flap and pulled the data cable from the obs wheel. The male connector snicked faintly in his suit's external control panel.

Through his helmet display, his view of the valley below and the sky above abruptly changed. The sky was brighter, free of the high gray cloud of mike's smudge pots. A time stamp in the lower right corner dated the image he saw to eight days before. Despite his decision, his heart pounded. This was a photograph. He sensed the traps laid by the technology: vortices of nostalgia and obsession, false beliefs that a thing could be grasped by freezing its image. He gulped a breath. He was man enough to be able to use it and set it aside.

How many other things did he fear and hate at his mother's bidding?

Available video appeared in his helmet display. *204:14:39* and after a long moment the second incremented.

By touch, Tomas worked a stick-wheel on the control panel. Time lapse, six thousand to one. He started playback.

A hundred minutes passed in every second of video. The main streets blurred with motion at the busiest times of day. The sky darkened appreciably when mike's aerosol cloud reached the vicinity.

Nothing much—wait.

For a couple of seconds of playback, the parking lot of the school filled with a crowd of people. What would lead so many people to stand around for three or four hours?

His fingers worked the stick-wheel, pausing, rewinding, zooming, playing back more slowly. His helmet display picked up the outlines of three chameleonskinned trucks. Two rows of implant stations stood nearby, powered by temporary cables laid on the asphalt. Uniformed mikes guided people from the crowd to the stations, and from there to the school's football field.

Tomas panned the view. At one end of the field, a wooden mockup of a Graywolf sat with its flank facing mikes and civilians at the other end. Though the civilians fired dummy grenades and missiles, smacking and splintering the wood, the launchers were real.

"Mike's here, in force!" Tomas said into the squad net. "Grenade launchers and anti-tank missiles, a lot of them. Impped skills and three hours of blank firing exercises."

"Where did you get that?" Alvarez asked.

"Video from the obs wheel."

"Video?" Cohen asked. "Did you watch…?"

Sgt. Johnson spoke. "You be certain, Neumann?"

"Absolutely, sergeant."

"Then we go back to platoon. On the double."

They crawled out of view of the town, adjusted their infrared ports to dump heat out the front of their suits only, and jogged back. Sgt. Johnson sought out Tomas and linked a cable between their two suits. "Send I and I the video."

Tomas did. The sergeant said nothing for a few seconds, then whistled. "We won't drive into this, idrin." About six hundred meters from the vehicles, the extreme range of the squad net, Sgt. Johnson spoke again. "Lt. Tower, do you read?" His voice carried urgency. He repeated the call several times, without answer. The paper tiger had to be listening to the squad, didn't he?

If he did, he didn't reply until the squad could make out the chameleonskinned machine guns of the Graywolfs at the head of the column. "Tower here. What, sergeant?"

"Mike has set an ambush in the town. We have video of civilians getting impped skills and testing fabbed anti-tank weapons. We can't go forward."

"Are you certain?"

"Two of us have seen it, including one of my sharper soldiers, Neumann."

Lt. Tower said nothing. Picked up by the lieutenant's microphone in the confines of their Badger's turret, Delacroix's muffled voice said, "Neumann?"

Finally, the lieutenant said, "Get that video to me. I can't call Capt. Marcinkus without an officer seeing it."

"Sir, maybe I and I was unclear. I and I've seen it as well—"

"It's not your career if we hugely deviate from our movement axis because we're spooked by phantoms. Get me that video. Tower out."

Johnson slumped his head for a moment, then shook it clear and beckoned the squad to hurry to their Badgers. Once inside, the infantrymen opened up all their infrared ports, lifted helmets, and mated air conditioning lines with the intakes on their suits. Sgt. Johnson entered Tomas' team vehicle, crowding the rear compartment even more than usual as he plugged a data cable from the wall into his suit and talked live to the lieutenant.

MacInnis writhed around and stuck his head out of the driver's compartment. "Neumann, did I hear this right? You watched video from an obs wheel?"

"That's right."

MacInnis double-took. "I thought it was against your religion."

Tomas shrugged. "The thing I most want to observe are you lot in civilian clothes on discharge day."

No one spoke for a moment, until Cohen chuckled. His actions released laughter from Lundergard and MacInnis, followed by the new guys.

"Cut the chatter!" Lt. Tower's voice echoed down from the turret. "We have orders from Capt. Marcinkus. The company will take a new route to the Grant River bridge. This will be longer than we expected, but the bridge will be destroyed at the same time. Everyone, strap in and prepare to move!"

Shouts of "yes, sir" filled the vehicle. Sgt. Johnson disconnected the data cable and moved for the ramp, then turned back to Tomas and gave a fist tap to Tomas' upper arm. "You did good, Neumann."

"I'm glad I could help the squad, sergeant."

"Was I not clear?" Lt. Tower called out.

Sgt. Johnson gave the underside of the turret a hooded glance, then trotted out. MacInnis shifted back into his usual position in the driver's compartment. The ramp closed behind him and the men strapped themselves into their seats.

The Badger lurched into motion. Alvarez spoke. "You bastards need to tell me something." His enunciation of *bastards* larded the word with a slight insult.

Cohen crossed his arms and turned to look at Alvarez. "What?"

"Why are you acting like Neumann did something great?"

Anger spiked in Tomas, but he also sensed sadness, partially masked by the anger like the surface of New Liberty under mike's aerosol cloud. The emotions flooded him. He couldn't respond.

"He violated a strong religious precept," Cohen said, "to save us from a potential ambush. Does that mean anything to you? Do you have any religious precepts?"

"Yeah. One," Alvarez replied. "Our team better be more important than anyone's god. I won't congratulate you for doing something you should have been doing from the day you joined us. You hear me, Neumann?" He glared at Tomas.

"I'm not asking for congratulations," Tomas said. He'd done the right thing. Maybe it would have been better for no one to know. He sought something more to say, to bring Alvarez to his side; but the other tucked his hands into his armpits, shut his eyes, and rested his chin on his chest.

"Haven't they set the explosives?" Iommarino said. He raised his voice over the burble of the river at the foot of the bluff. He stood next to a concrete structure showing a meter-high wedge above the ground. An alloy cable, thick as a fat man's thigh, ran from a hole in one side of the wedge to the top of the nearest tower of the Grant River bridge. He slapped the cable to emphasize his words.

"Over there." Cohen pointed to the river's sunright bank, six hundred meters away, where blurs of chameleonskin showed the bulk of the company's vehicles moving into defensive positions. A few tiny human figures worked at the cable anchorages near the foot of the tower holding the suspension cable on that side. "You only have to blow one anchor per cable for the whole thing to fall."

"Is blowing up the bridge going to be enough?" Monroe asked. "How high and steep are the bluffs?"

"Mike can't drive down," Tomas said. He stood at the edge of the bluff overlooking the river. A steep slope bearing pines dropped twenty meters over about fifteen meters of distance. A dirt trail forty centimeters wide switchbacked down the bluff, ending at a flat strip of sandy puddles before the river's main channel.

"You're certain?"

"I'm certain."

"Alright, idrin, enough sightseeing." Sgt. Johnson gestured. Four vehicles, two Graywolfs and two Badgers, sat hull down in tank scrapes. Beyond them, a quarter-circle of foxholes ran from the top of the switchback down the bluff to the sunleft shoulder of the road. "The engineers gave our task force some nice holes. Time to get to them."

The squad split into buddy teams and started toward the foxholes. "Sergeant, how close is mike?" Lundergard asked.

"Not as close as our scouts and rear guard." The sergeant sounded testy. "We be here until the entire battalion gets across."

Tomas and Iommarino settled into the foxhole nearest the road. The view out the firing port showed sparse tufts of grass all the way to the sunleft horizon. Interrrupted lengths of the road showed over rolling hills.

Above, mike's aerosol cloud covered the far half the sky. Icons superimposed on Tomas' view showed seven Crows, airmobile hussar transport thopters, wheeling to sunright. Their wings swatted the air when they passed over the foxhole.

In the silence after the Crows passed, the ground level wind moaned as it carried wisps of sand across the road's living asphalt. In lulls, the rumble of distant gunfire reached them.

"Is that them or us?" Iommarino asked.

Tomas angled his ear that direction. "That's mike. Hear that whoosh, though? Our antitank missiles."

"So mike's sending armor our way." Iommarino's voice sounded hesitant.

"He's sending everything our way. Maybe we'll be across the river by the time he arrives."

A few minutes later, the first friendly vehicles appeared in their helmet displays. Three Weasels from a scout platoon, one of which had a blank panel of chameleonskin. The icons representing the scout vehicles remained visible even when the Weasels dipped out of sight behind rolls in the landscape.

The Weasels slowed when they neared the foxholes. Although their identity beacons could not be forged, mike still could have patched up wrecked Weasels he'd found on the battlefield. But when the hatch on the lead Weasel popped open, Tomas' helmet display identified the head sticking out as belonging to the lieutenant commanding the scout platoon. "Soldier, where's the task force commander, Lt. Tower?"

"In the scrape behind us nearest the road," Tomas called. "If I may, what's going on?"

"Mike's tanks are on our tail. They knocked out one of us and nicked another. Three thousand meters behind us, before we lost sight of him. The terrain rolls too much. Keep your eyes peeled. He might sneak up on you." The scout lieutenant looked inside the hatch and swatted his hand on the turret. The lead Weasel lurched into motion and the remaining ones followed.

"How close could mike get to us without us seeing him?" Iommarino sounded nervous.

"Too close," Tomas said. "He knows the terrain, and we don't have obs wheels away from the road."

"He couldn't pop up right in front of us. We'd see his dust in the distance."

"Would we? Assumptions are a good way to end up dead."

Tomas pondered. "Even if he snuck up on us, he'd have to worry about fire from our Graywolfs. If our tanks and mike's start dueling, keep your head down. We're in the safest place we could be."

Iommarino gave him a look mingling incredulity with a dollop of fear. "You're not scared?"

Tomas looked him straight in the eyes. "I'm very scared, and I'm glad for it."

"Glad?"

"Because it reminds me not to take stupid chances." Tomas gestured out the firing port. "Now let's watch for mike."

Lt. Tower soon came on the task force net. For the benefit of everyone other than Tomas and Iommarino, he relayed the scout lieutenant's report that mike might be within three klicks and closing. He also reported another scout platoon was still beyond their perimeter and due any moment. "If mike gets here first, we'll hold the bridgehead as long as we can or until the scouts report they can't reach us. Stay calm, all of you."

Tomas peered across the landscape. At a hill's crest seven hundred meters out, patches of air shimmered. He grabbed his grenade launcher. Those shimmers had to be... but they didn't look like chameleonskin. Instead, sunlight dazzled in them as if they were a mist of water.

He zoomed in on one of them with his helmet display. The patch showed vertical streaks, like water from a sprayer. Below the vertical streaks, dirt grew darker, and tiny puddles formed on the ground. Water indeed, soaking into the soil.

Tomas yanked on Iommarino's arm. "Get down!"

A cannonade boomed from the far hill. It sounded louder than the gun of one Marlborough, or even a platoon of Marlboroughs. How many tanks had mike sent after them? The ground shook when mike's shells struck near the hull-down GF fighting vehicles, rattling dust out of the foxhole's walls and making the two men waver on their feet.

"I know why we didn't see mike's dust!" Tomas shouted but still could barely hear his own voice. "He's rigged up sprayers to wet the ground in front of his tracks!"

The two Graywolfs fired, and a missile whooshed from a Badger. The task force's vehicles were still in the battle. Mike would need fortunate hits to strike their turrets while the ground around their shallow holes hid the bulk of their hulls.

The reverse was true. The crest of the distant hill covered most of the front slopes of mike's tanks. The distance made Tomas' grenade launcher ineffective. He leaned it against the wall of the foxhole and picked up his rifle, in case mike had infantry nearby.

Voices shouted in the task force net. "Goddammit, how many tanks does mike have?" Lt. Tower's voice sounded high and thin. "A company? We've got to get across the bridge now!"

"Tower, we still have scouts outside the perimeter," said the Graywolf platoon commander, Lt. Lampenius.

"Four Weasels can't get past a company of tanks!" Lt. Tower sounded frantic. "We've done all we can. I'm ordering a withdrawal."

"Withdrawal? The scouts can get through, if we help them. We're relatively safe in our scrapes and can launch smoke over the whole area."

"I was given command of this task force," Lt. Tower replied. "We're withdrawing. Infantry, remount now."

A lull in the tank guns' fire let Tomas hear Iommarino's fast, ragged breaths. "Is he serious?"

"—We're on our way." Radio chatter from Alvarez partially masked Iommarino's words.

"He's in command." Tomas worked his suit's controls for the infrared ports. Open the ones in front, close the ones in back. He waved his hands over his torso and legs to confirm as he said, "He made a valid point. Better to write off the scouts than get us all killed or captured. The longer we wait to head for the bridge, the more time for mike to find a better firing angle against us. Get your infrared ports set."

Iommarino moved his hands closer to the infrared ports on his chest. "I got them. I can feel the heat."

"Did you close the rear ports?"

"Of course I—damn." Iommarino fiddled with the control panel, then waved his hands behind his back. "Damn. I almost forgot that? My back would've been covered in bulls-eyes—"

"We caught it," Tomas said. He clapped Iommarino on the shoulder. "Get going. I'll follow in a second."

Iommarino scraped over the loose rock. Pebbles clattered to the foxhole floor. Tomas looked out the foxhole's firing port. No mike infantry; not even vague smears of low probability calculated by the computers in his helmet and shilling. Maybe they would make it across the bridge. He turned and crawled out.

Guns boomed around him. He followed Iommarino around tufts of hardy grass, on a line that would take them about as far between the nearest Graywolf and the front of their Badger as possible. An armor-piercing shell shrieked into the dirt near the Graywolf, thirty meters away, kicking up dust but not detonating. Relief relaxed his shoulders. They would be able to remount without much trouble. The vehicles would then drop some thick smoke and call in harassing fire from the formations on the other side of the river. They could make it across in one piece.

The guns lulled again. Through the relative silence came the hydraulic whine of a Graywolf turret adjusting its position, followed by the thwock of a thopter's wings.

Thopter? Tomas looked up. A red icon flashed in his helmet display and warning tones sounded through his earbuds. Not GF— mike. An Immelmann fighter floated three hundred meters overhead, gliding from station to station like a kite. Flashes on its belly showed the muzzles of its machine guns. Tomas flinched and pulled his knees toward his chest. A second later, the sound of its fire reached the ground. It sounded like a flock of woodpeckers hammering a hardwood tree.

Dust kicked up behind the dropped ramp of the lieutenant's Badger, followed by twinned screams through the air and the squad net. Alvarez and Monroe had been the first members of the team to reach the vicinity of the Badger's rear compartment. Tomas' helmet display showed their icons, both dull red and throbbing. Side ports of their suits glowed in infrared.

"Shit! I'm hit!" Alvarez shouted. "Somebody, help me."

"Oh lord Jesus help me," said Monroe. His voice sounded tight with pain. "Help me lord Jesus. Please sweet Jesus."

Lt. Tower shouted more frantically than before. "Mike air on an antipersonnel mission. I don't have anti-air assets! Don't you bastards have any deployed?" Sounded like he spoke with the rest of the company's platoon commanders and had forgotten to close the channel to the task force. "I can't remount the infantry if you don't clear the sky!"

The Immelmann's machine guns fired again. Tomas' helmet display marked the target area, behind the other Badger on this side of the bridge. Alvarez continued to shout for aid. Tears choked Monroe's voice.

"High prob a mike tank platoon peeled off the end of their line," said a Graywolf crew chief. "We've lost them on lidar, infrared, and visual."

"I can't remount the infantry and mike's armor is trying to outflank us!" shouted Lt. Tower. "We have to save our vehicles and crews! Vehicles are withdrawing now!"

Tomas snapped his gaze to his Badger. Had he heard right?

Lt. Tower kept shouting. "Goddammit, MacInnis, that's an order and you'll be court-martialed if you don't lift the ramp and put this sonofabitch into gear!"

The Immelmann's machine guns fired another burst as Sgt. Johnson said, "Sir, we can hold until company drives off mike's bird. Sir. Sir?"

Lt. Tower made no reply. The Badger backed out of its scrape.

"Don't leave me and watch where you're driving you almost hit me!" Alvarez shouted. The Badger slewed sharply, a deft motion for a forty-ton vehicle, then shifted gears and moved forward, right at Tomas. He quickly crawled to the side. The Badger passed three meters from him. MacInnis knew how to drive. The Badger picked up speed and headed for the roadway leading onto the bridge, followed by the platoon's other Badgers from both sides of the road. Mike shells chased them but missed.

"How will we get across the river?" Lundergard asked into the squad net.

"Ride the Graywolfs!" yelled Iommarino with naïve confidence.

Cohen replied, "The Graywolfs will be prime targets for all those mike tanks. You don't want to ride a Graywolf when its reactive armor goes off." The guns of mike tanks fired to emphasize his words. Shells roared overhead.

"We aren't leaving yet." Lampenius, the Graywolf commander, spoke. "We're men with skills, not paper tigers." Some cheers followed his words through the task force net.

"Dammit, where's a medic?" Alvarez shouted. "I need a medic!"

Tomas glanced up. The Immelmann flitted from point to point in the air above, continuing to fire bursts at the ground. A burst shredded the chameleonskin roofing his former foxhole. He crawled in the other direction, toward the wounded men.

Alvarez writhed, clutching his left leg. A round had shattered his knee, but he'd managed to get a self-wrapping tourniquet around the middle of his thigh. He'd live. "You're not a medic!" he yelled at Tomas.

"You did a good enough job on yourself," Tomas said. "You don't need a medic."

"Wait! I need help!"

"So does he." Tomas crawled toward Monroe.

Blood stained the ground and slicked Monroe's tattered suit. His shilling telemetered signs of severe shock. Rapid pulse, rapid breathing, low body temperature. His slurred voice sounded like it came from far away. "Take me, lor' Jesus. Grea'-mee-maw, course you here by His throne...."

Grief washed over Tomas. "You'll be okay," he said, and the grief was chased by guilt.

"More'n okay. I'm in the arms of the lord." Monroe fell silent, and his icon in Tomas' helmet display darkened to deep red.

Tomas gripped his gloved hand. *I wish I could mourn you now, Monroe—*

An odd sound came from behind him. He let go of Monroe's hand and looked over his shoulder.

A loud twanging sound came from the anchorage, followed by the double-crump of nearly-simultaneous explosions at each of the cable anchorages on the far side of the bridge.

The twanging grew louder. The cables, pulled taut across the river, were now free to relax. The relaxing tension pulled them from the top of the tower on the sunright bluff. The sheared cables plunged toward the bridge deck. The deck writhed as it crumbled into the river below.

"They've blown the bridge!" Tomas shouted into the task force net.

For a moment, no one spoke. Even mike's tank guns fell silent. Then men erupted into babble on the task force net, some plaintive, some frantic, but a few—Johnson, Cohen, Lt. Lampenius, and Tomas—calm. "There's a switchback down the bluff!" Tomas shouted repeatedly, until most of the soldiers stilled their babble. "We can make it to the riverside and swim across."

"And abandon our vehicles?" Lampenius asked.

"Sir, seems to me we can fab tanks, but we can't fab brains to learn the skills to drive tanks."

"Good point—shit! Mike tank platoon, on our flank!"

Two Graywolfs swung their turrets and fired their main guns. Too late for one—a mike shell pierced the top deck near the bottom of the turret. The hatch popped. Two crewmen leaped out frantically as fire licked the edge of the hatchway. The men wore simple camouflage patterns, no chameleonskin, no infrared wicking. The sky silhouetted them as they scrambled for cover. Some of the main line of mike tanks fired their machine guns. One of the Graywolf's escaped crew toppled.

"We must abandon the position, sir," Sgt. Johnson said.

Lampenius grunted. "Agreed. What about mike's bird? A mass of men at the top of a switchback would be prime targets."

Wisps of sound came from across the river. A glance at the sky showed missiles streaking toward the Immelmann. Finally someone had answered Tower's call for anti-aircraft fire.

The Immelmann left its hover and accelerated to sunleft, spitting out a cloud of reflective particles in an attempt to confuse the guidance packages on the missiles. The missiles detoured around the reflective particles. The Immelmann lurched from side to side like a clumsy hummingbird. It avoided the missiles, but was soon a shrinking speck heading into the distance.

"All right, that settles it." Lampenius said, "Infantrymen, get down that switchback. We're going to destroy our vehicle, then follow you."

"I'll throw smoke canisters," Sgt. Johnson said. "We still need men with grenade launchers to cover us against mike's armor."

Tomas blinked. He was one of those men. But I need to get Alvarez—No. *We* need to get Alvarez across the river.

"Iommarino!" Tomas shouted. "Help Alvarez to the switchback!" No answer. "Iommarino, you can do this! The team needs you!"

"Yeah, yeah, I'm coming, I'm coming." Iommarino soon scrambled to them. He wrapped his arm over Alvarez' chest and started crawling, dragging the wounded man, all without meeting Tomas' gaze.

"Good job, Iommarino," Tomas said. A few dozen meters away, a canister arced end-over-end through the air. It clacked on the stony ground and spewed gray smoke. Another canister followed. The last functioning Graywolf chuffed out more. Tomas peered into the gloom and held his fire. He only had four grenades and didn't want to waste them. Soon a thick pall covered the area, obscuring the GF soldiers as they crawled and dragged their wounded to the top of the switchback.

The enemy could probably guess what the GF was trying to do. The mike tanks fired their machine guns through the smoke, wounding one man by luck. The number of GF soldiers at the top of the switchback dwindled. Tomas' helmet display showed icons of descending soldiers on his view of the ground between him and the bluff.

The surviving Graywolf fired one more armor-piercing round into the gloom. The blast from its gun's muzzle flashed like lightning amid the smoke. A few moments later, its hatch opened. Lampenius laid it quietly against the turret, then jumped to the ground and waved the crewmen out. "Forty-five seconds until it self-destructs," he told the task force. "Get down the bluff face before it goes."

The Graywolf crew, starkly visible in their camouflage uniforms, crouched and ran for the switchback. Their commander followed.

Tomas and the other man with a grenade launcher took turns bounding for the switchback. Tomas was first to reach the top of the bluff. He hid behind a shrub four meters from the top of the trail as the other man made his final bound.

The ground rumbled. Tracks clacked somewhere in the gloom. A vague shape, flickering with probability estimates aided by the lidar still functioning on the last Graywolf, coalesced out of the smoke. A Marlborough. Its gun traversed and elevated like a sniffing aardvark nose. Tomas aimed at the front drive wheel. Time seemed to slow in the moment before he fired. He ran for the trailhead. It took a few seconds for him to realize the grenade had telemetered a hit.

The rumble deepened and the clack of tracks heightened, soon followed by a colossal roar when the Graywolf exploded. Shards of metal whizzed over the edge of the bluff, some on steep trajectories. "Hunker, hunker!" Tomas shouted into the task force net. Men pressed themselves against the face of the bluff as metal splintered branches and clattered against the slope. "Go!" he yelled after the last fragments of the Graywolf's hull fell to the ground.

The men hurried down the slope. Tomas slung his grenade launcher over one shoulder and brought his rifle to his hands from the other. At the first switchback, he glanced back the way he'd come. The gun of a mike tank was visible above the bluff's edge. Though close to it, the men were safe; Marlboroughs couldn't depress their armament low enough to fire down the slope.

They could probably fire on the middle of the river channel, but that was a problem for a few minutes from now.

The men formed up on the sandy flat. "I'm the last one down," Tomas said. "Let's get across."

Sgt. Johnson spoke with his usual aplomb. "Idrin, start swim—"

"Sergeant," Tomas said, "with respect, impped skills are no guarantee of success on an open water swim. A soldier might know the motions but lack the knowledge in the bone of how to handle the current. I suggest we buddy up. The strongest swimmers buddy with wounded and the next strongest buddy with weaker swimmers. Before you get in the water, drop anything you don't need. We can fab it later."

"Good ideas, Neumann. Who be my strong swimmers?"

Tomas said, "I'm pretty strong; I'll take Alvarez. And men, if your buddy flails, take care of yourself first." He dropped the grenade launcher to the damp sand. He went to Alvarez while the rest of the men buddied up.

Alvarez clutched the thigh of his wounded leg with both hands. He thrashed his head side-to-side when Tomas approached. "I don't need help."

"Do I have to get the sergeant to order you?"

"Alright." Alvarez shifted his weight, then his upper body froze, head facing the top of the bluff. "Shit, we've got more mikes at the party."

Tomas glanced up long enough to see mike infantrymen at the top of the bluff, shouting at one another and drawing their rifles.

"Idrin, in the water, now!" Sgt. Johnson shouted. He fired his rifle at the top of the bluff. "Lieutenant, can we get some cover—"

"Working on it," Lampenius said. "Company, we need anti-personnel suppressing fire on the top of the bluff. Do you read? We need anti-personnel suppressing fire. Don't let them get down the bluff!"

Rifle fire came from the mikes atop the bluff, pinging the ground around the clearest targets, the Graywolf crewmen. A mike team started down the slope.

Tomas put his arm around Alvarez and lifted him to his good foot. They hobbled across the sand, Alvarez cursing with every step. The river babbled down the main channel. Blurs masked by spray showed where the first swimmers had entered the water. The river's current looked stronger from up close. Machine guns on the sun-right bank drummed out rounds against the mike infantry.

Tomas and Alvarez waded in. "Son of a whore it's cold!" Alvarez said.

Tomas grabbed Alvarez' right arm with his left and dove. He started a sidestroke, working the water with his right arm and towing Alvarez with his left. A few rifle rounds smacked the water nearby.

The river was indeed cold, the product of glacial melt from the icecaps covering New Liberty's dark face. The water seeped between the collar of Tomas' suit and the bottom of his helmet. Too long in the river and something would get them, either hypothermia or the extra weight soaking their suits. Glances at the bluffs showed the current rapidly pushed them downriver. Tomas adjusted course toward the sunright base of the bridge.

"Still with me?" Tomas asked Alvarez.

Alvarez didn't reply. Suddenly worried, Tomas checked his helmet display to see if the other's vitals had gotten worse. He almost asked again when Alvarez finally spoke. "Go ahead, say it."

"What?"

"Don't lie." Alvarez sounded resigned. "You caught me and you know it."

He wanted to feel guilty, Tomas realized. About what? "I want to hear it from you in your own words."

Machine guns and the main armament of tanks fired atop both bluffs. Tomas listened for the fire of mike rifles, or the smack of Marlborough machine guns striking the river, and heard none. The GF suppressing fire did its job.

"I talked so much shit about you," Alvarez said. "That your god outweighed our team. But shit, who am I to talk? My god has outweighed the team too. At least your god was something bigger than you. Mine wasn't. My god was nothing. It was me."

Tomas stroked and kicked, adjusted course. "You."

"Dammit, how much are you going to make me say? Me. My own fucking ego. All I've given a damn about is getting out of here. I kept my head down and didn't help anybody else. I didn't even help Monroe. I saw his wounds and the telltales on my helmet display—"

The shoals at the foot of the sunright bluff were too low to the river for Tomas to gauge the distance. "You couldn't have helped him."

"Shit, don't say that. I could've helped him just as much as you did. Human contact, a consoling voice." Alvarez' voice caught. "All I wanted him to do was die so I didn't have to hear his words as he hung on. I'm not like that. I'm no saint but I swear to god I'm not like that."

Tomas took more strokes. "Yeah, you're no saint. You're something better." He stroked again and his outstretched right arm brushed sand beneath him. He stretched his legs toward the shallow bottom, then helped Alvarez to stand up. "You're my squadmate."

"Shit."

"Listen to me." He put his arm around Alvarez and helped him hobble onto the shoal. A cool wind from darkward made Tomas shiver. "You've made the best choices you've known how to make. If you want to make different ones, I will gladly help you. If you want to make the same ones, I will gladly help you do that too." At the top of the bluff in front of them, GF machine guns and ordnance boomed out fire against the mikes across the river. Other men from the squad, as well as the Graywolf crews, crawled dripping and shaky-legged onto shore. "Now let's get dry."

14

The New Lieutenant

"Ten-hut!" Sgt. Johnson called. Tomas and the rest of the platoon came to attention as the new lieutenant took his place in front of them on the parade ground.

The new lieutenant surveyed them for a time. His brown eyes shared a palette with his tanned face and the dusty greens and khakis of the camouflage pattern on his garrison cap. He stood stiff-backed, with pressed camouflage fatigues and shined boots. Do we have another Academy grad?

"At ease. I'm Lt. O'Brien. I'm replacing Lt. Tower, who I'm sure you've heard has been reassigned." He studied them more. Tomas kept his face blank.

Lt. O'Brien smirked. "Every platoon I've served in has had a man with his ear to the rumor mill. I don't need to know who serves that function here, but I'm no paper tiger you can lie to. Play straight by me and I'll return the favor."

Tomas let out a breath. The new lieutenant had come up through OCS.

Lt. O'Brien delivered a brief speech. He'd reviewed the platoon's record. Any black marks on it were attributable to previous poor leadership. The platoon had good men and he was honored to lead them.

He then greeted each of the soldiers in turn. Tomas kept his eyes mostly forward, but occasionally let them stray as he tried to over-hear the new lieutenant's conversations. He'd studied their dossiers, Tomas realized, asking Cohen about his home region on Shambhala and talking with Iommarino about their high schools' rivalry in the McAuliffe city sports leagues on Challenger.

Yet he had little to say to Tomas. O'Brien mainly scrutinized him and muttered small talk. A measure of disappointment grew in him until O'Brien said, "Come with the sergeant to my office after we're done here." O'Brien then moved on to the next man in line.

Disappointment vanished, replaced with fear. Had he done something to irritate the new lieutenant already? In the rank ahead of him, Iommarino turned with boggled eyes and mouthed *what?*

Tomas accepted his fear and shrugged. He'd find out soon enough.

After the inspection, Sgt. Johnson waited in front of the platoon while the other soldiers left the parade ground for the shelters. Word had somehow spread about Tomas' orders, and each man took it differently. Cohen bumped Tomas' shoulder with his fist and mur-mured "Good luck," while Lundergard avoided Tomas' gaze and walked a long arc around the sergeant to keep at a distance.

"Sergeant, do you know what this is about?"

Sgt. Johnson showed a poker face. "I and I have an inkling."

"Sergeant, tell me."

"Better you hear it from Lt. O'Brien himself. Let's go."

The company's new base was a cluster of shelters bermed to the eaves with dirt. No windows here. Constitution stood a hands-breadth above the top of the innermost of the razor wire fences form-ing the base's perimeter, higher in the sky than anywhere else Tomas had seen it on-planet. The more intense rays of the sun compounded his nervousness, sending sweat streaming down his neck as he ap-proached the cluster of shelters housing the platoon commanders' offices.

The LEDs in the ceiling were fabbed to match the output spec-trum of Epsilon Eridani, Challenger's sun. After all his time on New Liberty, the light struck Tomas as too white, too austere. It made the text displayed by the tablet and stacks of paper on the lieutenant's desk too stark. It sharpened the lines of Lt. O'Brien's face and the scrutiny in his eyes.

Tomas snapped his heels together and saluted. "Private Neumann reporting, sir."

O'Brien returned the salute. "At ease. I'm sure you're wondering why I called you here. I've been reading your dossier. Coming into the GF, it was clear you were smart and had some good aptitudes. Your early record as an armored grenadier is solid. But since your return from the hospital in R-town.... Some men get wounded and they come back to the front fearful it will happen again. Others come back foolhardy, thinking death had its best shot at them and missed. You avoided both those traps."

"I had an excellent psychological and spiritual consultation at the hospital in R-town, sir."

"Whatever the reason," Lt. O'Brien said, "you've become an excellent soldier. Sgt. Johnson has written pages and pages of favorable reviews."

Tomas' eyebrows rose. Sgt. Johnson stood a little taller. "Don't let it go to your head, Neumann."

Lt. O'Brien went on. "Lt. Lampenius hadn't met you before the day you crossed the river, but he has great praise for your actions. Lt. Tower didn't say much about you... and all else being equal, that's another point in your favor." He leaned back and laid his hands on his desk.

"Favor? Sir, are you putting me up for a medal? Are we pitching hero stories to the media to fluff up the war effort?"

Lt. O'Brien crossed his arms and leaned back further. "You're telling me you think you deserve a medal?"

"Sir, no. I'm telling you, I did my duty because it was the right thing to do."

"Did your duty? You went beyond your duty. You violated your religious precepts and avoided an ambush that would have wrecked this company as a fighting force. After Tower blew the bridge early, you showed initiative. You gave the sergeant and Lt. Lampenius sound advice. You led twenty-five men across the river."

"Sir, I only made suggestions to my superiors."

"Well phrased." Sgt. Johnson chuckled.

More sweat dampened Tomas' nape. "Whatever I've done well, there are too many men in the GF who would've done as well in the same situation. I don't deserve more recognition than they do."

With a smile, Lt. O'Brien shook his head. "As it turns out, I am putting you up for a medal. But I didn't call you in here to talk about a new bauble for your dress uniform. I'm here to talk to you about a promotion."

Tomas took in the words and noted his feelings. "I'm flattered, and confused. The platoon has a full complement of corporals—"

"No, Neumann. Not corporal, or even sergeant." Lt. O'Brien regarded Tomas levelly. "I recommend you apply to officer candidates school."

Tomas blinked a few times, and his gaze wandered over the interior of the office. He'd never thought about OCS before. His thoughts churned in an effort to understand the hesitant feeling pooling behind the muscles of his face. He let out a breath. The hesitation gave him all the understanding he needed. "Sir, I'm flattered—"

"But you want to say 'no.' Neumann, I understand. I was in your position, only eight months ago. You're worried about maybe someday giving orders to your former squadmates? That won't happen. You won't get assigned to the Blackjacks, let alone to this battalion, company, or platoon."

Tomas observed his hesitation through the framework of Lt. O'Brien's words. "Thank you for the clarification, sir, but that's not what's holding me back. In fact, what you've said makes me even more hesitant."

"How so?"

"For me, the GF more than anything is the half-dozen of us in the fireteam riding in your Badger. I feel like I'd be skipping out on them for easier duty. Not that being an officer is easy, sir." He remembered Tower in the plaza in New Boston, coldly murderous one moment and passively apathetic the next. "I understand you have commitments and responsibilities we don't. But I have a bond to the team."

"There's a role you play here. You don't want to take that away from your team."

"Yes, sir."

Lt. O'Brien pursed his lips. "As your new platoon commander, I should be glad to have a man with that attitude riding in my Badger. But I'm disappointed you define your position in the GF so narrowly. At our best, we are a team that spans all our deployments, from here to the worlds bordering the Progressive Republic, and from the private who just took his shilling to the highest ranking general who's had his for decades. Being in our team means finding the role we are best suited to, and playing it for our sake and the sake of everyone else with this thing—" He tapped an index finger on the front of his fatigues, over the shilling riding on his chest.

Tomas' mind expanded from a realization of the truth of the lieutenant's words. The team would find another grenadier. If his actions were worth emulating, the team would emulate them even if he wasn't there. His duty to his teammates, both those living and those dead, was to do the most he could to win this war and affirm their sacrifices. If he could best do that by becoming an officer, he owed it to his teammates to follow the lieutenant's recommendation.

But what about after the war? "Sir, you make many good points. But I never thought about making a career out of the GF."

"You would be committed for five years," Lt. O'Brien said, and his voice grew softer as he added, "or the duration of this war if it runs longer than that. After your commitment ended, you could retire to civilian life and become, whatever you want, an Observer minister or anything else. Or it's thirty years to a full pension. Think about it, Neumann. If you need more information to make up your mind, ask me.... What's this?" An alert appeared on his tablet's display, just as Tomas' shilling throbbed.

Lt. O'Brien scrolled the display. "We're being ordered to start our patrol of our river frontage ahead of schedule. This is a readiness drill ordered by Capt. Marcinkus. He wants us out the gate in ten."

Sgt. Johnson showed no sign of finding the order challenging. "We will be in the Badgers in seven, sir."

The lieutenant pushed his chair back from his desk and reached for his earbuds and helmet in a wall-mounted case behind him. "See you there, Johnson, Neumann."

As they trotted to the squad's shelter for their helmets and suits, Tomas asked, "Do you have another inkling, sergeant?"

"All I know is what you know. Looks like Capt. Marcinkus wants us to keep ready."

"Ready for what?" Tomas asked. They reached the squad's shelter and Sgt. Johnson went to his locker without replying.

The patrol left on schedule. Despite the rushed departure, nothing out of the ordinary happened after they left the base's gate. They rode their Badgers up to the river, then spent the next six hours alternating between the hot, cramped rear compartment and foot patrols to the bluff's edge. On the sunleft side of the riverfront road, the engineers had rigged sheets of chameleonskin over tall alloy struts. While on the road, their Badgers were invisible to cameras and radars on mike's side of the river.

They were obscured to mike's birds, as well. The GF ran its own smudgepots, on the darkward side of each brigade's zone. Their aerosols rode the prevailing low-altitude winds. Whatever benefit they provided in obscuring GF movements from mike's aircraft was bought at the cost of black dust. The dust coated the Badger's windows and camera ports and wormed in through the breathing ports on the soldiers' helmets.

On a foot patrol to check a cluster of obs wheels on the edge of the bluff, about five klicks upriver from the blown bridge, coughs racked Lundergard. "Why the aerosols?" he asked. "Are our brass planning an attack and want to hide our preparations?"

Tomas watched eddies in the dark haze. "They're planning something."

"To attack we'd need to throw a new bridge across the river. Have you seen any prep for one? I haven't."

"Me neither." Tomas watched the far bluff for traces of movement. "But they might be planning an attack outside our zone. Or not planning an attack at all."

Lundergard coughed again. "You're no help."

"I don't like uncertainty either. But all we can do is be ready for whatever order comes down."

When Alvarez returned from the Reagantown hospital, recovered from his wounds during the river crossing, he reported a wide range of rumors had circulated the wards, like competing strains of infectious diseases. Peace negotiations with the Unity; a crushing defeat of, or by, the Progressive Republic in an SF action near Péngláishān; a massive reinforcement being prepared by the GF for New Liberty. Alvarez also told them about an odd duty he'd been assigned his last two days of rehab: he'd fed papers into a whirring, humming machine that spat them out unchanged. "What the hell was that about?" he asked the men in the squad's shelter.

"They were digitally capturing information from the papers," Tomas said. A perfectly sensible reason for Alvarez' task drove out his breath. "They're preparing to evacuate the planet."

"What?" Cohen asked with curiosity.

Tomas hefted his tablet. "It's easier to carry this into orbit than a million sheets of paper."

Alvarez shook his head. "That can't be it. They put all the paper back where it came from."

"Time will tell," Tomas said. His tablet chimed with an incoming message. "Later." He went to his bunk and called up his messaging app.

New message from Annike Neumann, Portage-du-Nord, Joséphine.

His heart quickened. Finally Mother had written back. Maybe now she was ready to give him some information about his father. Tomas forced himself to slowly open the message.

Dear Tomas,

I am relieved to read you survived your wounds. Yet every day, when I see a car on the Bois d'Orme highway slowing near the turn-off for the parsonage, I fear it's a 'family relations officer' (such a ghastly euphemism) coming to tell me you have been killed. When the car passes, I relax for a moment, until I imagine you returning to me after your discharge with your body whole, but your mind broken. I can tell when you try to hide things from me. I can read between the lines. You've hidden many things from me. When you hint this 'Peters-Stein Technique' helped you regain your mental wholeness, it's clear you are protesting too much. I don't know how broken your mind is now, or how much worse it will be when you return to me, but you at least will have a place to stay once the GF casts you away.

I've inquired about the Peters-Stein Technique. It's misguided foolishness. I don't know why they made up those absurd stories about your father and me.

I know you should have heard from me the full story of what happened to your father. Our family never went to Nueva Andalucia. We instead went to Challenger. Your father had grandiose dreams of bringing the Observer message to the underclass in the big cities. Yet some people don't want to be helped. Your father got a knife in the back for his grandiose dreams. That's what happened. Remember, Tomas, I have never lied to you.

In one of your earlier letters, you mentioned running into a Monsieur DuBois from Sainte-Therese. I don't know any DuBois family in that town. The only DuBois I know is the widow in Portage. Obviously she's no relation to him.

Please stay as safe as you can. I don't approve what you've done, but I want you to come home alive. I'll even care for you if you're broken inside. I'm the only person who ever loved you.

Love Mother.

Tomas kept the message open for a time, flicking the text up and down the display as he thought about what she'd said. Gooseflesh prickled his cheeks. She'd lied about Challenger, and his father's death at some petty criminal's blade. He must have died on Nueva Andalucia. Did she want to hide that fact because Nueva Andalucia hung in hostile space? Or had his father died in some circumstance too embarrassing to repeat? Tomas imagined a lurid story, an affair with an Andaluciana in a flamenco dress ended by pistol fire from a jealous husband with a waxed mustache—

None of it mattered. His father was dead. His corpse fertilized the soil of a planet in enemy space. Even if Tomas redeployed to Nueva Andalucia later in the war, he would never find his father's grave. He had no father. The thought hurt, but carried with it a restful feeling.

I thank you for what you were able to provide, he expressed to his father's memory. *Now I take that and build my own life.*

Tomas thought for a few more minutes, then swept away his mother's message and tapped the compose button on the messaging app. He scrolled through a directory of GF personnel on-planet and found the addressee he sought.

Dear Chief Younger,

I hope this message finds you well. I repeatedly think back on our session as a dividing line in my life. It's like a cocoon, where an insect transforms from a crawling worm to a winged flyer.

In light of the insights our session has given me into who I am and what I can do, I've decided to apply to officer candidates school....

15

The Final Mission

Lt. O'Brien stood in front of the platoon, outside the main entrance to the base's fitness building. "Men, I don't know what's going on, but it's big. You've heard the battalion commander is here? He's not alone. The brigade commander is here as well."

A hush settled over the men. A summons to meet that much brass had never happened. Not just in the two months since they'd crossed the river, but since Sgt. Johnson had joined their unit. The lieutenant led them inside.

A clump of officers stood under the folded-up basketball goal at the far end of the gym. Their voices echoed off the mycocrete walls as they spoke among themselves. Tomas studied the group, looking for nametags and rank insignia among the dazzle of khakis and greens of the GF's garrison-duty fatigues. He glimpsed a single silver star on the collar of the brigade commander, Brigadier Kanagawa, near Capt. Marcinkus and a host of other captains and majors. A silver oak leaf marked the collar of Lt. Col. Bar-Talab, the battalion commander, who stood near an incongruous figure dressed in light blue. An SF uniform? Tomas craned his neck for a better look at the SF man but couldn't get one.

"Ten-hut!" Lt. O'Brien said. The enlisted men formed ranks and saluted.

The officers returned the gesture. "At ease," Brig. Kanagawa said.

Tomas dropped his hand, and then his whole face fell. The SF man was Lucien LaSalle. Lucien squinted his way, then leaned his head back with a glower aimed at Tomas.

Brig. Kanagawa had a weathered face and gray hair at his temples. "I commend you on doing fine work here. The base has been tip-top from the moment Lt. Col. Bar-Talab and I arrived, and men, you have turned out smartly. I am honored to command your brigade."

The brigadier cleared his throat. "You are of course wondering why the sheriff is here." He tapped the single star on his collar to explain the slang. He had to be older than he looked to use so archaic a term; Tomas knew the word but had never heard it spoken. "There is a mission of supreme importance that your platoon is uniquely well suited to take part in. But for me to talk about it, I must warn you, requires a level of secrecy we don't normally ask of our enlisted men. We know you have the will to keep it secret, but the higher brass in R-town ordered me to hand out lethe capsules to each of you before you can leave this room." Knots of staff officers filed out behind the brigadier and drifted to the exits. "Do you commit to this, men?"

"Yes, sir!" Sgt. Johnson said. Tomas joined his voice with the sergeant's about halfway through.

"I didn't catch that."

"Yes, sir!" The platoon spoke in unison.

"Thank you, men. You might also be wondering why one of our Space Force colleagues has come down from orbit to be with us." Brig. Kanagawa gestured at Lucien. The latter looked uncomfortable and cast hooded looks around the room. "It all fits together. The War Ministry on Challenger has made a decision and both our branches have to work together to execute it. We are evacuating New Liberty."

Gasps and murmurs came from the men around Tomas. He sagged over his stomach. So many months, so many dead, for nothing?

Tomas took a breath. No. They had learned valuable lessons no amount of impped skills or peacetime training could impart. If he was accepted and passed OCS, the lessons he had learned would make him a better officer for the rest of his career.

The brigadier grew stern. "Quiet, men. Your mission is to reconnoiter the landing zone for the SF's transport ships. I now hand the floor to Lt. Col. Bar-Talab to fill you in on the details."

The staff officers shifted to face the lieutenant colonel. Behind him, a gangly lieutenant unrolled a tripod-mounted display and stretched to lock it into place. The pause gave Tomas time to wonder. Why do they need an armored grenadier platoon to do reconnaissance? What's out there the scouts can't handle?

Lt. Col. Bar-Talab had a stout body and a blunt voice. "Thank you, brigadier." A map appeared on the display. Near the top of the map, Tomas read the icons of friendly units, mike formations, and the Grant River dividing them.

The river curved to the lower left and ended in a fifty kilometer long zone of intermittent lakes, where Constitution shone strongly enough to evaporate the river. Beyond the intermittent lakes was nothing but sun-scorched desert. Bar-Talab pointed a laser at a geologic formation on the cooler side of the evaporating river. "This is the Paiute Plateau, about a hundred-forty klicks behind us. It's thirty klicks by twenty, and averages four hundred meters above our current altitude. Its sunward edge is a high mountain chain that rainshadows the plateau. It's hot, dry, and mostly empty of NLer settlement, according to Shir—Space Force monitoring. It's the best place our brass and SF's have found to get all our forces on the sun-left front off the planet."

The display switched to a more detailed map of the plateau. " 'Mostly uninhabited' is another way of saying there is a permanent settlement we need to look at more closely." He circled the laser dot over a temple icon situated in the mountain chain between dense forest on the sunward slopes and the high desert of the plateau. "This temple is the Novus Homo Observation Society." Lt. Col. Bar-Talab peered at the platoon. "I understand Private Neumann is an Observer?"

And the reason his platoon had been tapped for this mission? Tomas said, "Yes, sir." His voice echoed flatly off the walls.

"The next images are based on SF photography of the site, further processed to give you men the view you'll have on approach. If that's a problem for anyone, shut your eyes."

Tomas took a breath and opened his eyes wide.

The temple reached for the sky. Perched on a cliff overlooking a pass, mycocrete outer walls showed *taijitus* to travelers approaching from the plateau. An Observer facility, all right. Behind the walls, a grassy courtyard held a number of buildings and a gracile tower of nanotubes and alloys. The tower held a platform twenty meters square, and a series of meshwork stairways leading up to it. Banners hanging from the edges of the platform showed more *taijitus*. The top of the platform might be fifty meters above the desert floor.

"Sir," Lt. O'Brien asked, "do you have a rendition of the view from the platform?"

"Here's our best calculation." The image flickered. Though shimmering with heat, the sunleft and darkward edges of the plateau were visible. Bar-Talab said, "You see why we need to reconnoiter this facility. If mike had surface-to-air missiles in that courtyard, and a man with a rangefinder on the platform, we could lose SF ships and GF men. Another question?"

Capt. Marcinkus spoke with a rehearsed tone. "Why not destroy the facility from orbit?"

Bar-Talab opened his mouth to speak, but stopped. Lucien fidgeted and turned his head to Bar-Talab, who said, "Lieutenant, care to answer?"

"Gladly." To the soldiers, Lucien said, "We easily could. We already have a plan to destroy every other structure on the plateau that's potentially usable by hostiles." He sneered at Tomas and disdain dripped from his voice. "Sadly, the Observer lobby on Challenger is insidiously powerful. They'd rather put GF lives at risk than let us blow up one of their temples from a safe distance."

Tomas swallowed thickly. Sweat dewed on his nape. You make me the bad guy? Still mad I didn't lie for you at the tribunal?

Lundergard whispered to Tomas, "This shirley knows a lot

about your religion."

"He has it in for me. You heard about the friendly fire casualties we suffered near New Boston? He pressed the button."

Alvarez nodded. "SF exiled him dirtside, and he blames Neumann for it instead of himself. He's stirring shit. Won't work. Some Observer might be the reason for this mission, but Neumann is part of our team."

Capt. Marcinkus spoke. "You have connections in the War Ministry, Lieutenant LaSalle?"

Lucien blinked a few times. "Pardon me, Captain?"

"All I know is we have an order to leave the Observer facility on the plateau untouched unless mike's using it against us. I have no idea how that order was decided. Do you?"

Lucien looked belligerent for a moment, but then glanced at the sea of GF camouflage around him. "I do not."

Lt. Col. Bar-Talab said, "Alright, men. You will be departing tomorrow at oh-two-hundred. Along the way, you'll link up with a scout platoon from one of our sister battalions. Together, you will travel to the Observer facility, ETA oh-ten-hundred. If mike has forces present, the highest priority is to neutralize them. Next highest is silence them. We want to keep mike in the dark as long as possible about our plans. If he doesn't know what we're doing, our redeployment to the plateau will be easier and the odds of mike getting into surface-to-air missile range to bring down a shuttle will be lower."

The lieutenant colonel went on. "If mike has no forces present, then the highest priority is to maintain the neutrality of the facility's staff until the evacuation is essentially complete. Between you and the scout platoon, your task force will have three men from Observer backgrounds. Neumann, you and those two scouts will make sure we interface with the facility's staff in a cultural sensitive manner." Lt. Col. Bar-Talab studied them. "Pack anything you can't fab on New Nauvoo, because you won't be coming back to this base. Brigadier, anything further?"

Brig. Kanagawa shook his head. "Dismissed."

Lucien joined Lt. O'Brien at the head of the platoon. They

filed out the gym doors, pausing to take lethe capsules from the brigadier's junior staffers. When Tomas took the clear plastic bag containing the capsule and its neck chain, his name and rank printed on it, knowledge filed away in his mind by the skills imps came to his consciousness. Bite through the capsule and swallow. In five minutes, his recent memories would be scrambled, unknowable to both his own recollection and a mike brain scanner should he be captured. The capsules were properly printed with a use-by date and time. Just under ninety-six hours from now.

Tomas read the implication. If the capsules would be useless in four days, by then they would be off the planet. He tore open the bag, hung the capsule around his neck, and tucked it inside his shirt next to his shilling. He dropped the empty bag into the maw of a recycling unit.

The platoon members spent the rest of the afternoon in their shelters. Tomas took a few minutes to sift through his belongings and dismiss most of them as being replaceable. After that, he checked his mail. Excitement bloomed in him when he saw a new letter from Chief Younger——Lissa. *Dear Tomas*, it began. They'd moved to first names a few weeks before. He read her letter carefully, savoring her choices of words, then composed a reply.

He spent the rest of the day reviewing intel on the Observer facility. Intel lacked floor plans of the buildings, but the layout reminded Tomas of facilities on Pénglàishān he read about in his mother's old, hardbound volumes of the Observer Encyclopedia. A meeting hall, an office, and a parsonage built into a spur of rock. Broad-roofed breezeways connected all the buildings. From the size of the parsonage, the facility could have anywhere from zero to eight resident staffers.

He read further. There was probably at least one permanent resident. The facility's website stated *Visitors welcome daily, eight a.m. to eight p.m.* Video, from both orbit and obs wheels along one of the roads up to the plateau, showed a supply truck making weekly runs from the municipal fab in Hale Valley, the nearest town, sixty kilometers to dark-sunright of the facility.

Tomas felt some relief. A mike unit at the facility would have its own fab, and wouldn't need supplies from a town in GF territory.

Unless mike kept the supply truck coming to create an illusion of normalcy.

Around sixteen-hundred, Lundergard rose from a group of men playing a multiplayer game on their tablets, and strode toward the shelter's door.

"Where are you going?" Sgt. Johnson asked.

"I'm getting antsy. I'll just hit the fitness room—"

"Do some pushups in the corner. We will eat a late dinner in the mess hall, but otherwise, idrin, we won't leave until we board the Badgers."

"I'm not going to tell anyone we're bugging off-planet in a few days," Lundergard said with a frown.

Sgt. Johnson said, "Orders be orders."

Lundergard looked unconvinced. Tomas set down his tablet and said to him, "The orificers trust us not to voluntarily spill the information. But the rest of the company knows something's happening. They haven't seen us all day, right? If they now see one of us outside, the rest of the company will ask us what's going on. No matter how little we tell them, the rumormongers might glean the truth. Sequestering us is the best chance to keep the mission confidential."

After looking thoughtful for a moment, Lundergard grunted. He dropped to the floor between two bunks and did pushups.

Dinner came at nineteen-thirty. They trooped across the base, Lt. O'Brien and Lucien in front and Sgt. Johnson at the rear. Lucien wore an untailored GF uniform, so short that his shirttail quickly came untucked from his pants. Tomas glanced around, but this side of the base was empty.

The SSC enlisted personnel crewing the mess line asked the soldiers no questions beyond which meats and vegetables they wanted. Past the mess line, the officers led the men toward the far table. Tomas found himself walking alongside Lucien. He kept quiet. It wasn't his place to strike up a conversation with any officer, even one he'd known in his former life.

"Don't think I wanted to run into you," Lucien said.

"I hadn't expected to see you after the tribunal, sir."

Lucien glowered. "Don't rub my face in the tribunal. I didn't want you to lie, but you painted the truth in the drabbest colors possible. Why? Mudbugs closing ranks against Shirley? Are you envious I'm an officer? That I had a better life on Joséphine?"

Tomas stopped at the middle of the table, near his squadmates. At the table's head, Lt. O'Brien set down his fork and eyed Tomas and Lucien. Tomas said, "I told the truth as I best recalled it."

"Don't give me that Observer claptrap."

"You sound angry."

Lucien leaned toward him, lips pressed together. "You have to worship the goddam yin-yang symbol to figure that out?"

The soldiers around them watched, with clear sympathy for Tomas and wary dislike for Lucien. Lt. O'Brien came up. "Problem, lieutenant?"

"Ask your man."

O'Brien's voice became flatter, deeper. "I'm asking you. I know about the misplaced fire mission, and I know Neumann testified about it. What's your problem?" O'Brien looked down his nose at Lucien's collar. "You kept your rank."

Lucien sniffed out a breath. "Rank? You think that's my only concern? I got exiled dirtside. 'Mud sticks to your wings.' It's ten times harder to get a promotion down here."

O'Brien shrugged. "Looks like you have two choices. You can bitch about your fate, or you can work ten times harder to get back into orbit. I don't care which you do, so long as you do your job when we roll out."

With a haughty look, Lucien said, "Thank you for your advice, O'Brien. My dinner's getting cold. I'm going to eat." He took his tray to the far end of the table, isolated from the GF soldiers.

Tomas sat too, amid his comrades. Alvarez said, "Shirley has a task on this mission?"

Iommarino raised an eyebrow and glanced at Lucien. "He'll call in the orbital fire if we find mike's occupying the facility. That way he can't scapegoat any of us for getting the coordinates wrong." Iommarino laughed at his own words. Alvarez chuckled.

Tomas smiled weakly. He wouldn't argue with his squadmates'

judgment, but he himself had nothing against Lucien. He wanted Lucien to play his role in the next day's mission as best he could.

After dinner and a few fitful hours of sleep, Sgt. Johnson roused the squad an hour before departure. They pulled on their chameleon-skin suits with stiff motions and bleary eyes. Stepping outside didn't help; Constitution's reddish glow thumped on Tomas's mental sluggishness in the middle of the clock-time night, but couldn't dispel it. Along with his squadmates, he dragged his feet to the Badgers.

Near the vehicle storage sheds, the clanking of Badger tracks riding onto their road carriages quickened Tomas' thoughts. The platoon rounded a corner and went in. Now a little more awake, Tomas noticed the mechanics had worked on the platoon's Badgers while the soldiers had waited in their shelters. Thin alloy struts formed a frame over the turret and top armor of each vehicle. Mechanics clambered over the Badgers, unfolding bulky rolls of chameleonskin over the outside of the frame. On one Badger, already framed over, the chameleonskin showed a civilian motor home.

"We're going incognito," Tomas said.

Iommarino looked surprised. "That makes us irregular combatants. If mike captures us, he could shoot us on sight."

"There's an easy solution to that," Tomas replied. "Don't get taken prisoner."

Cohen chuckled and guided them to their Badger. In the chameleonskin covering each side of the vehicle, a hole gave access to a gray half-globe the size of a football. Finger taps on the chameleonskin above and below gave proof of framing struts holding the half-globe in place. The half-globe's translucent cover obscured some articulated devices inside it. "What's that?" Lundergard asked. No one knew.

The chameleonskin over the rear of the vehicle had a slit up the middle, like a stage's curtains. Inside the rear compartment, Monroe's old seat, the one between Cohen and Tomas, remained empty. After they filed in, Cohen said into the vehicle's net, "MacInnis, we're all mounted."

"Can't shut the ramp yet."

"Why not?"

"Waiting on a passenger."

Tomas' mood fell; he knew who that passenger would be. A moment later, Lucien and Lt. O'Brien came into view at the foot of the ramp. "This is your ride," Lt. O'Brien said.

Lucien took a step, then scowled. At Tomas, at the other soldiers, at O'Brien. "Is this the only one?"

"We outfitted it for your needs. It's the only Badger with an empty seat."

"Someone's skipping this mission?" Lucien asked.

O'Brien looked away. Tomas spoke. "His name was Monroe. He's skipping this and every mission, sir."

Lucien's eyes widened and he grew a little pale when Tomas' meaning sank in. He trudged up the ramp and strapped into Monroe's old seat, while O'Brien loped up the ladder on the outside of the vehicle to the turret hatch. His footsteps overhead rang through the hull.

At the appointed hour, the Badgers rolled out. Though it was a combat mission, the smooth flow of the road carriage tires on pavement lulled the men. Soon, most were dozing. Tomas occasionally opened his eyes enough to glimpse Lucien, bleary-eyed but awake, watching the displays and craning his neck to look around the compartment.

They met the scout platoon on schedule at a crossroads, then turned onto the road leading up to the plateau. The plateau's shadow caught them a minute before they started climbing a road slanting up the darkward rim. The view in the displays showed lamps on tall poles lighting up when their vehicles drew near. A meter-high guardrail hugged the edge of the road. It could stop a civilian car, but the massive fighting vehicles would plunge right through. Iommarino looked away from the display and squeezed his fists until his knuckles turned white. His nervousness tinged the entire compartment. Tomas, awake now, pushed himself into sitting upright.

Lucien, meanwhile, pulled out his tablet and scrolled through an app. His motions and the glow of the screen drew Tomas' attention. Many pages of text, control buttons, an SF logo.

Tomas remembered his thoughts about Lucien during dinner the night before. "Anything I can help with, sir?"

Lucien scowled. "You think I can't do my job?"

A nugget of anger formed in Tomas' gut, but he let it dissolve. "Sir, I'm certain you can do your job perfectly. I have nothing else to do right now and would be happy to help."

"My job is to scope out prospective landing sites on the plateau. The ground-penetrating radar modules on the sides of the vehicle are linked to my tablet. There's nothing you can help with."

Soon, they reached the top of the plateau. The side views showed dry, rocky terrain, interspersed by green tufts of cactus. Lucien looked bored at first, but he kept glancing at Tomas until he set his face and hunched over his tablet, swiping and tapping, as colored lines traced seemingly meaningless patterns.

"Whoa," Lucien said.

"We need to stop, sir?" MacInnis asked.

Lucien studied his display for a moment. "No. I've seen enough." He tapped a button, then drew a circle on his tablet's display. Once complete, the circle filled with bright warning red. "Unstable terrain," he murmured. "Easily could have missed it," he added, even more softly.

MacInnis switched one of the displays on the inside of the ramp to a forward view. In the distance, a faint gray smudge in the heat shimmer of the desert marked out their objective from the sandy brown palette of the plateau. As the last kilometers rolled by, the Observer facility grew more clear. The *taijitus* facing darkward were plainly visible at two klicks out.

The caravan of fighting vehicles turned from the main road onto a paved driveway leading to the Observer facility. The driveway climbed a slope scattered with boulders and shrubs. Tomas studied the forward view for traces of mike activity while his hand reached to the side of the compartment to be near his rifle and grenade launcher on their rack. The Badgers grumbled as they climbed toward the facility. The slope was empty of mike.

At the top of the slope, the gate in the facility's outer wall stood open. The black alloy gate rested its lower corner on the ground at the side of the track. The mycocrete wall looked pitted by years of windblown dust. *Taijitu* banners fluttered against the wall.

The disguised Badgers slowed to ease through the gateway. MacInnis deftly drove through, keeping the ground-penetrating radars' housings clear by a few centimeters on each side. The vehicles parked in a line facing the buildings.

The forward view showed a man standing just off the parking lot, on a paved walkway leading to the meeting hall. He dressed more casually than Tomas expected of an Observer minister—blue denim pants and a short-sleeved plaid shirt in a paler shade of blue. The task force's arrival seemed to have hurriedly brought him outside: his chest heaved as he caught his breath, and he reseated the arms of his sunglasses more solidly on his ears. Roughly Tomas' height, he had brown hair edged with gray and a narrow jaw.

"Neumann," said Lt. O'Brien, "leave the grenade launcher and your helmet in the back. Keep your rifle over your shoulder and your suit on plain gray-green. Along with the two scout Observers, greet him. The officers and sergeants will be right behind you."

The ramp dropped. Tomas watched the display as the viewing angle grew steeper and then too steep to watch. But by then, he'd seen enough of the man to know. Not an illusion, nor mistaken identity. New Liberty was a single wormhole from Nueva Andalucia.

"Neumann?"

"Sorry, sir. I'm on it." Tomas stood, slung his rifle over his shoulder, and tromped down the ramp. He parted the halves of the chameleonskin cloaking the Badger's rear. His heart pounded as he rounded the vehicle and walked toward his father.

The man's arms moved nervously, crossed over his chest one moment, at his sides the next. As Tomas and the scouts approached, he asked, "What can I do for the Confederated Worlds military?"

One of the scout Observers, a Pénglàishān native named Wong, glanced at Tomas and the other scout. His peer shuffled a half-step back.

Tomas studied his father. *He doesn't recognize me. Of course he doesn't, he left when I was five.* Words fled his mouth.

Wong stepped forward. "Our respects, *dàoshi*. On behalf of our officers—" Wong waved at the vehicles behind him, where the two GF lieutenants and Lucien gathered. "—we ask your permission to search your facility."

Tomas' father took off his sunglasses and squinted at the approaching officers and the fighting vehicles behind them. "This isn't Pénglǎishān. You don't have to call me *dàoshi*."

The heat of the pavement made Tomas' feet sweat. The man's eyes were deep blue and hooded on the upper eyelid, just like the man he'd envisioned in the skills imps' chamber. You're seeing things. How do you even know what your father looked like? A subconscious burble? And you have no evidence your family was ever on Nueva Andalucia....

"As you wish, honored sir," said Wong. "How should we call you?"

"Mr. Newman is fine."

Tomas' heart pounded more. He had to speak. His throat clenched to spew out his words. "Did you anglicize it from 'Neumann' when you came here from Nueva Andalucia?"

Everyone around Tomas drew in breaths and stared at him. Though aware of the others in passing, Tomas focused on his father. The man blinked, mouth open, face slack with surprise. "How do you know that?"

A dozen years of longing stampeded out of Tomas' subconscious. How many times as a small boy had he cried himself to sleep, wishing for even a minute with his father? Here he had one.

A few more blinks and his father recovered his wits enough to look for the nameplate on Tomas' suit. His eyes widened and he lurched back a step. "Tomas?"

"Mother said you were dead."

His father stepped closer. Tears glistened in his eyes and he reached toward Tomas. "I'm sorry she lied to you. She was always selfish. I should have known she would cringe from the stigma of divorce. Easier to pass herself off as a widow—"

"*She* was selfish?"

His father looked puzzled. "The divorce was her idea. We were on Nueva Andalucia and, and...." He turned his head to the officers standing behind Tomas.

Lt. O'Brien said, "I would be glad for the two of you to catch up, but we do need an answer to Pvt. Wong's question, Mr. Newman. May we search your facility?"

"Search?" Tomas' father looked at the fighting vehicles. The infantrymen stood on the pavement and the front chameleonskins had been furled to reveal the main armament of the Badgers and Weasels. "I would never harbor the militia. This place is a haven from the war."

"Your words are promising," Lt. O'Brien replied. "May we search your facility?"

Tomas' father shrugged. "You have my permission, but you'll find nothing." He gestured at the meeting hall.

Lt. O'Brien curtly moved his head in acknowledgment, then turned to the sergeants gathered a couple of meters behind them. "Your squads have their assignments. Johnson, you'll be a man down, any issues?"

Sgt. Johnson gave Tomas the warmest look Tomas had ever seen from him. "None, sir."

"Let's move."

With the rustle and creak of swaying equipment, and the scrape of boot soles on asphalt, the soldiers filed across the parking lot and fanned out to the different buildings. Lt. O'Brien, the scout commander, and Lucien went to the shadow of the meeting hall, a discreet distance from Tomas and his father. Lucien's expression cycled from smirks, to narrow squints, even occasional flashes of compassion, and who cared what he thought? Fate had opened a window for Tomas that would soon shut forever.

"Tell me what you're feeling," Tomas asked.

His father extended his hands toward Tomas, then dropped them when Tomas didn't reciprocate. "Like I said, the divorce was her idea. We thought Nueva Andalucia would be a fertile ground for spreading the Observer message. It shared a Roman Catholic cultural background with Sankt-Benedikts-Welt, so we knew how to pitch our message in terms the locals would understand. But the Andalucianos didn't heed it. We tried and tried, but we finally had to admit we weren't gaining converts. Maybe the saber-rattling coming from Challenger made them leery of foreigners. This was a year or two before the Confederated Worlds STL ship dragged the wormhole here from New Nauvoo." He caught his breath. "Your mother wanted to go back to Sankt-Benedikts-Welt, but I told her we had to revise our task, not drop it. So she left with you and I came here."

How many of his words were lies to Tomas or himself? Had 'we' done what he'd said, or did he try to spread responsibility for his bad decisions onto Tomas' mother?

Lies or truths, all he could do was accept his father as he was. "Thank you for that information," Tomas said, "but I'd like to know what you're feeling."

"Feelings? I'm surprised, of course. Aren't you? To meet you again, like this… and you joined the military…."

"Tell me more."

"I'm angry at your mother." His father's face showed mild bewilderment, as if he surprised himself by saying more. "She took you and then lied to you. That's wrong." His father's gaze fell to the pavement, and his shoulders hunched. "And I feel bad she never told you why she left me. That must have hurt."

Memories pushed into Tomas' consciousness, like lava seeping onto a world's surface. "I missed you when I was a child. I wished I could somehow have you back, even for a moment. I remember, after we moved to Joséphine—"

"Joséphine?" His father looked thoughtful. "She too couldn't face the shame of returning as a failure to Sankt-Benedikts-Welt."

Tomas glanced up at the *taijitu* banner fluttering from the deck of the elevated platform. The parallel with his active memory lifted the corners of his mouth. "I went into the Saint-Girard church, lurked in the corner, and I prayed to the crucified Christ behind the altar you were really alive and would come for me. Mother would have harangued me for months if she'd ever found out."

"I'm sorry you felt the need to pray to other people's god over what your mother did to us."

"It was years ago. I see the world as it is, now." Tomas looked into his father's eyes. "I know coming here was the best decision you could have made."

His father smiled weakly. "You need to understand something, Tomas. A man has to work for something bigger than himself. It's the only thing that gives his life any meaning. Otherwise he's sleep-walking and will wake up some day wondering where his life went. I had to come here. I had to spread our message and be an example of how to dedicate one's life to the higher truth within each one of us."

Spreading the Observer message by working alone with what-ever few visitors journeyed here? His father denied so much. The wind rustled sand across the parking lot and Tomas vowed again to accept his father as he was. "I understand," he replied. "For us soldiers, the GF can be that thing bigger than ourselves."

"Your mother never understood me when I told her that." His fa-ther lacked any sign of hearing his reply. "If she had, she would have known we had to keep bringing the Observer message to worlds that needed it, and she would have kept the three of us together. We're fortunate we had this chance to meet despite her." He slowly turned his head to take in the line of fighting vehicles. "What could have brought you here? I don't mean New Liberty. I mean here."

Tomas wished he could tell him, but the mission and the team outranked even family. "You know I can't tell you."

"But I'm your father." His face showed reconsideration. "Who's been out of your life for over a dozen years. I accept that you might be angry."

After a moment to gauge his feelings, Tomas shook his head. "I'm not."

"You're a better Observer than I am." Red rimmed his father's eyes.

"Thank you for the compliment. My commitment to my fellow soldiers is the reason I can't talk about why we're here."

His father shifted his weight. "Like I told the officers, the mili-tia's done nothing around here. Your ships—" He glanced into the sky. "—would see it if they had. All that empty desert...." He waved in the direction of the main gate and the asphalt road leading dark-ward across the plateau. After a time, he looked once more in the general direction of the SF ships in orbit. His gaze flickered over a tiny portion of the vast sky for several moments. Tomas couldn't read his thoughts.

Eventually, his father spoke. "I suppose the military has to see for itself the militia isn't here. Do your superiors doubt the competence of the spaceship fleet?"

"No more than the Space Force doubts ours."

His father smiled weakly, over an agitated demeanor. He turned his shoulders to look for the GF personnel working their way from building to building. Tomas followed his gaze and saw the purpose in his comrades' motions, purpose his father wouldn't see. Quiet chatter from the task force net came sporadically through Tomas' earbuds. "Meeting hall secure."

"Office building secure," Cohen said.

"Parsonage secure."

Lt. O'Brien broke in. "With the buildings secure, I want the scouts to go up to the observing platform to look for mike activity and set some obs wheels. Johnson, have you seen a way out of the facility on the sunward side?"

"No, sir."

"Take your squad out the way we came in, circle behind the facility, and scout that side. Shirley's orbital eyes show piney hills dropping down to the river, with no mike activity, but I want boots on the ground to confirm."

"Yes, sir," Johnson said. "Idrin, you heard the man. Foot patrol."

Sgt. Johnson and the rest of the squad came out of the office building and trudged along the walkway toward Tomas and his father. Iommarino stared at Tomas' father, and Cohen gave Tomas a compassionate look. "We'll take care of the assignment," he said to Tomas.

"You're certain? Sergeant?"

Johnson nodded. "You have bigger things to take care of."

I do? Tomas had longed for the chance to talk to his father every day between his arrival on Joséphine and his enlistment in the GF. Yet now that he had the chance, how little he could do with it. The questions that had gnawed at him for over a dozen years, variations on what happened? and why? now lacked importance. His father, watching the line of men walking between two Badgers on their way to the facility's front gate, was a stranger to Tomas, and vice versa.

"Son…." The word struck Tomas with a self-conscious tone, and his father's expression showed the older man knew how it sounded. "I want to talk more, but I need a few minutes in the restroom."

"I'll walk with you."

"You don't have to do that."

Tomas squinted at Constitution just above the parsonage's low shed roof. Even with his suit set to plain gray-green, the fabric was heavy and hot. "I would take a few minutes in the shade."

"Oh. Your uniform must weigh a lot. I'll get you a glass of water too. Follow me." His father led him down the walkway.

The office building was a long, low structure of reddish-brown mycocrete. Inside, cool air whooshed from the vents, and drawn window shades kept the interior pleasantly dim. Past a spotless reception area and near the beginning of a long, dark hallway, his father showed Tomas into his office. "Have a seat. I'll be right back with your water."

Soon, from someplace nearby on the opposite side of the hallway, came the thump of cabinet doors shutting and the gurgle of a cooler dispensing water. While he waited, Tomas looked around his father's office. It reminded him of his mother's study at the parsonage back home: behind a worn wooden desk, shelves bowed under the weight of books, among them a complete set of the *Observer Encyclopedia* and the leading missionary guidebook, *Showing Others the Way*.

Unlike his mother's study, though, dust stood thickly atop the books, and a tablet stood in a charging cradle on his father's desk.

From the doorway came his father's voice. "When I was your age, I loved the old books. Their weight, the rustle of their pages, the typefaces…. I can still remember where on the page certain passages from the *Tao Te Ching* could be found in the old hardback edition your grandfather gave me. 'Those who know the Tao are not extensively learned; the extensively learned do not know the Tao.' But the digitized version on the tablet is so much more convenient and powerful." His father looked pensive. "Here's your water. Please excuse me. I should only be a few minutes."

Tomas sipped the water. "Thank you. Father."

Another weak smile. His father pulled his tablet off its charging cradle and left the room. The sound of his footsteps faded down the hallway.

Tomas drank more water and listened to the task force's chatter in his earbuds. The scouts on the elevated platform saw a terrain free of mike for tens of klicks in every direction. They had mounted obs wheels and now ran the initial tests and calibrations. So far so good. The GF still had a great chance to get off the planet without mike finding out in time to interfere.

Somewhere down the hall came a dim sound, like hard objects clanging into each other. Not a typical latrine sound. And how long had it been since his father had left the room? Tomas rose from his seat and stood in the open doorway. Silence filled the hall.

Tomas padded in the direction his father had gone. Every door he passed was closed. He leaned his head toward each door, listening for sounds or voices. Nothing.

He paused outside a unisex restroom, the only one in the entire hallway. He held his breath and pulled out the earbud linked to the task force net. Still nothing.

Tomas frowned and kept going. Next to the nearest door on the opposite wall, a placard read *Storage*. A noise came from within.

After leaning closer, Tomas heard a voice, quiet and muffled. He cupped his hand around his ear. The voice was definitely his father's.

"Concerned citizen to Militia Headquarters Shermanville, do you read?" The voice was quiet and muffled by the door. "Concerned citizen to Militia Headquarters Shermanville. Come on, pick up. Come on. Concerned citizen to Militia Headquarters Shermanville, do you read?"

Tomas' heart slammed. His hand shook as he replaced the earbud in his ear. He pulled the rifle off his shoulder and to his hands, hoping the sound of plastic and metal hitting his palms would go unheard. He took a deep breath. A clammy feeling crawled over his skin.

He kicked in the door.

His father stood in a far corner, behind an open metal shelving unit in the middle of the room. Tomas saw his father between a small cardboard box and some electronic parts in a thick plastic bag. The older man's face was pale. His mouth hung open and his eyes were wide.

Tomas rounded the shelving unit and aimed the rifle at his father. In his left hand, the older man held a radio headset. Static hissed in the earpiece. His right hand rested on the controls of a hand-crank radio. The radio sat at the end of a shelf. On the tile floor between him and Tomas, metal and plastic desk accessories spilled out of a cardboard box with a crumpled corner.

"Turn off the radio," Tomas said.

"Tomas. Son. I can explain—"

"Turn it off." Tomas' voice sounded cold to his ears. The part of him that had acted behind the pillbox stirred again. He took a breath. He didn't expect to need it, but its availability straightened his back.

His father rocked a switch on the radio. The static in the earpiece cut off.

"Send the radio over."

His father held out the headset.

"Not the headset. Put the radio on the floor and kick it my way with your foot. Easy motions."

A nod, and then his father bent down. He shoved the radio with his foot. It came most of the way to Tomas and he left it on the floor between them.

"I can explain," his father said again. "The Confederated Worlds army is leaving New Liberty, isn't it?"

Tomas glared and said nothing.

"Not answering means 'yes.' The supply drivers from Hale Valley, and the people who come here for spiritual retreats, all talk about how outnumbered you are and how much territory you've yielded to the militia. People down here with telescopes can count the ships in orbit. Everyone knows the Confederated Worlds have sent away ships ever since the Progressive Republic declared war.

You're leaving. Why else come to the plateau? The militia has done nothing up here. Why else could the plateau matter to your superiors than as a place to leave without the militia seeing you go?"

"We can't stop you from speculating," Tomas said. "But we won't let you share your speculations with mike."

His father took a breath. "If you were leaving, would you have taken me with you?"

The answer came immediately to Tomas' mind. No. Impped knowledge told him civilians were to be denied transport in a withdrawal from a hostile planet. Beneath the impped knowledge, another thought emerged. *You should have thought of that when you abandoned me to Mother.*

"No. Don't try to deny it. I know what happens to locals the militia thinks collaborated with you. The mayor of Sunright Decatur was lined up against a wall and shot. I'm the nearest civilian to where you'll jump off the planet. The militia will find me and scan my brain. I'm a native of the Confederated Worlds. I knew you were here and I guessed why you came. If I didn't tell them, they'd kill me on the spot."

He reached out for Tomas. "Our work is too important. The Observer Way is rarely followed here, but that's all the more reason we have to keep doing it. A drip of water over ten million years can make a canyon. We—"

"We?"

"Come with me. The militia will welcome you. You can reveal everything you know to the Unity when their fleet returns to New Liberty."

The thought disgusted Tomas. "My loyalty is to the Confederated Worlds and the Ground Force." He stood taller. "Come with me."

His father's eyes widened. "What are you going to do with me?"

"I'm going to march you to Lt. O'Brien and tell him what happened. I suspect we'll keep you in custody until we depart. Mike can't fault you for failing to inform—"

"Yes he can!"

Tomas shrugged. "Then you should have succeeded."

"But, but, I'm your... father...." The older man's face fell.

Tomas squatted, bracing the rifle against his hip as he groped for the radio with his left hand. He took his gaze off his father for a moment—

Cardboard and plastic scraped on the shelf above his head. Tomas looked up and jerked his left hand between his head and falling boxes. The shelving unit leaned toward him. Footfalls and a glimpse of brown hair from the other side of the shelves showed his father had ducked around the end of the unit when Tomas had looked away.

The shelving unit tipped further. Tomas jumped up and stood against the wall to his right. The top of the unit crashed into his left forearm. He winced and the door to the room slammed behind his father.

Tomas squirmed backward. The top of the shelving unit pressed against his arm. Awkwardly, with his right arm squeezing his rifle into his armpit, he worked his shilling with his right hand through the fabric of his suit. "Sergeant! Lieutenant! Newman is unarmed but hostile. Repeat, Newman is unarmed but hostile. I prevented him from attempting contact with mike but he escaped my custody. Look for him. I will follow."

Finally he reached the end of the shelving unit. His breath hard, he ran to the door, yanked it open, ran out. The hallway was empty. At the end furthest from his father's office, a vertical sliver of daylight narrowed and disappeared as a door to the outside swung shut.

Tomas ran that way. He squinted when he reached the outside. Confused chatter and questions filled the task force net. He ignored them. A glimpse of motion around the corner of the parsonage caught his attention and he followed.

He found a patio of stone pavers and a round, raised firepit behind the parsonage. A sliding glass door gave access to the building. Behind the glass panes, thick curtains hung from floor to ceiling.

He could be hidden there, armed and willing to shoot.

He could have a radio there, too, and even now be trying to call mike.

Tomas tugged on the door handle. Locked. He reversed his rifle and butted it against the glass. Cracks formed like thin ice under a heavy footstep. He butted again, again. The crack pattern spread and the glass buckled away from the blows. He reached in and worked the handle open.

Once the lock snicked, he pulled back his hand, yanked open the door, and swept the curtains aside with his rifle muzzle. The room held a worn brown chair facing a video screen on the wall. The odor of smoked hashish came from a hookah in the corner. Empty.

Tomas went into a narrow hallway. The doors were all shut, except one to a bedroom. A queen-sized bed, neatly made; carpet with straight lines left by a vacuum cleaner. To Tomas' right, near a window looking out on the spur of rock, stood a closet door. A strip of light leaked out from beneath it. Tomas flung open the door and burst into the closet, muzzle up.

The scent of cedar hit him. A light in the ceiling was on, illuminating cedar planking and built-in storage on all four walls. Shoe racks, hanging rods, a floor-to-ceiling wardrobe. Small outdoors gadgets—powered binoculars, a GPS receiver, a self-folding tent—shared space with his father's shirts and pants.

Tomas glanced behind him, suddenly fearful his father was sneaking up on him. No motion, no sound. Where was he?

The wardrobe. Tomas moved as quietly as he could. He braced his rifle against his body and yanked open the wardrobe door.

No hiding man. No clothes. Instead, the rear panel of the wardrobe had been mounted on hinges. The rear panel stood open now, revealing a passageway eighty centimeters in diameter carved out of the rock. The scrabble of motion came from somewhere down the tunnel.

Tomas activated his shilling. "Mr. Newman is taking a tunnel. Presumably to the outside. I will follow."

"I'll get the idrin outside," Sgt. Johnson said. "We'll look for him and you."

Tomas crawled into the tunnel. The rough surface pressed his shilling against his chest. Dim light followed from the closet, and after a turn, it soon left him in darkness. The tunnel sloped down and wound through more turns. Tomas shoved aside a thought of the tons of rock around him on all sides. Alone in the dark, all he could hear was his breathing. His helmet, now stowed in the Badger, would be worth its weight in gold for its night vision capability right now. His father might have turned to make a stand and he would never know until it was too late.

After a couple of minutes, a glimmer of light came from around another turn. He crawled faster and rounded the turn. An entrance to the outside showed the side of a boulder and the trunks of pines rising from below.

Tomas scurried out and oriented himself. The facility's my-cocrete wall behind him lacked taijitu banners. In front of him, glimpsed between pines, the salty flats of the evaporating river lay a few klicks away, and beyond them, a dry rocky plain stretched toward the fat red ember of Constitution. "I'm behind the facility," he said. After looking downslope, he said, "Mr. Newman is in view."

A blue-clad figure hurried down the slope, amid clattering pebbles and thwacking shrubs. He kept his right arm straight, wavering a little to balance himself. His left hand held a small gray box to the side of his face. The box reached from mouth to ear.

Tomas raised his rifle's sights to his eye. "Stop!" he shouted. "Put down the radio! Hands up and come to me!"

His father glanced back in a blur of pale face, then kept running.

"Stop!" Tomas shouted again. He fired a burst over his father's head. Rounds smacked a tree trunk. The older man crouched, startled. He hesitated, but for only a moment.

The part of Tomas that had come out behind the pillbox stirred again, but it was not alone. Another part of himself, wiser, more mature, came out of his subconscious. The two merged together and filled him with certainty. He checked his father's direction of motion, then sighted again. Pale blue plaid filled the aperture. He fired.

His father sprawled on the slope, face down. The small gray radio lay a few meters from him. His elbows dug at the dirt and his right arm reached for the radio, but his motion ceased in moments.

Tomas stood and hurried down the slope. "We need a medic back here! Fifty meters my sunward. Now!"

His father's threat had been neutralized. Maybe the medic could get here in time. If medical corps finds them alive, they'll stay that way.

Tomas breathed hard. And if not? *I can still get that one minute with him if I hurry.* He ran faster and slid on his rump the last two meters downslope. He scrambled onto his knees next to his father.

The older man still lay on his belly, one cheek against the dirt and one arm stretched out for the portable radio. Blood soaked the dirt under him. Thick red wounds gaped on his back. He didn't move.

Tomas touched the underside of his jaw with the backs of two fingers. No pulse. He moved his fingers around, trying to find a pulse. None. His father's lifeless eye stared into the pine forest.

Footsteps of many men came from up the slope. Tomas turned to see a medic and his squad filing toward him. His squadmates looked shocked. Their gazes flickered from Tomas to his father. The medic rushed forward and knelt by Tomas' father.

Sgt. Johnson clapped Tomas on the shoulder. "Good work, Neumann. The other squad found the radio he used in the building. Lt. O'Brien and the scout commander checked its outgoing buffer. He didn't get a message off to mike."

"He had another radio," Tomas said. He gestured at the gray portable one lying in the dirt nearby. "I don't know if I stopped him before he could use it."

"We'll check it out too."

Cohen stepped closer. "How are you, Tomas?"

Had Cohen ever called him anything but 'Neumann?' Tomas welcomed the closeness implied by Cohen's choice of words. "I'm okay."

"Tell me more."

Tomas looked at his father. The medic leaned back on his haunches and dropped blood-stained hands to his lap. He'd shut his father's eyes along the way. "I'm angry at him for trying to alert mike. Sad, too, that he felt he had to. Sad I had to shoot him. I gave him chances to surrender. And all my life I'd wanted to talk to him, just for a moment, to hear what wisdom he could give me. From everything he said before he sneaked off to call mike I know there wasn't any wisdom and why did I think there was and is this what

I really wanted…." He dropped his rifle to the ground and hung his head in his hands.

"It's okay," Cohen said. "Let it out."

Tomas kept his eyes shut and took deep breaths. From the shadows of his subconscious, his twinned parts, the murderous and the noble, watched him with acceptance. He returned the acceptance to them. Beyond them, around them, he sensed the squad nearby. His senses expanded. He visualized the rest of the task force, up at the facility. Lissa in her office in the base at R-town and he hoped she would make it off-planet with the rest of them. And all the dead men: Voloshenko, Sharma, Obermeyer, Ryan, Monroe. Marchbanks. Their bodies rotted but they lived on as virtual souls, emulated in his memory and the memory of every other soldier who'd known them. He accepted all of them, just as they were, and he knew they accepted him.

He opened his eyes. "I feel those things, and I know I did the right thing. Thanks."

"I know." Most of the others nodded.

Most, but not all. Words caught in Iommarino's throat before forcing their way out. "The right thing? What the hell is wrong with you? Maybe he was a mike simp, but you killed your own father!"

Tomas gave him a level look. "There are things more important than family."

Iommarino recoiled. "What could be more important than family?"

"None of us chose our families." Tomas set the flat of his hand on his chest. "Every one of us chose to take the shilling."

OPERATION IAGO

1

Butterbar

The pair of orbital mirrors cast wintry light on the company's base. The physical fitness facility's walls of woodland camouflage rose above berms capped with sandbags. A curtain wall about two-and-a-half meters high hid the PT facility's entrance from a casual glance. Tomas approached, boots squeaking on the snow, when a voice came from someone standing behind the curtain wall, out of sight.

"We should let Papa Romeo have this bloody planet."

Tomas stopped. A moment to place the voice. The Scotiaman in the scout squad... Connor? Campbell.

The scout's voice continued. "It snows every tenth day and the terrain's uglier than that one Daughter of Astarte on Kahlenberg—"

"And the locals all talk like poofs," another scout said. This one put on an Ardenese accent. "*Forsooth*, let Papa have this *whoreson* planet."

The Scotiaman laughed, and the second scout chuckled at his own joke.

A third voice spoke up, belonging to Cpl. Nilsson, one of the scout squad's fireteam leaders. His voice lacked humor. "Papa can take the butterbar while he's at it."

The chill air bit the lining of Tomas' nose. He narrowed his eyes and angled his ear toward the front of the PT facility. Nilsson's records portrayed a better soldier than the one Tomas had seen while commanding the scout squad cross-posted to his armored grenadier platoon.

"Lt. Neumann's not that bad an officer," said the second scout. Tomas placed the voice. Gorthi, from Satyayuga. He even got the pronunciation right, *Noy-mun*. "For an armored grenadier."

Campbell said, "He's not a paper tiger."

"You think Academy grads are bad?" Nilsson said. "He's worse."

The others muttered words inaudible with distance. Tomas shuffled closer.

"Hear me out," Nilsson said. "Paper tigers got to the Ground Force Academy on family connections. They saw it as a shrewd career move before the war. But when the war broke out, they wanted to lie low, so they can go home to run for election or take over the family business. If they lie low, the better the chances we can lie low. Especially now, that the war's over and we lost."

He went on. "Now look at OCS grads. They survive battle and then volunteer for more. They believe the buncombe about truth, justice, and the Confederated Worlds way. They want us to believe it too. Even if it means we all get killed for nothing."

Only the faint crackling of cigarettes—a vile habit common among scouts—sounded for a moment. Tomas reached for his collar, glanced down. The chameleon cloth showed a yellow bar, signifier of his rank, clean and pressed in yesterday's laundry. He brushed away non-existent dirt from his yellow bar, then put on a stern face and strode around the corner toward the PT facility entrance.

Gorthi saw him first. "Ten-hut," the scout muttered to his peers. He straightened his back and pulled his hand from his pocket. A flick of his other hand sent his cigarette two meters against the wall of the building. Campbell dropped his cigarette and pivoted to face Tomas. Under their saluting hands, both scouts showed nervous faces, like boys expecting a scolding.

Nilsson leaned against the curtain wall. He eased to an upright position, dropped his cigarette. The cigarette sent up a plume of smoke and steam for a moment before Nilsson ground it into the snow. Although he saluted by the book, his hooded upper lids gave his pale blue eyes an impression of cool regard.

Tomas saluted back. His expression matched Nilsson's. "At. Ease."

Campbell and Gorthi relaxed. Nilsson's demeanor showed no change.

"Does your sergeant know you're lounging around?" Tomas asked. He scowled at each of them in turn.

"We're officially on PT for another eight minutes, sir," Gorthi said. His bulbous nose contrasted with the lines of his face, sharpened by training and action. "The company kinesiologist checked off our workout as being intense enough about ten minutes ago."

"What did you bribe her with?"

Campbell's eyelids fluttered. "Instead of catching our breath after a set, we start right away into a different lift, sir."

Tomas' scowl hardened. "You finished your workout, fine, but it sounds like some of you think our brigade's mission here on Arden is for nothing."

"Just letting off steam, sir," Campbell said.

"There's no steam to let off. It doesn't matter that Shirley Foxtrot couldn't keep the Progressive Republic space force from reaching Challenger. It doesn't matter the politicians on Challenger gave away half a dozen solar systems in the peace treaty. The only thing that matters is, our superiors ordered us to suppress pro-PR irregular military action before Arden votes to stay in the Confederated Worlds. That means there's another month left in our war—" A sports metaphor from one of the OCS instructors came to mind. "—and we're going to play till the whistle. Do you hear me?" He scowled at Campbell and Gorthi.

The two scouts nodded and said, "Yes, sir."

Tomas turned to Nilsson. The scout corporal gave Tomas the same flat stare he'd held throughout the encounter. "As you say. Sir."

Nilsson's attitude made it easy for Tomas to remain brusque. "I don't know how you ever made corporal. I've seen better men than you die." Memories from his tour as an enlisted man on New Liberty stirred in his subconscious.

Gorthi and Campbell looked shocked. Nilsson's expression remained unchanged.

Tomas turned up his glower. "Listen to me, Nilsson. You've got thirty-two days in the field until we leave Arden. I will be watching you every one of those days. If you malinger, or spread defeatism, or commit anything else colorable as an offense under the code of military justice, you'll be staring down a court-martial and facing years in a terraforming battalion before you get home to Midgard."

The flat stare buckled for a moment—a plea in the eyes, a petulant quirk of the mouth. Nilsson apparently hailed from Österbotter *and you should know those things about your men* and if Nilsson wanted to be treated with dignity he should view his superiors with respect—

The attitudes Tomas had taken in from his OCS instructors and skills imps clashed with his recollections of being a grunt and serving under officers, good and bad. *You aren't officer material*, part of him thought for the hundredth time.

Anxiety squeezed him, inside, where the men couldn't see. *What choice do I have now?*

Tomas inhaled the crisp air and refocused on Nilsson. "Do you understand me?"

"Yes, sir," Nilsson said. Then his gaze turned to the sky over Tomas' shoulder and a haggard look formed around his eyes.

Tomas turned. Arden's primary, a gas giant named Prospero, covered five degrees of the sky near the zenith. It looked like a child's ball held at arm's length, a round bruise in the cloudless blue sky. The weak rays of the system's red dwarf star, Sun of York, now turned half of Prospero's visible face into a purple and blue hemisphere, barely brighter than the shaded hemisphere of the gas giant's night.

He'd grown up on a gas giant's terraformed moon, and seen pictures of the rings of Saturn in far-off Sol System, but Tomas had never seen anything like the Ariel Band. Formed from zettatons of water and methane ice melted on Arden's surface and expelled at high velocity from the top of the space elevator during the terraforming process, the Ariel Band ringed Prospero far more densely, widely, and thickly than the rings of Saturn. In the distant future, long after the war had become a footnote in history texts, some of the ice might coalesce into another moon of the gas giant. For now, the trillion trillion chunks of ice masked Prospero's midsection, and glittered in the thin light of Sun of York like the diamonds of a wedding ring.

As it always did, the sight reminded him of Lissa.

I want to get home in one piece, same as all of you, part of him wanted to tell Nilsson and the other scouts. But an officer couldn't show such weakness to his men.

Especially now, given the unnatural features showing in Arden's sky. Not the two arrays of mirrors, tens of thousands of kilometers across, attending the planet at the gravitationally-stable L4 and L5 points formed by Prospero and Arden, gathering and focusing the wan sunlight onto Arden's surface. Instead, descending through the indigo sky under the now-edge-on L4 mirror, came six fuzzy glows of light, falling down the sky like lighted marbles in some clear but viscous liquid. Either they descended very slowly, or they aimed for landing points hundreds of kilometers away.

Why bother setting the buildings' chameleonskin to camouflage? The only ships in orbit are the Progressive Republic's. They have the coordinates of every structure on base to within a meter, and all the camouflage in the Confederated Worlds won't help us if they support their allies on the ground with orbital fires.

"Och, I've never seen Papa land so many in one go," Campbell said. *Papa*, from Papa Romeo, the phonetic alphabet letters for the initials of the Progressive Republic.

Six ships. Officially, the Progressive Republic denied it ever landed ships on Arden, let alone ships loaded with weapons, matériel, or combat advisors for the pro-PR insurrection active in the wild lands recently seeded with terrestrial life by Arden's ecological engineers. But under the terms of the treaty, Papa's ships held orbit over Arden, and the nearest units of the Confederated Worlds Space Force remained in dock in the Nuova Toscano system, two artificial wormholes and twelve light years away.

Six ships, and only one overstretched Ground Force battalion to deny them operational freedom over a million square kilometers of the planet.

Tomas turned to the three scouts. "You might have ten minutes more relief before the order comes for us to saddle up. Use them wisely. We'll be cooped up in our rides for a long time."

"Yes, sir," Campbell said. He and Gorthi shared a look, then went through the gap in the curtain wall toward their bivouac. Their cigarettes remained, brown shades of tobacco and filters littering the slushy snow.

Nilsson stood for a moment, fixing a thousand-yard stare on the distant points of the descending fusion drives. Tomas had seen that look on many a face. You could take a man's body out of combat, but part of his mind would always be there.

Nilsson took a breath, shook his head. With crisp, economical motions, taken without regard for Tomas' presence, he squatted near his dropped cigarette, and scooped it up with a handful of boot-dented snow.

A habit of security—leaving no spoor for a foe to trail him. Nilsson was a diligent soldier. Why was he so surly? Which side of him would come out on their next mission?

Amid cheap plastic chairs, next to a table perched on spindly carbon nanotube legs, Captain Bao waited in the conference room of company headquarters. An unrolled display, one meter by a meter and a half, lay on the tabletop, its corners glued down by blobs of reversible adhesive. Captain Bao's chin slumped against his hand while his gaze flicked from spot to spot on the display.

Tomas stopped inside the doorway. "Lt. Neumann reporting, sir."

Captain Bao looked up. "Come on in."

A step, a glance around. "Where's everyone else?"

"You're early, Neumann." Captain Bao turned back to the display. "Take a look."

Tomas approached the display. Earth tones and mottled greens mapped a million and a half square kilometers of Arden. In common with most of the territory of most freshly terraformed worlds, this region of Arden held scattered settlements of artisan farmers, ecological engineers, or followers of heretical branches of the local religion. Rumor had it some dabbled in quasi-intelligent computer code and other immoral practices shunned by worlds that remembered the causes of virtual fugue on Heinlein's World and Earth.

Thin black lines showed the roads linking the settlements to one another, the company's home base, and, via the one broad highway entering the region from the southeast, to Belmont, the planet's capital city. Thinner gray lines marked the wired communication net the Ground Force relied on during the times Papa Romeo's ships in orbit "accidentally" jammed radio communications.

A bright green line marked off a quarter of an annulus—like the last bites of a giant doughnut with Belmont in the hole. Inside the quarter-annulus lay the company's sector. A vast stretch, a thousand kilometers from the inner edge to the outer. Impossible to patrol even if the full battalion, or even the entire brigade, devoted itself to the task.

The company had help, at least on paper-thin graphical display. Each of the settlements had a powder blue icon representing a unit of the Arden Volunteer Constabulary. Icon size and a badge in traffic-light colors showed each unit's notional effectiveness. The same powder blue tinged the terrain around the settlements and sent arms down the roads. If the map could be believed, the Constabulary patrolled every stretch of road every day.

From the rawest privates to the officers on Captain Bao's staff, few of the company's personnel believed it. They spoke the nickname of the Constabulary, *ArChars*, with the contempt all line soldiers felt for local militias. Tomas held back from that judgment. The Constabulary existed to deny the settlements and roads to the pro-PR insurrection, and sometimes fix the rebels with observation and fires until the Ground Force could deliver the knockout blow. That's all they could ask of men with families and careers.

Staying home gave no guarantee war would leave you alone.

One other color rounded out the map's palette. Six gold spots marked Papa Romeo's approximate landing sites. Five of them formed a wavering line, roughly northeast to southwest, about four hundred kilometers from the company's base. Tomas looked for landmarks. The towns of Sempronius and Verona to the northeast. The Sycorax Hills. Another town, Eltham. The bright green of their sector boundary bisected the wavering line before its final point, near a town called Eastcheap, south of them in Bravo Company's sector.

The sixth landing site lay three hundred kilometers further to the west of the others. Only a single ecological engineering camp, abandoned since the start of the insurrection, showed anywhere nearby.

Footsteps and a conversation flowed into the room. Tomas turned to see the three members of Captain Bao's staff, the executive officer, the supply and support officer, and the first sergeant. The conversation dried up. All three looked weary.

"You look like I feel," Captain Bao said. "But we're going to get through this. Thirty-two days. We can sleep the whole way back to Challenger." He looked past the new arrivals to the entryway. "Lieutenant Landon, Staff Sergeant Khudobin, come in."

The last two, the company's platoon commanders other than Tomas, had little in common. Lt. Landon had an Academy degree and chiseled cheekbones. On the warm days of Arden's weather cycle, he wore short sleeves that showed lean yet muscular arms. Though commissioned after Tomas, Lt. Landon showed only confidence verging into arrogance.

Khudobin, in contrast, exuded a grunt's fatalism. His stubbled chin, at odds with his soft face, showed an expectation that anything that could go wrong would, at the worst possible time. He commanded a platoon because his superior, Lt. Kalus, lay in a medical tank in the hospital in Belmont after taking a sniper round through the head.

The crowd gathered near the table. Bao cleared his throat. "You all know why we're here. Six Papa ships came down jacob's ladder half an hour ago. Lt. Neumann is going to tell us his plan for dealing with them."

Tomas' head jerked up. "Sir?"

Capt. Bao raised an eyebrow. "You've studied the map more than anyone else, haven't you?"

Tomas blinked. Words failed him. Bao usually started a conversation and built a consensus from his platoon leaders. Why was he singling Tomas out this time?

"Come on, Newman," added Lt. Landon. "OCS intake knows what it's doing. Most of the time."

The others stayed quiet, but their faces lacked sympathy. Tomas dropped his gaze to the map and breathed deep into his belly.

"Landon and I split up these four sites." He pointed to the middle of the map. "My platoon will scout the sites near…" *Doesn't matter which. Pick two.* "Sycorax Hills and Eltham, his will take the ones near Sempronius and Verona. Khudobin will stay in reserve to give his platoon more time to recover from its recent action."

The staff sergeant let out a barely-audible breath.

Tomas pointed at the distant landing site near the ecological engineering camp. "This one is too far, at least until we scout the nearer sites. We tell the Constabulary units nearest to this site to do more aggressive patrolling in their immediate regions. If one can spare the men and vehicles to scout the landing site, so much the better—"

"ArChars?" asked Lt. Landon. "They aren't even scouts, for chrissake." With Kalus in the hospital, only armored grenadiers led the company's combat platoons.

Another deep breath, held for a two-count. "Perhaps I expect too much," Tomas said. He glanced up at the company's SSC officer, a blond Midgarder with soft brown eyes. "Lt. Haraldsdottir, can you spare a few fab cycles for a piece of equipment a Constabulary unit might want?"

She squinted. "Let me think."

Capt. Bao spoke up. "You want to offer the ArChars a carrot for reconnoitering that landing site?"

"If Lt. Haraldsdottir says she can spare the fab cycles, then, yes."

Lt. Haraldsdottir nodded. "They're always asking for better trace metal extractors than civilian fabs in their towns are allowed. We can squeeze one into the schedule over the next four or five days."

"No," Lt. Landon said. "Quite the bad idea. Don't you agree, Captain?"

Capt. Bao gave him an impassive look. "Give me more info and maybe I will."

Lt. Landon's face showed a certainty the captain would come to agree with him. "It's a point the Academy instructors hammered into us in counterinsurgency class. We have to assume at least some ArChars are rebel agents. If we give the ArChars equipment to make better vehicle parts or whatever, there's a chance they'll give it to the rebels."

Tomas frowned. "With these landings, Papa Romeo might be giving the rebels much more and better matériel than one metal extractor. Six ships could land two companies of tanks."

With a nod, Khudobin said, "Even if the rebels take a metal extractor, they couldn't fab enough stronger alloys in the next month to make a difference."

"I've heard the pros and cons regarding the site near the ecological engineering camp." Capt. Bao peered at the last spot on the map. "What about this one, near Eastcheap?"

"We alert the Constabulary units on our side of the sector boundary. And after Bravo Company steps on its own—" Tomas rarely used salty language, and especially not with a lady present. "—tail, whichever of Landon or I finishes our part of the mission first can help it."

Capt. Bao and the executive officer chuckled. The mood of the others lightened. Even Lt. Landon's usual smirk changed, to include Tomas within its circle.

A sad fact about human nature, that a strong way to build camaraderie among one's team lay in denigrating another.

After his chuckle faded, Capt. Bao rubbed his chin while his gaze roved over the map. "Good plan, Neumann."

"Sir? Thank you."

Capt. Bao looked up, taking in Tomas and Landon. "Now it's time to execute. I want to see your platoons roll out the gate within an hour."

2

Sycorax Hills

The platoon's main column rolled into a town named Navarre. Past a few outlying cottages, the road climbed the eastern slope of a low hill toward the bulk of the town. The snow of recent days had mostly melted, showing the dull green of hardy grass, except on the western sides of buildings and swales in the ground. Though the weather had warmed, they drove toward an indigo sky. Above the town, the L4 mirror showed a mere crescent of light under the dull red ball of Sun of York.

The cameras on the hull of Tomas' Badger sent to the video displays in the turret live footage of a few civilians working in cottage gardens. Many kept digging into the rocky soil, ignoring the machines rumbling by. A few looked up with unreadable expressions until the vehicles passed.

One of the platoon's two Weasels, the scouts' lighter infantry fighting vehicles, waited in Navarre's paved central square. Its turret's open hatch jutted up, and its rear ramp pressed into the living asphalt. Cpl. Nilsson and the men of his fireteam stood near their Weasel, in proper mode for dealing with friendly civilians: cee-skin set to an urban camouflage pattern, helmet faceplates up.

Tomas wished the other scout vehicle, commanded by Sergeant Hoch, had been the lead outrider when entering the town. Not simply to have a higher ranking NCO be the first to meet with the locals. The defeatism expressed by Nilsson and his men—Campbell and Gorthi stood together near the back of the fireteam formation, leaning toward one another in some private conversation—might leak out. Yet Tomas had realized too late which Weasel would be the first into Navarre. Nilsson would have known why, had he changed the column order for entry into the town. Tomas would have appeared even weaker to Nilsson and the others if he'd changed the order then.

In the square also waited a handful of Constabulary men in plain khaki uniforms and powder blue berets, standing in a loose semicircle around a few civilians. Most of the civilians wore typical dress, cargo trousers and multipocketed jackets. One in the front and middle of the crowd augmented his attire with a white wig and a purple sash over one shoulder, marking him as the mayor. Next to him stood a clerk holding a thick tablet computer.

Tomas' mouth scrunched. Civilians didn't need tablets stuffed with so many computer parts, regardless of Ardenite cultural attitudes.

The masses of both Earth and Heinlein's World had used even bigger computers than the clerk's, before they succumbed to virtual fugue.

Tomas ordered the platoon's vehicles to halt. The reactors quieted, and the infantry riding in the passenger compartments prepared to dismount. After the rear hatches clanged to the pavement and the last echoes of tramping boots faded from the interior of his Badger, Tomas pressed the button to open his turret hatch, and he and his gunner, Clayworth, a New Zionite—from the Mormon planet, not the Jewish one—climbed out.

The mayor stepped forward to meet him. "Leftenant Neumann, honoréd are the folk of our humble town that you of such renown have come to us."

"Thank you, Mayor—" The platoon's networked computers whispered the name to a speaker in his helmet. "Brown. The Confederated Worlds Ground Force is grateful for your welcome." Maybe that sounded lofty enough to Ardenite ears. "What can you and

Constable—Urbanowicz tell us about Papa's landing in the Sycorax Hills?"

The town constable stepped forward. A slender man, he had a long nose and narrow eyes. "I tell you, sir, every eye in town noted yon cullion's landing. His fusion exhaust renderéd incarnadine two-tenths the sky."

Ground Force encouraged its officers to respect local officials, even ones stating the obvious. "No doubt. From our observations at company headquarters, and your unit's initial report, we placed the landing at about thirty kilometers west-northwest of here. Do you have updated intelligence?"

"My brave and happy few have scouted the approaches toward Navarre from yon Sycorax Hills. We have not yet seen the vessel our enemy hath landed."

The Constabulary unit had avoided the landing site. As expected. Nearby, Cpl. Nilsson rolled his eyes.

Tomas said, "We'll operate on the assumption the initial location estimate is accurate. Tell us about the terrain near there."

Constable Urbanowicz frowned. "No doubt, your maps are accurate. I know not what I could add to them."

"Despite our maps," Tomas said, "your unit knows more about the Sycorax Hills than you could ever transmit to company headquarters."

"You speak more to the shortcomings of our wingéd spirits of the air and their wiréd cousins," Constable Urbanowicz said, "than to the strengths of mine unit, with only such augmentations of its organs of sense as the civilian fab can provide."

The constable angled for more hardware. Tomas eyed him coolly. "Go on."

"Hear, then, as I speak of yon Sycorax Hills." Constable Urbanowicz flourished his arm toward the west. "Their main ridge runs three score kilometers, the spine of a dragon-queen buried under two megameters of ice for half the universe's age, their foothills attending her like drones of her hive interred with their queen in the funerary custom of a barbarous people. Their lower hills have been touchéd by our acolytes of Demeter, our *johnny appleseeds* as those whose given tongue is Confed betimes name them, seeded with grass and brush and shrub, offering hearth and home to deer and bear alike. Their higher, further hills, though, remain near as deserted and clad in stone as the day we flung their covering waters to freeze in Prospero orbit. Yon cullion landed in that unconceivéd nursery."

Back in the *lycée*, Madame Martin's literature classes had studied texts from ancient France, not ancient England. Tomas shut his eyes while translating the constable's Elizabethan speech into standard Confed. The hills' extent, the fact that ecological engineering hadn't yet induced ecosystems at higher elevations, some detail about Papa Romeo's estimated landing site.

"Constable, I told you, we know all that." Tomas wrestled his voice into a warmer tone. "What we seek is detail finer than the standard maps. How much does the ground roll between the contour lines? What tricks of the terrain could an enemy use to his advantage?"

Constable Urbanowicz looked both hurt and graciously forgiving. "Sir, you needed only have askéd to be gifted with all my expounding. Most every grade in yon hills slopes gently from crest to vale. Marzanna's long eon of icy dominion wore down their sharper lines no less than those of Arden's every other district. Trees and brush lie thick upon the lower slopes. We prune them back to ten meters of the roadside, the furthest extent the chancellor of ecological engineering in Belmont hath permitted us. The ground providing root for Flora's bounty hath been turnéd for decades by worm and vole and fusion-powered auger, and will yield readily to the spade."

Limited visibility while driving through terrain suitable for entrenchment. Tomas raised his hand to pause the constable, then murmured into the microphone inside his helmet. "Drivers, gunners, vehicle commanders, we'll be moving through prime ambush territory at lower elevations." In his mind's eye, he saw a map, while the constable's description of the hills' higher elevations echoed in his memory. "After that, our chameleonskin better be working properly, because we'll have stark silhouettes otherwise." He turned back to the constable. "Thank you. Mayor Brown, I have some questions for you."

"Me?" Mayor Brown asked. "Bellona's bridegroom, I am not."

Speak Confed for once, would you? Tomas blinked his eyes wider. "I must ask you about the political situation here in Navarre. How loyal are the people to the Confederated Worlds?"

Mayor Brown's eyes widened and his head lurched back. After a moment, he recovered, leaning forward, wiping the air with his hands, shaking his head so fast the ends of his white wig arced away from his ears. "Sir, I assure you, every Navarrene is friend to this ground, and liegeman to the Constitution of the Confederated Worlds."

"Then why would Papa land so near?"

"Sir?" Despite the inflection in his voice, alarm in Mayor Brown's eyes showed he knew the answer to Tomas' rhetorical question. "Zounds, I lack all knowledge of our enemy's plans."

"As do I, yet I can still predict his intentions. Were Navarre as loyal as you say, Papa would not land here. The people would reject his attempts to foment rebellion and—" The city government and the Constabulary unit would be free of rebel subversion. Best not to say that without proof. "—he would miss opportunities to work mischief elsewhere."

Tomas swept his gaze around the square. Wary civilians huddled in doorways. They wanted this war to be over, no less than he did.

Yet they could want the war to end by voting to join the Progressive Republic.

He set the thought aside. "On the other hand," he said to Mayor Brown, "if the rebels dominated Navarre, then Papa would gain nothing by landing here. He would gain more by showing his strength near a town still up for grabs. How many Navarrenes are rebel sympathizers? How many have quit the town to serve with rebel formations in those thick forests in the Sycorax Hills?"

Mayor Brown swallowed thickly. "Sir, I assure you, none of our citizens would give any aid and comfort to our enemy."

Tomas set his fists on his hips and peered at the mayor. He lowered his voice. "They've threatened—you? your family?—to not cooperate with Ground Force?"

Mayor Brown's face froze.

"Even if you do as the rebels ask, if they win the plebiscite, at best you'll lose your job. At best. At worst, I don't have to tell you. Against a pack of armed men in a vacuum of legal authority, with Papa turning a blind eye to their excesses, you and your family wouldn't stand a chance."

Constable Urbanowicz puffed out his thin chest. "We're not such whippéd curs as you mind us to be, sir."

"Beaten dogs or not, I don't care. All I ask is you think hard about which side gives you the best chance of keeping you and your loved ones in one piece. Here's a hint, it's us. Here's another hint. The better you cooperate with us, the better your chances."

The mayor studied a seam in the living asphalt for a time, before a slow inhalation lifted his head. "Twenty to twenty-five young men have abandonéd the town for the ungovernéd wilds in the past ten tendays." He whispered. Tomas kept himself from looking around the square to gauge if any of those seemingly wary civilians in truth spied for the rebels.

Mayor Brown kept whispering. "Each of those young men has some sense, but too little for admission to the university in Belmont. Instead they waited in Navarre, tinkering with computers or working as freelances for ecological engineering, yet in their own minds, naught more than cagéd beasts pacing the rounds of their captivity. When they tunéd their wireless sets to the broadcasts of our enemy in orbit, 'twas like the siren's song beckoning an Odysseus from the mast of a ship whose sailors tied slip-shod knots."

Tomas turned to Constable Urbanowicz. "Twenty-five young men, from this town. Do your patrols encounter them?"

"Most oft we find only their spoor," the constable replied. "Betimes they harass us with rifle fire failing even to prick our vehicles' armor or our own. Marry, they have harméd some of the loyal residents of our western outskirts, with crops put to flame, livestock put to flight, vehicles wrecked, or assaults perpetrated upon our kith."

"They have entered the town, as well?"

Constable Urbanowicz put on a bluff face. "They've never undertaken a clash of arms against us. We may be few, and ill-equipped and trained compared to the likes of Ground Force, but we would outfight that scurvy lot and they know it."

"Twenty-five from Navarre have joined the rebels. Overtly, at least. How many from others, from other towns, are out there?"

After scratching his head, Constable Urbanowicz said, "We estimate at least a hundred are scattered among the length and breadth of the Sycorax Hills."

Tomas turned to Mayor Brown. "How many rebels are in Navarre?"

"Sir? Marry, none, as the constable hath already answered."

"No, the constable only said the rebels active in the wilds have never tested the town's defenses. My question is different. How many rebels live inside the town?"

Mayor Brown gulped. Despite the chill air, sweat beaded on his forehead. "Sir, I...."

Tomas leaned toward him. "Enough to render credible the threat you feel. You have given me answer enough." He swept his gaze over the assembled town officials and Constabulary men. "And now, each one of you will tell me if Mayor Brown and Constable Urbanowicz have spoken truthfully."

The mayor's clerk shifted his tablet computer, seemingly subconsciously, to shield his groin. "Each of us, sir? Gadzooks, if two or three corroborate the words already spoken, what need any other raise his voice?"

"If any one if you happens to be a rebel agent—" Tomas raised his eyebrow at the clerk. "—we need that you must answer to your masters for providing Ground Force good intel."

"My innocence of the crime of rebel service is as visible as the glittering ice boulders girdling brooding Prospero," the clerk said, voice huffy. "But should the plebiscite go our enemy's way, our innocence would avail us naught, when the rebel compels us to answer for our service to you."

Tomas shrugged. "To paraphrase one of the ancient presidents, if you don't hang together, then you will hang separately." He fixed his gaze on the clerk.

After a moment, the clerk bowed his head. "The mayor and constable tell you true."

"Thank you. What say you?" Tomas asked one of the Constabulary men. The man gave the same answer as the clerk. Tomas worked his way around the group, and got the same answer from each person in turn.

After that, Tomas stretched his hand toward the mayor. He shook the mayor's hand, then the constable's. "Gentlemen, thank you for the hospitality of the town, but now we must go."

Tomas went toward his Badger while the men remounted their vehicles. Before he climbed up the ladder, Tomas muttered a query to his helmet. Soon he had a voice link with Cpl. Yarborough, the platoon medic.

"Doc, I need a pain pill."

"Sir?" Cpl. Yarborough had the terse accent of one of the hardscrabble worlds settled by the last refugee wave from Heinlein's. "What's wrong?"

"Having to understand Ardenese gives me a headache."

A pause, then a chuckle. "Better you than me, sir, no disrespect. I'll be there in a moment."

While Tomas waited, Nilsson, Campbell, and Gorthi trudged up the ramp of their fireteam's Weasel. Maybe Nilsson would show some fighting spirit when they encountered Papa Romeo and the rebels. Riding around in a big moving target would bring a firefight to him whether he wanted it or not, and there might be a good enough soldier left in him to see that.

"Lieutenant," said Sgt. Hoch over the platoon's radio net, from the passenger compartment of the other Weasel.

With thoughts on Nilsson, Tomas said, "Yes?"

"You may recall, we're still on our road carriages."

Tomas took a moment to redirect his thoughts. For better speed and gentler wear on pavement, the vehicles had driven from company headquarters on road carriages. These were low, wide metal frames with two axles of run-flat tires reaching chest-height on a man. Power and control for a road carriage's steering and drivetrain came from hookups to the Badger or Weasel they carried.

The road carriages enabled high speeds in rear areas, but made the vehicles less maneuverable and easier to spot when in or near enemy contact.

"We'll disconnect just outside of town," Tomas said. "There's a refit station at the next intersection."

"According to the map."

"The town constable would have too much to answer for, if he let the rebels destroy it."

Sgt. Hoch drew in a breath. "You've got a lot of faith in the Ar-Chars."

The best-remembered piece of advice Tomas had gotten on officership while still an infantryman had independently come from two sources, his squad sergeant and his platoon commander. *Listen to your sergeants. They give you advice because they want you to be an officer worth following.* "Even if I didn't, the rebels have spies in town. If they see us roll out on our road carriages, their friends in the hills may expect us to still be riding them when we make contact."

Sgt. Hoch took a moment. "Not a bad idea, lieutenant."

High praise coming from an old non-com. Tomas hustled into his Badger's turret. Moments later, the fusion reactor under the crew compartment rumbled to generate more power. Its peers in the other vehicles grew louder, and the microphones on the outside of the Badger fed into Tomas' helmet echoes from the brick faces of timber-framed buildings ringing the square.

The vehicles pulled out in column—Sgt. Hoch's Weasel, then Tomas' Badger, the other Badger, and the Buffalo. The Weasel carrying Nilsson's fireteam would bring up the rear. First into town, last out. Lucky and lazy.

The jagged vee-shape of a St. Martin's cloak painted on the side of the Buffalo marked it as an armored, but weaponless, vehicle belonging to Supply and Support Corps, SSC. The Buffalo rode near the back of the column for safety—it held the only military-grade fab for three hundred kilometers. Without it, the platoon's ability to remain in the field would be limited by the stocks of ammunition and self-cooking meals carried in the infantry fighting vehicles.

The column rolled out of the square down a wide street leading to the west. The watchers from doorways and windows shrank back, and pedestrians on the sidewalks stopped and faced the street. The impassive faces of the Navarrenes hid the degree of their loyalty.

"Jumping cuesticks," said Clayworth, the gunner. His head swiveled to watch the video feeds from the side-mounted cameras, showing passing sidewalks and buildings. The view of the western outskirts of town in the main display in front of Clayworth silhouetted his long, narrow nose. "Every one of those jackholes is a Papa spy. I feel it in my bones."

"We don't know that," Tomas replied. The video feeds showed more wary townsfolk. One teen boy nodded from vehicle to vehicle, then lifted his shoulders and widened his eyes at the St. Martin's cloak on the Buffalo. "But quite likely there's at least one."

The column rolled on. After the last few cottages, barbed wire to the right of the road fenced off a sheep paddock. The barbed wire made a poor quality obstacle, for a soldier: four strands parallel to each other and the ground, with a total height of about one-meter-fifty. It must suffice for the sheep. The blues and reds of their genetically-engineered wool contrasted with the deep green grass.

To the left, they passed an ecological engineering yard showing rows of potted juvenile pines and firs. Like the grass, their needles showed a deep green, nearing black, to better catch the reflected red-tinted light of Sun of York. The Ardenites would plant them come peacetime, in some sparse landscape liberated within living memory from two thousand kilometers of ice. Come peacetime, regardless whether Arden voted for the Confederated Worlds or the Progressive Republic.

What difference did one world make? Did this young world justify the cost of towing a wormhole to it, and maintaining ground and space forces to defend it? Would it be so bad if the locals voted to join the Progressive Republic? To some politicians on Challenger, yes, but to the Ground Force personnel being asked to fight and die here?

Tomas pushed the thoughts from his mind. He had an assignment, and whether wise or foolish, he lacked standing to question it. Nor did it matter. For the next month, he had his platoon's effort to direct as wisely as he could. Forty people's lives to spend as dearly as possible. He returned his attention to the video displays, the maps, and the vehicle and telemetry data crowding the inner surfaces of the turret.

In the forward view, the Sycorax Hills appeared as a green fringe at the horizon.

At four thousand meters from Navarre's last cottage, the column came to a crossroads. At one corner of the intersection, five-meter-tall poles held up a thick sheet of chameleonskin. Twenty meters by thirty, the chameleonskin covered a space secured against foes more wily than sheep. Thick taut strands of electrified wire, not barbed but razor spiked, formed a double fence around the perimeter. A slab of reinforced concrete secured fenceposts and floored the enclosure. More coils of razor wire ringed the poles to dissuade sappers from climbing. With the coils of wire, cameras and microphones shared the poles. Wired and wireless relays would alert the Navarre Constabulary if anyone tried to cross the fence.

All this would secure the enclosure, if the Constabulary could be trusted.

The gate opened in response to the IFF transponder on Sgt. Hoch's Weasel. The gate telemetered its security log to Tomas' Badger as the rest of the column rolled in. Since the last Ground Force entry, no attempts to force the gate or the fence. According to the log, Constabulary personnel on patrol had verified the enclosure's security twice a day. By the book.

"Have some dismounts confirm the all-clear," Tomas told Sgt. Hoch.

The Weasel's rear hatch dropped. Sgt. Hoch's fireteam hustled out, chameleonskin dialed to transparent. The cee-skin wasn't perfect. The men could be glimpsed in distortions of the background, and motion blurred the outlines of their figures. Their terse words came through the platoon net. Ground undisturbed, latrine and kitchenette unoccupied and free of booby traps.

"All clear from visual inspection," Sgt. Hoch said. "Agrees with logged data."

"We are all clear," Tomas said. "Dismounts, you have twenty

minutes for comfort breaks. Crews and commanders, we're leaving our road carriages here and checking our rides' chameleonskin before you can hit the buckets."

The passenger compartment's hatch in Tomas' ride, Badger One, clanged to the concrete. Out tromped a dozen boots. The soldiers spoke among themselves with guarded humor, mostly about hot meals and the nearest Daughters of Astarte facility, far off in Belmont. Part of Tomas longed for that camaraderie again, but he was the only officer within three hundred kilometers. He had no comrades here. Only subordinates he had to lead.

Get back to work. He climbed out of his Badger and oversaw the disconnecting of vehicles from their carriages, the flipping down of carriage ramps, the churning of tracks. Once all five vehicles stood on the concrete, the crews ran diagnostics on the vehicles' cee-skin panels and set them to transparent. Up close, anyone could identify their outlines, from distortions at angles and edges, but it would be far tougher from across a thousand meters of battlefield. Or from orbit.

Tomas circled the vehicles, verifying each panel, and climbed up the sides to check the cee-skins on the turrets and decks. "Looks good. Take ten."

The vehicle crews headed toward the latrine. Tomas' gut churned, but he waited for everyone else to queue up first. As he approached the end of the line, he noticed Nilsson nearby, leaning against the track of his Weasel, his eyes closed.

"This is the last crapper for a while," Tomas said. "Better go here than think you can dig a cathole."

Nilsson cast a hooded gaze at Tomas. "I'm fine. My insides aren't wired that way."

Minutes later, a chain of bioreactors under the concrete turning his shit into sugar, Tomas called together the sergeants and vehicle crews. "Faceplates down," he told them. He pulled his tablet from a zip pocket of his uniform, and soon projected a map to their helmet displays.

"Here's where we're going." Using the tablet, he highlighted a golden smear in the treeless higher land twenty-five kilometers away. "We have three routes to get there. Left, right, or straight ahead." A backlight effect haloed parts of the road net. From the intersection, the crossroad was paved all the way to the next towns to north and south. Within ten kilometers either direction on the crossroad, narrower, gravel roads ran from the pavement up into the forested lower elevations. The road they'd taken from Navarre remained paved for two kilometers past the intersection, then turned to gravel at the edge of the forest. Tomas recalled the minor country roads around his home town on Joséphine. The gravel roads probably turned to rutted dirt shortly after the forest cover started.

"Papa in orbit saw us come to here. With our cee-skin to transparent, we can probably make it unseen to the edge of the pavement. Once we're on the gravel, though, we'll be kicking up enough dust for Papa to see from orbit—or rebels to see from the forest."

Cameras inside the helmets of the men around him provided visuals of their faces, which his display superimposed over the locations of their helmeted and cee-skinned heads. The sergeants looked glum, as usual. *Is my leadership that poor?*

Advice from an OCS instructor came to him. *Fake it till you make it.* "Still, if we move quickly enough down a path the rebels aren't expecting, we'll reach the Papa landing site before the rebels can take action against us."

The driver of Nilsson's Weasel worked the air with his jaw. "Sir, we'd expose our rear to any rebels in the forest if we drove balls-out."

"We'll chance it. It would take too long to clear the rebels from the forest before we scout the landing site. And even if the rebels tried blocking our exit from the hills, let them. We could fight through them on the way back here before Papa could focus against us whatever forces he might have brought down jacob's ladder. The rebels around here haven't faced Ground Force yet. We'd give them more of a fight than the Constabulary ever has. Got it?"

The driver shrugged. "Whatever you say, ell-tee."

Tomas widened his stance to take in all the men. "Our only risk is driving into an ambush on the way. Which route would the rebels expect us to take? Straight out from Navarre gives the shortest route to the landing site, so we'll take another."

"Sir," Sgt. Hoch said, "they could set up multiple ambushes."

Tomas peered at the sergeant. Did he have a point? *Again, fake it till you make it.* "That's unlikely. They have a hundred poorly-trained men armed only with whatever rifles they can cobble together from civilian fabs."

"Probably. But Papa Romeo might have given them anti-armor weapons. Or they might have improvised something more effective than rifles."

"If they've split up to cover each of the roads, all the more reason to pick one and drive to the hoop." Tomas put on a stern face for the benefit of the cameras inside his helmet. The expression clashed with a sudden burst of self-doubt. *Even if you assayed the situation correctly, sports clichés make you sound like some paper tiger.*

If the personnel around him saw his doubts, none let on. Relieved, Tomas spoke. "Here's the plan. We turn right at the crossroads, then left onto that gravel road into the hills. If we don't make contact on the way, we dismount the infantry and switch to line here." More swipes on the tablet, and a checkpoint appeared on the map at about three thousand meters from Papa's estimated landing site.

"Final thing. We're rearranging the column. Weasels remain at point and tail, and in the middle, it will be Badger Two, then the Buffalo, then me in Badger One. Now saddle up. We roll out in five minutes. Move!"

Some of the sergeants and crews shared questioning glances, yet all went to their vehicles without complaint.

The column sped northward on the paved road and made the left turn on schedule. At the gravel road, according to the mission schedule, the Weasels swapped positions, with the one carrying Cpl. Nilsson's fireteam taking point.

The vehicles slowed. Their tracks creased the gray basaltic gravel and flung crushed pebbles behind them. The rear-view display showed a thin smudge of dust rising behind them, and an analysis of the microphone data feed estimated the sound of their passage as audible for hundreds of meters into the dense forest at either hand.

Constable Urbanowicz had spoken truthfully about the terrain. Ten meters separated roadside drainage ditches from the treelines. Dense undergrowth covered the ground under the canopies of firs and pines. A few patches of snow remained at the bases of the shrubs near the forest's edges. Tomas worked the lidar—laser rangefinder—in search of human shapes amid the undergrowth. The tangle of shrubs returned only noisy data.

The terrain undulated as they drove higher into the Sycorax Hills. The metal detectors and the real-time video analysis modules in the lead Weasel showed only undisturbed gravel and rocky soil. No buried land mines, then. But Tomas refused to trust the machines. When the lead Weasel topped each undulation, Tomas checked the forward camera view it transmitted. His eyes told him the same story. No sign of rebel activity.

Did I guess right about the enemy only setting up an ambush on the straight path?

Around a bend, the road ahead still looked clear, and the lidar still failed to give conclusive data. The horizon showed a flattened gray elevation ahead. Almost through the forest, into terrain where no one could hide—

A crump rumbled through the ground. The video feed from the lead Weasel slewed, then pitched forward. "They opened a ditch under us!" yelled its driver over the platoon net.

"Ambush!" Tomas shouted. "Full stop! Infantry dismount! Gunners, cover your side! Prep anti-missile chaff!"

The column erupted with motion. The rear hatch of Tomas' Badger clanked to the ground while he slewed the turret to the right. Cpl. Meriwether, the infantry fireteam leader in his Badger, shouted at his men to get moving. The displays from other vehicles, combined with data feeds from men's shillings, showed the first man from the other Badger's fireteam running toward the drainage ditch to the left of the road.

"Missile, three o'clock!" someone called.

"Everyone, chaff!" Tomas ordered.

Voices shouted over the radio. Among them, his Badger's driver, Edelstein. "Chaff up!"

Out of habit impped into his head during vehicle command training, Tomas looked to the display showing the missile. Despite the glittering haze of reflective chaff, the missile appeared as a narrow, finned dart. That slender package had enough high explosive, precisely arrayed, to have a fair chance of penetrating a Badger's reactive armor. High above the trees, the missile seemed to hang for a moment, yawing like a sniffing dog, its lidar seeking out its target.

It stopped yawing when its nose pointed at Tomas' Badger.

"Corporal, get your men out now!"

Meriwether shouted again. The infantrymen nearest the hatch started out. A burst of machine gun fire from the woods to the right chewed up the gravel road a few meters away. The nearest men lurched back against their teammates coming out of the second row of seats.

"Goddammit, you got to move your asses!" shouted Meriwether.

The missile drew closer, falling ever faster. "Fire on the MG, both tubes!" Tomas said to Clayworth.

"But the anti-missile laser—"

"Never hits anyway! Chaff's up! Fire both!"

A moment of utter silence. Behind a thick steel mesh near Tomas' head, the barrel of Badger One's main gun jerked back. One round fired, its sound suppressed by the noise-canceling hardware in his helmet. The entire Badger rocked with the recoil. Near Tomas' hip, the autoloader clanked, carrying an antipersonnel round from the magazine to the main gun's breech. Another sound, like a thousand hornets stoked into rage, came from a long burst from Badger One's thirteen millimeter machine gun.

In the display, the missile wavered, its lidar presumably scrambled by chaff, then refixed itself on the Badger—

"Move your asses!" Meriwether shouted again. Boots stomped, men shouted—

The reactive armor on the side of the Badger roared. A moment later came a sharp ping, followed by shouts and screams both over the radio and from the crew compartment.

For a moment, everything seemed unreal, as if he held his breath and floated. Tomas couldn't think. *We're hit am I hit I don't feel anything—*

His impped skills pushed their way out of his subconscious and into his arms, voice, and senses. They dragged his conscious mind with them.

Badger One's diagnostic displays showed yellows and reds for hull integrity and the right-side drive wheels and track. Smells of scorched plastic hit Tomas' nose. The ruffling sound of automated fire extinguishers followed. The fusion reactor, the magazine, and both weapons remained functional.

Medical data telemetered from the men's shillings showed two infantrymen had been hit. More screams sounded through the vehicle.

You never got used to wounded men screaming. The echoes inside Badger One made the sound even more plaintive.

"Doc, crew compartment, Badger One!" Tomas said over the radio.

"Roger," Cpl. Yarborough said. His voice wavered. "Coming asap."

Tomas felt as if he wore blinders on all his senses. Impped habits worked through his arms and voice before his consciousness could second guess them. "Edelstein, status?"

"I don't know if she'll drive, sir."

"Clayworth?"

"We can shoot."

"Meriwether?"

"We in the ditch on the right side of the road. Who they get? Lemieux, Chen. Shit. Thought the reac knocked down that dart." More machine gun fire chattered from the woods, panging off the gravel. "We need cover fire to go anywhere."

"We'll suppress the rebel MG with both barrels," Tomas said. "Weasel Two, target the missile launch site."

No reply from the forward Weasel.

Lemieux screamed in barely-coherent Nouvelle-Quebeçois profanity, a stream of *maudits* and *ciarges*. Chen whimpered. His vitals showed the onset of shock.

"Where's doc?" Focus. "Suppress the MG!" Tomas said to Clay-worth. The enraged-hornet sound buzzed, and another shell clanked up from the magazine. Still no reply from the lead scout vehicle. "Weasel Two, put your autocannon on the missile launch site!"

"I can't do it!" replied its gunner. "We're ass-up in this goddam trap and I can't traverse the autocannon for shit!"

Tomas found Weasel Two's video feed on one display, and a re-mote view of it from the Buffalo in another. Weasel Two's rear third showed above the lip of the tank trap. It wasn't going anywhere, and the thin armor on its exposed undercarriage made a prime tar-get for the rebels. Not this moment's problem. At least Weasel Two's ramp had opened. Telemetered data showed Cpl. Nilsson and the rest of his fireteam in the tank trap, near an end that opened to the drainage ditch on the right side of the road. "Nilsson, go after that missile launcher!"

"Sir, there's an MG in the woods—"

Clayworth fired another burst from the thirteen into the for-est, followed by an anti-personnel round from the main gun. The round detonated somewhere amid the pines and firs. The micro-phones picked up falling trees. Judging from the gunner's scowl and a minced oath at a pop-up window on his display, the round had struck short of the MG. Still, his work had some effect; the MG stayed quiet as Meriwether's team crawled toward the treeline.

"You think I don't know that?" Tomas shouted at Nilsson. "I'm the only doing something about it!"

"Where there's one, there might be two."

"Get moving! Or do you want to hoof back to Navarre with noth-ing but your rifles for company and rebels chasing you every step?"

A moment of silence followed. "Understood," Nilsson said. His tone made clear his understanding came without approval. Even so, he followed up with orders to his fireteam.

"Badger One, on my way!" shouted someone. Yarborough. From the output of his shilling, Tomas' displays showed the medic ran at a crouch from the Buffalo's open rear hatch.

A microphone picked up another woosh from deep in the woods to the column's right. One of the displays showed another missile approaching the top of its arc.

"More chaff!" Tomas ordered. The hazes above the vehicles thickened. "Buffalo, shut your hatch! Clayworth, keep suppressing the MG! Someone, put fires on that missile site!"

The missile seemed to hover again, yawing as it sniffed for a target. It swept through a wider arc, from Tomas' Badger to the Buffalo. Unlike the first missile, though, it kept yawing as it started down its arc.

"Badger One, this is Badger Two. No sign of hostiles on our left. We have ordnance to spare for the missile site."

"*Baptiser le tabernac!*" screamed Lemieux.

Footsteps clanged on the ramp. "I'm here, I've got you," said Yarborough, followed by the muttered words, "Jesus God."

"Badger Two, go!" Tomas tensed as the missile flexed its fins toward his Badger. Getting closer—

The missile's fins spasmed. It tumbled in mid-air and detonated twenty meters away. Its armor-piercing projectile launched, leaving a streak across the display as it sailed into the woods to the column's left.

Small arms fire rattled in the woods to the right. He checked the infantry. Nilsson's team went toward the treeline in cautious bounds. No sign of rebels in front of them. The small arms fire came from Meriwether's men, fifty meters into the undergrowth. The rebel MG returned fire, joined by the trilling bursts of rifles fabbed according to Papa Romeo blueprints.

Badger Two slewed off the road to the left and straddled the drainage ditch, the front of its tracks on the gravel, higher than its rear. Its turret traversed to point its main gun in the direction of the missile launches. The barrel of the main gun angled upward, and Badger Two's slanted orientation gave it an even steeper angle, an even shorter range. Its gunner would try to drop antipersonnel rounds onto the missile launcher from above, not through, the woods.

Badger Two's gun boomed. The recoil rocked the vehicle and kicked up dust from the road. The barrel made an adjustment and out roared another shell.

"B-one, we need more cover fire," said Meriwether. "You got the MG coords?"

"Roger," said Clayworth. "Telemetered in."

The view beneath the forest canopy had already thinned from thirteen millimeter rounds and antipersonnel shrapnel. Clayworth fired a burst from the thirteen and another shell from the main gun. A second later, Badger Two fired its main gun at the missile launch site.

"*Criss mange l'os!—tiiii....*" Painkiller thickened Lemieux's voice.

The medic apparently forgot his microphone fed into the platoon net. "You'll live, you'll live, now, other man, Jesus God, where do I start?"

Meriwether whooped. "Good shooting, B-one! I make rebel MG operator dead or wounded. The other motherfuckers are pulling away!"

"Prisoners if you can get them!" Tomas said.

"Roger, ell-tee. Come on, team, we going to fuck them up!"

Tomas checked the displays. In front of Nilsson, the display showed flickering probabilities of cee-skinned rebels in the undergrowth. "Rebels are falling back," Nilsson said.

Nilsson's tone of voice had to be insubordinate. Tomas knew it, even if he couldn't hear it. "Bag some prisoners."

"Forgot my net, lieutenant."

"Then use your bare hands! Don't let them slip away!"

Nothing from Nilsson for a moment. Then his voice sounded distant, like he spoke to a man nearby and forgot his microphone fed into the platoon net. No. Nilsson knew. He wanted Tomas to overhear. "They're already taking their lethe capsules. But butterbar says to capture them." He spoke the last sentence in a goofy voice, mocking the order as he relayed it to his men. "Ahead careful. Watch for traps and trip wires." Then he cut the microphone feed.

You insubordinate—but Nilsson had a good point. The rebels might fall back as a ruse to get the infantrymen to hurry forward and blunder into booby traps or preregistered fires. As if to validate Nilsson, bursts of rifle fire came from deep in the woods. The men of Nilsson's fireteam went prone in the undergrowth. A few returned fire in sluggish bursts.

"Something airborne!" called the commander of Badger Two.

Tomas flinched. "Missile? No." He checked his displays. A pillar of light over the horizon to the northwest. "The Papa lander is going back up to orbit."

"What? No, sir, look closer!"

Another display showed probability curves flickering over beating wings. A cee-skinned shape rose from a clearing three hundred meters behind the last missile site. "Unidentified aircraft. Clayworth, the thirteen. Clayworth!"

"Sir?" the gunner said with a flinch. He looked up from the display showing the view ahead of the main gun to another with a wider field of view. "What the hades?" He aimed the thirteen millimeter and fired a few bursts as the unidentified ornithopter darted through the air on pumping wings. He checked the telemetry from the rounds. "Missed."

The unidentified thopter grew smaller. "Keep an eye up," Tomas said to the platoon, "in case that bird comes back."

The unidentified thopter kept going. It shrank to a small dot, then faded out of sight to the south, in the direction of Eastcheap.

3

After Action

The line of prisoners sat on the roadside, where the gravel faded out in favor of grass. Their helmets littered the drainage ditch. Zip ties bound their hands behind their backs, and their uniforms' cee-skin showed bright orange. The usual mix of facial expressions: some sullen, most scared, a few relieved their war had come to an end.

Cpl. Meriwether's boots crunched on the gravel. "Y'all going to open your mouths, or I'm a blow your hand off." He hefted his rifle with both hands. "We're going to stick our fingers in y'all's throats till you puke. Bite our fingers, I'm a blow your hand off. You motherfuckers understand enough Confed to get that straight?"

The prisoners kept their usual looks, and stayed silent.

"Not your hand," Cpl. Nilsson said. "Use a stick. There's a million of them." He waved toward the thinned woods between Tomas' Badger and the destroyed rebel MG nest.

Cpl. Meriwether nodded. "Aight. Carcetti, set us up."

Carcetti jogged down and up the drainage ditch toward the tree-line. The day had grown brighter, hotter. The polarized filter in the faceplate of Tomas' helmet cut the glare but did nothing for the beads of sweat rolling down his cheeks.

Carcetti entered the partial shade of shattered trees.

"Don't be dawdling," Cpl. Meriwether said to Carcetti over the platoon's radio net. "There ain't no Daughters in there."

Soon, Carcetti hustled back with four fragments of wood, twenty or thirty centimeters long and thicker than a man's thumb. Sharp edges and yellow-white wood showed the damage from the thirteen millimeter rounds that sundered them from their parent trees.

"The prisoners know in theory what you're going to do," Tomas said over the platoon net, "but they'll balk at the practice."

No one responded, but Cpl. Nilsson turned to Cpl. Meriwether with body language communicating a private message between the two. Tomas glowered at Nilsson. *You think I'm an idiot for figuring out something you already knew?*

—Maybe if you'd been a non-com before OCS, they would believe you know your stuff—

Carcetti loped up the side of the drainage ditch, then held out the sticks for Cpl. Meriwether and the other two unwounded members of the fireteam. Each took one. Cpl Meriwether then advanced to the first prisoner.

"Open your mouth."

The prisoner leaned back. His sullen look intensified. "Gadzooks! What foulness would you perpetrate, vile vassal of cruel Ares?"

"What I say a happen if you don't open your mouth?" Anger sharpened Cpl. Meriwether's voice.

"Ell-tee was right," someone muttered into the platoon net.

"Disfigure me and all here would know you serve the vain god of barbarous war, not the modest virgin goddess of the profession of arms! Lads, join my cry!"

The other prisoners kept silent. Cpl. Meriwether loomed over the prisoner. "Motherfucker—"

Tomas spoke up. "Pry the prisoner's jaw open." Tomas looked at the rest of Meriwether's fireteam. "Get at it!"

Two of the infantrymen hurried forward. Cpl. Meriwether turned to Tomas, a scowl projected onto his face. "Ell-tee, I said I'm a shoot his hand off—"

"We don't shoot prisoners." Though Tomas spoke to Meriwether, everyone in the platoon overheard.

Cpl. Meriwether froze his expression and his pose. He didn't agree, but he would follow the order. From his face, Tomas read some bound part of the corporal's psyche wanted to show itself—

You're their commander, not their counselor. Give them Lissa's business card after they demobilize.

"I've tried shooting prisoners before," Tomas said. Though his voice sounded off-hand, under the influence of the memory, his pounding heart rocked his torso. "It doesn't work. Now get them puking before it's too late."

Motion flowed into Cpl. Meriwether's face and body. "Aight, men, you heard the ell-tee. Pry his mouth open, now!"

Two of the soldiers moved to the prisoner. He thrashed his head when their hands reached for him. He wore his hair too long. A soldier backhanded him across the cheek, then grabbed a handful of hair and yanked his head back. The other soldier jammed his thumb and forefinger against the prisoner's chin and pushed down his lower jaw. The prisoner squeezed shut his eyes.

Cpl. Meriwether shoved in the stick.

Gagging sounds. Heaving chest. Meriwether yanked the stick out as the prisoner pitched forward and vomited.

While the prisoner lay on his side, sucking in breaths, Meriwether poked at the vomit with the stick. "Here's the capsule." He shoved a partial cylinder, a centimeter long and translucent, along the gravel and clear of the prisoner's vomit. "Stomach acid already got one end. Contents probably absorbed already."

Once the lethe compound crossed the stomach wall, it would take a minute to circulate through the bloodstream to the brain. By now, the compound had scrambled the prisoner's recent memories, of who or what had come down in the Papa Romeo lander.

"Next," Tomas said.

The other prisoners opened their mouths on their own for Meriwether's vomit stick. Despite the compliance, same results, all down the line. Capsules at least partially dissolved, lethe compound beyond the vomit stick's reach.

Tomas called to Yarborough. "We probably won't get anything, but I'll interrogate them while you scan them with the brain scanner."

Yarborough frowned. "The brain scanner in the Buffalo is intended for field diagnosis.... Lieutenant, I've never done intelligence gathering."

"First time for everything."

Yarborough's face implored. "Sir. I took a Hippocratic oath. I help the wounded, theirs as well as ours. I don't hurt anyone."

Tomas set his fists on his hips, then relented. "This isn't torture. I'll ask them questions. Whether they answer me or not, the brain scan will tell us something. Probably just that their lethe capsules kicked in before Meriwether purged them. But the more I learn from the prisoners, the fewer of us and them who'll get wounded or killed in the next month. I have to find out and you—" Tomas jutted his finger at Yarborough. "—are going to help. Does that shine a light on all the subtle nuances in your Hippocratic oath?"

The medic looked glum. "It does."

"What I want to hear. Nilsson, your team will relieve Meriwether at guard duty. On my order, bring prisoners one by one to the Buffalo."

Nilsson stood in profile to Tomas. He looked through the prisoners as he spoke. "Why us?"

"Because Meriwether's team is two down, and fatigued from a vigorous advance against an enemy MG emplacement." Tomas glowered at Nilsson for a second, then swept the expression over Campbell, Gorthi, and the rest of Nilsson's fireteam. All avoided his gaze. Good enough. Tomas turned to the medic. "Follow me—wait."

Motion in the woods. Tomas' helmet display outlined and tagged the cee-skinned figures of Sgt. Hoch's fireteam. Amid them came someone else, visible through normal light as a figure in orange, hands bound, shoulders and head slumped forward.

"We have something good," Sgt. Hoch said over the platoon net.

By the time Hoch's team reached the treeline, most of the Ground Force soldiers on the road watched. Some of the seated prisoners noticed the shift in attention and looked over their shoulders to see for themselves. Some looked relieved, others sad, when they saw their comrade. "Alack," said one of the seated prisoners, "these varlets have too seizéd thee?"

A scout smacked the side of the speaking prisoner's head. "Shut it."

The new prisoner remained quiet.

While the rest of his team marched the new prisoner to the end of the line, Sgt. Hoch stepped quickly to Tomas. A popup in Tomas' display showed Hoch wanted to talk privately.

Tomas switched to a private connection. The sergeant pointed over his shoulder at the new prisoner, using a thumb jutting from a loose fist. "We found him cowering in the woods." He lowered his hand, rotated his wrist, and opened his fingers. "One of my men saw him put this in his mouth."

The lethe capsule looked intact. "Did he swallow it?"

"I fished it from his puke. Thirty seconds in his stomach, tops."

Tomas smiled. "Good. Who knows?"

"My whole team, plus you. Why?"

"If the other prisoners find out he forgot to take his lethe capsule, he'll face some jailyard justice when we aren't looking. If we get good intel out of him, let's spare him a shanking. Find anything else?"

Hoch's voice flattened. "Fourteen dead arsefucks."

"I'll call the Navarre Constabulary to send out a human remains team."

"They won't bother," Hoch said. "They'll let the arsefucks fertilize the ecosystem." His voice sounded more lively as he went on. "Some blood spoor between the last missile site and the thopter's liftoff point. We swabbed samples." Hoch yanked down a zipper in the cee-skin over his chest and drew out four small plastic vials with rounded conical bottoms.

A wounded person got away. A local? A Papa operative? Tomas muttered voice commands to change his radio to the platoon channel, then turned to Yarborough. "Toss those in the DNA analyzer while I'm interrogating the prisoners."

Ten minutes later, while the DNA analyzer hummed in a crevice in the Buffalo's crowded rear compartment, Campbell and Gorthi marched the first prisoner over for interrogation. He sat on the road with a brain scan helmet strapped onto his head while Tomas towered over him. With a bloop of reversible adhesive, Yarborough stuck a tablet showing brain scanner output onto an inner wall of the Buffalo's rear compartment, at an angle where he and Tomas could see but the prisoner could not.

"I'm going to ask you some questions," Tomas said. "Reply or not, if you know the answer, your brain activity will tell it to me. You might as well tell me. Cooperation will benefit you while you sit in the prison camp. Better food, better billet, a few privileges."

The prisoner looked surly. "I am made of sterner stuff than you cross-garteréd minces out of Challenger. In a brace of fortnights, I and my entire rounded world shall be free. Till then, I shall eat your mealy bread and drink your stagnant water, and regard them as the first courses in Arden's independence feast."

Tomas raised his voice. "Name?"

… rank, identification number. From either training given by Papa Romeo, or a thousand years of war stories accessed through Arden's too-powerful computers, the prisoner rattled off the answers.

He quit answering when the next questions came up. Rebel unit designation, number of men, organization, equipment. When had he joined the rebels? What training did he have? Where lay his unit's base? How many fabs did they control, with what throughput, and for what weapons and matériel did they have blueprints?

Though the prisoner refused to reply, parts of his brain knew the answers and lit up. Like telling a man *don't think of an elephant* guaranteed he would think of one.

We put such effort into masking our selves, and our brains betray us anyway.

The brain scanner gave at least partial answers. First Navarre Independent Company. Thirty men. Assault rifles generated by a fab dug into a wooded hillside three kilometers to the southwest of their current location. Advice, encouragement, and weapons designs received wirelessly from orbit.

The MG had been fabbed a tenday earlier.

The rebels had never fabbed an ornithopter.

Tomas showed the prisoner a few photos of dead rebels, to identify the dead and suss out the rebel unit's hierarchy. The prisoner tried turning away, but his gaze kept returning to the photos with horror and despair on his face. *You thought this would be easy? Hikes in the woods, a few shots at us, and our low morale would crumble further and we would slink away? Blame your puppet masters in orbit for lying to you.*

Tomas remembered a trick from interrogation class at OCS. *Look at the scanner like it's the first time you saw a girl's honeypot. Make sure the subject sees your face, but not the scanner output, when you do. Even if the scanner output is all noise, he'll think you found some of his deep dark secrets, and he might as well tell you the rest.*

After asking one of his questions, Tomas peered at the tablet, then widened his eyes and held his mouth half-open for a couple of seconds. The falsity of his expression gnawed at him—the prisoner must have the perceptiveness to see through it, right?—but it worked: the prisoner waxed at length about how he'd come to join the rebels and where he had trained with them. He named one of Mayor Brown's aides as a supplier of information to the rebels.

Tomas jotted down the name, then kept going. "What, or who, came down jacob's ladder two days ago?"

The prisoner's newfound helpfulness evaporated. "I knowest not. Three days gone our leader of foot told us we would meet a ship descending soon from Arden orbit. An hour gone I lifted my hands in panic at thy approach."

The scanner corroborated the prisoner's ignorance. The lethe capsule had dissolved his memories of the ship's landing. His brain would yield no more intel.

One of Nilsson's men led the prisoner away. Before he returned with another, Tomas took a long drink of water through a straw connected to a canteen in his suit and checked his men's activity. At the column's front, men shouted and Badger Two clanked as it towed the lead Weasel out of the tank trap. Nearby, at Tomas' Badger, Sgt. Svoboda and another SSC man, Nunes, worked with Edelstein to repair the track and roller wheels on the right side.

Svoboda's face turned red and he grunted out a stream of expletives at a nut that resisted his wrench.

Edelstein spoke. "It would go better if you detached yourself from your desire for an easy task."

Nunes snorted. "Shove that Shambhala shit up your ass."

"Easy," said Svoboda, his voice suddenly thoughtful. "The missile damage we're repairing could've been on our ride." He looked toward Tomas and nodded.

The second prisoner arrived at the back of the Buffalo, and Tomas returned to work. Under the scanner, his brain revealed essentially the same intel as the first prisoner's. The contents and passengers of the Papa lander remained unknown.

As Tomas continued down the line, the same pattern played out again and again. However poor their overall martial virtues, the rebels generally had good lethe capsule discipline. The later prisoners provided slight wrinkles on the original narrative. Maybe the intel experts at GFB Belmont could piece together a broader story from the fragments Tomas would send them.

They came to the final prisoner, the one found by Hoch's team.

Not all the rebels had good lethe capsule discipline.

The final prisoner had a tired, dirty face, and brown hair matted down by sweat. "I knowest not who hath fallen from heaven," he said when Tomas asked about the Papa lander. But his brain knew. The scanner teased an image from the prisoner's visual memory: a man, pale of face and pink of cheek, one-meter-ninety, with green eyes and a thin ruff of orange-red hair. The man had spoken almost exclusively with the rebel company's now-dead commander, but the prisoner had overheard him a few times speaking flawless Ardenese. A happy memory kindled in the prisoner's limbic system.

"You like the fact the Papa operative had been impped with your dialect?" Tomas asked.

A horrified look crept over the prisoner's face.

"That's right," Tomas said. "The lethe capsule didn't work."

The horrified look deepened.

Tomas let him stew a moment, then went on, with as much false chumminess as he could put into his voice. "You and I both know you forgot to take it in time. Combat is disorienting and confusing, especially for virgins." The prisoner's face lifted slightly, until

Tomas darkened his voice. "But your comrades may decide you 'forgot' on purpose. Or that you didn't take the lethe capsule at all. What would they do to you in POW holding when they decide you wanted to give intel to Ground Force?"

The prisoner looked defiant. "My brothers in arms would know the honor of my intentions…." His defiance evaporated as his voice trailed off.

Tomas nodded. "If you answer my questions truthfully and quickly, I'll make sure you get into protective custody back in POW holding. What was the Papa operative's name?"

The prisoner stared at the dirt. His voice came softly. "Our commander hailéd him as 'our friend.' No other name for him enteréd my ears."

Tomas scrawled notes on the tablet. *One Papa operative landed. Name unknown.*

A thought came to him. He navigated to an Ardenese lexicon and followed internal links to a listing of Shakespearean villains. After a moment's scrolling, he nodded to himself, then added to the note. *I will refer to the Papa operative as 'Iago.'*

He asked the prisoner, "Did he bring an ornithopter?"

"Yes. A fine bird, cloakéd from beak to tail in chameleon's skin."

"What else?"

"A missile launcher, and fabricator code for all the anti-armor missiles we might wish to hurl against you." The prisoner's voice turned thoughtful. "Though one of my comrades noted our friend denied us code to fabricate the launcher, and bound it to fire only by our friend's leave."

Papa used the rebels as pawns, and would deny them any say in how Arden would be governed by the Progressive Republic. The prisoner's face showed a deepening glimmer of understanding. *How deluded were you, foolish boy, to think Papa would treat you as an equal?*

Another thought crept up on Tomas. *And you aren't a pawn of the top brass and spineless politicians on Challenger?*

Tomas pushed the thought away. He set his fists on his hips and leaned toward the prisoner. "Who are the rebel sympathizers in Navarre?"

The prisoner's mouth hung limply open.

"If you tell me their names, we will arrest them and they'll be kept in custody until after the plebiscite. If we have to pull their names out with this—" Tomas thumped the scanner helmet with his fingertip. "—it might go worse for them."

The prisoner swallowed, then rattled off names.

With a scritch, Tomas pulled his tablet off the Buffalo's sidewall, then opened up a frame of video from the ride out of Navarre. The young man counting the Buffalo's place in the column filled the tablet.

Tomas swung the screen to the prisoner. "Who's this?"

"I just now naméd him, sir—" The prisoner repeated the name. "My brother." The scanner verified he told the truth.

In the Buffalo's rear compartment, the genotyper pinged. Yarborough spoke softly. "Ell-tee, blood sample analysis is complete."

"Take the prisoner away," Tomas ordered a nearby scout. The scout jammed his hand into the prisoner's armpit and pushed up. The prisoner stumbled to his feet, then shuffled back to his place in line.

Tomas turned to the medic. "Show me what you found."

Yarborough swiped at a display, then pulled it on its mounting arm to show Tomas. "Blood from three people. Two have single nucleotide polymorphisms, snips, indicative of descent from Arden's founding population."

"The third is Iago."

"The Papa operative? Can't be. The man's estimated phenotype—his physical traits predicted by his genomic markers—disagree with the prisoner's description. Mean height estimate is one-meter-seventy. Curly brown hair, blue eyes. Not Iago."

"But not an Ardenite."

"True. His snips come from the ancient United States, not ancient Britain, but there's still a dozen worlds he might've been born on."

"New Madison or Galt's World, then." Members of the Progressive Republic.

"Or Challenger," Yarborough said. "He could be a Confed."

Tomas sloughed out a breath. A Confed from an American-settled world, serving with the Ardenite rebels? Who? How? Given the Papa blockade of the wormhole into the system, it could only be a Ground Force soldier or a Confederated Worlds government official stationed to the planet during the war. A deserter. But no word of a desertion had come to Tomas, either through official channels or scuttlebutt.

Unless they don't bother telling lieutenants.

A second thought came to him. *What if he came from Confed space after the armistice, and Papa let him through?* The thought brought up, like a slumbering leviathan beginning to wake, cold intuitions of something far more vile than desertion. Treason extending its tentacles to high offices on Challenger.

That can't be it. And no one deserted. Tomas put on a confident face before speaking to the medic. "We'll report your finding to company headquarters and let them figure out who it might be. But ten credits says it's a second Papa operative. That's all, doc."

Tomas stepped away. He opened his report and added more text. *Analysis of blood spoor from battlefield indicates a second Papa operative was wounded. I will refer to him as…* Tomas called up the list of Shakespeare's villains, found one that would do. *Claudius.*

Report amended, he turned his attention to his squad leaders and vehicle crews. "Status."

"Weasel Two is back on the road."

"Prisoners are ready to transport," said Sgt. O'Herlihy, the armored grenadier squad leader.

"Good job," Tomas said. "What about Badger One?"

Sgt. Svoboda spoke. His microphone picked up the pang and hiss of a portable sintering tool. "We've almost got her drive wheel replaced. The fab in the Buffalo is working on a replacement plate of flank armor and some parts for the right-side stabilizer, so call it two hours—"

"Scratch that, sergeant. We have to get rolling."

"Sir?"

"Once Badger One has its new drive wheel, we'll return to Navarre to arrest rebel sympathizers and hand over our prisoners to the Constabulary. We'll leave Chen's remains in the morgue there for the next human remains team to come out from Belmont. While we do those tasks, you should have enough time to patch her holes. Shouldn't you?"

"I should," Sgt. Svoboda began. His intonation presaged his next words. "Unless she's got damage I can't scope out here—"

"You can give her a full damage scan after the locals vote to remain in the Confederated Worlds," Tomas said.

After a moment, Sgt. Svoboda said, "Your order, sir."

Someone on the channel grumbled, words too low to make out.

"Who has a problem?" Tomas asked. He peered at the scout squad. Nilsson or one of his lackeys?

Sgt. Hoch broke a brittle silence. "Sir, there might be some concern about riding in a vehicle with damaged armor and a missing sheet of cee-skin."

"There shouldn't. The thopter took the keys to the rebels' missile launcher with it. Any rebels still in these woods have nothing more than rifles. Badger One can resist that, damaged armor or not. We'll face no threats between here and Navarre."

Tomas focused his attention on the silence filling the channel. No backtalk. Good.

"Svoboda, let me know the instant Badger One is ready to roll. Then we move out."

4

Eltham

Tomas shut his eyes for a moment. A rise in the road to Eltham lifted his eyelids, and a glance at the displays snapped them fully open. Judging by the changes in the external views, he'd dozed for ten or twelve seconds.

His heart thudded as he glanced at Clayworth. The gunner looked bleary, yet alert enough. Most important, Clayworth showed no sign of having noticed Tomas nod off. Good. However much men might grumble at an officer setting a hard pace, if they thought him a hypocrite, setting a pace for them he himself couldn't keep, the grumbling would double.

Through his cee-skin uniform, Tomas tapped an arrhythmic pattern on his shilling where it lay against his chest. Up went the gain on the neurostimulator entraining wakeful brain waves. In a few minutes, he would feel more alert.

They could all sleep after the plebiscite. Win or lose.

Three times as large as Navarre, Eltham occupied a hilltop giving a broad view in all directions. South and east, dark green fields near the town, dotted with sheep and dairy cattle, faded into gray basalt mottled with lichen. North and west, a forest canopy concealed boggy ground. Deeper within the forest, the bogs turned to a swamp of trickling creeks. Vehicles would be limited to the few causewayed roads through the swamp.

Somewhere in the swamp lay the Papa landing site.

Eltham's central plaza showed the expected façades—the storefront for the town's molecular fabrication facility, a stone-cladded town hall, a Constabulary station. A replica of an ancient timberframed theater dominated the northern side of the square. A breeze tickled the ends of varicolored pennants on the theater's roof.

The urges driving the embrace of virtual fugue had existed centuries before the computer technology enabling it. Perhaps those urges arose in the first human beings. The universe granted them one life, and they immersed themselves in another.

The vehicles formed a square with the Buffalo in the middle. Tomas set his cee-skin to a fixed urban camouflage pattern and raised his faceplate, then ordered the platoon to do likewise. He climbed out of Badger One's turret while the men dismounted and fell into ranks facing the local delegation.

The usual mix of town officials and Constabulary personnel waited for Tomas. The L4 mirror in the western sky had grown to half-full, and the L5 mirror to the east remained almost at maximum. Each mirror reflected enough light from Sun of York that together they cast double shadows, like stadium lights. A faint breeze touched Tomas' face as he approached them, yet still sweat trickled down his nape. The ports on the back of his uniform, open to dump waste heat, would glow in a sniper's IR scope.

Mayor Patel stepped forward. A slender man, slightly darker of skin tone than most other Ardenites. Jet-black hair with a precise part. His brown eyes were narrow and his cheeks, tight, and not from squinting at the deep blue sky. "Please find yourself welcome on this fine summer's day," he said, "though have you not receivéd Constable Turner's missive?"

"I have." Company headquarters had relayed a report from the Eltham Constabulary to Tomas via encrypted wired link during the platoon's recent, brief stop in Navarre.

Constable Turner came forward and aimed his tall, stout girth at Tomas. "You know we have scouted yon Papa lander long ere now. Yet you come anyway, leftenant?" He peered down his nose at Tomas.

A few grumbles leaked into the platoon net. Tomas ignored them. The constable acted as if he outranked a Ground Force lieutenant. Lessons from auxiliary affairs training at OCS reminded Tomas he had to stop the constable's behavior. "I also know we arrested two Navarre Constabulary soldiers and one official of that town's government as rebel agents. Ground Force is in no mood to take Constabulary reports at face value. Especially if I read your report right. You claim Papa landed a ship just to self-destruct it?"

Constable Turner puffed out his chest. "I claim nothing save that seen by the optical sensors of mine unit."

Optical sensors? Spare us the poesy and just call them 'eyes.' "Then maybe you need to check your—lenses."

"We did, afore and after scouting, as is ever our wont."

Tomas frowned. "Then you're mistaken about what you claim you saw. It makes no sense for Papa to land a ship just to destroy it."

"No sense 't'all, spratling? What meager knowledge have the skills witches stufféd into your head? The flotilla ten thousand kilometers above us contains fabricators capable of building a town as big as Eltham in a single cycle of the mirror's shutters. A fusion drive, a control mechanism, and a hull to house them both contain far less matter than our town. And, marry, for fuel, the flotilla above need only dip their scoops there—" The constable pointed up, a hair east of the zenith, to indicate Prospero. "—and partake of zettatons of hydrogen. Papa can sacrifice ships as casually as Mansa Musa could hand out nuggets of gold on his saracen pilgrimage."

His words plowed onward. "Yet even were the ship to cost Papa dear, it could still be a meet gambit, an it bought him some greater advantage. Has it not drawn you here against any need? What may Papa be about, in the places you now are not?"

Did Constable Turner know where Iago had flown to, and why? "I don't know. Do you?"

"I fall under suspicion of being in league with our enemies, merely because I know more of the ways of war than a whiskerless boy? You think distilling Athena's wine ere it was squeezéd into your head makes you Bellona's bridegroom?"

Mayor Patel gave Constable Turner a sharp look. The taller, stouter constable showed no sign of noticing, let alone being chastened. Someone over the platoon net chuckled.

"My orders are to find out what Papa is up to out there." Tomas waved toward the forested swampland to the west. "And perhaps you didn't hear me right. Yesterday we arrested two men of the Navarre Constabulary on good intel as being rebel agents. Ground Force already had a low opinion of—ArChars. Finding traitors in your ranks makes our opinion of you even lower. So I will assume everything the Eltham Constabulary tells me is rebel misinformation until I see it with my own *optical sensors*. Do you understand plain Confed enough to get what I'm saying?"

Constable Turner folded his arms and showed Tomas a stony face.

Mayor Patel stepped closer to Tomas, arms wide. "We have no traitors here, I assure you."

"I heard that in Navarre. And the skills imps squeezed enough knowledge into my head that I know Papa only landed near here because he thinks he can swing Eltham into his column."

Mayor Patel leaned in and angled his mouth up toward Tomas' ear. "Can we speak privately in my office? The ears of your wireless stopped up for a time, and no persons listening to echoes from the square's daub-and-wattle walls?"

The ears of my wireless stopped up? What did the mayor want to tell Tomas out of hearing of his men? After leaving the armored grenadier squad leader, Sgt. O'Herlihy, in charge, Tomas said, "Lead the way."

The way to the town hall went due east, into the dazzle of the L5 mirror, while the western mirror reflected enough light to cast a gray shadow in front of Tomas. Inside the town hall, clerks slunk away from their path.

The path wound down hallways of scuffed plasterboard. Tomas glanced behind him. The clerks returned to their duties and did not follow. Mayor Patel and Constable Turner seemed loyal—and even if they weren't, springing an elaborate trap on him would only lead to the devastation of their town, and if they were rebels they would know that—but even so, Tomas' hand drifted to the butt of his holstered pistol.

At the back of the building, they entered an office of dark paneling and dense tapestries over the two windows. A walnut-brown desk bore a single tablet, its screen dim.

Mayor Patel gestured at a chair facing the desk, then raised a finger to his lips. Tomas waited, silently, while the mayor went around the room. The mayor pulled back a corner of one tapestry. Stark daylight invaded the room and left an afterimage when Tomas blinked. The mayor peered out the window, then did the same at the other window.

He faced Tomas. "We have no traitors here, good leftenant, for we have turnéd them."

Tomas raised an eyebrow. "All the rebel sympathizers in the town are double agents?"

"Marry, not all, but those at the three highest levels of the rebel hierarchy. They relay to their bandit peers in the wetland and their one-time masters in orbit only such false information as we wish to be known." The corner's of the mayor's mouth lifted. Tomas read Mayor Patel's pride in his counterintelligence operation.

Tomas squinted. "You've never reported this to Ground Force."

Constable Turner snorted. "You would have us pour our precious knowledge into the sieve of Belmont?"

Anger hardened Tomas' features. "Who are you to say we are careless—or worse?"

"Who am I, leftenant? Your superior officer, betimes. I were a major in Ground Force intelligence on New Liberty, till the higher command needed scapegoats for the eruption of rebellion on that world. Not that someone with a mind dripping out fresh officer skills—"

"I served on New Liberty. Before OCS. An armored grenadier, Twenty-first Brigade." Tomas showed his palms in well-intentioned but powerless sympathy. "I saw the eruption of that rebellion first hand. I know the officer most responsible for it. I assure you, I will speak to my superiors to correct the record—"

Constable Turner laughed without mirth. "A true leftenant. Not

Bellona's bridegroom, but her ringbearer, a prepubescent lad dressing up in a man's uniform."

Tomas' back stiffened and anger curled his mouth.

The constable shut his eyes, bowed his head. "Your pardons, leftenant. My ill-treatment by some high in the Ground Force chain of command biaséd me against you. I take your urge to correct the injustice done to me as reflective of your own self and the idealism of youth. However, my years of service disillusionéd me so much that I know no good, and much ill, would come to you if spoke to your commanders on my behalf. Do not do so."

Any human organization acquired bureaucratic time-servers, like ticks on a dog. But unlike ticks, the time-servers could play politics. Indeed, they could do nothing else. Tomas had sensed these things before, but now a chill swept over him as he considered the constable's words. "Thank you for your advice." Tomas dropped his hands to his sides. "Now why do you think Belmont would be loose with your secrets?"

"The intelligence office at GFB Belmont is stafféd, not with angels, but with men and women. A man may mislay a file, or write a password on a slip of paper, or say too much in his cups whilst at liberty, and a precious secret be lost. And more, a man may seem loyal, yet willfully work against his master."

A character description from the Shakespearean glossary came to Tomas. "Like Iago."

Constable Turner blinked. "You have read our grounding texts?"

"No," Tomas said. "It's against my religion. But back to our business. Do you have a basis for suspecting a double agent among Ground Force planetary command?"

"In faith, no. I merely have a grasp of the capabilities of people, especially when defeat knocks away a man's unquestioning certainty his side is right."

Tomas studied Constable Turner's craggy face. "Then why trust me with this information? I lost the war as much as any traitor in Belmont."

"Because the missile that struck your track and side armor

yestern could neither know nor care if your heart cleavéd to the men who launchéd it. You know that so well as I."

Tomas stepped back to let his thoughts collect. The dark paneling cocooned him against the hot day outside. The tapestries smothered echoes of Constable Turner shifting his weight, Mayor Patel dabbing fingers at a tablet. The constable's words joined with his musings about the second man in the thopter. A conspiracy could reach far beyond GFB Belmont. He would keep secret the Eltham leadership's counterintelligence success. Despite his upregulated wakeful brainwaves, his eyelids drooped at his relaxed certitude.

Another thought pried them open. He only had their word for their loyalty to the Confederated Worlds. They could be rebel agents in steadfast guise.

"You speak truthfully, Constable Turner," Tomas said, because he either did, or should be lied to. "Now we must plan our joint operation to reconnoiter the Papa landing site."

"You have no need to double-check our sums...." Constable Turner narrowed his eyes. "Still you trust us not?"

Tomas put on a pained look. "Haven't we just shown each other our true faces? You know the swamp, the wetland, better than me. More, if rebels lie in wait for us along the approaches to the landing site, we want all the skilled men we can muster to punch them in the mouth."

"We've heard of no such rebel plans," the constable said.

"Your counterintelligence operation may be good, but are you sure it's perfect?"

Mayor Patel spoke. "Marry, that's a fair point."

Constable Turner grunted. "Have you more?"

Optical sensors came back to Tomas' mind. "Here's another one. If we do not scout the site, then Papa would infer you have already done so, with effectiveness full enough for Ground Force to trust. Is that a card you want to tip him?"

A breath rustled out the constable's nose. "All well spoken, leftenant. We shall align our force with yours. Let us meet at Constabulary headquarters with your sergeants and mine to plan."

Half an hour later, a woman in the uniform of the Constabulary

Auxiliary guided Tomas and his squad leaders through the stone-walled corridors of Constabulary headquarters. She left them in a tall, windowless room. Ceiling panels of diffuse light smeared reflections on large displays glued to the walls.

Constable Turner and his staff waited near one of the displays. Waiting with them was a civilian, a woman of about twenty standard years, wearing a rumpled khaki vest and matching cargo pants. Her black hair, her brown eyes, and the shape of her face all showed a family resemblance to the mayor. Presumably his daughter.

Tomas had little grasp of women. The sexual frankness of Daughters of Astarte; the deep perceptiveness of Lissa. Little grasp, but enough to think he knew their main types. From her demeanor, the mayor's daughter seemed distinct. Bookish, his schoolteachers might say. A cold fish, a soldier on liberty might describe her. She struck Tomas as a person for whom understanding other people mattered far less than solving some puzzle of things and ideas.

The constable made introductions. She was indeed the mayor's daughter, Beatrice Patel. She spoke to Tomas in a smooth but absent-minded voice while her hand remained at her side. Tomas hesitated, then extended his to shake hers.

Beatrice blinked—Tomas read it as she rousing herself from absentmindedness—and raised up the back of her hand to be kissed.

He froze, then awkwardly raised her hand to his lips.

Introductions complete, Tomas realized no one had explained Beatrice Patel's presence in a military planning meeting.

Constable Turner waved his hand at the wall display. It mapped the portion of the swamp where the Papa ship had landed. At ten meters to the centimeter, the few roads showed as lines thick as a stylus point. Nearly solid green covered the perimeter of the map, marked only by roads. In the middle, though, no roads traversed a terrain denoted in various shades of green and blue forming a pattern like a tortoise's shell or a giraffe's pelt. Sluggish waterways surrounded low islands for hundreds of meters in every direction from an angular red shape: Papa's landing point on a small island.

"They picked a touchdown site we can't drive to," Tomas said.

One of the constable's staffers spoke. "Papa also quenchéd by the wetland the fire of the ship's fusion drive. It scouréd yon island but sparéd the rest of the wetland's ecology. Many an Ardenite would think favorably of him for avoiding a forest or heathland fire."

"The landing site was chosen as a propaganda play?" Tomas shrugged. "There's an easy counter. Don't tell many an Ardenite." He turned to Constable Turner. "You couldn't drive there either. How did you get to the site?"

The constable pointed to spurs of road in the southwest corner of the map. The spurs led to powder blue squares at nearby waterways. "Here and here we dock our riverine vessels."

"You just leave them out in the open?" Sgt. Hoch said.

"Solid concrete, thick as a man's arm is long, forms the superstructure of the docks, and algorithms uncrackable till Sun of York leaves the main sequence seal them. The lock on each vessels' manual controls are encrypted likewise. Never will a rebel bandit purloin them."

Tomas quirked his mouth at the thought of the computer power involved. But computers themselves did not entomb cultures in virtual fugue. "Show us how you scouted the landing site."

Powder blue dotted lines sprung onto the map. They ran from the docks down different watercourses, some running straight at the landing site and others looping wide, so the lines converged on the site from three directions roughly equidistant around the compass. Small blue wedges flowed down the lines toward the angular red shape. Most stopped a few hundred meters from the Papa landing site. Some disgorged powder blue mites onto islands.

"We kept gunboats on station in the waterways, and debarkéd ordnance teams onto drier land," Constable Turner said, "should the vessel have proven hostile."

More blue wedges flowed on toward the landing site. "How many men scouted the ship?"

The men of the Eltham Constabulary cast nervous glances toward Constable Turner. The constable opened and closed his mouth, not sure what to say.

Beatrice Patel rolled her eyes, then turned to Tomas. "The constable uséd my drones, leftenant."

Constable Turner gritted his teeth. A cold itch crawled over Tomas' nape. He stiffened his back to smother it. Behind him, Sgt O'Herlihy gasped.

Drones? The peoples of both Earth and Heinlein's World had built masses of robots in their last vibrant years. Tomas remembered the amphitheater at his mother's parsonage, open to the sky, and her many sermons denouncing autonomous machines. Handmaidens of virtual fugue. Constable Turner spoke of them as harmless? As tools fit for an unmarried woman to build and use?

Tomas blinked at the wall-mounted display to give his thoughts time to settle. He remembered New Liberty, Shermantown, the remote sensors that had to be quickly accessed by someone in his squad. He'd overcome his own prejudices, instilled in him with his mother's milk, against watching recorded video and spared his unit an ambush in unfavorable terrain. How were Miss Patel's drones any different than those remote sensors?

The drones moved under their own power. Perhaps even their own volition.

The Observer faith had lost adherents and allies throughout the Confederated Worlds, but most people still viewed autonomous machines as an abomination. Even though Tomas had shucked some of his mother's more stringent teachings, a pit of revulsion in his gut told him he had not shucked this one.

Sgt. Hoch muttered, "We give these isolated worlds too much freedom."

Another thought came to Tomas. He lifted his hand to silence Hoch. Perhaps *drone* had a meaning in Ardenese that speakers of plain Confed mistranslated. To Constable Turner, he said, "Their pilots remained on the gunboats, or debarked to the islands to control the drones remotely?"

The constable's face looked pained. "Such details are petty niceties in the greater picture, are they not?"

Beatrice rolled her eyes again. "Come, leftenant, I know the mewls of Challenger must tell the old ladies and church fathers of Pengláishān and suchlike planets that robots are a sin against one god or another. But strategist Athena and berserker Ares each in their own way care only for the soldier who best delivers fires upon the focus point. Whether from an arméd man or a machine built for the purposes of war, those belligerent gods will accept a hecatomb. I should think a man in the profession of arms would know this to his bones."

The enormity of it struck Tomas. He had to say something. "Those drone boats are fully autonomous."

She raised an eyebrow. "Yes. Have not my words been plain? No matter."

"No matter." Tomas glowered at the constable. "Is the use of autonomous machines your idea, or the mayor's?"

Beatrice stepped forward, eyes sharp. "You think me a bystander in the doings of men? I have a talent for cybernetic engineering. My world is in a moment of need, against foes notorious throughout the settled spheres of man for their tinkering with machines and bodies. I offeréd my talents for the benefit of the Constabulary. Constable Turner accepted my offer."

Constable Turner reared back and waved his hands, palms out, in a slow, conciliating gesture. "Yes, leftenant, I did. You are a good man, I sense, and took in the simple pieties of Sankt-Benedikts-Welt or wherever else might be your homeworld. But those pieties would serve us poorly if we parroted them in blindness of the facts."

"Facts? You better start giving me some."

"I have but three score men, skilléd craftsmen with families started or desiréd, who are aware of yon Progressive Republic's reputation as a wielder of greater technologies and better developer of new ones than the Confederated Worlds. They see as plain as I, Arden would accrue no benefit were it to transfer its allegiance to the Progressive Republic."

Tomas gave Beatrice Patel a cold look. "It's not the opinion of men I'm worried about."

She pressed her lips together and narrowed her eyes. "You are a dunderheaded addlepate who thinks the filteréd glasses clouding his vision show him the truth of the world."

"Miss Patel," Constable Turner said, with a tone of exasperation.

"Yes, Miss Patel," Tomas said. "Tell me why a cybernetic engineer would prefer Arden remain in the Confederated Worlds over joining Papa Romeo?"

Beatrice set her fists on her hips. "The Progressive Republic wields those greater technologies in the service of a monolithic ideology. It has smashéd flat the variations of every world it has absorbéd. It would do the same were it to overmaster Arden. Our language and culture would vanish. My work in cybernetic engineering would be dismisséd as deviationism and my mind forcibly reconfiguréd to match the template of yon gray empire of conformity."

"My men know the truth of the Progressive Republic no less than Miss Patel," the constable said. "They will resist with all they have. Miss Patel's engineering projects amplify their abilities, nothing more."

Tomas' face scrunched, but the constable's logic held. To a point. "I'd give you that, if you remotely controlled your drone boats. But Miss Patel says they travel courses of their own choice. Free of any man's control."

"Control?" Wise sadness tinged Constable Turner's voice. "Think you, leftenant, that conscious control is a boon when we are in the crucible with an arméd foe? From your face, I see you know from bitter experience the clash of arms drowns out thought."

Tomas nodded slowly. His remark to Meriwether replayed itself in his head, now with the flippant air burned away. *We don't shoot prisoners. It doesn't work.*

"Hence, the skills imps pour their distillate of Athena into soldier's minds," the constable said, "and many hours of training pump that distillate through the warp and woof of their bodies. All such is done to make a soldier the very like of an autonomous machine, observing and acting without cognition."

"Perhaps we make soldiers into something like a robot," Tomas said. "But you've made a robot into something like a soldier."

"No," Beatrice Patel said. Constable Turner gave her an imploring glance to which she shook her head. "I am loyal to the Confederated Worlds, but I refuse to bat my eyes and play at being impresséd by the gasbaggeries of a man who attests the same loyalties." She faced Tomas and lifted her chin. "My robots are better than a soldier. Easier to build and train for battle, easier to deploy to it, and easier to sacrifice in strategem."

Constable Turner cut in. "Leftenant, Miss Patel and I have spent enough words. Let us show you the deeds of our drone boats, and I'll wager twenty confeds you shall see they pose neither you nor any man the scantest risk of virtual fugue." He turned to one of his staff members. "Pop up video windows of the drones' examination of the landed vessel."

On the map, the blue wedges had stopped at the ends of their dotted lines. Twenty meters separated them from the angular red icon denoting the Papa ship.

The staffer tapped on his tablet. Video windows appeared to the upper left of the map, tethered by arrowed lines to the drones' blue wedges. Each window held a partial view of the Papa ship overlaid with graphics and alphanumerics providing data from the drone's other sensors. Together, the windows showed nearly every square meter of the Papa ship.

From his knowledge of standard Papa ship designs, Tomas expected sharp angles. Instead, the Papa ship leaned like a moldy bag of oranges on an islet of baked, blackened soil. One landing leg dipped into muddy water. The landing leg looked wrong—too squat and distended.

The whole ship looked wrong. Even if it were a new design, it should have a standard axis to provide the illusion of gravity when under thrust, and another to provide the same illusion by rotation when coasting. Though if designed to go solely from orbit to dirt and back, under thrust the whole way, it would only need one direction to be *up*.

But how could Papa fit a deck perpendicular to the line of thrust into the misshapen mess of this ship?

A drone on the ship's far side shot video of the exposed underside. Where Tomas expected to see the paraboloid fusion drive exhausts, instead broken ion cages and jagged slabs of hull plating dangled toward dried mud crazed with cracks.

This ship wasn't heading back to orbit.

Another sign confirmed it. What from a distance had appeared as a band of glowing lights came from blue flames rising from nozzles around the lower reaches of the ship, near the engines.

"What's the flame chemistry?" Tomas asked the Constabulary staffer.

A few taps on a tablet, and spectral analysis appeared. Essentially pure water, extremely hot.

"It's flaring off its hydrogen," Tomas said.

"Another benefit of sending drones to spy out the site," Constable Turner said. "Should the flares have turnéd to weapons, the drones would have left no widows or orphans."

Tomas saw the logic of his words. Yet their logic was like lichen on the surface of kilometers-deep emotional rock. His disdain and fear remained intact.

"We scannéd every square centimeter of yon vessel, in wavelengths from radio to ultraviolet. She held neither man nor poweréd machine. From her cracks leakéd vapors of melted plastics and metals, suggesting she had set internal fires upon landing as part of self-destruction."

"Perhaps," Tomas said.

"Perhaps the prejudices of thy upbringing blinker thy eyes," Constable Turner said. "Bootéd feet on yon islet, and glovéd hands on the hull of yon ship, would have told us nothing more than did Miss Patel's drones."

"We'll see about that." Tomas glanced over the map. "Here's our plan. We go out in column, Ground Force forward and Constabulary at the rear, and split the task force here—" He pointed at a fork in the road southeast of the docks. "Weasel Two, the Buffalo, and a Constabulary vehicle will continue with me along the east-west road on the south side of the swamp, and the other vehicles will take the north-south road on the east side. The infantry will dismount at the docks and ride the boats—the manned boats—to the Papa ship along these routes." Through the watercourses, he traced lines converging on the angular red icon. Gray lines sprung up on the map as his fingertip passed.

Constable Turner cleared his throat. "The drones can carry your men—"

"Your boat pilots need practice, against the day the robots stop working." Tomas turned a sharp stare from the constable to Beatrice Patel. Constable Turner drew back. Beatrice returned an unyielding look.

Tomas' finger then hovered over the map, drawing in air a circle about half a kilometer in radius around the Papa ship. His finger dipped to slash across the infantry boat routes. "They'll wait at this distance until the vehicles have taken up covering positions here and here." With his fingernail, he popped points on each road about fifteen hundred meters from the ship. "When we're ready, the infantry will close on the target. Sgt. Hoch, your team will remain in reserve. The armored grenadier fireteams will cover." A smirk tightened his mouth. "Cpl. Nilsson will be first to land on the islet. Any questions?"

Silence replied.

Tomas looked around for a clock. "We'll roll out of the square in an hour, at twenty-thirty. That puts us at our assigned positions just after sun-off. Dismissed."

Moments later, he and the sergeants exited Constabulary headquarters into the bright light of late afternoon. They walked without words, until Sgt. O'Herlihy drew in a pensive breath.

"Something to say, sergeant?"

O'Herlihy took a moment to speak. "Sir, how could you take it so easily?" His mouth curled down in disgust. "Robots?"

Tomas stopped and faced him. "It seemed I took their revelation easily, sergeant?"

"You didn't push back when the constable, and that pushy politician's daughter, kept peddling their lies."

Tomas reflected on the recent encounter. "What the Eltham Constabulary is doing is as much a sin to my upbringing as it is to yours. Yet the constable and Miss Patel are on our side and we'll work with them."

O'Herlihy glanced around the square. "Wish they weren't. On our side, sir."

Tomas stopped. He leaned into O'Herlihy's space. "Clarify that. Now."

"Sir, all I mean is, I'd rather the Ardenites voted to join Papa. If they stay with us, their cultural poison will spread. Planets in the Confederated Worlds will fall into virtual fugue because of them. But if they join Papa, when the next war breaks out, we can melt Arden's surface back to rock and all the Ardenites' robot fab blueprints with it."

A next war. Tomas suddenly felt weary. He paused with his hand halfway to the brain wave synchronizer controls on his shilling. "If they join Papa, they'll have ten times the robotic abominations they do now. Today, we're going to keep Arden in the Confederated Worlds. We can start curing the locals of their obsessions in a month."

Nothing would cure Beatrice Patel, Tomas realized, but he masked his face to remain the image of confident leadership for his sergeants. He pumped up the wakefulness stimulation to his brain, then strode toward the vehicles waiting in the square before O'Herlihy could reply.

At the vehicles, the sergeants went to their squads while Tomas checked out his Badger with Clayworth and Edelstein. With the turret hatch open and the platoon's radio chatter coming through his helmet, Sgt. Hoch's briefing of his squad carried to Tomas. "Nilsson, your team gets to kick the tires on the Papa ship."

"Me? Why?" Nilsson's tone darkened. "Oh that's why."

"You got a problem, take it up with the ell-tee."

"Why? So he can shit on me more for thinking he's a slotted dick of a butterbar?"

"Zip it," Sgt. Hoch said. "Get ready. We roll out at the start of twilight."

The platoon, augmented by two Bawsons, the Constabulary's thinner-skinned and lighter-armed infantry fighting vehicles, rolled out three minutes late. Grumbles about "slowboat ArChars" crossed the platoon net as the vehicles navigated the twisting streets leading to the road into the swamp.

Three minutes late, and the light of the twin mirrors already had perceptibly dimmed. Millions of panels composed each mirror, with each panel being electrically conformable from a reflective, daytime surface structure to an absorptive, photovolatic, nighttime one. Scattered at random on each mirror, a thousand panels a second changed to their nighttime conformation. In half an hour, the entirety of each mirror's Arden-lighting face would be fully dark.

By the time the column entered the woods, the mirrors looked like flickering coals in a dying fire. The Ariel Band, girdling Prospero and glinting with the feeble red light of Sun of York, by far outshone them.

Tomas and Clayworth's displays lit up the inside of Badger One's turret. Tomas' gaze roved each display, forward, sides, rear, other vehicles, and jumped to every sudden change in an alphanumeric value or color-coded indicator. No sign of rebels, or Papa operatives. With gain cranked to maximum, ground penetrating radars and seismic echoers searched for tunnels under the road ahead ready to be collapsed by remote-controlled bombs. None. Tomas' eyelids felt heavy and he turned his wakefulness brain wave inducers up one more notch.

The platoon split at the fork in the road. A minute later, Tomas' half of the formation turned off the pavement for a short trip down a gravel lane. The vehicles' weight pushed the gravel into the soft soil. Foliage whipped by their passage danced like green dragonflies in the night vision displays.

They stopped at one of the docks. It glowed in infrared as it radiated away the day's absorbed heat, but even in the wan visible light of Sun of York, no one could mistake it. A dull gray block, eight meters high, twenty deep, thirty long. One of its long sides faced the gravel lane. The watercourse beyond it showed reflected light of the Ariel Band.

Constabulary men went to one end of the dock. A roll-up gate clattered into the dock's interior. Cameras mounted inside the dock showed in Tomas' display an elevated walkway along one of the long walls, the one on the landward side. The walkway ended at a small, windowless room in a back corner.

More roll-up gates showed on the wall opposite the walkway, one for each of four boats. Their sterns abutted the walkway and their bows, bristling with sensors, nearly brushed the gates. The boats' top decks lacked protuberances, save for a castle barely larger than a shower stall and having a pair of ring-mounted thirteens on top. Constabulary men traveled the walkway and climbed aboard the two nearest boats.

Tomas spoke by radio to Constable Turner. "Are your drones at the other dock?"

"Nay, leftenant. Look on the two farthest boats, and you shall see our handiwork."

The two boats in question looked the same as the others. Their thirteens pointed toward the ceiling. Renewed wariness of autonomous machines flooded Tomas. "You have given robots the ability to fire large caliber machine guns?"

"Nay, nay. Their armaments are fíréd remotely, by operators in yon control room." He appeared to mean the windowless room in the corner. "We have progresséd too little in our researches to grant our machines the autonomy of fire."

Yet, Tomas inferred. His next breaths sounded ragged. He shut his eyes to calm himself. The Ardenite obsession for robots could be dealt with another day. "No matter, since we'll use the manned boats. Are your crews ready?"

"Within moments, leftenant," the constable said. A reactor in one boat thrummed to life. Its peer soon joined it.

To the sergeants, Tomas said, "Get the men onboard."

Moments later, dismounted infantrymen flowed past his scopes. Ports in their backs glowed in the infrared where their uniforms dumped waste heat. From nowhere, fear gripped Tomas. He peered past the men, suddenly convinced some Papa operatives prepared an attack. There, that flicker of green, was that—?

A pair of swamp sparrows darted from reeds at the water's edge. You need some sleep.

On the deck of one boat, O'Herlihy walked between rows of men seated against side railings. He checked cee-skin and heat vents, and chatted with each soldier in turn. The scouts on the other boat slouched against the rails. If Nilsson did anything to lead them, Tomas didn't see it.

"The riverine detachment is ready," the constable said.

Tomas blinked at a sandy feeling in his eyes. The glow of displays in the otherwise dark turret made him squint. "Roll up the gates and head out."

More clattering gates. The watercourse came into view beyond the boats' bows. The first boat, with O'Herlihy and the armored grenadiers, eased out of the dock and into the channel. The second followed, riding up and down the first boat's wake as it fell into position behind the other.

Tomas said to the constable, "Button up the dock for our departure."

The gates rolled down. A rustle punctuated the hum of their motors when they entered the water. Constabulary men hurried out, with two waiting outside the land-side gate to shut and seal it. Tomas pressed his lips together in sudden unease. Yes, the security promised by the algorithms would resist brute-force cracking by a rebel at the gates, even if advanced Papa hardware augmented his capabilities. But the promise could be undone if a rebel agent in the Constabulary unit compromised the private key.

If the rebels somehow sabotaged the boats, it's even more important we get to our support positions. The last two Constabulary men ran to their peers in their Bawson. "Roll out!" Tomas ordered as the Bawson's ramp swung shut.

They reached their support position without incident. The paved road canted up a slight rise. Around them stood trees short and sparse enough to partially hide the vehicles while still allowing indirect fire by the main gun. Clayworth aimed Badger One's main gun at the Papa ship while Constabulary riflemen fanned out to the perimeter. The Weasel covered the road to the west with its thirteen. An encrypted radio burst came in from the other vehicles to the east of the swamp.

Position reached. Ready to support.

His main display showed a map with the boats at their jump-off positions. In the side displays, the boats' cameras showed the dark swamp. All ready. Tomas gave the order for them to advance, then switched the main display to the forward camera in Nilsson's boat.

Dark islets drank up light between waterways glittering in the light of the Ariel Band. The infrared view showed the same features in reverse, the water dark, the reeds at the waterline and the moss streamers dangling from the cypresses bright. The boat crept forward along a winding course. Metal detectors pinged the water for mines. None. An overlay on the display showed a red outline—the Papa lander as scouted by the Constabulary. At a distance, the Papa ship itself went unseen in both visible and infrared. Only after the boat turned the final bend did the ship appear.

Under the red outline, alloy shards of the Papa lander slumped on the islet. Tomas imagined a dumping site for the wreckage of a spaceship battle. The fragments, some half the size of Tomas' Badger, showed a mottling of dark grays accented with black scorching. The shards of the lander looked darker in infrared, too. Spectral analysis at gaps between the slumped-together fragments showed carbon and nitrogen oxides, cold and sluggish.

"Looks like it self-destructed after all," Nilsson said over the net. "Probably right after the Ar—den Constabulary scouted the site."

Sgt. Hoch's voice sounded firm. "*Looks* won't cut it. Get your boots on it."

"Like it matters," Nilsson said.

In contrast to Nilsson's apathy, the boat's Constabulary crew acted with precision. Almost machine-like, except that a sense of higher purpose guided them. The boat moved ahead with a bare whisper of sound. Thirty meters to shore. Twenty. The pile of rubble rose high overhead. Ten. In a pocket formed by two massive alloy slabs, the Papa ship's fusion drive bays showed stalactites of rusting metal and crumbling ceramics above the scorched and blackened islet.

"The ground beneath yon whoreson interloper slopes too gently for our stern to touch," said the boat's pilot, "but our bow's angle will fit it like the very twin." He nudged the boat to the right and cut the engine to nearly nothing. With a squelch, the underside of the bow scraped on the baked ground.

"Where's a ladder?" Nilsson asked. Indistinct words in the rhythm of Ardenese answered him. A crewman ran to the bow with a rope ladder, hooked it to the railing, and then flung it over to unfurl as it went.

Nilsson called his men over and assigned an order to descend the ladder. "...then Gorthi, Campbell, and me at the rear. Go to it."

Men went down. The ladder's rope uprights and metal steps clanged against the boat's hull with each man's motions. When Nilsson descended, Tomas switched his view to a bow camera mounted near the waterline. Nilsson stepped off onto muddy ground, then gave the ruins of the fusion drive a wary look. "At least if they go off, we won't even know it."

The men grunted. Tomas scowled at the display. The Papa lander had self-destructed so completely, it would never fire its engines again. Nilsson needed to change his attitude.

"All right, let's make sure the locals didn't send blind men here," Nilsson said. His hands flitted, as if of their own volition, over his infrared ports, checking, double-checking, triple-checking the ports were closed, and thus invisible to an infrared scope.

The boat pilot's voice broke in. "Zounds, what be those behind us?"

Tomas' fingers switched the main display to the boat's stern camera, just in time to see muzzle flashes from about fifty meters away.

Large caliber rounds smacked the boat and pinged off disjointed slabs of the Papa lander.

Tomas peered at the boat's stern camera view. More muzzle flashes backlit two gray mounds barely peeking out of the water.

Papa had landed something hostile.

"Down, down!" shouted Nilsson. More rounds pinged and squealed off the Papa lander's rubble as his men dropped to their bellies on the dried mud.

"I'm hit," groaned one of the scouts.

The twin thirteens on the boat turned toward one of the gray mounds and fired. A crewman shouted over the din. "Damage we've taken to the screw, and a man has lost his arm! Medic, hie thee here!"

The thirteens and the gray mounds kept firing. The thirteens tracked their target, but the gray mounds zigged and zagged as they returned fire. Boats, submarines, what had Papa landed?

"Many a hole belowdecks!" the same crewman said. "We're taking on water and—argh! Medic!"

The boat's thirteens fired again. The camera's night vision mode showed bright green shards flying off one of the hostiles. The Papa object rolled to its side. The barrel of its machine gun jerked through the air. It fired a burst striking high on the Papa ship, then smacked the water and fired its next burst into the depths of the river. The muzzle flash in the water lit up a cigar shape, about two meters long and eighty centimeters in diameter. Paddles mounted like duck feet near the back of the cigar shape thrashed the water in an apparent effort to hold station. A submarine.

Tomas intuited more. The Papa submarine was a robot.

"Constable Turner!" he shouted into the radio. His voice snarled as he went on. "Now do you see the price of relying on Miss Patel's 'engineering projects?'"

The damaged hostile slipped below the surface. Over the radio chatter, the boat's gunner shouted in triumph. "Struck down, you floating cur! Now your infernal twin—curséd luck!"

The other robotic submarine kept firing while its peer sank. It aimed higher, at the boat's castle. At the thirteens' mounting bracket. Tomas checked diagnostics from the boat. A cut in the control line. Failsafes swung the machine gun pair free of its broken controls to aim straight up.

"We have no armament!" the boat's gunner shouted.

The remaining robotic submarine traversed its machine gun to aim at the boat's waterline and slid closer to its target.

"Badger One," called the boat's pilot, "your ordnance, please!"

"I have a firing solution," Clayworth said.

"Do it," Tomas said.

Badger One's main gum boomed. In the silence generated by his noise-canceling earbuds, Tomas felt the Badger wobble.

When he could hear himself again, Tomas said to Clayworth, "Something's wrong!"

Light from the gunner's display cast a cold blue sheen on Clayworth's face. "The right-side stabilizers malfed."

A clammy feeling gripped Tomas' gut. He'd said it so confidently on the roadside in the Sycorax Hills. *She needs a better refit than we can give her here.*

No time for feelings. Through the boat's microphones came the shell's shriek. It sailed over the Papa lander and detonated harmlessly.

"We need thy help, Badger One!" called the boat's pilot.

"Goal tend it!" Clayworth's hands lunged from control to control. "With one stabilizer gone, I can't drop shells close enough."

"Can a man aim the thirteens manually?" Tomas asked the boat pilot. "Get someone up there! Hoch, deploy your reserve!"

The boat's microphones picked up another burst of fire from the robotic submarine. The boat's microphones picked up a panging sound, but no muzzle flash in any camera—

Another crewman shouted. "Yon cur bites at our underbelly!" the pilot said. "Manual aim would help us less than a tinker's dam! Zounds, much more and we'll sink!"

A drawn in breath, then Nilsson spoke. "I got it."

Never before had Tomas heard so much focus in his voice.

"Nilsson?" Campbell's voice. "What are you—?"

A splashing sound. The locator chip in Nilsson's shilling showed he'd slipped into the water on the boat's portside.

The robotic submarine fired another burst through the bottom of the boat. Rounds zinged off metal belowdeck. The bow and stern cameras showed slanted views of the swamp and the Papa lander. The boat listed to starboard.

"All hands, abandon her!" the boat's pilot called.

A new voice cried out, keening at the edge of panic. "Two men badly wounded and water up to my knees! To help them both is beyond me!"

The boat's microphones picked up more rounds fired below. A few more bursts could bring the boat down. Where was Nilsson? What did he hope to do?

Again came the pounding tempo of a machine gun burst directly under the boat. Water muffled the sound. Nilsson's locator chip showed him somewhere under the boat. How close to the robotic submarine's machine gun muzzle? Another burst. More rounds fired. Slower, different in pitch.

Nilsson's locator chip showed him rising from the bottom of the watercourse to starboard of the boat. His head poked above the surface and he thrashed it from side to side, sucking in breaths. A few moments later, his voice came over the radio net.

"I shot up its power source. It's belly up on the bottom. Not going anywhere." He glanced at the boat leaning toward him. His eyes widened at the bulk tilting toward him. He gulped in a breath and swam hard for the cluster of men huddling next to the Papa lander's fusion drive exhausts.

Nilsson staggered out of the water. Gorthi held out Nilsson's helmet, but he waved the offer aside. Instead, Nilsson went to the bow ladder. He spared a glance, but nothing more, for a moaning, bleeding scout and a Constabulary man laid out with feet crossed and arms folded over his chest in a hasty funerary repose.

Nilsson climbed the ladder. He winced as he grasped each rung. The boat's pilot waited, one hand on the railing, the other around a man with lolling head and a tourniqueted stump in place of his right arm.

"Put him over my shoulder," Nilsson said.

"Certain are you?"

"Just do it, will you?"

The boat's pilot guided the wounded crewman over Nilsson's shoulder. The ladder wobbled as Nilsson descended, one arm on the ladder and the other wrapped around the wounded man. The other scouts ran to help him lay the wounded crewman on the ground next to the injured scout.

The boat's pilot followed Nilsson to the islet. He stopped beside the dead man and slumped to his knees. "Old friend," the pilot began. Sorrow choked his next words. "How couldst thee, so good of heart, be struck down?"

Nilsson gripped the hand of the injured scout. He spoke to the boat's pilot without turning his head. Tomas couldn't see his face, but he remembered Nilsson's thousand-yard stare. "That's war, pal."

A rushing sound came from the distance. A glance at the map

showed the boat with Hoch's fireteam arriving on the scene. From Hoch's boat, a camera showed the damaged boat twisting onto its starboard side. Its bow lifted off the islet and its stern slumped to the bottom of the watercourse. The slosh of water filled every microphone, and waves kicked up by the settling boat lapped at the pocket of dried mud and slumped alloy where the men huddled. A wave elicited obscenities from the wounded scout. The wave nudged the feet of the dead Constabulary crewman.

The wrecked boat's bow camera remained above the water's surface, aimed at the sky. In Tomas' main display, brighter than Prospero, brighter even than the Ariel Band, the white dot of a Papa ship crawled along its orbit.

5

Refit-in-place

Tomas trudged from his Badger toward Eltham Constabulary headquarters. Though still a twilit morning, the mirrors at L4 and L5 had halfway brightened, heralding one of the hottest days of Arden's four-day summer. The thick stone walls of Constabulary headquarters chilled the interior of the building. He shivered once as the front door shut itself behind him.

By the afternoon, though, after hours in the Badger's confined turret on the journey back to company headquarters, he would long for this cool moment.

A woman from the Constabulary Auxiliary, with a powder blue cap clipped to her curly brown hair, stood up from her desk and saluted. "Welcome, leftenant." After he returned the salute, she added, "How may I assist you?"

"I need to call my company commander on the landline."

"I shall guide you." Her skirt rustled with quick, narrow steps.

They soon arrived at the comm room. She tucked her skirt under her legs as she sat at a keyboard facing a bank of a monitor, a handset, a camera, and a headset. Keys clacked as she opened a secure connection to company headquarters. After the night's action, the faint plastic tinkle of the keys sounded ominous. He shut his eyes and breathed deeply.

She cleared her throat. With a gesture at the monitor, she said, "There you are, sir. I shall return to my station, but press yon button—" She pointed at controls near the keyboard. "—should you need assistance."

"Thanks."

She vacated the chair and he slumped into it. The monitor showed the comm room in company headquarters, dominated by the brigade standard painted on the far wall with the company's designation under it. An enlisted man hustled onto the screen. "Sir, I've pinged Capt. Bao. He'll be here in a mo."

Tomas fumbled for the headset and took a moment to adjust it. Then he pulled his tablet from its hook-and-loop binding on his thigh and held it near a wireless interface. A few swipes later, he said, "My full write up on last night's action is on its way."

"I'll route it to the captain's inbox. Here he is now." The enlisted stepped away.

"Fill me in," Bao said as he pulled a chair up closer to the camera.

"We reconnoitered the Papa lander. The site was only accessible by boat. The vehicles remained in support positions about fifteen hundred meters away. Constabulary had previously scouted the Papa lander and expressed the belief it was a decoy sent to self-destruct. However, when our lead boat approached the Papa lander, two autonomous submarines attacked it with large caliber MGs. We suffered one scout wounded. Constabulary had two boat crew wounded and one killed."

Bao pinched the bridge of his nose. "Autonomous submarines. Robots, you mean. PRs showing their true colors."

How to bring up Miss Patel and her *engineering projects*? Tomas set the question aside. "Yes, robots. The gunner on the Constabulary boat destroyed one and Nilsson neutralized the other. We salvaged them for intelligence to examine."

"Go back. Nilsson did as much damage as a pair of thirteens?"

"He went into the water and destroyed its ability to fire and maneuver."

"All that? Does he merit a commendation?"

Tomas drew in a breath. Nilsson had closed with a weapon that could have torn him in half with a burst of fire, shot out its power supply, and probably saved most of the boat's crew. Commendable, indeed. Worthy of the Cross of Valor.

An intuition made Tomas light-headed. Nilsson hadn't given his fullest effort before because he hadn't been recognized for his service. A commendation would show Nilsson his true value, even here and now on this sideshow planet after the war had been lost.

"I'll review my report and make a recommendation, sir, when we get back to company today."

"You won't be coming back today."

Had he heard right? "Sir? By the original plan—"

"Yes, you would return after reconnoitering your two sites. I'm amending the plan. You are to remain in Eltham until further notice."

Tomas frowned for a moment. "Very well, sir. May I ask why?"

"For one, your last report on Iago and Claudius had them in an ornithopter heading south, toward the town of Eastcheap in Bravo Company's sector. A civilian recently reported to the Constabulary a possible sighting of their thopter a few kilometers north of Eastcheap. The report describes a nearly transparent aircraft taking off from woods known to shelter a rebel formation. It's likely our Papa operatives are active there."

Bao sniffed out a breath like a chuckle. "Like you said, Bravo Company is going to step on its dick when dealing with them. When they call for help, you'll be ready to roll to their rescue. You're a lot closer to the hot zone now than Landon or Khudobin are or will be, and you have some grasp of these Papa operatives' tactics."

"You make sense, sir."

"Also, Sgt. Svoboda reported to Lt. Haraldsdottir overnight, and she reported to me, that your task force has overexerted itself."

Tomas stiffened his back. "If the sergeant can't keep up the pace, he should tell me directly."

"Didn't he? I heard via Lt. Haraldsdottir that Svoboda recommended you take a day in Navarre for repairs after your encounter with the enemy in the Sycorax Hills. Is that true?"

"Sir, yes, but as last night's encounter shows—"

"Your ordnance malfunctioned?" Bao peered at something off-screen. "Not the gun, but the right-side stabilizers. That's the side that took the missile impact in your prior engagement?"

"Sir, entering the Sycorax Hills, I adjusted the column to put Badger One in the crosshairs rather than the Buffalo."

"Indeed you did. A respectable decision. You kept the Buffalo and your SSC personnel fully functional in the aftermath of Sycorax Hills. But not your Badger."

Tomas sat, frozen. From parts of his subconscious, self-criticism whipped him, more forcefully than Bao's understated words. "Go on, sir."

"You have some fine traits. Pushing the men and the vehicles can certainly be appropriate, under the right circumstances. But both have limits we should keep within until the times grow most dire. Those times have not come yet."

Dark feelings rose into Tomas' throat. "Will they come at all this month, sir?"

"You mean, is Arden worth fighting to keep in the Confederated Worlds?" Bao held his gaze firm for a while, until his face fell. "Damn if I know. But there's something more important to you and me than whether this fringe world stays with us or not. We each have to look in the mirror and see an officer who upheld the honor of the Ground Force in all he did. That will be worth pushing the men to their limit. It'll be worth pushing ourselves there, too."

"Thank you for your words, sir."

"Let Sgt. Svoboda repair and maintain the vehicles. Give the men some time to air out their socks. Even if Bravo Company comes running for help today, I'll hold off ordering you their way until tomorrow morning."

"Understood, sir."

Bao reached off-screen for the video conference controls, stopped. "Anything more?"

Tomas' chest tightened. It had to be said, but how? "Yes, sir. I must tell you something I left out of the report. The Eltham Constabulary is using robots."

Bao blinked. "Robots? What sort?"

"Drone boats. Their thirteens are human controlled, but in all else they're autonomous." Another thought came to him. "And that's just what they've told us about. They might have other autonomous machines tucked away somewhere." Other machines, that like the boats could also fail to scout as well as men, and bring more casualties down on his overstretched platoon....

Bao sucked his teeth as he thought. "Technically, the legality of robots is up to each member world. But, Christ, it's unsavory. This is the first I've heard of Constabulary units dabbling with it. You think this is unique to Eltham?"

"There was no sign of it in Navarre. Judging by the people involved, I think it reflects a peculiarity in this town's politics. Any recommendations for dealing with it?"

"Don't alienate the locals. If you haven't already?"

"Hopefully not, sir."

Bao rubbed his eyes again. "Then accept what they're doing, for now. If Arden stays with us after the plebiscite, we can change the situation then."

"I had thoughts along those lines. Thank you for clarifying them."

With a squint, Bao asked, "You aren't going to cause an incident by letting your out your inner Observer, are you?"

Anger spiked behind Tomas' face. He managed to speak calmly. "I checked that box during enlistment solely out of habit."

"I don't care what you believe. Just keep the Constabulary on our side through the plebiscite." Bao ended the call.

Bao's words stung as Tomas left the Constabulary office for the platoon. Since late in his deployment on New Liberty, he'd settled every other conflict between his upbringing and his service in favor of Ground Force. He wouldn't stop now.

He called the platoon to order on the plaza near the parked Badgers and Weasels. The L4 and L5 mirrors shone at full brightness, overexposing the men's faces. They showed relief at the announcement of a day's rest. Even Sgt. Svoboda and his men looked pleased, despite being assigned a day of repair and maintenance of the platoon's vehicles. If only every man would take such pride in being useful.

"That's it," Tomas said in conclusion. "Sgt. Hoch, Cpl. Nilsson, come talk with me. Everyone else, dismissed."

As the others trudged away, Hoch and Nilsson came up. An unasked question crinkled Hoch's brow. Nilsson looked wary. Medical wrap swaddled his hands like thick bluish-white gloves.

"Corporal," Tomas said, "You did well out there. How are your injuries?"

Nilsson shrugged. "They still sting. Medic says the burns will heal today."

"I've never seen anything comparable to what you did. When you said you shot up its power supply, you left out you reached in and ripped out hot wires to ensure the thing was taken out of action. All while underwater for a minute." Tomas affected an amazed look.

Gaze flat, Nilsson said, "I swam a lot, growing up on Österbötter."

"I did too, on Joséphine," Tomas said. Nilsson looked unmoved. "What I'm saying is, you acted above and beyond the call of duty out there."

"Above and beyond. Doesn't seem that way to me. Two guys got hurt. One got dead."

"No matter what, you couldn't have saved that one crewman from the boat. But without your action, once the robot submarine sank the boat, it would have turned its machine gun on your fireteam. Combine your fireteam and the boat's survivors, and you saved ten men from death or severe wounds."

Nilsson avoided Tomas' gaze by studying the flank of Badger One. After a time, he said, "I just did my job."

Memories stirred in Tomas. The hemp field. Staying in his foxhole too long. A part of himself wanting to die. Did an inner demon haunt Nilsson the same way? But an officer couldn't lift the rock off a man's subconscious to see what crawled beneath. Or, in front of his men, off his own. "You did much more. I'm going to recommend you for the Cross of Valor."

Though he didn't move, Nilsson's next breaths came fast and ragged. "Sir, respectfully, I ask that you do not."

"I understand your modesty, but I assure you, we saw what you did and you've earned it. Right, sergeant?"

Hoch nodded. "I've already complimented Cpl. Nilsson on his actions last night."

Nilsson drew his head back and down. "The sergeant's compliments are enough for me."

With a question plain on his face, Tomas glanced at Hoch. *Will Nilsson come around if I make the commendation despite his unwillingness?* Hoch shook his head.

Tomas said to Nilsson, "Think about it. Dismissed."

Nilsson stalked away, brooding. He slipped between parked vehicles, going in the direction of soldiers' chatter heading toward a far corner of the plaza.

Once he was out of earshot, Tomas said, "What's his problem?"

"I don't know. He got assigned to my squad just before our transfer here. His record before that looks good. Solid but not outstanding soldier."

"Where did he serve?" Tomas shut his eyes to aid remembering. "Kahlenberg, at least. Some hard fighting there, I heard."

"All fighting's hard fighting, sir. But you know that." Hoch quirked his mouth. "Maybe he doesn't see a point anymore."

Tomas' doubts about their mission rose up from his subconscious like bats at sunset. He swatted them away. "We might have lost the war everywhere else. We still can win our part of it here."

"I suppose so."

Tomas set his fists on his hips. "You think our cause is lost?"

Hoch shrugged. "I have no clue what these people—" He waved at the buildings across the plaza to take in every resident of Eltham, every citizen of Arden. "—think and feel. They watch us with shaded eyes and talk to us in their thick dialect I don't know how you can understand, but what truth are they hiding? 'We put up with you now but will vote you out?' 'We want to vote for you, but if the rest of Arden doesn't, we'll be fucked by the new Papa regime?'"

Tomas put on an authoritative tone. "The opinion polls show a hefty majority support the Confederated Worlds."

Hoch's face showed resistance. "I don't trust what comes officially out of Belmont. For damn sure the locals don't."

"If you want to know what the Ardenites are thinking, you have a day to find out. But first, we have to talk to the constable. Back inside."

The Auxiliary woman led them to the same room as the previous day's planning. Constable Turner and his aides, and Beatrice Patel, pondered the map and strata of overlapping message windows laid on it.

All turned when the Auxiliary woman announced Tomas and Hoch. "Leftenant, sergeant, welcome." Constable Turner sounded less energetic than he had the day before.

"Doing a post-mortem?" Tomas asked. "What have you come up with so far?"

One of the aides spoke. "We need scanners with wider eyes and ears, ringéd all around our boats, to espy such hostile machines sooner and at greater distance."

"I shall add the same to my drones," Beatrice said. She seemed chastened by the previous night's events.

"Your drones?" Tomas said, voice cutting. "The same ones that scouted the scene three days ago and fooled you into thinking the ship was only a decoy?"

Beatrice lifted her chin. "Our drones misséd nothing a human eye would have seen."

Tomas glowered at her, then turned on the constable. "If you had landed men on the islet, you might have found what we did when we worked through the wreckage—a crane heavy enough to drop a fab into the water. You might have found that fab in the water and destroyed it before it built one robot submarine, let alone two. If you'd done that, right now we might not have men in the infirmary." Tomas softened his voice. "You might not have one in the morgue."

Constable Turner looked glum. "We intend our robots to save men's efforts, and their lives."

A touch of pride flowed into Beatrice's face and voice. "Many a time ere now they have."

"You're probably right," Tomas said. "Yet they will be more effective when they complement, not substitute for, men's efforts.

Take that to heart, and your man would not have died in vain."

The constable studied Tomas. "You do not castigate us for our perceivéd sins?"

Tomas weighed his words. "Whether or not I approve of robotics, one of my tasks is to help you be more effective as a fighting force. That includes optimally using your equipment, which includes your drone boats—" Tomas raised his eyebrow at Beatrice. "—and your other robots."

She touched her mouth before speaking. "Other robots, sir? Marry, we have none other."

Tomas shook his head. "Spare me the denials. Look, I haven't and I won't tell Ground Force, or Constabulary command in Belmont, what you're doing out here. The way I see it, your robots are just another combat arm. I want to help you use it properly. Something I learned even before I enlisted is, the purpose of all other combat arms is to put the infantryman in sole possession of the battlefield."

Constable Turner nodded. "Forsooth, we have developéd a variety of autonomous machines—"

"Good sir—" Beatrice said, then clamped shut her lips.

"He has surmiséd the truth. What good would come of telling him the hawk he sees is a handsaw?" To Tomas, the constable said. "We welcome your advice in the use of Miss Patel's engineering projects."

"I'll give it. But first," Tomas said, and then nodded his head in conciliation to Beatrice, "you have to tell me what types of robots you have."

She looked thoughtful for a moment, then sighed. "A fair trade, leftenant. Good sir, if I may?" She gestured at the wall-mounted display. The constable nodded minimally. Beatrice undid the flap on a wide pocket in her cargo pants and pulled out a tablet. A few taps, and windows appeared on the wall-mounted display.

"In faith, we have developéd a drone Bawson and supply drones. These last may be new to thee." She pointed at an image of a wheeled robot about one-meter-fifty long and fifty centimeters wide and tall.

A closer glance and Tomas revised his understanding. One robot on four knobby run-flat tires at the front, serving as an armored and powered tractor, with two cargo bins towed behind it.

"These are programméd to take on ammunition and matériel from the fabricator in a Buffalo or the Constabulary's version, the Wisent, and deliver the same to men in the field, without putting men of the supply element at risk of fires."

"Sensible. But go back." He gestured at a window showing a photo of a seemingly normal Constabulary infantry fighting vehicle. "A drone Bawson?"

"Again, sir, it lacks autonomy over its thirteen or its missiles, but it will direct itself to where it would best allow a remote operator to direct its fires. It responds also to commands spoken by the ranking man in the passenger compartment."

They went on throughout the morning to discuss how her robots—her *engineering projects*, she called them—could be more effective, in themselves and in cooperation with soldiers and other robots. A break for tea and bitter coffee, then a discussion of safeguards and other requirements for giving the robots control over their armament. After that, Beatrice discussed some other robots she worked on that were not yet ready, including a drone pygmy thopter, a child's toy she wanted to adapt for espionage, demolition laying, and rifle fire.

They wrapped up in late morning. "Thank you for showing me all this. Yet I still hope I never have to work with your robots," Tomas said.

"Ell-tee speaks for me," Sgt. Hoch said.

Beatrice shrugged. "As you wish, leftenant. But do you not say, 'hope is not a planning factor?'"

Tomas chuckled. "Very true. But now I know if I must work with them, they'll do their jobs."

6

Joint Operation

New sounds joined the road noise coming from the groundcar's wheels: the whir of a window and the rustle of wind.

From his seat in the back, Tomas looked at the driver from Bravo Company. "What are you doing?"

The driver steered the car with one hand. With the other, he fished a cigarette from a pack. "Having a smoke, ell-tee."

"I presume you know it's against regs to open a window in a groundcar in territory not fully secured?"

"The territory is secured, ell-tee, from Eastcheap up to your company's boundary." The driver spoke around the cigarette, now between his lips. He glanced down and groped in the console for a lighter.

The land on either side of the paved road held rolling hills and a few isolated cottages. Each mirror showed an oval of light, a harbinger of the coming two days of autumn. In the distance, the woods where Iago and Claudius' ornithopter had last been spotted covered the hills in dark green. "If it were secured…." Bravo Company wouldn't have sent a driver to pick Tomas up for a joint operation planning session. "…your superiors would have told you. Did they?"

"Ell-tee, it's only open a crack—"

"The window would stop a round from a civilian hunting rifle and slow down a round fired by a Papa-spec'd weapon. That crack will stop nothing. Shut the window, or do you want a reprimand from your superiors?"

The driver looked hooded eyes at Tomas in the rear view mirror. His shoulder moved, indicative of some action in his arm. The window motor whirred again. The window shut and the road noise abruptly cut out.

A click soon broke the silence, followed by a rustle of burning paper and tobacco. The driver exhaled a cloud of smoke at the rear view mirror.

"And put that thing out."

"What? Ell-tee, are you serious?"

"Only approved psychoactives when on duty. Nicotine is off the list."

The driver's eyes hooded again. He stubbed out the cigarette and drove in silence the rest of the way to Eastcheap.

The groundcar pulled up at a large building showing walls of large, uneven chunks of basalt holed by a few tiny windows. A smaller structure of concrete block walls bulged from one side of the main building. The officers of Bravo Company had borrowed a wool merchant's office on the northern outskirts of the town. Captain Carlton from Bravo headquarters, along with two platoon commanders, Lieutenants McClernan and Beauchamp, waited in a meeting room inside the smaller structure. The inner face of the concrete block walls had been painted grayish-blue. Interior windows showed the large building was the merchant's warehouse: stacked bales of gene-dyed wool nearly brushed the ceiling.

After making his way through introductions and handshakes, Tomas said, "Lt. Beauchamp? *Vous-etes á Jósephine?*" You are from Jósephine?

Beauchamp peered down his long, narrow nose. "Couronnement." The planetary capital. "You are from the planet too? *Newmaw* is not a typical *jósephinais* name."

"My family moved from Sankt-Benedikts-Welt to the town of Portage-du-Nord in my early childhood."* *

A frown. "I don't recall you from Ground Force Academy—ah."

Tomas knew the tone in which Beauchamp spoke the last syllable. Your ancestors did not terraform Jósephine with mine, so spare us both embarrassment by minding your place.

And if my place in this mission will be to save your backside? How about I shirk it—

And put at risk the infantrymen and vehicle crews he's supposed to be leading?

Tomas stood taller, then spoke to Capt. Carlton. "Sir, shall we get started with the briefing?"

Carlton raised a fleshy hand. "In time, in time. From Sankt-Benedikts, you say—?"

Tomas gritted his teeth and tersely answered Carlton's small talk. Either Carlton missed the signs of Tomas' impatience or showed his power by disregarding them. Twenty minutes passed before Carlton said, "Here's the plan."

On a map of the woods north of Eastcheap, a faint red smear depicted the probability distribution of the Papa operatives and rebels' locations. Low precision. Very sloppy. Bravo Company, the local Constabulary, or both did a poor job patrolling the woods. A brown line showed a gravel road running north-south through the woods, roughly parallel to and about eight kilometers from the paved one Tomas had just traveled.

"Lt. McClernan will deploy here," Carlton said. He dragged his finger to draw a curve entering the woods from the southwest. "He'll drive Papa and the rebels this way." Carlton's finger stubbed the map and drew a straight line to the northeast. "Lt. Beauchamp will then target Papa and the rebels' left flank, to drive them to the northwest. The lieutenants will keep hounding their flanks to force them ever northward." Carlton's finger zig-zagged along the map. "As beautiful as Grant's 1864 campaign against Lee."

Tomas could look up the ancient history later. "What role is my platoon to play, sir?"

"Yes, yes, Neumann. We know the rebels are aware of the sector boundary." A pop of Carlton's thick fingernail summoned a line of fluorescent green dots and dashes. "That's why you will set up a blocking position here." Carlton indicated a ridgeline running east-west, perpendicular to the gravel road, about six kilometers into Bravo Company's sector. "You shall be the anvil for my two hammers. With three platoons, we can surround and annihilate the rebel formation and kill or capture the two Papa operatives."

Tomas rubbed his chin, then pointed at the zig-zags up the map. "Are Papa and the rebels weak enough to push back?"

"Our intelligence says so," Carlton said.

Tomas frowned at the faint red smear.

"And our platoons are pure armored grenadier," Beauchamp said. "We haven't made the mis—the decision Bao did, to commingle scout and armored grenadier squads."

Carlton nodded. To Tomas, he said, "We assume good defensive preparation at the blocking position will make up for your platoon's weakness." He checked his chronometer. "Time for dinner."

The others shuffled toward the door as Tomas asked, "Sandwiches or field rations?"

"What?" Carlton looked surprised. "You come all this way and we feed you Buffalo shit? No, no, that won't do. There's a good restaurant here in town."

"In town?" Tomas peered at Carlton. "Sir, all it would take is a single rebel agent catching sight of me and realizing I'm not from Bravo—"

"There are no rebels in Eastcheap. Everyone here is loyal. Right, McClernan?"

"Right," McClernan muttered.

Carlton kept a magnanimous expression on his face. "Besides, even if the rebels somehow saw you and somehow put together your role in our plans, they would expect you north of the sector boundary, not at—" He jabbed his finger at the map. "—that ridgeline."

Tomas clamped his lips together for a time. "You've given the order, sir."

"After dinner, Neumann, we'll find you a bunk for the night. In the morning, we'll share radio call signs and the like before you sending you on your way."

"I assure you, sir, I'm willing to work late and travel back to my platoon tonight."

Carlton shook his head, grin wry. "No doubt, but there's no hurry. Iago and Claudius are cooped up in the woods. From there, they can't cajole or threaten the good citizens of Arden to vote for the Progressive Republic in the plebiscite. Get back tomorrow, get to the position tomorrow night, and all will be fine."

"Sir, with all due respect, the greater we delay, the more time the Papa operatives can ready the rebels for action."

The grin faded. "Tomorrow is time enough, lieutenant."

Perhaps the Bravo Company lieutenants knew how to persuade their superior. Tomas looked to McClernan and Beauchamp with a help-me expression. Fear flashed briefly on the former's visage, then gave way to a stolid front. The latter arched one eyebrow to repeat the message given by his earlier tone of voice.

In a private room at the restaurant, the waiters brought traditional English fare. Warm beer, fish and chips, chicken tikka masala. While Carlton reminisced about food and drink from half a dozen worlds, McClernan played yes-man and Beauchamp talked down his nose in favor of pinot noir wines and beef bourgignon. "Jósephine has the finest cuisine in the Confederated Worlds, is it not so, New-maw?"

Tomas peered at the waiters for signs they paid too close attention to the Ground Force officers. If the waiters did spy for the rebels, they had been well-trained to allay suspicion. "I haven't eaten on enough worlds to know." Beauchamp narrowed his eyes. Tomas hurried on. "But wherever a man is from, home cooking is the finest cuisine of all."

Carlton raised his beer mug. "Well spoken, Neumann." At least by gabbing about food and drink, Carlton and his junior officers would not let slip any military secrets.

A different driver returned Tomas to his platoon the next day. Outside of Eastcheap, Tomas cycled his attention from the woods slipping by to the left to a survey map of those same woods on his tablet. He mapped out the likely paths of Bravo Company's platoons and the rebel formation. If McClernan and Beauchamp could keep contact with the rebels, and move quickly in turn to flanking positions, Carlton's plan could work. The ridgeline picked out by the captain as the blocking position had a treeless southern approach. Move the Badgers and Weasels into hull-down positions on the reverse slope of the ridgeline, dig in the dismounts, and the treeless area would become a cauldron for the trapped rebels.

If McClernan and Beauchamp could move quickly in turn.

A grim thought came to Tomas. Brigade had a database of command metrics on everyone who led a combat unit. Any officer could look up the performance of any of his peers.

Tomas opened up the app on his tablet, entered the names of Carlton, McClernan, and Beauchamp in the search box. When the results came up, his nose wrinkled. Carlton was the worst company commander, and McClernan and Beauchamp two of the worst three platoon commanders, in the entire brigade. If Tomas believed in deities, he could imagine some malevolent god of war cackling with delight that Carlton's most competent platoon commander, Gutierrez, would sit this operation out.

You don't need to invoke a malevolent god when you could chalk it up to bad luck.

So, assume McClernan and Beauchamp would move too slowly. Tomas picked out features on the map and looked out the car window to try to find them in the terrain. At some places the rebels could, if they rapidly broke contact and maneuvered faster than Bravo Company's platoons, outflank the flankers. Imagine a Badger, rolling forward through the woods, expecting the rebels' exposed flank to be in front, when the rebels already occupied positions to the Badger's flank or rear. Smart missiles, RPG teams, what other capabilities could the rebels have, thanks to Iago and Claudius?

You can't control what the rebels will do. You can't control what Bravo Company will do. You can only control what you do. Get to your assigned position and get ready.

The next morning, Tomas' platoon took its positions along the ridgeline an hour before the L4 and L5 mirrors brightened. As they fully illuminated, the mirrors revealed flattened ovals partially occluded by the foliage of the woods. The night before had cooled nearly to freezing. Mist had settled over the treeless gentle slope in front of the platoon. A southerly wind picked up, rustling the needles of the pines and firs over his headquarters, a cee-skin lean-to hacked into the northern slope of the ridgeline about twenty meters west of the dirt road. On one of the supporting poles, he used a dab of adhesive to stick up a small videoloop of Lissa, laughing. For a few days, home sweet home.

Tomas knelt under the lean-to with Hoch and O'Herlihy. Between them, an unfurled map slumped over a box of field rations. Tomas tapped his finger at a spot on the map near Eastcheap. Red and blue pinpoints marked telemetry reports of Ground Force and rebel fires. "Bravo has started driving the rebels our way. It'll take them a couple of days to reach us. We're going to use that time wisely. O'Herlihy, the armored grenadier squad will improve our position. Behind the ridgeline, I want deep foxholes sandbagged by the book. In front of the ridgeline, I want some low profile foxholes for pickets. Those need to be rigged to collapse by remote control when our pickets fall back to the main position behind the ridgeline. The cee-skin covering each foxhole will be tight and bright. Got it?"

"Yes, sir."

"Hoch, your squad is going to patrol forward. One dismounted fireteam, twice a day." Nilsson would lead one of each day's patrols. With luck, his heroism in the swamp and two days' rest in Eltham had returned Nilsson to fighting trim.

Hoch frowned and glanced over his shoulder, in the direction of the treeless field in front of their position. "That's a lot of clear zone to cross, sir. We might be seen. That would tip the rebels that we're here."

"We'll minimize that chance by moving your patrols laterally around the clear zone and staying under forest cover. Papa in orbit won't see you. Stay clear of any rebels you happen to see in the woods. Observe, don't engage."

Tomas pointed at the map, at the colored pinpoints in the southern part of the woods. "If we don't patrol, our only intel on rebel activities will come from Bravo Company. Do you trust Bravo, Hoch?

Me neither. By patrolling, we'll know on our own if the rebels are closing."

"Understood, sir. We'll send out the first patrol within the hour."

The day passed, then the next. The patrols made quick time—the woods held the regular sparseness of recent planting, with spaces between pines and firs wide enough for ecological engineering trucks, or fighting vehicles, to pass. Numerous trails criss-crossed the woods. No sign of rebels.

It fit with the telemetered intel from Bravo Company. The red and blue spoor of firefights crept northward on the map. McClernan and Beauchamp advanced slowly. The firefights inflicted few casualties, a wounded rebel here, there a POW who took his lethe capsule in good time. The rebels maneuvered on flatbed trailers towed by small, four-wheeled, all-terrain vehicles. Larger and man-driven versions of Beatrice Patel's resupply drones. In addition to rifles manufactured according to Papa's molecular fabrication code, the rebels had a few mortars, a few grenade launchers, but nothing heavier.

Full winter came the second day. Tomas' breath steamed and fallen snow chilled his boots as he reviewed the work done by O'Herlihy's squad. He ordered Sgt. Svoboda to fab anti-aircraft rounds for the Badgers' main guns, in case Iago and Claudius' thopter happened to fly their way. After night fell, Tomas oversaw O'Herlihy lead the squad through rehearsal of a fall-back from the forward foxholes to the ones behind the ridgeline, then he worked with the Badger and Weasel gunners to register the coordinates of the forward foxholes for fire from the thirteens.

A Weasel gunner frowned. "O'Herlihy's men have rigged them to collapse. Why do we need to register fires on them?"

A cliché from OCS came to Tomas' mind. "Belts and suspenders. We don't know what's going to happen. Our best intel says we outnumber and outgun the rebels, but that assumes Bravo has gotten an accurate count." Someone sniffed out a breath. "Even on the off chance Bravo's number is accurate, the rebels could still break contact with McClernan and Beauchamp and throw everything they have at us. Therefore, we will be tactically flexible."

After the meeting, the gunners trudged from his lean-to back to their dugouts. Cold air bit the lining of his nose as Tomas watched them tromp across the snow. Ariel Band-light glittered on the snow lying undisturbed on taut cee-skin foxhole covers. Their preparations would be enough, if Bravo Company pulled its weight.

Tomas ducked back into his lean-to, left his helmet near a back corner. He stuffed a chemical heat stick into the foot of his sleeping bag, then crawled in and zipped it up from the inside. He mimed a kiss at the videoloop of Lissa. Moments later he fell asleep.

Voices in his helmet woke him. He opened his eyes to dark gray. Still night, Ariel Band-light reflected off snow. He unzipped his sleeping bag and pulled the helmet on. Cold air clinging to the helmet's interior padding set his mouth to trembling. "Neumann."

"Nilsson. Major rebel activity at about six thousand meters south-south-east."

Tomas flipped down his helmet's faceplate. The helmet projected Nilsson's fireteam as tiny man-shapes coming closer through the trees to the east.

"Nilsson, report to HQ when you come in. Hoch, O'Herlihy, you too."

A few minutes later, sleeping bag rolled up and wedged in a corner, all four men squatted under the lean-to. Tomas turned to Nilsson. "Fill us in."

Nilsson beamed over photos and recorded audio while talking about what his patrol had seen. A dozen infantry fighting vehicles, fabbed copies of Papa's scout IFV, occupied the north slope of a ridge and faced south. From the infantry carriers, three-man teams had dismounted. Two riflemen and a grenadier per team. The RPG tubes strapped to the latter's backs were unmistakable, glittering in the light of the Ariel Band.

"The Papa operatives are there too," Nilsson said. "Photo 17."

Tomas muttered a voice command to his helmet. The photo appeared inside his faceplate. An ornithopter, cee-skin set to snowy woodland, with infrared vents glowing in night vision.

"Bravo doesn't know the rebels have all this," Hoch said.

Tomas checked the map. "Bravo also doesn't know where the rebels are."

Bravo Company's intel reported the main rebel force occupied a valley twelve hundred meters southwest of the slope occupied by the rebel IFVs seen by Nilsson. To Bravo Company, the rebel IFVs didn't exist.

A closer look at the map showed Beauchamp's platoon moving in line toward the valley from the east. "Beauchamp has no clue he'll expose his right flank to the rebels."

Tomas set his cee-skin to transparent in case some unseen rebels happened to be nearby, then scrambled out of the lean-to. He ran to the main comm center, a foxhole that held one end of a wired connection the platoon had laid down along the roadside during the nighttime journey to the current position. His footsteps crunched the brittle top layer of the snow. A few meters from the comm center, his helmet automatically made a low-power wireless connection to the wired transceiver. "Call Beauchamp," he muttered as he jumped into the foxhole.

The wired connection led to company headquarters. One of the enlisteds answered. "I'll connect you, sir. It may take a minute to get to him through Bravo HQ."

Tomas pulled his tablet from an inner pocket of his uniform, called up the joint operation's status. His heart thudded as a blue line, Beauchamp's platoon, crept toward the rebel kill zone. *Come on, answer—*

"Beauchamp here. I'm busy, Newmaw."

"I have intel on a rebel formation flanking your line of march. Three platoons of Papa-type scout vehicles and multiple RPG teams dug in on a ridge to your one o'clock, waiting for you to expose your right."

After a pause, Beauchamp replied, "What do you mean, intel? You're six thousand meters north of that ridge."

"Our scout squad has patrolled south of our position since we arrived—"

"*Vive l'Empereur!* You're supposed to remain hidden in your position! You put our whole operation at risk!"

"There's no sign rebels have seen us. But we've seen them. I repeat, three platoons of scout IFVs, and dismount element equipped for anti-armor activity."

A few harsh breaths hinted at Beauchamp's reaction to the news, until the sounds of him shifting his body and sighing came over the connection. "Your scouts jump at tricks of Ariel-light on the snow. The rebels have no IFVs."

"Maybe they fabbed them while Carlton took us to dinner." Tomas softened his tone. "Regardless of how or when the rebels did it, my scouts saw it."

"Scouts? Barely better than ArChars."

"I'm forwarding my scouts' photoreconaissance to you. Take a look—"

"—Beauchamp out."

The only motion came from the progress bar filling in as the tablet sent Nilsson's photos. Would Beauchamp even look at them? Tomas stared at the map and watched Beauchamp advance closer to the rebel formation.

The enlisted at company headquarters cleared his throat. "Should I hold the connection to Beauchamp open, sir?"

Tomas sloughed out a breath. "No. Neumann out."

He tucked his tablet away, then trudged back through the snow to the lean-to. Though his eyes only saw the shades of pale gray in the night around him, his mind's eye returned to the blue line on the map. It wasn't Beauchamp who advanced. Forty men advanced. Men who trusted Beauchamp to lead them. Many would die, or suffer wounds, or be taken captive. The survivors would curse Beauchamp, in their cups or in sweat-drenched sheets, for the rest of their lives. Curse Beauchamp and all Ground Force officers with him.

Back in the lean-to, Tomas summarized the conversation with Beauchamp.

O'Herlihy shook his head. "Paper fucking tiger."

Tomas looked to Hoch. The scout sergeant's face showed his thoughts echoed O'Herlihy's. Men were about to die, and nothing more could be done.

Nothing?

You can only control what you can do.

Tomas leaned forward. "Sgt. Hoch, how soon can we roll out?"

Hoch's eyebrows jumped upward. Moments later he overcame his surprise. "Soon enough, God willing."

The other men didn't follow. Tomas spoke to each in turn. "Nilsson, your fireteam cannot rack out yet. O'Herlihy, your squad's work the past two days may have gone to waste. We're going to crash the rebels' party."

He then opened a channel to the entire platoon. "Everyone, mount up, double-time! We're going to drive as fast as we can at the rebel formation and hit them before they can hit Bravo Company. Move! Move!"

Within moments, men stirred in their foxholes and dugout shelters. Five minutes later, the platoon's position swarmed with activity. Men zipped up their uniforms as they ran to the vehicles waiting to the rear of the main foxhole line. Ramps clattered to the ground and clouds of steam rose from snow melting near the vehicle's waste heat vents. After men tromped aboard their rides, drivers flicked ceeskin to transparent, causing Badgers and Weasels to seemingly vanish in a blink of the naked eye. Over the radio came terse readiness reports.

Tomas took his seat inside the turret of Badger One and checked the telltales from the other vehicles. The last red status indicators winked out on his displays, leaving only greens and a few yellows. Nothing likely to cause a breakdown. "Platoon, roll out!"

The vehicles rolled forward in column. Their tracks clanked and, as each crested the ridgeline, it presented a silhouette that a rebel patrol with a lidar could easily pick up. Tails of slush flew from the tracks of the lead Weasel. Unruffled snow under the vehicles' passage glimmered in the infrared from vented waste heat. Could Papa in orbit detect the platoon's traces?

Even if Papa could, he only had ten minutes to warn Iago, Claudius, and the rebels.

Ten minutes. Tomas glanced at the map showing Beauchamp and McClernan's locations, and those of the rebels. If Bravo Company moved as slowly as usual, Tomas would engage the rebels in time and Beauchamp's platoon would be safe.

A nervous chuckle bubbled out of Tomas' throat. Now would be the one time Beauchamp moved at top speed.

The column left the treeless zone. The sparse arrays of pines and firs, dark foliated columns dusted with snow, flashed by in the view from the side cameras. The regularity of the trees' pattern gave a strobe effect, reminding Tomas of the gene-teched soybean and hemp fields of artisanal organic farms on New Liberty. Above the crowns of the trees, the Ariel Band remained the brightest object in the sky. Tomas checked the time. Fifteen minutes till dawn.

They entered a part of the woods where the snow showed an undulating surface. When he glanced at the map, Tomas remembered scout reports regarding the terrain here. Boulders peppered the ground beneath. No matter, the vehicles' suspensions could handle the terrain.

His belly turned cold and hollow. Even with a yellow telltale from the left-side hydraulics on Weasel Two?

Just as the thought crossed his mind, that vehicle's status display flashed red in front of Tomas. A voice shouted over the platoon net. "We've thrown the left-side track! Repeating, Weasel Two has thrown its left-side track! We can't move until we fix it."

Tomas rocked in his seat as Badger One slowed. Under normal circumstances, a platoon on the move would stay together if one had a breakdown. But these circumstances were not normal.

"Buffalo, stay with Weasel Two and help with repairs. Yarborough will dismount and catch a ride with Badger Two. Weasel Two, if you can get rolling, drive toward the sound of our guns. Everyone else, once Yarborough's on board his new ride, keep going, full speed!"

The Buffalo stopped, then executed a three-point turn and rolled back toward Weasel Two at the column's tail. A vague shape, bulky with a pack on its back, ran from the Buffalo. Yarborough heading to Badger Two. The Buffalo's forward camera showed Weasel Two's dismounted scouts gesticulating to one another over the thrown track as their breaths streamed into the cold pre-dawn air.

No time to gawk at the repair job. The rest of the platoon had to find firing positions. Tomas' finger led his gaze across a map—*there*.

A slight upslope to provide both partial cover and extra elevation of the main guns. Eight hundred meters from the rebel IFVs. He highlighted the upslope with a circling finger and swiped a copy of the map toward the gunner's display. "Clayworth, can you fire from there?"

After a second's thought, Clayworth said, "That'll do, sir. Quite nicely."

Tomas sent the same map image to the other vehicles. "Drivers, we will form a line there. Weasel One on the right, Badger Two on the left. We're going to fire the guns as the infantry dismount. Infantry will screen the vehicles. Engaging rebels with small arms is secondary."

"What about Iago and Claudius' thopter?" Hoch asked.

"Unless it fires on us or Beauchamp's platoon, it's a secondary target. Preserving Bravo Company is our highest priority."

"Sir, this is a golden opportunity to hamstring the Papa operatives—"

"Ground Force is spread too thinly as it is. We can't afford to lose an entire platoon, let alone two. Everyone, you have your orders."

The column broke apart. Each vehicle rolled into its assigned position. Edelstein lowered Badger One's ramp and the infantrymen hustled out under the lash of Cpl. Meriwether's harsh whisper.

Tomas' gaze tracked the line of dots representing Beauchamp's platoon. Nearly even with the middle of the enemy formation. "Pick our first targets from the rebel center."

Badger One's turret slewed. With a hydraulic whine, the main gun lifted. "Round one lined up," Clayworth said. The other Badger's gunner soon reported his readiness as well.

"Fire!"

A noise-canceled moment, the recoil of the gun past his head. When he could hear again, Tomas said, "Line up the next—"

A roar echoed through the woods from the rebel formation. In Tomas' display, muzzle flashes, strobing like lightning, silhouetted the barrels of rebel guns aimed at Beauchamp's vehicles.

Badger One's turret slewed, slinging Tomas' thoughts with it. *Beauchamp, you arrogant fool—*

"Ready!" said Clayworth.

"Fire!" Tomas said. "Keep going down the line! Don't wait for my order!"

The Badgers' guns pounded. Armor-piercing shells shrieked over the intermittent trees toward the rebel formation. The thirteen on Weasel One poured rounds through the woods, to keep down the heads of rebels guarding their rear on foot. Hoch, O'Herlihy, and Meriwether's fireteams rushed forward.

Telemetry and night vision video showed flame and smoke rising from IFVs in the center of the rebel formation. The next volley of rebel fire sounded raggedly through the forest. Even if Iago and Claudius had implanted into the rebels' heads all the skills needed by an IFV gunner, the rebels lacked the training that drove impped skills from the top of a man's head all the way through his muscle and bone. Surprise clearly shook them. Clayworth and Badger Two's gunner both kept firing. More rebel vehicles erupted with smoke and flame.

Tomas opened encrypted radio channels to Bravo Company. The rebels knew Tomas was nearby; radio silence had no more value. "Beauchamp, McClernan, we've got the battle Carlton wants! About eight to ten rebel IFVs remain effective. Beauchamp, wheel your formation to your right! McClernan, close as fast as you can on the rebels' right flank, here—" He circled with his finger part of the map showing the two rightmost rebel IFVs, zoomed in, and swiped the map region to send it to McClernan. "Move!"

"What's going on?" McClernan asked. "I hear fire, Beauchamp, why are you engaging the targets from such a distance?"

Beauchamp shouted to his platoon in Confed spiced with *joséphinais* curses. "One Badger down. *Vulve de Pauline!* Throw up smoke, the rest of you! Dismount your men!"

"Beauchamp?" asked McClernan, into a noise-canceled silence giving way to the sounds of battle.

He didn't grasp the situation. Tomas said, "The handful of rebels in the valley are a decoy! They have an armored grenadier force on the ridge to the northeast of where you think they are!"

"Neumann? Why are you breaking radio silence? You're firing?

But you're out of range.... Where are you?"

"Engaging the rebels! Do you want to fight them or do you want Beauchamp's platoon to be destroyed?"

"Uh, uh.... roger, we'll engage rebel right at coords Neumann sent."

"Two rebel cans are turning on us!" Edelstein called from the cockpit below the turret. "Make that three. The rebels have our positions!"

"Smoke and evade!" Tomas checked the map to keep himself from thinking about armor-piercing shells penetrating his Badger. Hoch, O'Herlihy, and Meriwether pushed forward. No sign of rebel dismounts in their way. "Fireteam leaders, can you get RPG launchers in position?"

"Will do," said O'Herlihy.

"Sir!" Hoch said. "They're turning our way! We've pulled Bravo's dick out of the meat grinder. And we're a hundred meters from the Papa thopter! We'll capture it if we can, destroy it if we can't!"

Badger One lurched as Edelstein put it in motion. A rebel armor-piercing shell whistled overhead. Tomas refocused on the radio traffic. "Negative, Hoch! The rebel dismounts will turn against Meriwether and O'Herlihy's grenadiers. Screen their fireteams!"

Silence responded.

"Hoch, do you copy? Screen the grenad—*ach*!"

A keening sound filled Tomas' earpiece. Papa jamming. He muttered at his helmet to lower the volume of keening to a whisper. "Edelstein, find a clear channel!"

He jostled against his harness as Edelstein braked hard behind another irregularity in the terrain. "Trying, sir."

Tomas watched the display mapping the dismounted infantry. The colored icons representing the men flickered, then showed probability smears generated by computers in Badger One. A moment later they disappeared entirely. Papa jammed their data channels as well as voice.

How can I command?

You can't. Do you trust the men to know what to do?

Yes, but—

—if they don't know what to do, whose fault is that?

Slotted skills, practiced in training, overrode his self-doubt. Tomas reached up to the inside of the turret hatch and pulled down the eyepiece for the fiber optic binoculars. As he oriented himself to the view, a hiss echoed through the woods from roughly the location of Meriwether's fireteam. A rocket-propelled grenade.

He turned the binoculars in time to see a flash from a rebel IFV. Between flickering panels of cee-skin, smoke poured from the rear seam between the hull and the turret. The rebel vehicle's hatch lifted slightly, shaking with the labor of the man trying to open it. It clattered back to the turret. Flame flared through the ruptured seam, and more smoke billowed out.

A Badger's gun boomed from deeper in the woods. Someone in Beauchamp's platoon? Another Badger fired. Not from Beauchamp. To the right.

Tomas panned the binoculars. Smoke bloomed from the side of a vehicle at the right end of the rebel formation. McClernan's platoon had joined the fight.

Both sides had about equal numbers of effective vehicles, but Ground Force had the advantages of surprise, better training, and positions on the rebels' flank and rear.* *Relief flowed through Tomas' chest. Press the advantage, and the rebels will panic and try to flee.

The relief turned chill. *Even in a panic, a rebel could fire a lucky shot.*

Clayworth fired. Edelstein rolled Badger One to a new position. Against a jolting background, Tomas panned the binoculars back to the center of the rebel line.

The L4 and L5 mirrors had brightened slightly. In the dim light of dawn, its cee-skin laboring to match the flicker of flames from nearby rebel IFVs, Iago and Claudius' thopter sat in a clearing.

Its wings beat, once, in preparation for flight.

They're getting away again—

Small arms fire rattled out of the woods near the thopter. Hoch's fireteam. Bullet holes spangled the cee-skin of the thopter. Its wings beat again, in quickening rhythm.

"Clayworth, put a round on the thopter! We have dismounts at close range."

"Sir, I'm sighting on one of the ashfreak vehicles—" Clayworth fired the main gun.

The thopter's wings beat faster and its legs sprung out of a crouch. It leaped up and hovered for a moment.

The autoloader chugged as it pulled a shell up from ammunition storage. "Thopter's off the ground!" Tomas said. "Switch that round for an antiair!"

"Switch? Will do." Clayworth's fingers thumped the gunnery control surfaces. The autoloader groaned and clanked, sending the armor-piercing shell back to storage.

Hoch's fireteam put more rifle rounds on the thopter. Too little too late. The thopter would fly off—

In the dim light, the thopter showed only a faint shimmer. It hovered for a few wing beats, then wheeled toward Hoch's fireteam.

The thopter's nose lit up with twin gouts of flame. Machine gun fire.

The foliage of the trees around Hoch's fireteam writhed. Trunks splintered and wedges crashed to the ground. The thopter's machine gun fire continued. The sound reached Badger One's external microphones, a constant buzz of hundreds of rounds pouring out within a few interminable seconds.

"Clayworth, where is that antiair shell?"

"Coming, sir!" The autoloader chunked and whirred.

The thopter stopped firing. After a moment's hover, it banked hard and its wings pounded the air. Tomas lost sight of it for a moment, then panned across it and refocused. Slewing and banking, the thopter headed east, toward Belmont.

"Clayworth!"

"Yes sir!" The turret traversed, the main gun elevated. The noise-canceled moment of firing. The thopter banked left and the shell burst in air to its right.

"Goal tend it! The other antiair round, sir?"

"Yes!" They might never get a better chance to bring down the two Papa operatives.

The autoloader clanked again. Clayworth aimed, fired. The shell burst, but the cee-skinned blur of the thopter kept on. Reflections of the knife-edge glare of the L5 mirror sparkled on its wings for a few downbeats, before its angle changed.

The rebel IFVs noticed the thopter's flight. One pulled out of the line and drove in a shoddy serpentine behind the rebel formation, heading east. The blur of its cee-skin clashed with the spray of snow and slush kicked up by its tracks. Another pulled out of the line, then a third.

"Clayworth, anti-armor!"

"On it, sir!" A moment later, Clayworth fired an armor-piercing shell at the first withdrawing IFV. The left-hand track jumped off its drive wheels. The turret hatch popped open and men with cee-skin set to camouflage, not transparency, jumped out.

Through the din of battle, Tomas noticed an absence of sound from his helmet. The jamming had stopped.

"This is Lt. Neumann!" he said over the encrypted connection to Beauchamp and McClernan. "Papa operatives have fled by air and rebel vehicles are withdrawing to east. Engage them!"

"Roger," said McClernan. Beauchamp made no reply, but his remaining two effective Badgers turned to fire on the rebel formation.

Tomas switched to his platoon's net. "Report!"

Badger Two and Weasel One were fully operational. Crewmen and dismounts from Weasel Two and the Buffalo had gotten the scout vehicle's track back on its drive wheels. The two vehicles hurried toward the action.

"O'Herlihy?"

"No casualties. Rebel dismounts are surrendering."

"Meriwether?"

"Ell-tee, we got us some dead arsefucks. All's good."

"Hoch?"

No reply. Tomas looked for effectiveness data from the shillings of Hoch and his men. The data connections were rebooting.

"Hoch?"

A shaky, unfamiliar voice came on, one of the privates in Hoch's fireteam. "Oh Christ oh Christ—"

"Private!" Tomas said, with a sinking feeling.

The private caught his breath before his next words. "Sergeant Hoch is dead."

7

Peters-Stein Technique

While Nilsson's fireteam stood guard over the prisoners, Sgt. Svoboda and his men gutted the captured rebel IFVs. Diamond-tipped saws groaned through alloy, and the stink of hot metallic flecks quenched by slushy snow pervaded the area. Behind the ridgeline held by the rebels at the start of the battle, the platoon's Badgers and Weasels formed a square around the Buffalo. Its fab ran full-speed, turning ground covered by slushy snow into thick mud under its cooling vents. The air above the Buffalo shimmered with heat.

The fab beeped to alert the SSC team, and Tomas, of completion of its first product. Tomas went over. The fab bay door parted to reveal a spool of two hundred meters of data cable and a controller box. A closer look showed two independent levers, a telescopic arm, and interfaces for power and data cables. Tomas called up schematics of the driving controls of a Papa IFV.

In his mind, Tomas rotated the controller box and matched it with the driving controls. "You'll weld it in place above the control sticks?" he asked Svoboda.

"No, ell-tee. Adhesive will hold long enough to get these rustbuckets—and the prisoners onboard—to Eastcheap."

"How are you going to route the data cable?"

"Through the turret. We're sawing off the hatches and ripping out the ammo storage and loading hardware. From there, we drill one hole, then fish the cable to the driving controls. The arsefucks in the back won't be able to unplug the controller. Only downside, we'll have to open the Badger and Weasel turret hatches to connect the other end of the cable to the master output from our drivers."

The prisoners would ride with hands and feet bound... and few mistakes were as deadly as underestimating an enemy, even a defeated one. Removed from the panicked conditions of battle, some of the captured rebels might rediscover their courage and try to take over the hacked, slaved IFVs carrying them to captivity. But with only four men fully trained to drive a twenty-ton vehicle, and those busy driving their own IFVs, the platoon had no better option. "Good work, sergeant."

The fab chugged, whirred. Tomas glanced at the number of intact rebel vehicles and multiplied by the time the first control hardware had taken to fab. "Four hours to get them all done?"

Svoboda raised his hand. "If I say five, I have a chance to come in ahead of schedule."

"Five it is. I've added all the value I can here. Carry on."

Elsewhere inside the square of the platoon's combat vehicles, Tomas found their casualties. Yarborough checked palm-sized monitors adhered to the skin of the platoon's wounded. Only four wounded men, three with wounds so minor a couple of days at company headquarters' infirmary would see them recovered. The fourth, a freckled, redheaded scout from Challenger, lay on a heated pad. Narcotic glazed his eyes and thick bandages smothered the stumps of his left arm and leg. Cline, his name. He deserved to have his name remembered. The thopter's machine gun had shredded his humerus and fibula. The main hospital in Belmont would grow him replacement limbs in a week or two, and he would need at least as long to learn how to use them.

Cline's war was over.

So, too, was that of three other members of Weasel One's fireteam. Their body bags lay nearby, ready to be hooked onto the Buffalo's exterior racks for transport back to the human remains team at company headquarters. Panels in the bags' smart fabric picked up data from their shillings and identified the dead. Sgt. Artur Hoch, Reorganized Catholic Church, Sankt-Benedikts-Welt. Pvt. Isaac Morgenthau, Transstellar Union for Traditional Progressive Judaism, New Zion/Kapteyn's Star. Pvt. Trajan Shorter, no known religion, Garvey's World.

Tomas let out a slow breath. An Observer saying came to memory, spoken by a part of him echoing the tone and timbre of his mother's voice presiding at a dozen funerals. The words brought little comfort. *He who walks in the Way is prepared for what life brings him, and for what death brings him.*

He stared at the identification panel on Sgt. Hoch's body bag. Cpl. Nilsson had become the ranking member of the scout squad.

After a moment, Tomas knew what he had to do. He wished Lissa was here. For a couple of breaths, he savored the wish, and memories of her, then set them aside. He trudged up the muddy, torn slope toward Nilsson and the prisoners.

Forty rebels sat, the overriden orange cee-skin of their uniforms in stark contrast to the plowed and blood-spattered snow. Hunched, hands bound behind their backs, they cast wary glances up at the men of Nilsson's fireteam. The scouts' uniforms showed wintry camouflage. Their breaths streamed into the chill morning air and they held their rifles at easy alert.

Nilsson stared at and through the prisoners, and started when Tomas approached. He straightened his back. "Morning, ell-tee."

"Good morning." An inhalation of cold air bit the lining of Tomas' nose. "Sgt. Hoch is dead."

"I know."

"That makes you acting sergeant of the scout squad."

Nilsson kept staring through the prisoners. A wind skittered through the pines and firs. "I can't say no."

The part of Tomas that had harangued Nilsson for weeks flared up. He viewed it with compassionate amusement. As if anger would make a difference in the scout's behavior now when it never had before.

Time for another approach. Tomas' heart slammed at the breach of protocol forming in his voicebox. He spoke, voice low and tone friendly and curious. "What happened on Kahlenberg?"

Nilsson's aloofness wavered. "Sir, I don't know what you mean."

"Hoch knew something happened before you joined his squad." Tomas spoke matter-of-factly. "He didn't know what, and now, he's dead, while you got to sit out this fight with mechanical trouble."

Emotions churned behind Nilsson's face.

Is this how Lissa would do it?

No. But it's how you're doing it. An intuition came to Tomas. "So who is dead because you fouled up?"

Nilsson's mouth clamped shut. His face paled.

"We'll get to *who* later. Tell me how. Accidental discharge of your weapon? No, no. Against regs, you smoked on a patrol. When you tossed away the butt, you revealed your position—"

"I didn't," Nilsson said through clenched teeth.

"You got a buddy killed—"

Sweat dewed on Nilsson's forehead.

"—no, it was his own fault. Your fault. His fault. Your fault. His fault."

Nilsson's eyes darted from side to side.

Behind Nilsson, Campbell and Gorthi gave Tomas wary looks. With a confident wave, Tomas beckoned them closer as he kept talking to Nilsson. "You fouled up and he got killed. He fouled up and you lived—"

Nilsson's head vibrated. A snarl lifted his upper lip. "Fuck you! It was all my goddam fault and why are you throwing it in my face? You think I don't fucking know I fucking killed Carvalho you fucking butterbar!?"

Campbell gasped. Gorthi shuffled a half-step away from Nilsson, his demeanor showing fear of the blast radius of an officer's anger.

Tomas kept his voice calm. "Sounds like it bothers you your actions led to his death. Would you like to do something about it?"

Nilsson glowered back. "You're going to give me some fucking pep talk? Win one for the nipper? Or some Midgarder myth, Carvalho's saving a seat for me in Valhalla, even though I'm from Österbötter and my ancestors have been Lutherans for fifteen hundred years? Carvalho's dead and it's my fault and there's nothing I can do about it—!"

His snarl collapsed. The muzzle of his rifle pointed at the ground. "I should be dead, not him." His eyes shut half-way. Tears welled up in them. "A dismounted patrol. Broke away from the column to take a piss and must have tripped a sensor. Goddam Unis got me with my dick in my hand."

He slumped to his backside on the ground. Rifle at his side, knees up, head between them, voice muffled. "They march me toward their lines. First Ni-Achterhooks Regiment, they are, and I hear them gabbling in Dutch or German or whatever their fucking language is. Something happens behind their column. Their squad leader sends men scurrying back and forth through the undergrowth. The ones near me get distracted and I make a break for it. They don't even shoot at me.

"I should have known right then."

Nilsson's torso rocked, and his voice grew even quieter. "I run through the woods towards our lines when I hear the Uni ambushers open up with rifles and remote controlled mines. My squad was coming for me." His torso rocked more. "Carvalho was coming for me. After I reached our lines they told me he was dead." His rocking torso sped up and swept through a wider range.

"Keep doing that," Tomas said. "Keep rocking your torso. Don't stop!" He cycled his right wrist in a join-in gesture at Campbell and Gorthi.

After a moment, the two scouts echoed Tomas' words.

Nilsson kept going. His torso rocked, plainly driven by the pressure of a long-tamped emotion. His eyes showed a touch of trance, a state where judgments from his consciousness could not interfere with his actions.

In the background, other men of Nilsson's fireteam drifted closer. McClernan's armored grenadiers stole puzzled glances from the guarded prisoners. Even a few of the captured rebels looked up.

Tomas narrowed his focus to Nilsson. "Faster. Stronger. Turn it up. You can do it. Turn it up!" Campbell and Gorthi added encouragement. Another scout—Bridges, Tomas remembered—joined in too.

Nilsson bucked. His backside scooted on the snowy ground. His forehead nearly brushed the snow on his forward strokes, and for a moment on each backward one, his contorted face showed itself fully to the sky. Grunts forced themselves out of his mouth. His bucking became even faster, his grunts, even louder. Just a moment more—

"Freeze that!" Tomas said.

Nilsson stopped at the top of a backward stroke. In the wintry daylight, lines of rigid muscle etched his face.

"When did you first feel this feeling?"

With a slurred and babyish voice, Nilsson said, "I'm four. Father is coming home early from work at the Terraformering-Departement and he told me when he left in the morning he would play with me when he got home. He almost never plays with me. All day I'm excited."

His tone turned sad. "Just before he came home I crap my pants. I don't know why. I'm in the bathroom, Mother is cleaning me up, and then he's standing in the doorway arms folded and glowering.

"'What have you done? Shit yourself? How can I play with a boy who shits himself?'

"'You said you would!'

"He just shakes his head. 'You're too much of a baby to play with.' I cry—" Nilsson's voice blubbers and tears run down his cheeks. "He says, 'And now you prove you are too much of a baby.' He walks away. The den door slams and I keep crying and crying...." The blubbering overwhelmed Nilsson's voice. The only sounds he made were dull sobs.

Tomas' hands clenched. What was the next step? He sought through his memories of undergoing the Peters-Stein process, and Lissa's discussions of leading the process for other men, seeking a checklist to follow. None came to mind.

Don't let the perfect be the enemy of the good. Improvise. You have to, for Nilsson.

And for you.

"We'd like to show you another way of handling that situation,"

Tomas said. "If you choose."

Nilsson found a space between sobs for words. "How could there be another way?"

"I don't know either, but one exists. May we show you?"

With a series of quick, slight nods, Nilsson assented.

Tomas looked at Campbell, Gorthi, and the other scout, Bridges. "I need someone to play his mother, and someone else to play his father. And someone to play him."

"Play his mother?" Gorthi said with a sour expression.

"Act out the role...." Tomas trailed off when he realized Gorthi understood the standard Confed idiom well enough. Instead, Gorthi lacked the willingness to play a woman's role.

"I'll do it," Campbell said. "Act his mother's part."

"I'll play Nilsson," said Bridges.

Tomas turned to Gorthi. "You can play the role of his father."

"No."

Tomas frowned. "You heard how his father acted in that situation. Do you need more to play the role?"

"No. No. Ell-tee, no. I don't know what you're doing but, are you trained in psychology? Sir?"

Tomas shrugged. "No. I conclude you don't want to take part." Tomas pressed his lips together. Who else could do it? He had to lead the process. Lissa hadn't been a role player in the troop of actors helping him back on New Liberty.

His previous thoughts came to him. *Improvise. Don't let the perfect be the enemy of the good.* He lifted his chin. "I'll play his father's role. Places." He gestured at Campbell and Bridges. They shuffled their feet in the snow, getting into position close to one another.

Tomas pointed at Campbell and Bridges. "Was it like this?" Tomas asked Nilsson.

From his sobs, Nilsson looked up with red-raccoon eyes. He shook his head at Bridges. "No, I was more...." His mouth gaped for words, gave up. His shoulders slumped and a hangdog look came over his face. Hope teetering on the edge of fear.

Bridges shifted his body and matched his shoulders and face to Nilsson's. Nilsson nodded.

Campbell patted Bridges' shoulder and started talking. He pitched his voice higher and more comforting than Tomas had ever heard it. "There, there. It was an accident. Your father will know that."

Tomas checked Nilsson's face. A dread look stiffened his features. Tomas nodded at Campbell and Bridges, and mouthed *that's it, keep going.*

He turned his attention back to Nilsson. "First, we're going to act it as it was." From Campbell and Bridge's positions, Tomas guessed the location of the imaginary bathroom's door. He took a few steps that direction, and a strange sensation smeared through the back of his mind. Parts of him separated, like schoolboys choosing sides for a game of cricket or ultimate flying disc, into two poles. Anger, frustration, and the burdens of what for middle aged pogeys passed for manhood flowed into the upper right quadrant of his chest. The bundle of feelings shot tendrils into his shoulder and up his neck into the lower right side of his face.

Tomas strode into the scene and gave the bundle of feelings control of his speech. "Christ damn it!" he said to Bridges as the child-Nilsson. "You shat your pants?"

"Father, I didn't mean to—"

"You're four years old! Old enough to control your shit… and your piss." A calm and conscious portion of Tomas noted the latter words in passing, as the bundle of feelings kept talking. "You're disgusting, I tell you! You want me to play with you and then you shit your pants?"

Tears burst from Bridges' eyes. "Father, please, you said you would—"

"I promised to play with a boy, not a baby! Christ, I need a drink." Tomas stalked away, back to his starting position. The bundle of feelings imbuing the role of Nilsson's father receded, and the calm and conscious portion of himself came to the fore.

"Was it like that?" Tomas asked Nilsson.

Vulnerability naked on his face, Nilsson stared at the scout playing his younger self. "Yes."

"Now, we're going to show you a different way it could have

happened. Are you ready?"

Nilsson's torso rocked slightly as he shook his head. "How could it be different?"

"Let's find out." Tomas went directly to Campbell and Bridges, spoke in a stark whisper. "We're going to report our feelings and ask about the other's feelings. That's all. Follow my prompts and my lead." He stepped back, then looped around to the bathroom door. The bundle of angry and frustrated parts regained their former strength—

—and the wide eyes of the scout playing the young Nilsson froze them. His expression balanced on a knife edge between innocence and fear. "Father, I'm sorry. I had a poop accident. I feel sad and scared."

The bundle of angry feelings bucked as Tomas calmly said, "Please tell me, son, about being scared."

"Because I know you're angry. I tried to be good, father, really good today because it's a special day you said you'd play with me, please, I'm sorry."

Tomas' intuitions put words in his mouth before he could think about them. "I'm angry and frustrated at the people I work with. That's true almost every day. And I can't tell them—no, I *don't* tell them, out of fear I'll lose my job. I don't tell them when I feel angry and frustrated. I don't even act on those feelings to them. Instead, I act on my anger and frustration to you—and your mother."

Campbell sucked in a breath. Something in his face showed Tomas his words had pierced the role and spoken to the man behind it.

Tomas continued, in character. "And today was especially bad. I wanted to leave early, which was like a magnet in my desk for extra work. Every village wants a forest seeded in their vicinity, and animals, but only the safe ones, but how can you have an ecosystem without wolves? It frustrates me. These people have connections with the planetary parliament and I can't tell them to buzz off and let us do our jobs."

More intuitions informed him of Nilsson's father's thoughts. "I deal with all that and I really want a drink. I feel guilty because I promised I would play with you instead. In response to the guilt I want a drink even more. I feel glad because your accident gives me an excuse to get angry and renege on my promise. In response to the gladness, I feel even more guilt and want to drown it in yet more drink." Tomas sloughed out a breath. "I made a commitment. I will fulfill it as best I can."

Still deep in his role as the young Nilsson, Bridges said, "Thank you, father." He came forward and raised his arms for a boyish hug.

Anxiety—*I'm an officer, he's a sweatie, and we're in a war zone*— yielded to the power of the role. Tomas wrapped his arms around the scout and clapped his back.

When they disconnected, the bundle of feelings that had galvanized the role of Nilsson's father lay loosely near the bottom of his consciousness. Tomas backed out of the scene and the calm side of him remained buoyant. Fully in his role as facilitator, he said to Nilsson, "Now it's your turn."

Nilsson shook his head. "I, I—" He looked up with sudden certainty. "I'll do it." He strode toward Campbell and Bridges. The latter backed away a few steps away, to give him center stage.

Tomas walked the looping, slushy path he had taken times before. Anger and frustration reflooded the upper right side of his chest. A detached part of him noticed those emotions reflected more than just the urge to get back into character. He recalled Nilsson's tone of voice when saying *butterbar*, and the anger ratcheted up.

When Lissa led a person through the Peters-Stein technique, she used a team of actors, strangers to the person. Tomas suddenly realized why. No personal feelings could interfere with the playing of roles, the way they would now.

The flooding emotions twisted his face and gave a harsh timbre to his voice. "Christ damn it!" Tomas shouted. "You shat your pants again?"

The part of Nilsson that had remained a frightened boy for fifteen standard years showed plainly on Nilsson's face. Bridges said something inaudible but in an encouraging tone, and Nilsson's fear subsided. "Father, tell me what you're feeling."

"What do you think I'm feeling? I have a son who can't control his shit and his piss! Are you so dense you don't know? You bring shame to me and your mother!"

Nilsson wavered. "You make me feel... No, I feel... very small."

"You feel like a baby? You should!"

Nilsson shrank back, against the outstretched hand of Bridges against his shoulderblade. Bridges murmured something, and Nilsson's courage regrouped enough to speak. "Father, I mean, I feel helpless. I don't want to do anything you think is shameful, yet I can't control myself enough to always avoid those things."

His words flowed faster. "I pooped my pants today, and I broke out of column to go pee and get captured by the Unis on Kahlenberg, and I don't know why I do those things but I know they push you away and Carvalho away and, and...."

The bundle of anger in Tomas' chest thawed. The detached part of him next spoke. "Tell us more."

"Merciful God, that's why I do them. To make you angry and to get him killed so I can feel small and helpless because inside that's the only way I know how to be...."

Nilsson fell to his knees and dropped his face into his uplifted palms. "Merciful God. Merciful God." He repeated the oath, over and over, in a choked whisper that finally trailed off. He remained unmoving for long moments.

After a time, he settled back on his ankles and dropped his hands against his thighs. He sniffled a trickle of clear snot back into his nose. "I don't want to die for this planet and its funny-talking locals. Except when I want to." He wiped his nose with his sleeve. "Part of me wanted that robotic minisubmarine to rip me apart, so I could get away from—" He waved his hand backward above his head. "—everything I've done wrong and carried around for nearly my whole life."

"I had the same sort of part," Tomas said. "It kept me in a foxhole too long. My friends saved me before I could die of shock."

Nilsson barely seemed to hear. "Why do I want to feel helpless and small?"

"'Why' is just a river in Egypt." He'd heard Lissa say that. She didn't know what it meant either. Tomas crouched on the snow near

Nilsson. "Take a moment to be with that small and helpless part of you. It might have something more to say."

Nilsson's shoulders slumped. He dropped his gaze to the torn snow near his knees, then shut his eyes. His belly bulged in and out with deep breaths. The breaths grew shallower, slower. His eyes remained shut.

"It's safer. Because I feel small and helpless, I don't try to connect with other people. With mother, with father, with anyone. What would be the point? I'm too minuscule for anyone to want to connect to. If I try to connect—" He winced and writhed his shoulders. "—they'll reject me and I'll feel disappointed." His face shuddered. "Merciful God, the disappointment is inside me. I can't escape it. And when I try to escape it...."

He looked up at Tomas, then settled back on his ankles. The thousand-yard stare flitted over his face. Tomas imagined him thinking of Carvalho.

"....it finds situations where it can come out." Introspection showed on Nilsson's face, and his gaze darted with thought.

Tomas waited until his eyes slowed and his face showed a willingness to be spoken to. "What do you feel now about leading the scout squad?"

"I'm scared." A passing frown creased his eyebrows, and Tomas read that his words were so honest they surprised him. "I'll be responsible for eight men. I'm scared that I'll fuck up and get them killed. Any of them. I don't know how I could live with myself. I know, war throws dice to claim its victims, and I could do everything right and the rebels or Papa could still get them."

His voice trailed off. Tomas let him gather his next words.

"And I'm scared I wouldn't risk fucking up. The war's lost and whether Arden stays Confederated or goes to Papa doesn't matter. There's nothing left to die for. Us scouts, hell, the whole platoon should just button up our rides or dig into foxholes and keep our heads down until after the plebiscite. But though I know that up here—" He tapped his fingertip to the top of his helmet. "—I can't shirk my duty. I enlisted with my eyes open. I gave a damn on Kahlenberg, at least until the Unis got Carvalho. And not giving a damn now fills me with guilt. Even though giving a damn raises the chance one of my men will be the last Ground Force to die for a mistake."

"I understand all those feelings," Tomas said. "Can you embrace them? They can help you lead the squad to the best of your abilities, if you let them be your allies."

Nilsson spent a few moments lost in thought. "I can, sir. I will."

Satisfaction washed through Tomas. Nilsson meant what he said. But Tomas' regard turned inward and the satisfaction turned sour. *You understand those feelings because you too feel them all. This isn't about Nilsson. Those feelings can help you better lead the platoon. Will you put your Confeds where your mouth is?*

From the line of damaged but drivable rebel IFVs came triumphant whoops from the SSC team. Some stubborn aspect of the drive-by-wire installation process must have just yielded. The platoon had come a step closer to reentering action.

Tomas nodded to Nilsson. "So will I."

8

The Thopter

Fiber optics shunted the bright sunlight of a summer day into the conference room at company headquarters. Tomas led in O'Herlihy and Nilsson. They stopped just inside the door. Captain Bao leaned over a map unrolled across the main table.

"Lt. Neumann reporting, sir."

"At ease. Come in."

Tomas strode to the main table. The last few steps he peered around Bao, trying to read the map. *There.* A red dot. "The Constabulary found Iago and Claudius?"

"About ninety minutes ago, an ArChar patrol spotted a thopter covered in cee-skin land near an abandoned ecological engineering facility, Camp Cordelia, in what's now a mature forest. Fifty klicks from here. And let me answer your next question. There were no loyal Ardenite or Ground Force aerial assets in the vicinity."

The Papa operatives, then. If the Constabulary reported accurately. "Spotted how?"

"Eyeballs and radar."

Tomas looked more closely at the map. Rolling hills striped with ragged strips of forest. Camp Cordelia occupied a treeless hilltop. "How many rebels in the area?"

"ArChars say twenty or thirty. They take potshots at ArChar patrols, but otherwise keep a low profile. Till now, at least. We'll see if Iago and Claudius spur them into action."

"That's been the Papa agents' M.O. so far. Shall we start planning, sir? My squad leaders are eager."

Bao nodded at O'Herlihy and Nilsson. "I'm glad to hear that. But planning? You don't need my help. You've hatched some reasonable plans all on your own, Neumann, and the way you improvised north of Eastcheap to keep that dipshit Josie lieutenant from driving into the sausage grinder impressed the hell out of me. Get the data you need from the map, roll out, and plan on the fly."

Tomas blinked at the unexpected compliments. Yet a hesitation in Bao's demeanor told him the captain had an agenda he didn't want to share. "We will do that, sir. Ah, perhaps my squad leaders can start reviewing the data while you brief me further?"

Captain Bao raised an eyebrow. "Great way to divide the labor. Come to my office."

The captain's desk held plastic models of ancient fighting vehicles, with uneven decals and incompletely snapped-together seams showing hand assembly from hundreds of small parts. Tomas took a seat facing the main gun of some ancient tank the color of sand. "What, sir, is...."

Bao's raised hand stopped him. A metallic sound of surfaces gliding over each other came from Bao's side of the desk. The captain pulled out a gray plastic box the size of a young child's fist and squeezed a button with his thumb. He set the box down on his desk, roughly equidistant between them. A green LED glowed on the box's top.

"I hope to Christ I'm paranoid and this damn thing isn't necessary," Captain Bao said.

"It's built to jam eavesdropping devices?"

A curt nod. "The joint operation started me thinking. The Papa operatives crossed into Bravo Company's sector, so we were stuck with Carlton. But of Carlton's three lieutenants, Beauchamp and Mc-Clernan are the worst two. Why did they take the field against the rebels north of Eastcheap?"

Tomas looked past the ancient tank to the green LED on the jamming device. "At least one of them had to."

"But not both."

"Maybe Lt. Gutierrez needed to patch up his platoon, the way Khudobin stayed here while we reconnoitered the Papa landing sites. Or, maybe Bravo's duty calendar assigned Gutierrez to reserve duty. I can tell from your face neither of those are true."

"Platoon readiness scores logged right before the joint operation had Gutierrez ahead of Beauchamp and McClernan. And according to the calendar, Beauchamp should have been in reserve for the joint operation."

Tomas said, "Carlton is a worse company commander than I thought."

"It wasn't Carlton."

"Sir?"

Captain Bao leaned forward and dropped his voice. "I have it from someone at battalion that brigade headquarters expressly ordered Carlton to assign the mission to Tweedledum and Twee-dledee. Brigade headquarters. Planetary command. Someone sitting behind our side of the chessboard wanted Papa and the rebels to win north of Eastcheap." Bao's voice fell further. "Someone at brigade HQ wants Arden to go to Papa."

Tomas' breath caught. After a moment, he spoke. "Sir, I see how that could be, but what's the old saying? Never attribute to malice what can be explained by stupidity."

Captain Bao admonished him with his eyes. "There's another old saying. Hope is not a planning factor." His face sank. "And I haven't even gone to the worst possibility."

Tomas' gut soured. "Someone at brigade is a Papa spy."

"Again, I hope to Christ I'm wrong." Exhaustion sapped the captain's voice. "But we have to minimize the damage if I'm right."

"Absolutely, sir. Anything more?"

Bao shook his head. "Godspeed—sorry, you're an Observer."

Tomas flicked his hand at the air. "Feel free to ask your deity to aid me. I take no offense."

"Regardless, Neumann, good luck."

A few minutes later, Tomas returned to the conference room.

O'Herlihy and Nilsson spoke in low voices and drew lines on the map with their fingertips.

Nilsson straightened up and faced Tomas. "Ell-tee, we have some ideas—"

"We need to scout the site before we can plan our attack. If you've copied over all the relevant data, let's get moving. Every second we dawdle gives the Papa operatives more time to fab rifles for their rebel allies—or weapons worse than that."

O'Herlihy grunted. Nilsson frowned, puzzled, but soon his face showed he recognized the situation had dimensions not yet revealed.

Within an hour, the platoon rolled out of the company base. Five blurs of transparent cee-skin in a warm summer afternoon. After going through the nearest town, the road passed through uninhabited fallow land. On his main display, Tomas called up a map of the area where the Papa operatives' thopter had landed. At low power, radio traffic between the vehicles would go unnoticed by Papa in orbit. "O'Herlihy, Nilsson, sorry to have to smokescreen you at company headquarters. Tell me your plans."

"It's Nilsson's plan, sir," O'Herlihy said.

"Nilsson?"

"Yes sir. I can't speak for anyone else, but I know my scouts are getting tired of chasing the Papa operatives. That's why we should try to capture them, or if nothing else, knock out or capture their thopter."

Tomas' mind went back to the woods near Eastcheap. From his memory came the frantic voice of the scout reporting Hoch's death. "What other reasons do you have for targeting them and not the rebel cadre?"

"I would be glad to pay the Papa operatives back for Hoch, Morgenthau, and Shorter. But that would only be a bonus. The thopter is heavily armored and armed, and the Papa operatives riding it are the command and control element for every rebel cadre they meet. Capturing them has a huge benefit. Even only knocking out their thopter helps by reducing their mobility to ground vehicle speed and terrain limitations." Nilsson's voice sounded clear. "It's the right kind of risk to take."

"How would we pull it off?" Tomas said.

"We follow the road to—" Nilsson gave the coordinates of a crossroads eight klicks as the crow flew from Camp Cordelia. East of the intersection, one road went east over a low, baretopped hill. To the south, the other road ran into a valley angling within a thousand meters of the camp.

"At the crossroads, the vehicles split into two groups. One goes due east, then turns off the road while hidden from view by the baretopped hill." A spotter at the abandoned camp could observe the road where it crested the hill. "That group loops around the hill, crosses the main road, and heads south on a gravel road toward the camp. I measure seventeen klicks to go that way."

Nilsson went on. "The other group has a shorter path, ten klicks on a treeless plain parallel to the southbound road, hidden behind the line of hills on the near side of the valley. Paralleling the angle of the southbound road, that line gets our group within two thousand meters of the camp without being seen. Another dirt road leads to Camp Cordelia."

Tomas tapped the display to call up a line-of-sight analysis. The vehicles could stay mostly hidden at first. Still…. "I'm sure they've put up cameras and microphones along both roads approaching the camp."

"Me too. That's part of the plan. Papa will know we're coming when one of the vehicles on the dirt road has a breakdown, and both sets of vehicles delay for ninety minutes."

Badger One rolled along the living pavement. "Don't keep me in suspense."

"At the crossroads, we dismount some infantry. I'll lead one scout fireteam, plus the men with grenade launchers from O'Herlihy's squad. We can make it eight klicks across open country in ninety minutes, if we hustle and avoid any rebel patrols. We'll have help with avoiding them, because once we fake the breakdown, the rebels would send men out the dirt road to try exploiting our problem."

Tomas saw the plan. "If the Papa operatives stay near the camp, you'll close on them."

"And if the Papa operatives fly to support the rebels, we'll pick up the thopter by sight and sound—"

"—Your senses are that sharp?"

"The skills imps slotted in what we need to look for. Refringence from the wings. So if we see the thopter flying toward the dirt road, we'll come in behind it. Either way, if we can get men with grenade launchers into position, we can cripple or destroy the thopter. We might even catch one or both Papa operatives on board."

After a moment's thought on prior engagements, Tomas said, "Usually at least one operative dismounts. Still, I like the idea. I agree, it carries some risk, but it's worth the possible reward. And if the plan gets foiled, we'll pull the vehicles back to the reverse slopes of the hills, here and here." He tapped the map. "Nilsson, anything to add?"

"No, sir."

"Then it's a go." Tomas opened a channel to all the vehicle crews to outline the plan. Then, in a private channel to Edelstein, he asked about ways to create fake evidence of vehicle damage. "Something an enemy could pick up by camera or microphone."

Edelstein took a moment to reply. "Can I call the Buffalo to fab something?"

"How quickly can they fab it?"

"I'll ask." Edelstein took a few moments to call the SSC team riding in the Buffalo, then finished answering Tomas' question. "They're fabbing antiair rounds, but they can spare a few cycles for us."

At the crossroads, dense forest filled the quadrant in the direction of Camp Cordelia. The platoon stopped to dismount Nilsson's fireteam and the RPG operators from the armored grenadier squad.

"Switch your team net to Nilsson's," Tomas told the men with the grenade launchers. "And triple check you're connected to Nilsson's team and nothing else. Nilsson's your leader in this mission. You have to be able to communicate with him. And we don't want your helmets sending radio signals five klicks to speak to your home fireteams. A signal that strong, the rebels might pick it up and triangulate to your team going cross-country on foot."

Tomas then split the platoon's vehicles into two groups. Weasel One, carrying the last two fit scouts from Hoch's fireteam, would lead Badger One on the easterly route. The other two fighting vehicles and the Buffalo would take the cross-country route parallel to the southbound road, then go up the dirt road toward the camp.

Speaking of the Buffalo... "Edelstein!" said Sgt. Svoboda over the platoon net. He hurried over from his vehicle. A gray lump the size of a man's two fists seemed to float in front of the transparent cee-skin tailored over him.

Tomas waited for him with Edelstein. "What's this?"

Svoboda took a parting blade to the cee-skin hiding the left track of Badger One. "An adhesive, ell-tee." He shoved the lump into the part near one of the drive wheels, then peered in, made fine adjustments by feel, peered in again. "Edelstein has the control code. When deployed, the adhesive will goop up the drive wheel and stop the track. Crude, but we could fab it quickly."

Tomas envisioned the track stopping so quickly it jumped off the drive wheels. "How crude?"

"She shouldn't throw the track," Svoboda said.

"Shouldn't?"

A final adjustment, and Svoboda stepped back from the Badger. "We can't work miracles, ell-tee." After he sealed the cee-skin, motion blurred near his waist, fabric parted with a scritch, and into view came a small spray canister, the size of a can of beardstop foam. "This will melt the adhesive."

He offered it to Tomas, who declined with a raised palm. "B-one is Edelstein's lady. He gets the honors."

"Of course, ell-tee," Svoboda said as Edelstein took the canister.

As Svoboda scampered back to the Buffalo, Tomas said, "Men, mount up. Nilsson, ready?"

"Yes, sir!"

"Head out."

Blurs of motion marked the men remounting the vehicles. A dappling effect at the edge of the forest showed Nilsson's team entering the woods at a brisk pace. The ramps clanged up and the vehicles lunged into motion.

The low hills flanking the valley filled the forward camera view when Edelstein turned off the road to the left. Badger One's suspension smoothed out the rolls of the ground. Tomas remembered a boat ride on the Friedland River, during a windy Harvest Fête one of his last years back home on Jósephine. The one time he'd ever gotten drunk at home, on the seasonal batch of beaujolais nouveau, with the river far choppier than usual. The memory combined with the expectation of action to turn his gut queasy.

His gut kept troubling him as Edelstein led the group of vehicles across the main road and onto the dirt road leading to the abandoned camp. Clumps of forest stood at either hand. Tufted grass and a few pine seedlings filled the center of the road, and more grass and seedlings had colonized the edges. Gravel rustled under the tracks and dust drifted into the air.

If the rebels had cameras and microphones along the dirt road, they knew fighting vehicles came their way.

A red x on the map showed the "breakdown" point, three klicks from the camp. Presuming the rebels had small off-road vehicles, like the ones the rebel decoys had used to lure Beauchamp and McClernan in the woods near Eastcheap, they could deploy against Tomas' group within minutes. The red x grew closer. Just over a high point in the road, more exposed than he would wish, and with dense woods on both sides.

They topped the high point. A red x appeared in the middle of the dirt road seen through the forward camera display, projected by Badger One's software. No rebel would expect Ground Force to choose to halt—

"Here!"

"Deploying adhesive," Edelstein said.

A shriek of alloy against alloy erupted from the right track. Badger One slewed as Edelstein stopped it. As Tomas caught his breath, Edelstein said, "Diagnostics check out. The adhesive did its job without breaking anything."

Further ahead, Weasel One stopped. A few lurches and it backed up, putting the standard halt-in-column separation between it and

Tomas' Badger. Weasel One's axial camera relayed to Tomas' displays that its thirteen covered its sight line down the dirt road toward the abandoned camp.

"East team, we have a breakdown," Tomas radioed. Though encrypted, the signal strength would alert rebel listeners. To the vehicles in his group, he said, "Infantry, dismount to a defensive perimeter. Meriwether, leave a man back. Edelstein, get out and spray the antiadhesive. Once you're done, get back on board. At that point, Meriwether's man will pretend he's trying to repair our breakdown."

Ramps dropped. Boots clomped out. Men crouched and trotted into the woods at either side. The computers in the turret took telemetry from their shillings and projected ghostly figures onto the camera views in Tomas' displays.

Meriwether was the man back.

"Your men don't need you?" Tomas asked.

"Sheeit. Those motherfuckers better know what to do, or after this Ima fuck them up worse than the arsefucks can." He waited outside the Badger as Edelstein clambered out of the cockpit and back through the infantry compartment.

Moments later, Edelstein and Meriwether were at the gummed-up drive wheel. Meriwether's head swiveled, checking the woods on that side of the Badger for rebels, while Edelstein worked inside a slit in the cee-skin. From a hull-mounted microphone came the hiss of the spray canister and the dripping sound of dissolving adhesive.

Tomas checked the side and forward sensors of both vehicles. The woods remained silent and free of human motion. Above, high clouds as white and puffy as pulled cotton drifted across a deep blue sky. Perhaps the rebels didn't know they were here.

Perhaps the rebels had already come and bided their time.

Footsteps thumped on the Badger's rear ramp. "Drive wheel is clear," Edelstein said over the radio. The Badger's interior added muffled echoes to his voice. He clambered into the cockpit, then yanked the safety harness over his torso and snapped the buckles.

"Easy," Tomas said. "Take the time to do it right."

"I did, ell-tee." Edelstein snapped the last buckle into place.

"Now I'm ready to wait."

Minutes elapsed. Edelstein took rhythmic breaths and counted as he exhaled, cycling through the numbers one to ten. In the turret, Clayworth shook his legs and swept his fingers past the buttons on the gunner's controls. "Where the hades are the ashfreaks?"

Tomas doubled checked the camera feeds and the sensor outputs. Still no hostiles.

A harsh whisper came over Meriwether's team net. "Arsefucks!" said Carcetti. "About a dozen, riding a train of flatbed carts pulled by a little all-wheel-drive off-roader. They're stopping about four hundred meters out at your three o'clock."

"Should I open up on them?" Clayworth asked.

"No. Both of you," Tomas said after adding Weasel One's gunner to the circuit. "Look oblivious till I give the word." To Carcetti, he said, "Keep an eye on them. Stay hidden."

Carcetti activated a small camera. From blurs of cee-skinned motion, Badger One's computers extracted the probability smears of the dozen rebels as they climbed off the flatbed carts. Two of them went to a bundle under a tarp on the rearmost flatbed. One pulled the tarp back. Four grenade launchers lay there, with painted cee-skin set to shades of gray in a woodland pattern. The two rebels adjusted the cee-skins to transparent and strapped grenade launchers over their shoulders. Two more came up and took the remaining grenade launchers. Enough to punch a hole in a Weasel or Badger.

The rebels split into four groups, each group made up of one grenadier and two riflemen. Without a spoken word, the groups fanned out in the direction of Badger One.

"Come on, cheap machine," Meriwether said aloud. His deep voice carried so well, Tomas imagined any rebels in reserve at Camp Cordelia, thousands of meters away, could hear it. Surely those in the woods could. Meriwether slammed the hull of Badger One with the heel of his hand. "Gimme something I can use."

A rustle of movement and exerted breath came from Carcetti. "I'm tracking the arsefucks," he whispered. "Still moving your way."

The probability smears in the turret displays abruptly widened and narrowed, and some cut out entirely. "Lidar getting fouled by underbrush," Clayworth said.

Tomas watched the skyward view. A broad oval of reflected sunlight, a few puffy clouds, and low above the woods, a flash of reflected light and a rhythmic pumping distortion of the deep blue—

"Papa operatives approaching by air," he said. "Get ready. It won't be long before they spring the rebels on us."

Tension thickened inside Badger One. Outside, Meriwether stooped sideways, his head and left shoulder inside the slit in the cee-skin and his rifle slung over his right. Feigned exertion filled his voice. "Now don't make me get mad...."

The thopter descended into a small clearing near the rebel cart train. Soon now.

Would Nilsson be in position in time?

Carcetti whispered, "The team I'm tracking stopped to wait. Oh shit."

Tomas' gaze roved the displays. Nothing live nor synthesized by algorithm gave him any information.

"What happened?" Clayworth asked.

"They might have found Carcetti," Tomas said. "The rebels might decide their secrecy is blown and go ahead and strike now."

"No, Papa gives the ashfreaks a short leash," Clayworth said. "Near Navarre they could only fire missiles while the operatives remained on the ground."

"The Papa operatives are men, not algorithms," said Edelstein. "They can change their minds, if they're willing to feel the feelings that change brings up."

"Get ready to do your jobs," Tomas said.

Carcetti's murmur came through the net. "They looked my way, but gave up and moved on. The grenadier is setting up. A few seconds now."

"Oh, come on," said Meriwether. He backed out of the slit in the cee-skin. "This shit just ain't funny. Where the powered wrench at?"

A calm washed over Tomas. He had able men with him inside Badger One, and another good crew in the Weasel. They had native aptitudes cranked up by the skills imps. He had led them here, but within moments, the best leadership he could provide would be to trust them—

Four rocket-propelled grenades wooshed in a single blur of sound.

"Now!" Tomas shouted.

Meriwether jumped into tall grass at the roadside and ran at a crouch toward the woods. Edelstein raced Badger One backwards over the high point in the road, then spun in place to turn the forward armor and turret toward the rebel teams. Chaff drifted in the air above the vehicle's line of motion. The chaff detonated one rebel grenade. The others arced by, control fins hard over at the command of their guidance packages, seeking Badger One and missing.

Plastic clicks of the control wheel under Clayworth's hand aimed the main gun and thirteen at the rebel RPG teams in turn. The noise-canceled moment of firing the main gun, the zipping sound of bursts from the thirteen. Weasel One trained its thirteen on the rebel RPG teams as well. Downrange telemetry returned empty green circles, half-filled yellow ones, and a few solid reds to Tomas' map display.

The sound of a rifle firing bursts in automatic mode came over the net. "Got one!" said Carcetti. Telemetry popped another filled red circle onto the map. "Oh, what's that?"

Tomas heard it too, from the external microphones on the right side of the Badger. A two-note drumbeat of Ground Force RPGs, deep in the woods, interspersed with the distant rattle of a half-dozen friendly rifles.

Nilsson's team.

A glance at the map gave a visual of telemetry. Rocket-propelled grenades struck cee-skin, alloy, and plastic. The splotches of grenade strikes outlined the side and one wing of the Papa operatives' thopter.

Clayworth zipped out another burst of fire from the thirteen. Rounds smacked trees and foliage near one of the positions formerly held by one of the rebel teams. No sign of casualties.

"More antipersonnel fire, sir?" he asked.

Tomas took in the map with a glance. "Put an anti-armor round on the thopter! Weasel One, keep suppressing the rebel RPG teams!

Nilsson, we're going to drop ordnance on the thopter, keep a safe distance!"

"Roger!" replied Nilsson.

Clayworth fired the main gun. The autoloader clanked up the next round from ammunition storage as the shell shrieked over the nearest trees.

On the map, a livid streak joined the splotches of grenade strikes. The shell's plasma jet had pierced the thopter's roof.

Another moment of silence, another jerk of the breech past Tomas' head, and the next shell shrieked away. A second livid streak joined the first. Just before the second armor-piercing round hit, a spike in the thopter's fuselage temperature suggested fires within.

"Arsefucks are running!" Carcetti called over the net.

"Roger that!" one of the scouts called from the woods near Weasel One. "Sounds in the underbrush in front of me, heading east." Weasel One panned its thirteen back and forth. Bursts pounded the forest, but telemetry showed all the rounds missed flesh.

From patchy lidar, probability smears of retreating rebels bloomed and faded on Tomas' display. The pattern of smears flowed steadily eastward. Behind them, the thopter's outline glowed with fire. A side display showed a camera feed from Nilsson's team. Black smoke gouted between shreds of cee-skin on the thopter's roof.

"Any sign of rebels or Papa operatives around the thopter?" Tomas asked Nilsson.

"No, ell-tee."

"Confirm that, then investigate the thopter." He opened up the full platoon channel. "O'Herlihy, I'm sending you tracking data on retreating rebels. Come over here and pursue them." Tomas swiped his finger across a display to send the tracking data. "And peel off the Buffalo to Nilsson's position."

"On my way, ell-tee. I'll give Sgt. Svoboda the word."

Tomas tracked the pattern of rebel probability smears flowing into deeper woods further to the east, near the limit of the platoon's lidar range. Even if the rebels, and their masters, eluded capture for a time, what did the Papa operatives leave behind in the wrecked thopter?

9

The Masks of Iago

The thopter crouched like a wounded, molting bird. Nilsson's team had ripped off the thopter's cee-skin. Jumbled coils of it littered the ground under the fuselage. Except where damaged by fires, the cee-skin held its transparency, blurring the ground. As Tomas entered the clearing, he raised his hand to shield his eyes from the blur and avoid an eyestrain headache.

Bullet holes pocked the thopter's alloy skin, but their damage was only cosmetic. The killing blows had come from above, dealt by Clayworth's armor-piercing rounds. Yet from the ground, even those showed only as pinholes venting thin smoke streams.

The thopter looked bigger than two men would need to fly from one rebel camp to the next. It measured twelve meters from pointed nose to broad tail, and three across at its widest. Enough to house, what? A high-throughput fab? Racks of coffin-like tanks for advanced skills implantation? A rebel platoon of airmobile hussars? A Papa one?

Tomas shook his head. Enough speculation. Time to find out.

A thin line on the thopter's flank near its nose marked the entry hatch. It remained tightly sealed despite the thopter's damage. Nilsson waited near the hatch. Close to him, Gorthi's hands caged a gray plastic ladder. He tapped it back and forth the few centimeters between his hands, as if too hot to hold. Presumably the ladder had been hurriedly fabbed by the Buffalo.

Sgt. Svoboda waited nearby, his uniform as transparent as the infantrymen's. His tools—stuck by polarized adhesive to his hips—lacked cee-skin, and seemed to float in the air. A closer look showed among his tools a cutter with a circular, diamond-edged blade, and a laser knife.

Nilsson nodded up at the thopter. "We're waiting for you, ell-tee."

"Open it up."

With more taps, Gorthi moved the ladder. It clattered against the alloy of the hatch. Gorthi put his boot on the bottom rung and pushed its feet into the soft ground.

Sgt. Svoboda went up a few rungs. He twisted the cutter off his hip, gripped the trigger and the stability handle, and started to work on the vertical seam on the hatch's right side. The cutter keened as he brought it closer to the fuselage. When he touched the diamond edge to the alloy, the keen turned to a growl and the cutter bucked away from the fuselage, kicking the safety shield toward his helmet.

"They covered the entire thopter in high strength alloy?" he muttered loudly enough for his in-helmet microphone to pick up.

Svoboda tried the cutter at lower speed. No kickback, but no penetration. Adjusting the angle gave the same poor result. He twisted the cutter back onto his hip and pulled off the laser knife from the other. He worked the laser knife for long minutes, generating a white-hot glow and the hiss of ablating alloy. When he pulled the tool away to expose the worksite, Tomas winced. Svoboda had opened up a slit no more than a centimeter long, and probably shallower than that. He would need hours to force the hatch this way.

Sgt. Svoboda twisted the laser knife back onto his hip, then readied the cutter. Tomas frowned, but when the spinning blade stopped bucking and its high pitched whine changed into a buzz, he understood. Svoboda worked the cutter blade's edge under the top layer of the fuselage and through softer metal beneath. Hot flecks of the top layer spewed downward. Most fell straight to the ground and smoldered like live coals. A few clung to the ladder and sent up curls of black smoke. Nilsson and Gorthi brushed the ladder free of hot cuttings, and smothered those on the ground with darting stomps of their boots.

Working steadily, Sgt. Svoboda went up and down a few rungs to extend the cut the full height of the hatch and start on the horizontal seams at top and bottom. He climbed off, moved the ladder to the left of the hatch, then mirrored his earlier actions. He made faster progress on the left side, yet slowed down as he worked on the last cuts. Nilsson called men from his squad to prepare for something hostile coming out of the hatch.

At the end, as he cut the last centimeters of the bottom seam, Svoboda dipped the blade in and out of the cut. "Stand clear in case it falls."

"Or gets pushed out," Nilsson said.

Sgt. Svoboda pulled the cutter blade away from the fuselage and jumped off the ladder in one motion. The cut-out hatch remained in place.

After the unpowered blade of his cutter spun down to silence, he said, "I swear I cut through all the way around."

"I'll try something," Nilsson said. He called out the names of some of his men. "Be ready to fire on anything coming out. If nothing does, the rest of you, follow me inside." He gripped his rifle by the barrel and went three rungs up the ladder. High enough. He pushed his rifle butt against the hatch.

The hatch slid inward. A booming *clang* sounded through the opened hatchway, then silence.

"Cover team, stand down." Nilsson reversed the rifle in his hands and climbed up. With one hand, he clutched a grab bar inside the hatchway, and with that handhold, pulled himself into the thopter. The rest of his maneuver team followed.

In Tomas' faceplate, his helmet overlaid the outlines of the men inside on his view of the thopter. Their voices crossed the platoon net. "Secure."

"Secure."

Near the thopter's nose, a man said, "Cockpit? Secure."

"Check feet." The outlines of men hesitated near the middle of the thopter.

"Step lively."

"Careful, careful."

"What the hell is that?" said a man near the thopter's rear.

Nilsson drew in a long breath. "I have not a damn clue. Ell-tee will tell us. Keep going!"

After more chatter in the platoon net, Nilsson spoke again. "Ell-tee, thopter is secure. If you would, come on up. All the way back. There's stuff we need you to see."

Tomas climbed up the ladder and in. He stood in a narrow walkway defined by bulkheads to either side. In the middle of the left-hand wall, an open doorway led to the cockpit. At the end of the right-hand wall, another open doorway gave access to the thopter's main cabin. A few pinholes pierced the right-hand wall, and intense heat had softened its base into a rippling pattern. Along the wall's base, spent firefighting foam crumbled into powder, and some added itself to the haze of foam particles suspended in the air. Tomas sneezed.

The thopter's interior stank of burnt meat.

We got one of them.

But Nilsson's scouts have seen men burned to death, haven't they? What do they want to show me? Something more horrific than usual, that their consciences want to off-load onto an officer?

Tomas went forward, over the uneven footing of the fallen hatch. He glanced to the left, into the cockpit, then double-took.

The only thing that made it a *cockpit* was its size and location at the thopter's nose. No windows, no displays, no control surfaces, no keypads or keyboards. Not even any apparent camera or micro-phone for a computerized autopilot to pick up visual or verbal com-mands. Just a small, rounded room of bare walls. One of Nilsson's scouts knelt inside. With a knife blade, he pried at a panel in the wall.

Tomas went in. "Fill me in, soldier."

After a quick glance over his shoulder, the scout resumed his task. Effort strained his voice. "My sensors picked up a magnetic field under here. Induced by a trickle of electrical current. It's the only electrical activity left on the thopter." The scout grunted, and the panel popped off.

Inside, held in place on the end of a telescoping arm, rested a keyboard with a small built-in video display. The scout reached for it—

"Leave it alone," Tomas said.

"Sir?"

A mix of half-remembered physics from school on Joséphine and coursework in OCS came to Tomas. "There might be a data store connected to that keyboard, right?"

"Yeah, sure."

"Intel would want that data store intact, right?"

The scout leaned his weight back on his ankles. "Of course, sir. I see that. You're saying me touching this keyboard could do something to the stored data?"

"The electrical current might mean a processor can pick up inputs from the keyboard. Iago and Claudius might have rigged the system to wipe the data store if the wrong key is touched. Or if the panel is opened."

In the image of the scout's face overlaid in Tomas' faceplate on the scout's cee-skinned head, the man's eyebrows lurched upward. His voice came hurriedly. "Sir, I didn't think—"

"Neither did I. Don't touch anything else. Intel will get what it can."

Tomas took a last look around the room—one narrow bunk folded into a niche in the bulkhead to the right of the door, with a locked drawer built into the bulkhead below it—then went deeper into the thopter. The fuselage formed a single space, filled with jumbled and scorched equipment. Holes riddled the doors and walls of metal cases. Thick stainless steel, combined with dense arrays of coils and fins mounted low on some of the cases' walls, indicated much of the equipment had been refrigerated.

In the middle of the thopter, a fist-sized hole in the ceiling let in double beams of light from the L4 and L5 mirrors. Above the reactor mounted in the thopter's belly, a large section of the floor had burned away, showing melted alloy ribs dusted with firefighting foam like snow fallen on a fence. Tomas eyed the damage, and skills implanted in fighting vehicle command school helped him assess it. The armor-piercing jet of molten metal had led to a hydrogen fire in the thopter's belly, either by directly rupturing and igniting the hydrogen tank or by wrecking the failsafes and heating the area around a vent or valve.

Along with the odors of melted plastic and heated metal, the stench of burnt flesh came more strongly.

Nilsson's men had turned a rope ladder on its side and stretched it into a vee shape, running from the ceiling forward of the gap in the floor to a spot of adhesive on one of the structural ribs, then back up again to the ceiling near the thopter's rear. The rope ladder traversed half a dozen ribs, each of which had a half-meter length swept clean by passing boots. Tomas turned sideways. He extended his feet from rib to rib, his hands from rope ladder rung to rung. Below him, parts of the dead reactor still glowed in the infrared. He sweated even before his helmet popped a high temperature warning into his vision.

At the back of the thopter, Tomas took two steps onto intact flooring before letting go of the rope ladder.

Faceplates up, Nilsson and two other scouts waited near a couple of large pieces of intact equipment. They stood near a stainless steel sarcophagus. A medical tank. The way Nilsson and the other scouts held themselves back from the medical tank, it served some other purpose. Presumably something visible in the large metal case near it made that purpose clear.

Tomas drew in a breath before stepping forward. "What's Papa done this time?"

Nilsson slowly turned his head. His face held a stark look. He lifted his hand toward a window on the face of the large case. "We hope you can tell us."

Tomas lifted his faceplate and leaned toward the case. He cupped his right hand around his eye. The edge of his hand touched cool glass and blocked stray reflections from the beams of mirror light. Even so, he could barely see inside the case. Dim shapes, smaller than soccer balls and with lumpier surfaces. With his left hand he patted his zip pockets, trying to remember which one held a penlight—

Hard plastic touched his left hand. "Here you go, sir," Nilsson said.

Tomas thanked him. Penlight on, press the bulb against the glass, and take a look.

Faces with slack muscles and gouged-out eyes stared back at him. The heads looked shrunken, dried out... no... there was no head underneath. Just faces and scalps, like masks, hanging loosely on an array of rounded knobs. The faces and scalps lacked eyes and teeth. They included lips, noses, ears, and hair.

Filaments emerged from under each skin mask. Their tips stuck to the cut edge of the skin. A tissue maintenance device, Tomas guessed, presumably failed from lack of electrical power. The intel dossier on Papa capabilities had told him nothing about biological technologies.

Tomas flicked the penlight beam around the inside of the case. Near the bottom he found a familiar face. Though the thawing conditions made all the faces pallid with purple mottles, one looked even more pale than the others. Bright red hair topped it. Iago, as revealed by the brain scan of the last prisoner in the Sycorax Hills.

And the other face? Hair curly and brown, if Tomas remembered right. Mounted on a shorter body, so he expected a more round face.

Shorter?

An intuition crystallized in his subconscious and bubbled up. Even height could be changed. Tomas realized the other cases held arms and legs.

The face you labeled 'Claudius' won't be here. The medic got its description from genomic analysis.

That was the face Iago was born with.

Tomas stepped back from the case and turned his attention to the radio. "Sgt. Svoboda, we've got a big job for you inside the thopter. The Papa operative left biological materials we need to get to company headquarters before they rot. They're stored in freezer cases we damaged during the fight. If you can fix the cases, great, but if not, get their contents on ice. If you can't do that, preserve them as best you can. Once the biological materials are stable, figure out how to get the thopter back to company. If you have to call the company SSC platoon for a flatbed with off-road tires, make the call. If you can do all that, you'll have given us a huge intelligence windfall."

"We'll be right there, ell-tee," Svoboda said.

Tomas rubbed his eyes. The remembered masks of skin stared at him from inside his eyelids.

"Ell-tee?" Nilsson asked. "Did we hear you say, 'Papa operative?' There's only one?"

Thumb pointed at the case, Tomas said, "These are his disguises."

Nilsson frowned, puzzled. "How—?"

"I don't know, either. That's why we need Svoboda to preserve as much of this as possible, and get the thopter back to company."

Nilsson peered at the case. "Captain Bao won't have it very long. Something this big, brigade headquarters in Belmont will want to see."

Brigade headquarters. Workplace of whoever had ordered Bravo company to foul up near Eastcheap. Tomas looked at the array of skin masks inside the case without seeing them.

A treacherous officer at brigade headquarters could do far worse than send a few men to their graves.

Even if you knew by name an officer who committed treason, what can you do about it here? Nothing.

"It will indeed, sergeant. It will indeed."

10

The Road to Belmont

A vibration from his wristwatch woke Tomas. Diffuse blocks of light came through the partially opaque windows of the male junior officers' bunkhouse. In the bunkhouse's open interior, beds with tightly-tucked sheets, and plastic chests with drawer locks blinking red, showed Landon and the company's staff officers had already risen and left for their day's duties.

His wristwatch vibrated again. He leaned over the side of his bed and pulled out his tablet from underneath. A notification window on the tablet provided more details.

Meet Capt. Bao in comm room, asap.

Tomas yawned, blinked. He made his bed, then rummaged in the drawers for a clean uniform and garrison cap. After dressing and setting the uniform's cee-skin to woodland camouflage, he left the bunkhouse.

A late-summer morning had come. In the sky, both mirrors had reached their full daytime reflectiveness. Their rays already made Tomas sweat and squint as he crossed the company's main base. The mirrors themselves showed elongated ovals, rather than the rounder shapes of the previous day. By evening it would be cool. By tomorrow it would be autumn.

The sights and sounds of activity drifted to Tomas from a

distance—the crack of bat and ball from the cricket field, Sgt. Khudobin calling the cadence as his platoon jogged a track ringing the PT facility, mechanical grinding and tearing from the SSC warehouse next to the company's main fab.

Near the latter sat his prize. A huge tarp covered Iago's thopter, yet the aircraft's shape could not be mistaken. The thopter remained on the flatbed trailer on which an SSC team had carried it back from the battlefield near the abandoned camp. Glimmers of motion told Tomas that men in cee-skin set to transparent guarded the thopter, the only men wearing transparent cee-skin in the entire base.

Iago would want his thopter back.

So too would his masters in orbit.

The offices of the headquarters platoon crouched in silence behind bermed dirt, sandbags, and cee-skin. The only motion outside them came from an infantryman in woodland camouflage standing guard at the entrance, who snapped a salute as Tomas approached.

Inside, under the glow of fluorescent panels, Tomas found the comm room. Door ajar, he rapped his knuckles on the frame surrounding the translucent glass panel. "Neumann reporting, sir."

"Come on in."

Tomas pushed open the door. Capt. Bao occupied one of the chairs facing the main videoconferencing equipment. He looked over his shoulder with a wince. "Sorry to have to wake you. I meant what I said about you deserving to sleep in."

"0645 is late enough to wake up." Tomas glanced past the captain, at the videoconference display and the spines of cameras and microphones mounted just above it. "Battalion wants to talk to us?"

Bao shook his head. Tomas read the gravity in the gesture before the captain said, "Brigade."

Tomas' chest tightened as he drew in his next breath. "Do we know who?"

"Col. Healey, brigade executive officer, and Maj. Tatarinova, intelligence officer."

"They aren't officially in the chain of command to direct our deployments...." Tomas trailed off.

"Or Bravo Company's?" Bao's face looked shrewd. "There might be a whole cabal at Brigade out to give this planet to Papa. Either or both of Healey or Tatarinova could be part of it. Be careful what you tell them."

"I will. Why are they calling? The Papa thopter?"

"The fact Healey is on the line and they're skipping battalion HQ to talk straight to us tells me they have something more than an attaboy for you. Ready to open the link?"

Tomas took an empty seat facing the videoconference equipment. He shifted his weight in search of a more comfortable position on the seat's thin padding, but couldn't find one. He gave up when the display started counting down 3... 2... 1....

Healey sat tall. He'd let a few gray hairs grow at his temples to accent a grizzled brown mass of hair. He peered down his narrow nose. "Captain, lieutenant, good morning. We want to start our conversation with Maj. Tatarinova asking you about the bird you captured yesterday."

"Of course, sir," Capt. Bao said. "Major, what would you like to know?"

Tatarinova wore wheat-yellow hair pulled back in a bun. Her gaze pierced out from the screen. "Were you involved in the operation, Capt. Bao?"

"I authorized Lt. Neumann to reconnoiter suspected Papa activity and engage if he saw fit. I then directed our SSC element to retrieve the thopter from the field."

Her voice took on a frosty edge. "In other words, you were not involved in the operation."

"No, ma'am."

"Thank you for clarifying," she said. "I'll direct my further questions to Lt. Neumann." She turned her attention to Tomas. "Though your report is rather thorough, I need more information." Her imperious blue eyes glanced down at some off-screen notes. "Lieutenant, you mentioned the discovery of computer systems on board the thopter. However, it is not clear whether you tried accessing those systems in the field."

"We did not. One of the men cracked open an access panel to a manual data entry device, but I stopped him before he touched anything. It occurred to me Papa might rig his computer systems to delete their contents in response to attempts at unauthorized access. I emphasized that point to the men."

"Very good." Her gaze followed a checklist. "You stated a conclusion that among the thopter's equipment damaged in the engagement were holding tanks for reversibly graftable legs. On what did you base that conclusion?"

"In view of the intact heads and the damaged tank of arms we found, it seemed likely Iago had a tank of legs, as well." Tomas' throat felt dry. "Further, we have intel that Iago may manifest at different heights, which head and arm swapping could not achieve."

Tatarinova's gaze scolded him. "Next time, lieutenant, let my team draw the conclusions. You provide us the facts."

"Yes, ma'am." Tomas arched his back to let his uniform separate from the sweaty skin between his shoulder blades.

She asked for a few more details regarding the thopter's damaged interior. Tomas answered truthfully. Even if she spied for Papa, any lies he might tell to misinform her would be exploded once someone from her team took a close look inside the thopter.

After expressing satisfaction with his answers, she leaned back and nodded to Healey.

He cleared his throat. "Captain, lieutenant, as you can probably guess, we want the bird brought to Belmont."

"It's still loaded on the flatbed we used to bring it from the field," Bao said.

"Great," Col. Healey said. "One thing to bear in mind. Presumably, Iago wants it recovered or destroyed. He might have data on board he doesn't want Maj. Tatarinova to extract. We would also get a public affairs boon if we display it to the Ardenites living in Belmont."

"We completely agree," Bao said. "We've guarded it the entire time we've held it."

Healey went on. "Of course. You may not see it, living and working in the countryside as you do, but ultimately, the plebiscite comes down to Belmont. Forty percent of all Ardenese live within twenty klicks of the space elevator base. We have a strong presence here, and the rebels are inactive. Polling suggests we have a clear majority of Belmont's residents on our side, however, there's enough sympathy here for Papa that, if you add it to the swaths of the countryside where the rebels have the upper hand, the planet-wide plebiscite will be a close thing."

"You have a bigger picture than we do," said Capt. Bao.

"We're not running down you, your company, Lt. Neumann, or his platoon. You're both doing yeoman's work out there to keep the rebels from intimidating those small towns into voting for Papa. That's important. But the biggest bang for the buck will come here in Belmont."

Healey gestured at someone off-screen. "We're already setting up with the local government a pro-Confederated Worlds rally." Over the video feed of Healey and Tatarinova appeared a flyer. Ardenese text in a color scheme of Confederated Worlds red-white-and-blue. Music, ceremonies honoring Ground Force, soliloquies from several Shakespeare plays, and speeches by the governor and Brigadier Ibáñez. Taking place in Confederation Square, between the governor's mansion and Arden Parliament House, at noon next Oneday.

"We expect thousands of Belmont residents to attend." The flyer disappeared from the screen. "Putting the bird on display as part of the rally would show the locals that Papa's efforts to suborn the plebiscite are increasing, yet failing. That makes us look like the stronger horse. Plus, we'll gin up some disgust regarding Iago's body part swapping equipment. Summing up, we want the bird brought here. With a security detail."

Bao looked thoughtful. "I'll talk with my platoon commanders. I can spare a platoon for the day it would take to deliver it and bring it back."

Col. Healey raised his eyebrow. He gestured at Tomas. "There's no need to talk to anyone. Lt. Neumann is the clear choice."

Just as Beauchamp and McClernan were north of Eastcheap? Tomas read from Capt. Bao's features that he had similar thoughts.

Bao said, "That would ultimately be Col. Rogers' decision." The brigade's operations officer, the one who formally directed unit deployments.

"Yes, yes. Operations already approved. They will send you the official word after we end our call."

"Sir, if I may. Neumann's platoon has seen a lot of action the past tenday. They're the most understrength of my platoons and their vehicles are overdue for maintenance. I would suggest we give Lt. Neumann and his men a rest. Instead, I could send Sgt. Khudobin's platoon to escort the thopter to Belmont. They're the freshest platoon I have, and they would greatly benefit from some light field work, which a security escort would provide—"

Healey shook his head. "That won't do. We need Neumann. You saw from the flyer that we're honoring Ground Force personnel? Lt. Neumann's platoon will be among them."

The thought of being a center of attention in a dog and pony show made Tomas wince. "Sir? I don't know that I've done anything commendable."

"You bagged Iago's bird, didn't you?"

"You'll have it on display. I don't think my presence would add—"

"People need heroes, lieutenant."

"Sir, all I've done is sit in the turret and tell men what to do. If I look heroic, it's because the entire platoon executed to the fullest."

Healey smiled. Perhaps he tried to look avuncular, but the smile failed to reach his eyes. It looked like a mask intended solely to persuade. "You want your men to get the credit they deserve. Don't worry. They will. We know every man has done his duty to the utmost. Your record since Iago came down jacob's ladder shows it."

Memories of self-doubt and poor leadership from the time before he led Nilsson through the Peters-Stein technique filled Tomas. He raised his hand while his mind sought the right words of protest—

"And I'm not talking about capturing the bird. Your platoon scored an intelligence success in the Sycorax Hills. You'd agree, major?"

Tatarinova mused for a moment, then nodded.

"And your—" Healey looked somewhere off-screen. A muffled voice said something. He nodded and turned back to Tomas. "That's the name. Nilsson. He kept his team and some ArChars from getting gunned down by those Papa robots. Robots." Disgust creased his face for a moment. "We have to be careful how we play that to the Ardenites, but still, it's heroism. Civil affairs will dress it in that Harry England and St. George business and the locals will buy it."

Healey refocused on Tomas. "I haven't even gotten to the best part. You showed a lot of initiative in the woods north of Eastcheap. You saved at least one of Bravo's platoons and severely damaged rebel capabilities in that region." He leaned forward and put on a look of false chumminess. "Plus, Capt. Carlton's first response was to write you up for failure to follow his orders. Just between the four of us, that's another point in your favor."

Tomas drew in a breath to buy a little time. "Thank you, sir, for the compliments. I do take the view, though, that my platoon and I were only doing our jobs."

"Which makes you and them even more worthy of commendation. It's settled, gentlemen. Lt. Neumann's platoon will escort Iago's bird to Belmont. We want to see it here before sunset today. That assumes the rebels won't delay you in any attempt to get the bird back."

Healey raised a finger. "Now, I understand your concerns about rest and refit. We'll take care of that. Once here, we'll give you top priority for fab cycles, and your men will have a few days to relax. When did they last visit the Daughters of Astarte? When did you?"

New Liberty. He would never forget Persephone's narrow room. He thought of Lissa, and guilt warmed his cheeks—

"Don't tell me. I don't need to know. Now, the major might—"

Businesslike, Tatarinova shook her head. "If I needed that information for my dossier on the lieutenant, I would have it by now." She gave Tomas an implacable look that, for a moment, convinced him she did have it.

"Quite," Healey said. "Back to business. Lt. Neumann, you have about thirteen hours to get here. That should be enough time at highway speeds, even if you take a circuitous route. Assuming the rebels don't block you along the way. That's all we have. Captain, lieutenant, anything further?"

"No, sir," Bao said. The communications staff at brigade ended the call. The screen darkened.

Tomas stood and faced Capt. Bao. "I'll get my men ready for this assignment. We can roll out within an hour. Anything further?"

Bao stroked his chin and stared at the dark display. "Tell your sergeants what to do, and trust them to get their men ready. I want you back in this room as soon as you can to call ArChar units whose zones you'll be driving through along the way."

"For what purpose?"

"We should assume Iago has bounced a message off his orbital assets to every rebel between here and Belmont. To get the thopter there in one piece—and more important, to get your platoon there in one piece too—we want to route you around any rebel hotspots. The ArChars should know what those are."

Tomas nodded.

"Also, will you want help? You have an undermanned platoon. If the ArChar units could add some of their vehicles and men to your escort, that might dissuade small rebel formations from engaging you."

"That's a suggestion?" Tomas asked. "Not an order?"

Bao looked glum. "I don't trust all my fellow officers at brigade headquarters. How can I trust an ArChar? I'll leave it to you."

Tomas thought out loud. "Papa in orbit will see the thopter when we're driving. They'll know we're heading to Belmont and they'll alert any rebels near our line of travel. If we stay away from rebel hotspots, then we won't need the Constabulary to ride with us. It's only if our line of travel has to go through rebel country that we would want the Constabulary alongside."

With a sour face, Bao said, "It's rebel country where the ArChars are most likely to be traitors."

Tomas angled his head in thought. "Even if they were traitors, they don't want to die, at the rebels' hands, or ours. I'll order them to ride in screening positions. If the rebels attack the formation, they wouldn't spare any allies they have in the Constabulary if they could recapture or destroy the thopter."

Bao bobbed his head in agreement. "Good idea. One last thing before you alert your sergeants. If it comes down to saving the thopter or saving your platoon, save the platoon. Tatarinova already has an intel report on the thopter. More intel would just be extra sauce. I need you and your men whole and healthy for the next two weeks. After the plebiscite, I want you all to go home and live long and fulfilling lives. Too many of us haven't."

A cool, quiet feeling rotated inside Tomas' abdomen. The captain's words called up memories of men who'd died on New Liberty, and men who'd died here. "I hear you, sir. If you'll excuse me?"

Bao's face hinted at the same sort of feeling. "I'll wait here for you."

The memories clung to Tomas' awareness as he made his way out of the headquarters building. He accepted their presence, but he lacked the time to fully experience them. Outside, he took a moment to offer them up to the twin ovals of sunlight to east and west. They seemed to evaporate in the bright day, to condense somewhere in the cooler and darker recesses of his subconscious. From there they could return, at the proper time.

Not now. He breathed deeply into his belly, then strode toward his platoon's bunkhouses, in search of O'Herlihy and Nilsson.

11

GFB Belmont

Within twenty hours after arriving at brigade headquarters with the captured thopter, the mood at GFB Belmont oppressed Tomas.

The effect on him started after rolling in through the main gate. Knots of MPs held up his platoon and the flatbed truck holding Iago's thopter while they bickered about which route his platoon should follow to the intelligence company's warehouse. When the platoon finally arrived there, Tomas found Maj. Tatarinova waiting, her mouth pursed in impatience. In a cool voice, occasionally masked by clanging alloy and the shouts of men working to unload the thopter, she asked him questions about the journey.

"No trouble. We routed around rebel hotspots. I'm sure Papa in orbit saw us, but looks like they couldn't get their lackeys on the ground in position to try recapturing the thopter." Tension bled out of his shoulders. The major seemed more personable now than she had during the videoconference early that morning.

Her voice remained aloof. "Tell me what happened yesterday when you tried to log into the thopter's computer system."

"Log in? No one in my platoon ever tried." He squinted. "Didn't I answer that this morning?"

"I'll ask the questions, lieutenant." She lowered her eyebrows.

Tomas shuffled a half-step away from her. Sweat dampened the inside of his collar. *Why is she asking the same question? Did I make her suspicious?*

Another part of him answered. *It's her job to be suspicious. And if you ask an unexpected question, a liar might not remember his previous lie before he answers.*

He stood taller. "Pardon me, ma'am. Ask away."

As Tatarinova continued querying him, from behind her, Tomas received more hints of low morale at GFB Belmont. The men wrangling the thopter off the flatbed waited for a crane truck. Although a cee-skin tarp still draped the thopter, no one worked to remove it. Instead, the men leaned against the flatbed or sat at stools near a workbench. Tomas strained to hear them without disregarding Maj. Tatarinova.

"Where's that crane?" someone asked.

"What? You're in a hurry? Let's hope the crane truck needs a part they can't fab till tomorrow."

"Hell. You think—" The first man's voice dropped as he glanced at the major. "—Maria Martinetta will take 'technical difficulties' for an answer? If the crane doesn't come soon, we'll get ordered to lift the thopter to the ground with our own damned hands."

The crane truck arrived moments later. The men roused themselves with grumbles. They took longer to release the cee-skin tarp from tie-down brackets on the flatbed's edge than they should have. Three men rolled up the tarp unevenly and dropped it along the side of the warehouse.

After the crane arm swung into place over the thopter, men on the flatbed rigged chains from the crane down the sides of the thopter, then crawled underneath to connect the chains with carabiners. They worked with a combination of speed and inattention that made Tomas grit his teeth. Excess chains clanked on the flatbed and flopped like dead snakes.

"...no more questions, lieutenant. A clerk should be along shortly to guide you and your men to your bunks." Maj. Tatarinova glanced at her wristwatch. Angry surprise flashed in her eyes. "He should be here already."

The crane lifted the thopter. As it swung the thopter over the flatbed, an excess in one of the chains caught on a tie-down bracket.

"Hey!" Tomas yelled. He waved his arms at the crane truck's driver.

The crane kept moving. The motion of the thopter pulled the caught chain straight, then tight. The carabiner holding that chain with its mate from the other side of the thopter came loose. The second chain rattled like a downpour on a metal roof when it hit the warehouse's concrete floor. The other sets of chains holding the thopter groaned. The aircraft shuddered and dropped, pulling the crane arm with it.

Maj. Tatarinova stalked toward the crane truck's cab. "Stop! *Mudak*, stop! What the hell are you doing? *Pizdets*!"

The cab cab door swung open and the driver climbed down to the floor. He held out his palms to her. "Major, I didn't hook the chains up! Blame those idiots!" He waggled his hand at the men near the flatbed.

"I'll blame every last one of you. *Ldi na khuy*! If you want to see sunlight during the rest of your duty on Arden, get the thopter down on the ground in one piece!"

The clerk finally arrived. He cast wary glances at Maj. Tatarinova as she continued to berate the warehouse crew. Though no one knew the meaning of her Russo-Gardariki exclamations, their undoubtable obscenity made the clerk wince. He hurried Tomas out of the warehouse to discuss the bivouac plan away from the major.

After getting the platoon's vehicles and men settled for the night, the clerk led Tomas to a male officers' dormitory. A one-story building of concrete block, the dormitory had a single long corridor, off which branched shorter hallways with four rooms on each side and a communal restroom at the end. Down one of the hallways, the clerk pointed. "Last door on the right. Follow me, sir."

Before he reached his room, Tomas passed an open door on the left. Raucous voices burst out of it. He glanced in.

In the space vacated by a folded-up murphy bed, six lieutenants crowded around a rickety table piled with playing cards, poker chips, ashtrays, and beer bottles. The lieutenant facing the door looked up, his eyebrows as bushy as woolly caterpillars. "Mate, deal you in?" he called.

"Thanks, no," Tomas replied, over the clank of glass on clay chips and some ball-busting chatter. "I just got onto base and it's been a long couple of weeks in the field. I'm going to turn in."

"Just got onto base?" another poker player asked. His face tapered to the tip of his nose. "You're with the unit that captured the Papa operative's thopter?"

Tomas nodded. "That was my platoon."

The chatter around the table quieted. In the silence, another lieutenant picked up a cigar between thick fingers and puffed on it. "You too good to lose money to us pogeys, is that it?" Smoke curled out of his mouth and nose.

The poker player with the tapered face glowered at the cigar smoker. "I'm no pogey. I've led my platoon in the field—"

"We're all pogeys to Gunner von Gunnerson." The smoker pointed the lighted end of the cigar toward Tomas. "He thinks if he's the little butterbar that could, he'll keep his commission when the brass start shitcanning the rest of us."

Tomas folded his arms and leaned against the doorjamb. "What are you talking about?"

"Don't play that country mouse act on me," the cigar smoker said. He puffed a cloud of blue-tinged smoke in Tomas' direction.

"You don't get much R-mail in the field?" said the lieutenant with the bushy eyebrows. R-mail, the rumor mill, scuttlebutt. "The brass need scapegoats. They can't admit they lost the war. So they'll blame the defeat on junior officers."

"Just on GFA grads," someone said.

"More like, just on you slotted dicks," muttered the poker player with the tapered face.

"Christ and the robbers," another man said. He shot annoyed looks around the room. "It's not about scapegoats. There's a secret codicil in the armistice. GF has to cut its active duty personnel in half, or Papa will resume hostilities."

The cigar smoker turned his glower away from Tomas. "Secret codicils? That's a two minute minor for talking out of your ass. Goddam, think. If Papa cut GF in half, we'd be so weak, they'd resume hostilities anyway."

"Like we matter," said the slotted dick. "If Space Force is strong enough, we could be disbanded and Papa would do nothing. If Space Force is too weak, we could conscript every male citizen and Papa would still win."

"Shit," said the poker player with the tapered face. "Hey, slotted dick, which strap-on does Shirley Foxtrot use when she pegs you?"

The lieutenant with the bushy eyebrows pitched his voice to cut through the conversations. "Enough." He looked up at Tomas. "If poker's not your thing, at least stay ten minutes and have a beer."

"Thanks, but I don't drink."

Another silence ensued. The man with the tapered face broke it. "You don't have to insult us."

The cigar smoker eyed Tomas. "You're serious? No shit? Huh." To the bickering men around the table, he said, "Gunner von Gunnerson is drunk on ambition. Fuck him. Whose deal?"

In the hallway, the clerk cleared his throat. Tomas let him lead the way to his assigned room. Full bed, a small kitchenette stocked with a fresh loaf of bread and sandwich meat, entertainment console with headphones and wraparound glasses. Tomas shut the door and climbed into bed. Nearly eleven. He closed his eyes—

For the next three hours, poker players on their way to and from the restroom slammed their palms on his door, rousing him from shallow sleep.

The next morning, similar attitudes dogged him through his PT routine, breakfast at the officer's mess, and his meetings with rec center personnel and vehicle maintenance crews. In the repair shed, one of the mechanics ran his gloved hand over Badger One's patched and dented right side. He spoke softly to the vehicle as he went. "Poor baby. Carrying men into harm's way and getting fired on for nothing. How many of those men didn't come back? Arden's not worth it. I wish the orificers would see that...." The mechanic looked sheepish when he realized Tomas had overheard.

"Arden may not be worth it," Tomas said, "but Ground Force is. I only ask you give me, and her—" He tapped his hand on the hull. "—work you can be proud of."

The mechanic mumbled, "Yes, sir." He avoided Tomas' gaze.

The presence of others failed to brighten his mood. A few Constabulary officers and men in powder blue uniforms hurried along. From their expressions as they glanced his way, they recognized him, but all avoided him. Rebel sympathizers disheartened at the capture of Iago's thopter? Or loyalists who anticipated, from the mood of the GF personnel around them, Papa victory in the plebiscite and re-education camps for them and their families under the new regime?

By the end of lunch, Tomas wanted to get away from people. An autumn wind sighed across the base, bringing with it rain clouds like bruises in the southern sky. Someplace quiet and indoors. The poker players might be lounging around his hallway at the officers' dormitory. The rec center would be too crowded.

An odd thought came to him. He strode toward the chapel under the encroaching clouds. He opened its door as the first fat raindrops splatted on his shoulders.

The vestibule bore thin gray carpet and corner tables holding vases of drooping flowers. Notecards said the flowers had been given by the local chapter of the Constabulary officers' wives' association. The only sounds came from the whisper of the ventilation system and the panging of rain on the roof. He crossed to a tablet mounted on the wall near a pair of doors leading to the chapel proper. As he expected, the afternoon schedule was free of organized services, and at that time, no one used it for informal worship or meditation.

A thousand years before, a few hundred communities of intense belief had left Earth to build new worlds away from the gleaming hedonic maw of virtual reality. The vast expenses of slower-than-light interstellar travel to, and terraforming of, the lifeless worlds of all known extrasolar suns represented costs so high that no export to Earth could pay for them. Only communities that sought infinite, transcendent benefits—a heaven, or a utopia—would pay those costs. Those communities had terraformed and settled each of the Confederated Worlds, and those of the Unity, and those of the Progressive Republic, and perhaps even others in deeper space, all in the service of higher callings: the rejuvenation of an old, settled religion; the rebirth of a long-dead one; or the raising to spiritual import of one's ethny or one's culture.

It said something about the human condition, that the descendants of those pious founders were now as secular as the people of the Earth walled up in the technological catatonia of virtual fugue.

Enough philosophy. 'Wise talk is plain; beautiful talk is foolish.' Tomas swiped through the tablet's menus for the controls to the chapel's décor. With the touch of a button, he could summon symbols and artwork to most of the surface area of the chapel's walls, tailored for any of the religious communities recognized by the Ground Force's chaplaincy.

...Manichean, Conservative.

Manichean, Reformed.

Mithraist.

Observer.

Orthodox, Russian.

Orthodox, Syrian....

Tomas tapped the *Observer* button, then went through submenus relating to various meditations. He specified one particular image he wanted displayed. An hourglass icon spun on the tablet's display, then froze with a ping and a glow of light. *Décor ready.*

He pulled open a door to the chapel proper. A small space, it could seat perhaps forty, in two banks of pews on either side of a center aisle. Smaller than the amphitheater at his mother's rectory on Joséphine, but, he assumed, about as well attended.

Also like home, an image of a gas giant loomed behind the podium. Here, though, not Napoléon, primary of Joséphine, but rather Prospero, as seen from a high latitude of Arden a thousand kilometers beyond the northernmost Ardenite settlement. A virtual image, assembled by computers from binary data. Though consciously he had long since set aside his mother's extreme tenets about recorded or synthesized audio and video, a sense of wrongness still set some of his mind's parts to shivering.

He took a breath and studied the image of Prospero. Between glittering portions of the Ariel Band, the gas giant turned to the display its darkened face. Prospero's shadow turned the central swath of the Ariel Band from diamond to coal.

He sat in the front pew. Eyes closed, he paid attention to his breaths. His thoughts churned and led his mind down rabbit trails, until he remembered himself and gently brought his mind back. Did he even remember how to meditate...? *come back.* The bad attitudes.... *come back.* Iago and the rebels want us dead.... *come back.* My parents.... *come back. Come back. Come back....*

With a start, his attention returned to the chapel. Lamps along the walls had brightened, and the image of Prospero had progressed at time-lapse speed to show a half-full face. The Ariel Band glittered through its full visible width.

Tomas took a last breath, then rose to leave.

A Constabulary officer sat in the back pew. He had a down-turned mouth and large eyes underlaid with purplish bags, which together gave him an air of recent worry. When had he come in? Clearly he waited for Tomas. Why?

Slowly, Tomas approached. The Constabulary officer stood up.

"Lt. Neumann, prithee, I wouldst have a word. Throckmorton, I am clept, of the rank of cornet. Attachéd I am to the Constabulary's planetary command, with particular duties to liaise with thy brigade's headquarters." Cornet Throckmorton extended his hand.

Tomas shook it. "I'll talk with you. Perhaps we should move elsewhere—"

"Good sir, an it shan't defame a place sacred to thee, I'dst rather we spoke here."

"I am an Observer. To those of my tradition, the sacred doesn't lie in places and things." And if Tomas assumed the chapel almost never had visitors, Cornet Throckmorton would know it for a fact.

"Marry, marry. Then, an it please thee, perhaps we couldst sit?"

Thee, not *you.* The cornet used the Ardenese informal second-person pronoun. Did Throckmorton think himself Tomas' friend? Or did he want Tomas to think that? Tomas sat in one of the nearby pews, then scooted to make room for Cornet Throckmorton. Once the cornet had settled, Tomas asked, "What do you have to tell me?"

Throckmorton spoke in a low voice. "Good sir, marry, but I

have news most foul I must tell. Yesternight there came to me a brother Constabulary officer, his face maskéd. He spoke to me with pompous words of 'freedom' and 'independence.' Though he naméd not the Progressive Republic, plain it was he sought to sunder the bonds between Arden and the Confederated Worlds and launch our planet into a new orbit round Papa's realm."

The ventilation system kicked in. The noise widened Cornet Throckmorton's eyes and lifted his gaze to the ceiling. Warm air whispered out of the vents. After a moment, he turned his gaze back to Tomas. "Needless to say, I fearéd what could befall me were I to cross him. For a brother Constabulary officer to mix himself in treachery made clear to me he could enact all manner of stealthy violence. I replied as noncommittally as I could. He took it as assent. He invited me to a meeting of the Constabulary's like-minded officers, to be held tonight. He gave a location in Belmont's finest neighborhood, though I am certain that is only a drop-point from which I would be taken to the true undercroft. I fearéd I had come in so deep I couldst not refuse to meet."

A faint smile glimmered on Cornet Throckmorton's face. "Though I did best him in one way. As I have said, he maskéd himself, but he spoke much and I have a strong ear for voices. I mark him as Ensign Redvers, a staff officer of the Belmont Constabulary."

Tomas studied the cornet's face. He seemed sincere, and why would he lie? "Why did you seek me out to share this news?"

"Thy reputation proceeds thee, good sir. Thou hast met my cousin—Constable Turner of Eltham."

Eltham lay days, and a huge psychic gulf, in the past. "I don't follow."

"When he spoke of thee, it was of an officer committed to do all things to the letter of rule and custom. Clearly to him thou wart posesséd of exceeding loyalty to the cause of the Confederated Worlds. Thy triumphs against the rebel ambuscade near Eastcheap and in the capture of Iago's thopter have further augmented thy reputation as an officer of merit."

"I'm also a lieutenant in an armored grenadier company. Why did you come to me with this news, and not someone in the brigade staff? Or Maj. Tatarinova?"

Cornet Throckmorton's eyes tightened. "Thou knowest not?"

"I know morale around here is low. It seems every junior officer expects Papa to win the plebiscite, and is too busy ducking his share of the blame to try stopping it. That low morale goes up the ranks?"

"Marry, good sir, but there is so much more. Suspicions I have that blanch mine eyes when the clock strikes oh-dark-thirty, and would freeze thy young blood."

Gooseflesh stippled Tomas' cheeks. "You think some GF officers are in league with Papa." Tomas' mind reeled. A shiver ran over his chest and face. An objection stilled it. "Such a claim demands evidence."

"Indeed," the cornet said. "I would not utter such things to thee had I no inkling of their truth. I shall tell thee this. It came the day prior to your meeting with Captain Carlton in Eastcheap. I had cause to visit thy brigade's operations office. I approachéd the door as a Ground Force enlisted came out, so he held the door for me. In I went, not taking care to be quiet but evenso making little noise whilst I passéd through the waiting area, alone. Then I overheard a man talking in an office down the hall. For I heard only a single voice, I conclude he spoke with another by telephone. He was Ground Force, I must assume, but my familiarity with your voices is so much lower than that with my peers'."

Tomas folded his arms. "What did he say?"

Cornet Throckmorton put on what was meant to be a Confed accent. "'Carlton is to use Beauchamp and McClernan? But their effectiveness and their competency metrics are—Yes, I see. Yes, I will. And Gutierrez to be kept too far back to provide an effective reserve.'"

His next words came in his usual voice. "Alack, I heard no more, for I realizéd I had heard quite enough. I went with mincing steps into the water closet and waited until more voices sounded in the waiting area. When I went off to the duty that brought me there, enough Ground Force personnel were about that none would suspect I had been lurking among them before the first had come in the door."

Tomas leaned back. If the cornet's words could be believed, at least two officers, at least one of them in brigade operations, had ordered Carlton to use his two worst lieutenants in the operation north of Eastcheap. They had wanted defeat.

Defeat meant dead and dying Ground Force soldiers.

At minimum, Throckmorton had overheard ineptitude. At worst, treason.

Tomas reached out and gripped the cornet's upper arm. "Have you told me everything you know about that bit of treachery? Do you know of more incidents like that one?"

"Marry, sir, I do not." Cornet Throckmorton pulled his arm from Tomas' grip. "I have no more to tell thee. I must away before my inattention to my tasks scheduléd for this time is noted. Please, if thou wouldst, remain here five minutes whilst I may amble onward without raising suspicion."

"Yes. Go, cornet. And thank you for coming to me. Better to know bad news than deny it."

Cornet Throckmorton took his leave and slipped out of the pew. Moments later, from the vestibule came the thin thud of the outer door shutting itself.

Behind the podium, Prospero now hung three-quarters full. The thought of resuming his meditation tickled Tomas' mind, but he knew it to be impossible right then. Righteous anger bubbled in his chest.

Hoch. Morgenthau. Shorter. Someone had sent those men to their deaths in an effort to give the planet to Papa.

That someone had to be found, and punished.

By a lieutenant from an armored grenadier company?

If no one could be trusted, who else?

Tomas left the chapel a few minutes later. He paused at the tablet in the vestibule long enough to swipe the tablet to a random setting, *Troth of Midgard, the*, before heading outside.

12

Need to Know

The next morning, Tomas visited the repair sheds to check progress on the vehicles, when his wristwatch vibrated and his tablet buzzed in its holster. *Maj. Tatarinova requests your presence, her office, your earliest convenience.*

His heart thudded. What now? He sent her a stalling reply, the mechanics needed him right then, he would visit later. The reply shamed him as he composed it. Whatever her true loyalty, he would have to face her eventually. He reflected on how best to approach her while the mechanics wrestled alloy sheets and reactive armor blocks into place. Men cursed and welding torches hissed in counterpoint to his thoughts.

His tablet guided him to her office shortly before noon. Her assistant showed him in as soon as he mentioned her name.

Maj. Tatarinova sat at her desk, scrolling and swiping through documents on one tablet and typing notes and drawing arrows one-handed on another. "Sit, please," she said, then kept working for a few more seconds, presumably to finish a thought.

She looked up, her blue eyes as cold as ever. "I need to ask you about a crime that has occurred."

Tomas froze. A crime? "Of course, I will answer, but I've witnessed no crime, and all due respect, isn't criminal investigation the

MPs' bailiwick?"

"Not even the MPs have jurisdiction over this one. No Ground Force personnel were involved, and the crime occurred off-base, in Belmont." She tapped the tablet of documents, spun it, and slid it across her desk. "He was found dead shortly after dawn today, with time of death estimated as about midnight last night. Do you know him?"

Cornet Throckmorton, with the glassy eyes and pallid face of the dead, against a sterile white plastic sheet. Civilian garb—a starched Edwardian collar, creased horizontally—covered his neck. "No. Some local civilian? I don't know any Ardenites living in Belmont."

Tatarinova reached forward and swiped. A photo of Cornet Throckmorton in the Constabulary uniform filled half the screen, with the content of his ID card, name, rank, the rest, taking up the remainder.

Tomas took a moment to speak. "There are quite a few Constabulary I've seen in the countryside and around the base. I can't say if he is, was, one of them."

"You are a capable young officer," Tatarinova said. "I am curious why you choose to lie to me."

"Lie? Major, I—"

"From the late cornet's accounts, we note he paid for his lunch yesterday at the south mess hall within a few minutes of you paying for yours. Soon after, according to his calendar, he attended a meeting on the west side of the base. His fellow attendees say he was five minutes late. In the interim, a security camera noted him going to the east side of the base, near the chapel."

Tomas feigned a shrug. "About lunch, like I said, I've seen quite a few Constabulary around the base. And what does it matter that he took a long way to get to his meeting?"

"Not simply a long way. Had the cornet walked at a firm pace, he could have taken a route from the south mess past the chapel and reached his meeting on time. I have more. As I suspect the cornet knew, and you as well, out of respect for freedom of worship, the chapel is not monitored by cameras or other devices. That said, the facilities staff logs adjustments to the décor. At some point while the cornet would have passed by the chapel, its décor had been set to *Observer*."

After forming a false frown, Tomas swept it from his face with a look of mildly exasperated understanding. "Oh, when I enlisted, I checked that box out of habit. It's been a long time since I've followed my parents' spiritual tradition."

"No doubt."

Tomas' mouth felt dry. "How many Observers are stationed here? Not many, I realize, we tend not to enlist or receive commissions, but I'm sure there are some—"

"Seven, other than you. The whereabouts of four of them during the time in question have been accounted for. Of the other three and you, the circumstances of lunch at the same time as the late cornet, and your recent interaction with—" She peered at the tablet with her notes and connecting arrows. "—his cousin, Constable Turner of Eltham, point to you as being of the greatest interest to him, and within twelve hours of his death."

Tomas sat frozen. The skills imps hadn't slotted into his head anything suitable for this situation. *When do you ask for a lawyer from the JAG—?*

"I have enough evidence to remand you to the custody of the Belmont City Watch," Maj. Tatarinova said. "However, I have no desire to do so. As I said, you are a capable young officer. That you choose to lie to me hints at things I must learn more about."

"He followed me into the chapel. I never saw him before. Or after."

"Yes, thank you for finally telling the truth, but that's of little import." Tatarinova peered at him, and a hint of crow's feet at her eyes heightened the intensity of her gaze. "That you lied suggests you have cause to mistrust brigade headquarters and the brigadier's staff. Including me."

Can you trust her? Dissemble. "Major, there's a lot of R-mail out in the field. It runs rampant when we feel we're risking our lives and losing our friends without guidance from brigade."

Tomas paused before his next words. Could he extract information from the major?

He had no choice but to try.

"For example," Tomas said, "there's a lot of rumor going around about Bravo Company near Eastcheap. Captain Carlton assigned his two most understrength and poorly-led platoons to the operation, while leaving his best platoon in reserve."

Maj. Tatarinova's hand hovered over her note-taking tablet. "Go on."

"Maybe that makes sense. You're familiar with the ancient stories about Napoléon and the Imperial Guard? Of course not, you're not a Josie. Anyway, while Captain Carlton's choice for the reserve could have made sense, he kept them sixty kilometers away. It would have taken them two hours to get to the site where Iago tried to destroy Carlton's other two platoons."

The major looked thoughtful, then scrolled through her notes. "Carlton is the worst company commander in the entire brigade, but if you're saying he willfully guided his two platoons to ruin...." She stared at her notes for a time. When she next spoke, her voice showed the first unease he had ever heard in it. "You're saying he was ordered to do so."

In response to her words and tone, relief bloomed in Tomas. The bloom soon withered. Were she a conspirator, who better than an intelligence officer to have control of her voice sufficient to feign ignorance of it? Tomas carefully selected his next words. "Rumor has it."

She pierced him with her gaze. "The wisest thing you can do is trust me."

"With what?"

"With the facts you conceal. Carlton was ordered to mismanage the operation near Eastcheap. Who ordered him? By the chain of command, the order would have come from Rogers, the operations officer. Though we all know a superior can be gulled by a shrewd subordinate, or that subordinate could pass off an order of his own devise as coming from the superior. If you know something about the operations staff and share that with me, I can focus my inquiries and have a better chance of finding the truth. Or in your mistrust of brigade staff, would you rather do it alone? Untrained and unskilled? Where a single misstep can spook a target and cause intelligence leads to shrivel up?"

Her words made sense. "First tell me what happened to Cornet Throckmorton."

"You bargain with me?"

"Things you tell me might jog my memory of my meeting with the late cornet."

"You do bargain with me. Very well." Maj. Tatarinova reviewed the tablet of files relating to the cornet. "The cornet was found dead in one of Belmont's tony neighborhoods. As you may have surmised from the medical examiner's photo, he was strangled with a garrote while dressed in civilian clothes. The Belmont City Watch has no inkling why he was there or who might have wanted him dead."

Time to tell her what he knew. "When he spoke with me in the chapel, he said a Constabulary officer had approached to invite him into a pro-Papa conspiracy—"

"Who?"

"The man wore a mask, but the cornet claimed to recognize his voice. Ensign Redvers, from the Belmont Constabulary's staff."

The major's eyebrows rose. She quickly typed a one-handed note.

"To avoid rousing the conspirator's suspicions, the cornet agreed to meet him last night in a fine neighborhood of Belmont. The cornet expected the plotters to lead him to the real meeting place."

Tatarinova frowned. "Is that all?"

"Yes."

"Why did he not alert my office?"

Tomas' heart pounded. You've already placed your bet. Time to go all-in. "He was aware of a conspiracy within brigade headquarters. He overheard someone in operations discuss by phone the deployment orders for Capt. Carlton. Those orders were chosen for Carlton to fail. For Ground Force soldiers to die."

"Did he identify the operations staffer? The person on the other end of the call?"

"No and no."

Maj. Tatarinova leaned back. "You have given me good information to work with. While I do so, you must not speak of these matters to anyone. Also, you must not investigate on your own. Do either of those, and you are likely to scare our targets, if they are guilty, or tip off the true guilty parties if they are someone else. Lastly, watch yourself, especially if you go into the city."

"Yes, ma'am."

"Dismissed." Tatarinova turned her attention to her notes before Tomas left the room.

13

Dog and Pony

Later that afternoon, Healey's assistant, a Captain Singh, asked Tomas to come to the executive offices to discuss matters related to the commendation ceremony at the rally. Tomas kept himself from rolling his eyes until after the call ended. A makework meeting about a dog-and-pony show. A stiff wind pushed him across the base under a clear blue sky, to a one-story building made of pre-fabbed modules. The Confederated Worlds and the brigade's flags snapped in the wind and their guidewires panged on their poles. He went inside.

Tomas hung his windbreaker in the reception area, on a rack near a wall of framed still photos and video loops. He stifled a childhood misgiving and looked at the photos and videos. It wasn't the depictions that mattered, after all, but what their selection said about Healey's staff.

Brigadier Ibáñez had the largest photo, in the upper center of the wall, with a long-range shot of the entire brigade on a parade ground almost as large and immediately below. Groups of soldiers held two large banners, one a Confederated Worlds flag, the other showing the brigade's logo and the text 19^{Th}* Armored Grenadier Brigade – Rarely Equaled*.

Tomas read a caption below the brigade's photo. Taken on Challenger, two years ago, at a time when Tomas had ridden in the back of a Badger on New Liberty and OCS had never crossed his mind.

Capt. Singh came up from the rear of the building. His turban and pinned-up beard suggesting he came from Navi Ambarsar. "Lt. Neumann, welcome." He looked past Tomas, at the photo of the brigade. "It's good from time to time to think of the fine soldiers we've lost along the way."

"Hopefully they gave their lives for a good cause."

Singh said, "The honor of the Confederated Worlds is the best cause there could be. Wouldn't you say so?"

Tomas' eyes widened. Did Singh doubt his loyalty? "Of course, absolutely. Nothing better."

His response seemed to dispel any doubts Singh might have had. "Come on back. The XO can't meet with us, but he's authorized me to tell you everything you need to know for the ceremony. Day after tomorrow will be here before we know it." Singh started off. He walked around a parallelogram of sun glare on the carpet, where the light from the L4 mirror came through a west-facing window.

"I'm sure Col. Healey has a lot on his plate." Tomas walked through the sun glare. His feet felt hot through his socks and boots.

"It takes a lot to keep the brigade running properly." Singh pushed through a swinging gate in a waist-high railing, then down a corridor. They stopped in a small room, darkly paneled in fabbed walnut, with serviceable chairs of nanotube composite legs and soft plastic webbing. "Have a seat."

Tomas did. On the wall, a bright rectangle showed a map of the base and the nearby parts of Belmont. Confederation Square lay two kilometers away. The map showed the site of the stage, at the north end of the square. The crowd would fill the rest. A small mound, lush with a lawn, provided a base for immense flagpoles in the middle of the square. In front of the stage, a bird-shaped icon marked where Iago's captured thopter would be displayed to the spectators.

A wider glance showed the lumbering bulk of Parliament House to the east, across the square from the wood-veneered facade of the Arden Planetary Shakespeare Company Theater. Behind the stage, government offices lined the square's north side.

"What do I need to do to prepare my platoon for the ceremony?"

"Just follow the book. Dress grays, unloaded weapons with cleared chambers. For the sweaties, I mean. You're an officer, how you carry your sidearm is up to your sense of honor. Do make sure the men are sober. Both Col. Healey and Col. Kleinfelter from civil affairs will be torqued if the VIP locals near the stage see sweaties staggering or vomiting."

"I assure you, my men will be up to standard." By eye, Tomas traced a path along twisting streets from the nearest gate of GFB Belmont to Confederation Square. "How are we going to travel the two klicks?"

"SSC fabbed up a luxury autobus to transfer you from the base to here." Singh highlighted a point on a street running east-west a block north of the square. A pedestrian alley led from that point, between government buildings, to the rear of the stage. "It's a short walk. We'll sit you at stage left, behind Arden political and military leaders and most of the brigade's staff."

Tomas frowned. "That's a lot of high value targets."

"Rebels? Yes, you've been in action against them, out in the countryside. We aren't worried about them. In the case of an attack, we'll get the big boys and girls into the buildings between the square and the street where your bus will stop. Their wattle-and-daub cladding is on top of material like the body armor in your field uniforms. Hardened against small arms fire. Your platoon can evacuate there as well. But we don't expect an attack. All our intel projections say the rebels lack the ability to project enough force into the middle of Belmont."

If Tatarinova considered an attack unlikely, Tomas could breathe a little easier. Still. "But if there is an attack, the GF can't just hide the VIPs in the government offices. We would have to engage the rebels. Unloaded weapons means my platoon couldn't."

"Exactly, exactly. We've thought of that. We're not all pogeys, lieutenant, and even if you think we are I don't take offense. We will assign an armored grenadier platoon to put dismounted infantry around the perimeter of the square and park its vehicles at the mound."

"Which platoon?"

Singh winced. "ArChars. I know, not our first choice either, but part of this event is to show the Ardenites that the Confederated Worlds considers them equal partners. Behind the scenes, we did insist the ArChars put up the best platoon from their best company on the planet. On the off chance a few rebels somehow make it to the square and try to launch an attack, these ArChars should be able to handle it."

Could Ensign Redvers have a say in which Constabulary platoon was the best? Tomas clamped his jaws together, lest he accidentally say something.

Singh raised his eyebrow at Tomas.

Your face can betray you even if your words don't. Tomas' thoughts scrabbled for a reply. "Whose stupid idea was that? Even the best Constabulary platoon is worse than our worst one."

"Brig. Ibáñez himself insisted. We know it stinks. Healey objected on behalf of all you guys who deal with ArChars day by day. But the sheriff stuck to his position. Make the best of it."

A cold feeling washed over Tomas' face. Forget a rogue staff officer. What if Brigadier Ibáñez were behind the efforts to give Arden to the rebels?

Tomas blinked the thought away. Time to answer Singh's question. "Brass. It's not his backside naked in the breeze."

"He'll be on the stage with you."

Tomas rolled his eyes, sniffed out a breath. "Cold comfort if a rebel assassin gets past the Constabulary platoon, looks for targets, and my shiny collar is the first one he sees. Alright, I'm done venting. What more do I need to know?"

"About the rally? Have your men at the gate on Oneday by eleven-hundred. Your performance evals will look like shit if you show up late. Yeah, it's a dog and pony show, but VIPs and brass want it."

"Anything else I need to know?"

Singh's mouth twisted up and he nodded. "There is something else. It should be simple, though. Both the XO and civil affairs need your help with it."

"It?"

"There are a lot of small-town mayors who've come to the city for the rally. Tonight, we're hosting a party with the ArChars and the planetary prime minister, to welcome those mayors to Belmont and give them a chance to meet a Ground Force hero in person."

A sour look formed around Tomas' mouth. "And since you couldn't find a GF hero, I'll have to do."

"It won't be that bad. Tonight, twenty-one-hundred, in Belmont. I'll send you the address. A ritzy part of town."

"Ritzy?" Tomas' legs stiffened.

"Oh, you heard about that ArChar officer who got strangled last night? That was ten blocks from the site. You'll be fine. And, after all, taking a ride to a nice neighborhood is better than getting shot at, isn't it?"

Tomas managed to put on a dark-humor smile. "Unless that ride and getting shot at are the same thing."

Tomas made it to the party without getting shot at. A driver from the brigade motor pool drove him in a nondescript civilian sedan through the night's first minutes of full darkness. After taking winding streets flanked by mature live oaks and laser-cut stone walls, the driver slowed at an open gate guarded by Constabulary men with rifles slung over their shoulders. A few seconds to confirm security credentials, and the guards stepped back and waved the driver through.

A driveway led to a manor house clad in more laser-cut stone. The driver stopped and Tomas climbed out. The night had a cool edge, probably the last cool night for three or four days. He approached the manor house's pair of tall and wide front doors. Flickering lamps on either side of the door cast a dim umber light on the landing and gave the laser-cut blocks an oily sheen.

Inside, a grand hall three stories high ran from the front doors to the back of the house. A single pane of self-healing glass formed the back wall of the room. The glass reflected clusters of people in Constabulary uniforms, GF dress grays, or civilian clothes featuring starched collars or flowing skirts clumped around sitting areas scattered through the grand hall. People conversed and a string quartet played in the back corner, yet somehow the honey-colored walls stopped echoes.

Tomas started across the parquet floor. He craned his neck looking for familiar faces. None. Familiar uniforms, then. There. He started toward a cluster of dress grays and a few civilians. Wait, two full colonels? Not a circle he wanted to break into. He backed away—

"Lt. Neumann!" said one of the colonels. Stout, with ruddy cheeks, the nameplate on his chest identified him as Kleinfelter, the brigade's civil affairs officer. "Come, join us. The prime minister has heard of your exploits and wants to shake your hand."

Tomas shuffled forward. The prime minister had a patrician demeanor, with a high forehead and a narrow nose. Tomas extended his hand and the prime minister took it in a crushing grip. "Well met, good sir. Your service to our planet is like to the true ring—" He flicked his middle finger from his thumb against air. "—of the crystal chalice holding Arden and her sister Confederated Worlds."

Preoccupied with his worries during the drive, Tomas hadn't prepared himself to listen to Ardenese. A compliment, he realized. "I'm just doing my job."

"Your modesty would become a maid, good sir, but a strapping man has no need of it. You have marooném an enemy operative in deep woods hundreds of kilometers distant, and offeréd up full proof the Progressive Republic has violated the pact of peace. The good citizens of Arden have taken note of our foe's false dealings, I assure you."

"The people of the Confederated Worlds will take note of it, too," Col. Healey said. "Lt. Neumann has helped make clear how deceitful an enemy we face."

"Thank you, gentlemen." Perhaps he could slip away—

The prime minister pressed his hand to Tomas' shoulder. "I would know more about your world and the faith of your upbringing. We are so newly inducted into the Confederated Worlds we know little of our sister cultures. I hear tell you come from

Joséphine?"

Tomas gave a potted biography, born on Sankt-Benedikts-Welt to Observer minister parents, and his mother's decision to relocate to Joséphine upon being—widowed. The prime minister nodded and pressed on, with questions about both worlds and the Observer faith. Tomas answered and occasionally glanced to the side in hopes Healey or Kleinfelter would extricate him. They didn't, and the prime minister's intense demeanor drew his attention back. Tomas saw and heard people around him, but only as blurs and fragments of words he did his best to ignore.

"You are a strapping man, indeed. Those who see you on the overmorrow shall pull with great vigor the lever for the Confederated Worlds. Marry, had I not already counted myself one of them, I would have upon our audience tonight. For Shakespeare, Arden, and St. George!" The prime minister gave Tomas' shoulder a final clap, then released him and turned to a group of Ardenite civilians coming toward them.

Healey beckoned Tomas closer. "Good work, Neumann. I know you're a forthright type who doesn't take easily to all this gladhanding. Get a drink, some hors d'oeuvre, and keep mingling." He patted Tomas' upper arm and gently guided him away.

After a few relieved steps, he glanced around, unsure what to do. He double-took at a familiar face. Slightly swarthy. Face narrow through the eyes. Every strand of black hair in place. Was that—?

"Leftenant!" said Mayor Patel of Eltham. "Pleaséd I am, to say I knew thee before thou art come to thy merited station." He held out his hand as Tomas came closer.

As they shook, Tomas said, "I'm pleased to see you again, mayor."

Patel squinted back. "Marry? Thou seemst less pleaséd than thy words comport." He lowered his voice. "Hast thou reflected on thy time spent in and near Eltham, and come to think less of our ways of resisting our mutual foe?"

The robots. "Not in the least. If I seem ill-at-ease, it's not with you. It's with—" *Subterfuge and deceit.* No, unutterable. Tomas waved his hand at the space.

"Thou art a gentleman who relishes quiet over the bombards of social speech. Not unlike my Beatrice, I should think."

The mayor's daughter, tinkering with her military robots....

Tomas perked up. "Did she come with you?"

After a few blinks, Patel said, "No. As I said, she shuns such circumstances. She remains in Eltham, working on—" He glanced around. No one seemed close, but still he spoke in euphemism. "—her engineering projects."

"That's regrettable." In a nearby knot of conversation, someone laughed.

Mayor Patel glanced at Tomas' left hand. "Sir, ken I well my daughter's departure from the narrow ways trod by nearly all the fair ladies of Arden. Ken I likewise her chosen way rebuffs many a young man who could make a meet son-in-law." He looked up, more stern of face and posture than Tomas remembered from Eltham. "But you, sir, are an off-worlder, and, zounds, a base-courted one, to inquire of my daughter as if the ring on your left hand were but a bauble."

Tomas frowned in puzzlement. "Mayor, my regrets, I spoke unclearly." He glanced at a passing waiter. No sign the man paid any notice to his words. Tomas returned his attention to Mayor Patel. "I want nothing from Beatrice."

Disgust filled Patel's face. "'Tis an unfair thought to seek what lies twixt a maid's legs."

What? Tomas blinked, then raised his palms in supplication. "It sounds like I misspoke, and I don't even know how. All I mean to ask is, how go Beatrice's engineering projects?"

Patel's upper body relaxed, yet his tone of voice remained wary. "What are those to you?"

"They could make the difference between disaster and triumph, come the day after tomorrow and in the plebiscite to follow. Of all the people around Belmont, I don't know whom I can trust and whom I cannot. Yet I know your family's loyalty to the Confederated Worlds is unwavering."

A pensive look crossed Patel's face. Tomas guessed at his thoughts. A Papa victory in the plebiscite meant a re-education camp, or worse, for small-town government officials like him. Who would then marry the daughter of an enemy of the people?

"Tell me what thou wouldst ask of her."

Tomas lowered his voice. "I want her to come to the rally. She should bring as many of her—engineering projects as are appropriate in a crowded urban environment. She should pick ones that would not attract attention from the massed people. Or my superiors. Or Iago. Also, Constable Turner should detach a squad of his best men, in civilian clothes, to accompany her. Would you relay that message to her?"

"I shall, good sir," Mayor Patel said. "And at this very moment. Good evening." He slipped away, toward a door leading to the dark gardens behind the manor house.

Tomas watched him go, until an intuition jerked his head around. Had someone been eavesdropping? He glanced sidelong at the clumps of people around him and at waiters passing by. All seemed intent on their tasks.

You jump at shadows.

He continued glancing around the space as his heart slowed its pace. Better to jump at shadows than be shot from them.

14

The Rally

The men of the platoon assembled outside their bivouacs at 0800. The brass buttons of dress uniforms, and the bayonets on rifles, gleamed in the summer morning light of the two mirrors. Sweat trickled down their motionless faces. Tomas walked among them, checking his reflection in the uppers of their black dress boots, peering at eyes for signs of hangover. They were ready for parade.

Would they be ready for action?

"O'Herlihy, Nilsson, follow me." Tomas went to open space in front of the assembled men. The squad leaders followed him. "Good job getting them ready."

"Thank you, ell-tee," O'Herlihy said. "We just followed the book."

"We're going to deviate from the book." Tomas unbuttoned his jacket and reached into the empty pocket over his heart. "I can fit a loaded magazine in here. They should each be able to do the same."

O'Herlihy's mouth gaped.

Nilsson glanced at the soldier's chests. "It might leave a bulge, ell-tee." He bent his leg to lift his left foot to waist height. He tapped the inner side of his leg, just above the ankle. "They'll hide better in their socks. And that way, each man can carry two."

You could never have enough ammo. And the lumps in their

socks would be symmetrical, which would look more normal. "Very good."

"Ell-tee?" O'Herlihy recovered his voice. "What am I missing? We show up, look pretty, then ride back here. What do we need ammo for?"

"Hopefully nothing, but hope's not a planning factor. Do you know where Iago is? Do you trust everyone who says there are no rebel sympathizers in Belmont? And if there are rebels afoot, do you want to leave security solely to the Constabulary?"

And if there are traitors in Ground Force—? They wouldn't dare openly attack their comrades.

"We'll tell them. Privately," O'Herlihy said.

"Anything else, ell-tee?"

Tomas nodded at Clayworth and Edelstein, as polished as the infantrymen, but unarmed. "Tell all the Badger and Weasel crewmen, Sgt. Svoboda's team, and Doc Yarborough to carry two magazines as well. If the rebels do attack, every round is precious, and the more we have, the better. And one last thing—someone hand me two for my socks."

O'Herlihy gestured at Tomas' right hip. "Don't you want to carry more rounds for your pistol?"

"If it comes down to how many rounds I can fire, then I haven't guided the men properly. Sixty more rounds for the men beats two dozen more for me. That's all for now. We will reassemble here at 1030 for the walk to the gate."

At the appointed time, and after Tomas slid two thirty-round magazines down his socks, the platoon set out across the base. The thin metal cases chafed the bumps of his ankle bones by the time they reached the bus.

A tall vehicle in an urban camouflage pattern, its interior held plush seats giving views out of high windows. The driver wore a Ground Force private's uniform, with the jagged y-shape of a St. Martin's cloak, the SSC logo, on the shoulder. Tomas took a seat up front and pinged the driver's shilling. Pvt. Evans, skills impped for all classes of transport vehicles, native to Chaffeeland, one of the smaller, less settled continents of Challenger.

Tomas asked him the most probing questions he could without rousing his suspicions, how life in the wilder parts of Challenger compared to the big cities like McAuliffe, where he had served before Arden, the like. The driver's answers rang true.

He's not a Papa agent with a forged shilling, but he could still be a traitor.... Tomas fell silent and watched the driver as he steered the bus through Belmont's twisting streets. Glances at the nav display near the steering wheel told Tomas the line of travel agreed with the map Singh had shown him.

Tomas still leaned forward from the edge of his seat.

A glance out the window further tightened his shoulders. The bus drove down commercial avenues, lined with tea rooms and handicraft artisans' shops. Pedestrians and customers looked up. The urban camouflage pattern of the bus could not be mistaken. Tomas remembered the rebel sympathizer in Navarre. His gaze jumped from face to face, looking for the same expression of someone gathering intel for the rebels. The bus moved too quickly for Tomas to find that expression.

The crowds thickened near Confederation Square. Many of the people on the street wore starched collars or long dresses with lace at the neck. Government employees, he guessed, released from their offices for a few hours to bolster the crowd. Though how many of the government employees spied, or worse, for the rebels?

A block before the square, the bus turned left. Constabulary personnel manned a set of barricades. Tomas couldn't see any verification, yet soon enough the Constabulary pulled the barricades aside and let the bus proceed.

Ground Force MPs, overseen by civil affairs personnel, guided the bus to its parking spot. Tomas quietly released the catch binding the flap of his holster. He stepped off the bus with his right hand resting on the loose flap. A glance showed Ground Force personnel and cars parked angle-in on both sides. Government buildings turned their backs of white plaster and walnut-brown synthetic timbers to the street. Looming above them, to Tomas' left, soared the upper stories of Parliament House. A clock tower showed a quarter till noon.

As he returned his gaze to the street, a blur along the edge of a roof made him double-take. Tomas took another look at the site of the blur. Nothing.

A young-looking captain with a dolorous face and thick unibrow glanced at the same site, then came to Tomas. "Escobedo, with Civil Affairs. I hear you were worried only ArChars were providing security. You weren't the only one."

"Sharpshooters?" Tomas asked.

Escobedo nodded.

Tomas went on. "Who greenlighted them?"

"Col. Rogers in operations. Who else?"

The squad leaders came out of the bus, followed by the first soldiers. "Form up your squads," Tomas told them. To Capt. Escobedo he asked, "Which way?"

Escobedo pointed at a passage between two government buildings. At most two men could walk abreast, if they were willing to brush sleeves with each other and the walls. "It leads to a courtyard where another civil affairs soldier waits to guide you to the back of the stage. Other than the courtyard, your path has no branches, just some twists and turns."

A twist or turn could lead them into the sights of a traitor's weapon, or one of Iago's. But Tomas had no choice. He glanced to the squads, formed up to process in column. "Nilsson, O'Herlihy, follow me." He started out.

In the alley, walls of white plaster and dark timbers formed a narrow canyon. The windows facing the alley remained closed, and no one lurked behind the alley's bends or at the roofs' parapets. The sliver of blue sky visible at the zenith, reflected at steep angles by the windows, taunted him with the hope of freedom and the fear of a grenade dropped from the roof. The cramped space inside Badger One's turret would be far more comfortable, and far more safe.

The courtyard held four picnic tables and a fountain trickling water over the stone bodies of two naiads. A civil affairs lieutenant, a woman whose facial features and accent suggested she came from Zion-against-Babylon, waited. "Jah be with you, Lt. Neumann. Your way be through here." She gestured at one of the courtyard's exits.

Despite the blessing, Tomas' mood remained clouded as he led the platoon. The next alley resembled the first. A blur of sound, the chatter of thousands of voices, came to him. Echoed by the facades of the buildings fronting the square, the crowd's sound boomed when Tomas emerged from the alley's final stretch.

A metallic framework a few meters in front of the alley's mouth stretched to left and right. Tall near Tomas' position, it stair-stepped down toward the pavement as it extended toward the center of the square. A set of risers, higher in the back, to make everyone on stage readily visible to the crowd.

If the rebels are here, they'll shoot at the brigadier and the colonels before they aim at you.

Another civil affairs lieutenant, this one a man with bland good looks and a mainland Challenger accent, looked up, checked his tablet, came forward. "Lt. Neumann—did I pronounce that correctly?"

"Close enough."

"We have your platoon standing on the back three rows, stage left." He pointed. "The band will play a mix of local favorites— Variations on a Theme of Ralph Vaughn Williams, that sort of thing—and some Confederated Worlds classics, then Brig. Ibáñez will call you forward to commemorate your unit. Forty minutes on your feet after that. Any questions?"

Tomas shook his head. "Sounds simple."

The lieutenant looked stern. "You think it's just a dog and pony? Lt. Neumann, this is as important as the combat mission you performed to capture that thopter. Great work, by the way. Don't know what meat Tatarinova might have picked off its bones, but we dressed it up like a Thanksgiving turkey. The crowd's going to think you're the bravest man alive and they should vote to stay Confederated Worlds."

Tomas had no idea what the lieutenant's metaphors about the thopter meant—Challengerites ate synthetic meat like anyone else, didn't they? "Three rows at back left, you said?"

"There's a stair up at the back corner. Get going." The lieutenant waved that direction in emphasis.

Tomas went. Nilsson and O'Herlihy's squads fell in behind him. The crowd noise echoed off the building fronts to his left. At the back corner of the stage, he made a right turn onto the stairs. The metal treads clanged under his boots. As more of the platoon's men turned onto the stairs, their unison march set the stage to vibrating.

At the head of the stairs, about halfway to the front of the stage, he glimpsed the crowd as he turned toward the back rows. He climbed the risers amid a sea of Ardenite faces, mostly men with sweating cheeks above high starched collars, perched on arrays of folding chairs. Small town mayors or minor bureaucrats, he guessed. Mayor Patel nodded at him. From the gesture, Tomas read that Beatrice had brought her engineering projects.

The last three rows of risers waited for them. Tomas faced the government buildings, his back to the crowd, while he oversaw the platoon's entry. Once all were in place, he gave the commands. "Attention! Order arms!"

Rifle butts clapped against the risers. The men stood fixed. Pride in their performance—not the chickenshit of drill, but their actions in the field that led them here—filled Tomas as he turned toward the crowd in the square.

At the front of the risers, the lowest level—still two meters above the pavement—held a podium sprouting a microphone and video cameras. Just behind the podium, in two rows of six chairs, sat high-ranking brass and local politicians. Brigadier Ibáñez and the prime minister sat in the center of the front row. On the prime minister's side of the formation sat an Ardenite in an ornate Constabulary uniform, presumably the High Constable of the planet, along with unfamiliar locals in civilian dress. Next to and behind Brigadier Ibáñez sat a number of bird colonels, staff officers: Rogers, Kleinfelter, and others Tomas didn't know. One of the chairs on the Ground Force side stood empty.

In front of the stage, the thopter's fuselage lay belly-down, landing legs broken. Its wings drooped on the ground. The crowd would have a clear view over the thopter at anyone standing at the podium. The damaged thopter looked artificial in the bright light of midday. A panicked thought crossed Tomas' mind, *the locals will think it's a fake and this whole plan will backfire—*

He took a breath.* As far as displaying the thopter goes, either civil affairs knows what it's doing, or it doesn't. You have other things to worry about.*

Tomas studied the scene. A waist-high wall of blue plastic formed a semicircle screening the thopter from the crowd. Just outside the wall, a squad of Constabulary personnel stood with rifles against their dress blue shoulders. A squint showed Tomas the insignia of the Parliament House guards on the squad's sleeves.

More Constabulary personnel occupied the center of the square. Constabulary fighting vehicles, Bawsons and Stoats, chopped up the view of the grassy flagpole mound. Infantrymen stood in formation in front of the vehicles, while on the mound behind the vehicles, a group of officers spoke among themselves.

Between the two groups of Constabulary personnel thronged the crowd. More people filled the back corners and the sides of the square. More spilled into the streets leading away. Starched white collars and dresses in muted colors dominated the front of the crowd, interspersed with locals in casual garb, collars folded down and blouses paired with skirts. Further back, casual attire predominated, though a few government employees or upper-crust Belmontese who'd apparently arrived late mixed in.

What would rebels look like? Casually dressed, resentful of the elite? Or garbed like government employees to masquerade as supporters of the regime? Tomas picked out individual faces to study, despite the long odds of seeing a rebel's thoughts plain on his face.

Though long, he had better odds of seeing a rebel than finding an answer to his other question. What would Iago look like? He had fled with a single face and set of limbs, but any image of those body parts had been lost when the thopter's data storage had self-destructed. He could be anyone, anywhere. He might not even be here—

Hope is not a planning factor.

Tomas looked up at the buildings on either side. People stood behind windows in the upper stories of Parliament House. The men had flashes of white at their necks, the fancy collars of government workers or even members of the planetary parliament.

Above the spectators inside Parliament House, at the edge of its roof, faint blurs occasionally caught Tomas' gaze. More GF sharpshooters, moving their limbs slightly, but faster than their cee-skin could adapt. A civilian might think of the blurs as floaters in the eye and pay them no more attention. A first glance across the square at the roof of the theater showed nothing. A closer look revealed another blur of motion near the roofline.

Who assigned the sharpshooters? The same person who had sent the worst platoon commanders on the planet against Iago north of Eastcheap? Or someone worse?

Another motion, much closer, turned Tomas' head. At the front of the stage, on the far side from Tomas, the band director stood. The musicians brought their horns to the ready. The band director's baton slashed the air, and the first notes of a song swept through the square. During the first few bars, the crowd's chatter subsided and its members grew more still.

Tomas knew little about music. With recordings barred from the house by his mother, his only childhood exposure had come from a local amateur orchestra's Bonapartist anthems during the Harvest Fête and on Coronation Day. The band's first piece seemed totally unfamiliar. A few minutes of pastoral, melancholic music drifted through the square. The well-dressed locals stood rapt, and their example led the rest toward the same state.

The second piece Tomas had heard before, somewhere during his service, from a band practice or some parade. Brassy, upbeat, some GF anthem. The crowd's attention slipped, but most remained focused enough for the movements of a few individuals to catch Tomas' eye. A local loped past one of the Stoats, lifting a cloth cap to scratch his head as he did so. Young boys slipped down a side street as one of their number cradled something illicit in his hands.

Tomas' gaze kept roving. No sign of rebels, nor of Beatrice Patel. Had he misread the mayor's nod?

If you were the rebels, when would you strike?

The final bars of the second piece echoed off the facades around the square, then faded from hearing. The prime minister pushed himself from his seat and went to the microphone.

"Friends, Ardenites, countrymen and -women, lend me your ears." His voice boomed from amplifiers mounted high on the faces of the government offices behind the stage. "This glorious day brings me great honor. My duties lead me to commend the actions of our friends from the rest of the Confederated Worlds, bound to us by their commitment to the freedom of our world against encroachment by our enemies. Our enemies think they may renege on their affirmations of peace without consequence. They think falsely. Our enemies' transgression is proven—" He chopped his hand in the air, in the direction of the thopter. "—to all within sight and sound."

Because Papa couldn't jam wired communication links, viewers across the planet saw the rally live.

"The Progressive Republic has violated the instruments of concord, like a barbarous chancellor so confident in powers calléd up from the vasty deep as to dismiss a solemn pact as a scrap of paper. For such violation, it will pay a steep price, now and for decades to come."

What steep price? Tomas mulled the question while the prime minister kept talking. Though Papa had handed the Confederated Worlds a *casus belli*, a justification for war,* *in the form of the captured thopter, the politicians on Challenger would do nothing. Shirley Foxtrot had lost the war. Renewed hostilities would lead to further defeat by Papa's space force, and the imposition of even harsher conditions by the victors.

The prime minister continued. "Now, the time has come to thank the men who have servéd up this proof—" He gestured again at the thopter. "—of the Progressive Republic's machinations. It is my extreme honor to be the citizen of Arden to commend Third Platoon Task Force, Alpha Company, Third Battalion, Nineteenth Brigade, Confederated Worlds Ground Force for its actions near Camp Cordelia on Threeday last, which resulted in the capture of yon air vehicle uséd by operatives of the Progressive Republic in the furtherance of insurrection against the rightful government of our world and in violation of the instruments of concord. Lt. Neumann of the aforesaid platoon task force, please come forward."

Tomas made his way through the array of minor Ardenite politicians seated in front of him. His heart slammed. *Want a good time to strike? Wait till the prime minister and a Ground Force officer who scored a coup against you are together, front and center.* The stage creaked under his last, slow steps as Tomas approached the prime minister.

An aide stepped forth with an opened jewelry box. The prime minister lifted from it a silver St. George cross pending from a blue ribbon. "Hereby I bestow upon thee, and by extension, each member of thy platoon task force, the Unit Medal of Prince Henry for meritorious service to the world and people of Arden." He widened the ribbon and raised it to go around Tomas' neck.

Tomas held his breath and ducked his chin. He looked up, eyes darting from side to side around the prime minister. The square looked peaceful as the prime minister rested the ribbon on the back of his neck. The St. George cross pressed lightly against his chest.

Maybe he did start at shadows. "Thank you, Your Excellency," Tomas said.

The prime minister shook his hand. "The people of Arden and I do not stand alone in commending thy meritorious actions. Thy brigade commander hath more to say."

Brigadier Ibáñez stood, then pulled down the hem of his jacket to smooth out wrinkles. A few steps later and he stood near Tomas and the prime minister. A tall man, with a few grays artfully salting his grizzled brown hair, he projected age and authority. An aide trailed behind him.

A cold feeling gripped Tomas.

Want a better time to strike?

Especially if someone leaked you an advanced copy of the program?

Ibáñez's voice boomed. The microphone echoed his words around the square. "Lt. Neumann, it is my honor to bestow on your platoon task force the Ground Force Meritorious Unit Award for its actions in the capture of the Progressive Republic thopter."

The aide pulled a ribbon from an inner pocket of his jacket. A pinch activated the adhesive backing. Ibáñez took it from him and deftly held it by the edges as he moved it toward Tomas' chest.

Tomas stood taller. From the corner of his eye, near the flagpole mound, the Constabulary vehicles rotated their turrets.

"Get down!" Tomas lunged forward and wrapped his arms around the prime minister and Brig. Ibáñez. He pulled them down behind the podium. Wait, was the podium armored—

The Constabulary vehicles opened fire.

The crowd screamed. On stage, the assembled politicians and Ground Force officers cowered, some quicker than others. Bullets panged off the thopter, smacked the walls behind the stage, tore open starched collars, dress blue jackets, arms and chests and heads. Screams of fear and pain filled the air.

Tomas lifted his head enough to look back at his platoon. "Get off stage!" he shouted over the din. "Take cover behind the thopter!" He looked for the squad leaders, caught Nilsson's eye. "Behind the thopter!" Tomas jerked his thumb at the grounded aircraft in front of the stage.

"Got it!" Nilsson shouted back. He yelled and shoved his men to get them moving. Crouched figures in dress gray pushed through the panicked crowd of small-town mayors between them and the stairs. A few soldiers lowered themselves off the side of the stage, climbing down struts and beams until they were low enough to jump. A few more squeezed between risers and dropped through the gaps into the area under the stage. Nilsson crouched and went along the risers from man to man, urging them to get to cover.

The Constabulary machine guns continued to fire, sounding like a hive of a million bees stoked into rage.

"Gah!" Nilsson's face contorted. His right arm dangled from his torn and bloody upper arm. He shoved his left hand into his armpit and staggered toward the stairs.

"I've got to join my men!" Tomas yelled to the prime minister and Ibáñez. "Follow me below the stage, then get yourselves into the buildings behind us!"

Before they replied, Tomas crawled toward the back of the riser. A figure in dress gray lay in his path. Col. Rogers. He lay clawing at his throat as blood bubbled out his mouth and nose.

Tomas kept crawling. Something poked him in the hollow between his neck and breastbone. The points of the St. George cross hanging at his neck. He worked the ribbon over the back of his head, then stuffed the medal into his back pocket.

The shriek of Constabulary machine guns abated. Relief brushed Tomas for a moment, only to be swept aside by foreboding in the instant before a Bawson fired a missile. The detonation of its warhead followed almost instantly, and echoed off the facades.

More screams from the crowd. Tomas' heart pounded. Not aimed at the stage. A side of the square… Parliament House.

Time to get to his men. He crawled over the back of the riser and held on by his fingertips. His arms burned for a moment, then he let go and dropped half a meter to the living asphalt. Bullets screeched off the higher risers. Garbled Ardenese came from the stage above him, but the tones of rage and fear and pain were clear. Blood dripped down the edges of the risers and puddled on the asphalt. Tomas' vision constricted, to show him just enough to make his way from under the front of the stage to his men gathering behind the thopter.

Most of the men already crouched there, Nilsson's squad to the right, O'Herlihy's to the left. They pulled magazines from their socks and drove them into their rifles. Ready for action, but too tightly bunched.

"Spread out!" Tomas called to the men. He gestured to show lines running from the ends of the thopter to far under the stage. "Hold fire till I give the word!"

The men started to fan out, but while they all remained close, Nilsson said through gritted teeth, "And carry your rifle like all you have is the bayonet. If the arsefucks think we're unarmed, let's keep them that way until we can punch them—ugh."

The men hustled to positions under the risers. Tomas went to Nilsson. Still conscious, he stanched his bleeding right arm as best he could with his left hand. Blood still oozed out of his shattered upper arm. He nodded toward his socks. "Good call on packing magazines, ell-tee. Did you know something?"

"Enough to want to be armed when I'm around high-value targets."

Tomas looked around. He could see nothing under or over the

thopter. From the lack of fires coming from the other side of the thopter, he guessed the Parliament House guards lay dead or dying. Presumably surviving civilians in the crowd between the thopter and the flagpole mound had gone to their bellies. A glance to either side showed civilians crawling toward the square's exits. Many lay still, either too frightened to move, or grievously wounded. Or dead.

A Stoat's thirteen chattered. Tomas flinched as bullets struck the thopter, the stage, and the government buildings behind them. Someone groaned and thudded onto the risers.

A Bawson fired a second missile. As the explosion of its warhead echoed away from Parliament House, rubble clattered to the ground.

Now what? Tomas glanced toward Parliament House. Holes gaped where the upper story windows had been. A portion of the roof had collapsed, and bullet holes dotted the remnants of the parapet. A strip of damaged cee-skin and a trickle of blood down the facade marked a dead sharpshooter slumped over the parapet.

Where was Mayor Patel's daughter and her robots?

Nilsson's face looked clammy. Come on, where was doc? Nilsson wore his shilling, and it still worked, right? Couldn't Yarborough see that?

Even if Yarborough could, he had a hundred other wounded to triage.

More machine gun fire banged out from the rebel fighting vehicles. As the last burst's echo faded from the square, an amplified voice boomed out from one of the Bawsons. "Fellow citizens!" More thirteen millimeter rounds burst out from the rebel fighting vehicles, pounded the stage and the government buildings behind it. "Ere now you have labored under the yoke of the foreign oppressor! The Arden Provisional Government hath brought the struggle for self-determination to the very heart of the intruder's puppet regime!"

One of the Bawsons fired another missile at Parliament House. The warhead's detonation thundered through the square.

"Even now, the false knaves who claim to represent Arden are dead, dying, or put to flight! The coarse soldiers of Challenger lay broken on stage or cower beneath it!" Another burst of fire pinged off the thopter, thudded into the government buildings. "Rise, fellow citizens, and wash away your foes in the flood of righteousness!"

The sliver of crowd visible under the thopter remained prone. A few kept crawling. More lay still than had moments earlier. Newly wounded or frightened, Tomas couldn't tell.

At least no one heeded the rebel's call to action.

A plan bloomed in Tomas' mind. A withdrawal into the government buildings behind the stage. From windows in the upper levels, they might have a chance to fire on dismounted rebels. The buildings' front faces were hardened against small arms and the rebel vehicles' thirteens... but high explosive warheads would tear them open.

Stay put? The rebel vehicles again fired their machine guns. The thopter's hull rang with bullet impacts. More rounds, higher, into the crowd on the stage. More screams. The air stank of blood.

Motion under the stage caught Tomas' gaze. Campbell waggled the fingers of one hand, then flexed them in a starburst. Tomas repeated the gestures to Nilsson. "What does that mean?"

"Dismounts. Opaque cee-skin." Nilsson grunted and jammed his hand deeper into his armpit. Sweat beaded on his forehead.

"Stay with me," Tomas said. Mere words, but the only thing he had. Tomas crouched and went under the stage. A few meters underneath, he went to his belly behind a prone scout. The scout held his rifle sideways, in shaking hands.

"Good job," Tomas told him. Then he saw the rebels.

A platoon's worth of rebels walked through the crowd of supine civilians, faceplates down and cee-skin set to an urban camouflage pattern. Still a contrast against the theater's facade behind them. The rebels held their rifles without aiming.

Suddenly, words boomed from the other side of the risers. Tomas glanced over his shoulder and saw another rebel platoon facing O'Herlihy's squad. "Challengerites! Your war has been ended! Ken we well your rifles have empty chambers. Throw your rifles down and set your chameleon skins to the Dutchman's shade!"

His men looked to Tomas with uncertainty in their faces.

"Fire!" he shouted.

Bursts roared from his men's rifles. Hot spent casings clattered to the pavement. Tomas turned and crawled toward one of the stage's support struts, drawing his pistol as he went. His men fired again. A third of the rebels were down, wounded or dead, but about fifteen still stood or knelt. None had yet reset their uniforms to transparent. He sighted the rebel who had called for their surrender and fired, two shots. The second caught the rebel in the chest. The rebel crumpled.

His men kept firing. More rebels fell, but the rest regained their wits enough to lie prone. One by one, they quickly winked out of view.

"We got them!" one of the armored grenadiers said.

"Sheeit," Meriwether said. "We ain't done with them if they still got their vehicles."

The rebels fired a burst from a thirteen. Not at the Ardenites on the stage, but under the nose and tail of the thopter. The rounds kicked up fragments from the living asphalt a few meters in front of the men. The men had formed their lines well enough to use the thopter for cover. No problem.

Until the rebels drove their Stoats just far enough to see the lines of men in dress gray. Or the Bawsons loaded antipersonnel missiles, targeted to his position, into their racks.

A Stoat's track clanked with a movement just begun. Repositioning for a better shot. Tomas gritted his teeth when a deep crump sounded through the square, followed by a metallic clatter. Moments later came another crump, another clatter.

In a lull, the next sound was flapping, as if from a flock of birds.

Relief washed through Tomas. The meeting in Eltham Constabulary headquarters. Drone pygmy thopters.

A Stoat's thirteen fired another burst. An odd one, it cut off early with a crump. More crumps followed in quick succession. A moment later, a strangled roar came from the vicinity of the flagpole mound and echoed through the square.

Blurs of movement came from the supine crowd to either side of the stage. As Tomas' heart slammed, time seemed to slow, giving him an eternity to make sense of what he saw. Rebels looked backwards, lifting their heads just far enough above the motionless civilians to see what had just happened to their vehicles.

The men fired before Tomas could give an order.

Rebels shouted in confusion. A few fired wildly at the stage's underside. Tomas' men fired more bursts, striking motionless civilians and cee-skinned rebels.

More flapping sounds. More crumps.

The surviving rebels slithered backward. Against the ever-changing background of cowering civilians and buildings along the side of the square, their cee-skin couldn't keep up. Tomas' men fired at the blurs of motion. At the back of the formation, a rebel rose to a crouch and hurried away. Two more joined him. Gorthi raised his rifle and fired. One rebel fell, arms jerking outward, dropping his weapon as he tumbled to the ground. Another one clutched at a wound in his side yet kept moving. The third kept running, unscathed, while other rebels crawled away faster.

A glance showed the same situation on O'Herlihy's side of the stage.

"Bound by teams!" Tomas called out. "Capture the rebels if you can, shoot them if you can't."

"But the thirteens!" O'Herlihy said.

He hadn't decoded the sounds of Beatrice Patel's robots and the sight of the rebel retreat. "Are neutralized!" Tomas replied.

O'Herlihy shook his head.

Tomas couldn't blame him. But they had to get moving before the rebels could escape. "Come with me, I'll show you!"

Tomas hustled to the thopter. O'Herlihy didn't follow. Tomas grabbed the bottom edge of the side hatch and clambered up. He pressed his cheek against the fuselage under the top of the thopter, then popped his head up for a moment.

A score of miniature thopters crawled over the rebel vehicles, like black alloy and nanotube birds come to roost. The machine guns drooped, pinched in the middle of their barrels, melted by shaped charges carried by the miniature thopters. One Bawson's missile launcher looked like a torn flower of alloy. The turret of the other Bawson looked ripped open, as if cleaved by a giant's axe. The shaped charges had pinched the barrel in the act of firing. Flame gouted from the cleft. Despite the distance to the destroyed Bawson, the air under the stage stank of melted plastic and burned flesh.

Tomas ducked his head and yelled to O'Herlihy. "The vehicles are neutralized. Move by bounds, now!"

The scouts moved first. Gorthi and other men fired over the heads of cowering civilians and rebels while Campbell led the first bound. The Stoats and Bawsons remained silent, confirming what Tomas had seen. Campbell's men dropped to the pavement behind Ardenite bodies.

O'Herlihy's team bounded out next. Gorthi's team advanced as well. Single shots rang out from the covering groups. A few more rebels stood up and ran toward the edges of the square.

One civilian stretched out his suited leg and tripped a rebel. The rebel stumbled and dropped his rifle as he fell to the pavement. Another civilian, this one in casual clothes, picked it up and fired a burst into the rebel's chest. He then dropped the rifle and held out his hands. "Shoot not! I side with you, good Challengerites!"

"Get down!" Gorthi shouted. Other scouts fired at blurs of movement while Campbell's team rushed forward.

Tomas took another look over the thopter. Beatrice's flying drones flapped their wings and lunged for perches on the Stoats and Bawsons. A crump and a hiss of smoke trailed up from a Bawson's side. A shaped charge. The tracks on that side hung loosely on damaged drive wheels, matching the heap of track visible on the Bawson's opposite side.

The rebel crews were trapped inside their vehicles. Immobilized and disarmed, they could be ignored. The only question would be if the rebel dismounts could slip out of the square before his squads could capture them.

Tomas went back to Nilsson. The scout corporal looked pallid. Sweat beaded on his face. "The rebel thirteens and missiles. Haven't heard them."

"Remember Eltham? Mayor Patel's daughter came today, with some of her robots. Neutralized them."

Nilsson's face gained a faraway look. "There's a sweet sound."

Was he losing consciousness? Tomas pressed his hand to Nilsson's chest. "Stay with me."

"I am." Nilsson's eyes moved. Tomas followed his gaze toward the back of the space under the stage. Yarborough hurried over at a crouch, with the handle of a Constabulary first aid kit clutched in his fist.

"Good ears," Tomas said.

"What?" Nilsson said. Yarborough knelt beside him. Nilsson noticed him for the first time. "Finally, doc."

"I've been busy." Yarborough's voice sounded tight.

Nilsson said, "Ell-tee, I didn't mean doc. Can't you hear it?"

Tomas cupped his ear with his hand. Rumbles came from all the square's approaches. He knew the sound. Badgers and Weasels.

Someone at GFB Belmont remained loyal.

A voice boomed from one of the approaching GF vehicles. "Attention, all civilians and rebels! Confederated Worlds Ground Force has assumed control of the area. Any attempt to leave the square will be construed as rebel activity and will be met with deadly force! Rebels, dial your cee-skin to orange and surrender now! Anyone sporting transparent cee-skin sixty seconds from now will be met with deadly force! Good citizens, remain calm. Medical personnel will attend to the wounded, and the rest will be free to leave after screening by Ground Force personnel."

Orange figures, arms raised, popped into view along the edges of the square. Tomas' men approached, rifles ready, and ordered the rebels first to their knees, then spreadeagled face down on the ground. A few solitary rounds of rifle fire echoed around the square. More orange figures popped into view and dropped to the pavement. From the center of the square came the crump of more shaped charge detonations.

O'Herlihy and his fireteam trotted toward the rebels' fighting vehicles. His men clanged rifle butts on the vehicle hulls and shouted at the rebels inside. "Pop the hatch! Out one-by-one, slow, hands up! We'll shoot if we have to!"

Tomas went around the thopter to join his men near the rebel vehicles. On the pavement nearby, a civilian couple sat up. The woman, in a smudged blue dress, huddled against the man. He brushed her hair with the back of his hand. "Ease thy fears, my lady. Yon Challengerites have taken or slain all those who so barbarously attackéd us."

A realization hit Tomas. He walked toward the flagpole mound. He drew his pistol as he went.

Hatches clanged. Half a dozen rifles swung up to cover the rebels as they climbed out and descended the ladders on their vehicle sides. O'Herlihy counted them. "That wraps it up, ell-tee—"

Tomas extended his index finger to silence O'Herlihy. He went past a Stoat and scanned the crowd. Most remained on their bellies, though a few peeked up. Heads turned. A cloth cap—there—no.

Another man in a cloth cap peered around, then bent a gangly arm to reach under himself, for something inside his jacket—

Tomas rushed forward, to just outside the kicking range of the man's long legs, and aimed his pistol at the man's back. "Freeze, Iago!"

The man stopped moving, with his hand still underneath him. "Such is not my name. Why clept me by it?"

"It's our code name for a Papa operative loose on Arden for two tendays."

"Papa operative? How blinded in your lust for blood are you? Your comrades said civilians would be free to depart. What derangement of your senses makes you think I am anything but?"

Had he misread this man? Was Iago still somewhere in the square, biding his time until he could slip away amid a crowd of civilians?

Tomas said, "They'll prick your finger to draw blood. Takes a few minutes for a genomic analysis. If it fails to match a blood sample gathered in the Sycorax Hills, then you aren't—"

The man rolled onto his side and pulled his arm out from under his torso in the same movement. A pistol in his hand—

Tomas fired. Three rounds, painfully loud in the now-quiet square. The civilians around them flinched and wailed.

Three red blooms splotched Iago's chest. The pistol tumbled

from his hand and clattered to the pavement. A nine millimeter. Its blocky shape and long barrel matched the specs for a standard-issue Papa officer's sidearm. Blood oozed from Iago's mouth.

Kick the nine millimeter aside. Step closer. "Time to talk."

"You think you won, connie?" Blood gargled Iago's voice. "Flesh is weak. Machines are strong. Ever stronger." Iago's chest convulsed, lifting a few centimeters off the pavement in a vain reflexive grasp at one more breath. A final gurgle and he sank back to the pavement. His now-lifeless eyes stared past Tomas to the mirror visible over the smashed lintel of Parliament House.

Footsteps. Tomas looked up. Four solid men in civilian clothes, but their carriage and darting eyes suggested disguised soldiers. Arranged in an arc, they paused and parted. Beatrice Patel approached.

Tomas bowed. "Thank you for coming to Belmont, Miss Patel, and demonstrating your—engineering projects."

"I am pleaséd to serve the people of Arden, and the Confederated Worlds." Pygmy thopters leaped off the crippled Bawsons and Stoats. They took up station above her, hovering on swift beats of their wings. "As, it appears, are you."

More movement, from an armored car parked with other Ground Force vehicles. Maj. Tatarinova strode his way as a couple of privates rushed toward Iago. One carried a portable brain scanner.

To the privates, Tatarinova said, "Any chance?"

One of the privates, crouching at Iago's neck, looked up. Blood slicked the private's hands. "He's dead, ma'am."

"*Pizdets.*"

"He drew his pistol," Tomas said. "I had to shoot him."

"I cannot fault you," she replied. "But I don't know how to identify his contact at GFB Belmont."

Another intuition made Tomas look to the stage. The thopter and the podium hid the dozen chairs set aside for the highest ranks. He didn't need to see the chairs—he remembered who had sat there.

Tomas shook his head. "Don't worry, major. We don't need him for that."

15

Aftermath

That afternoon, the executive offices at GFB Belmont swarmed with activity. Casualty reports, readiness reports, civil affairs assessments, prisoner interrogation transcripts, communications to and from loyal Constabulary units, and more flooded in following the rebel attack. With a frantic air, most of Healey's staff tapped and swiped at tablets. Inside an office with an open door, Captain Singh worked, generating the thick clack of an old-fashioned keyboard.

No one gave a second glance to Tomas and Maj. Tatarinova as they went to Col. Healey's office.

"The colonel is very busy," an enlisted aide said. He had smooth skin and clear eyes, and Tomas instantly held him in contempt as a pogey. "Can it wait?"

"No."

The aide's aplomb wavered at Tatarinova's curt word. "Major, lieutenant, if you would give me a moment?"

"Of course," Tatarinova said. Before the aide could offer a seat, she and Tomas sat in chairs facing the aide's desk and the door to Healey's private office. As they waited, Tomas called up on his tablet floorplans of the building, and searched for nearby windows and doors that led to the outside.

The aide came around his desk. "He'll see you now." He led

them to Healey's office and hovered by the door.

Healey remained seated behind his desk. "Major. Lieutenant. Quite a surprise. I'll talk with you, but I'm busy as hell right now."

"No doubt," Tatarinova said. She glanced at Tomas. Tomas pressed his hand to the aide's shoulder, guiding the man out of the room. He shut the door on the aide before the man could react.

Tatarinova and Tomas took seats opposite Healey's desk. The major crossed her legs and folded her hands together on her knee. As she did, the window behind the executive officer caught Tomas' eye with a sunny sky puffed with high clouds.

For how many people had that day's summer sky been the last thing they'd seen?

Tomas returned his attention to Healey as Tatarinova spoke.

"We're here because Lt. Neumann noticed you were absent from the stage at today's ceremony."

Healey hesitated for a moment, then nodded. "I'm glad I caught up on paperwork this morning, because it would have bitten me in the backside if I'd waited till after the rally."

"Assuming you would have survived it," Tatarinova said, voice cool.

A sad shake of his head as Healey spoke. "That's a hell of thing that happened."

"Typically, the XO would attend a ceremony such as today's."

"I cleared my absence with Ibáñez." Healey leaned back, a little too artfully. "I don't know what you are getting at, major."

Her eyes resembled cold amethysts. "I think you do."

He swallowed. "No, I don't. I wasn't there? So? Neither were you."

"Were that all, I would not be here. Yet your absence today led me to spend the last three hours investigating a number of other things. The minutes of meetings between you, Rogers, and Ibáñez in the weeks immediately after the armistice indicate you advocated taking no action against rebels in the countryside, or against Papa landings."

"What of that? I wanted to preserve our forces. I didn't want the brigade to overextend itself trying to contest every settled square kilometer of Arden." Healey gestured at Tomas. "The lieutenant will see my point."

Tomas folded his arms.

Tatarinova went on. "For another example, according to communication records, either you or your aide made a phone call to one of Rogers' assistants shortly before Capt. Carlton received orders, direct from Rogers' office, to deploy his weakest platoons against the rebels near Eastcheap."

"I call operations a lot."

"Operations, perhaps. But not that particular assistant." Tatarinova sat taller. Her back was as rigid as a statue's. "Just now he proved a fount of information when I interrogated him with a brain scanner. That call came from you."

Healey opened his mouth as if he suddenly remembered. "Oh, that's right. I'd reviewed the records of those two lieutenants, Beauchamp and McClernan. Poor performers, true, but they just needed to be trusted with an operation to have a chance to prove themselves. Boost their confidence. Even if them becoming better officers wouldn't make a difference in the vote next week, we have to think of Ground Force's future."

It almost sounded believable. Then Tatarinova spoke. "There is one more thing. You left your office for two hours yesterday. There is no record of you being seen elsewhere on the base. However, someone in civilian clothes and matching your sex, height, and build exited the pedestrian street to downtown Belmont and returned shortly before you were next seen in your office. Where did you go, colonel? With whom did you speak?"

Healey blanched for a moment, then regained his composure. "How did you put that together? I knew there would be some data fragments, but you don't have the advanced computers of the Progressive Republic to piece them together." His nostrils flared with an inhalation, and he fixed them with a level gaze. "So be it. Being found out doesn't matter. What matters is that it had to be done."

Tomas could hold his tongue no longer. "You had to work with Papa and the rebels to send your fellow Ground Force to the hospital or the grave?"

Healey gave Tatarinova a *would-you-believe-this-butterbar?* look. When she didn't respond, Healey returned his attention to Tomas and knowingly shook his head. "You're a lieutenant just out of OCS. Still, you've led your platoon through enough action that you too have sent your men, in your words, to the hospital or grave. You've grasped a key insight into leadership. To achieve a worthy objective, you must pay a cost, in the lives of your men."

"I never...." Tomas trailed off, as memories of recent engagements struck him.

"You rearranged your column in the Sycorax Hills," Healey said. "To protect your Buffalo, sensible, but your actions caused the fireteam riding in your Badger to suffer one KIA, and another man still laid up in the hospital here. You left your position north of Eastcheap to engage the enemy, against orders, and sent three scouts, including a long-serving sergeant, to their deaths. I know men in your command were killed or wounded in the swamps near Eltham, and I'll wager your orders caused—"

"My orders served the mission assigned to me. Not treason."

"Treason?" Healey waved his hand in artfully confident dismissal. "Is it treason to surrender when you're surrounded by hostiles and cut off from your source of supply? In the Academy, I learned the answer is no, and I assume in OCS you learned the same. The scale is bigger, but the same principle holds true here. From the moment the Papa ships came through the wormhole, Arden was doomed to fall to them. Our brigade could only delay the inevitable."

"The plebiscite—"

"The plebiscite? Lieutenant, think clearly. Even if the voters of Arden sided with us now, the only way here from the rest of the Confederated Worlds is through Papa space. During peacetime, Papa would send the ships he wanted, and the messages he wanted, to Arden at will, while delaying or blocking Space Force transit. And even if the ships and messages Papa would send failed to turn the Ardenites to his cause, what will happen when the next war will break out? Because it will. What will happen, lieutenant?"

Tomas knew the answer immediately. "The Papa fleet would

have orbital supremacy. It would land multiple full-strength brigades against our undermanned one."

Healey chopped the side of his hand against his desk. "Another war with the Progressive Republic is inevitable. They saw how ineffectual Shirley Foxtrot is. They smell blood in the water. Papa already has machines more advanced than ours, and he will build more and build them faster. Papa doesn't want peace. He wants a breather. He'll catch his breath long before the feckless fools on Challenger will catch theirs. We need to switch to a war economy, on all the Confederated Worlds, as soon as possible, and rapidly resume hostilities, to have a chance of crushing Papa before he has a certainty of crushing us. The politicians don't see that. They have to be made to see it."

Healey leaned forward. "To make that switch and beat the drum for renewed hostilities, we need a cause that will overcome the petty greed of the electorate. Civilians want the never-ending tap of pleasures from the molecular fabricator rather than the bracing challenge of war. That's where Arden comes in. To lose Arden to the plebiscite would annoy a few voters. To lose Arden because Papa sent in face-swapping agents and advanced military vehicles in blatant disregard of the terms of the armistice, that would enrage the masses."

Intensity, almost madness, danced in Healey's eyes. "Lieutenant, your actions made that less likely, but don't despair. It's not too late. We can pull our units out of the field and give Papa the last week before the vote to strongarm small settlements and half the neighborhoods of Belmont into voting for him. We want Papa to score a hollow victory by winning the vote. The thirst for revenge is more satisfying to the human soul than all the pleasures of the fabricator. The people of the Confederated Worlds will see that. We will get the war we need."

Healey's voice grew solemn, but the intensity in his eyes remained. "Yes, some Ground Force soldiers unwittingly gave their lives, so that the Confederated Worlds may reach the ultimate victory. Their sacrifice will be commemorated, after the Unis and Papa have been vanquished."

His words swirled through Tomas' mind, until they fell into orbit around a single thought. The rebel attack today killed eighty people—Ground Force, Constabulary, and Ardenite civilians—and left three hundred wounded. Tomas leaned forward. "Did the General Staff order you to find out the rebels and Iago's plan, so you could hide in your office and not risk your own skin?"

Healey dropped his hands below his desktop. His confident expression wavered. "General Staff will exonerate me."

Maj. Tatarinova spoke. "Perhaps it will. I cannot. You are under arrest, Col. Healey, for treason and espionage for a foreign power. You will accompany Lt. Neumann and me to the guardhouse pending a court-martial."

Epilogue
Departure

Tomas waited in the departure lounge at the space elevator station in Belmont. Most of the platoon's men lay about, using their rucksacks as pillows. Music on headphones, letters from home displayed on tablets. A few of the men stood at the tall windows along the wide, incurving wall. Outside, the car of the climber train on which they would ride to stationary orbit gleamed in the double sunlight of the mirrors. Gorthi craned his neck to peer upward. Perhaps he wanted to see the top car of the climber train, or the ribbon climbing a hundred thousand kilometers toward Prospero and the Ariel Band.

"What's taking them so long?" Campbell said.

O'Herlihy replied. "They have to off-load our replacements."

The gate doors opened. Men from Tenth Brigade trudged out and passed under a sign, *Welcome to Arden*. On both sides of their path stood a row of women from the Constabulary Auxiliary. The women hung lanyards around the new arrivals' necks. Datachips on the lanyards fell against the men's chests. The datachips held the complete works of Shakespeare and fifty productions of his plays recorded over the past thousand years. Text and audio-recorded glossaries of Ardenese words and concepts filled the balance of the datachips. Finally, at the escalator down to ground level, the last

Auxiliary women took hold of the men's hands and welcomed them to the planet.

Nilsson sniffed out a breath. "A better greeting than we got, ell-tee."

"And all because of the work we did," Tomas said. He glanced at Nilsson's right arm. "How's the new limb?"

"Good as the old one. I've been diligent about rehab." Nilsson glanced at the window. The Cross of Valor at his neck dazzled with reflected light. His expression grew more serious. "I won't miss this planet. Except when I will."

"My thoughts too."

They would have six days on the climb up to the orbital station and a waiting Space Force transport. Three weeks under thrust, spin-gravity, and deceleration, interleaved with wormhole transits before reaching Challenger. They would be cooped up within a few dozen meters of each other for much of that time. Still, this moment held a charge of imminent, irrevocable sundering. Crossing the telescoping bridge to the climber car would transform the bonds grown between Tomas and all his men, Nilsson most of all.

"At least we survived, ell-tee."

Tomas nodded. "Most of us." He waited a moment. "What are your plans after we get to Challenger?"

"Accept a discharge as soon as I can. Then home to Österbot-ter. I have family connections, I'll get a job with the Terraformering-Departement. Maybe a field team. It'll feel strange walking in wilderness without getting shot at."

"You'll get used to it," Tomas said. "A girlfriend waiting for you?"

Nilsson quirked his mouth. "Not waiting."

"Her loss."

Nilsson chuckled. It soon faded. He gestured at Tomas' ring finger. "You're lucky, ell-tee."

Tomas thought of Lissa, in their temporary quarters on the station above Challenger. Soon after came memories of their first meeting, then their second. "More than you know."

The ends of the Auxiliary lines curled away from the escalators, to open the path between them to the departure lounge. A voice came over the loudspeaker. "All passengers bound for high orbit are askéd to prepare for boarding. A single queue, please, forméd to pass twixt the bracéd lines of the fair maidens and dames of the Auxiliary."

The rustle of forty bodies moving, rising, and hoisting rucksacks smothered the echoes of the boarding announcement. Tomas stretched and lifted his own rucksack to his shoulders.

"Shouldn't you be at the head of the line, ell-tee?"

"It'll take us six days to make the climb. I'm in no hurry."

They flowed toward the rear of the forming line of figures in urban camouflage. Nilsson's face showed he had a question long before he spoke. "Ell-tee, if I may, are you staying in the Ground Force?"

Tomas shook his head. "They have me another four years, if they want. I can't resign my commission yet."

"That's a shame. After that?"

The line moved its first steps forward. Tomas' pace fell in with the rest. "I think I'll make a career of it."

A BODYGUARD OF LIES

1

The Rally

The wall of the subway station entrance cast a narrow shadow on the steps. Tomas emerged from the station into the yellow-orange light of Epsilon Eridani. Though bright, the steps remained cool underfoot all the way up to the street.

At the top of the steps, long, skinny signs hung from poles flanking the entrance. *Firstlanding Square South*. On his side of the street, skyscraper walls of curved concrete and vast sheets of mirrored glass towered above the sidewalk. A step brought Tomas into glare reflected from more mirrored glass cladding an upper floor of a high-rise across the street.

He squinted and turned his head, and the sounds of downtown McAuliffe city pummeled his ears. Rustling feet, the whisper of automobile tires and the squeak of brakes, and conversations over phones and wearable communicators flooded him.

He felt more exposed in downtown McAuliffe than he had on any battlefield.

Tomas took a breath. He would follow through on Rolston's invitation. Forrester's campaign rally would help him decide about the candidate, one way or the other.

He started along the sidewalk toward the square. He held his shoulders back and chest up. Civilians in the latest fashions—one exposed shoulder, sequined necklines plunging to the breastbone, oversized sunglasses doubling as video displays, earbuds curling like cooked plastic shrimp, and those were just the *men*—loomed in front of Tomas, then veered away at the last moment. They smoothly continued their conversations, as if skills imps had planted in their brains how to walk crowded streets without noticing the people around them.

Tomas slowed. How could he find Rolston and Unzai in this crowd?

The only answer came from a man's step on his heel. "Keep moving, tourist," the man muttered as he walked by.

Tomas picked up his pace to keep with the flow of pedestrians. He neared a walnut-brown awning and cramped chairs and tables of a sidewalk café. Half a dozen youthful men in garish clothes stood near a pair of tables, shouting and gesticulating at someone the crowd hid from Tomas.

A few more steps, and he found Rolston and Unzai.

Rolston's garrison cap sat low on his forehead, nearly touching the top of his augmented reality glasses. The position of the garrison cap accented the sharp lines of his eyebrows and the venom in his green eyes. "Sit you down, each be-damned one of you."

One of the men, with bulging eyes, in a shirt speckled and iridescent as a trout, slapped the back of his hand against a friend's shoulder. "A warmonger *and* a stupid Endeavourite."

Another of the men, his teeth partially exposed in a sneer, cocked his head and flicked it back. His voice dripped with smug superiority. "We don't sit down for some lieutenant or whatever from a continent covered in *lichen*."

Rolston's hands clenched into fists. Next to him, Unzai tapped his fingers on his pointed chin and muttered something too quiet for Tomas to catch. Rolston's angry gaze remained locked on the sneering man. "You don't sit down for me? True, you don't. You only kneel. For the Progressive Republic. So you can catch their pubes in your teeth when you—"

Tomas hurried to them. He extended his arms and pressed his palms against Rolston's chest and the sneering man's. He alloyed his voice with steel. "Enough. Both of you."

The sneering young man took a half-step back and swatted at Tomas' arm with his hand. "Or what? You're another warmonger? Hiding a gun to brandish at me?"

"We can take these swine with our fists," Rolston said.

"We could." Tomas turned his head. "But we will let him go. He has his right to speak, just as we have ours."

Rolston shrugged away from Tomas' hand. "Maybe by law. But by justice? We earned our right to speak in the mud and blood on New Liberty and Navi Ambarsar."

"You volunteered," the sneering young man said. "You got what you deserved."

Tomas narrowed his eyes and fixed the sneering man with a scowl. Man? Boy. A cocooned boy, with enough income to drink overpriced coffee and buy clothes handcrafted by a tailor. As if he could know even the tiniest fraction about the soldier's life to dismiss Tomas, Unzai, and Rolston.

"What I deserved?" Rolston clenched his fists and leaned forward. "A back stab from you?"

Tomas squared his shoulders to the sneering young man. On the other side of Rolston, Unzai did the same.

The young man's gaze flicked from side to side. He shifted his weight to his heels, and his sneer curdled into mild fear.

His companion in the speckled, iridescent shirt leaned closer. This one looked toward the subway station and his eyes bulged even wider than before. "Let it go."

The young man's eyes turned in the direction his companion watched. Tomas glanced that way as well.

Five men approached, wearing blue jackets and matching pants. On their hips, secured by instant release adhesive, rode handled batons. An armband ringed their right sleeves, showing a red cross barby against a blue field. These five men wore garrison caps, similar to Rolston's, but coming to a flat vertical face over the wearer's forehead. On each flat face of their caps stood the dark disk of a camera.

Passing civilians veered wide around them.

The five men in blue belonged to the Restoration Party's security organization. A thug squad, some of Forrester's opponents called the bluecoats. The RP's militia, planning street battles if Forrester lost the upcoming election, said others.

The young man and his companions quickly sat down. Their rigid backs did not touch their chairs. Their gazes and voices remained amongst themselves.

Rolston adjusted his cap to a jaunty angle. "Good afternoon, team leader," he said to a bluecoat with crow's feet around humorless eyes, and white stripes of rank flanking the cross barby on his armband.

"Good afternoon to you, captain—" The bluecoat team leader nodded to Thomas and Unzai. "— citizens. All well?"

Rolston glanced at the young men seated at the nearby tables. His mouth puckered as if to spit cherry pits into the young men's ornate hairstyles. "Well enough."

The bluecoat team leader squinted at the young men, then nodded with an air of finality. "We'll see you at the rally, captain?"

"All of us." Rolston lifted his hands twenty centimeters to indicate Unzai and Tomas.

"Glad to hear it." The Restoration Party security team walked on toward Firstlanding Square.

Rolston glanced at the lower left corner of his vision. "It's 1545 already? If we don't go now we'll be far from the stage." He led Tomas and Unzai down the sidewalk. The RP security team provided a wake shield. This time, no pedestrians loomed in Tomas' path.

"Unzai, Neumann," Rolston began. Despite being raised here on Challenger, he pronounced Tomas' name correctly enough, *Noymun*. The thick soles of Rolston's black service-dress shoes clacked on the sidewalk. "Why the civvy garb, you two?"

Tomas reached inside the collar of his polo shirt and scratched his nape. His topsiders muffled his footfalls. "You know regs forbid appearing in uniform at partisan political events."

"That's right," said Unzai.

Rolston clapped his hand on Tomas' shoulder, squeezed the blue cotton of Tomas' polo shirt. His green eyes danced. "Right, I can trust you two to follow regs. But the regs are a guide, not a lifeline to cling to. Neumann, I've heard your stories about New Liberty and Arden. You've deviated from regs to better pound the Unis or the PRs. Now I'm doing the same."

"The same?" Tomas said.

"Right, not all the same. You poor married bastards lack my grasp of fashion. Unlike you, if I wore civvy garb, I'd look too much like our lilies of the field back at the café." Rolston laughed.

Tomas pressed his lips together. He'd left Lissa at home with the boys for this. "You know there are cameras everywhere. What if some higher rank sees video of you?" On the other side of Rolston, Unzai nodded.

Rolston gave a jaunty shake of his head. "Higher ranks will attend the rally in uniform. The GF brass is pro-Forrester—"

"I know," Tomas said, though all he knew was r-mail, rumor. His mouth felt dry. "But we're supposed to appear impar—"

Rolston laughed again. Tomas gritted his teeth. "Relax, Neumann. If the brass call me on the carpet for taking sides while in uniform, I'll tell them you tried to stop me."

They walked on. Challenger's rapid rotation shrank the shadows of highrises as Epsilon Eridani neared the third noon of the calendar day.

Soon the skyscraper vista opened up to Firstlanding Square.

A ring of streets defined the square's perimeter. They climbed steps to a footbridge held up by stylus-thin strands of nanotube alloy. Above the crowded streets, sinuous highrises stretched glassy faces into the sky.

Tomas surveyed the highrises, then relaxed. Peacetime. The buildings lacked sniper nests.

He, Rolston, and Unzai reached the far end of the footbridge. Two men in gray-black windbreakers and shaded videoglasses, Confederal Police, studied a pair of Restoration Party bluecoats. The bluecoats stared back.

Down the steps from the footbridge, concrete slabs paved most of the square. In two ranks of raised planters, cypresses extended branches like high thin clouds. Ten meters beyond the inner row of planters, the concrete slabs stopped at a four-strand railing. Beyond lay a zone of rippled, reddish-brown basalt. Five standard centuries earlier, the first ship to land on Challenger had softened that rock with the heat of its fusion drive. The LZ remained a monument to the planet's terraformers.

At the railing, a small sign showed the cross barby and an arrow pointing to the right.

Readily visible from two hundred meters across the square, a crowd faced a stage. Behind the stage, rising above the foliage of cypresses, a huge backdrop showed another cross barby, the Restoration Party's logo, against a red-white-and-blue ripple evoking the Confederated Worlds flag. A lectern near the front of the stage looked tiny beneath the flag. Next to the logo stood the words *Forrester for President 3018. Honor Restored.*

Halfway between the small sign and the stage stood a line of bluecoats. The nearest one shifted his position to intercept Tomas, Unzai, and Rolston. A chemical sniffer, like a tiny alloy lizard, rested on his shoulder. The bluecoat's eyes seemed as wide as the camera lens on his cap. He had a smooth face and a voice of naïve confidence. "Good afternoon, captain, citizens. Have you already selected Forrester as your first preference on the ballot?"

"Yes, absolutely," Rolston said.

Tomas shook his head. "Not yet." He leaned toward O'Brien of the Outworld Alliance Party.

The smooth-faced bluecoat stood taller. "That will change when you hear Forrester speak. He understands our problems and our only acceptable solution better than any other candidate." He gestured toward a line of waiting people. "Please queue up for a security screen."

Rolston leaned forward and stretched his palm toward the young man. "We can set that aside, can't we? You approve us."

"I would if I could, captain."

A temporary railing ran from the rippled basalt field to the outermost row of cypress planters. The queue led to the only passage through the railing, a security scanner crewed by more men in shaded videoglasses and dark windbreakers.

Tomas said, "ConPol doesn't trust you to provide security?"

The smooth-faced bluecoat shook his head gravely. "We don't trust them. Captain, gentlemen, please proceed."

Tomas, Rolston, and Unzai started forward. Angling toward the rear of the queue a few steps ahead of them went a solitary man wearing a tan, baggy, plastic jacket. He faced away from them, showing only a thick mop of brown hair and a sharp facet of cheekbone.

Unzai tapped his fingers on his chin. His voice carried a disbelieving tone. "That young fellow's listened to too much of Forrester's rhetoric. ConPol wouldn't intentionally fail to protect Forrester."

Rolston's eyebrows arched. "Don't be you naïve, Unzai. The older parties and the senior bureaucrats all hate Forrester. His every word gut-punches them with a reminder they surrendered rather than risk their precious capital cities to orbital fires." He waggled his hands to indicate both McAuliffe, the planetary capital, around them, and Confederal City, the capital of the Confederated Worlds, four kilometers east across the lake. "They can't stomach that. They'll pull every string they can to get ConPol looking the other way if an assassin comes after him."

"You think they could be that duplicitous?" Tomas said. Rolston's brow crinkled. "Double-dealing?"

"Think it? I feel it in my bones."

They reached the queue and shuffled forward. From the slow progress of the queue and the focused motions of the personnel at the security scanner, the Confederal Police seemed serious about security.

When they neared the scanner, Tomas' impression grew stronger. Ahead of them, the scanner hummed for long seconds around the man with the baggy jacket and sharp cheekbones. A sharp glance between two ConPol agents, and they beckoned the man aside for handheld scanning. He held his arms straight out to his sides while ConPol swept wands over his body. His mouth turned down. "I haven't done anything. You're singling me out because I got my jacket from the fab utility. That's class warfare...."

His voice faded as Tomas and Rolston took turns going through the scanner.

"There's a good spot." Rolston pointed at one of the cypress planters, about a dozen meters from the stage. They wound their way through the growing crowd, and stopped under the cypress' canopy. A faint citrus scent came from the leaves. On a nearby platform two meters above the ground, audio and video technicians chatted among themselves and prepped their equipment.

The crowd filled the space for a while longer, under the watchful gazes of Restoration Party bluecoats and ConPol agents standing near the front of the stage. Rolston's earlier comment about military personnel in uniform proved true. Amid the civilians stood noncoms and junior officers in Ground Force service gray and officers in Space Force deep blue.

Personnel from each service mostly clumped together. Two lieutenants provided a rare exception. Though their uniforms differed, they matched by wearing white turbans and beards pinned under their chins. Their long noses made them look like brothers. The turbans and beards suggested they were Sikhs from Navi Ambarsar, a world lost to the Progressive Republic at the end of the war.

A few minutes before 1600, the halves of the backdrop parted. The first notes of an old patriotic song, *Challenger, Gem of the Spaceways*, played from elevated speakers. The crowd hushed and focused on the stage.

Instead of the candidate, out came four men, two in suits of gray and two, of blue. Not the services' dress uniforms, but civilian suits cut in Ground Force and Space Force style. The men had unlined faces and wrinkled eyes produced by decades of rejuvenation treatments.

"The budget cuts and finger pointing pushed them into early retirement," Rolston said.

The retired officers took measured steps forward and stopped in a gapped line just behind the lectern.

From the speakers boomed an announcer's voice. "Ladies and gentlemen, please stand at attention, and gentlemen, remove your hats, as together we sing the Confederated Worlds anthem."

The crowd stirred in compliance. Tomas clapped his hands

against his sides as the anthem began. Rolston held his cap over his heart and sung along with gusto. "....Confed'rated Worlds, we stand on guard for thee!"

As the final word echoed around the square, the halves of the backdrop parted again. Two aides, one man and one woman, scurried out and held the backdrop halves. The announcer said, "Ladies and gentlemen, your next president, Roderick Forrester!"

Cheers and applause erupted from the crowd. Cameras and parabolic microphones swung toward the stage. Forrester emerged from the backdrop and strode toward the lectern.

His aides dropped the backdrop and hurried after him. Forrester stood head and shoulders above them—almost exactly two meters? No. Assuming the retired officers stood not much taller than average, recalibrating Forrester's height when he reached them put him at a meter-ninety, still taller than the average man raised on Challenger.

Forrester shook the hand of one of the Ground Force retirees and laughed at something the other one said. Forrester's teeth gleamed in rows as regular as the line of cypresses.

He took his hand back from the Ground Force retiree, then turned to say something to one of the former Space Force officers. After a brief clap on the other Space Force retiree's shoulder, two steps brought Forrester to the lectern. His dark-blond hair, swept back, remained fixed against a sudden breeze sighing through the square. His hazel eyes gleamed as he waved to the cheering crowd.

Toward the sides of the backdrop, at the height of the cross barby and the campaign slogan, chameleoncloth panels woven into the fabric came to life. Each showed a closeup of Forrester captured by a camera around the rally. A tan suffused his clear skin. The few wrinkles at the corners of his eyes, and the few gray hairs at his temples, implied he combined the wisdom of years with the vigor of relative youth.

Tomas looked away from the video panels. The immense closeups were too much to take in, even if they only magnified a sight he could have seen with his naked eye.

At the lectern, Forrester pointed his hand at someone in the crowd and nodded. His head swiveled to Tomas, Unzai, and Rolston, and he smiled as if he saw old friends. In a moment, he looked toward someone else.

Tomas clapped more quietly. "Do you know him?"

"What?"

Tomas raised his voice over the crowd noise. "Do you know him? Or he you?"

"Never met him," Rolston said. His mouth remained slightly open. "Yet."

The smile of recognition had to be some politician's trick. Tomas pressed his lips together. A leader like Forrester aspired to be should abstain from such tricks—

A thought bubbled up from Tomas' subconscious and relaxed his mouth. *The skills imps implanted into your brain a dozen skills or more for managing enlisted men. He's the same as you.*

Somewhere in the crowd arose a chant, "Honor restored. Honor restored...." The chant built for a few moments, and Forrester's smile beamed at the crowd. Finally he pushed his hands down through the air. The chant died out. Forrester nudged the lectern's microphone closer to his mouth.

"Fellow citizens, good afternoon." Even without the microphone, his deep, resonant voice would have carried to Tomas. "I am deeply honored to see so many Challengerites before me who know the struggle we face...."

Forrester continued his speech. From time to time, Rolston nodded, and occasionally emphasized the gesture with a poke in the ribs or a whisper to Unzai or Tomas. Overhead, a two-man ornithopter with the ConPol logo on its side hovered on slow beats of its mechanical wings.

"....There are *those*," Forrester said, and his enunciation of the last word drew echoes of disdain from the crowd, "who say I'm blind to the reality of the Unity and the Progressive Republic. *They* say I can't see the reality of the human galaxy since the end of the war. *They* say New Liberty belongs to the Unity."

Forrester looked at the brothers in turbans. "*They* say Navi Ambarsar belongs to the PR. And because I say otherwise, *they* call me blind."

Voices in the crowd hissed. Someone shouted "Shame!"

Forrester's words tugged at parts of Tomas, like a magnet summoning iron. But other parts of Tomas, metal alloyed with the mud and blood of New Liberty and Arden, remained immobile.

"But *they* are the ones who are blind!" Forrester said. "For I have seen the Progressive Republic far more clearly than *they* ever will! I saw its weapons rend my ship. I spent two years as its prisoner. The Progressive Republic lifted its mask and I stared its inhuman monstrosity in the face!"

Tomas shuddered. He remembered a scene like this, on Arden. Crawling under dripping blood. Pursuing the elusive PR agent—

"Its malevolence will not rest until its tyranny enslaves every citizen of the Confederated Worlds! In the sight of the god I worship, I swear I shall not rest until the Unity and Progressive Republic's threat is broken for all time!"

Someone passed behind Tomas. An elbow brushed Tomas' back. "Pardon me," said a slightly familiar male voice.

"Sure," Tomas said while focusing most of his attention on the stage. Then an intuition pricked him. He glanced over his shoulder. The voice belonged to the man with sharp cheekbones and baggy plastic jacket. He wormed through the crowd toward the nearby cypress planter.

The crowd erupted in applause and cheers. Rolston glanced around, then pumped his fist and shouted "Hoo-rah!"

Tomas craned his neck to keep an eye on the man in the baggy tan jacket. Sweat suddenly bloomed on his forehead, and not from the rays of Epsilon Eridani.

"Pardon me," he said to Rolston and Unzai. He sidled through the crowd, following the man in the baggy jacket. He stopped with a screen of spectators between them, slicing his view of the man into vertical strips.

The man stood on tiptoes, with his belly against the flat concrete ledge rimming the planter. The bottom of his jacket dangled between the planter wall and his leg. Something bulged in the jacket's front pockets. With an intent look in his eyes harmonizing with the sharp angle of his cheekbones, he dug through the planter's loose soil with both hands.

He rose from the planter holding a transparent bag. Soil clung to the thick plastic and obscured the object inside. A bluish-gray shape, a thin cylinder about twenty centimeters long.

The man brushed the dirt from the bag, then plunged it into one of his jacket pockets. Suddenly, his thick mop of hair flowed with his head, as if he sensed he was watched.

Tomas jolted his gaze up to Forrester. From the corner of his eye, he glimpsed the man's sharp cheekbone and newly hunched shoulders.

"The path stretches before us." Forrester's voice echoed from the speakers. The man's shoulders eased back and down. The weight of hands, and more, in his pockets pulled taut his jacket.

Forrester continued his speech. "The way is long and difficult. But it is far more dangerous for us to heed the fool's counsels of the complacent, to hide our heads in virtual realities, and do nothing to gird against the Unity and Progressive Republic's renewed aggression!"

The man snaked closer to the stage. His jacket sleeves rippled, as if his hands worked at some intricate assembly in his pockets.

Tomas' peripheral vision fell away. His eyes became a scope locked on the man. "Out of the way," he said to the people around him. "Move it." He pressed hard on elbows and shoulders.

Angry looks and muttered curses followed him. He barely noticed. He craned his neck and peered after the man. The man kept his head facing the stage and his hands in his jacket pockets. He worked at something behind the jacket's closed zipper.

"For aggress they will!" Forrester's hand chopped the air. "The Progressive Republic and the Unity have not chosen peace, but a truce! Which they shall break the moment they conclude us too weak to defend ourselves!"

The man stopped behind a clump of spectators six meters from Forrester. The edges of Tomas' vision turned gray and spotty. Tomas shoved through the crowd. No apologies. Too focused to speak.

Forrester's voice thundered. "Elect me, and I vow to put forth every effort to defend us from our enemies and neutralize the threat of our domestic foes!"

Tomas came within a few steps of the man, behind him and to his right. The man's hand emerged from his jacket pocket. A dark blue pistol. The man wrapped his left hand around his right, thumbs aligned under the slide—

Tomas lunged forward. Knee into the back of the assassin's legs, left hand on far shoulder, right arm reaching under the assassin's arms. The pistol roared as he toppled the assassin backward over his knee. Another shot, another, high into the air over Forrester.

His ringing ears muffled the crowd's screams.

The assassin collapsed. Tomas jumped on him. His right hand clutched the assassin's right forearm, keeping the pistol aimed into the air. His left hand pushed the assassin's head against the concrete.

Pain bloomed around Tomas' right eye. He winced. The assassin pulled back his left fist for another punch.

Tomas grunted. He shoved the assassin's head harder against the concrete. He shifted his left knee into the assassin's neck. "Drop the pistol!"

The crowd had backed away. A glance at the stage showed the now-empty lectern. ConPol in dark windbreakers crouched around two of their peers lying on Forrester. From somewhere at ground level, dimly heard through the ringing in Tomas' ears, male voices shouted at one another with the intensity of soldiers in combat.

The assassin dropped the pistol. It banged against the small bones of Tomas' hand as it tumbled to the ground. The assassin's face turned purple, yet he sneered at Tomas. "We lost," the assassin hissed. "This time." He gnashed his teeth together in a brief but complex rhythm—

Bluecoats arrived first. Young men, their eyebrows low in a look of brittle toughness. The tips of their batons turned tiny circles through the air. "He swallowed a lethe capsule!" Tomas said. "Empty his stomach before it dissolves!" Otherwise, the assassin's memories of the recent days would evaporate into a mist no brain scanner could read.

The assassin barked a laugh. "Lethe capsules. You want to fight the Progressive Republic and you think lethe capsules are state of the art?"

The young bluecoats gave each other puzzled looks. Finally, the one with team leader stripes on his armband said, "How can we empty his stomach?"

Boots clomped closer. "With your baton, virgin." The speaker's voice sounded like some gruff uncle. He had blond hair like a wheat field after harvest on some planet where people chose to grow food by farming. Enough wrinkles edged his authoritative gray eyes to mark him as a few years older. His armband showed more stripes than the team leader. "That's how we did it dirtside in the war. Make him puke."

The young team leader nodded. He stepped forward and aimed his baton's tip at the assassin's mouth.

The older bluecoat sharpened his voice. "You aren't having sex with your high school sweetheart for the first time. You're banging some off-base whore. Like this." He wrapped his hand over the young team leader's and shoved the baton into the assassin's mouth.

The assassin gagged. Muscles clenched under his jacket and he twisted his head to the side.

His vomit hit the concrete. One of the young bluecoats hot-footed twenty centimeters back in a vain effort to keep his boots clean. His comrades chuckled.

The older bluecoat poked the toes of his boot through clumps of vomit. "Where's that damn capsule?" He toed the assassin's ribs. "How long ago you swallow it?"

"What did I tell you about lethe capsules, morons?" the assassin said.

Without rancor, the older bluecoat kicked the assassin in the belly.

The assassin gasped for breath. "That's a violation—undue force—"

The older bluecoat drew his foot back for another kick.

"That's enough, sergeant," Tomas said, and how did he know the older bluecoat had been a sergeant? The older bluecoat stepped back. His gray eyes remained unabashed.

"Listen to the civilian," a deep voice said. Three ConPol agents now waited nearby.

The older bluecoat looked up at them. "About time you showed up."

One of the ConPol agents, with the dark skin and coiled hair of a Garvey's World native, shot the older bluecoat a cold look, then stepped toward the assassin. "You are under arrest for the attempted murder of a candidate for confederal office. You will be taken into custody and subjected to interrogation augmented by brain scanning." To his fellow agents, he said, "Grab him."

The other two ConPol agents went toward the assassin's sides. The Restoration Party security team stepped forward, threatening to block them.

The chief agent swept back a panel of his jacket and set his fist on his hip, near a holstered pistol. His other hand pulled videoglasses from his eyes. He glowered at the older bluecoat. "Do I look like I want to take shit from a pack of boy scouts?"

The older bluecoat's face turned unreadable. Definitely a former sergeant. He stared back at the chief ConPol agent, then slowly turned to his men. "We did our job. We know what really happened, even if ConPol try to take the credit. Let them take him."

The Restoration Party security team stepped back. The ConPol agents lifted the assassin to his feet. One ConPol agent cuffed the assassin's hands behind his back, and another shackled his ankles together with a short chain.

The assassin's forehead crinkled. He looked around—the ConPol agents, the crowd, the stage. His thick mop of hair gave him a dull look.

Tomas' breath caught. The assassin acted as if he recognized nothing. As if he had no idea what brought him here.

Inhale. A breath in Tomas' chest, the next one in his belly, and he could think. The assassin must have taken a week or so to select cypress planters and hide the parts of his pistol. A lethe capsule could erase memories that far back, even a little further. Yet even if he'd taken a lethe capsule, the assassin must have planned to shoot Forrester for months, and that memory would remain.

A cold feeling trickled down the inside of Tomas' chest. "He didn't swallow a lethe capsule."

The chief ConPol agent kept most of his attention on the assassin's puzzled face. "We'll make that call." The chief agent nodded to the two men guarding the assassin. They walked the assassin away. The stunned crowd quickly vacated their path, then slowly refilled the space left in their wake. Wide-eyed gazes returned to the stage.

Forrester stood at the lectern. ConPol agents and Restoration Party bluecoats reached for his elbows, like fretting wives or timid subordinates urging retreat. Forrester kept all his attention on the crowd.

"Fellow citizens!" Forrester's voice boomed from the speakers. "Fellow citizens, you have seen our enemies in action!" He jutted his finger at the assassin and the ConPol agents escorting him away. "They see the threat I pose their heinous plans! He is not the first, and will not be the last, to try to bury me. But I am not the message! I am merely a mirror dazzling our foes' shifty eyes with the light of truth! For I am merely one of millions of true sons of the Confederated Worlds—joined by true patriots such as this man!" He extended his hand toward Tomas. "And we will do whatever is needed to keep our worlds strong and free!"

Forrester's words echoed around the square. After a moment, someone in the crowd broke the silence with slow applause. Others joined in then, with livelier applause and a few ragged cheers. Even so, the civilian faces around Tomas still showed shock.

And surprise. A man with a lined face and a collar pin from the KIA families association came closer to Tomas. His hands probed for Tomas'. "You saved him. Thank you, sir, thank you."

Other faces turned to Tomas. Eyes wide, lips parted, as if they beheld a worker of wonders.

Tomas wanted to squirm. He shrugged. "Anyone would have done the same, if they'd noticed the assassin."

The older bluecoat stuck his baton back onto the adhesive strip on his pants. "But you're the one who did." He suddenly angled his head, looking like he listened to someone through an earbud. "Sir? Yes, he's with me." He nodded once, a crisp bob of his chin. "Yes sir."

He turned to Tomas. "Forrester would like you to join him on stage."

Tomas blinked. His head swiveled, scanning the crowd for Rolston or Unzai to deflect Forrester's interest in him. *Keep me out of politics!*

Someone in a gray jacket and trousers pressed through the crowd. Energy flashed in Rolston's green eyes. He clapped Tomas on the shoulder. "Neumann. I'm tingling with awe. What about the shooter got under your skin?"

Tomas shrugged. "I can't tell you. I just knew."

The older bluecoat leaned his square head toward Tomas. "Sir, Forrester is waiting—"

"Waiting?" Rolston gaped. "Neumann, what in the hell is holding you back? Climb you up there!"

"I don't want to get involved in politics," Tomas finally said.

"When you stopped the shooter, you stuck your hand in the monkey trap." Rolston leaned toward Tomas' ear. "When Forrester wins, you'll ride the promotion fast track. Give you me just one hand up, when you get a chance, is all I ask you. Remember you us little people, will you?"

"I—what? I'm going back to work on Oneday same as you."

Rolston chuckled. "Oneday, perhaps. But you won't be staying long."

Tomas rotated his upper body, trying to pull his shoulder from under Rolston's hand. "It's two weeks till the election. He won't remember. If he even wins."

Rolston lowered his hand to Tomas' upper back. "You saved his life, Neumann. He will remember. Not if he wins. When." He shoved Tomas toward the stage.

Tomas took two steps before he could think. Forrester's voice boomed from the loudspeakers. "Here he comes! The hero of the hour!"

A thousand eyes seemed to cast smoldering rays onto Tomas' skin. Applause and cheers struck him like a stiff rain. He trudged forward until he stood near the edge of the stage.

On stage, two bluecoats came forward. They bent their knees and extended their banded arms toward Tomas. He lifted his right arm, but then surprise froze it in mid-air. Forrester strode around the lectern. "I'll help him," he told the bluecoats.

They stepped back. Forrester reached down from the edge of the stage. He and Tomas grasped forearms and he pulled Tomas up.

"Thank you for saving my life," Forrester said. Though low in volume, and competing with the cheers of the crowd, his voice still resonated through Tomas' mind. "What's your name?"

"Tomas Neumann."

"Law enforcement? Military?"

"Ground Force."

Forrester beamed, though a wry note pulled down the corners of his mouth. He moved his head closer to Tomas' ear. The spectacle of the rally, the noise of the crowd, all receded. "I know my old comrades in Space Force dismiss your contributions. It pains me to say it, I dismissed them too, years ago. But interservice rivalry is part of what led us to defeat. Undoing it will be part of what will restore us our rightful place in the galaxy."

"I'm glad to hear that, Mr. Forrester. I agree completely." Tomas' memories of mud and blood softened. *To get to the destination this man sees for the Confederated Worlds, the price in lives and pain is worth paying.*

A glint filled Forrester's eyes. He spoke with leonine certainty. "I see I can rely on you."

2

Reassignment

Figures with concealed faces pierced the back of Tomas' wrist with pins and he woke up. His right hand groped for his watch and tapped it to silence. He blinked open his eyes. The bedroom curtains attenuated the light of the bioluminescent cypresses at the curbside in front of the house. Shades of gray painted the ceiling and walls in the colorless palette of 0500.

He swung his legs out of bed. Lissa lay on her side, breath reedy in her nose. She shifted her limbs at his motion, yet remained asleep. At least she faced him. The night before, he'd gone to bed before her, while she glumly drank a glass of riesling and watched the election results from outsystem. *She gets a little time after the boys fall asleep and she watches content she can read the next morning. She needs downtime, fine, but when the idea of making love stiffens her back—*

His bare feet touched the cool floor of nanofabbed wood. Tomas made his way through the living room and kitchen. His foot came down on a toy car. The toy rolled across the living room floor. *She could tell Stefan to put away his toys—* His legs tensed and he angled his head, listening for sounds from upstairs, but the boys stayed asleep.

Four minutes after waking, he lifted his kettlebell off its rack in the garage. He took it to the workout mat in the corner, between a tool rack and boxes of Stefan's old toddler clothes, too big yet for Artur. First, a set of swings—

His watch prodded his wrist again. He'd turned it off, not set it to snooze. Hadn't he?

He stopped the kettlebell at the bottom of its arc, lowered it to the workout mat. He squinted at the watch face. Not an alarm— an incoming call. *From: Brig. G. Echevarria, 1ˢᵗ** Armored Grenadier Brigade.*

The caller identification kicked Tomas in the back. The brigade commander? Skipping two layers of channels to call a mere battalion staff officer over an hour before dawn?

Don't make him wait any longer. Tomas swiped his finger across his watch face, then held his wrist close to his mouth. "Good morning, sir. Sorry about the audio-only. I'm in the middle of my workout—"

"Get you to a video screen."

Tomas gulped. "Right away, sir."

He padded into the kitchen. In the gray light before the day's first dawn, disassembled baby bottles and breastpump hardware cluttered the countertops like the phantoms of spent smoke canisters and rocket propelled grenades littering a battlefield. He went to a tablet mounted on the wall between the cooktop and the oven. He pulled it away from the wall on its flexing arm, then tapped and swiped. His finger motions made the tablet wobble on its arm. Video appeared in the tablet's display. "As you asked, sir."

Echevarria sat in front of ornately-molded walnut bookshelves bearing a golf ball embedded in transparent plastic and a crude statue of a man's head and torso carved by tinsnips and pliers from the lid of an ammunition case. The brigadier wore a civilian polo shirt tight across his chest and around his upper arms. He leaned his head on his elbow, his elbow on a desk. His brown eyes looked like slits, despite heavy blinks and a steaming coffee mug near to hand. "You know why I'm calling, Newman, so I'll get to the point—"

"Sir? With respect, sir, I don't know. I look forward to as much information as you can share."

Echevarria squinted. "Don't play you the innocent with me. It's too be-damned early in the morning for that."

Tomas racked his mind for some clue. His voice sounded rushed. "Did Forrester win?"

Echevarria's eyes remained slit-like. Tomas imagined a boulder stared at him. Then the brigadier reached for his coffee. "You watched the election returns last night?"

Tomas shook his head. "I sacked out around 2530."

"You checked the results this morning?"

"No. I knew Rolston would tell me when I got to battalion headquarters, if I hadn't heard before then."

Echevarria shook his head in ponderous shakes. "You really don't know. Listen you, it's not my job to tell some battalion staffer what's happening in the worlds, so I only say this once. The last votes didn't come in from Arden until sometime between 2800 and midnight. The outworld voters who ranked their local candidates first mostly ranked Forrester second, and he got more first- and second-place votes from here than the peace-at-any-price party wanted to believe."

Tomas tried to follow the details of the preferential ballot. Too early in the morning. He shut his eyes and nodded. The details didn't matter. "Forrester won."

The brigadier wrinkled his nose. "Why else would I be calling? You put him up to this, nay?"

"Put whom up to what, sir?"

"Two hours ago, General Olafson called me. Woke me out of a fine sleep, he did. I dreamed of beefier Badgers and Graywolfs for my armored grenadier and armored battalions when he roused me."

General Olafson? The Chief of Staff, the Ground Force's highest ranking officer? "What did he ask you to do, sir?"

Echevarria raised an eyebrow like a black and gray caterpillar. "You still want to tell me you didn't put Forrester up to this? An hour before Olafson called me—barely an hour after the acceptance speech—Forrester called Olafson. Forrester wants you assigned to his office as his special assistant for Ground Force affairs."

Tomas rested his hand on the countertop. He shut his eyes and a glowing green rectangle drifted across his eyelids. How could he get out of this? "I'm flattered, sir, that he should think of me—"

"Drop you the act. You asked him for the job, nay?" Echevarria's mouth looked sour. "All the cameras caught you two talking in plain sight on stage after you stopped the gunman. You seized your opportunity."

Eyes wide, palms facing the camera, Tomas said, "Sir, I first heard of the President-Elect's job offer when you mentioned it to me a moment ago." He spoke a little more slowly. "I speak the truth. And I speak the truth when I say, I don't want to work for Mr.—President-Elect Forrester."

Echevarria angled his head down. His gaze seemed so intense it seemed it could singe his eyebrows. "You think you have a choice?"

Tomas froze. A mouse trapped in a room with big cats, hoping to go unseen. From upstairs came a throaty shriek. Baby Artur needed milk or a clean diaper.

"Do you?"

Tomas' back stiffened. "I belong with my battalion, and your brigade, improving our combat effectiveness. I wouldn't add a fraction as much value working in an office in Confederal City after Forrester takes office."

The baby kept crying. Every few moments, he paused to catch his breath. Each time, part of Tomas hoped the baby would soothe himself. Each time, the rest of him would castigate himself. *Hope is not a planning factor.*

On screen, the brigadier dropped his thick hands to the desktop. "It doesn't matter what you want. It doesn't matter what I want. It doesn't even matter what Old Man Olafson wants. He was ired beyond belief to be roused from his beauty sleep, I say, and if he told me true, he pushed back at Forrester for a good ten minutes to work through proper channels."

Tomas let out a breath. A faint warm pleasant glow entered his chest. "I'm pleased the Chief of Staff agrees with me."

"Bah. Olafson pushed back for he wanted Forrester to pick a horse from his stable, not some unknown battalion staff officer who splashed across our screens a month ago. What be-damned noise is in the background?"

Artur kept crying. Lissa's footsteps plodded up the stairs. "My baby, sir."

"Get you your wife to soothe it."

"She's working on it, sir."

"Good." Echevarria nodded like a teetering boulder. "Because you ought ready yourself right now. Report you to Forrester's transition office by 0900."

A ball of dread formed in Tomas' belly. "Today?"

"What did it sound like, captain? Yes, today!"

"But Forrester isn't yet commander-in-chief—"

Brig. Echevarria's gaze grew even more stony than usual. "He's going to be. All his campaign speeches about restoring honor, you know what that means."

"A bigger budget for both forces." More ships, more equipment, better pay and benefits for volunteers—

"And promotions. And opportunities for better housing, choicer assignments, all of that. For you, and me. So you will go today, and every day until he leaves office, and today and every day, you will do the best be-damned job you can. Hear you me?"

Tomas dipped his head and slowly blinked. "I will do any assignment to the best of my ability."

"You will do more than that. You will put in a good word for me with Forrester every chance you get. And if you foul up, and Forrester sends you back to me, I wouldn't keep you. I'd pack you off to Nuova Toscano. Good luck slowing down the PR army if they push through the wormhole and get orbital supremacy."

Tomas' mouth hung open. He closed it and lifted his shoulders. "Your orders are clear, sir."

"Good. I've already told Lt. Col. Sokolov you've been reassigned from his battalion staff. Today, 0900. The Hotel Transstellar in Confederal City. Look you up the address. Echevarria out."

Tomas stepped back from the display and shut his eyes while the afterimage faded. He nibbled at his lower lip. Echevarria's words rattled around his mind and soured in his gut.

He knew regardless of merit, a man had to play politics to rise to brigade command. But to see it so blatantly... the sour feeling in his gut intensified. Politics didn't matter. Only readying the Confederated Worlds' forces mattered, against the day the PRs renounced the peace treaty and started the next war.

That's all that matters to Forrester, too.

Tomas relaxed, until another thought speared him through the shoulders. He had about three hours to get sixty kilometers across the capital cities. He reached for the display to call up directions—

"What's going on?"

Lissa stood in the open way from the living room. She held Artur at her hip. His thick hands groped at the hem of her loose, milk-stained nursing blouse. A blond lock, an escapee from her hairband, dangled toward a wary eye.

"I've been reassigned."

She remained still for a moment, then slumped her shoulders as a breath escaped. "We've barely settled in here—"

"Not a transfer," Tomas said. "Forrester wants me to serve as an assistant. The brass ordered me to start today."

She clutched Artur closer. His head squashed her breast, yet her gaze remained fixed on Tomas. "You want to work for Forrester?"

"No, love."

"Then say no."

He peered at her. "I've already gotten the order."

"Go today if you have to, but get out of working for that man. Please."

Tomas dropped his hands to his sides and widened his stance. "What's bothering you? I know you ranked him low on your ballot, but he's the President-Elect. It's not yet official, but he'll be my commander-in-chief. I took an oath to go where I'm ordered."

"Does that man only want you because you saved him from the assassin?"

Tomas shrugged. "That's the only thing that makes sense to me. Plenty of bluecoats have as much military experience as me."

She stepped closer. Her free hand cradled Artur's head. "That lone gunman was no lone gunman. Whoever wants Forrester dead won't stop after one failure. They won't stop if you're in their way." Intensity burned in her eyes. "You could turn me into a widow and leave two young boys fatherless!"

"That won't happen. He has—" A double layer of ConPol and Restoration Party security. Yet the risk to Tomas was only a rationalization. He could tell from the tight line of her mouth. His hands rose to his hips and his elbows jutted out. He leaned forward. "What's the real problem?"

"The risk to you isn't problem enough?" Lissa said.

"Regardless of my assigned duty, there's risk every day I hold my commission, and you know that. You knew it when we got married, before I shipped out to Arden." He padded across the cool tile and reached for her shoulders. "You accepted the risk then."

Lissa backed away from his touch. "You say you stand for high values, service, duty, but you just want an excuse to leave me alone with these two—" She jostled Artur. "—and my career and everything else I have to deal with. And you'll get that excuse in spades, won't you? Working in Confederal City till all hours, never seeing Stefan awake, leaving me to get up in the night to feed Artur. What do the boys and I get out of it? A chance to fake smile and say we're so proud of you?"

The dimly-lit kitchen seemed to press on him, like the gray walls of a maze's cul-de-sacs. Since Artur's birth, they'd had variations of this argument dozens of times.

But never before when the President-Elect waited for him.

"We all have our jobs," Tomas said. "I'm going to get ready for mine." He strode past Lissa toward their bedroom. He did not look back.

3

Transition of Power

On a floor of the Hotel Transtellar given over to office spaces, Forrester's transition team worked out of a set of adjoining suites. Shortly before 0900, a young man with a caesar haircut and a Shambalese accent ushered Tomas into the corner suite.

Floor-to-ceiling windows gave views to south and east. Presumably reflective coated on the outside, and armored in the middle. Forrester's team would have taken anti-surveillance and anti-sniper measures before they occupied the space.

So why did Forrester want Tomas assigned to him?

It would come clear soon enough.

Tomas glanced out the windows. A Daughters of Astarte temple adorned with classical columns stood catercorner. In the distance, marble-white Confederal government buildings—Congress surmounted by obelisks, the Foreign Ministry's four cylinders, the white mountain of the Defense Ministry—towered above the jumbled roofs of civilian buildings. Sharp-edged shadows showed Epsilon Eridani hung just west of the zenith. At a conference table, Forrester and a group of aides, five men in jackets and ties and a woman in a pantsuit stood over bundles of smartpaper. The top sheet of each bundle showed a photo of a politician and bullet-pointed lines of text.

Forrester looked up. His dark-blond hair moved like a helmet. "Neumann, you're a sight for sore eyes." He crossed to Tomas, shook his hand. Forrester gripped strongly and gave a slight twist to Tomas' forearm. "Stay there. I need a minute to see this—" He waggled his hand at the tabletop. "—to a break point. Then I'll tell you what I need you to take a look at."

"As you wish, sir."

One of the male aides spoke. Deep lines ran down from the corners of his mouth. He peered over the straight top edge of semicircular smartglasses. The expression added to his dour tone of voice. "Mr. Forrester, while I appreciate you have an important task for the captain here, we need to bottom out on a vice-presidential selection very soon."

"We will."

The aide went on. "It's customary to select a vice president from a prospective coalition partner. We have a majority in the Senate of the Worlds, but not in the House of the Peop—"

Forrester's voice contained a steely core. "I'm aware of that." Then he smiled and looked up. "Neumann, who would you pick as my vice-president?"

Tomas' mouth fell open. The room suddenly seemed glaringly bright. The Constitution empowered the President-Elect to select a vice president from among all presidential candidates who had received at least one second-place vote out of all the instant-runoff ballots cast across the Confederated Worlds.

The President-Elect, not a young Ground Force captain! "Sir, I don't follow politics closely—"

Forrester waved away Tomas' objection. "You don't need to. After you ranked me first on your ballot, you ranked someone second, after all. Who?"

"Thank you, sir. I ranked second O'Brien from the Outworld Alliance Party."

The aide blinked. "O'Brien." He reached to his right for a smart-paper bundle. "O'Brien is a man of principle. He's moderately popular across most worlds other than Challenger, and he supports a strong defense. Definite pluses. That said, I see a few minuses." He picked up the bundle and held it face-out in front of his chest. "He and the OAP have very few supporters on Challenger. That makes his share of the House of the People too small to give us a majority. Also, on a number of outworlds, primarily the ones dominated by single-planet parties affiliated with the world's dominant religion or ideology, he's very unpopular."

Forrester stared at the aide. "I see. Tomas, why did you rank O'Brien second?"

With a jolt, Tomas stood taller. "He doesn't know me, but I knew his son. The best platoon commander I served under, in the war. His son recommended I apply for OCS. His son set me on the path to my commission."

"It appears O'Brien raised his son to be a fine man," Forrester said. "Have you seen him since you went to OCS?"

Pressure welled behind Tomas' eyes. He swallowed down a lump in his throat. "I heard he died fighting the Progressive Republic on Navi Ambarsar."

Forrester peered at the aide. "True?"

"Yes, wait, I believe so, let me confirm...." The aide pushed back pages in the bundle. His fingers slipped like a man climbing a slippery slope. "Yes, a son, Ground Force.... this can't be right."

"What?"

"A Congressman's son enlisted? Then went through OCS? That can't be right."

"My research team took its eyes off the ball?" Forrester spoke evenly, but a hard look formed in his eyes.

"No, no, we double-checked everything, that must be true, it just surprised me, Mr. Forrester, a man like O'Brien having a son enlist instead of attending one of the military academies. I agree—" He gestured to take in the other aides, who nodded even before he kept speaking. "—We agree with Captain Neumann that O'Brien is a fine man. Again, though, there are multiple factors we might want to consider, Congressional vote math—"

Forrester aimed a taut-skinned palm and splayed, stretched fingers at the aide. "We'll look at this issue later. Now I'll show Neumann what I need him to do."

"Mr. Forrester—" The aide bowed his head. "You're right. We can table this for an hour. A break might freshen our perspectives."

A hooded stare from Forrester emphasized his next words. "Yes it might." He turned to Tomas and the stare vanished. "Neumann, come with me."

Forrester led the way out of the conference room and through the office suite's narrow hallways. Tomas strode quickly to keep pace. Junior aides pressed themselves against the walls. Women demurely looked away from Forrester, and mens' adam's apples bobbed under freshly beardstopped faces.

In response, Forrester nodded and greeted each by name without slowing down.

Finally, Forrester and Tomas came to a door guarded by a hard-faced bluecoat. The crisp tailoring of the security man's uniform and the smooth round third eye on the front of his cap clashed with his thick features and nose distorted by at least one break. The bluecoat snapped his heels together and opened the door.

The room beyond was small and windowless. A lighting panel in the ceiling bloomed with yellow-white light, the spectrum of far-off, interdicted Sol. The light showed a circular table and two chairs, all with stylus-thin legs of nanotube alloy. On the table sat a blank smartpaper, next to a box the size of a child's fist. A green LED on the box blinked at the sedate pace of an endurance athlete's resting heart. Tomas recognized the box as a scanner and scrambler of eavesdropping devices.

The guard shut the door behind them. In the small room, Forrester's presence felt even greater than it had on stage at the rally.

"We're hidden in here from prying eyes and ears," Forrester said. "I appreciate you being willing to switch duty assignments with three hours notice."

Tomas drew a breath. He wanted to cut to the chase, but Echevarria's warnings weighed on him. "First, if I may, Mr. Forrester, I want to thank you for the opportunity to serve. I understand Chief of Staff Olafson resisted your request, but I assure you, Brigadier Echevarria and I are eager to comply."

"Superb. Glad to hear that about you and the brigadier. As for

Olafson, he only resisted because he didn't see a way for your glory to shine on him."

Tomas shrugged. "I don't know about glory, sir."

"Your perceptiveness, quick thinking, and physical ability saved my life from that shooter. That looks like glory to me." Forrester fixed Tomas with an intense expression of his hazel eyes. "Which brings us to why I asked for you to be assigned to me."

Forrester tapped out a quick, dense pattern on the smartpaper. Black lines of text and a full-color image appeared, oriented toward Tomas. A thick mop of hair, sharp cheekbones, a confused expression. The would-be assassin.

Forrester popped a fingernail against the smartpaper. "It's been a month and we know next to nothing about this bastard. Jordan Walters, 22 years old, born and raised in a middle-class neighborhood of McAuliffe city. He was a volunteer for one of the soft-on-defense, submissive-to-our-enemies parties in the '14 and '16 elections, then dropped out. Between the '16 election and Firstlanding Square, we have no clue about anything important. Where did he get the pistol? Who might have helped him?"

Tomas squinted at the smartpaper. "ConPol has held Walters for a month."

"ConPol." Forrester sniffed out a breath. "Two days after this bastard's assassination attempt, Assistant Director MacAdams from ConPol showed my team and me all the background info I just summarized. He said he'd share more info after they extracted it from Walters' brain. A brain scan should take, what, an hour?"

"In the field, with freshly captured prisoners, about that," Tomas said. "Intel would spend more time, and brain scans were only part of a test battery."

"Then a day or two. But it's a month later, and ConPol hasn't shown us a damn thing." Forrester straightened himself to his full height. "Your first assignment is to go to ConPol to find out what they know about Walters. Your second assignment is to find out what you can about ConPol. What do they know about this bastard? What have they not shown me? And if they're keeping something hidden, why?"

Tomas blinked. His mind roved over the problem. "I'll do all I can, sir. Though ConPol might refuse to share information with a mere Ground Force captain."

Forrester's chest puffed out. He leaned toward Tomas, eyes intense. He raised one finger and said, "You are no longer a mere Ground Force captain. Now you work for me."

Epsilon Eridani set and rose and set again before Tomas reached a waiting room down the hall from Assistant Director MacAdams' office. MacAdams' assistant, a tall and sturdy woman, seemed genuinely to regret the delay, once a coworker confirmed Tomas acted on Forrester's orders. "The AD is extremely busy today, or he would have seen you by now," she said. "Here, have a seat. Coffee?"

Tomas waved a hand. Almost a decade since he'd left his mother's house, his mother's strict interpretation of the Observer faith, and he still avoided stimulants. He spoke with more energy than he felt. "Just water, thank you." Not this woman's fault a chain of ConPol bureaucrats had sent him from office to office before he finally made it here.

Here was an elevator lobby strewn with overstuffed brown armchairs. Carpet as white and plush as cloud lay under his black shoes. Accent lights shone down on framed oil paintings showing people, mostly men, most in ancient garb. Copper plates on the bottom of each frame showed embossed names. Montagu. Pinkerton. A woman in a long dress, Boyd. Legends in spy craft, presumably. One name, Fouché, under a painting of a man with slender fingers and a long, narrow nose, seemed familiar. Probably from the Bonapartist catechism he'd rolled his eyes at, as an offworld-born boy growing up on Joséphine.

The swishing sound of her skirt marked the assistant's return. "The AD will see you now." She led him down a lengthy hallway to a corner office, then beckoned him to enter.

"Come in, captain. Have a seat."

MacAdams looked like a bowling ball in a gray suit. Across his craggy face he wore a wraparound strip of smartglass. Reversed texts and images, unreadable to Tomas, scrolled along the bottom of the smartglass. A rigid nanotube mesh hung down near the ends of the strip and covered MacAdams' ears. He splayed his hands on his hips and pointed his elbows away from his body, nearly brushing the side of his desk. He rocked up on the balls of his feet. A ConPol ID card hanging from the front pocket of his suit jacket bobbed with his motion.

Tomas sat facing the desk. MacAdams went behind it. The room seemed too narrow for a ConPol assistant director, though the windows gave views north and east toward the lights on top of Congress's obelisks and the lighted windows of hotels and mid-rise office towers toward Lake Liberty. On MacAdams' desk, video loops of presumably his wife and children, along with stacks of smartpaper, filled the sides. Sol-spectrum light from ceiling panels glossed the relatively empty central region of the glass desktop.

MacAdams lifted a bundle of smartpaper and set it atop another closer to the edge of the desk. His hands swept across the desktop's empty center. "First off, congratulations to your boss. I speak for everyone here at ConPol when I say we look forward to working with him after his inauguration. So though he's not officially president yet, I want you and him to know I can spare you a few minutes. He sent you about Walters?"

"Forrester wants an update on your investigation."

MacAdams grimaced. "He could have called instead of sending you. You've spent a long time today waiting to hear this, but there's simply nothing to tell you." His gaze briefly met Tomas', then slid away.

"Perhaps you could recap what you do know." Tomas reached into his jacket pocket for his phone and stylus. He put a mild expression on his face. "There might be something you told Forrester that didn't make it into our notes." Rather than snap the phone into its rigid state, he slowly and quietly unrolled it.

MacAdams inhaled. "Right, of course, that can happen to anyone." He nudged a framed video loop further from the line of sight between him and Tomas. "Here's what we know about Jordan Walters...."

As MacAdams gave his recap, Tomas tapped his stylus on his phone, checking off items already noted by Forrester's team. Walters' old political allies disclaimed any knowledge of the shooter's recent activities, and ConPol lacked enough evidence for a brain-scanning warrant to confirm or deny their claims.

"What about his recent political allies?" Tomas asked.

"He doesn't have any." MacAdams leaned back in his chair and stretched his arms wide. "Everything points to him becoming a loner after the '16 election. Doesn't prove, but fits with the story, he hatched this plot on his own." MacAdams dropped his forearms to his chair's armrests. He rocked his body back and forth in an exaggerated nod.

"What did his brain scan reveal?"

MacAdams stopped rocking. He rubbed his palms together, then returned his forearms to the armrests and hunched forward. "Nothing."

Tomas narrowed his eyes for a moment. "Meaning he used a lethe potion."

Tension eased from MacAdams' shoulders. "Exactly. As you may know, after the potion hits the brain, it scrambles memories, which foils efforts to verify verbal questioning by use of fMRI and related technologies—"

"I do know," Tomas said. "I've interrogated prisoners in the field who've used it. Plus I've been trained in proper use in case I were ever captured and questioned." He stared at MacAdams. His few lingering doubts about being a mere captain asking questions of a senior ConPol bureaucrat evaporated. He could see through a smokescreen about lethe potions. And Forrester backed him. "I also know the highest safe dose of the lethe potion is normally only effective to scramble about a week of memories."

MacAdams turned rigid for a moment. He blinked, and a wave of relaxation oozed down his limbs. He blinked again, then reached for a stack of smartpaper near the side of his desk. He squared it up in front of himself. MacAdams interlaced his fingers and set his hands on the smartpaper stack. "Yes, well, normally, but it appears he may have developed a new formulation. Longer term memory scrambling without the dangerous side effects."

Tomas arched an eyebrow. "Walters developed it? The dossier we have is silent about him having drug development expertise."

"Perhaps some domestic terrorist organization helped him." MacAdams hurried the words. "By scrambling his memories far enough back to hide his dealings with that organization, it would remain in the shadows."

"If a terrorist organization helped him, but you know nothing about it, what leads you to conclude it was domestic one? I'm sure both the Unity and the Progressive Republic have spies under cover on their embassy staffs. Plus the technical expertise to create the long-term lethe potion and the easy-assembly pistol."

MacAdams reached to the side and pulled a framed videoloop of his family toward the center of his desk. He shook his head and deepened his voice. "Trying to kill Forrester puts their politicians in the crosshairs, if we can prove up their involvement. I don't know the leading Uni and PR politicians, but I know their type. They value their own skins too much to put themselves at risk of assassination. That's why we're focusing on domestic leads."

He separated his hands. MacAdams' expression flashed with surprise, as if he just noticed his fingers had intertwined. He masked the surprise by glancing at the text crawling across the bottom of his glasses, then spoke. "And this case is one of the reasons we want your boss to move quickly after his inauguration to push through the Investigation of Terroristic Activities bill. That bill would give us a lot more capabilities to bring Walters' coconspirators to justice. I know your boss is leaning that way, but we want him to see how important it is, what a high priority it should be to pass it."

Tomas nodded slowly and stroked his fingers along his jaw. It made sense for MacAdams to play the situation in a bid to increase the power of his bureaucratic fiefdom. It made sense the foreign powers would not get involved.

"I'll give Forrester that message," Tomas said. Abruptly he stopped moving his fingers. "And I'd also like to receive all the raw data you've collected from interrogating Walters and investigating his known ties."

MacAdams blinked again. "That's an interesting request." He shoved another bundle of smartpaper toward the center of his desk, strengthening the wall he built between himself and Tomas. Then he met Tomas' gaze. "But interrogation data regarding assassination attempts on presidential candidates can only be given to personnel with top-secret security clearances. Does that apply to you, captain?"

Tomas folded his arms. "No."

"You can talk to your boss about gaining that clearance. If you choose to pursue it, let my assistant know, and we'll expedite our review. Depending on what we might have to do to help Congress pass the legislation we need, maybe we can get you cleared soon after your boss' inauguration."

Two months away. A blast shield seemed to slam into place behind Tomas' eyes. MacAdams stalled. Did he do so on his own initiative, or at the request of his superiors? No matter. "I'll do that." He rose and extended his hand toward MacAdams. "Thank you for your time."

MacAdams came around the desk and shook. "Glad to. Look forward to working with you and your boss. He acts quickly and forcefully, we respect that. He's already chosen his vice-president." MacAdams tapped the strip of smartglass.

"I hadn't heard. Who?"

"O'Brien. An unexpected choice. What do you think?"

A deep breath flowed into Tomas' lungs. Forrester had decided—today—based on his suggestion? He felt like he rode an ornithopter in the moment it leaped off a pad and started flapping its wings.

"I agree," Tomas managed to say. "An unexpected choice."

As seen from Forrester's offices in the Hotel Transtellar, a faint glow edged the eastern horizon, between the lights of Confederal City and the light-polluted gray-black sky. Tomas rubbed his eyes. The third dawn of each calendar day always got him tired, even after a standard year on the planet. MacAdams' stonewalling compounded his tiredness.

"The President-Elect is ready," one of Forrester's interns said.

One more eye rub, then blinks and head-shakes. Time to get more alert. Tomas followed the intern to the secure, windowless room.

Forrester sat half on the edge of the table. He seemed to fill the space. After the intern shut the door, he turned to Tomas. "What did MacAdams tell you?"

"Next to nothing. He's stonewalling us."

"Where do you see that?"

In his memory, Tomas replayed bits of his meeting with MacAdams. "He said they've discovered nothing, but he won't share raw data because I don't have a top-secret security clearance. Though he'll expedite his review for me to get that clearance, after you ensure passage of the Investigation of Terroristic Activities Act."

The few wrinkles at Forrester's eyes grew smoother. "He's playing one of this town's standard games. Typical bullshit."

"If I may ask, do you support that bill?"

"Sure you can ask. I support it. I'm also pissed off at MacAdams for playing this game. I can only pick one fight at a time, and it won't be with MacAdams and ConPol, and he damn well knows it. We need this bill to improve our ability to deal with enemy agents. They're out there." Forrester waved at the walls. His gesture took in the city around them. "I'm sure of it."

Tomas' gut churned. "There's something else I must tell you. MacAdams has no evidence, yet is convinced Walters was part of a domestic terrorist organization. He immediately rebuffed my speculation that Walters was backed by a foreign party."

Forrester's hazel eyes narrowed. He stared at the far wall as if his gaze could burn a hole through it. "Incompetence or worse?"

"I don't know, sir."

Forrester's stare eased. "I don't have enough rope to hang him. Yet." He drummed a few notes with his palms on his thighs. "There's your next task."

Tomas stood taller and nodded.

"The party's security service gets real-time feeds from its personnel's third-eye cameras. Those cameras capture gigabytes of video data every second. We've ordered a team to dig through that data for appearances by Walters." Forrester winced.

"You worry he avoided being seen by the bluecoats?"

Forrester shook his head. "We have so many personnel active in the city, someone has seen him. What bothers me is, despite all the reasons I hate the Progressive Republic, I envy them their acceptance of advanced software for national security purposes. I'm sure the PR's software could find Walters in seconds. It's taken the party's security service nearly four weeks and there are still more gaps than filled portions of their timeline on Walters."

He leaned toward Tomas. "I want you to review our surveillance on Walters. Look for where he went and whom he might have met. This will be an ongoing project. You're going to be getting chunks of data over the next few months. I'm not expecting instant results, but any lead you can give to party security will be followed."

Part of Tomas longed to be back at battalion headquarters. Despite that, a certitude filled him. He would execute this assignment to the best of his abilities. "I'll be glad to do it, sir."

"I can see that. I can also see you'll be glad to do the other tasks I'll assign you."

Tomas peered at Forrester. "Which tasks, sir?"

Forrester slapped his hand onto Tomas' shoulder. "When the time comes, I'll show them to you."

4

Special Representative

The negotiating chamber occupied the uppermost twenty meters of one of the Foreign Ministry's cylindrical towers. The chamber was a sphere fifteen meters in diameter. It rested on thick, rubberized coils grown into a mycocrete floor. Sheets of glass rose from the floor to above the top of the chamber and gave long views in all directions, from the mansions of Confederal Heights to the north, to Lake Liberty and the wilderness preserve beyond it to the east, to the crowded towers of McAuliffe city to the west casting their shadows onto Lake Freedom's choppy surface.

On the mycocrete floor, near the stairs up to the chamber, a Foreign Ministry staffer touched his earbud. "The Uni team is coming up the elevator."

The Foreign Minister himself, a man with uplifted hair salted with gray, nodded and started toward the stairs. He glanced back at Tomas and hesitated. A frown creased his face. His voice flowed like sour honey. "You'll disappoint the President if you don't follow us, yes?"

The Foreign Minister had gained his position as part of some backroom deal between his party and Forrester's. That did not mean the Foreign Minister liked Forrester. It especially meant he did not like Tomas, added to the negotiating team at Forrester's order for the obvious purpose of monitoring the Foreign Minister and his junior diplomats.

A few staffers and junior diplomats chuckled. The sound fluttered off the mycocrete and glass. Tomas scrutinized one of the junior diplomats. The chuckles drained away.

Tomas followed the diplomats up the stairs.

The negotiating chamber's main room filled the middle of the sphere. Diffuse panels of Sol-spectrum light made up the ceiling. In the middle of the room stood a rectangular table carved from a single piece of bioengineered oak. The table's long axis stretched nearly the full diameter of the chamber, perpendicular to the line between the two doors into the room. The table's short axis allowed the shaking of hands above the lacquered surface. Eleven plush chairs held station on each side. Around the periphery of the room were sitting areas, liquor and cigar cabinets, and twin buffet tables.

The Foreign Minister stood behind the chair in the middle of the table's near side. The junior diplomats and staffers took up positions flanking him. The lower a rank, the further from the Foreign Minister. A junior diplomat gave Tomas a cold glance over his shoulder and hurried to one of the last chairs. Like his superior and his peers, he stood behind the chair.

Tomas took the last chair on the left. Like the others, he stayed on his feet. He pulled out his phone, snapped the display to its flat and rigid conformation, and balanced it on top of the chair's backrest. He pulled out his stylus and peered at the people on his side. Some of them gave him hooded glances and turned their shoulders away from him.

President Forrester's words came back to Tomas. *The less they want to see you, the more you want to see them.*

A thin green flame seemed to warm his chest.

Moments later, all the diplomats looked up, and Tomas' gaze followed them. The far door slid open. Uni diplomats filed into the room, led by their ambassador. His long, narrow nose and down-curved mouth gave him an air of disapproval.

They came from similar stock as most citizens of the Confederated Worlds. A product of the kinds of people on ancient

Earth with both access to wealthy patrons and fanaticism sufficient to make slower-than-light journeys to lifeless but terraformable worlds. Most of the Unis had pale to medium complected skin, eyes from blue to light brown, straight or loosely curled hair ranging in color from blond to rich black. Cousins of the Confederated Worlds' citizens, to one way of looking. Populations diverged for centuries, long enough to acquire incompatible goals, to another.

The most vicious wars in history had been fought between similar peoples.

Most of the Uni diplomats wore suits, except for one in the khaki dress uniform of the Unity ground force. A military attaché, at least as a cover story. His jacket cuffs showed four gold stripes in a three plus one pattern, a major. A mustache filled his upper lip. His brown eyes exuded confidence. He took up a position toward Tomas' end of the table, two seats closer to the center.

Once the Unis stood at their positions, a wave of ritual introductions and handshakes flowed out from the center of the table. The Uni major's name sounded like *Aaron Wez*, but the dossier on Tomas' phone display spelled the surname *Aranjuez*. A trace of a Spanish-descended language accented the major's Confed.

Tomas squinted at the Uni major. A memory from New Liberty gnawed at Tomas.

The Uni major peered back.

After finishing introductions, the Uni ambassador spoke. "First, it is our wish to extend to President Forrester our congratulations upon his taking office. It is true we find some of his rhetoric intemperate. It is further true we are disappointed he insisted you and I meet before I present my credentials to him. That said, it is our assumption that he strikes these poses for domestic consumption, and that he is willing to settle any disputes between our polities in an amicable spirit, seeking compromise before confrontation. Or, as an ancient figure held in regard by both our societies, Winston Churchill, put, "'jaw-jaw" is better than "war-war."'"

The Uni major, Aranjuez, nodded along. Tomas agreed, to a point. *War is a foul business, but 'compromise' does not mean 'submission.'* Tomas shifted his gaze to the Foreign Minister.

"Well said, Mr. Ambassador." The Foreign Minister worked his jowly face into a chummy expression. "You understand domestic politics. One must throw the rubes red meat to get out the vote, yes? I assure you, we can work around the public's limited grasp of affairs to achieve mutually acceptable resolutions to our disputes."

The Foreign Minister had to say that... but the thin green flame returned. Tomas scratched a few notes with his stylus on his phone display. The Foreign Ministry's junior diplomats squirmed in their seats.

The diplomats spent the rest of the morning discussing two main points of dispute. The first related to the numbers and types of observation ships to be stationed near wormhole mouths in neutral stellar systems. In practice this meant Alpha Centauri, home to Heinlein's World, as the unknown minds, human or computer, governing Earth forbade ships to enter or leave Sol system.

Like Earth, the vast majority of Heinlein's World's citizens used advanced brain/computer interfaces to live in virtual realities, in fantasies of infinite wealth, power, and adventure. Virtual fugue. No matter how much Tomas fell away from his mother's spiritual beliefs, he would always shudder, his mouth always curl, at the thought of what the people of Earth and Heinlein's World had done to themselves.

But when it came to his duties, the only thing about Heinlein's World that mattered to Tomas was the wormholes it had created and towed to a dozen neighboring star systems, before its creative and pioneering spirit burned out. The current government of Heinlein's World paid no attention to small, unarmed squadrons holding station near wormhole mouths located at the gravitationally-stable Lagrange points generated by Alpha Centauri A and B.

Heinlein's World paid no attention, but the Confederated Worlds and the Unis did. Presumably, both sides planned first strike options through wormholes into and out of the Alpha Centauri system. But an observer could send a warning of an enemy attack through the wormholes to Challenger or Europa Regina (the Uni capital world) at light speed, faster than canned spam could cross normal space in a ship.

Perhaps it would make a critical difference in watching for a Uni first strike if the Confederated Worlds Space Force had eight ships instead of six, or ships capable of accelerating at seven gees instead of five. More likely, these were bargaining tokens to be spent resolving the other main point of dispute.

"It is apparent that allowing Confederated Worlds intelligence agents onto New Liberty would impinge our sovereignty and disregard the wishes of a Unity member world," the Uni ambassador said.

The Foreign Minister bent his head toward the murmuring lips and shielding hand of the diplomat to his right. He nodded, then turned to the ambassador. "You mentioned ancient beliefs shared by our two states. These include human rights traditions, yes? Which include allowing the peaceful expression of minority cultural and political beliefs, yes?"

The corners of the Uni ambassador's mouth curved down even further. "It appears you imply the people of New Liberty oppress their brethren who formerly assisted the Confederated Worlds occupation during the recent war."

Down the table from the Uni ambassador, a troubled look formed on Maj. Aranjuez' face. A familiar look. Tomas suddenly felt light-headed. Could it be—?

The Foreign Minister raised his eyebrow. The expression seemed so false, Tomas imagined he'd learned it from an actor. "You heard about the Reagantown massacre, yes?"

"It is the case a few hotheads unfortunately chose to settle old scores in the days following your withdrawal from New Liberty and its system."

"A few hotheads." The Foreign Minister's tone dripped with doubt.

The Uni ambassador raised his voice a notch. "Within a week, the majority of New Liberty citizens, and all Unity regular forces deployed to New Liberty, restored order. Including respect for the basic rights of persons formerly assisting the Confederated Worlds occupation."

"So we are told, but we have never seen for ourselves." The Foreign Minister extended two fingers and opened his mouth to continue speaking.

A staffer bustled in. The Foreign Minister changed his gesture to a just-a-moment open palm. The staffer whispered something to him.

He nodded, then turned to the Uni ambassador. "We will spend many more hours before we close this dispute. Lunch is ready to be served. You would take a break, yes?"

"If we ever close it," the Uni ambassador said. He sloughed out a breath. "Lunch is one thing we can agree on."

Within moments, waiters pulled carts in from the door behind the Foreign Minister and filled the buffet table at the side of the room. They clanged serving trays into place and thumbed the switches of heating elements. They opened lids and steam bloomed out from curries of farm-grown vegetables and vat-synthesized meat.

The two sides merged into one line, Foreign Minister and ambassador first, everyone else following in pecking order. Maj. Aranjuez disrupted the flow by hanging back for Tomas.

He extended his hand. "Captain Neumann. You are of course famous for saving your new president from assassination, but having seen you across the table, you seem more familiar."

Tomas shook. Each applied a solid grip. They disconnected hands and Tomas beckoned Maj. Aranjuez to serve himself.

Tomas' heart slammed in his chest. He knew the major's voice. "Perhaps we met on New Liberty."

Maj. Aranjuez' eyes grew sharper. "I met more Confederated Worlds Ground Force personnel on New Liberty than I preferred. I was taken prisoner. I spent years surrounded by Ground Force guards instead of seeing your infantry as probability spreads on the displays of my Bismarck."

Despite having smeared his face with beardstop that morning, the follicles on Tomas' jaw stood up. "We had almost reached New Boston when we ambushed an armored grenadier column. A detachment from a Nuevo Andaluciano regiment. We destroyed the company commander's Bismarck. He took shrapnel through the gut. I tracked him down in the tall tufted grass north of the road—"

"*Madre de dios.*" Maj. Aranjuez paled. "You are him?"

"Apparently so."

The major's eyes moistened. He sucked in a breath and his face firmed. "I would have died if you hadn't captured me. Thank you."

"You're welcome." Tomas shrugged. "Though any of us would have done it for any other. We were merely enemies. I did not hate you then. I do not hate you now."

Maj. Aranjuez paused a serving spoon full of some chickpea dish above his plate. "You speak, how does one say, off the record? And for yourself, not President Forrester?"

"Yes. And yes."

They went down the rest of the buffet table in silence. Seating areas around the room's periphery held knots of three or four diplomats. Maj. Aranjuez lifted his chin to point at Tomas' seat at the far end of the table. Far from everyone else. His voice insisted. "Would you follow me, captain?"

A crisp nod. Tomas followed Maj. Aranjuez to the seats. The major moved his fork quickly to his mouth, and his jaws quickly gnashed white chicken protein. After a minute, he wiped his mustache and mouth with a slow motion of his napkin. "Your pardons. I learned to eat quickly in the prison camp. The sight of all you *contrapelos* brings that habit back out of me."

"I never learned what that word meant. Though knowing soldiers, it was an insult."

Maj. Aranjuez sniffed out a chuckle. "We called every Confederated Worlds personnel a *contrapelo*. It is the Nuevo Andaluciano word for a man, how does one say, aligned in the wrong direction?"

Tomas grinned and nodded. "As I said, I know soldiers."

Maj. Aranjuez tore a hunk from a flat, puffy piece of naan. He lifted an eyebrow. "How did you hear this word?"

Tomas frowned. "Your soldier. Don't you remember?"

"My soldier?"

Memories of tufted grass, and permanent twilight to sunward, and his heart pounding and breath roaring through his helmet. "When I dragged you back to our lines, I ran into one of your riflemen looking for you. We surprised each other within two or three meters distance."

Memories of the Uni rifleman—*why didn't he kill you? why didn't you kill him?*—sobered Tomas. He went on. "We couldn't talk to each other—he could understand Confed, of course, but I wasn't impped to understand Nuevo Andaluciano—but he grasped you had a better chance of living if you reached my unit and he said *medico* enough for me to finally figure it out. We let each other go our ways. I hope he made it home. Do you know?"

Sharp lines creased Maj. Aranjuez's face. He set down his fork and shook his head. "I don't even know a man tried to rescue me. I must have lost my memory of the event. I am glad you told me this."

"You don't remember him?" Tomas asked. "He asked you if you were, what was it, *rasgudo?*"

"Our word is *rasguñado*. Wounded. I still don't remember."

Tomas squinted. How could the major forget a thing like that? Then up came a memory of Lissa, speaking to him in happier times about her work. Psychogenic amnesia. The mind defends itself from unbearable memories in all sorts of ways.

A big breath filled Tomas' torso. *Tell Maj. Aranjuez about Lissa's work….*

Objections pricked him, deflated him. Despite their personal history, the major could not trust the wife of a Ground Force officer to keep his file privileged. Brig. Echevarria's warning stirred in Tomas' mind as well. Forrester would take poorly to an officer he trusted forging a personal bond with a Uni officer and likely spy.

Maj. Aranjuez spoke. "I will ask the Nuevo Andaluciano veterans' association about your story. Perhaps I will learn about the man." A weary look touched his eyes. "Every day I am reminded how stupid was the war. Our societies have so much in common, yet we fight and die over a planet of no consequence."

From across the room, forced chuckles erupted from the Uni ambassador and the Foreign Minister. The corners of Tomas' mouth curled up. "You speak off the record? For yourself, not the ambassador?"

Maj. Aranjuez said, "I would forge a lasting peace with the Confederated Worlds. I do what I can to remove obstacles to that peace."

Tomas' gut turned sour, and his mouth puckered in regret. "I would prefer peace between our polities too, but hope is not a planning factor."

All traces of ease fled Aranjuez' face. His haggard look returned Tomas to that twilit battlefield on New Liberty. His voice dropped to a coarse whisper. "Our worst foreign policy mistake ever came in inducing the Progressive Republic to join us in making war against you. The faction then dominant on Europa Regina thought it best to, how does one say, ride the lion—?"

"The tiger."

"That faction won its short-term goal. You abandoned New Liberty and Kahlenberg. The Unity returned to the pre-war status quo." He leaned forward over his empty plate. His eyes glimmered like brown diamonds. "And the Progressive Republic advanced toward its long-term goal: the domination of all human-settled space."

Whether a diplomat or a spy, the major would tell the story most favorable to the Unity, rather than the truth. Tomas stiffened his back. "The PRs certainly achieved domination of some Confederated Worlds. Navi Ambarsar, Bridge to Total Freedom, Nanissáanah—"

"You see the surface and think it the truth." Maj. Aranjuez' mouth twisted and he dismissedly shook his head. "By the terms of our treaty with the PR, we granted it the right to deploy advisors and expeditionary forces in our star systems. That treaty soon comes up for renewal. Those of our leaders who still think the Confederated Worlds are the greater threat seek to renew it. But we who know better realize the treaty's renewal will allow the PR to seize worlds from both you and us, when the next war comes."

Tomas folded his arms and leaned back. "Then don't renew the treaty."

Aranjuez rolled his wrists to turn his hands palms-up. "We can only do that if Forrester's words turn from warlike to peaceful, and if the Confederated Worlds' actions turn to match."

Across the room, the Foreign Minister stood. He clinked his fork against his glass until all the room's conversations fell silent. He nodded at the Uni ambassador as if the ambassador had seduced his wife. "My esteemed colleague and I will resume our negotiations in five minutes."

After a brief lull, the knots of conversation bloomed like the last flowers of a growing season, in some part of some world that had seasons. Into the louder ambient, Maj. Aranjuez raised his voice. "If you work with us on this, you need not worry about your border with us, when the PR attacks. But if you decline our offer, you'll be outnumbered and pressed upon from two sides, when the PR attacks."

Tomas' mind churned through the idea, then stumbled on one point. "*Us*? You only speak for one faction on Europa Regina. How strong is your faction?"

"If Forrester tells us, and shows us, he wants peace with the Unity, then very strong indeed." Maj. Aranjuez stole a glance across the room. The ambassador and the other Uni diplomats were on their feet, readying themselves to resume their seats. "Give Forrester this message."

The message of a diplomat, or a spy? Even if true, a message making clear the PR's supporters dominated the halls of power on Europa Regina? Tomas' jaw hardened....

...then relaxed. Maj. Aranjuez' message would be merely one shard of intelligence to add to the mosaic. The more intelligence, the better Forrester would lead the Confederated Worlds through the challenges the PR would throw at them.

Another notion stirred in Tomas. He recognized it as a foolish one, but part of him could only believe he had saved Maj. Aranjuez on New Liberty because Maj. Aranjuez was a man worth saving. Honest, brave, potent, honorable. A man who spoke truthfully. Part of Tomas believed, even though he could not know the truth.

"I will," Tomas said. "But I can promise nothing more."

Maj. Aranjuez' leaned forward a final time. "If he is a wise leader, you need only give him my message, and he will agree."

The glow of displays filled Forrester's face with pale, steel blue light, matching the expression on his face. "You know why the Uni attaché told you this. Don't you?"

They were in Forrester's private office. Not the austere but opulent Sutherland Office shown in broadcasts to the people of the Confederated Worlds, or used to meet with cabinet ministers and leaders of Congress. No picture windows looking over the Executive Mansion's gardens, no sitting area near a gaslog fireplace, no sculptures and paintings of illustrious predecessors like Finzi and Sutherland himself offering olympian stares from their niches.

Forrester's private office lacked windows, and the only way in came through a disguised side door in the Sutherland Office. Upon his inauguration, the private office had been stripped to the walls and rebuilt. Tomas assumed it resembled the control deck of a Space Force vessel. A wall of video displays, jumping with news reporters and small groups of pundits from half a dozen worlds, faced a curved black desk studded with tablets and communicators. Behind the desk, in a pod-like chair tailored to his hips and torso, Forrester leaned back and cradled his hands behind his head.

Tomas blinked. The air conditioning purred, but sweat still trickled down the side of his face. "Perhaps you could fill me in, sir."

"The Unis are scared of us," Forrester said.

At the side of the desk, rumpled in his Space Force service blues, Maj. Sharma nodded at Forrester with soft brown eyes. In his Satyayugan accent, he said, "Absolutely right."

Sharma had served in the war with Forrester, been taken prisoner with Forrester, survived the POW camp with Forrester, labored ever since for Forrester. Tomas wondered if Sharma had ever disagreed with his patron.

Tomas set the thought aside. "I understand how that could be."

"Could be? Come on, Neumann, you Observers pride yourselves on seeing things as they are. Those bastards see we would defeat them, next time. It's plain as day. We have them on the run, looking over their shoulders!"

"When the enemy is in trouble, pursue him," Sharma said.

Forrester lunged forward in his chair. He drummed his hands against his desktop. He showed his teeth and a cold gleam flashed in his green eyes. "Time to press the advantage! Dim the fire of my speeches? Hell no! It's time to make it brighter!"

More sweat trickled down Tomas' forehead and wicked into his eyebrow. Then a cooling wave flowed through him. Forrester had heeded him when selecting O'Brien as vice-president. Forrester could heed him again.

"Mr. President, pursuing a fleeing enemy is a sound tactical rule of thumb."

Forrester's smile froze. "But?"

"Even sound tactics can work against us, depending on the strategic situation."

A faint creak came from his chair. Forrester folded his arms in a languid motion. "Show me your cards."

Tomas' adam's apple bobbed. "Yes, well, together the Unis and the PRs outnumber us in both ships and ground formations. They have access to six wormholes leading into Confederated Worlds systems. Space Force can do a lot, but even that might be too many holes in the dike for it to plug."

"Go on." Forrester's face revealed nothing.

"We all agree the PRs are the greater threat." Tomas glanced at Maj. Sharma. The Space Force major's face mirrored the President's. "If we could turn the Unis neutral, we could focus our defenses, and eventually our offensive power, against the PRs. After the PRs were weakened, then we'd be in a much stronger position in our disputes with the Unis."

Forrester inhaled. He shut his eyes and rested his fingertips on his forehead, under his swept-back cut of sandy blond hair. The tiny muscles around his eyes twitched for a few seconds.

His eyes snapped open. "Plausible reasoning, Neumann, but no. We look at some army leaders at Space Force Academy, did you know?"

Tomas mouth worked. "No."

"I always looked up to Frederick the Great. You know his history?"

Memories from OCS came up, dragging with them a heavy feeling that broke loose and sank into his gut. "He held out against foes on all his landward sides."

"Exactly." Forrester's voice filled the room. "Because of his army's superior organization, he could mass his forces against each of his enemies in turn. He wasn't surrounded—he had interior lines. As do we!"

"Interior lines can give a commander victory," Sharma said.

Tomas' mouth pressed together into a tight line. The energy of his thoughts pried his lips apart. "The technology of his day made it difficult for his opponents to coordinate their actions. His successors a few centuries later thought they could emulate him, but their opponents had armies an order of magnitude larger, and better command and control links between their field formations and their high commands. The German grand strategists of the twentieth century completely failed to account for the advances in technology up to their day. As a result they suffered two devastating defeats."

Forrester eased back in his chair. His voice turned quiet, like an ambuscade before a foe blundered into it. "This isn't the twentieth century, Neumann."

At the side of the desk, Sharma swung his head from side to side, like the pendulum of some archaic timepiece.

Sweat dewed on Tomas' neck, yet a chill flowed up his arms and legs. Echevarria's words came back to him. "That's very true, Mr. President. And I lack expertise in grand strategy."

"Indeed you do." Forrester paused, then pawed his hand sideways through the air. "Where do you stand on the review of Party security video?"

Tomas' mind lurched toward the new topic. "I've been working through it as it comes. The last batch arrived a few minutes before I came up here."

"Anything so far?"

A band seemed to tighten around his chest. "No, Mr. President. What I've seen to date of Walters' public behavior before his attempt on your life shows he concealed his plans."

"Look at the rest. You can show me the final results in two days?"

Two days? If he worked past 2100, hours after the offices neighboring his in the basement fell silent, and his boys would be enjoying a few minutes outside in the day's third dawn before Lissa readied them for bed. Tomas swallowed down his worry. "Easily, Mr. President. If that's all, I'll see myself out." He waited a moment, then turned to the door leading back to the public office—

"There's a shorter way." Forrester pointed the opposite direction, past the wall of video displays. A shelving unit held copies of rigid-bound books, the antiquated kind, with ink printed on dumb-paper. "Push in to disengage the magnetic contact, then swing the shelving unit out. Ends in the basement. Check the peephole before you go into the basement hallway."

Tomas pushed on the shelving unit. A faint thud and it swung a few centimeters toward him. Forrester's instruction to check the peephole at the bottom made the back of his neck prickle. "I will, Mr. President."

A few minutes later, unseen on the way, Tomas reached his office. If he stretched out his arms, he'd bump the walls. Ceiling panels poured out artificial white light. A glance at his wristwatch gave the time as 1530, about halfway through Epsilon Eridani's second descent of the day. When he approached his desktop display, twenty times larger and much higher resolution than any tablet, its unlock screen bloomed to life.

Type in password, show retina to scanner, gesture like a coach calling a play, press finger to print reader. The display opened up to walls of text. He cleared messages sent his way—three from Rolston, forwarding dirty jokes and links to photos of girls in flimsy clothing—Tomas shook his head, then opened the last video files sent by Restoration Party security and his notes on Walters' publicly visible activities.

The rest of that day, and most of the next, he watched the surveillance video. At 2050 the next day, he leaned back in his chair and rubbed his eyes. He'd reviewed every frame of bluecoats' video containing Walters. Nothing. The would-be shooter had lived his day-to-day life without any obvious outward sign he plotted to assassinate Forrester. Unless he took note of bluecoats around him, and only conspired with allies when out of sight of third-eye cameras.

Tomas rubbed his eyes again. Tell Forrester that, and the president would ask how thoroughly he'd reviewed the video. Of course

Walter wouldn't reveal a sign of his intentions in front of a bluecoat.

Time to look for non-obvious signs.

Each frame of video included date, time, location, and direction stamps relating to the capture of the image. He'd added each location to his notes. Time to plot all those on a map....

Good thing Challenger had progressed part of the way toward virtual fugue. Software should be able to do it. He hunted and pecked for the name of the plotter program, read through its instructions, fed it the location data. He pressed *enter* and a progress window showed *0%... 1%....*

He went down the hall, past the nearly invisible door to the hidden stairwell. He'd gone by the door for weeks and assumed only a closet or storeroom lay behind it. He took a piss, drank a cup of water, then went back to his office. *87%....*

Finally, the map bloomed across the screen. It distorted the layout of the capital cities to overemphasize the Barber Park neighborhood of downslope McAuliffe, southwest of the Lake Freedom dam. Streets named after Challenger terraformers, most long dead even after lifespans extended by rejuvenation treatments. Plain mycocrete buildings. Walk-up apartments above cafés and the molecular fabrication utility's storefronts.

Why this neighborhood? One of the buildings showed a bright red x: Walters' apartment. Hundreds of red dots surrounded it, most in clusters of twenty, thirty, more. Walters had been a creature of habit—frequenting this café, that by-the-slice pizzeria, a parkour gym, and the mol fab utility's storefront on Schmidt Avenue.

Would he meet with other plotters in one of his usual places? Or someplace where no one knew him? If the latter, near or far from his neighborhood?

A hunch turned Tomas' gaze to the map's isolated dots. He zoomed in, one by one. A few dots he dismissed as random encounters on the sidewalk between Walters and Party security. Others he gave a closer look. Near the flying disc golf course in Barber Park. Outside a fish-protein sushi bar near downtown McAuliffe. A doubleton, five minutes apart, the first dot at the front door and the second twenty meters down the street from a café entrance on the west side, near the space elevator station. More.

He called up the video snippets from the isolated dots. Walters trudged through the capital cities, hands deep in jacket pockets against the region's high altitude and its quick slices of darkness. Alone, usually, though he accompanied seven people roughly his age to the fish-protein sushi bar. Nothing but the fabbed plastic clothes on his back and a pair of smartglasses over his eyes.

Except at the café near the space elevator station. New Portland's Finest Coffees & Teas. Tomas squinted and shook his head. How had he missed it during his first pass through the video data?

On his approach and departure from New Portland's Finest, Walters wore a tan backpack.

Tomas played the video a dozen times. The same backpack? Laden differently, as if he'd stuffed something into it in the café? His fist clenched and the muscles around his mouth grew rigid. He couldn't tell.

He scoured the video more, looking for suspicious faces. None triggered his suspicions, but he at least had a lead.

He opened up the messaging app and typed a message to the Party security video custodian. *I need every frame you have from this city block and the interior of New Portland's Finest from three hours before and three hours after these two clips. IDs and dossiers on every person in those frames. As soon as you can.*

Tomas hit *send* and eased back in his chair. His intuition throbbed with certainty.

In that café, someone had given Walters the improved lethe potion and the easy-assembly pistol.

The next batch of Party security video would show that someone's face.

5

Secret Meetings

Late the next day, Tomas worked his way through the Executive Mansion's quiet halls toward the Sutherland Office. Glimpses through open doors showed cluttered desks and windows giving views of sky growing in brightness. Though almost all employees had departed, the bustle of the workday seemed to slowly settle over the offices, like the dust of a maneuver zone kicked up by a Badger's tracks.

At least one other employee remained. In an anteroom before the closed door to the Sutherland Office, Forrester's assistant, a mousy woman whose lips never seemed to meet, sat behind a spartan workstation. The workstation showed bare, shellacked cherrywood, save for a large display, three neat-edged bundles of smartpaper, and affirming photos captioned with quotes from the Jewish and Christian Bibles. Her fingers collated the edges of another bundle of smartpaper.

She looked up with a beaming smile. "Welcome, captain. He and the other gentlemen are waiting for you."

"Other gentlemen?" Tomas checked his wristwatch. 2120. "If his last meeting is running over, I can wait—"

"Captain, he expressly told me to send you in."

Tomas frowned. "Who's with him?"

Her beaming smile weakened. " 'Every idle word that men shall speak, they shall give account thereof in the day of judgment.' Please go in."

He padded across the carpet toward the door. He turned the knob and pushed the door a dozen centimeters. Forrester's confident tone of voice reached him, although the president's words could not be made out.

Tomas rapped his knuckles on the door's cherrywood veneer. Forrester fell silent. "Neumann, get in here. There's someone you need to meet."

He opened the door all the way, stepped in, and shoved the door to get it closing. He squared his shoulders and face to the room just as the door thudded closed. A clang resonated from the door's armored alloy hidden by the veneer.

Tomas started. Forrester and the other gentlemen occupied one end of the sitting area. Forrester stretched out on a plush red armchair in Terraforming Age style. He crossed his legs at the ankles and his hands dangled over the chair arms. To his left, the Chief of Staff sat at the end of a couch. The Chief of Staff balanced thick bundles of smartpaper on his knees and showed no sign of noticing Tomas' arrival.

The someone Tomas needed to meet could only be the third figure. Gray-blue eyes regarded Tomas with a smirk. He lifted a hand. The silk sleeve of his suit jacket slid back to reveal cuff links of golden beryl. He spoke *joséphinais* in a deep and smooth voice. "Tomas, *bon soir*," good evening.

Lucien LaSalle. It seemed like blast doors ponderously shut themselves behind Tomas' face. He replied in Confed. "It's been years since home. And our encounters on New Liberty."

A furrow briefly touched Lucien's brow, soon cast aside as a politician's mask returned. "Yes, years. Too long. We need to catch up sometime. There's an exquisite patisserie in Confederal Heights, it almost makes me believe I'm back home."

Tomas exhaled. "I'll send you my contact info." Lucien would forget the offer to meet for pastries within a minute after he left the room.

"Don't send it in here directly from phone to phone," Forrester said.

Lucien said, "You are a wise man, Mr. President." He turned to Tomas and his eyebrows jumped to include Tomas in his circle. "We're the only four—wait, five—" He gestured toward the door. "—who know I'm here."

"My assistant is the soul of discretion," Forrester said. "And Neumann saved my life, so I know he too can be trusted."

"Indeed." Lucien blinked heavily. "Tomas heeds more rules than I've ever abided by." To Tomas, he said, "The president's concern, of course, is someone in my party's leadership could access my phone's data logs and see a short-range transfer took place at coordinates on the XM grounds." He used the insider jargon for the Executive Mansion, *XM*, as if he'd spent decades working the levers of power.

"Your party?" Tomas asked. He'd been expecting to talk to Forrester about Walters, not meet the scion of an arrogant old Joséphine family and muddy his boots with political skullduggery.

"I was low on our list at the last House election. Small wonder you didn't notice my name. The Democratic Terraformer Party."

A party popular across the younger worlds. Advocates of more Confederal support for local terraforming and an increase in artificial wormhole construction and placement.

Tomas nodded, then looked to Forrester. "How can I help, Mr. President?"

"Take a seat." Forrester chopped his hand toward the unoccupied end of the Chief of Staff's couch. "Keep your eyes open."

Like a Badger traversing its turret to lock its main gun on a target, Forrester's gaze swiveled to Lucien. "It's clear what I need."

Lucien ticked off items on his fingers. "Votes for the Investigation of Terroristic Activities Act and some related legislation. Votes for an increased military budget and legislation relating to resulting personnel needs."

"What do you want in return?"

"A heightened support for terraforming projects and expansion of the Confederated Worlds wormhole network." Lucien's voice flowed like a deep, broad river.

Forrester stared at him, then laughed. "You picked up that ne-gotiating ploy from your old dad? The first guy to name a number becomes the bitch? You can't gull me like you can the average josie whose ancestors labored for yours to build a throne for an emperor who'll never come."

Tucked between his hip and the arm of his chair, Lucien's fist clenched. Its mottles of purple and white contrasted with the chair's cool gray upholstery. Lucien stretched out his fingers, then squared his shoulders to Forrester. "As you wish, Mr. President. I'll name numbers. But before I do, please bear in mind, the only way I can get the party's executive committee and rank-and-file to support my takeover bid is if I can deliver results bigger than the party leader-ship's greatest dreams."

A hooded look formed in Forrester's green eyes.

Lucien kept his shoulders wide and his chest up. "Double Con-federal support for terraforming projects. Add at least two synthesis arrays to the exotic matter factory and increase the rate of wormhole network enlargement to match."

"Two?"

"Two."

Forrester leaned back and cradled his head against interlaced fin-gers. "That's a hell of a high price for your support. But worth pay-ing. If you can deliver."

Lucien smirked. "I can deliver."

"I've seen your dossier." Forrester aimed his chin toward a sheaf of smartpaper balanced on the Chief of Staff's knees. "You're the youngest member of the Democratic Terraformer bloc in the House of the People, and many more senior people were below you on the list. You clearly have allies in the DT executive committee, but you must also have created a lot of resentment in people passed over in your favor. And the executive committee will fight against any backbench rebellion you could foment against them."

A languid, back-handed flick of his wrist, and Lucien made clear his view of Forrester's objections. "A third of the executive commit-tee will support me, because they think they can channel my ambitions to work in their favor. Another third will support me, because they will believe I'll deliver on all those promises. And I will hound out the last third, and raise people loyal to me in their place."

Forrester shifted forward. He tapped the fingertips of his hands together, and angled his head to look up from under pensive brows. "I'm going to look at your offer and get back to you within two days. The Chief of Staff will guide you to the private gate."

Lucien stood. "I think you'll find it a good offer, Mr. President. Tomas, *au revoir.* I'll be in touch." He followed the Chief of Staff out of the room. Confidence trailed Lucien like a subtle, expensive cologne.

Forrester looked at Tomas. "You see what I need from him?"

"Yes," Tomas said. Lucien promised to deliver the Democratic Terraforming party to Forrester's coalition, if Forrester promised to support his bold demands.

"Can he make it happen?"

Tomas rolled his shoulders, turned up his palms. "I don't know what goes on inside the DT executive—"

"I'm looking for your view of him. I know you are the same age and grew up in the same town on Joséphine. I know during the war you encountered him a couple of times on New Liberty. Why do you think I had my assistant show you in?" Forrester tapped his black synthleather shoe on the carpet. "From what you've seen of him, can LaSalle make happen what I need?"

Tomas' lips puckered. A loathing of Lucien built up over a dozen years of his childhood and adolescence returned to Tomas. "He's a small-town heir to a founder's land grant."

"You're a small-town boy who passed OCS with flying colors and got a rapid promotion to captain as a reward for keeping Arden in the Confederated Worlds. Not to mention foiling a would-be assassin whom scores of ConPol and party security personnel watched walk by." Forrester raised his eyebrows. "You still only see what you want to see?"

Tomas leaned away from Forrester. The arm of the sofa pressed against his side. He had nowhere to hide. No option but to face the truth. Lucien could have coasted through life as a Josie from a founder family, prosperous and lazy. Instead, he'd volunteered for Space Force, with his eye even then on his political ambitions. Lucien had overcome a checkered wartime record to become his party's youngest House member. Shrewd and quick enough to butter up Tomas as soon as he saw him.

"He's ambitious and politically adept." Tomas frowned. "But he's never pursued anything more than his personal gain. He lacks principle."

Forrester chuckled. "That makes him look bad?"

"Mr. President?" Tomas blinked to dispel the air of naivete created by his words. "Yes, of course, politics involves compromise. It just struck me as odd for so principled a man as you to treat his lack of principle so lightly."

The wrinkles at the corners of Forrester's hazel eyes accented their sudden glint. "It's better for me he lacks principle. If he's motivated by nothing more than self-interest, then I need only aggrandize his self-interest until I see I no longer need him. With idealists, though, goddam." Forrester's features seemed to draw inward. He slowly shook his head. "At any time, idealists can get hypnotized by their perfect visions and lose sight of a deal that's good enough. They can get stubborn, or foolish, or any of a dozen other damn things, and burn down everything you've built with them."

His face transformed to a practical expression. "You've given me some superb information on LaSalle. And you had something on Walters?"

"I have a strong lead as to where and when he met with a co-conspirator. I asked Restoration Party security for all the relevant data."

"Superb. I know I can count on you." Forrester scowled at the crown molding on the wall behind Tomas. "How long will it take them to show you that data?"

"A month, at least. Perhaps five or six weeks."

"Six weeks?" Forrester's voice knifed through the room.

Tomas winced. Party security seemed competent. The limitations of hunting pertinent information from the data flood determined the long time frames. The president shouldn't punish anyone working for Party security for being slow.

"Maybe the PRs could do it faster using their computers," Tomas said.

Forrester chuckled. He swept his foot over the Confederated Worlds flag pattern in the carpet. "If you have that much free time, I have another project where I can use your eyes."

6

War Footing

The wash of pale blue light from the displays lit up Forrester's firm expression. "Ready," he told Tomas and Maj. Sharma. Not a question. He strode toward the door back to the public office.

Tomas glanced at his wristwatch, 1025, a few minutes before the day's first sunset, then looked up and saw Forrester and Sharma's backs. Tomas hurried after them.

Glimpsed through the Sutherland Office's westerly windows, Epsilon Eridani plunged toward the horizon. Challenger's sun stretched the long shadow of a sofa toward the painting of Sutherland with a wormhole departure ship behind him.

Forrester went to his usual armchair. Tomas and Sharma stood behind him. Forrester paid them no attention, and spoke presumably at someone he saw in his smartglasses. "Today! The committee's a whore's twat! Ram the bill through it! ConPol wants the bill, Democratic Terraforming wants it, and I want it! If ConPol had the Investigation of Terroristic Activities Act four months ago, they'd have Walters' coconspirators on trial by now!"

After listening a moment, Forrester's mouth hardened and jutted forward. "…Wavering? You give them the carrot, ConPol leadership is supporting this, and they'll stay in line. And if they don't, we'll give them the stick."

A few voices and the rustle of a numerous moving bodies percolated through the open doorway from the assistant's station. Forrester glanced that way, then returned his attention to the other party on his call. "Don't say that. It's more ominous if they figure it out on their own. You got it? Tell me you got it. Another meeting coming up. Forrester out."

The president turned to Tomas. "Time?"

"1028."

"They're early. Like they should be."

Sharma's head bobbed. "They know what's best for them."

Forrester twisted in his chair to take in both Tomas and Sharma. "Between your two branches, there are fifteen generals coming in. Watch their reactions when I lift the curtain on my proposal. I need to know who will see eye to eye with me on this, and who won't. If any of them blink, I want to see their fingers removed from the levers of command, one way or another. With your help."

"Yes, sir!" Sharma said.

Tomas' mouth felt dry. Over the past few days, Forrester's hints about a great proposal and expected opposition from the senior brass woke Tomas in the lighted hours between midnight and 0330, and kept him awake amid sweaty, wrinkled sheets. "Understood, Mr. President."

"Good." Forrester stood up. He turned his shoulders to the door, held them wide. He lifted his chin. Commanding confidence filled his face. "Show them in."

His assistant opened the door. Ground Force and Space Force generals filed in. The four-stars, each force's chief of staff, led the way, Gen. Olafson for GF and Gen. Bar-Yuek for shirley foxtrot. Behind them followed five men and a woman in Ground Force service gray dispersed among seven men and two women in Space Force service blue. All had careful hints of maturity, a few crags of face, a few gray strands of hair. Toward the back, the two-stars looked around the room with wide eyes.

Forrester shook Bar-Yuek's hand, then Olafson's. He gestured at the couches and armchairs filling this end of the office. "Take a seat, gentlemen and ladies."

As Forrester and the generals sat, Tomas glanced from face to face among the Ground Force generals in front of him, people decades older and four or more ranks above him. None glanced back at him. Through the last rays of Epsilon Eridani shining straight into their faces, they squinted at Forrester.

Unease writhed in Tomas' belly. With a word to Forrester, he could tip the trajectory of each general's career. Even that of Old Man Olafson himself.

"You might be wondering why I've invited you here today." Forrester sat like a king assured of his throne. "We stand at the cusp of a new era. The history of the Confederated Worlds—of all human space—hinges on my next words." Forrester stared at the generals. His hazel eyes burned. "We must double our forces in the next six months."

Tomas' eyes widened. Chairs squeaked and upholstery rustled with cautious movements. The Ground Force brass cast sidelong glances at one another. The glances snowballed together and flowed toward Gen. Olafson.

Olafson lifted his hand twenty centimeters. The Ground Force brass fell silent, turned rigid. A second later, whispers from the Space Force side ebbed away.

"Mr. President," Olafson said, "That will violate the peace treaty."

Forrester peered down his nose at Olafson. Spite laced his voice. "The correct answer is, 'Thank you, Mr. President, for giving me more men and fab cycles to work with.'"

Olafson folded his arms. His ruddy cheeks were like twin shields turned toward the president. "Thank you for enlarging our *skith* so we can stick it in a sausage grinder, more like. Odin's eye. Both opponents are at the net and we're caught flatfooted. You want to try hitting a winner against the odds. The right play is lobbing the ball over them to give ourselves time to recover."

Forrester rested his finger on the side of his smartglasses. Looking something up. Then he pulled the smartglasses from his face. His hazel eyes narrowed further. "You love tennis, don't you, general? Here's how I see it. If the PRs and Unis are at the net, we're going to smash the ball into their goddam faces before they can lift their rackets."

"Mr. President." Olafson's face scrunched as if he had heartburn. "They outnumber us already. If they catch us violating the peace treaty, they'll double their forces and we'll be even further behind them."

"They won't see what we're doing." Forrester kept his voice at medium volume but it still filled the room. "Unless someone here tells them."

Olafson swallowed, then leaned forward. Ceiling panels brightened slightly with the dimming natural light. Sol-spectrum light glossed in Olafson's gray-speckled hair. "There are a million ways a force buildup could leak. Line items in the budget. Counting heads of men going up the space elevator for intake at GFB Challenger Orbital Station 1. Odin's eye, even an increase in recruiting trips to small towns on the outworlds could tip them off."

Forrester turned his head and raised a look-at-this-guy eyebrow to Tomas. Tomas' mouth tightened. Then he gave his head one crisp nod. He saw and heard Olafson, indeed.

Bar-Yuek spoke. His voice sounded surprisingly pinched for a man risen to Space Force's chief of staff. "The Investigation of Terroristic Activities Act will help ConPol run better counterespionage. We can keep our buildup secret."

Olafson snorted. "To do that, ConPol must catch every PR and Uni spy. The PRs and Unis only need one."

Epsilon Eridani now lay just below the horizon. Diffuse orange-red light tinged Forrester's clear, tanned face. "I see that. So what?"

"Mr. President?" Olafson angled his head a fraction of a turn away from Forrester. His eyes looked wide under arched eyebrows. "As we both recognize, if the PRs and Unis found out we doubled our forces, they'd double—"

Forrester's hand jutted out, pointing at Olafson like some martial arts blow. "That's where you're blind. For two years, I saw them with their helmets raised. I saw their faces. I. Saw. Their. Faces!"

His gaze roved the room, peering into each face like a ground-penetrating radar searching for the hidden caches of an enemy. No one breathed.

"They have no goddam spine. If we double our forces, we call their bluff." His lips curled in mockery. "Their ambassadors will shake their heads like schoolmarms and shove a copy of the treaty at me, and tap their fingers at the clause limiting our forces. Then they will do not one goddam thing more."

Bar-Yuek quirked his mouth from side to side, the look of a man with something to say. Yet he kept his lips together and shared a quick glance with his highest ranking subordinate.

Olafson's upper body remained rigid. "Underestimating the enemy is a good way to end up defeated. Or dead."

Forrester's voice rose. It echoed off the secreted plasterboard, the crown moldings, the paintings of his illustrious predecessors. "The PR fleet scored a single lucky victory to gain orbital supremacy over Challenger. Will that happen again, General Bar-Yuek?"

Bar-Yuek blinked rapidly. "No—" He cleared his throat, and his voice sounded deeper. "No. I assure you, it shall not."

"I know why it will not," Forrester said. "Providence sides with us, and our foes know it too." His voice filled the room, dispelling doubt. He looked at Tomas. "Isn't that right, Neumann?"

Every pair of eyes in the room burned into him. Olafson's face seemed as faceted and armored as the front slope of a Graywolf battle tank. Tomas stared at the flag pattern in the rug below. A line from the Bonapartist catechism, taught in every school on Joséphine, came to him. *The moral is to the physical as three is to one.*

You already look like a junior fool in over his head. Say that and you remove all doubt.

Forrester arched an eyebrow.

Sweat dampened the small of Tomas' back, instantly felt like ice. "I've seen outmanned and outgunned forces outfight their opponents, Mr. President."

"Seen it? You did it, on Arden. How many of your so-called superiors can say the same?"

Tomas' gaze flicked over the impassive faces on the Ground Force side of the room, avoiding Olafson. His mouth felt dry. "I can't say, Mr. President."

Olafson sniffed out a breath.

Forrester stretched himself to his full seated height. His gaze pierced the generals. "That's all for now. You'll give me progress reports every month. Don't try to bullshit me—I have men behind me who can see through your lies." He jerked his thumb toward his shoulder, in the direction of Tomas and Maj. Sharma.

"Willfully drag your feet and heads will roll. But give me twice the forces with the same effectiveness per man and per ship, and you'll get every reward I can offer. Dismissed."

The president stood and stalked toward his private office. Moments later, the door thudded shut behind him.

The generals stood in a daze. Each turned to the ones nearby with plaintive eyes. Like Tomas' sons, aware of something amiss and craving assurance from a more forceful personality. A Ground Force three-star leaned his weight away from Olafson and shared a sullen look with one of his subordinates.

Was Olafson that forceful personality? Or Forrester?

Ruddy cheeks and hair speckled with gray loomed in the corner of Tomas' eye. "Captain, a word, now."

Tomas lifted his chest. "Yes, general?"

"We all know his plan is reckless. The PRs and Unis are going to return his serve harder than he expects. The risks are plain. Tell him that."

"I agree, general, the president's course of action carries risks. Yet an effective leader takes risks to pursue the mission objective. I did when I led fireteams and platoons." Parts of him separated, one lifted on an unnaturally high trajectory by Forrester's magnetism, the other settling downward under Gen. Olafson's narrow-eyed glare. Tomas gave the elevated part his voice. "I assume you did when you told the civilians Ground Force could take control of New Liberty if they towed a wormhole there."

Olafson's nostrils flared. His eyes showed wide whites. His pupils danced, his gaze skittering over Tomas' face for some toehold, finding none.

A ball of warmth bloomed in Tomas' gut. "Forrester takes risks to pursue the largest mission objective of all."

"Odin's eye." Olafson jabbed at Tomas with his index finger. "He will lead us off a cliff. You think you'll have a safe landing because you're a thousand meters up his ass? You'll be spattered on the rocks with the rest of us, more like."

Tomas stared back. "I'll do the duty asked of me by my commander-in-chief. Will you, general?"

Olafson's face grew red. A deep furrow creased the skin between his eyes. He gnashed his teeth. Frustration, Tomas read, that a mere captain could defy him, thanks to Forrester's shield.

"Tell him or don't," Olafson muttered. "The blood will be on your hands." He pivoted and trooped out.

One day two months later, Tomas sat in his basement office. He pored over Restoration Party security dossiers compiled on Ground Force generals and composed notes to the president. A familiar name crossed his screen and dredged up his memory of the telephone call from the morning after the election.

Given the centrality of Ground Force combat elements stationed at GFB West McAuliffe to any defense of the capital cities against PR and/or Uni ground forces, strategic planning should include Brig. Echevarria—

Knuckles rapped his office's open door. He turned. Irina, a junior assistant assistant staff member. Two years out of college—barely younger than Tomas—she seemed a girl in a curvy woman's body. She wore a cross barby pin on her tight sweater, just below her left shoulder.

He lifted his gaze to her face and kept it there.

"Captain Neumann," she said, "we're going to lunch." In the hallway behind her, men and women, all in their twenties standard, mingled with relaxed limbs. In casual bantering tones they chatted among themselves about an electronic communications security bill up for vote that afternoon in the Senate of the Worlds.

Irina leaned her head against the door. Her fingers trailed down the door's edge. "Come with us."

Lunch? Tomas stomach rumbled. He had a sandwich in the fridge, mol fabbed meat and cheese between slices of mol fabbed bread.

Lunch. Time away from data displays. Time with people his age. With a woman who asked for his company, instead of giving him sullen looks and feigning rigid-backed sleep when he came to bed....

He pressed his lips together. He'd sworn his fidelity to Lissa, before whatever gods he might worship, before the witnesses at their wedding, and before himself. He would not put himself in temptation's way. "Wish I could. Too much work." He lifted his hand to indicate the data display behind him.

"But we all have too much work," she said. "Are you sure?"

"He's sure," said a young man's voice behind her. His tone combined arrogance, impatience, resentment, and fear.

Behind Tomas, a ping sounded from the speakers. Tomas glanced over his shoulder. A popup showed the first lines of a message from RP security's video archivists. *Sorry we're so late, but we finally have background info and images gathered on everyone at New Portland's Finest the same time as Walters....*

"I am," Tomas said to Irina. "Perhaps another time." He glimpsed her drooping shoulders in the moment before he turned back to his display.

Finally, data on who might have given the pistol and advanced lethe potion to Walters. His hands jumped to the keyboard and raced through the keystrokes needed to open up the video files and party security dossiers on everyone identified in them.

He spent the rest of the day, and most of the next three, reviewing the files. Passers-by whom a bluecoat's third-eye camera happened to catch. Regular customers of the café coming in for their afternoon beverages. Bank records, somehow acquired by party security under the recently-passed Investigation of Terroristic Activities Act, gave purchase times and amounts. No one of interest.

Late in the third day, Tomas perked up. Party security identified a man, roughly Walters' age, whose social media stream advocated advanced computers, more immersive virtual reality, and even robotics. The cameras caught his wide, timid eyes glancing about when he entered the café—

—and his mop of curly hair low over his eyes when he slunk

away six minutes later. Not enough confeds in his account to buy a cup of coffee, Tomas read in his slumped shoulders.

Despite his intuition, Tomas gave a closer look to the man with the timid eyes. The man entered and exited New Portland's Finest over an hour before Walters. He could have hidden a parcel containing the pistol and the advanced lethe potion somewhere in the café, somewhere only Walters would know to look.

Hidden in six minutes? Not much time. Especially when one of the few snippets of video from inside the café came from a bluecoat waiting to order a coffee drink. The man with the timid eyes shuffled forward in line, fumbled with an old phone when time came to pay, then trudged around the bluecoat on his way to the front door. The video snippet accounted for the last four minutes of the man's time in New Portland's Finest.

As for the first two minutes…. the man went into the café around 1700, when Epsilon Eridani remained above the horizon. All the previous video suggested the weather had been hotter than usual that sunlit slice of that day—men unbuttoned their cuffs or bunched up their sleeves at their elbows, and many women tied their sweaters' sleeves around their waists. Tomas checked the weather almanac for that day. 24°C. Balmy for Challenger's thin air and the capital cities' altitude on the shield volcano called Mount Kennedy, whose glaciers at even higher elevation typically fed cooling winds.

In the video, the man with timid eyes dressed for the warm weather as well. He entered New Portland's Finest wearing a tee shirt tucked into narrow-legged trousers. A belt cinched tightly enough to scallop the waistband.

The man with timid eyes could not have hidden the pistol under his clothes.

The video from the café was a dead end.

Tomas leaned back and shut his eyes. Grit seemed to rasp under his eyelids. Months of investigation come to nothing—

Not quite. The *video* was a dead end. What might he find if he visited the café in the flesh?

7

Boots on the Ground

The next morning, even before Epsilon Eridani rose in the east for the first time, Tomas felt weary to his bones.

Artur's cry pierced his ears. Stefan raised his voice to be heard. "Daddy, I need go poop."

Tomas looked down. In his left arm, Artur caught his breath, then cried again. Through Artur's diaper, Tomas felt the squish of soft baby stool. "I'll go with you. Lissa, take Artur—"

"I'll help Stefan on the potty." Her chin rested on the heel of her hand, her elbow on the kitchen table near a half-eaten breakfast roll filled with meat and cheese. A strand of untucked hair partially occluded one of her drooping eyes. "You don't change enough diapers."

Tomas shook his head. "Stefan might do better with a man helping him."

"Not once a week. Change Artur." Lissa pushed herself out of her chair and shuffled across the kitchen's tile floor. She yawned and reached for Stefan's hand. She spoke to their elder son in tones of nurturing sweetness. "I want to see how much poop you can put in the potty."

Stefan nodded his head with a three-year-old's seriousness. "I go all my poop." Mother and son left the room.

Tomas took Artur upstairs, toward the changing table. Up the narrow stairway, near the framed photo from their honeymoon, his watch prodded his wrist.

What now? His head drooped. He stopped on the stairs, then sloughed out a breath. The call could wait. Artur's tears eased, but a red raccoon look splotched his eyes. Tomas hurried the rest of the way up to the nursery.

Pajama pants off, diaper off. Squishy stool greeted Tomas, everywhere, from the top of Artur's rump to the underside of his penis. The corners of Tomas' mouth pulled up. *Where's that container of wipes—don't squirm, son—another wipe—I said don't squirm—how did he get stool there?—the last wipe in the container?*—Tomas held Artur between his left hand and his chest, dangling the baby's bare bottom over the floor of mol-fabbed wood, then hurried around the room. *Where are more wipes? Did a bit of stool just drop from his bottom? Did I just step in it?* His watch prodded his wrist. Artur's face crinkled and he drew in a breath. *No, don't cry.* Tomas scowled around the room. *Where does she put those wipes? And the diapers?*

Lissa came into the room. She rolled her eyes cool as sapphire, then regarded him as she took quick steps around the room. She grabbed wipes and a diaper by muscle memory, then took a wide step over the bit of dropped stool. Her eyebrows formed a strong, low line. She held out her arms. "Give him to me."

Ten minutes later, Tomas ducked into the master bedroom. Lissa's disdain swirled down the hallway outside the bedroom, and a few tendrils wisped inside.

He caught his breath and glanced out the window. In the backyard, wisps of the day's first dawn revealed traces of color in toys left out overnight.

She shouldn't let the boys.... He inhaled deeply. Lissa did the best she could.

Time for him to do the same. He tapped his watch. The video display on the dresser bloomed with color. Forrester's assistant filled the screen.

"Good morning, captain. The president wants you to be at the following address at ten o'clock." The address appeared. Somewhere in Finziburg, south of and downslope from Confederal City. Tomas fed the address to his calendar and navigation guide. "He'd like you to observe and write up a report for delivery to him tomorrow."

Her mousy features looked even more placating. "I understand this may disrupt your day's plans. Remember, 'he that is faithful in that which is least is faithful also in much.' Goodbye."

Reaching the address in Finziburg required a change of subway lines near the white mountain and a ride on the intraregional through the Southcrest nature preserve. Beyond the transparent sound-baffling walls on both sides of the track, a few narrow roads and thick bundles of data trunks showed amid the dense stands of oaks and maples. Epsilon Eridani sank in the west. A gloom welled beneath the canopies of the trees, and stirred up hibernating memories of forested battlefields on New Liberty and Arden.

He shook his head to settle the memories. The train pulled into the intraregional station in Finziburg. He took a bus and straphanged near the door. At every stop after the bus left the station, he checked his watch and tapped his foot. He let out a breath when the bus reached his destination at 0956.

The address held a long mycocrete building, fifteen meters high. A pedestrian door and small flanking windows broke up the plain gray wall. Above the door and windows loomed the words *CC Telecom*, the capital cities' communications utility.

Between the street and the building, a parking lot held blue jeeps and trucks. Bluecoats milled around. One squinted at Tomas, then pulled his baton from its adhesive and approached.

Suddenly, the bluecoat cocked his head, suggesting he heard something on a hidden earbud. He started. He jammed his baton against his leg and hurried forward. His gaze roved over the nameplate on Tomas' service uniform. "Captain Neumann, please come with me. The task force leader is waiting for you."

Stripes ringed the task force leader's cross barby armband. His blond hair resembled the stubble of farmer's crop. Gray eyes were narrow pits in his square face. Around him, bluecoats with smoother faces deferred to him.

Tomas nodded. "Good to meet you again."

The old sergeant, last met in the aftermath of the attempted assassination in Firstlanding Square, dipped his chin once in greeting. "Likewise, captain. And I understand you know Captain Rolston?"

"Neumann!" Rolston stepped forward from the dropped tailgate of one of the trucks. His Ground Force service gray stuck out from the mass of blue uniforms around them. He clapped his hand on Tomas' shoulder. "Thanks for giving me a leg up on this one."

"Remind me again what 'this one' is?"

Rolston's eyebrows arched, like suspension cables holding up the bridge deck of his smartglasses. "Your hands are in so many pies you forget which one this is? The president is signing a new cybersecurity bill into law today. We're putting part of it into effect."

He jerked his thumb toward the back of the truck, then tugged Tomas by the shoulder in that direction. Bench seats lined the truck's cargo area. A lieutenant with wide ears and a long, pointy nose sat near the tailgate, with five enlisteds nearby. Their service gray sleeves bore the cone-of-arcs logo of the Signal Corps. On the floor, between the benches, lay three small crates.

The lieutenant lurched to his feet and saluted. His garrison cap nearly brushed the ceiling. "Captain, captain, are we ready?"

"We are, Yeungling," Rolston said. Yeungling was the name on the lieutenant's nameplate, not the nickname *youngling*. "Come on out, and bring in our cargo." Rolston's cheeks tightened and his green eyes grew lively. "And look sharp. Captain Neumann can put in a good word for you with the president. Or a bad one."

A high-pitched, staccato laugh burst from Yeungling's mouth. His hand fluttered up to stop it. He took a deep breath, then jumped up out of the truck bed. Yeungling ordered the enlisteds to bring the crates and follow him. At least he had enough of a commanding presence to order about pogey sweaties.

Tomas' thoughts weighed down his eyelids. *You were a butterbar once, too.* Yeungling looked gangly, and Tomas would hate to rely on him to fire a sidearm, but everyone had a role to play. The tip needs the spear behind it, the pogeys said, and they had it right.

Rolston and the bluecoat task force leader led the way to the glass front door. Tomas followed a step behind, trailed by Yeungling and the Signal Corps sweaties. A third of the bluecoats followed, while the rest dispersed around the parking lot and the sides of the building.

They entered a reception area. On the far wall, two doors stood between them and the deeper parts of the building. CC Telecom's name and logo hung on a plain white wall above a receptionist's station. The receptionist herself, a woman with pale skin and pouty lips, stood near the front door, blocking the routes deeper into the building.

Rolston angled his head. His voice held mirth. "You had your ear to the ground, nay?"

Her narrow eyes peered through smartglasses, and studied the Ground Force enlisted and the mass of bluecoats still coming in. "How may I help you?"

"We're here to put into effect one of the clauses of the new communications security law." He touched her elbow. "We'll find our way, don't let us bother you—"

The receptionist's gaze landed on Rolston's face. Her eyes remained narrow. "I don't know anything about a new law."

The bluecoat task force leader stepped forward, barely seeming to move. His tiny gray eyes did not blink. "Tell the senior company official on site we're here."

She leaned back. Her right hand checked the top button of her blouse. "Very well. Please wait." She scurried behind the reception station, touched the side of her smartglasses. She soon murmured words too quietly for Tomas to hear.

Five minutes later, a man in a short-sleeve dress shirt and gray rep necktie hurried in. He ran his hand through his brown hair, then tried to stand tall. "Sirs, how can I help you?"

"We're here to put into effect one of the clauses of the new communications security law." Rolston's voice lacked mirth.

"The new law?" the site manager asked. "The president signed it?"

Tomas frowned. Of course Forrester had signed it. First thing, probably. That explained the delay till 1000 to implement whatever the crates concealed.

Rolston's head turned side to side. "It becomes law today."

A cold sensation touched Tomas' gut. He slipped his phone from his pocket. Holding it with both hands close to his hip, he snapped it into its rigid conformation. Public news sites. Executive Mansion news feed. Silent.

Tomas scrolled through Forrester's calendar for the day. *CS law signing ceremony, Sutherland Office, 1300.*

The site manager licked his lips. "Even though he's signed it, there's still the regulatory process. I can't speak for corporate headquarters, but I'm sure they'd be willing to work with the Defense Ministry, the Confederal Police, concerned citizens like the Restoration Party—"

"Assassins." The task force leader's voice thudded. "Terrorists. Uni and PR spies. They're everywhere. We're here to stop them. Are you?"

The site manager ran his hand through his hair, licked his lips. "I, ah, please, wait here."

Mirth bubbled in Rolston's voice. "We will."

He went around the receptionist's station. "Get me corporate headquarters," he said in a harsh whisper. A wide-eyed glance in Tomas' direction showed he knew he'd spoken loudly enough to be heard.

Tomas shuffled his feet. He leaned toward Rolston and the bluecoat task force leader and muttered, "Forrester hasn't signed the bill into law yet."

Rolston arched his eyebrow. He nudged his elbow into Tomas' ribs. "Rules don't bind the one who writes them." He turned to the task force leader. "CC Telecom corporate headquarters will fall in line?"

The bluecoat leader's face was a broad shield. "Already has."

"Would you check?"

"I don't need to."

Tomas stepped back. He rocked his weight from foot to foot. Not yet a law? Formal regulations weeks away? Bluecoats throwing their weight around at CC Telecom corporate headquarters? Rules mattered.

Even if following them made it more difficult to track down people like Walters and his unknown coconspirators?

He mulled the question, without an answer, until the site manager came back around the receptionist's desk. The site manager licked his lips and said, "Corporate has considered your request and is happy to comply. Please, follow me."

The site manager led them through one of the doors off the reception area. They passed a control room filled with hardwired panels and employees plainly trying not to look at the Ground Force and bluecoat personnel. A stairwell down led to a basement, stuffy and echoing with cooling fans.

One of the basement's rooms held racks of computer equipment connected by thick bundles of data cables. The bluecoat task force leader and some of his subordinates boxed the site manager against the wall just inside the door. Rolston turned to Lt. Yeungling. "You know what to do. And remember, Forrester's got his eye on you!"

Yeungling gulped, stumbled. Rolston grinned as Yeungling and the sweaties took the crates toward the depths of the room.

"What does he know to do?" Tomas asked.

"Every voice, video, or text message sent to or from anyone in the capital cities goes through here." Rolston lassoed the air with an upraised finger. "We're installing a filter to look at or block communications to or from anyone. Or everyone. Lookback period depends on storage capacity, but probably days, weeks."

Tomas weighed the idea. "Six months ago, that would have helped us find with whom Walters might have acted."

"Might? Would've. That pistol he had, no way he acted alone." Rolston beckoned him to follow, then led the way between equipment racks like red-lit and fan-humming shelves of a dumbpaper library.

Yeungling and his men worked at a rack. They slid equipment in and out, snicked cable connectors into place, watched diagnostic results scroll across their phone and tablet screens. Tomas lacked any idea of what they did, but they moved crisply and spoke in assured tones. Even Yeungling seemed more confident.

Good men pursued this mission's objective.

They wrapped up around 1230, deep in the period of late morning darkness. The Ground Force personnel returned to their truck and the bluecoats dispersed to their civilian vehicles at the edges of the parking lot. Tomas waited alone at the bus stop, rode alone to the train station, made his way alone through the transferring crowds at the White Mountain subway stop.

He checked his schedule. Clear—Forrester didn't need him the rest of the day.

Instead of taking the line to the Executive Mansion, Tomas found the intercity to McAuliffe. He took a seat on the train, then pulled out his phone and plotted his route to New Portland's Finest.

The eastern horizon glowed, lit from below by Epsilon Eridani, as Tomas walked toward the café. A street of two- and three-story buildings, set back behind broad sidewalks. Small cars, mostly two-seater hatchbacks, slipped in and out of slanted parking spaces along the curbs. Bioluminescent cypresses washed out all but a handful of the brightest stars and the blinking lights of a space elevator car climbing up the invisibly dark and thin cable to orbit.

Inside New Portland's Finest, Tomas glanced around. A few late-morning patrons looked up from their conversations or their data displays. Narrow eyes regarded Tomas, then turned away. At the tables near the back of the line, shoulders hunkered and voices dropped.

Tomas stiffened his back to the civilians behind him. A display case near the counter held a few forlorn pastries and one salad packaged with protein strips. A smartpaper stuck to the display case's window read *Due to reduced production by the molecular fabrication utility, many menu items are unavailable. We are attempting to restock from other sources. We appreciate your patience.*

Lissa had grumbled about shortages, too. Tomas' eyebrows lifted. Of course. Increased construction of ships and other equipment for the forces required more mol fab techs then Challenger's skills imps could provide.

Though short, the line moved slowly. A drawling customer

asked for food items absent from the display case, then dithered over a coffee order. By the time Tomas reached the counter, he felt the presence of other people behind him at a wary distance.

"Sparkling water," he told the clerk, "and I need to speak with the manager."

The clerk blinked repeatedly. His mouth gaped like a fish on a riverbank. "The owner? Yes, of course, sir, of course, I'll send her right out."

Tomas found an empty, small round table and took three swallows of sparkling water before the manager came from a back room. She wore pale makeup and dark eyeliner. After a hesitant step, she strode forward and rested her hands on her hips. Elbows wide, she lifted her chin. "What's this about?"

Tomas set down his drink. He snapped his phone to its rigid conformation. "This man was here on a Sixday afternoon about three weeks before the election. Roughly 1800. Eighteen o'clock." He showed her a picture of Walters. "Do you recall seeing him?"

She peered down her narrow, aquiline nose. Her nostrils flared. "That's the man who tried shooting Forrester?"

"Yes."

Her eyes showed whites incongruous against her eyeliner and brown irises. "What are you accusing me of?"

"Nothing," Tomas said. "Should I?"

Her hands fluttered up, as if to placate him and shield herself at the same time. "I didn't even rank him on my ballot and I don't approve of you space navy types dragooning all the mol fab techs, but I swear, I would never help someone try to kill a presidential candidate."

"Few people would. We suspect Walters met with at least one other person to further their conspiracy to assassinate Mr. Forrester. Met without your knowledge, of course." Tomas leaned his weight forward. "I need to know which of your employees worked here that date and time."

She shrank back. "A few minutes, please."

"I'll wait here." Tomas sat and the owner padded back to the office.

A few minutes stretched out. Tomas finished his sparkling water, then checked messages. Irina again invited him to lunch.

He left her message open for a long time, before a thought refocused him. What took the owner so long?

Tomas peered at the entrance to the back office. The Solspectrum lighting panels seemed to flood the room with stark white light.

Had the owner been involved in Walters' conspiracy? Did she even now warn her fellow conspirators? Would they send a team of operatives after him—

The front door chimed. Tomas jolted and snapped his head around. Two women, with studded and buckled handbags tucked over their shoulders, talked to one another with barely a glance around.

Tomas took a breath. Walters' conspiracy would select a neutral site, not one that would naturally lead interrogators to one of its members. The owner's work logs of the meeting date would tell him nothing. The café was a dead end.

And he had a bladder full of piss.

He left the table, followed the restroom signs to a hallway running across the back of the café. The air felt cooler near the men's room entrance. *Because it's dimmer here. And you're calming down.* He found the urinal and relaxed even further. Wash hands, splash water on his face. He stepped back out.

The air really was cooler in the hallway.

He stood in place, arms away from his body and fingertips splayed. He turned his head to angle his ears toward the dimness at either end of the hallway. To the right. A draft feathered over his fingertips. A voice.

"—that's why I gotta keep this shitty job."

Tomas padded closer.

Another voice, deeper and scornful, spoke. "You got more than tobacco in that thing? No fricking way they're gonna draft men for the forces. And only guys living off mol fab freebies? You think those are the kind of guys with the chops to crew a Weasel or a Graywolf?"

At the end of the hall, behind stacked boxes of cups and plates and beverage slurry pouches, stood an emergency door, propped open by a chunk of mycocrete. Wires twisted in the air, underneath the door handle's words *alarm will sound.*

"They can skills imp anyone to do anything. I tell ya, they got a draft in the works—"

Tomas pushed the door open and strode through. "We want to impose conscription?" he said. "I hadn't heard."

The two men scrambled to their feet. Tough to see in the dim alley, lit only by a few straggly lights over the service docks of stores, but plainly both men wore khaki pants and green polos with the logo of New Portland's Finest. The shorter one dragged on a cigarette as if to draw strength from the smoke. The taller one, pudgy and bearded, dropped his cigarette and stood stiff-backed. The stink of burning tobacco bit Tomas' nose.

The shorter one exhaled a stream of smoke. "Wait, you aren't boss lady."

"I know where to find her. What's your name?"

A sullen drag on the cigarette. "Fuck off. You ain't drafted me yet."

Tomas turned to the taller man. "Where'd you serve, scout?"

The taller man's eyebrows jumped. "How, uh, New Lib, sir."

"Where? I was sunright of Reagantown my whole time there."

Some dredged-up memory left its trail on the tall former scout's face. "Sunleft. Wasn't there long. Three weeks in the field and I got sent back to R-town for a new set of these." He tapped his legs. The look on his face became even more faraway.

Two new limbs wasn't enough to get a man a medical discharge. He'd gotten hit worse, in body or in spirit. Tomas put on an easy smile. "Which one of you jimmied the door's alarm?"

"He did."

The shorter man's hands turned to fists. His eyes hardened at the former scout. "Ya told me you were done with that army shit. But this go shows up and you tell him everything."

Tomas squared his shoulders to the shorter man. "Were you working here on the Sixday afternoon three weeks before the election?"

"Fuck off."

Behind Tomas, inside the hallway, someone slid boxes. The emergency door scraped on the chunk of mycocrete as the owner swung it open. "I can answer," the owner said. She brandished a tablet in the air. "He was." She scowled at the two men. "You're smoking on the job, which is against the employee handbook, and hacking the door is a fire code violation, you realize that?"

The former scout looked sheepish. "Yes, ma'am."

The other, shorter man scrunched up his mouth. He dropped his cigarette and ground it out with his foot.

The owner jutted her finger at him. "You're fired." She aimed her feet at the tall former scout. "As for you, I'll give you one more chance, but if you smoke on the job again, or hack the emergency door again, you're on the street with him. Clear?"

"Yes, ma'am." The former scout stepped on his cigarette. "I'll get back to work now." He hunched his shoulders and went back inside the café.

For a moment, a bony, thrashing dark green bundle covered the shorter man's face. "Fuck all of you." He flung the polo shirt at Tomas' feet, then stalked up the alley.

The owner cleared his throat. "I have the complete list of employees working at eighteen o'clock that day. I can beam it to you."

"Please," Tomas said. A smile creased his mouth as he watched the shorter man stalk along the alley.

He didn't need the list. He knew the route Walters' coconspirator had taken into the café.

8

The Coconspirator

Two weeks later, in his basement office, Tomas loosened his necktie and unbuttoned the cuffs of his sleeves. The closed door trapped warm air in the room, but rebuffed Irina and the other young women working down here. Forrester had assigned him to review test data on an anti-missile laser system considered for deployment on Ground Force's fighting vehicles. Forrester's hazel eyes burned in Tomas' memory. "The CEO is a diamond-level member of the Restoration Party, but if you tell me this goddam laser thing is smoke and mirrors, I'll tell the CEO to get out of my sight."

The earlier versions never worked. So far, the new anti-missile laser system looked about as ineffective as the old. Tomas frowned. Brig. Echevarria's summary praised it. On the other hand, Gen. Olafson panned it with particularly sharp words—

The incoming message indicator pinged. Tomas glanced at it. *Video data from alley and nearby streets ready for you.*

Tomas perked up. Quicker than he expected… probably because there wasn't much. A short time window, a narrow search area. He sloughed out a breath and checked the clock. How had it gotten to be 1840 already? His stomach grumbled.

Forrester wanted his report on the anti-missile laser by noon the next day. He glanced at the number and sizes of the test data files.

Five hours in the morning would be plenty of time to study the rest and write up his assessment. He would feel especially productive doing that tomorrow if the video from the alley came up empty.

He opened up the video files. Restoration Party security had tagged eleven people on foot near the alley's mouths around the time Walters entered New Portland's Finest. Most of the video came from a bluecoat who'd laid his cap near the window of a barbershop. The people at Party video archiving had stitched visible light and night vision data into ugly but coherent information.

Hovering tooltips gave the name of each tagged person. Tomas opened up the dossier on each. Unexceptional citizens, with no obvious whiff of conspiracy. The video corroborated the dossiers. Here, a Montessori teacher holding a folded jacket over her arm as she walked along the street. There, a recipient of the mol fab minimum allotment, shoulders slumped as he looked in the windows of handcrafters' shops. Another, a cellist lugging his cased instrument through the front door of his walk-up apartment building.

Tomas' brow crinkled. Eleven people.

Why had video archiving sent files on twelve?

He opened up the last video file. The first frame showed the green blur of someone caught moving in the darkness between bioluminescent cypresses. The body size and shape strongly suggested a man. The tooltip showed *subject not identified*.

How? Didn't Party security have dossiers on every citizen of the Confederated Worlds?

Coldness wrapped itself like an icy belt around Tomas' waist. He pressed *play*.

The night vision image of the man remained a blur, impossible to identify. He came closer to a bioluminescent cypress and flickers of visible spectrum data entered his shape. Freeze the video when he's directly under a cypress—

Tomas' finger stumbled. He paused the video a second after the man passed under the bioluminescent cypress. The angle of light in the paused frame partially shadowed his face. Enough that Tomas couldn't be sure.

He had to be sure.

Tomas rewound the video a second. He paused it nearly at the perfect spot. Imperfect, but good enough to see the man.

Civilian clothes, striped trousers and a half-buttoned short sleeve shirt, could not disguise him. Brown hair, mustache. Maj. Aranjuez.

Gooseflesh crawled over Tomas' skin like ants. By a strap, held at the side of his body, Maj. Aranjuez carried a large backpack.

An intuition punched Tomas in the gut. His hands pounded the keyboard. A moment later, a video frame of Walters popped up in a separate window. Walters, walking away from New Portland's Finest, ten minutes after Maj. Aranjuez passed through the cypress' illumination.

Walters hadn't added something to his backpack inside the café.

He'd swapped backpacks with Maj. Aranjuez.

Tomas' gaze flicked over the two images. That strap, that zipper, that frayed thread…. The same backpack.

He sagged back in his chair. *If I could, I would forge a lasting peace with the Confederated Worlds.* The lie of a diplomat. Of a spy. Of an assassin.

Tomas clutched his chair's arms. His arms shook. One deep breath, another, and still his arms shook.

A thought slid into place, like ice breaking up on the river near his home.

He called Lissa. Her image appeared on his display, overlaying frames of Walters and Maj. Aranjuez. Her image didn't belong here.

She looked haggard. "I'm getting the boys to bed. Make it quick."

"I'll swing by the house for a few minutes, but then I have to come back in for work."

"What else is new." Her look grew more intent. "Something more? No? Then I'm going to take care of our sons." Her image blinked out.

Tomas took another deep breath. His emotions remained steady. He could do what needed to be done.

Ten minutes at the office found a diplomat's directory from the Foreign Ministry. Names, message addresses, residences…. A schedule of the evening's diplomatic events, start and end times, and expected attendees…. According to the Foreign Ministry's schedule, Maj. Aranjuez would spend the evening, from 2200 to 2500, at a reception in downtown McAuliffe.

Ten minutes at home and Tomas left with a full magazine in his sidearm.

About 2530, Tomas waited in a wooded lot on a broad, quiet street in Confederal Heights. Epsilon Eridani lay nearly an hour under the western horizon. The scattered light of bioluminescent cypresses failed to penetrate to Tomas' hiding place.

He yawned and rubbed gritty eyes. On a normal day he slept by now. But this day was not normal.

Footsteps clacked on the sidewalk, coming from the direction of the nearest subway station, heading toward the sprawling house Maj. Aranjuez shared with four other Uni diplomats and two housekeepers. Tomas' eyes opened wider.

Tomas stepped lightly through the grass. A glance down showed his service gray uniform to be a vague dappling in the darkness under the trees. He approached a waist-high iron fence and laid his hand on the gate. Beyond the gate, the sidewalk ran along the fence. Between the sidewalk and the street loomed a massive oak. The oak's lowermost branches nearly brushed the ground, then curled up. Its foliage shadowed the light of bioluminescent cypresses down the block.

The only light between Tomas and the oak came from a phone display. The phone's user looked to be walking under muscle memory. The screen lit his face bluish-white. Brown hair. Mustache. An idle look in his brown eyes as he tapped the display.

Tomas drew his pistol and swung open the gate. Two steps later, he stopped in the middle of the sidewalk. Over his raised pistol, he said, "Don't move."

The whites of Maj. Aranjuez's eyes flashed. His shoes scraped to a halt. Then, calmly, he moved his hands away from his body. The phone display glowed in his left hand.

"Put the phone on the ground, then slide it toward me with your foot."

Maj. Aranjuez squinted. "Captain Neumann. *Madre de dios*, you are causing the, how does one say, diplomatic accident?"

"You must know all about diplomatic incidents," Tomas said. "Phone on the ground, slide it toward me."

Maj. Aranjuez stiffly bent his knees. "What do you mean, I must know?" He rested the phone screen-up on the sidewalk, then stood.

"You traded backpacks with Jordan Walters at New Portland's Finest a week before the assassination attempt on Forrester. The phone."

Maj. Aranjuez took a deep breath. A breath to gird himself for a plan of action. Deftly he tapped the phone with his foot. The phone skittered two meters along the sidewalk. It stopped ten centimeters from the tip of Tomas' right shoe.

Tomas stepped back. He squatted down, gaze and pistol covering Maj. Aranjuez, and groped for the phone with his free hand. He stood and shoved it into his pants pocket. He waved the pistol toward the iron gate. "Go in. Slowly. Hands visible. No sudden moves."

Maj. Aranjuez went through the gate. He complied with Tomas' requests yet still seemed dangerous, ready to plant his foot on the turf, pivot, and strike without warning. Tomas kept the pistol aimed at the major's spine.

"Stop here," Tomas said in a small clearing in the wooded lot. Maples and elms surrounded them. A breeze rustled the leaves. "Turn. Hands visible."

Maj. Aranjuez followed the order. He glanced around the small clearing. The tips of his mustache jumped, almost too quickly to notice. When he faced Tomas fully, his expression was serious. "You know my role in the attempt on candidate Forrester's life. I have not been declared *persona non grata*. Your Foreign Ministry has not demanded my expulsion. Your president has not rattled his saber against the Unity. Therefore, I conclude you alone know my role. It's also plain you didn't bring me here to kill me—"

"Don't be so sure." To Tomas' own ears, his voice sounded earnest.

Maj. Aranjuez stamped the ground with his foot. "The soil is soft enough to turn, but you have not dug a shallow grave." The tips of his mustache jumped again. His face returned to seriousness, slowly this time. "And you are a gentleman too honorable to kill in cold blood."

Tomas swallowed. Bluff called. "True or not, I have the handgun. Tell me your game."

"My game?"

"You want peace between the Unity and the Confederated Worlds, yet you attempt to kill a presidential candidate. Which is your true objective?"

"Both."

Tomas held the pistol steady. "Go on."

"I and many of my peers on Europa Regina and here on Challenger want peace between us and you. This is the truth. It is also the truth that peace is impossible so long as Forrester is your president."

Stiffness wrapped Tomas' torso. "Forrester knows what he's doing."

Maj. Aranjuez leaned back his head. White teeth gleamed in the gloomy light. His staccato laughter rippled through the air.

"Quiet."

Maj. Aranjuez lowered his head and caught his breath. "I assure you, he does not."

Tomas' eyebrows lowered. A scowl formed in the muscles around his mouth. "Everyone slanders his political rival as an idiot or a lunatic—"

"It is not slander if one speaks the truth. Forrester is neither an idiot nor, technically, a lunatic. But he does not know what he does, nor why."

Tomas held the pistol steady, yet he angled his head and peered sidelong at the major. The breeze rustled the leaves. Tomas' voice took on a haggard tone. "What in the hell are you telling me?"

Maj. Aranjuez glanced at Tomas' pocket holding his phone. "You might better believe me if I showed you."

"Show me what?"

"Give me my phone, and you will see."

Tomas shook his head. "Talk me through how to access whatever it is."

After a pause, Maj. Aranjuez rolled his wrists. "Very well. First, log in by swiping...."

Tomas kept the pistol aimed at Aranjuez' chest with one hand and worked the major's phone with the other. Slowly, with frequent glances at Maj. Aranjuez, his thumb traced a pattern across the lock screen. More instructions led Tomas to a secure connection to the Uni embassy's servers.

"I must authenticate with my voice and retina," Maj. Aranjuez said.

A glance at the display corroborated Aranjuez' words. "No touching." Tomas stretched his arm to bring the phone toward the major. "Close enough?"

"Yes." Maj. Aranjuez raised an eyebrow. "First, though, I must have your word you will only open the document I direct you to, and none other."

A golden opportunity to gather intel from inside the Uni embassy. Tomas knew he would not take it. "I give you my word. Before you, my religious tradition, and my own conscience."

The lines of Maj. Aranjuez's face softened. He said a few words in Nuevo Andaluciano. A flash of light strobed over his open eyes. "We are in. Go now to…"

Tomas followed the instructions. They led him to a single document deep in an encrypted, password-protected part of the Uni embassy's server.

He squinted at the name. "What's 'Plan 827?'"

"It means nothing to you?"

"I've never heard of a Unity operation using that format of name." Gooseflesh stippled his jaw and cheeks. He trembled like a maple leaf in the breeze. "But the PRs…."

"Open that, please, captain. If you promise to speak quietly, you may read aloud."

Tomas opened the document and skimmed the cover page. "Written in 3011—" During the war. "—by an official of the PR's

Fourth Intelligence Directorate—that's foreign covert actions, isn't it?"

"It is indeed the PRs foreign covert actions directorate."

"Classified *highly secret*." Tomas swiped to the next page. "Mission Objective. By applying skills implantation to select Confederated Worlds POW in our custody, said skills implantation sessions forcibly expunged from their memories by administration of lethe potions, we will amplify destructive leadership traits in said POW, thereby weakening CW's post-war threat."

Aranjuez's arms hang loosely by his sides and his mustache tips turned up.

Tomas' mouth suddenly turned dry. He flipped through the next pages, reading to himself. He still aimed his pistol at Maj. Aranjuez' chest, but barely noticed the major, even out of his peripheral vision. The document on the major's phone compelled all his attention.

"Tell me what it says."

Tomas arched an eyebrow. "As if you don't know? The PRs selected our POWs who scored highly on tests of interpersonal influence and social skills. Thirty-eight POWs. The PRs then found the prisoners' weak points and used skills imp technology to boost them. The PRs injected the prisoners with lethe potions after each skills imp session to cause the prisoners to forget the skills imp process. So they wouldn't realize their personality changes were chosen by the PRs. The prisoners didn't consent."

"In a few pages, you'll find a list of your thirty-eight POWs."

Tomas's thumb suddenly felt thick and clumsy, an arthritic sausage. He swiped to the list. His gaze roved it. His breath caught. "He's on it."

A sudden urge drove him to an individual dossier page. "'Major Roderick Forrester, CWSF. Interpersonal influence test scores and observations of this subject in interactions with other POW suggest potential to win elections or otherwise achieve high office. Difficult to provoke, but can be goaded into rage. Harbors grudges. Strongly rejects disconfirming evidence. With a properly molded subconscious, he could become our best asset.'"

"Everything Forrester works for is at the behest of the PRs," Maj.

Aranjuez said. "We have known this since he first announced his candidacy. My faction on Europa Regina authorized all means for neutralizing his threat. Hence, the assassination attempt. Hence, the seized opportunity to worm through his defenses by talking to you. Hence, the further seized opportunity right now to show you Plan 827."

Tomas pictured Forrester under cold light, naked and gripped by a dozen strong hands, writhing and fighting as the PRs dropped him into a skills imp tank. Yet even if he'd resisted them, they would still reach their desired outcome. "Forrester is a PR pawn." Tomas dropped his hand holding the major's phone. His hand holding the pistol soon followed. "If this document is real."

"If?" Maj. Aranjuez frowned. "I would have prepared a complex forgery for the chance you would somehow uncover my meeting with Walters and hold me at gunpoint to find out why?"

"I need to verify it. I'm going to send a copy to my phone."

The frown deepened for a moment. "Very well. Regardless of the tests you apply to that document, you will find it genuine."

Tomas returned his sidearm to its holster. He pulled out his phone and beamed the Plan 827 document from the major's phone to his. As the document transferred over, a thought gnawed at Tomas. Even if Maj. Aranjuez told the truth, then what? Forrester had been duly elected. The Constitution lacked a provision for countermanding a president skills impped to serve a foreign power's interests. Forrester was commander-in-chief and Tomas had sworn an oath to follow his every lawful order.

His phone chimed. Transfer complete. He would face the question of what to do after he determined the document to be genuine.

Tomas looked up and took notice of Maj. Aranjuez. Aranjuez rested one knee on the soft grass and tied his shoe. After Maj. Aranjuez returned to his feet, Tomas spoke.

"While I verify the document, I will keep our conversation secret. But in exchange, you will take no action against the president. And if I find it to be a hoax, I'll turn all this over to ConPol to have you expelled from the Uni mission."

"I agree to all your terms," Maj. Aranjuez said. "You may meet me in this same manner—preferably, using kind words, rather than a handgun—whenever you have your answer."

"Very well."

Mirth stretched Maj. Aranjuez' mouth into a curled-up line. "Before we part, may I offer you some advice in spycraft?"

"What advice?"

"You should always pat down a prospective hostile," the major said, "especially when they may have a pistol holstered at their ankle." Maj. Aranjuez lifted and rotated the foot clad in the just-tied shoe. He pulled up the pants leg. A tiny holster and pistol formed an unmistakable black shape against the gray light of 2600.

Tomas shuddered.

"My phone, captain, and I'll return to my billet." Maj. Aranjuez held out his hand. "I will abide by your verification, though I find it easy to agree."

"Easy." Tomas wobbled on his feet.

Maj. Aranjuez leaned forward. His quiet voice rang with pure certitude. "Because you will confirm the Plan 827 document is what it purports to be."

Tomas handed Maj. Aranjuez back his phone, then stalked away into the deepening night.

9

Peters-Stein Technique

The next afternoon, just after lunch, while Epsilon Eridani still climbed toward the zenith, Tomas came toward the Sutherland Office. An analysis of Ground Force morale waited on his phone. The Plan 827 document weighed on his heart. It had to be a forgery, though how could he find out without raising suspicions about how he had gotten it?

A crisp inhalation, then a head shake to clear his mind. The door to Forrester's office stood full open, and his voice carried a tone of smothered fury. Tomas reached for the edge of Forrester's assistant's station.

"Capt. Neumann," the assistant said, "Please go in."

Tomas cupped his hand behind his ear and raised an eyebrow.

The assistant's mousy face looked unperturbed. "I asked him if he was certain, and he said yes. 'Be ye angry, and sin not: let not the sun go down upon your wrath.'"

Tomas drew a deep breath, then strode into the Sutherland Office.

At the far side of the room stood the large ceremonial desk. The desk's broad, bare top looked like a dance floor. Only a small tablet interrupted the smooth surface of gleaming bioengineered walnut. Behind the desk, Forrester leaned back, arms crossed. His chair yawed in rapid cycles, bringing his face and torso forward, then sending them back. Hidden from view, Forrester's legs must have been pumping like the hydraulics of a Badger's turret.

A chill washed over Tomas. Could the Plan 827 document be authentic?

From under low eyebrows, Forrester stared at a video display unrolled from a nearly invisible slit in the ceiling. He glanced away from the display enough to notice Tomas, and pushed his hand against the air, then crooked his finger.

Tomas closed the door and stepped forward. He gave a sharp-angled glance at the video display. A male politician, long nose and ears, and the caption *Rep. Martin McLaren, Protestant Union Party.*

"You gave me votes to pay for more ships," Forrester said to McLaren. "Now you block me from manning them?"

"You budgeted for ships, Mr. President," McLaren said. "Not their crews."

Forrester's face turned rigid, except for rapid blinks. "Do I look amused?"

A wisp of a smirk lifted the corners of McLaren's mouth. "Mr. President, the Protestant Union's opposition to conscription has nothing to do with you. It's solely about freedom of conscience."

Conscription? A draft would provide the Confederated Worlds forces with enough manpower to resist any PR aggression. Plan 827 had to be false.

"Don't shit on my plate," Forrester said, "and call it chocolate ice cream. Your Bible is like any other holy book, you can look for a quote out of context and color it any way you want. Like 'render unto Caesar.'"

McLaren gravely shook his head. "My party's leadership conferred well into the night about your proposed bill. We cannot allow young men to be compelled to kill."

The rigid expression on Forrester's face softened to one of—conciliation? Tomas frowned. When had Forrester ever been conciliatory?

Forrester's tone of voice matched his expression. "You make a good point. Freedom of conscience, why, that's important. Yours isn't the only religion to say 'thou shalt not kill.'"

McLaren's eyebrows crinkled. A wary breath widened his nostrils. "That's true."

"Though a lot of civilians don't realize only a tiny fraction of each force's personnel actually pulls the trigger. So here's a compromise. We'll amend the bill to give draftees a conscientious objector option. They can serve in non-combat functions. Medics, engineers, mol fab teams riding in those unarmed vehicles, what's the Ground Force model called again, Captain Neumann?"

"Buffalo."

Forrester nodded. "The enemy targeted Buffaloes, didn't they?"

Tomas' eyes widened. He lifted his shoulders in an exaggerated shrug. "We did the same against the enemy on New Liberty."

"All those mol fab techs with targets on their backs. But at least they were never ordered to kill." Forrester theatrically turned away from wartime reminiscence and refocused his mild expression on McLaren. "So you see, there are many ways a conscientious objector can serve in combat and never take a human life."

McLaren blinked a few times. "Mr. President, that's a step in the right direction, a spirit of compromise, but even conscription into a non-combat role is a violation of young mens' freedom of—"

Forrester slammed the flat of his hand on the table. He stood up and his desk chair spun away toward the back wall. "I knew your position had not a goddam thing to do with freedom of conscience or religious precepts. You and your party leadership want your coddled brat sons to go to private colleges to spend four years drinking and fucking while young men, from families who truly love the Confederated Worlds, will respond to the draft board." Forrester gestured toward Tomas.

Tomas stiffened his back and stared at McLaren. However, he aimed his other senses to Forrester, straining for some confirming or denying detail about Plan 827 possibly borne in the sound of the president's breaths or the heat from his face.

Forrester addressed McLaren. "Whether it's feeding shit into a mol fab hopper or killing and dying in the mud of some foreign world, those true young patriots will serve without complaint, and your brats will spit on them when they return home. You think you'll look good if you tell the voters you rejected a conscription bill with a conscientious objector option?"

McLaren crossed his arms. He drew a deep breath. A smirk again touched the corners of his mouth. "We'll know when we count the votes, Mr. President. Would you excuse me, I have important bus—"

Forrester stabbed his finger against the tablet display. McLaren's voice and image evaporated. The display retracted into the ceiling.

Forrester's hands clamped the edge of his desk. His arms trembled and his fingers turned white. His eyes narrowed as if to laser a hole through the portrait of Pres. Finzi across the room.

Tomas hesitated, then moved a step forward, close enough to reach out for the desk. "Mr. President, you're right, the public—"

"Goddam, Neumann, that's not the point!" Forrester expelled his next words through clenched jaws. "The point is that cockbiter. Defied. Me!" Forrester swept the back of his hand across the desk. The tablet spun through the air and landed near an antique sidetable bearing a glass statuette of the STL ship that brought the first terraformers from Heinlein's World to Epsilon Eridani.

Forrester went around his desk to the sidetable. "Goddammit, I'll show you to defy me!" He lifted the statuette and flung it at the far wall. The statuette struck between the door and the portrait of Finzi. Glass fragments tinkled outward. The statuette clattered down the wall and thudded onto the thick carpet. The gypsumboard wall showed a gouge the size and depth of Stefan's fist.

"Fuck you!" Forrester screamed. His contorted red face glared at the empty wall. His chest heaved, then a little slower, then a little slower still. He noticed Tomas. "What, Neumann? You have a fucking problem?"

Difficult to provoke, but can be goaded into rage. No, mere words, they proved nothing—

Tomas eased out a breath. "No, Mr. President."

Forrester's face showed he didn't believe Tomas. "You want me to be a plaster saint who can turn the other goddam cheek?"

"No, sir. I've seen my share of reactions to stressful situations."

"You're damn right this is combat. Civil war fought with voting booths and opinion polls. That fucker thinks he's defended against that, but I'll show him." Forrester paced over the Confederated Worlds flag motif in the carpet.

"Yes, sir." More thoughts unfurled. Tomas' face slackened while his intuitions raced ahead. Even if the Plan 827 document was a forgery, Forrester suffered some psychological wound, and Tomas could recommend a cure. And if Plan 827 had reprogrammed Forrester, Tomas knew how Forrester himself could find out and undo the damage.

Forrester's pacing slowed. He glanced about and sank into his usual chair in the office's meeting area. Heavy breaths lifted and sank his chest.

Tomas took a nearby seat. He studied Forrester's face. Yes, this moment gave him the best chance he might ever have. "If I may, Mr. President, there are ways you could be even more effective as a leader. Both against political rivals and, if it comes to war, against the PRs and the Unis."

A moment of rapt features and wide eyes showed part of Forrester wanted to learn more. However, his hazel eyes squinted, so quickly and firmly that the rapt moment seemed an illusion raised by Tomas' hopes. Forrester asked, "What are you talking about?"

"My wife, Lissa, is a psychological counselor. She has a strong practice helping veterans integrate their wartime experiences into their psyches."

Forrester's eyebrows crinkled. "Don't smokescreen me with buzzwords. Lay it out in black and white."

Tomas spoke faster. "Only you can know how your mind responded to ship combat—and the PR prison camp—but if it looks to you that your mind's response *then* is holding you back *now*—"

"You're saying...." Forrester's face glazed over. His torso wavered. Forrester looked like a man intoxicated by drink or drugs.

But the president had been stone sober—

"Mr. President?" Tomas heard the alarm in his voice. Forrester must hear it too.

Forrester's dead gaze stared straight ahead. Sweat sheened on his forehead.

Tomas' breath stuck in his chest. Forrester suffered a heart attack? An epileptic seizure? Tomas opened his mouth to shout for help. *How soundproofed are the walls?*

Like a video skipping a frame, Forrester's attention came back to the room. He glowered at Tomas. "You're saying I look crazy."

"Mr. President?"

Forrester scowled. He swept the back of his hand across his forehead. Sweat flattened and darkened wisps of hair near his hairline. "Why is it so goddam hot in here?"

"I—ah—" Tomas hooked his fingers inside the collar of his shirt and pulled it away from his skin.

"You're goddam right I don't look crazy!"

Tomas' chest tightened, yet somehow he drew a breath. Offhandedly as he could, he said, "Crazy? I simply thought you'd rather spend money on new ships and Ground Force equipment than office repairs."

Forrester's eyes remained narrow for a moment. Then his shoulders eased and he chuckled. "Not my proudest moment." He nodded toward the damaged statuette. "Good to know you'll keep what you saw under wraps."

"So would Lissa," Tomas said. "She's very strict about counselor-patient privilege—she never even tells me—"

"She specializes in veterans' issues? I have no issues from the war. I hate the PRs and the cowardly civilian politicians who surrendered to the PRs. My hate is proper and healthy. It lights the path I tread to restore the Confederated Worlds' honor. I won't be seen in a situation colorable as leading me off that path."

"She could come here," Tomas said. "The cover story would be she's visiting me."

Forrester's voice filled the room. "I don't need therapy. McLaren's hypocrisy made me see red, that's all." He peered at Tomas. "Captain, you've been a straight shooter since you've started working for me that day in Firstlanding Square. Don't bullshit me now."

"Sir?"

"I just told you I don't need therapy. Do you believe me?"

If Forrester were unwilling to look into his psyche, no therapy in human space would be effective. "Yes."

A squint emphasized Forrester's next words. "Don't tell me you believe me, then bring up your wife's job again. Next week, next month, next standard year, I don't want to hear it. I don't need therapy."

"You know what you need, Mr. President. I won't bring it up again." Tomas waited a moment, then lifted his tablet. "I have the analysis of the Ground Force morale survey—"

He spent the next twenty minutes talking to Forrester. The president listened attentively, his hazel eyes lively with understanding and perceptive questions. He understood that Ground Force did not want a war but would fight to the utmost if the PRs started one.

Tomas relaxed. Forrester again showed himself to be the right leader for the Confederated Worlds' hour of need. A PR pawn? Impossible. The Plan 827 document? A forgery. Tomas chest felt buoyant as he finished the meeting and walked to the door.

He glanced once at the smashed statuette on the carpet, then quickly looked away.

Two mornings later, Tomas hung onto a strap as the subway approached the Firstlanding Square transfer station. The elbows and backs of morning commuters hemmed him in. Too crowded to even work on his phone, not that he could get anything done. His thoughts roved over Forrester's behavior after the phone call with MacLaren of Protestant Union, his encounter with Aranjuez, and the Plan 827 document.

To verify the document, he would have to work alone. If he took it to anyone, the other might question how a Ground Force captain, lacking any military intelligence background, acquired a copy. A question he had no desire to answer.

Over a businessman's shoulder, he glimpsed a scrolling newsfeed in the man's smartglasses. *Protestant Union joins Democratic Terraformers in support of conscription bill....*

The subway car decelerated. Tomas leaned into it, somehow

managed to avoid bumping anyone around him. Six months riding the subway and he still felt clumsy. He flowed with the crowd out of the subway car and into the station.

Near the stairs down to the Confederal City line, the usual pattern of foot traffic slowed, shifted, like a river around a dam. Two men in Restoration Party uniforms stood at the head of the stairs. Gimlet eyes studied the commuters, and hands rested on baton handles. Tomas expected a nod to his service uniform, but the Restoration Party men only dispassionately scanned his face.

Halfway down the stairs, his phone rang. He knew the tone and vibration pattern.

He stopped along the handrail and fished the phone out of his pocket. "Lissa?"

Haggard eyes stared from the screen. "Come to my office. As soon as you can."

"I'm on my way to work—"

"You need to come here and do something about this." Her nostrils flared. "Are you involved in this?"

"What's going on?"

Her expression opened slightly. "You're not involved. Good. They might listen to you. But come here. Now."

She usually didn't intrude on his working day. But she couldn't assume he would disrupt his schedule based on *they* and *this*. "I'll check my schedule and head your way when I have a few clear hours."

"No. Now. Please."

"I can't ask the president to reschedule me. I'll be there as soon as I can. Love you."

Tomas swiped to break the call. He took a couple of breaths, then continued down the stairs. One foot, another. He stopped.

Calling him on his way to work. Her troubled expression. Something big happened.

He checked his schedule—no meetings with Forrester or anyone else important. The outbound subway would be much less crowded, giving him some space to work. In his scheduler he blocked out the next three hours of the morning, then worked his way against the crowd of descending commuters to catch the next outbound train.

Just before 1000 he strode up the street from the Westside subway station to Lissa's office. The street held professional offices, cafés, and the shops of handcrafters who lacked the revenue to afford downtown real estate, all tucked into two and three-story buildings of swooping pigmented mycocrete. The street looked nothing like the urban battlefields of New Liberty or Arden. Still, habit drove Tomas' gaze over the windows and roofs, watching for hostiles.

A breeze chilled the backs of his hands as he rounded the last turn before Lissa's office. Against the bright pastel buildings and the green-black living asphalt of the street, two blue figures contrasted. They stood on the sidewalk in front of the door leading to Lissa's office.

Tomas scowled. What brought Restoration Party security here? Someone had broken into Lissa's office? But she would call the police. He glanced up at her office window. The curtains blocked his view, except for a slender triangle of darkened office revealed by one pulled-back corner.

On the sidewalk, a third figure completed the scene. A civilian male in a bright blue plastic jacket. His wide ears and hunched shoulders emphasized he lived off free mol fab cycles. His voice rasped at the bluecoats. "What do you mean, Mrs. Neumann is unavailable?"

The elder of the two bluecoats turned his square head to the civilian. Tomas recognized the old sergeant. His eyes seemed smaller and narrower than Tomas recalled. "We mean you won't be seeing her today. Go home."

The civilian blinked slowly. "But I have an appointment."

The old sergeant rocked up on the balls of his feet. His palm landed on his holstered baton's handle. "The Investigation of Terroristic Activities Act calls on private citizens to investigate potential crimes against Confederal security."

Tomas stopped a meter and a half away. "Crimes against Confederal security? He has a therapy session scheduled with my wife."

The old sergeant turned his head to focus his cap-mounted camera on Tomas. "We've recently investigated the Protestant Union Party for the same potential crimes. Your service grays don't give her immunity. I will say, she's not the only one. We suspect a lot of psychological counselors aid our enemies, and today we've investigating hundreds of them."

Tomas blinked. Hundreds? Lissa was innocent, but perhaps a few of her colleagues…. "What evidence do you have to investigate anyone?"

The old sergeant shifted his weight from foot to foot like a boxer. "A lot of soldiers and spacemen get psychological counseling. Don't know why, I served and my conscience is clean. Veterans and active duty military know a lot of secrets and might spill them. Psych counselors say their work is confidential, as if they're real doctors, so we don't know what they learn, and we don't know what they might share against the rules of their profession. A lot of opposition to the President's plans came up recently. The best explanation is foreign powers are stoking opposition up. Psych counselors might be helping them."

Tomas pushed out his chest. "I should not have to do this, but do you know I work directly for Pres—"

The old sergeant's gray eyes blinked once. "I know who you are, Captain Neumann. That's why your wife's getting away easy."

Sometimes, an officer did well to overlook a non-com's insubordination. But this man had given up his stripes. Tomas leaned forward into the old sergeant's space. "Let her patient through."

"I can't do that. We don't know what secrets he would share—"

"Let him through." Tomas leaned forward, rocking the former sergeant onto his heels.

The younger Restoration Party security man cleared his throat. "Team leader."

The old sergeant turned to his underling. The younger man lifted a tablet. For a few moments, the two men muttered and swiped through text and photos. Then the old sergeant smiled coldly and faced Tomas.

"I wouldn't say this about all officers," he said, "but captain, you are a man of your word. We don't need to investigate your wife. Or this particular ex-soldier, Zachariah Smith, formerly of the Third Airmobile Hussar Brigade—?"

The man nodded. Then his face froze. "I'm going to my appointment." He hunched his shoulders and ducked his head. A step past the two men to the door.

The old sergeant raised his voice. "Still, a lot of terrorists pay for their crimes through frauds. Some by fraud on the molecular fabrication utility. Some by fraud on the Veterans Benefits Bureau. And first thing when agencies investigate fraud..." Gray eyes flicked up and down like a knife slitting the cheap plastic jacket.

The ex-soldier, Smith, halted. He plunged his hands deeper into his jacket pockets.

"...they freeze suspicious accounts. Without a job, you need a mol fab account. And vet bennies? Even if you got cleared of fraud, you know how long it takes pogeys to fix their data entry mistakes." The old sergeant's lips curled up. "But if you move along you'll show us you're no terrorist."

Smith hunched his shoulders, like a timid turtle trying to reenter a bright blue shell. A northerly breeze lifted wisps of hair dangling over his wide ears. He swallowed once, then shoved his hands deeper into his jacket pockets. He stalked past Tomas with wounded eyes.

In the window above, the curtains shifted again.

The old sergeant gave Tomas an impassive look. "Captain, I did you a favor. Too bad Smith didn't take you up on it."

Tomas scowled. Everything he'd just done for the departing man meant nothing. Restoration Party security could block entrance to Lissa's office long after his duties in the executive offices compelled his departure. Not just Lissa's. The offices of hundreds of other psych counselors around the capital cities.

Who had given the bluecoats these orders?

Don't pretend you don't know. Forrester.

An intuition froze solid in his gut. Tomas knew more than who. He knew why.

Tomas lifted his chin. "I'm going to see my wife." He went around the two men to the door. They said nothing, and the younger one shuffled back a fraction of a step.

On either side of the door, security cameras lurked in shallow recesses. Tomas stared at the one on the right until the door's magnetic seal released with a thud.

At the top of the stairs, her office door swung inward. Lissa clutched the edge of the door. "You couldn't even get my client past those two thugs."

"I did." Tomas' voice sounded weary in his ears. He put his hand on her shoulder and guided her deeper into her office. "But this is bigger than you and a client."

She twisted her shoulder away from his hand, then faced him. "You think I don't know that? Everyone in the counselors' association is talking in our online forum. Restoration Party paramilitary members invading my colleagues' offices, pulling clients out of sessions, even stealing confidential patient files. What is your boss doing?"

The frozen intuition sent icy tendrils up Tomas' throat. Forrester's moment of fugue when Tomas brought up psychological counseling. Forrester's decision to suppress counselors' treatment of veterans.

Forrester acted out of a suggestion implanted by the PR skills imps to cover their tracks.

No, Plan 827 couldn't be real—

Anger rimmed her blue eyes. "I deserve an answer, Tomas."

Semiconciously, he cobbled one together. "He must have some intel that someone, maybe just one or two of your peers, is acquiring and giving away military secrets."

"You know that's ridiculous." A flicker of doubt crossed her face. "But even if it were true, one or two suspects is not enough to justify disrupting the work of hundreds of people."

"It will blow over. Eventually any guilty parties will be found and prosecuted. Ride it out."

She peered at him. "Ride it out? How about you tell your boss to call off his dogs?"

And drive Forrester to dismiss him? Echevarria to send him off to Nuova Toscano or Arden to try defending them if the PRs chose to attack? His hands fell like dead meat against his thighs. "There's nothing I can do."

"Nothing you can do? Or nothing you will do?"

"Be happy with what you have."

She sniffed out a breath. "Be happy? With an empty office?" She waved her hands at a chair and couch. The cushions bore wear patterns imposed by a thousand backsides.

"You're free to treat civilian patients—"

"I've specialized in military and ex-military patients since—" She gave an implacable stare.

Since he'd been a psychiatric casualty on New Liberty. She seriously played that card? "You can develop a new speciality," he said.

She blinked. Her face hardened. "If I told you to resign your commission, you'd shout me down. But you tell me to throw away my career and expect me to bow my head?"

"An officer serves a higher purpose—"

"So my career means nothing to you? What am I? A caretaker for your boys? An imitation Daughter of Astarte?"

His face turned into a brittle shell. "Caretaker for the boys? They spend half their waking hours in the base Montessori school."

Lissa's eyes widened. "At least *I'm* there for the other half—"

"The base Montessori is only an option because of my commission!" The brittle shell cracked, releasing molten anger. "And sex? When was the last time we had sex?"

Her nostrils flared. She lifted her head, looked down her nose. "The last time," she said.

Tomas set his fist on his hip. A skeptical expression flowed into his face. "It's good you have no patients today. You can rethink that threat while I go back to work."

Tomas exited the intercity train at Confederal City Central Station around 1100. So deep underground, so uniformly bright the Sol-spectrum ceiling panels, the surface would surprise him with cypresses in full bioluminescence and the sky a light-polluted shade of black.

Who's going to the surface? Take the Blue Line to Executive Mansion—

A thought, clinging to his awareness like a burred seedpod, became more insistent. He had time to take a trip two stops up the Red Line. He'd gone that way every morning between the election and the inauguration, to the Hotel Transtellar.

Catercorner from the Hotel Transtellar stood the capital cities' largest temple of the Daughters of Astarte.

He had two hours clear in his schedule. The only work waiting for him revolved around validating the Plan 827 document. He could go to the Daughters.

Guilt constricted his throat. *You affirmed you would be faithful to Lissa—*

—And she affirmed she would cleave to me. How many of your brother officers have desires unslaked in the marriage bed, and sate them with the Daughters? More than you think....

Within two minutes, Tomas rode the subway northbound on the Red Line.

After debarking, smartpaper signs led him from the platform up to the street at Nuova Toscano Boulevard and First Avenue. The midday darkness made him glance furtively around.

Midrise buildings curled across their lots, with mycocrete buttresses plunging like roots into the volcanic soil. Potted gardens and loading docks huddled between the buttresses. Bioluminescent cypresses made glass panels glitter like the scales of fish in the river he swam in his youth.

Three blocks north on First, the marble-white needle of a Confederal Government office building poked into the sky. A block down Nuova Toscano to the west glimmered the cold surface of Lake Freedom. Across the lake, the skyscrapers of the McAuliffe lakefront glowed like the light-decorated holiday objects of a dozen religions.

To the southeast rose the Daughters' temple.

The Daughters of Astarte had a temple on almost every Ground Force base, but those had the same warehouse look of every other military or civilian contractor facility. This one, though, did not blend in with the buildings around it. Its straight lines and lintels sculpted with reliefs fit with how he imagined ancient temples on Earth. From the sidewalks of both streets, broad steps led up to column-lined porticos. Screened by the columns, red walls held revolving doors of mirrored glass.

Blue motion on the sidewalk pulled Tomas' attention. A bluecoat strolled toward him. The bluecoat touched his fingertips to the edge of his cap, drawing attention to the third eye camera. "Good morning, captain."

Tomas coughed and turned his head. Too late. Restoration Party security now knew he had come here. Face tight with mirth, the bluecoat strolled past.

Of course Restoration Party security would watch the temple. Observing who went in and out gave them intel on half the power brokers in Confederal City, whether single, married, or widowed. Still Tomas hunched his shoulders and swiveled his head.

Another thought let him stand a little taller. Even if they took notice of a mere Ground Force captain, they wouldn't share that intel with Lissa.

He nodded to himself and jogged up the steps.

In the portico, two statues on plinths flanked the approach to the revolving door—statues of the goddess, breasts and belly swollen with pregnancy, head back, eyes closed, face contorted. Each statue's raised and spread knees channeled the eye to her dilated honeypot.

He wrenched his gaze toward the revolving door.

Inside, he entered a maroon vestibule half the size of his house. Thick carpets, deep chairs, upholstered panels on the walls. From chains mounted in the four corners of the ceiling, in the center of the room hung a round glass bowl, two meters across and filled one-third with water. A candle floated in the bowl. Its light shimmered in the water.

If you're going to do this, sign in. The vestibule's back wall held an array of four closed doors. Tomas went to the furthest of the four. He looked around for a wall-mounted tablet. What he'd taken for part of the upholstered paneling suddenly glowed—a disguised screen displaying text.

Welcome to the Daughters of Astarte. Your donation will help us minister to the spiritual needs of people throughout the Confederated Worlds.

His finger hovered over the screen, then he tapped and swiped. How much to donate? Maybe some Executive Mansion staff meeting would cater in a lunch and leave leftovers for him to scavenge. If not, he could go hungry today, then pack sandwiches for a couple of weeks and make some excuse why.

A hundred-fifty confeds from his personal account. He tapped *confirm* before he could think further.

A moment later, the door opened. His stomach flopped and his nape itched. He went through.

A cozier version of the vestibule greeted him. A single couch faced a wall of thick floor-to-ceiling curtains. On a table next to the couch, a dozen roses, pink with purplish tips, stood in a vase shaped like a snifter. He breathed in the concentrated scent as he sat. Piano notes trickled down from speakers hidden in the ceiling. The music brought to mind soft rain on a warm night—

The curtains rustled. Tomas stood and removed his cap.

"You're quite the gentleman, Captain Neumann." The Daughter wore a long but form-fitting dress. Blond hair fell past her shoulders like an asymmetric waterfall, hiding one ear. "May I sit with you a moment?"

Tomas gestured at the couch with his left hand. A reflection flashed in his wedding ring. He jerked his hand, held it behind his back while she sat.

After he joined her on the couch, she held her left hand palm-up in her right. "You can reveal your ring, if you want. Many of our congregants are married. It doesn't bother us."

He avoided her gaze. "Tell me something about yourself."

Knees together, she shifted her legs to brush against his. "I'm—"

She suddenly angled her head. A distracted look formed on her features. She raised a hand to him, nodded at—he guessed—a message coming to her through an earbud hidden under her hair.

A final brisk nod. She stood and a faint pout formed on her face. "My apologies, captain. I would have been blessed to share our sacrament with you, but another requests that honor. May the goddess bless." She pecked his cheek with dry lips and slipped between the curtains.

Another? Tomas frowned at the curtains. Perhaps this was a sign to leave.

Since when do you see divine portents?

The curtains rustled again. Another Daughter stood there, her lean left arm bent at the elbow. A bracelet of polished stones, round like robin's eggs or yellow as calisson candies, slid down her wrist. She wore a thin dress of pale yellow, hemmed just below the knee. An attractive woman, her teeth too large to be beautiful, but Tomas' *biroute* came to attention within three beats of his heart.

"Persephone."

The first hundred times he'd made love with Lissa had in truth been *ménages à trois*, with Persephone living in his memory, guiding his hands, his mouth, his *biroute.*

"I'm sorry," he said, "you wouldn't remember me—"

"Of course I do, Tomas." She stepped closer. "You think I have shared our sacraments with so many congregants, I cannot remember them? Yes, in truth, I have forgotten most. But some I remember."

His heart ached with longing. A simpler time, it seemed, when he rode in the infantry compartment of a Badger, when he knew his enemies, when his sole concern was survival. He romanticized the past and knew it. Still, to see her again....

The longing abruptly changed its flavor. An intuition dipped him in a bracing certainty.

He would remain faithful to Lissa.

Persephone leaned back. Her eyebrows crinkled for a moment. She nodded then, and a wistful smile crossed her lips. "You have bonded with a good woman, I can tell. What unhappy circumstance has brought you to us?"

Tomas leaned back in the couch and shut his eyes. He stretched his arm to the side and patted the cushion. "I'll tell you everything."

She sat, and he did. His first two meetings with Lissa on New Liberty during the war. Their marriage. His graduation from OCS as a lieutenant, and his promotion to captain after his actions on Arden in the aftermath of the peace treaty. Two young sons, Lissa's transition to civilian life, his continued service under the threat of budget cuts and forced decommission. Through it all, she listened, with eyes clear and face free of judgment.

Sexual congress was not the only sacrament the Daughters offered.

He kept talking. Foiling Walters the assassin in Firstlanding Square—

"I had a shock when I saw you in the news videocasts about the assassination attempt." Her eyebrows dipped for a moment. "What led you there that day?"

Tomas scratched his chin as he thought back. "One of my colleagues invited me. Said I needed to hear for myself what Forrester promised." Promises gamed up by the PRs? Again, it seemed unreal.

"You simply happened to be at the place and time to stop the would-be assassin." Her lips parted and her tongue dabbed her upper teeth. "Go on."

"I made a favorable impression on him—"

"You did save his life."

Tomas shrugged. "—and after the election he had me reassigned."

"You work in the white mountain, then."

"No, the Executive Mansion."

Persephone scrutinized his face. "How far removed are you from President Forrester?"

"I don't follow you. On the table of organization? I don't really know. He assigns me irregular tasks—"

Persephone's fists balled pale in her lap. "You work directly for him? You see him daily?"

"Not daily. Two or three times a week." He reached for her tense hands, then thought better of it and rested his hand on the upholstery. "You think ill of him?"

She pressed her lips together. "The Daughters take no position on the political questions of the day."

"I'll rephrase. And I assure you, I'll keep your answer in confidence. What do you think of him as a man?" An insight came, so obvious he wanted to slap his own cheeks. "He's a congregant, isn't he?"

A glimmer of her usual world-wise serenity returned to her eyes. "One would expect that. One of the most powerful men in the Confederated Worlds, a bachelor lacking any aura of homosexuality, would seem the essence of our congregants." The glimmer faded. "But we haven't shared with him our sacrament in over five years."

Tomas drew in a heavy breath. His mind roved over the timeline. "Was his last visit before or after the PRs repatriated him at the end of the war?"

"After." Persephone peered at him. "What do you know about that time in his life?"

Tomas' chest tightened. "I know his experiences in the POW camp changed him. Do you know the same?"

The human urge to spill one's secrets and thereby be truly known by another showed in her face. She glanced down at her fingers tracing a seam in the cushion until the urge camouflaged itself. "My vows to the goddess bind my tongue. I've talked too much, Tomas. Let's lay political questions aside. Tell me more about you. The things you told me on New Liberty that I've forgotten, the things you never told me at all…."

His chest relaxed. He talked to her, and part of him marveled at a woman paying attention to his words. Yet a greater part of him mulled the things she had inadvertently revealed about Forrester. The POW camp had changed him greatly, in some internal psychological dimension revealed only when he lost himself in the sexual and emotional connections of the Daughters' sacrament.

He didn't need a trustworthy expert on PR intelligence operations to vet the document given him by Aranjuez.

Plan 827 was real.

"Thank you for offering me your sacrament," he said. "I will never forget you. But I must get back to the Executive Mansion."

"We all must answer when a higher purpose calls, whatever that higher purpose may be. I'm blessed to have had the chance to meet you again." She looked older and wiser and more lovely than their prior meeting during the war. Despite that—because of it—his fidelity to Lissa reaffirmed itself.

Persephone went on. "Did you come in the front door or through the tunnels?"

"Tunnels?" He grinned. "I just answered your question, didn't I?"

"If you came in from the street, we insist you go out that way, so the bluecoats can match a departure to your arrival. You have spoken as if you will not return, but should that change, we have two tunnel entrances. One leads to what appears from the outside to be a maintenance closet off the elevator lobby in the Hotel Transstellar's atrium. The other—"

He raised a hand to silence her. "Keep your secret." He hesitated, then kissed her cheeks. His thoughts about Plan 827 pressed in on him. "Because I must keep mine."

10

Intelligence Reports

At 1525 one day a week later, a reminder flashed onto Tomas' desktop display. *Suth Offc. Attendees: Pres, Gen. Olafson, others? 5 min.*

Tomas tossed his sandwich wrapper into the trash and wiped his mouth. The meeting's terse description had appeared on his calendar shortly after he arrived at the Executive Mansion that morning. No subject line, no intended agenda. Another example of Forrester's unpredictability.

The PRs might have changed Forrester's tendencies, but they couldn't control what he would do.

Tomas mulled Plan 827 while his hands organized notes on his tablet and his feet trod the faded carpet of the basement corridors and time-worn stairs. The PR document had nothing to do with the implantable suggestions of the thriller stories Lissa watched late at night, where plucky secretaries and schoolteachers foiled assassins triggered to act by a spymaster's catchphrase. Plan 827 spoke only of personality traits. The PR skills imps might have made Forrester more prone to rages, but at what target? More prone to harboring grudges, but against whom, and why? More prone to reject evidence clashing with his made-up mind, but what evidence would still persuade him?

A tendency made an outcome more likely, but could not guarantee it.

Perhaps the PR had been too clever by a half, and given Forrester the tendencies he most needed to defeat it in the next war.

He reached the assistant's station and filed away his thoughts. Four figures in Ground Force service gray, one of them a woman, stood near the window. In the midst of them stood Gen. Olafson, arms folded, looking out.

Gen. Olafson turned. His ruddy cheeks glowed like the barrel of an overfired gun. "Forrester sent for his ball boy."

Tomas' upper back stiffened. "Good afternoon, sir." He turned to the assistant. "Should I—?"

"Please go inside." She smiled her mousy smile, showing her small teeth. "Maj. Sharma has already arrived. 'Where no counsel is, the people fall: but in the multitude of counselors there is safety.'"

Tomas opened the door to the Sutherland Office, slipped through, and shut it behind him.

Forrester sat at the head of the meeting area. He leaned over the arm of his chair and looked over the upper rim of his smartglasses toward Sharma standing to his left. Forrester straightened his posture. "Olafson asked for this meeting, captain. Any guesses why?"

"No, Mr. President." Tomas racked his thoughts. "Perhaps some concern about tomorrow's anti-conscription rally?"

Forrester shook his head. "The Confederal City police assure me they'll keep those spoiled brats out of sight."

"Very well," Tomas said. "Regarding Gen. Olafson, I'll review my notes—"

"Don't bother. That old bastard wants something and will feed me a line of bullshit to try getting it. All you have to do is help me see through it as it comes up."

Tomas nodded. "Of course."

Forrester touched the side of his smartglasses to activate a microphone. "Send them in."

Moments later, his assistant opened the door and waved in Olafson and the other Ground Force officers. Olafson led them into a line across the width of the sitting area. The woman stood at one end of the line, a colonel with blond hair and gimlet eyes marked with crow's feet. She looked familiar.

Olafson spoke. "Mr. President, thank you for taking the time to meet."

"If one of my chiefs of staff requests an urgent meeting," Forrester said, "he probably has something important to show me. With me are Maj. Sharma and Capt. Neumann."

The colonel's eyes widened. Tomas recognized her then.

Olafson introduced the others on his team, ending with "—Col. Tatarinova."

Tatarinova said, "Pleased to meet you, Mr. President, Maj. Sharma. I've previously made Capt. Neumann's acquaintance."

Tomas nodded to her. "Good afternoon, ma'am."

Forrester lifted an eyebrow in Tomas' direction.

Tomas leaned toward him and muttered, "She served in military intelligence on Tenth Brigade staff on Arden."

Forrester's eyes darted across the windows. "Military intelligence," he murmured. "Hmm." He looked at Olafson and waggled his fingers at the sofas and chairs defining the meeting space. "You and your team look for your seats. Then show me what you have."

After everyone sat, Olafson nodded. The bright light of midday flooded the room and washed out the gray speckles in his brown hair. "Good to hear you want to hit the court. We're here to talk about the military buildup. As you may recall, a few months ago I warned you about the possible repercussions. I regret to say those repercussions have come to pass. Both the Unis and the PRs have started building up their forces in response."

Forrester's expression flattened. "What shows that?"

Olafson's squint showed he tried to read Forrester's mood, and failed. He glanced at Tatarinova. "The colonel has the complete dossier."

Tatarinova sat straighter, on the edge of her chair. "Thank you, general." She took a rolled-up tablet from a pocket of her skirt and snapped it flat. Her gaze tracked down the display. "First, we have human intelligence from Europa Regina that Unity politicians authorized a military buildup and Unity civil servants implement it. Other humint from Unity space reports increased ship traffic from Unity spacedocks and to Unity training facilities and forward bases."

"Two times zero is still zero." Forrester looked bored. "You better show me more than that."

"Second, humint from the Progressive Republic shows no evidence of a buildup. In fact, our assets report the PR is reducing its forces."

Forrester glowered at Olafson. "You're wasting my time with this shit?"

Tatarinova's gaze drilled into Forrester. He turned back to her with a raised eyebrow. She stared back unflinching. "Because we know all our humint assets in PR space have been turned by PR counterintelligence, we conclude the PR feeds them false information."

She went on. "Signals intelligence from the PR supports a finding of a PR military buildup. Our sigint team in the embassy has observed an eighty percent increase in encrypted military traffic through public networks on Brotherhood of Humankind and throughout its star system."

"They've cracked the code?" Forrester asked.

"No, Mr. President."

"Then you have no goddam clue what the PRs are talking about."

Olafson shifted in his seat. The other Ground Force personnel tugged at their collars and gave Tatarinova wincing glances. She lengthened her neck. "A traffic increase of such magnitude suggests an increase of similar magnitude in the number of ships, squadrons, ground formations, and personnel."

"Or that they're hoaxing you." Forrester folded his arms and slouched backward. "They know you know your humint assets are compromised, so they're using fake signals to show you the story you want to believe."

"The president can see that," Sharma said. "Why can't you?"

For a moment, Tatarinova looked rattled. Then she gave Sharma a quick, dismissive glance, and refocused on Forrester. "Our monitoring posts at the wormhole mouths leading from Navi Ambarsar to Arden and Nuova Toscano have observed comparable increases in sigint. Our resupply ships to Arden bear a full panoply of passive sensors which they use when traversing Navi Ambarsar system. Even if we assume the PRs practice good signals discipline and reduce their exposure when our resupply ships pass through the system, still they generate more encrypted signals than they did either six months or one year ago."

Forrester studied her through hooded eyes, but did not speak.

Tatarinova scrolled down her tablet. "We observe comparable increases in signals activity from the Unity as detected by our sigint team in the embassy on Europa Regina, and through the wormholes to New Liberty and Kahlenberg." She moved her hands to the tablet's bezel and, her chin raised, regarded the president.

"That's it?"

"Yes, Mr. President."

Forrester spoke in Sharma's general direction. "That's all she can show me." He gravely shook his head. "The data *supports* and *suggests* and is *compatible* with a PR and Uni buildup. I'm sure it does, if you have a vision in mind, and you look for evidence matching it."

Tatarinova's eyes flashed. "Mr. President—"

"She's examined all the evidence," Olafson said, while holding his palm toward Tatarinova, "whether favoring or disfavoring this conclusion. And her record shows she calls the balls in or out based on where they land relative to the line. Nothing else. Captain Neumann can attest to that."

Forrester gave his head another grave shake. "Don't shine the spotlight on him to hide your bullshit. You've looked for reasons to not build up our forces for months, and now, what's before my eyes but a set of those reasons?"

"We have hard data," Olafson said. "I'll send it to your man Neumann there, if you want to verify it. What do you have?"

"I don't need your story verified. I have harder data." Forrester looked smug. "ConPol's Third Special Analysis Branch has been updating me for months on our enemies' lack of response."

"ConPol!?" Olafson's cheeks looked even ruddier than usual. "Loki's *skith*! Your pardons, colonel," he quickly said to Tatarinova. "Mr. President, anything you're told by ConPol is hardly harder data.

They have few assets for interpolity intelligence gathering and analysis. ConPol's effort is a short lob within reach of the opponent at the net, more like."

Forrester leaned forward and rested his hands on his knees. His necktie dangled like a waiting sword. "I also have the hardest data of all, general. For two years, I saw the PRs up close every waking moment. I know them better than you—" He pointed a finger at Olafson. "—or her—" The finger moved to Tatarinova. "—or any of the rest of you—" He backhanded the air in the direction of the other Ground Force general staff officers, like a man shooing a fly. "—ever will."

"Believe him," Sharma said.

For a long moment, Forrester glared at Olafson. "Are you going to waste any more of my time? If you're even thinking about it, then maybe I should be thinking too—about what kind of senior leadership Ground Force really needs."

Olafson stared back. The people in the room spent a second as immobile as the portraits of Sutherland and Finzi. Finally, Olafson stood up. His subordinates and Col. Tatarinova did the same.

"We'll see ourselves out, Mr. President," Olafson said. He stalked away without a backward glance. The other officers followed him out.

After the door thudded shut behind the departed Ground Force brass, Forrester harrumphed. "Can you believe that? The old man cherry-picks data backing up his story and then acts like *I'm* full of shit?"

"Unbelievable," Sharma said.

"Damn right." Forrester swung his gaze to Tomas. "You saw it too, Neumann, didn't you?"

Tomas' chest tightened. A plausible story from a military intelligence officer whose competence he'd seen first-hand, versus some branch of the domestic police and counterespionage force he'd never heard of?

Strongly rejects disconfirming evidence.

"The colonel's report fits with Gen. Olafson's prior advice against a buildup," Tomas said.

"You're looking through soft filters at the old man." Forrester spoke calmly. "Don't look alarmed, I can see why you'd be loyal to your highest ranking officer, even if he's willfully blind about the Unis and PRs. Just don't be too loyal."

"I won't, Mr. President."

Forrester checked something in his smartglasses. "I have nothing more for you today, Neumann. Unless you have something I need to know—?"

"I don't. Farewell." Tomas bobbed his head and headed to the exit.

He had nothing Forrester needed to know. Yet. But whatever tendencies the PRs might have grown in him, Forrester would still listen to reason. If he opposed Olafson because of faulty intelligence, he would change his mind if he saw it was faulty.

All Tomas needed was proof.

By late the following afternoon, he almost had it. As on his previous visit to ConPol on the day after the election, Tomas spent hours in waiting rooms, shunted from one ConPol official to another. In contrast to his previous visit, instead of rising higher up both ConPol's headquarters building and its table of organization, Tomas bounced around on a downward trajectory. When ConPol officials took time to meet him, between tense messages and phone calls regarding the massive anti-conscription protest snarling traffic throughout Confederal City, they spoke of ConPol's Special Analysis Branches in terms mixing mystery with disdain. Assuming they knew the Special Analysis Branches even existed.

By 1640, Tomas went down a dingy basement corridor. A lighting panel flickered over his destination. Third door on the right after passing the last stairwell. No markings on the frosted glass door, no nameplate by the frame. Could this really be the source of Forrester's 'harder data'?

Toma activated the recorder function of his phone and slipped it into his pocket. Then he rapped his knuckles on the frosted glass.

A woman's muffled voice bade him enter. Confusion touched her voice.

Tomas opened the door and put on an affable smile. "Is this the Third Special Analysis Branch?"

The first room inside the door had no windows. Spindly tables heaped with stacks of smartpaper, old printed books, and handwritten notes scribbled across any object that would take ink. The room smelled musty. Further doors off the perimeter of the first room held what he took as cramped offices. Most of their doors stood closed.

The Third Special Analysis Branch hadn't fallen on hard times. It had never known good times.

A woman with crossed arms leaned against the doorway of an office nearest the front door. Her voice confirmed she'd invited him in, matching all the way to the touch of confusion in her voice. "What do you want, captain?"

"Yes, I'm Capt. Tomas Neumann, from President Forrester's office. He needs more information—"

Her arms remained crossed. Confusion evaporated, replaced by disbelief. "The president sent you? Here?"

"Yes."

"Really, why are you here?"

From the far side of the room, motion bustled out of one of the few open office doors. A long man, not simply tall, but with face, ears, nose, arms, hands all elongated. "You said Capt. Neumann? The man saving the president from the assassin?"

"I'm Neumann."

"Scarlatti, branch director. How do you do, how do you do." The branch director's hand enveloped Tomas'. Tomas imagined his arm to be a bundle of brittle reeds. "You work in his office? He needs more information? I'm pleased to hear he reads our reports. Some people—" He cast a droopy-eyed gaze at the woman with crossed arms. "Some people don't appreciate the value of what we do down here."

Her eyebrows arched. Tomas read in her expression she wanted to roll eyes but stopped herself. "There's no way Forrester cares what we do," she said. "I'm going back to my office to polish my résumé and network with human resources people at other agencies." She retreated to her office and uncrossed her arms long enough to shut the door.

The branch director shook his head, his nose like the pendulum of some archaic clock. "The kind of people I'm stuck with. Assistant Director MacAdams doesn't see how much value we add and sends me the dregs of ConPol's other branches. But the president sees our value! Whatever we can do for him, tell us, and we'll get right on it!"

"He needs more information about the PR and Uni military staffing and budgeting your branch reported."

"Military staffing!" The branch director's exuberant eyes turned glassy. His mouth slackened. "Military staffing. Do you have the report ID number?"

A chill shivered down Tomas' back. A part of him responded with a nugget of OCS wisdom. *Fake it till you make it.* "Let me look it up." He pulled out his phone and snapped it to rigidity. Careful to keep the screen away from the branch director, he scrolled through his messages and faked a scowl. "Where did my assistant put it? You'd think the XM would only hire the best of the best, even for clerical jobs."

The branch director nodded in sympathy.

Tomas went on. "If you would, show me all your reports on the PR and Uni militaries and I'll figure out which one."

The branch director winced. "I would be glad to, captain. Anything we can do to help the president make better decisions, that's why we're here, gathering puzzle pieces and putting them together. Rest assured, that's what we do, and please tell him that—"

"I will." Tomas put a slight edge into his voice. "After you show me the reports."

The branch director turned his head. He pressed his lips together and his fists churned the air in front of his abdomen. "I don't know what reports you mean, captain."

Tomas wavered on his feet. "How could Forrester know about the work you do if you didn't send a report to the XM?" Spots swam in his vision. He took a deep breath. Had Forrester conjured his 'harder data' out of thin air?

Slender fingers at the end of elongated palms fluttered in front of the branch director's face. "Perhaps it was a footnote in a more general report on the foreign polities. Even so, of course I read and approved it before we sent it, it must simply be that I forgot, we work so hard and prepare so many documents—"

Tomas felt more grounded. "One of your analysts prepared it?"

"Yes, yes, we have a number of people who have the foreign polities on their desks. Of course that's it. A footnote. One of many, on one of many reports, I read and approve everything, I'm sure you realize that and President Forrester would realize that too."

The branch director had entered cover-his-backside mode. Tomas raised a palm. "Relax. Plainly, you work incredibly hard. No one expects you to remember every word of every report you send. I speak for the president on that." He glanced at the doors around the perimeter of the front room. "One of your analysts? Perhaps we could speak to him?"

"Yes, yes." The branch director's fingertips danced on his chin. Then he pointed at one of the closed office doors. "Cromer. We'll talk to him. Young, but he has a knack for the work."

Four of the branch director's loping strides, and five of Tomas', brought them to Cromer's door. Like a woodpecker's bill, the branch director's knuckles rattled the door. Two seconds later, a muffled male voice said, "Come in, chief."

The branch director opened the door. The office beyond felt even more cramped than Tomas'. If he wanted, he could touch the side walls with bent arms. The branch director looked like a stick insect trapped in a small box.

Cromer sat near the back of the room, facing them. From above smartglasses perched on the tip of his nose and under low, brown bangs, he squinted at Tomas. Behind Cromer, a rack of video displays filled the back wall from the top of an ordered desk to near the ceiling. The side walls held large sheets of smartpaper showing blocks of handwritten text full of precise squiggles of shorthand.

He lifted his head to flip his bangs in Tomas' direction. "Chief, who's this?"

"Captain Neumann," the branch director said. "He works directly for the president."

Cromer's eyes flashed their whites. "He does, now? Captain,

how do you do?"

"I'm here because President Forrester needs more information about PR and Uni military preparations," Tomas said. "Did you add a footnote on that topic to a recent report? Your chief couldn't remember."

Cromer aimed a glint in his eye toward Tomas. "I did. I'd be happy to talk about it with you two, but chief, did you see the alert from AD MacAdams? He needs the branch directors to get up to speed on today's anti-draft protests. The protests are edging into riots. The AD wants you and the other branch directors to brainstorm a response."

The branch director shook his head. "My work is never done. Captain, would you excuse me? The AD needs me and I strive to always be a team player. You can tell the president that."

"He'll understand," Tomas said.

After the branch director left, Tomas shut the door. Cromer waved to his office's single guest chair, a thinly-cushioned hunk of extruded plastic on the right-hand wall.

As he sat, Tomas glanced around the office, mulling tactics to get what he needed from Cromer.

"How did you get stuck down here?" Tomas asked.

"Bad luck. My friends from the University of Challenger got plum gigs—a couple are in the basement at the XM right now—but me, I'm stuck working for that idiot." He stretched out his arms toward the door in mockery of the branch director's elongated limbs.

Tomas nodded as if he agreed. "The branch director seems the type to never read the reports he signs."

Cromer guffawed. "If you told me he didn't know how to read, I'd believe you. I don't know how he keeps his job. The rest of us debate whether it's because he's some politician's mentally challenged cousin, or MacAdams and the other ADs forgot he's down here."

"So the report on PR and Uni military preparations came solely from you."

Cromer angled his head to reflect the overhead light from his smartglasses into Tomas' eyes. His voice sounded cautious. "That's right."

"I'm just trying to learn the lay of the land. Most of the intel coming in says the PRs and Unis have been rapidly building up their forces in the last few months. You have friends working in the XM, you might have heard that."

"There and elsewhere," Cromer said. Tomas read *elsewhere* as meaning the white mountain, the Defense Ministry.

Tomas nodded. He slipped into lies like a hermit crab donning a shell. "A number of us welcomed your footnote to the contrary."

Cromer's lips parted in a lazy smile. "I'm not sure what you mean."

"You're not now?" Tomas asked. He arched his eyebrow for emphasis.

Another guffaw from Cromer. Traces of laughter percolated through his first few words. "I know from my friends at the XM what kind of story the president wants to hear. It couldn't hurt my career to tell that kind of story, just like it couldn't hurt yours to echo it."

"It couldn't hurt at all," Tomas said, "provided the other side can't blow it up."

"The forces' general staffs? Why should I worry about them? I hear how Forrester is. When he finds a story he likes, he sticks with it, even if every two-star in both forces tells him he's wrong."

Tomas bobbed his head in half-agreement. "You heard right about the president. But Confederal City doesn't resemble the civics class textbook, where the president decides and the bureaucracy acts."

For a moment, Cromer's face suggested he thought Tomas a fool. "Did I mention I graduated from the University of Challenger now?"

"You think you're cynical. Are you cynical enough? Let's say the president settles on a policy. His subordinates, from the general staffs to the assistant directors and on down, can cripple that policy in a thousand ways."

Cromer shrugged. "Then RP security will pay a visit to those subordinates and persuade them to do their jobs."

Perhaps he was cynical enough. Tomas shook his head. "Unless they're too secure to be threatened by the bluecoats. Here's what I'm getting at. When your conclusions become crucial to the president's foreign policy, the other side is going to scrutinize your conclusions with an eye to destroying their credibility." Tomas leaned forward and stared at a spot between Cromer's eyes. "For us to properly defend your conclusions, we need to know how you reached them."

For a moment, Cromer looked introspective, until another guffaw split his mouth open and leaned back his head. "You really want to know now?"

"More than anything."

Mirth lifted the corners of Cromer's mouth. "I cherry-picked four bits of data, three from the Uni desk and one from the PR. That's all."

Tomas suddenly felt as brittle as the extruded plastic chair. "Did you see any countervailing evidence?"

"Did I now? Sure as your hell and mine I did. But telling the same story as everyone else won't get me promoted out of this cave, will it now?"

Forrester based his assessment of PR and Uni military preparedness on the brazen lies of an ambitious youth. "You didn't give us much to work with."

Cromer waved away the concern in Tomas' voice. "The forces' general staffs will never find out what I just told you. You alerted the branch director. As soon as he realizes AD MacAdams doesn't need his opinion on whatever riots are happening around town, he'll start reading the reports for the one with my addendum. By tomorrow morning, he'll have memorized my addendum so well anyone would think he wrote it himself. And if someone presses him on the conclusions in the addendum, he'll baffle them with bullshit until they assume he must know what he's talking about." Cromer shook his head to flip his bangs away from his eyes. "Have I made it worth your while, captain, to come down here now?"

Tomas stood and extended his hand for a parting shake. The narrow walls, a phalanx of identical screen savers, and the ambition and contempt for the truth visible in Cromer's eyes made him want to flee. "You have indeed."

Outside Third Special Analysis Branch, Tomas stopped recording audio on his phone. He hurried through the dingy basement corridors, back toward the front entrance on the street level. The sooner he got to the Executive Mansion, the better.

Halfway to the entrance, his wristwatch tingled his skin. Urgent message. He snapped open his phone and words from Forrester's assistant appeared on screen.

He wants you here at 1830. Both forces' general staffs attending. Highly important. 'I must work the works of him that sent me, while it is day: the night cometh, when no man can work.'

Palms suddenly slick with sweat, he put away his phone and stalked toward the front entrance.

In the lobby of ConPol headquarters, the thin light of bioluminescent cypresses came through the front windows. Tomas checked his watch, 1740, a few minutes after Epsilon Eridani descended below the western horizon for the third time that day. He might beat enough of rush hour to make it to the Executive Mansion and play for the President his recorded conversation with Cromer before the meeting with the general staffs took place.

Why did so many people linger in the lobby? Their suits and coats muffled the echo of his footsteps on the polished basalt floor. They spoke among themselves in tight whispers. The crowd proved thicker near the front doors. Not yet 1800, normal quitting time, unless ConPol pogeys left early most days.

"Pardon me, excuse me," he repeated, punctuating the words with discreet touches to people's elbows and shoulders. Startled people moved out of his way.

The last person near the front doors, a man with thin strips of mustache and beard on his angular face, stepped back and glanced over the chest and shoulders of Tomas' service dress. He spoke with an Endeavourite accent. "Be you careful out there, captain."

The inner door parted. Tomas went through with a puzzled frown. Quick steps brought him to the outer door, which remained closed for a second. What was the problem? The inner door closed and the outer door slid open. A glitch—

A crowd's chant hit his ears. "Peace for our time! Not another war! Peace for our time! Not another war!"

Tomas slowly descended the marble-white steps of ConPol headquarters. The steps ended at a small paved plaza, ten meters deep and lined with statues of law enforcement virtues. Squat myocrete cylinders formed an anti-vehicle barricade between the plaza's far side and the sidewalk. In the gaps between myocrete boulders stood ConPol agents and Confederal City police in helmets and riot shielding, facing the avenue.

The crowd filled the street. The pools of light under the foliage of cypresses showed them to be mostly men, mostly young. Tomas crossed the plaza and took a closer look at the protesters. Most wore the fashions of their generation—though barely younger than Tomas, they were their generation, not his—wide lapels, bare shoulders, garish colors, intricate work in beads and fringing. Handcrafted garments costing a week of Tomas' salary, sold by boutiques near the University of Challenger campus.

"Peace for our time! Not another war!"

A few smartpaper signs, held up on sticks, showed slogans and animated images. *How can a free society enslave its young men to fight?* read one. *Die for Forrester? I have better things to do* read another. Other signs identified protesters belonging to *Mothers of KIAs for Peace* and *Veterans Against the Draft.*

"Peace for our time! Not another war!"

Tomas stopped just behind the line of riot police. A ConPol field agent, bulky with armor and face covered with a thick visor, turned to him. "Sir, we don't have need for Ground Force. We have the protesters contained."

"I have to get to the Executive Mansion," Tomas said. "It's urgent."

On the avenue, the chant continued. "Peace for our time! Not another war!"

"In that case, sir, I suggest you wait inside the building until the protesters move on."

Tomas stood taller. "You want to tell President Forrester he can't send a courier to one of his own agencies?"

The ConPol riot policeman leaned back on his heels. "Sir, I'm sure you're brave. But these kids aren't the Unis or mike on New Lib. Let them blow off steam, then head out."

"Peace for our time! Not another war!"

"Thank you." Tomas nodded to the riot policeman, then went to the nearest mycocrete cylinder. A high bend of the knee put his foot on the upper surface.

"Sir. Sir!"

Tomas jumped from the mycocrete cylinder to the sidewalk. He squared his shoulders and started up the avenue toward the nearest subway station.

"Peace for our time! Not another—!"

The crowd members nearest Tomas reacted first. Eyes widened. A ragged male voice shouted "Slave-driver!"

Chin up, gaze forward, Tomas kept walking.

"Slave-driver! Slave-driver!" the ragged voice kept chanting. "Come on, join me, don't turn into cowards at the sight of a Space Force uniform! Slave-driver! Slave-driver!"

Members of the crowd glanced out of Tomas' sight, toward the man with the ragged voice. The pale light of the bioluminescent cypresses shadowed large swathes of their faces, burying their eyes.

Ahead of Tomas, past a cypress in a mycocrete planter box, a man in the crowd shuffled forward. The people flanking him edged up alongside him. The man was a leader, whatever his formal rank, if any, in one of the protest groups.

Step aside, let me go on my way, and you can protest the conscription law all you want.

The man took two steps to the center of the sidewalk, then turned to Tomas. The light of a cypress caught him in the face. Dark eyes, a face vaguely familiar. A crucifix pendant glimmered against the brightly colored patches of his shirt.

Tomas kept up his pace and direction. He touched his fingertips to the front crease of his garrison cap. He kept his voice polite. "Good afternoon, citizen."

The man with the crucifix pendant raised his hand in a stop gesture. "Where are you going? Captain." He larded the word with contempt. Protesters near the man joined him on the sidewalk. They packed the sidewalk behind him, blocking Tomas' path. The bearers of the Veterans Against the Draft sign came closer.

Tomas stopped about two meters from the man. That voice…. "I wasn't always an orificer," he said.

The man set his fists on his hips, jutting his elbows to the sides. "OCS? You chose to lord over men just as good as you who don't have jewelry at their collars." Behind him, a bulky man, his clothes a fabbed knockoff of the fashions around him, repeatedly smacked his fist against the palm of his other hand, all the while eying Tomas.

Tomas kept his gaze on the man with the crucifix pendant. "No. I went to OCS to stop sharing a foxhole with you."

The man's head jutted forward. His fists opened and his hands slid over his hipbones to dangle at his sides. "Neumann?"

"Iommarino. This isn't the time or place I'd expected a platoon reunion."

The protesters around him shifted their weight to their heels, yet Iommarino stood his ground. "I lost track of you after you went to OCS. I should have guessed you'd make it through and stay in after the war."

"I assumed everyone from the platoon returned to civilian life," Tomas said. In his mind's eye, faces unremembered for weeks, even months, fixed him with thousand-yard stares. "The ones who survived."

Urgency kicked him in the back. "Though we clearly disagree on many issues," Tomas said, "I would enjoy reminiscing. But right now I have urgent business."

Iommarino shook his head. "Too bad, Neumann. We've taken over the streets of Confederal City to keep the government from doing urgent business." His words steeled the spines of the protesters behind him. They shuffled forward, and the bulky man reballed his hands into fists.

At the end of the block, lights at the subway entrance outshone the intervening cypresses. "Step aside while I pass."

Iommarino rolled his lips between his teeth before speaking. "We served together, and you're too low a rank to have mattered when the forces pushed for a draft. That's why I'll tell you this. Go back inside ConPol. Wait a couple of hours. We'll all be just fine."

And if I press on?

The bulky man wedged his shoulder forward and muttered to Iommarino. Iommarino held up a hand to delay him.

Sweat dampened Tomas' nape. Words came to him in a rush. "You want to avoid another war?"

"Of course."

Tomas drilled his gaze into Iommarino. "So do I."

The bulky man and some of the other protesters crinkled their faces. Plainly they assumed all the forces' career personnel looked forward to wars.

Iommarino's expression showed he knew better. "That's your urgent business? Then go." He turned to the protesters and swept his arms in the direction of the street. "Give the captain room to pass."

His sweeping arms impelled most of the protesters toward the street. The bulky man planted his feet. "We have a plan."

Iommarino stared him down. "I'm deviating from it. Give him room."

The bulky man quirked his mouth, but stepped back.

A distant rustle, what might have been the sound of a train pulling into the subway station, carried to Tomas through the crowd noise. He strode toward the subway station, with a moment for one look back at Iommarino. "I'm serious about reminiscing sometime. We shared experiences no one else can understand."

"Experiences no one else *should* understand," Iommarino replied. "I'll pray to St. Maurice for you!"

Tomas raised his left hand in acknowledgement. A metallic flash of his wristwatch in the bioluminescent glow reminded him to check the time. 1802. Twenty-eight minutes to make it to the Sutherland Office.

He strode even faster toward the subway station. The protesters nearest his path backed away.

11

Case White

Forrester sat in his usual chair in the Sutherland Office's meeting area. He scowled at something in his smartglasses. "Where the goddam hell are the general staffs?"

"This tardiness is unacceptable," Sharma added.

A few minutes before 2000. The curtains were closed against the darkness of early afternoon. Sutherland and Finzi stared down from their paintings as if they too disapproved the lateness of the general staffs.

"The protesters have snarled traffic all around the white mountain," Tomas said. He felt like he'd finally caught his breath after hurrying in ten minutes before. He rolled up his phone and stood taller. "Mr. President, perhaps now would be a good time to tell you what I found—"

"Protesters are no excuse. The generals could see their way through that mob of coddled crybabies if they wanted. Time to unleash the hounds." Forrester touched the side of his smartglasses, activating a link. Restoration Party security, Tomas guessed.

"Forrester here. Put the plan into motion. Level 2. Enough to intimidate them. None of them have the stomach to fight back. They'll piss themselves when we show force and cringe whenever they look in a mirror for the rest of their lives. You'll see what I mean. Forrester out."

The president scowled at the door to his assistant's station, then lurched out of his seat. He paced and muttered. "Damn, I hate this office. In there—" He waved toward his private office, the ship's cockpit with video displays. "In there I could do something about these spoiled brats acting out. As if they can derail destiny. Today is a galactic historical day."

"Mr. President." Tomas spoke with an insistent edge. "I need to tell—"

Knuckles rapped the door. Forrester's fingers immediately jumped to the audio button on the side of his smartglasses. "Yes? They're here? Show them in." He glowered at the door, eyebrows low over his hazel eyes.

Forrester's assistant swung open the door. Into the room filed figures in service blue uniforms. Space Force. Gen. Bar-Yuek led in a column of staffers. Bar-Yuek lifted his hand to shake the president's.

Forrester's hands remained at his sides. "Where's Ground Force?"

Gen. Bar-Yuek opened his mouth and blinked. A frown soon formed on his face. "We last saw them clustered by the windows in Olafson's office, watching the protesters. Olafson told us he would wait to leave until the crowds thinned out."

"How did you get here?"

"We took alleys and side streets to the nearest car ferry, then through downtown McAuliffe to the northernmost bridge back across Lake Freedom. On behalf of all my officers, I apologize. I didn't recognize the magnitude of the delay the protesters would cause. Don't blame anyone else. I take full responsibility."

Forrester brooded. "No one foresaw the delay. At least you looked for a route around the blockage." He chopped his hand at the seats nearest the windows. "Sit and rest your eyes until Olafson finally shows up."

"Of course, Mr. President." Bar-Yuek moved to his seat. An unasked question made its way onto his face. "We'd be glad to use the time to prepare for the meeting. If you could share the agenda."

Forrester returned to his usual seat. He crossed his legs and lounged back. "We'll wait until your mudbug colleagues arrive." Forrester glanced over his left shoulder. "No offense, Neumann."

"None taken." Tomas remained rigidly standing. Between his shoulder blades, his back itched. He couldn't mention the recording to Forrester now, with Space Force in the room. After this meeting, after the president dismissed Sharma, he could play the recording to Forrester. The president could change his mind about the intel without losing face....

After fifteen minutes, Forrester's assistant knocked and opened the door. Harsh voices in the next room cut off, sign of some disagreement within the Ground Force general staff. When Olafson led the way in, the lines of his face seemed years deeper compared to a few months ago. Behind them came the rest of the Ground Force general staff, two thirds of them newly promoted over the last few months, including Tomas' former brigadier, Echevarria, now a major general and commander of the Challenger military district.

Forrester stood. Olafson stiffly extended his hand.

The president clamped Olafson's hand and twisted his forearm. "You're late."

Olafson spoke through a wince. "Didn't your underlings—" he glanced at Tomas through narrowed eyes. "—tell you how thick the crowds were between here and the Defense Ministry?"

"Gen. Bar-Yuek made it here fifteen minutes ago." Forrester shoved Olafson's hand out of his grip.

Olafson grimaced, stepped back. One of the lower ranked Ground Force generals apologized for the delay and glanced disapprovingly in Olafson's direction. Echevarria complemented the cut of Forrester's suit, then gave Tomas an appreciative nod.

Everyone took their seats and turned their eyes to Forrester. He remained on his feet. Somehow he seemed even taller, his dark-blond hair reaching even further toward the ceiling. His recent anger at Olafson's delay drained from his tanned face, replaced by a look of intense confidence.

His deep voice filled the room. "Now that you're all here, the time has come to reveal my plan. The history of the next millennium will hinge on my next words. You will be remembered as the men and women who changed human history."

The Space Force general staffers glanced at one another. Echevarria's cheeks and eyes tightened and the corners of his mouth rose. A Ground Force general staffer sitting next to him raised his eyebrows and nudged his elbow into Echevarria's side. Olafson crossed his arms and watched Forrester through hooded eyes.

Forrester went on. "Nine months ago I said we would double our forces within a year. Space Force is on track to make that happen." He nodded at Bar-Yuek. He looked past Olafson down the line of new staff generals. "Ground Force has lagged, but still will have an additional six armored grenadier and two airmobile hussar brigades ready by the target date. Good job."

He stood taller. His gaze swept over both lines of general staff officers. "Your forces will be ready for war within three months. A war we will launch. A war we will win."

A cold feeling crushed Tomas, like thousands of kilometers of ices pressing down on the rocky core of some unterraformed world. The cold poured into his nose and mouth. It clutched his voice box in icy talons. He had to speak, but couldn't.

Olafson's face showed crinkled eyes, wide with fear. The lower ranked staff officers said nothing. Even Echevarria at the far end of the line remained silent, although the corners of his mouth turned up, and a sheen of ambition glazed his eyes.

Bar-Yuek cleared his throat. "Very bold, Mr. President. Preventative war is justifiable under interpolity law. Sometimes the best defense is a good offense. Strike our opponents before they can prepare a blow aimed at us."

"You see it," Forrester said. "Superb some of my chiefs of staff have their eyes open."

Tomas' voice remained frozen.

"I've named the plan 'Case White,'" Forrester said. "Here's what I've roughed out so far. Space Force will send a resupply mission to Arden, traversing the Navi Ambarsar system, as is permitted by treaty. We will send armed ships to escort our relief mission."

Olafson found his voice. "Which gives the PR a *casus belli*."

"A ground for war? No shit." Forrester's gaze hardened. "The

PRs will fire on the relief ships." He looked at Bar-Yuek and sadly shook his head. "It's a mission with low odds of survival. I would love to ask for volunteer crews, but if the PRs have lucky spies, they might glimpse the call for volunteers and take a closer look. The relief ships' sole purpose is to radio back through the wormhole to Nuova Toscano for help. And then our strike force, bigger than anything the PR will be prepared for, will sweep through the wormhole and crush the PR fleet at Navi Ambarsar, then strike deeper into PR space."

Bar-Yuek nodded. "Mr. President, Space Force will do its part. We fabbed enough ships in secret to surprise the PR, once we fully crew them with skills impped conscripts."

"I saw that." Forrester fixed his stare on Olafson. "Will Ground Force show us what it can do?"

Olafson shook his head. His haggard gaze remained locked on Forrester. "Ground Force won't get a chance. Your strike force is a weak serve and the PRs will smash the return down our throats. Odin's eye! Every bit of intel we've gathered makes clear the PRs and Unis have built up more than you think."

The fine wrinkles around Forrester's eyes deepened. "Time for you to stop talking."

"Is today a galactic historical day?" Olafson asked. "The day the Confederated Worlds sealed its doom, more like. The day that led to a million soldiers and spacemen and civilians dying for a cause lost from the beginning. The day that set the Unis and the PR on the path to dividing up our worlds."

Olafson raised his finger at Bar-Yuek and swept it around the room. "If you assist him in doing this, then the Confederated Worlds' defeat will be on your hands no less than his. You must join me in what I'm about to do." Olafson stood up and swelled out his chest. "Pres. Forrester, I refuse to follow this order."

Muscles churned behind Forrester's fixed expression. The churn broke out of his control. His head shook and red splotched his face. He stalked to Olafson, shot out his arms, pushed the general. Olafson stumbled backward into his chair. Eyes wide, he clutched the arms.

Forrester leaned to ten centimeters from Olafson's face. "Everyone saw you refuse my righteous order! Do you think, since I haven't been able to demote you from your office before, your way is clear? Look twice!" As he shouted, saliva flew from his mouth. Forrester pulled back his right fist—

Tomas hurried forward and touched Forrester's elbow. "Mr. President."

"What, Neumann?" Forrester's eyes boiled with rage. "I'll blacken a goddam traitor's eye if I want!"

"The dignity of your office…." The words sounded weak as they left his lips.

Yet they somehow worked. Forrester backed a step away from Olafson. His mouth widened to scoop in breaths. "You're right. He's shown himself a traitor more than my fist could."

Olafson stared back at Forrester. "Whether I'm a traitor or a hero is up to my peers to decide." He extended his hand to indicate the Ground Force and Space Force generals. "Every last one of you knows this man's plan will destroy everything we swore oaths to defend. Join me in refusing to implement it."

"You heard Gen. Olafson," Forrester said. His gaze darted from general to general around the conference area. "Join him, if you want."

No one stirred. On the Ground Force side, Echevarria folded his hands and stared at the portrait of Finzi on the far wall.

Bar-Yuek crossed his arms and shook his head at Olafson like a parent expressing grave disappointment. "I cannot speak for all my brother and sister officers," Bar-Yuek said, "but I have received a lawful order from my commander-in-chief."

The rest of the Space Force staff nodded or murmured in agreement.

A raised vein snaking across his forehead, Olafson set his mouth in a tight line. He spat out his next words. "What I should have expected from Shirley Foxtrot." He took a breath and turned to his subordinates. "At least you're on my side."

The Ground Force staffers looked caught. A few tried glancing at one another, a few at Forrester, but none met Olafson's gaze.

Maj. Gen. Echevarria turned to Forrester. His face formed solemn lines, except for an eager glint in his eyes. "Mr. President, I will do as I'm commanded. Regardless of who might be the chief of staff."

The rest of the Ground Force staff let out breaths. They all looked at Forrester now. The ones closest to Olafson turned their shoulders away from him, excluding him.

"You're abandoning me?" Olafson's shoulders drooped. "After everything I've done for Ground Force? For you?"

All avoided his gaze. "He's the commander-in-chief," one of them muttered.

Forrester nodded. He stared down at Olafson. "You have your answer."

Olafson's shoulders drooped even further. "You'll have my resignation in the morn—"

"Tonight." Forrester spoke softly, yet his voice filled the room. "And I don't need to remind you to keep your opinions out of the public eye."

Olafson inhaled sharply. In his features, beaten pride mingled with disbelief. "I'm done." His spine straightened and he walked to the far door. When he passed Echevarria, he turned up his nose.

Tomas' knees wobbled. He had only been in the same room as Olafson three times. He did not know him, and given the gap in their ranks, could not know him. Olafson had been as distant, and as fixed in place, as Napoléon, the gas giant primary above the settled face of Joséphine. Decades of Ground Force service—a decade as the Chief of Staff—gone in an instant.

Would Forrester bring him back, after Tomas showed the defects in the intel from Third Special Analysis Branch? Would Olafson even come back if asked?

Questions to be answered when time allowed, later. First, Tomas had to avert the rush to war.

Forrester touched his unruffled hair with the flats of his fingers. "We'll look for Ground Force's next chief of staff later. Right now, we all know what I envision for Space Force. Don't worry, Ground Force, I can see a role for you too.

"We know the PRs have three regiments of ground forces on Navi Ambarsar," Forrester said. "We don't know the number of administrators they sent to crush dissent on the planet, but it's bound to be thousands. As soon as Bar-Yuek gives us space supremacy, Ground Force will land and destroy the PR administration. Every one of their government employees gets rounded up. A prison camp at first, then ship them up the space elevator when you have time. And if a climber car suffers an accident on the way up, well, it's war time, and *accidents happen.*"

"Indeed they do," Sharma said.

Tomas frowned. Even though PR government employees were legitimate targets, to kill surrendered prisoners would give the PRs a propaganda victory.

His blood ran chill. Plan 827 had worked too well.

Forrester went on. "It should only take a small detachment to round up those PR swine. The rest of Ground Force will fix the three PR regiments so Space Force can blast them from orbit."

"We'll do our part," Bar-Yuek said. "No problem."

Tomas rolled his eyes. Easy for the head of Shirley Foxtrot to say. A fire control officer gets a call from the ground and a tech sergeant presses the button. No problem, except for the Ground Force infantrymen doing the hard work fixing those three PR regiments.

And the PR relief ships coming through from Galt's World.

And the Unis, obliged by treaty and prodded by the PRs and one of their factions to act, threatening to strike at New Nauvoo, or Challenger itself.

Forrester's hazel eyes gleamed. "I foresee our enemies will attempt to counterattack. Now that we have cleaned house on the Ground Force side, I have only extreme confidence in your ability to take my plan and see three or four or five moves ahead. We have the relative strength advantage to make this work. A few weeks of bold action, mostly by Space Force, will compel the PR to yield. At that point, the Unis would sue for peace. At least Navi Ambarsar and New Liberty will be returned to the Confederated Worlds." His deep voice resonated through the room. "Victory is ours for the taking."

Nods and murmured agreement came from both sides of the conference area.

"I want detailed plans on my desk in a week," Forrester said. "Meeting adjourned."

The staff officers filed out of the room. Forrester watched them go like a lion watching his pride. After the last one left, Forrester turned to Sharma and Neumann. "I don't need you any more tonight. Head on home."

Sharma headed for the door. Tomas' throat felt dry. "Mr. President, if you would, I need a few minutes of your time."

Forrester raised an eyebrow. "My real office. Follow."

Inside the dim room, Forrester made his way to the captain's chair facing the video displays. The darkness pressed on Tomas. Forrester's voice pierced him. "Five minutes. Starting now."

Tomas' planned words fled from mind. He blinked uselessly in the dark. Forrester inhaled heavily and anxiety crawled across Tomas' back.

"The intel from Third Special Analysis Branch is defective," Tomas blurted.

Forrester's breathing ceased for three seconds. Finally, he said, "You better have a strong hand to show me."

"No video to show, Mr. President, but I have audio. From the branch director and the analyst who determined PR and Uni preparedness." Tomas pulled his phone from his pocket, snapped it open. He set it down on a worktable and pressed *play*.

The faint bluish glow revealed a pensive cast to Forrester's features as he listened. The five minute mark passed as the branch director's pompous voice claimed to have forgotten Cromer's addendum. With each moment, Tomas relaxed more and more. Forrester's forehead creased when Cromer admitted to cherry-picking details to catch the president's attention.

In the recording, a creaking door announced Tomas' departure from Third Special Analysis Branch's office. "The recording is complete, Mr. President." He pressed *stop* and rested his hands on the worktable, flanking his phone. He glanced at Forrester, then looked away for a long moment. He repeated the head motions to show his willingness to listen, but only when the president wished to speak.

Forrester stared at the video display in front of his command chair. His expression lacked its usual extreme confidence. Tomas inhaled, and the breath buoyed him with relief. Forrester would listen—

Suddenly, Forrester's hazel eyes flared at Tomas. "Did you fake that recording?"

Tomas flinched. "What? No. Mr. President, I assure you, I would never—"

"Olafson put you up to this? Or that Gardariki twat of a bird colonel?"

Tomas raised his palms. "Mr. President, I serve you, no one else. I want to help you make the best decisions you can, whether for war or peace."

"You counsel peace."

"There's a time and place for a preemptive strike. Navi Ambarsar in three months may not be it."

Forrester leaned back. He steepled his fingers and shut his hazel eyes.

Sweat trickled down Tomas cheeks. A good sweat, though, a sweat of alert action. The president at least considered how Cromer had damned himself and the evidence of no foreign response to the buildup.

Forrester sat taller and opened his eyes. "You see facts and figures and think you see all. Don't look at what I just said as an attack. Most people cannot envision the truth beyond their sight."

"Mr. President?"

"One batch of intelligence reports comes with the imprint of authority. Another batch comes with an aura of self-interest. Yet authority may err, especially if no one sees a way to challenge its errors. And even if its motives are suspect, self-interest may still report the truth."

A pit grew in Tomas' stomach, as if he hadn't eaten for days.

"I can envision the truth beyond facts and figures." Forrester gazed through Tomas. His voice filled the cramped room, echoing back from all sides. "Third Special Analysis Branch shows the truth, even if it doesn't see it itself. Olafson and his cronies, wittingly or not, lie. When the war begins, we will win."

A fanatical confidence filled Forrester's face. "Since childhood I knew I was capable of greatness. My time in the PR prison camp confirmed I am more. More than greatness. I am destiny."

"The PR prison camp—"

A sharp look from Forrester's hazel eyes reminded Tomas of the suppression of veterans' counselors, and the lenience shown to Lissa. Once. Tomas shut up.

"I am destiny," Forrester said. "How else could I earn the fervor of the million stalwart patriots who've joined the Restoration Party? How else could I win election? How else could every element of my plan come to fruition? There is no other explanation. Providence has chosen me to bring the Confederated Worlds to supremacy over the settled galaxy. Or prove it deserves annihilation."

Tomas felt smothered in crash gel, like on a Shirley Foxtrot transport launch. A transport struck by a missile. Disintegrating around him, and powerless to move—

"For if we lose, the Confederated Worlds would prove they are unworthy of me, and deserve whatever suffering the Unis and the PR would inflict on them."

Tomas' mouth hung open. *Did Forrester just say—*

"Again, Neumann, take no offense. You are a decent man who looks for peace by preparing for war. But you see only facts and figures. You are blind to the reality. We will never arrive at peace with the Unis and the PRs. A century ago, when our only contact with the Unis passed through the Alpha Centauri wormholes, and the PRs still struggled to build a biosphere on Brotherhood of Humankind, we had peace. Those days are irretrievably far behind us, out of sight. We will never have peace again. Not until only one polity stands where three now struggle. The only question is war later or war now. By electing me, Providence has answered. *Now.*"

Forrester stood up and stretched, as relaxed as if he'd just been bull-shooting about last night's ultimate flying disc game. "Head home, Neumann. Spend some time with your family. When the war starts, every night will be a late one." Forrester's eyes narrowed enough to emphasize the conversation was over.

Tomas trudged down to the basement and paced through quiet hallways. The faint glow of the day's final sunrise came through the windows. He stopped at his office door—

Cold dread flowed down Tomas' chest. He heard nothing but the rushing of his own blood, and his vision shrank to a narrow circle surrounded by gray. Forrester would send hundreds of thousands of men to their deaths and preside over the division of the Confederated Worlds among the Unity and the Progressive Republic.

What can I do?

The narrow circle of his vision constricted even further. He fled his office door, down the hallway, down another, down another.

Nothing.

A panicked part of him thrashed like a drowning man. It propelled him further through the basement. *Nothing.* Bare mycocrete stairs, a rail of unpainted nanotube alloy smooth under his hand. *Nothing.* More hallways, bare walls. *Nothing....*

He put his hands on his knees and took deep breaths. This wasn't battle, where he could end up dead in three seconds. He had three months. Enough time to take stock, decide on a plan, and act.

What plan—?

The one I'll develop later. Tomas looked up and down an unfamiliar corridor. Huge equipment hummed somewhere ahead. *After I figure out where I am.*

Tomas pulled out his phone. A few swipes brought up floorplans of the executive mansion basements. Storage spaces, offices for junior personnel. No utilities able to generate the giant hum. Where had he gotten to?

He walked on. After a dozen meters, he found the source of the hum. To the right, an opening showed a glimpse of a fusion reactor, furnace and boiler units, a guard in chameleonskin set to urban camouflage—

Tomas froze.

The guard jutted his head forward. Most of his face showed a warm, weathered tan. A splotch of youthful pink ran from his left cheek across his mouth and tapered to a point along his right jaw. He came out of the reactor room. "Do you have some business here?" His empty hands stayed at his side, near a holstered pistol.

"I don't," Tomas said. "Walking, deep in thought, I took a wrong turn and ended up down here."

"This is a restricted area, captain." The guard studied Tomas's face, then noticed the nameplate on Tomas' service uniform jacket. His eyes jolted wide. "Capt. Neumann! The officer who saved the president from the assassin." The guard saluted. "Truly an honor, sir."

Guard? Tomas returned the salute. "I only did my duty, soldier." Tomas nodded at the pink skin of the man's face. "Just like you did yours."

"My beauty mark, captain? Came by it on Kahlenberg. A Uni shell fragment redecorated my face a little. Too bad the medics couldn't rejuvenate my whole face or—" The soldier's expression darkened.

Tomas read the rest in his face. The shelling that mutilated his face left a comrade of his dead.

How many men will end up with the twin burdens of guilt for surviving and shame for losing, if Forrester gives the PRs their desired war?

Behind the guard's shoulder, ceiling panels poured out light in the visible spectrum of Sol, banishing shadows from the reactor room. The fusion reactor comprised a platform holding five barrel-shaped housings. Hydrogen fuel, cooling, and energy transfer piping, all as thick as a strong man's upper arms, ran from the housings into the platform. Each housing contained a polywell. Tomas recalled the specs of the polywells under the infantry compartments of Badger IFVs, and made a few guesstimates from the size of these and the demands of the executive mansion and offices. Enough to power the entire complex. "This post is a far cry from Kahlenberg."

The soldier shrugged. "Captain, it's easy duty. Never been shot at once down here. Honest enough work for a generous wage. My son gets to see me hold down a job like a real man. Too many of us who served can't say that."

A thought came to Tomas. It sent shivers over his skin and stippled his face. His body wavered as if he stood at the edge of a chasm. It wasn't—it couldn't—how—?

Tomas refocused on the reactor room and the former soldier. "Very honest work." He studied the reactor and parts of his mind clashed. *You might need to know* I'm not really serious *must look at all the options*— "Does that reactor power the entire facility?"

"You have an eye for equipment, captain. We're connected to the city grid, but only tap it if the main reactor is down for maintenance."

Tomas nodded. "Carry on, soldier. We appreciate all you do. Now, if you could just point me to the way out?"

The soldier chuckled. "Of course, captain. Just head that way—" He gestured, and kept talking. Up, left, right... Tomas forced his wandering mind to pay attention. He turned back the way he came, repeating the directions like a mantra. The thought clamoring for his attention was wrong and the repeats kept it outside the doors of his consciousness. Up, left, right....

A few minutes later, he emerged from the Executive Mansion employees' entrance into the early evening light of Epsilon Eridani. No one else trod the walkway from the building entrance to the Challenger Boulevard gate. Here, in sunlight, the thought seemed unreal. He had better options. Easier ones. Safer ones. One of those might work.

Tomas squinted at the gatehouse, where three bored guards chatted among themselves, their rifles slung over their shoulders. *Only three*—

His mouth suddenly felt arid. His hopes crashed against cold black boulders of intuition. The easier and safer options would fail. The blood of hundreds of thousands, the fates of worlds, would be on his hands if he tried them. He had one option.

Him, alone?

More intuitions flooded him. Enough people would help him, if he knew how to ask.

And he knew someone who could teach him how to ask.

The guards paid him no attention. The world seemed brighter than ever, as if Epsilon Eridani entered one of its variable phases. He went through the gate and headed toward the subway. With luck, he would have a short wait at the central station for a transfer to the Red Line.

12

First Approaches

High in a cloudless sky, Epsilon Eridani poured sunlight over Nuova Toscano Boulevard and First Avenue. Only a few cars and taxis plied the streets.

Tomas paused five meters from the subway station. The Daughters' temple loomed to his left. No one trod the steps to or from the temple. Tomas nodded to himself, then glanced down the sidewalk. A Restoration Party bluecoat strode casually in Tomas' direction. The bluecoat's third-eye camera showed a deep black disc on the man's cap.

Perfect. Tomas ducked his chin toward his chest and turned his face away from the bluecoat. He climbed the steps with choppy strides. Just what a man trying to visit the Daughters unnoticed would do.

In the vestibule, Tomas went to one of the doors. The tablet mounted in the wall next to the door came to life.

He didn't want their sacraments. *Let me in without donating.* There should be a way. He tapped corners of the screen.

An intuition froze his finger. He was a man coming to partake of the sacrament, at least as far as Restoration Party security would know. If the bluecoats found otherwise, the hundreds of thousands of dead could include him.

Doubt washed through him. *You don't have to attempt what you're thinking.*

A vision of a grassy plain arrayed with a hundred thousand headstones came to him.

Tomas swallowed. He keyed in a donation. A hundred--seventy-five confeds.

The door next to the tablet swung open.

Into a sitting area same as the previous one. Thick red curtains walled off three sides. He went to the couch. While he waited for a priestess, he scripted his request. *You're lovely, but I'd really like to spend time with Persephone.*

After five minutes, he checked his wristwatch. After ten minutes, his foot tapped a fast rhythm on the floor. A priestess should be here by now. Blood roared in his ears. Unless ConPol or the bluecoats picked up his thoughts between the Executive Mansion and here? A long-distance brain scanner? Could the black ops side of ConPol have such a thing—

A hand pulled back a curtain. Tomas sucked in a breath, then relaxed when he saw a familiar bracelet sliding down a woman's slender arm.

Persephone came in and let the curtain fall into place behind her. "Tomas. After our last visit, I did not expect to see you again."

"That was a year ago. Things have changed."

Persephone joined him on the couch. She took his hand between hers. "You were true to your interpretation of your wedding vow, then." She peered into his eyes. "You still are."

Tomas covered her hands with his free one, as softly as Stefan did after being reminded to play gently with baby Artur. "I'm not here to partake of your sacrament."

"What brings you to me?"

"You remember that other person we talked about?"

Her eyes widened for a moment. "Yes."

"You were right about—"

"You need not have come to me to tell me that." Fear tinged her guileless face.

"There's more. Much more. So much more that I have to act, but

I need help. Your help."

Persephone had likely spoken her next words to a thousand congregants, but never before in a tone so sexless. "Let's go someplace more private."

She led him through the curtain. The thick fabric brushed his arm. She took his arm and walked with him along a winding corridor of more red velour to a flight of stairs.

His experience of smaller temples, ministering to Ground Force personnel on New Liberty during the war, led him to expect a single flight of stairs and a cramped room. Instead, she guided him up multiple flights of stairs railed with wide, honey-colored balustrades of what might even be wood harvested from once-living trees.

On the fourth floor, she guided him through twisting hallways, to a room the size of a pogey general's office. Floral print wallpaper covered the walls above deep brown wainscot. Near the door stood a kitchenette, a wet bar, and a seating area for a half dozen people. To the back of the room, a pony wall surmounted by curtains concealed a king-sized bed.

Persephone gestured for him to enter, then followed and shut the door. It snicked shut. She tapped keys on the door and a deadbolt thudded home, like a round chambering in his pistol. She smiled at Tomas. "We're secure."

"How secure?"

For a moment, she looked to be marshaling soothing but empty words. Then she gazed on his face and her expression turned alert and businesslike. "We have to keep some of our secrets, but I can tell you, this room is swept for listening devices and cameras, it's hardened against eavesdropping and intrusion, and we jam wireless data communications in and out of the temple. Is that secure enough?"

"It will do."

"For what serious matter do you seek our help?"

Tomas squared his shoulders and stared into her eyes. His words sounded half-unreal as he spoke them. "I must organize a coup d'état."

Her eyes widened. Her hand covered her neck. "How can you say such a thing?"

He showed her his open palm, then pushed down through the air. "Listen to me."

Persephone's head jittered. "The ancients left that behind in the petroleum age. It's like religious wars and torturing people for information. A coup. The ancient Americans got one thing right, the military stays out of politics—"

Tomas deepened his voice. "I would if I could."

She blinked. The muscles around her eyes showed she could listen with at least a sliver of an open mind.

He clutched her wrists. "Pres—the incumbent wants to launch a war. Almost every intelligence report shows we would lose. He has one contrary report that makes him think he can win. I showed him that one report is faulty. He refused to believe me."

"Why?"

His chest swelled a bit. Her question showed she trusted him to speak the truth.

Time to lie.

"I don't know. Perhaps his time in the PR prison camp unhinged him." Tomas jostled her arms. "*Why* doesn't matter. If he remains in office, vast numbers of men will die and the Confederated Worlds will be conquered. He must be stopped."

She leaned her body closer. "Yes, but... he didn't listen to you but he might listen to someone else. Someone more...." She trailed off. Her face showed she wanted to salve Tomas' ego.

"Someone more than a mere captain? There was someone, as a high a rank as you could imagine. The incumbent forced him to resign an hour ago."

"Olafson?" she muttered. "That's not important. There must be an answer other than what you propose. The PR prison camp unhinged him. You guess that. We know it."

"Know?" Did the Daughters have a copy of Plan 827?

"After he returned to the Confederated Worlds, he sought our sacrament. Once."

The smashed statuette in the Sutherland Office came to mind. "What happened?"

"He failed to perform. It is more common than one might think, and we think no less of a congregant for it. Our priestess applied various techniques to arouse him. These failed. Then he attacked her. We defused the situation and forbade him from ever visiting again."

"I see."

"Something unhinged him. A psychological counselor could perhaps rehinge him."

Tomas shook his head. "I suggested that to him months ago. Immediately before the bluecoats investigated every counselor in the city on trumped-up charges of espionage." He noticed he still clutched Persephone's wrists. He let go and stared into her eyes. "He won't choose peace."

"Then force him to choose peace."

The easy and safe ways. His intuitions had told him they would fail, but he hadn't yet followed the logic to those conclusions. He gestured at a loveseat in the sitting area and raised his eyebrows in a question. She nodded and sat. Tomas followed a half second behind.

"How would you force him to choose peace?" he asked.

Persephone looked thoughtful. "You could leak his plan to start a war to one of the pacifist parties in Congress. They supported today's protesters, after all."

"It wouldn't work. ConPol or the bluecoats would hunt down the leak." Tomas tapped his breastbone. "If they found me, I don't know if they would drag me to prison or shoot me in the street in front of my house." Tomas pictured Lissa, red-eyed and hysterical, pressing the boys' faces against her, and Capt. Krishnalingam and wife running out from the house next door.

Countercurrents of higher purpose swirled within him. "It would be worth the risk if it would stop him. If."

"How could it not?"

"I've seen him break opposing politicians and remold opposing parties. Against that, I don't trust politicians to act on principle. True, a leak would give the Unis and PR advance warning of his current plan. But if ConPol or the bluecoats catch me, he would propose another plan for his lackeys in the general staffs. A different path to the same result."

Persephone eyed the floral print on the far wall. "Impeachment?"

"Impossible. He remains popular enough."

"The protests—"

"On the subway here, I heard the silent majority muttering about spoiled brats. Many people will still take his side. And again, it would rely on his enemies in Congress to stand firm against the pressure he can bring."

She drew in a deep breath, then gave Tomas a level look. "Then shoot him."

"I could kill him if I wanted. I could easily smuggle a pistol into the Executive Mansion, then get close enough to guarantee two rounds to the chest. In ten seconds he would be dead. My arrest and either prison or death would be guaranteed as well."

"That wouldn't be worth it?"

Tomas vigorously shook his head. "Even his death would be no guarantee. Assassination rarely achieves its desired policy. Killing him would only make him a martyr, like some ancient American president worshiped as a saint on New Liberty. O'Brien becomes president? A wave of public opinion would join Bar-Yuek and Echevarria in maneuvering O'Brien to war."

He took a deep breath. Again he shivered, even though he saw no way around the conclusion. "Neutralizing him alone accomplishes nothing. All his loyalists would have to be cut out of power at the same time. That requires a coup d'état."

She settled into the loveseat cushions. "Perhaps. But what do you seek by telling me this?"

"I need allies. Military, police, and government personnel to take necessary actions at the necessary time. Personnel I can trust."

She looked pensive. "Not me."

"You for the active phase of the coup." He set his face to show he lacked any desire for denials. "But you have dossiers on thousands of candidates, don't you?"

Persephone's hand fluttered toward her mouth. Her bracelet clanked toward her elbow. "Tomas, I don't know what you mean."

"My last visit, you hinted something was amiss about—him.

This visit you confirmed it."

"Never, but we priestesses talk—"

"About one man of the hundreds, thousands? denied your sacrament over the past years?"

"He is the incumbent."

"He wasn't then." Tomas drilled his gaze into her. "You agree he must be stopped. You agree a coup is the best option. For a coup to succeed, I need the Daughters' knowledge of the secret hearts of powerful men, to know which ones I can safely invite to join me."

Persephone's hands writhed together. Suddenly, they dropped into her lap, and her face showed clarity. "I said too much last year. You are right that we notice things about our congregants that could help you in your task. But what we know we cannot share."

His nostrils flared. Tomas shut his eyes and took a slow breath. "Do you believe the PRs will allow you to keep your secrets? Or even give you freedom to practice your faith?"

"We're priestesses, not politicians. Societies work best when each person knows her role and does not transgress it. We minister. We do not command."

His spine grew rigid and cold. "If you won't help me, I'll do this on my own. Without what you know about the personnel I need to invite to join, I'm much more likely to ask the wrong man. If I do that, I will be denounced to ConPol or the bluecoats. I'll end up dead." Their wartime encounter on New Liberty came back to him. Sadness when she mused on Ground Force soldiers dying on that planet. "Hundreds of thousands of men will end up dead. Will your goddess let you speed them to their deaths?"

Her eyes narrowed. "Such stirring words. But words—even from you, a man I know better than most—words are foolish things. Actions are the only true measure of a man." She stood up. One hand reached for his. She stretched the other toward the gap between the curtains and the visible slice of the king-sized bed. "Would you prove yourself by sharing the sacrament with me?"

His penis throbbed at the thought of her. His first lover, come back into his life, next to a bed softer than the cold one waiting for him at home....

Dread washed through Tomas. She asked something monstrous. Despite the tension and lack of passion at home, he would not accept Persephone's offer. A coup could only hold its gains if the public believed the coup's organizers sacrificed for the greater good, rather than sought pleasures of the world.

If the coup's organizers believed the same about themselves.

Tomas pushed himself off the loveseat. He brushed nonexistent lint off his pants. "If I haven't proven myself by coming here, then you cannot help me. Thank you for your time. Don't worry, I won't tell anyone about the Daughters' capabilities—"

Her bracelet clinked. Persephone touched her forefinger to his lips. Tears pooled in her eyes, then glistened in her lashes after she blinked. "You have confirmed your words. I will work with you. Tell me the names, and I will copy over to you any dossier on Ground Force and Space Force officers and government personnel we have. But you must keep these secure."

"I will guard your secrets as my own. In encrypted and biometrically-locked storage."

She said, "Not every name will be in our files—"

His eyebrow lifted. A tiny bubble of humor leavened his mood. "I'm not the only officer who declines to take your sacraments?" The bubble burst. "Names. Bar-Yuek. Echevarria." Tomas added the names of all the general staff officers from the meeting, then widened his net. "Sokolov and the other battalion commanders at GFB West McAuliffe. Everyone on the brigade staff." An intuition made him blink. "And Olafson." The former Ground Force Chief of Staff had proven himself an opponent of Forrester, and even in retirement he might have influence over other high-ranking officers.

He would have disgust for Tomas. How could he overcome Olafson's negative opinion of him?

With insights from the Daughter's dossier.

"That's all? Let me make sure I have everyone." Persephone quoted back the list from memory.

He let out a breath. "You do."

"And if they join your cause? You would have to meet to discuss the matter? Do you have a secure location that can be reached out of sight of the bluecoats?"

An anxious feeling gripped him. He shook his head.

She took his hand. Her eyes seemed as large as the temple, as large as all the Daughters' temples combined. "You do now."

The taxi slowed to turn off the winding road. Metallic letters floated on extender arms jutting from a low wall of gray basalt blocks. *Confederal Heights Country Club*. Smaller letters below spelled out *Members and invited guests only.*

The taxi turned onto the driveway. Between the entrance and exit lanes stood a guardhouse. Tomas held his breath, expecting a challenge from a guard. Most club members had their own cars, didn't they? Only a guest would come by taxi—

The taxi driver accelerated past the guardhouse. No one came out. A far cry from the golf course at GFB West McAuliffe, where a heavily guarded entrance limited entrance to officers only.

The taxi wound its way along an oak-lined, curving driveway, toward a sprawling clubhouse partially occluded by trees. Every ten meters along the driveway, cameras mounted on posts tracked the taxi.

The driveway ended in a circle looping under a roof covering double doors into the clubhouse. A club employee, short yet with a high forehead and elongated face, stood with his jacketed arms at his sides, formal and alert.

"Wait just outside the gate," Tomas told his taxi driver. Tomas read the meter, rounded up, added twenty. He reached into his pocket and unclipped stiff banknotes with unpracticed fingers. "Here's a hundred-forty Confeds. Another hundred when you get me back to the subway station near the executive mansion. I'll call you when my work is done."

The taxi driver raised his eyebrows at the cash. He swiped the banknotes from Tomas' hands and counted them by pushing back corners with his thumbs. He nodded once.

Tomas climbed out of the taxi. The back of his long-sleeved polo shirt untucked itself from his civilian chinos. He stood tall and tucked his shirt back in one-handed. The shirt's fabric felt sodden with sweat. A deep breath, then he turned to the double doors.

The man with the long face stayed unmoving. "Sir, perhaps you failed to notice the sign?"

Time-honored wisdom for officers in over their heads came to him. *Fake it till you make it.* "Sign?"

"The sign informs we only admit members and invited guests."

"Oh, that? You're a stickler for the rules. Good man. General Olafson invited me."

The man blinked slowly. "Your name, sir?"

"Tomas Neumann." He spelled his surname, then put on a bluff face.

"I did not see a guest of the general's, nor any guest by that name, on today's list. Perhaps an oversight on my part. Wait here." The man retreated to a kiosk near the doors. A display hidden to Tomas cast a warm gray tinge on the man's face. His gaze flicked up and down the screen. His frown deepened. He returned to Tomas with a pained look on his face. "My memory was accurate. The general invited no one, nor is your name on today's list."

Tomas rolled his eyes. "Someone misentered the data. The general will be highly annoyed if he must be interrupted on the tennis court or in the locker room for me to be allowed in."

Gen. Olafson would be highly annoyed, indeed.

The man pressed his lips together. "Sir, come with me." He started off along the circular driveway, away from the main doors, then along a path running parallel to the clubhouse's windowless, gray, basalt block wall. Thick hedges hid the path from the grounds. From the distance came the metallic clink of golf clubs and shouts of "pull!" from a laser skeet range.

The path turned toward the building. It stopped at a plain alloy door painted to match the basalt wall. The man pressed his thumb on a wall-mounted pad and stared unblinking at a spot on the wall above it. The door made a soft click.

Inside this part of the clubhouse was a suite of small offices, worn carpet, and scuffed gypsum board. Employees in the club's uniforms bustled to and fro. A woman carrying a tablet hurried past Tomas and down a short hallway. A double door opened at her approach, giving a view of a wide, opulent hallway.

They kept him away from members and approved guests. But at least he'd entered the building.

The man led Tomas to the largest of the offices. A cramped place, with smartpaper piled high on a small extruded desk. The man beckoned Tomas to sit in a chair facing the desk. Tomas did, and his knees brushed the privacy panel under the desktop.

"Please wait here," the man said. "We'll alert the general of your arrival as soon as we can." The man left.

Within a few seconds, Tomas tapped his foot on the thin carpet. His pants leg brushed louder against the desk. Would Olafson even see him? If the general would, he would have at least a few seconds to persuade Olafson to listen.

High on the wall, the minute hand of an analog clock ticked along. Still no sign of Olafson. Tomas fidgeted in the chair. On the bright side, every second he waited meant Olafson had not yet refused to meet him.

Hope is not a planning factor.

From down the hallway came the clatter of the door to the members' area of the clubhouse. The man from earlier spoke. "Sir, we have no objection to bringing your guest—"

"Guest?" Olafson's voice. "A gate crasher, more like. Loki's *skith*, I'll be damned if I parade him around as if he is a guest. Where the hell is he?"

"This way, sir." Footsteps became audible. Tomas stood at parade rest, filling the space between the desk and the wall.

Olafson appeared in the doorway. His attire seemed wrong, even for a weekend—polo and chinos, hair damp from a shower, the smells of soap and cologne. Even seeing his resignation happen, his new civilian status had not reached deep into Tomas' view of the world. "You have one hell of a lot of nerve."

"Sir, my apologies if I cut short your tennis game."

Olafson's face tightened. He glanced over his shoulder at the club employee. "Leave us alone."

"As you wish, sir." The man backed out, then reached for the door. Olafson held out his hand to keep the door open.

"What does your boss want with me? I turned over every classified file I had, then cleaned my damned office."

Tomas raised his hand. "Sir, perhaps we could speak someplace more private." Tomas mouthed *more secure*.

Olafson scowled at the room's close walls, and at Tomas. "We'll speak here, captain."

Chatting voices heralded club employees passing through the hallway outside. Tomas shook his head. "What I need to tell you, neither of us wants overheard. Sir, please, someplace private."

Olafson squinted at Tomas. His ruddy cheeks seemed redder than usual. "Follow."

He led Tomas out the employee entrance and toward the sounds of running feet and thwocking tennis balls. They reached a five-meter high fence overgrown with ivy. At a gate of alloy mesh, free of ivy and so fine and dense it looked like a gray haze, Olafson's stiff fingers tapped a passcode. The gate opened itself.

The ivied fence surrounded six tennis courts laid side-by-side. Two couples played mixed doubles at the far end. Between points, a man at the service line raised his racket in greeting to Olafson.

Tomas' gut tightened. "Sir, I asked that we speak someplace secure."

"You said *private*." Olafson gestured at the nearby empty courts.

But not too private. The presence of witnesses, especially witnesses whose country club membership suggested powerful connections, shielded Olafson.

Tomas' eyelids drooped. He had a strategy from the Daughters' thick dossier on Olafson, but would it crack the general's suspicion? "Sir, when I said we didn't want to be overheard, I didn't simply mean other people." He gestured at the couples at the farthest court. "Listening devices as well."

"The club protects its members' privacy. There isn't a recording device anywhere on site, other than the phones in our pockets. Odin's eye, are you recording this?"

"No, sir."

"'Sir?' Your boss shitcanned me, you realize that?" Olafson

peered at him. "Leave your phone here."

A chance to build trust. "I would if I could, sir. There's something on it you need to see."

"Do I need to see it now?"

Tomas pulled his phone from its pocket and lay it camera- and microphone-down on the rubberized court surface. Its edge touched one of the net posts. "Not now, sir."

Olafson peered again at Tomas. Then he led the way to benches between the two courts nearest the gate. Tomas sat. Olafson remained standing and pulled out his phone. "You aren't recording this, but I am. If anything happens to me—"

"Nothing will, sir."

Olafson folded his arms and narrowed his eyes. "Say your piece."

"The president did not send me. He doesn't know I'm here. I apologize for intruding but this seemed the safest way to approach you."

Olafson squinted. "Approach me? You want me to grovel my way back into the white mountain?"

"No, sir. The reasons for your resignation were absolutely right." Tomas glanced over his shoulder at the couples in the far court. They rallied in the middle of a long point. Despite their attention being on their game, he lowered his voice. "The president will lead us to disaster. The intel he cited, about Uni and PR weakness, is utterly broken."

Olafson's mouth soured. "You had a chance to agree with me. You backed your boss."

"When you and Col. Tatarinova came to the Executive Mansion, I didn't even know the president had intel contrary to yours, let alone that it was faulty. I researched on my own and showed him irrefutable evidence. He refused to believe me." Tomas leaned forward. His voice turned into a harsh whisper. "And even worse is, I know why he refused."

The thwock of a racket against a ball sounded, followed by the patter of feet and the thwock of a return stroke. Finally, Olafson said, "Go on."

Tomas' back itched between his shoulder blades. "When the PRs held him as a POW, they programmed him to seek high office and guide the Confederated Worlds into disaster."

After a moment, Olafson angled his phone closer to his mouth. "For the record, Captain Neumann is attempting to entrap me into treasonous activity."

Hot pressure built up behind Tomas' eyes. "Sir, I have proof. On my phone."

"Proof? Of what must be the most guarded secret in the settled galaxy? How the hell did Forrester's ballboy come by 'proof?'"

"From the Uni spy who recruited the would-be assassin during the election campaign. Thanks for asking."

Olafson's eyebrow lifted.

Tomas said, "I'll show you the proof." He rose and crossed the tennis court, running his fingers along the net cord. He picked up his phone and decrypted the Plan 827 document as he walked back. He held his phone out.

A skeptical downcast look showed on Olafson's face. Yet he returned his phone to his pocket and reached for Tomas'. He scrolled through the document with thick swipes of his stubby fingers. His eyes widened at the pages with Forrester's name. "This reads like a real PR document. If it's a forgery, it's well done." Olafson squinted at Tomas. "Odin's eye, what trickery are you trying to work on me?

"Sir, I have to stop him from launching a war we cannot win. I will do whatever I can. But a mere captain, and on top of that an advisor of his? Who would join me? But many Ground Force officers still respect you. I need you—the Confederated Worlds need you—to help me stop him."

Olafson kept his arms folded for a time. "This must be a trick. If your boss can't abide by me being powerless but still free, I will be damned if I'll commit an unforced error and put my *skith* on the chopping block."

Gears seemed to grind inside Tomas. After reading the Daughters' dossier on Olafson, he'd been certain he could persuade the general. Now, in the face of Olafson's implacable stare, the certainty evaporated. Yet he had nothing else.

Tomas took a deep breath and lifted his left foot to the bench. Olafson's brow crinkled.

Tomas rolled up his pants leg in wide bands doubling back on themselves. His calf showed smooth pink skin lightly tufted with hair. Near his knee, the fabric became too thick to fold further. He slid the pants leg over his knee, partway up his thigh. *Come on, just a little further, make obvious the contrast between new skin and old—*

"Where did you come by that new leg?" Olafson sounded more curious than cautious.

"A healing tank at GFB Reagantown."

"New Liberty."

"Yes, sir."

"That wasn't a question."

"Of course, sir." Tomas slid his right sleeve from his wrist up to his elbow. "The hospital there also fixed up my right arm."

"You took both wounds in the same action?" Olafson looked pensive. "The Valkyries nearly carried you to Valhalla."

"Two of my buddies risked their lives to get me to the medics in time." Tomas' eyes thickened with moisture. Ryan and Cohen, the hemp field, the mike dismounts. His conscious mind had forgotten that day for months. "I can't pay them back. All I can do is keep a hundred thousand men from dying for a mistake."

Olafson nodded at Tomas' exposed calf. "Roll down your pant leg. The people in the distant court might wonder what's going on."

A long enough demonstration? It would have to be. "Of course, sir." Tomas slid the fabric down his leg, then unfolded it the rest of the way. He pushed his foot off the bench and stood at parade rest. "I've said all I can. I realize you may need a day or two to think about it, but please, no longer than that. On Oneday night, at twenty-five o'clock, go to a blue door off the lobby of the Hotel Transtellar, First Avenue and Nuova Toscano. Stairs down and follow the graffiti of Astarte. At the Daughters' temple, ask for Persephone. She'll guide you to me. In only three months, the next war will start. I—we—have to plan what must be done as soon as possible."

Olafson crossed his arms. "You would go through with—what needs doing—if I said no?"

Tomas drew a breath and stood tall. "To the best of my abilities."

"You said the odds would be against you."

"Yes, sir. But the Confederated Worlds need me to act, despite the odds."

Brows furrowed, Olafson sat on the bench. He stared at the net post on the near side of the court, but clearly didn't see it. Tomas stood rigidly as nervous energy fired the muscles of his legs, arms, and torso, like a charge seeking a ground.

Olafson's gaze returned to Tomas. His broad face concealed his thoughts. "Odin's eye, you asked a lot. I'll take that day or two. Now get out of here, and do not come back."

13

Strategems

The next Oneday night, around 2450, Persephone led Tomas to a sacrament room on the uppermost floor. In layout and furnishings, the room resembled the one they'd spoken in on his previous visit. Here, though, on both sides of the sitting area, red velvet curtains hid the walls.

Persephone went to the curtain on the right-hand wall. Her bracelet jangled and her hand disappeared through a gap between the curtain's velvet panels. A hum sounded near the ceiling and the curtain bunched up toward the ceiling, exposing the wall behind it.

A flat keypad blended with the wall, next to a revealed door. The door had a recessed handle and a glowing green dot.

"Wait here," Persephone said. "This door is unlocked. If Olafson comes, we'll lead him to the next room and tell him to come in here."

Tomas touched her elbow. "Thank you for hosting this meeting, and however many others may come. I know the Daughters risk much—"

"They risk nothing. I've done this on my own initiative. If you are found out before you succeed, my sisters will survive by sacrificing me to the incumbent."

Tomas took in her words. "I didn't know you risked so much."

"To save a hundred thousand men from meaningless deaths is

worth the risk." She turned haggard eyes to the wallpaper. How much did a Daughter grieve a congregant who later died in battle? Multiplied by a hundred thousand.... She gazed solemnly at him. "May the Goddess bless you. You have this room as long as you need it." Persephone left through the front door.

The solemnity lingered over the room. A few minutes later, when it began to fade, curiosity took its place. Tomas went to the full-length curtain on the room's left-hand wall. He groped behind it. A thin vertical gap under his fingertips—a rectangle with smoother texture than the rest of the wall, the size of the handle recess on the other door—

He peeked behind the curtain to confirm this wall also had a door.

This entire line of sacrament rooms might interconnect.

Behind him, hardware buzzed and clicked at the adjoining door on the room's far side. Tomas' head jerked around. He checked the handle near him for the red glow marking the door locked. Yes, locked. He hurried across the room to the far door.

The door swung into the room. A white polo shirt with an emblem over the heart, a kangaroo holding a tennis racket. A broad face, ruddy cheeks, hair salted with gray.

Tomas let out a breath. "Thank you for coming, sir."

Olafson came in and took a step to the right. He stopped and his gaze roved the room. Finally, tension bled from his shoulders. He shut the door and turned to Tomas. "I almost didn't, captain. In the hotel lobby, I saw the blue door and the first time walked by it. I didn't know if I could trust you. I still don't know."

He went on. "But I realized something. Yes, if I trust you and you betray me, I'll end up dead. But if I don't trust you, and this damned fool war starts because I didn't do what I could, I'll enter Valhalla in shame, when I see the men there who died for Forrester's folly." He extended his hand.

Tomas met his grip. "May we both do all we can, sir."

"Stop the 'sir.' I'm not your superior anymore. I'm an old man whom no one will listen to, more like."

"I don't think so, s—general."

Eyebrows raised, Olafson glanced around the room. "How did you get the Daughters to join you?"

"Elements within the Daughters also seek the neutralization of the incumbent."

"Elements. The Daughters as a whole are opposed? Neutral?"

"Neutral," Tomas said.

"Only to be expected." Olafson's voice sounded world-weary. "Women usually aim to make the best of their situation, rather than try to change it. Like our wives looking the other way whenever we make our donations here."

Tomas grimaced in passing. "Near enough." He gestured at two armchairs facing each other over a coffee table. "Have a seat, please, and let's get started."

They sat. On the table between them lay two tablets, thin clients only displaying data from their phones, caching nothing. A bottle of aquavit, an opened and fizzing bottle of sparkling water, and two glasses completed the tableau.

Olafson pulled the cork from the bottle and poured a shot. He looked more relaxed than Tomas could recall from any of their prior meetings. "You know what I like about the Daughters?"

Tomas poured himself sparkling water. The drinks had waited for him and Persephone. Had he ever told her he didn't drink alcohol? "They know our wants."

"Close, but still out. Our wives know our wants too, once we're married long enough. But the Daughters satisfy our wants, without negotiating or complaining." Olafson lifted his glass. "*Prosit.*" He flung the liquor down his throat, then returned the empty glass to the table with a sharp clack. "What's our goal for tonight?" He asked the question with the air of a rigorous professor.

"Mission planning and recruit selection."

"You've thought that far, at least." Olafson peered at Tomas. "Start. The mission?"

Just like any other planning meeting, but his sweaty palms and dry throat told him the truth. Tomas sipped sparkling water and took a deep breath. "Our objective is to displace the incumbent's control of the machinery of government with our own. Three prongs to that.

First, take him and his most powerful loyalists into custody. Second, block physical access to Confederal City until the first prong is achieved. Third, control communications in and around the capital cities until we have the situation under control."

Olafson continued to sound professorial. "How will you and I do that?"

"We must persuade key personnel to join us."

"Key personnel? How many? There are tens of thousands of Ground Force, Space Force, ConPol, police, and bluecoats in the capital cities, at GFB West McAuliffe, and atop the space elevator who could interfere."

Tomas swallowed thickly. "We, ah—" He coughed and sipped more sparkling water. He would pass the test if he relaxed. "A few men who can act are worth more than ten thousand kept out of action. The space elevator takes days to return personnel to the surface. We'll have won or lost by then. Space Force won't use orbital fires against targets in the capital cities."

"Good point," Olafson said. "That still leaves a lot of GF in the white mountain and GFB West McAuliffe."

"By controlling communications, we can keep most loyal personnel in the dark. Blockading the bridges and major roads will keep the few loyal units able to act away from the scene. Despite all that, if we identify a loyal unit which could still act, persuading a key person in the chain of command to sit on his hands could immobilize the entire unit."

Olafson squeezed shut his eyes. "We need a communications expert inside the white mountain and another inside the executive mansion."

"Not the XM." Tomas said, "I can neutralize the entire building and grounds."

An eyebrow flickered up. For a moment, Olafson looked impressed, but a moment only. "What about civilians? Have you taken them into account?" He squinted at Tomas. "I wouldn't rely on soldiers to fire on civilians."

"We wouldn't need to," Tomas said. "We'll shut down civilian communications as well. Every civilian data transfer—audio, video, voice, text—sent by or sent to anyone in the capital cities goes through CC Telecom's facility in Finziburg. One team can shut down all communications, except for our sides', for as long as we need to prevent any civilians from organizing resistance."

Olafson scowled at the aquavit bottle. "We'll need more." He poured another shot. A whiff of pungent liquor bit Tomas' nose.

"How many more?" Tomas asked.

Olafson gulped aquavit. He set down his glass and counted on his fingers. "A team to shut down civilian communications, another to shut down military comm in and out of the white mountain, a third to shut down military com at GFB West McAuliffe.... Bridges and roads aren't enough. We need a team to shut down the subway system by neutralizing its control center."

Tomas felt pinned. "I should have thought of that."

"Good thing you aren't playing singles." Olafson kept counting. "Teams to take into protective custody key personnel. Key personnel being the incumbent, the heads of the RP militia and ConPol, the chiefs of staff, the defense minister, the interior minister.... We need dependable men to perform these tasks. One task per man. Doing so keeps things need-to-know during the planning stage. That keeps everyone safer."

If ConPol or the bluecoats caught a hint of the plan, a single brain scan could send everyone to prison or a shallow, wilderness grave. Tomas set down his glass of sparkling water. "One task per man also means all the tasks can be completed simultaneously. Speed is of the essence. Delay gives resistance time to mobilize, concentrate, and deploy against us. Prominent resistance will give timid supporters of the status quo enough backbone to join the resistance." His shoulders slumped. "Can we find that many dependable men?"

"Dependability doesn't require trustworthiness," Olafson said.

Tomas' eyebrows crinkled. Then he got it. "You brought up need-to-know. If we get the right superior officers, the men leading the teams don't need to know the higher purpose behind their orders. Their superiors could even hint that the orders are based on ConPol or GF intel. Orders to protect the targets from hostiles."

"Make the rank and file think we're loyal." Olafson turned professorial again. "Will that work?"

Tomas' shoulders slumped again. "Not to make the highest ranking arrests. I'll arrest the incumbent, but anyone else on our side, who might believe his order comes from on high, could stop believing if a cabinet official or general staff officer tells him otherwise."

"We'll need men of strong allegiance to our cause to make those arrests," Olafson said.

Tomas shut his eyes for a moment. From his memory, pages from the Daughters' dossiers appeared inside his eyelids. "I guarantee we can find them."

Olafson's ruddy face showed no response. "Say we can. Say we seize all our objectives at zero hour. What then?"

"We organize a transitional government." Tomas had thought through this. "With our control of mass communication, we tell everyone in Confederal City and throughout the Confederated Worlds we acted to remove treasonous forces from high levels of the government. We will oversee a transition back to an elected government after our work is done."

"What do we mean by remove?" Olafson arched his eyebrow like a question mark, then formed his hand into a pistol shape and bent his thumb.

Tomas shook his head. "A trial. With the Plan 827 document as Exhibit 1."

"You want to take the risk of an acquittal? Or even a conviction that spills our dirty laundry?"

As opposed to killing Forrester, leading to resistance by the bluecoats and revulsion from the general populace? "It's the least bad option, general."

Olafson's mouth pinched. "One document forensics expert with loyalty to the incumbent can throw up enough chaff to discredit the Plan 827 document."

Tomas straightened his back. "Are you letting your anger at the incumbent cloud your judgment?"

"Are you letting your year of working for him cloud yours?"

They stared at each other for a moment. Then Olafson rolled his wrist in a shrug. "We can table this till we've recruited the rest of the core team. Because if we don't get the right team, planning our victory parade is moot. Which gets us to our next agenda item."

"Deciding who to recruit."

Olafson leaned forward. He extended his index finger. "Burn this into your mind like a two hundred kilometer-per-hour serve. Every approach to a potential recruit exposes us to betrayal."

Tomas brought his glass closer to his face. The fizzing bubbles and mineral smell relaxed him slightly. "Yes, general."

"That's all you have to say? Loki's *skith*, this is a damned big problem."

An encrypted storage on his phone held hundreds of dossiers. "Perhaps not as big as you fear," Tomas said. "Go on."

"What happens when we start talking to a man about 'political reform' and he realizes we mean a coup? He'll decide our talk is one of three things. Maybe we're really a sting operation by ConPol or the bluecoats. Maybe we're idiots stumbling toward a firing squad. Or maybe we've got a viable shot at overthrowing the incumbent. In any of those cases, his most sensible response will be to report us to the regime."

Tomas frowned. "I understand the first two, but the third?"

"Yes, the first two are pretty obvious. Better a sure chance of even a slight reward than being almost certainly the defendant in a show trial for treason. But think about the third."

He sipped to buy time. "I'm thinking."

"How would he conclude we've got a viable shot at overthrowing the incumbent?" Olafson's face showed he knew the answer. "Because we would hint we have a huge number of personnel already on our side. So if he's shrewd enough for us to want to recruit him, he's shrewd enough to realize if he joins, he'd divide up the spoils of victory with a huge number of other people. Instead, if he reports us to the incumbent, many of his rivals for promotions will get implicated in the plot and court-martialed or forced into retirement, freeing him up for advancement."

"I hadn't thought of that." Tomas shook his head. "Though, general, you may overestimate most men's ability to think through all the consequences."

Olafson pressed his lips together. "It only takes one."

Tomas thought a moment. "So we limit our approaches to those personnel who would respond to pleas to patriotism... enough sense to avoid starting a war we're likely to lose...."

Olafson looked like he suddenly suffered heartburn.

"General?"

"Patriotism and sense. How many men like that can you find at GFB West McAuliffe, or in the white mountain?" Olafson emphasized his question with a stare, then poured himself another shot of aquavit.

"I found one." Tomas bowed his head at Olafson.

Olafson downed the shot, thudded the glass back to the tabletop. "My motives aren't as pure as that. Yes, what's best for the Confederated Worlds is for the incumbent to get his hands pried off the levers of power. But if he weren't an arrogant prick, I'll be honest, even with the document you showed me, I might not be here."

"So we play to self-interest. Or personal ties. Or both."

Olafson looked pleased. "By personal ties you mean friendship?"

"That's one avenue," Tomas said. "I know Academy grads tend to stick together, and those of us who came up through OCS do the same in response. But not the only avenue. We tend to like people like us, so having a common homeworld and professed religion would help. I know Midgarders like you are fairly prevalent in the officer corps—"

"—and our faith wins converts from Ground Force personnel native to other worlds." Olafson rubbed his chin and peered at Tomas. "What's your homeworld? Challenger?"

"Born on Sankt-Benedikts-Welt. Grew up on Joséphine. I'm not enough from either place to create a strong tie with someone from either world. My professed faith is Observer, which is little help either."

"That's a hell of an understatement, captain."

"Then we go back to self-interest," Tomas said. "We persuade the candidate his best interest lies in siding with us."

Olafson puffed out a breath. "You were right a moment ago.

Many potential candidates will only see the stars in their eyes. We can promise everyone an overnight promotion of three ranks, then renege after the transitional government takes power." He leaned forward, reached for the aquavit bottle, stopped short.

"And?"

Olafson slowly picked his next words. "Self-interest doesn't always come down to more money and rank. Every man has some emotional button you can press. Half the time, money and rank are only symbolic of the shot of emotional liquor a man really wants. We'll look for men nursing a grudge—passed over for a promotion, assigned to some miserable post, like that. Press their emotional buttons and they'll join the coup even if they get nothing out of it." Olafson poured a shot of aquavit, then glanced at Tomas. "You have second thoughts about that."

Tomas' face twisted. "I'd rather we didn't emotionally manipulate personnel to join us."

"Didn't you say you'd do whatever it took to overthrow the incumbent?"

A jolt of guilt struck Tomas. Then he laughed. "Touché. You're right. Playing those tricks runs counter to how I was raised and how I try to live my life, but it's necessary."

Olafson extended his index finger straight into the air. "But remember, some men may have been passed over for good reason."

Tomas frowned. "General?"

"Some men are bad leaders. Some men don't know how to play the political games required to get those promotions. Some men are too socially awkward for anyone to follow. We have to recruit influential leaders—they may not always hold high formal ranks—and rely on them to bring in everyone else." Olafson downed the shot of aquavit. "When it comes to the good men passed over for promotion, I'll make the initial approach."

"You think I fall short in some way?"

"If they were passed over in the last year, they're looking for someone to blame."

Tomas' mouth opened in a half-smile of realization. "And they'll blame an upstart who wormed his way into the incumbent's good graces. Have we laid enough groundwork? Time to name names."

"Let's start with the combat side," Olafson said. "To seal off Confederal City during the operation, we need at least part of the brigade stationed at GFB West McAuliffe."

Tomas mulled the situation. "The simplest candidate to get the brigade—to get every GF unit close enough to act—would be Echevarria."

Olafson's eyes narrowed. "Not Echevarria."

"If we could get him, we need no one else from the combat side."

"You saw how he turned on me in the meeting last week. Not him." Olafson shook his head. "We don't need him. We can get almost the same effect from one of the brigade staff officers. If brigade ops gives an order, battalion commanders will assume it's from Echevarria. All's good. Hell, one battalion might do, if it's in the right spot, ahead of any forces loyal to the incumbent. The loyalists would think twice before firing blue on blue. You were on a battalion staff out there, right? Would your old battalion commander, who was it, listen to you?"

"Lt. Col. Sokolov. Yes."

"Sokolov?" Olafson looked sour.

Tomas guessed at the source of Olafson's distaste. "He is cautious, if that's what worries you."

"Timid, more like. He might listen to you in the bright light of day, but could we rely on him to roll out of the barracks at zero hour?"

An intuition bubbled in Tomas. "I know what to say to make that answer yes." He rubbed his eyes. Awake later than usual of a night. "As for everyone else, I've gathered some information on all the key players at brigade," Tomas said. "I'll send it. Take a look, then we can make the decision."

Olafson grunted. Tomas swiped at his tablet and sent copies of the Daughters' dossiers to Olafson.

The next forty minutes passed in silence. Tomas reread the dossiers, with a new judgment acquired from Olafson's shrewdness. Men once plausible candidates Tomas now deleted from his list. He reread the Daughters' dossier on Echevarria. Relief trickled through him that he hadn't pushed harder for Echevarria. *Extremely ambitious. Extremely self-serving.*

At the end of the time, Lt. Col. Sokolov and Lt. Col. Quisenberry, the brigade's operations officer, remained at the head of his list.

When they compared notes, Olafson agreed. Tomas would make the first approach to Sokolov, then to Quisenberry.

"The brigade is just one of the formations we have to infiltrate or neutralize," Olafson said. "We need technicians to disable or subvert transportation and communication infrastructure, plus reliable men to make the arrests—"

On they went for hours, quietly reviewing the Daughters' dossiers on dozens of men, then engaging in bursts of debate regarding which to approach, and how to approach them. Maj. Hamilton, head of the military police detachment at GFB West McAuliffe, passed over for promotion. What about Rolston, now a major, on Echevarria's staff at the white mountain?

A friend, yes, but *wait you a minute.* "If you don't want Echevarria, don't pick Rolston," Tomas said. "They're both Endeavourites."

Olafson nodded. "Good eye. Endeavourites tend to stick together. Except if not him, who's our communications tech?"

Tomas remembered a name, though the spelling eluded him when he searched the Daughters' dossier. He tried a variant, then another before he found him. "Lt. Yeungling installed the comm control systems at the CC Telecom facility in Finziburg."

"A lieutenant?" Olafson scrolled through the dossiers on his tablet, then shook his head. "Loki's *skith*, he's even younger than you."

"You use the assets you have," Tomas said.

"Hmm." Olafson scowled at the tablet. "He might do. Make the approach…."

They continued for a time. At the end, with the tablets wiped and their phones encrypted, Tomas stood and stretched. His wristwatch showed almost midnight. Three hours of good progress made. "We have our candidates."

Olafson took a final shot of aquavit. He slammed the empty glass onto the tabletop. "The hard part will be contacting them."

"I thought the hard part would be getting the operation ready in three months."

A hardbitten grin, and Olafson clapped his hand on Tomas' shoulder. "Get out of here, get some sleep, and get back to your day job. We can meet here again?"

"Same time once a week."

Olafson departed out the adjoining door. Ten minutes later, a priestess led Tomas to the vestibule. The candle floating in the suspended bowl threw guttering light onto the ceiling and the upper paneling of the walls. The light of just-risen Epsilon Eridani, refracted through the sky and down the mycocrete canyons of the city, came through the windows and the revolving door. Outside, on the sidewalk at the foot of the steps, a bluecoat walked slowly toward a man in shabby civilian clothes with wide ears. The man hunched his shoulders away from the bluecoat and hurried up the stairs toward the vestibule.

Act the same. Tomas ducked his head and went out the revolving door. His feet pounded a quick staccato on the steps. He detoured slightly around the man with wide ears. From the corner of his eye, Tomas saw the man cast a quizzical look at him.

On the sidewalk below, the bluecoat stopped and panned his camera up and down Tomas' body, then settled on his face. Long enough to identify him. Which was what Tomas wanted. He pressed his lips together and whipped his head away, pretending to be a congregant of the Daughters embarrassed by being seen. Pretending to be what the bluecoat expected.

Even after the bluecoat passed, Tomas hid his emotions. Inside, though, confidence warmed his chest. He'd fooled the bluecoats this time. He'd fool them every time again.

Tomas entered the Sutherland Office and double-took. A conference table stood along one wall, between the portrait of Sutherland and the door to Forrester's private office. Unrolled sheets of smartpaper covered the tabletop, like layers of lava poured out by a hundred eruptions of a shield volcano. The bodies and limbs of three figures in service gray mostly blocked Tomas' view of the smartpaper sheets. Blotches of green, blue, brown, dotted with gray.

Maps, but of which world?

Tomas greeted the figures in service gray. Ground Force officers, three or more ranks above him. Two returned the greeting, then returned to discussing the mapped scenario in low voices.

The third, a Col. Levy, whose long nose gave him a patrician look and whose accent suggested an origin on Shambhala, said, "Captain, where's the President?"

"I don't know his schedule, sir. I only received last minute notice of this meeting myself." At least the meeting would occupy Tomas' attention. Better than staring at the walls of his office and rehearse for the twentieth time his upcoming approaches to Sokolov and Quisenberry.

"He's ten minutes late."

Sokolov?—No, the colonel talked about Forrester. Tomas turned up his palms. "Most likely, his prior meeting ran over."

Nearby, the door from the president's private office creaked. Forrester came through and palmed the door shut behind him. His hazel eyes remained intense, but with a smolder, not a burn. Purplish bags slumped under his eyes. Already he'd fit multiple late nights into his schedule, and many more to come before the war would start.

Tomas studied his face. He did not hate Forrester. *Dragged by the PRs to the skills imp stations, to be turned into the thing he most hated.* Pity and indignation stirred in Tomas, uselessly. The emotions' charge could not go to ground. The pity and indignation could be felt, but not acted on.

A victim like a plague carrier, requiring quarantine through no fault of his own.

Forrester paid no attention to Tomas. He turned to one of the Ground Force officers, a three-star from Midgard. "Show me your plan."

The three-star spoke with a pompous voice. "As you can see from the map, Mr. President, Papa has three regiments on Navi Ambarsar. All based near NA city." The three-star tapped a squat finger three times on the uppermost sheet of smartpaper. "We will land—"

"A moment." Forrester looked at Tomas as if he'd just noticed him. "Captain, step closer. I want you to take a look."

"Captain?" The three-star's voice held a note of disbelief.

"He's ridden in a Badger, top and bottom," Forrester said. "Have you?"

Col. Levy and the other senior officer, a two-star, grudgingly made space for Tomas. The three-star ignored him and spoke to Forrester. "Getting back to business, we will land our four brigades around the city and tighten the noose. The PRs can't block all our units. Space Force will have orbital supremacy and provide fire support to the brigade with the clearest path to NA city. A simple plan, but certain to work."

Forrester ran the backs of his fingers along his jaw, then his hazel eyes scowled at the map. "Our brigades and PR regiments have roughly equal strength. Yes or no."

"Yes," the three-star said. His voice leaked annoyance at such a basic question.

"One brigade advances," Forrester said, "while the other three fight at even odds. Against an enemy who knows the terrain and has planned a defense to use it."

Tomas' practiced gaze surveyed the map. Rolling hills covered with decades-old forests surrounded Navi Ambarsar city on three sides, with the wide Bhagatbani River on the fourth. *Give me five years in that terrain and I could prepare a defense against eight brigades, not four...*

"Their purpose is to fix PR units so they can't plug the hole the fourth brigade will pour through," the three-star said.

Forrester scowled. He flung his hand over the forested hills. "Looks like difficult terrain for Graywolfs and Badgers." He aimed his gaze at the river. "And can our fighting vehicles swim?"

"Mr. President, we will have the advantage of numbers—"

"Bah. This plan is shit."

Col. Levy crossed his arms. The three-star gave Forrester an acid look. "You won't come up with a better one."

Forrester loomed over the three-star. "I won't? You're right, I won't. Captain Neumann will."

Tomas' breath caught. Plan an operation? For a war that should never start? For a commander-in-chief he had to unseat from power?

"Are five minutes enough, captain?" Forrester's face exuded confidence, just as he had a hundred times before. More pity touched Tomas. Though a PR pawn in the greater game, Forrester truly sought what he believed was best for the Confederated Worlds.

Like a switch closed inside Tomas' subconscious, he decided. "Yes." He stepped closer to the map and the higher ranks yielded him room.

Navi Ambarsar resembled most recently terraformed worlds. The capital city held the space elevator, spaceport for fusion-powered surface-to-orbit ships, or both, along with most of the planet's people. Smaller towns dotted a map circle centered on the capital city, and terraforming facilities, where plant and animal techs raised and released the creatures of self-sustaining ecosystems, defined the circle's circumference.

On Navi Ambarsar, an ellipse replaced the usual circle. The ellipse's long axis, and the highest density of towns, ran along the Bhagatbani River. The thickest concentration of terraforming facilities came at the mouth of the river, where it emptied into the planet's vast northern ocean.

Tomas turned to the three-star. "How many units can we land at one time?"

The three-star pretended not to hear. "Six battalions," Col. Levy said.

"Two brigades," Tomas said to Forrester. He returned his attention to the map. A wooded, hilly plateau about a third of the way from NA city to the river mouth.... "I've got it."

"This'll be rich," the three-star muttered.

"We land two brigades near the mouth of the river. They advance toward NA city, capturing PR officials as they go. The PRs will send a force to stop them. The enemy force will travel at night and under maximum concealment to minimize detection by Space Force in orbit."

He pointed to the wooded, hilly plateau. "After the PR force passes this plateau, we'll land the other two brigades between the plateau and NA city. Those two brigades will occupy the plateau. The PR force will be trapped between the first two brigades, the second two brigades, and the river. Our four brigades will neutralize it, then turn against the weakened defenses of NA city."

The three-star harrumphed. Col. Levy angled his head and looked thoughtful.

Forrester's deep voice filled the room. "A superb plan."

"Thank you, Mr. President." Tomas kept his voice low-key. Superb? Who knew. Serviceable off the top of his head, at least.

Serviceable, but were it put into action, it would be mooted if Space Force lost orbital supremacy to the PR fleet. Better to file it away for some future year, after the Unity switched allegiances and the PRs gave the Confederated Worlds a *casus belli*.

"Don't try to hide in the woodwork, captain. You've proposed the better plan I've seen today. General, general, colonel, take his plan and make it work."

The three-star's mouth tightened. He inhaled through flared nostrils, then looked to calm himself through an act of will. "Roger, Mr. President."

Forrester jutted his finger toward the three-star's face. "His plan is better because Captain Neumann is a better man than the lot of you. He saved my life. He has unquestionable love for the Confederated Worlds. Remember that. Meeting adjourned."

The three-star and the others tromped out of the room. Tomas stood still despite his wobbly legs. *Imagine if Forrester only knew—*

The president would find out the truth soon enough.

Forrester turned his body toward his private office, then glanced back with surprise. "Neumann, you're dismissed too. Keep up the good work."

Guilt needled him through the chest. Tomas fought against the guilt, pushing back his shoulders and pushing out his chest. "I'll do my best, Mr. President."

14

Recruiting

Tomas' words to Forrester echoed in his mind as he traveled westward under the capital cities to the subway stop outside GFB West McAuliffe. Epsilon Eridani had just risen, lighting up the hours of early evening. The star cast a long shadow of the security cabin at the main gate.

At this hour, Lissa fed the boys in their small home in the junior officer's tract of base housing. He could have dinner with his family for the first time in weeks. Just go in the main gate, turn right, then five hundred meters down cypress-lined streets.

The gate guard waved a telemetry wand over his chest to pick up data from his shilling, then matched the telemetry with the output of retina and fingerprint scanners. "Thank you, sir."

Tomas went through the pedestrian turnstile gate and sloughed out a breath. He went a block past the turn for his house, then headed to the left, into senior officer country.

Half a block from Lt. Col. Sokolov's house, Tomas paused on the sidewalk and sent Sokolov a follow-up message. *Are you still available for a discussion? I'm near your house.*

Moments later, the reply came. *Meet me in the garage.*

Sokolov's house rambled across a wide lot. A driveway ran along one side, between the house and a tall fence of engineered wood. Tomas followed the driveway, through the shade of the fence. The house's mycocrete wall muffled the sound of a piano and two female voices, one girlish and plaintive, the other maternal and gruff.

The garage's open door showed two vehicles, a family sedan and a tall utility with a thick tow hitch. Sokolov, clad in civilian cargo pants and a loose, striped shirt, leaned on the utility's back bumper. He rattled ice cubes in a short, wide glass containing two fingers of brown liquor.

He nodded in greeting to Tomas. "My best staff officer, returned from the XM. Get yourself a drink." He hooked his thumb toward a back corner of the garage. "Then tell me what's going on."

A minute later, with a glass of sparkling water in his hand, Tomas pitched the coup to Lt. Col. Sokolov.

He didn't use the word *coup* at first. He didn't even use Olafson's euphemism, *political reform*. "What sort of r-mail are you hearing about possible future operations?"

Sokolov's eyes widened, jutting his bushy eyebrows toward his high hairline. He stared at his house for a moment. The piano's distant tinkle trickled to them, indicating his wife and daughter remained out of earshot. Sokolov then craned his neck to look down the driveway and toward his neighbor's fence. "There are some big rumors," he murmured. "Working at the XM, you might know if—"

Tomas nodded solemnly.

Sokolov lowered his voice even further. "The president is going to start a war?"

Tomas nodded once more.

"What are our chances?" Sokolov's face showed he expected the worst.

Tomas drew a constricted breath. "Poor. Most intel indicates the PRs and Unis are too well-prepared. The president found one piece of evidence to the contrary and clings to it."

"No one's tried to persuade him to stand down?"

"I tried. I couldn't succeed. No one could succeed." Tomas leaned closer. "If you can keep a secret, sir, I can show you why."

One could rely on some men, if asked to keep a secret, to spill it at any and every opportunity. Not Sokolov. Whatever Sokolov's other flaws, Tomas believed his next words. "I give you my word." Sokolov nodded firmly enough to sway his pendulous earlobes.

Tomas pulled out his phone and opened up the Plan 827 document. He sat quietly on the narrow and rigid bumper, sipping sparkling water and ignoring the growing ache in his backside, while Sokolov read. Let the candidate convince himself Forrester had to be removed from office.

Five minutes later, Sokolov handed back the phone and scowled. "Something has to be done."

"That's why I came to you, sir."

Sokolov didn't seem to hear. "Take this document to someone in Congress. There must be a party immune to bluecoat intimidation."

"There probably is, sir. But it won't have enough votes to impeach the incumbent." The ache in Tomas' backside gave him an excuse to stand. "He must be removed from office another way."

Sokolov's bushy eyebrows jumped toward his high hairline. Realization formed on his face. "What you're saying... we could all get shot."

He said *we*. Tomas relaxed slightly. Sokolov sympathized with the cause. Yet sympathy meant nothing unless it led to action.

Tomas nodded to himself, then set up a rehearsed lie. "If he remains in office, we enter a war we cannot win. And our current postings here on Challenger won't shield us. He's expressed concern about First Brigade. We're the last line of defense. That's an awesome responsibility."

"One we've earned." The tone of Sokolov's voice showed he tried to convince himself he could ride out a war in safety here on Challenger.

"My thought too. But he's concerned we, I mean, brigade and all the battalion headquarters personnel, haven't proven ourselves. I've told him otherwise but I can tell he's not convinced." Tomas paused to make the lie even more potent. "He's going to rotate us all out to Navi Ambarsar or New Liberty after the war starts, to get that combat experience."

Sokolov lifted his glass toward his mouth. The ice cubes clinked against the glass. He took a swallow, then with the back of his hand nudged a dribble of liquor from the corner of his mouth.

Tomas looked away. The Daughters' dossier clarified an assessment Tomas had long held. Sokolov feared defeat. Not because he feared wounds or death, even though a battalion HQ could fall under the guns of enemy fighting vehicles breaking through. Instead, Sokolov feared being proven unworthy of command. He feared shame.

Tomas could give Sokolov Lissa's business card after they removed Forrester from office. For now, he would exploit Sokolov's weaknesses for the greater good, and swallow his qualms about doing so.

After several ragged breaths, Sokolov asked, "What would I need to do?"

"Not much. When you get the signal, set up roadblocks on the Confederal City sides of the Lake Freedom bridges and on the main thoroughfares in from Confederal City Heights and Finziburg. No one is to pass the roadblocks until you receive the all-clear. That's it."

"That's it?"

"Your role, like everyone else's, will be safe."

Sokolov stared at the ice cubes at the bottom of his nearly empty glass. "What comes after?"

Tomas said, "We remove from office persons compromised by—" He lifted his phone to signify the Plan 827 document. "Then we oversee free and fair elections."

From the house came the muffled slam of piano keys and harsh female argument. Sokolov showed no sign of noticing, and instead continued staring into his glass. A cool dark nugget congealed in Tomas' gut. Had he misjudged Sokolov? The Daughters had misread him?

Sokolov looked up. His face showed an expression of commitment. The congealed nugget melted even before Sokolov said, "Count me in."

* * *

Tomas' next approach came the following morning, to Lt. Col. Quisenberry, the brigade's operations officer. Before the 0700 dawn that most Challengerites considered the start of the day, Tomas pulled on running shoes. He went to the base's main rec field, stepped onto the gritted track ringing it. The banks of lights illuminated a solitary figure jogging around the track's far curve.

It should be an easy pitch. If Quisenberry joined the coup, he would only need to order the battalion commanders other than Sokolov to stay in their barracks. His role would be even safer than Sokolov's. If the coup failed, Quisenberry could easily feign ignorance, confusion, or fear had led him to keep the brigade out of action.

The Daughters' dossier on Quisenberry showed a man of deep conviction. A check of his Ground Force Academy record showed a philosophy major from New Zion—the Mormon planet of that name, not the Jewish one—whose classmates were now brigadiers, king pogeys working in the white mountain, or recent retirees in upper management for companies or government agencies. Did Quisenberry resent being passed over on the promotion chain? Or did he view his more successful classmates with pity or contempt, for pursuing the brass ring over dedication to truth?

Tomas finished stretching. The solitary figure came closer. Small, widely-separated eyes and a wide mustache confirmed it was Quisenberry. Tomas jogged onto the track and fell into formation next to him.

It took a lap for Tomas to learn Quisenberry knew the rumors about the push for war. Quisenberry pulled off the track to read the Plan 827 document. At first, he absently mopped sweat from his eyebrows and chin, but then seemed to completely forget the towel in his hands. His gaze roved like a scanning machine over the text. A nauseated expression gripped his mouth and throat.

Tomas exhaled as if he caught his breath from the lap. *He's disgusted the PRs did this. That's what we want.*

Quisenberry ducked his head and rested one hand on his knee. He gulped a few breaths, then straightened up. "That's horrifying. If it's true."

"It's true," Tomas said. His voice dropped at the end of the last word.

"You've checked everything? Your source for this document, the content, everything?" The sickened look returned to Quisenberry's face.

"I have." Tomas filled his voice with maximal confidence. "My source was in position to acquire it. The content fits the PR intelligence service's style sheet. And it fits with my direct observations of the incumbent."

"Does it? You're certain? At first read, it does look like captured PR data I read during the war." Quisenberry rested his hand on his chest and his face tightened with nausea. "But you have to be certain. For what it would take to correct the problem, you would have to be certain." He snapped his gaze to Tomas' face. "You want my help to correct the problem, don't you?"

"Yes."

Quisenberry winced. His head shook from side to side. "I need a copy. A few days to verify it. Then I could join you. But not unless I prove beyond any doubt this is genuine."

Tomas gritted his teeth. If Quisenberry were sloppy, and copies of Plan 827 circulated, ConPol might find out. A chain of brain scans could lead them back to Quisenberry, then to Tomas, and unravel everything.

"You can do that completely by yourself?"

"I worked in intelligence during the war. I know what to look for. And how to maintain operational security."

And if any other candidate had doubts about Plan 827's veracity, Quisenberry's work would banish those doubts.

"I'll give you a copy," Tomas said.

Quisenberry looked relieved.

Five seconds with their phones completed the transfer. Five minutes later, Tomas and Quisenberry left the track. They headed in opposite directions, Tomas walking toward the sky paling in the east. His spirit rose with the dawning star. Success. With key personnel joining them, and nearly three months to plan, they were certain to remove Forrester in time.

15

Change of Plans

Tomas spent the next two months navigating his double life. Days, evenings, and weekends in the Executive Mansion, going between his cramped basement office and the cockpit, Forrester's private study off the Sutherland Office, to help the president prepare for the war he conspired to prevent.

Oneday nights, he found excuses to leave the XM, and met with Olafson, Sokolov, Quisenberry, and the others at the Daughters' temple, to plot Forrester's overthrow. Much to do and few men to do it. When they crossed one item off the checklist, two more appeared.

Few men, and none of them perfect. They kept their flaws: Sokolov fretted about the risks, and occasional doubts about the Plan 827 document's authenticity slipped out of Quisenberry's mouth. But all men had fears and doubts when in their foxholes waiting for H-hour. Even Tomas felt those doubts, riding on the subway around civilians cocooned by their smartglasses and earbuds. One slip-up and he would end up dead or in prison, his boys as fatherless as he had been—

There's an easy solution. Don't slip up.

One Fourday evening around 2120, as a rising Epsilon Eridani's illumination reached all the way to the western sky, Forrester and the chiefs of staff stood at the conference table in the Sutherland Office. Bar-Yuek's voice droned from one piece of Space Force jargon to the next. Behind them, Tomas rubbed his bleary eyes and yawned.

Forrester glanced over his shoulder. "Head in the game, Neumann."

Tomas straightened his back, widened his eyes. "Sorry, Mr. President. Didn't sleep well last night."

An arched eyebrow heightened Forrester's amused expression. "A late night, ah, religious ritual?"

Tomas' breath caught. Forrester knew about his Oneday visits to the Daughters. The president assumed them to be what they appeared. Giddiness bloomed in Tomas' belly. He stifled the emotion with a dour head shake. "Lissa nagged me for working so late these weeks."

Forrester chuckled. "You make me even more glad I've never married." He turned back to Bar-Yuek. "To confirm, the armed relief force is ready to trip the wire?"

"Yes, Mr. President."

"Their backup is fully deployed to Nuova Toscano system?"

"Not fully. Elements of the strike force are still en route. They should arrive within a week. The complete strike force will conduct final drills and finish preparations."

Forrester looked thoughtful. "So they will be a month ahead of schedule."

"That's right."

Forrester turned to Ground Force's new chief of staff. "What about the liberation force's readiness?"

"The first two brigades are on station above Nuova Toscano. The next two brigades are shipping in. Expected arrival tomorrow. Like the Space Force elements, they'll need some time to plan and train."

"How much time is 'some?'" Forrester's voice made the new chief of staff shrink. "Five days? Or a whole damn month?"

"Fi-five, give or take."

Forrester looked serene. "In sum, everything is ahead of schedule. We'll be ready ahead of the target date, and every day we wait makes our enemies another day stronger. We're going to move the start of the operation up a month."

Tomas' breath caught. The plotters already lagged the initial preparation schedule. Chopping a month of the schedule meant they must accelerate. But how? The schedule had so little slack....

The Ground Force chief of staff tapped his lower teeth with his thumbnail. "The first four brigades will be ready, but their replacements won't be. We can't keep the four brigades in combat forever. They will need to be rotated off the front line after, at most, two months. I can't guarantee their replacements will be ready."

Forrester glowered.

Tomas saw a chance. "What have you been doing all this time, general? There's a continuing flow of conscripts into the system and up the space elevator to the intake station." If he compounded the chief of staff's pragmatic hesitation with anger at a mere captain questioning his leadership, the chief of staff might dig in his heels, even against Forrester's powers of compulsion.

The Ground Force chief of staff narrowed his eyes to firing slits. "Captain, just because you went through basic doesn't make you an expert on the logistics of new recruit intake and training. I don't want to just win the first battles on Navi Ambarsar. I also want to win the whole damn war."

Forrester's voice contained an edge of steel. "Space Force will win the war."

The Ground Force chief of staff shot Tomas a cold look, then faced Forrester. "Mr. President, no disrespect to Gen. Bar-Yuek, but if we're going to carry the war to PR space, we'll need Ground Force to land on those PR planets and eliminate opposition."

"If you can't pacify the planets we'll conquer," Forrester said in an offhand tone, "Space Force can. It's simple. We demand the local population send PR officials up the space elevator, or else we destroy civilian targets from orbit."

Bar-Yuek's eyes flashed. A moment later he dropped his gaze to the tabletop.

Tomas, too, looked away. *Destroy civilian targets? One of the atrocities of ancient warfare, left behind in the petroleum age—*

An atrocity to fuel the PR's propaganda machine. The steel of Tomas' resolve hardened. Yet another reason he had to overthrow

Forrester.

The Ground Force chief of staff shook his head. "Mr. President, you'll need boots on the ground—"

"I won't. Space Force intelligence officers will brain scan every PR official sent up. From that information, we put together the local PR org chart. Too many holes in the chart, and we bomb civilian targets."

Silence reigned through the room. The Ground Force chief of staff finally spoke. "Is destroying civilian targets from orbit a precedent we wish to set, Mr. President?"

"If those civilian populations don't turn over PR officials when they see only our ships in orbit, then they are as active an enemy as any uniformed PR." Forrester jutted out his chest. He set his hands on his hips and held his elbows wide. "Either you pacify PR planets, or Bar-Yuek will. Your choice." Forrester stood even taller. "Either way, the tripwire fleet will launch next Fiveday. One week from tomorrow."

The meeting ended. Tomas found himself in his office without any memory of going down two flights of stairs. The familiarity of his office gave him enough comfort to breathe.

A week? Part of him wanted to cry out. Another breath and he let the useless wish evaporate.

We'll do what we must. Within a week.

He spent the next hours thinking. Contact Olafson and the others after he left the XM, to schedule an emergency meeting at the Daughters' temple? And risk detection? Would a few extra days cross off enough necessary tasks to justify the risk?

Tomas' gut knotted. They hadn't figured out how to neutralize the capital cities police, or Restoration Party security. Or ConPol, but ConPol did investigations and intelligence, not armed action. ConPol's reaction time was slow enough to ignore. And police wouldn't climb out of their squad cars to face armored grenadiers backed by Badgers and Graywolfs.

The bluecoats watching the Daughters' temple might investigate further if they noticed him changing his schedule. Might notice Olafson and the others had appeared in public near the temple the same time as Tomas for months. He would break the news to them on Oneday.

After that resolution, he returned his attention to his work. Reviews of Ground Force readiness metrics. A dinner of leftover sandwiches catered in for a lunch meeting. Analysis of hardware modifications proposed for the next generation of Badgers. He shook his head. *A tank's a tank and an IFV is an IFV, the designers should stop trying to turn an IFV into a tank....*

He left the Executive Mansion grounds a few minutes before 2500. Darkness had come again. No pedestrians plied Challenger Boulevard at this hour. He plodded toward the subway station, dogged by worry. Only a few cars passed with the whisper of tires on dry pavement.

A long black sedan, tinted windows glossing the light of bioluminescent cypresses, pulled up to the curb in front of him. Three doors opened. Men in dark suits and mirrored videoglasses climbed out. Faces grim, they started toward Tomas.

Gooseflesh crawled over his face. He stopped walking and shifted his weight toward his heels. Behind him squeaked the brakes of another car. His eyes widened. A glance over his shoulder. Another black sedan. Out climbed three more men. All dressed like ConPol.

Down his torso swept a wave of calm. He widened his stance, bent his knees, shifted his weight forward. He gave the men approaching him from the front a look of bemused confidence. *I'd be glad to cooperate, but do you realize who I am?*

One pulled a ConPol badge from an inner pocket of his suit jacket. "Tomas Neumann, captain, Ground Force?"

"Yes."

"Come with us."

"What's this about?"

"Come with us."

An innocent man would protest. "Go with you? For what?"

"Under Confederal law, I'm not free to answer those questions. Please come with us."

Then threaten. "I work directly for President Forrester."

"We're aware of that, Capt. Neumann." The mirrored video-glasses obscured the ConPol agent's expression. What did they know? Tomas tightened his core muscles against a spike of panic.

The ConPol agent said, "Please come with us."

Behind Tomas, one ConPol agent shifted his weight. Another inhaled slowly and loudly. The ConPol agents would take him away, willingly or not.

He shrugged. The other two ConPol agents from the front car took positions at his shoulders. Their leader went to the front passenger door. "You'll sit between us," one of the other ConPol agents said.

Moments later, the car pulled away from the curb. Tomas sat in the middle of the rear seat. His feet on the drivetrain hump pushed his knees toward his chest. The ConPol agents crowded him with bulky arms and thick cologne.

The spike of panic turned cold, like an iced blade through his gut.

They knew about the coup.

His stomach soured. His throat burned. With each breath, a constricting band seemed to ratchet tighter around his chest. How did ConPol find out? Betrayal by one of his fellow plotters? Even if all of them remained committed to Forrester's overthrow, a single careless action could leave enough thread for ConPol to unravel the entire plot.

The cold spike melted, and seeped through his abdomen. There would be no trial. Publicizing a half-dozen prominent officers plotting a coup would lead the public to wonder. *Wouldn't military men be in favor of war? What did they know we don't?* Forrester could not risk such thoughts arising in two hundred million minds.

Decades in a prison? Or a bullet to the back of the head? Either way, Tomas would disappear.

Lissa would never understand what he had done. She would go to her grave hating him.

The boys wouldn't even be able to do that. They would have longings in their souls they couldn't even perceive. The same longings he had felt without a father—

Tomas lost track of their route. The car entered a commercial district. The bioluminescent cypresses colored the pavement pallid blue, like the flesh of drowned men. They turned into an alley between a handcrafter's bakery—imagine, people paying triple price for something available from the municipal fab—

Good job. Fill your mind with garbage thoughts. You can survive this.

Fear hollowed out his gut. Thinking about surviving argued he wouldn't. How else can you spoof a brain scanner?

—and a Feldenkrais parkour studio. A glimpse past the ConPol agent on that side showed high padded obstacles inside the studio's darkened windows.

Moments later, the car entered a parking garage. Plain mycocrete, slender nanotube alloy pillars vertically striped with pulsing light strips. Empty. No witnesses. They wound their way to a gray alloy garage door. It rolled up as they approached. Tomas counted the articulated slats. Twelve. There were twelve. Those twelve slats were the most important fact in the settled galaxy....

They drove in, followed by the trailing car. The two cars pulled up near a metal door with a small, thick window. The engines' whisper cut out. Behind them, the garage door clattered to the cold mycocrete.

The agents flanking Tomas forced him out of the car under the watchful gaze of the lead agent. At the metal door, the lead agent showed his badge and his retina to someone on the other side of the window. "I have Capt. Neumann," he said.

A buzz sounded near the doorknob. The agents hustled Tomas down stark corridors of plain mycocrete. With every step the cold feeling seeped further down his legs. Never again to breathe fresh air, to warm his skin in sunlight... to hold Lissa's hand....

The lead agent showed him into a small room, and took up a blocking position inside the door. Two people and a large chair surmounted by a helmet crowded the space. One of the two people, a black-haired woman with videoglasses pushed up over her hairline, perched on a stool next to the large chair and checked something on the large chair's side. A control panel, presumably.

Tomas' throat tightened. In OCS, the lectures about brain scanning focused on technical tricks for interrogating prisoners in the field. If you interrogated a prisoner before he could timely take a lethe potion, his brain would give you truthful answers regardless how his voice answered your questions. One lecture discussed ways to try defeating a brain scan if you couldn't take a lethe potion. *White elephants, think of an elephant, what was it?*

One lecture, followed by a test that every officer candidate failed....

One breath pushed back the panic. Somehow, his subconscious mind dragged a checklist out of his memory. *The first way to defeat a brain scan? Don't get scanned.*

The other person came forward from a shadowed corner. Short, stout, craggy face. Tomas glanced at the ConPol ID card hanging from the front pocket of his suit jacket before speaking. "What's this about, Assistant Director MacAdams? None of your people have told me."

MacAdams put his hands on his hips and pointed his elbows away from his body. He rocked up on the balls of his feet. "Because I told them not to. We've caught a whiff of serious malfeasance going on among high ranks of the military. We want to see what you might have heard about."

Tomas blinked in mock surprise. "I haven't heard of anything, but I'll answer your questions." He looked around at the bare mycocrete walls, dark gray outside the narrow cones of harsh white light provided by the ceiling's recessed lamps. Shadows obscured whatever expression might be on the face of the ConPol agent at the door. "Perhaps we could start someplace more comfortable?"

MacAdams shrugged. "Even if we started somewhere else, we'd end up down here anyway. No matter someone's innocence or guilt, I can only get the truth here. Nothing personal, captain. I'd start here with any Ground Force personnel, from a private freshly poured out of the skills imp tank, all the way to, say, a former chief of the General Staff." MacAdams gave Tomas a flat stare. He then gestured at the brain scanner. "The technician will give you instructions."

The black-haired woman swung up the scanner helmet by its

mounting arm. "Sit, captain. Breathe deeply."

The cold spike in his gut reformed, then twisted. Tomas' limbs seemed to carry him of their own will to the scanner. He screamed inside.

A thin breath leveled off the panic. The checklist, the next item, what was it? *Fill your mind with chaff.* The OCS lecturer had talked about nonsense phrases, and now one heard years ago floated back into Tomas' consciousness. Hazy and indistinct, how did it go, *sense her said the censor?*

The scanner chair seemed to tug at him with a heightened gravity, to make him drop into the seat. Instead, he lowered himself. A bluff pose, but his next inhalation barely swelled his chest. *Maybe they'll see your agitation as simply nerves at being brain scanned.*

Another part of him answered. *Hope is not a planning factor.*

The technician swung the scanner helmet back into position, then receded behind the seat's thick curved siderest. A note of honeysuckle perfume lingered in his nose. A hum in the helmet echoed around his head. The brain activity pickups drew power.

Though quiet, the sound seemed to pierce his skull. His face froze. He needed chaff. Any thought to spoof the scanner.

Tomas' mind spun up two lines of elephants receding into the distance. Males and females, fifty clones of each, all pale as milk. The male and female at the head of the line stepped closer and bowed to each other with flourishes of trunk and ears. They danced a branle, steps Tomas half remembered from a ball during a Harvest Fête on Joséphine nearly a decade before. His next inhalation reached deeper into his belly.

Seated on a stool, MacAdams rolled closer. The stool's motor hummed and its wheels squeaked on the mycocrete floor. MacAdams stopped in front of Tomas, under one of the stark spotlights. The light from above deepened the shadows of his wrinkles.

"Your name?" MacAdams asked.

In his vision, MacAdams' face seemed to detach from his shadowed body and float toward him across the darkened space. "Tomas Neumann."

Side by side, the male and female elephant faced the same direction and mirrored each other's movements. Quick steps apart, then together, then a forward kick of each front leg in rapid succession....

"Planet of birth?"

"Sankt-Benedikts-Welt."

"Planet of residence as of your 18th standard birthday?"

The male elephant now wore a white tunic and pants under a rich blue jacket. The female wore an ankle-length gown. "Joséphine.
"

"Any other worlds you lived on before you turned 18?" MacAdams' voice droned.

"Nueva Andalucia, I'm told. My mother took me to Joséphine by age five." Wait, why say so much? And which step of the branle came next?

MacAdams showed no surprise at hearing Tomas had lived on a Unity world in his early childhood. "When you enlisted in Ground Force, where did you undergo initial skills implantation and occupation assignment?"

"GFB Challenger Orbital Station 1." The elephants shuffled their feet, the proper steps forgotten. The male looked like Napoléon, the ancient man, not the gas giant around which Joséphine orbited. His legitimate heir could still come and claim the empty throne in the palace in Couronnement, the planet's capital.

Legitimate government—

MacAdams continued with innocuous questions about his enlistment and service. Route of travel from Joséphine to the facility orbiting Challenger at the top of the space elevator. Formations served in and locations deployed to during the war. The male elephant could come to Couronnement and claim the throne and all *joséphinais* would shout *vive l'empereur*....

After a wheezy breath, MacAdams said, "Tell me about Plan 827."

It's—A burst of sweat stuck Tomas' shirt to the small of his back. "Plan what?"

"Plan 827."

"I've never heard of a GF operation by such a code name." Echoed by the scanner helmet, his voice struck his ears false.

Still out of Tomas' sight, the technician's fingers clacked on control keys. MacAdams sniffed in a breath and looked her way. Her fingers stopped and she murmured something.

MacAdams guided his stool toward the control panel. Tomas watched him go out of sight, blocked by the siderest of the chair. He breathed in to quash tendrils of cold creeping up the inside of his chest. *I gave a truthful statement, that can't be enough to arrest me!*

Tomas glanced about, craving some clue to his fate. The ConPol agent near the door remained in the shadows. Expression unreadable.

Quiet words, inaudible over the hum of the helmet. The technician's tone revealed puzzlement. MacAdams' firm tone answered her.

Wheels squeaked with motion. The technician rolled into view. She stopped in front of Tomas and turned to him. Atop her head, her videoglasses dazzled in the spotlights. Her gaze, still bearing traces of puzzlement, turned to Tomas. "Assistant Director MacAdams has asked me to ask some further questions."

From out of sight to Tomas's left, MacAdams' wheezy breath emphasized her words.

A moment later, MacAdams' fingers tapped out a long string of keys on the control panel. What could that mean?

The technician crossed her legs and nested her fingers around her top knee. She glanced in MacAdams' direction. "Sir, I have experience with this scanner model—"

"Quite alright, I'll take care of it. Need to keep current on the equipment." A pause, then MacAdams' fingers clacked another long string. "Ready to proceed, miss."

She pulled her videoglasses down over her eyes, then squinted at something only she could see. To Tomas, she asked, "Do you know or suspect one or more Ground Force officers have met secretly with foreign agents in the last few months?"

His chest felt buoyant. In his mind's eye, the elephants interrupted their branle to lean together and entwine their trunks. ConPol suspected espionage, not a coup. "No."

"Capt. Neumann, have you met Maj. Rodrigo Aranjuez, Unity

Army, currently posted as a military attaché to their embassy?"

Tomas frowned. It took a moment to remember the truth, a moment more to construct a lie. "I have. Once. A diplomatic meeting, shortly after the president's inauguration."

His next inhalation went a little deeper. Could he spin ambiguous brain scanner results as an effort to conceal classified information from people of unknown security status? If he could, he might walk out of this room a free man.

MacAdams' fingers typed more. The technician read something in her videoglasses. "To confirm, you met Maj. Aranjuez once during the president's term of office. This is correct?"

He lifted his chin and looked for her eyes through the videoglasses. The lead elephants bowed to one another and circled to the back of their respective lines. "Correct."

She read the next question from her videoglasses. "How would you rate Pres. Forrester's efforts in defending the Confederated Worlds against Progressive Republic aggression?"

Tomas blinked. ConPol didn't know Forrester's plan to trigger war. He could not say it aloud. "Pres. Forrester is doing an excellent job."

"If the Progressive Republic started a war in the coming months, would we win?"

"Yes."

The technician looked at the next text in her videoglasses. Her cheekbones became shields and her eyes, narrow loopholes. She glanced toward MacAdams in his hidden position at the control panel. MacAdams' only sound remained the steady noise of his breath, slightly louder and more wheezy than a moment earlier.

She took a breath and made her voice more calm. She peered at Tomas. "Are you aware of any military personnel contemplating extralegal regime change against Pres. Forrester?"

Tomas's face felt like a hollow shell. All the blood inside seemed to drain. He put on a shocked look. "What? Extralegal regime change? You mean a coup? I can't imagine it. No. No." Tomas shook his head. "If I had even a hint someone thought about a coup, I would tell you."

Out of sight to Tomas' left, MacAdams' breath sounded heavier, and the control panel keys clacked loudly for long seconds. Tomas let out a breath. *Capt. Neumann, sorry for the inconvenience, we'll drive you to the nearest subway station—*

The control panel whirred, the sound of an ejecting data stick. Stool casters squeaked on mycocrete. MacAdams stepped into view. His hand fondled a small object in a front pocket of his suit jacket. He said to the technician, "We have enough information from Capt. Neumann." MacAdams pulled his now-empty hand from his pocket. "Power down the machine while the agent and I take Capt. Neumann upstairs."

The technician came toward Tomas and lifted the helmet off his head. Her honeysuckle perfume touched his nose. His heart ached. To recline with Lissa's soft curves against him, just for a moment.... Never again.

The technician went to the control panel. MacAdams cracked his knuckles and scowled at Tomas. The lead agent emerged from the shadows. "Follow the assistant director," he said.

MacAdams went to the door, swiped a touchscreen on the wall next to the frame. The door opened. The glow of the hallway seen around MacAdams' silhouette seemed harsh, like a mortician's worklight.

"I said, follow the assistant director."

Tomas trudged out of the room on tired legs.

MacAdams ahead and the lead agent behind, Tomas went through the hallways to an elevator. The doors parted. MacAdams went first. The lead agent's presence behind Tomas herded him in. The door slid shut and the elevator rose.

Tomas tried to swallow. The motion seemed to pry open his throat. What waited for him a level above? A holding cell? A loading dock for transport elsewhere? An execution chamber with remote control acid sprayers and drains in the floor?

Bing. Tomas started. The elevator climbed past the first level above. Bing. Bing.

Maybe the roof. A waiting ornithopter, flexing its wings, to transport him to a prison camp or a shallow grave in the wilds of the continent of Endeavour—

Bing. The elevator slowed, stopped. Bing, and the doors opened. MacAdams led the way out.

Accent lights shone down on the framed oil paintings of ancient spies. Carpet stretched away from the elevator, white and plush as cloud. Tomas hesitated, as if he would drop through the carpet to distant ground the instant he set foot on it.

They were in ConPol headquarters, near MacAdams' office.

The lead agent shoved his shoulder. "Keep moving."

Tomas' bladder suddenly felt swollen. His bowels churned. He followed MacAdams down a dark hallway. One of the paintings, Fouché, caught Tomas' eye, and Fouché's role in the Bonapartist catechism coalesced from the mists of memory. Fouché, one-time secret police chief for Napoléon himself, later conspiring against his emperor.

The hallway seemed interminable. Offices empty for the night passed on the left. Through open doors, the windows showed the low skyline of Confederal City, dominated by the dazzling white obelisks of the Capitol.

They came to MacAdams' office. The assistant director paused in the open door, then said to the lead agent, "Wait outside."

The agent nodded. He turned his back to the door and settled into a ready stance.

"Come in, captain. Have a seat." Ceiling panels lit up as Tomas went toward the center of the office. The windows gave views north and east toward the Capitol and the lighted hotels and office towers along the Lake Liberty shore.

The door snicked shut. MacAdams pressed buttons in the door handle, then went to his desk. "The door and walls are soundproofed." MacAdams sat behind the desk, in a chair that made him look tall. He took a wheezy breath. "I can discharge my pistol in here, and the agent would never know. I said, have a seat."

Tomas' gaze jerked to the ceiling. Firefighting sprinklers, not sprayers for flesh-dissolving acid. His peripheral vision turned dark and spotty. He studied the floor. More plush carpet, no drains for blood.

A ConPol assistant director wouldn't soil his own office. Would he?

Tomas sat and drew in a breath. Steadier, he looked across the desk.

MacAdams tapped the lock of a desk drawer. He pulled out an anti-eavesdropping box pressed a button with his thumb. He set the box down on his desk, roughly equidistant between them. A green LED glowed on the box's top face.

Unless the box was a hoax, nothing would be overheard.

MacAdams said, "I know everything."

Tomas sucked in a breath. Fear mingled with relief. He could shrug off the burden of lies and go more calmly to his grave—

A lesson from OCS, used effectively on a prisoner he'd taken on Arden, came to Tomas. MacAdams might be bluffing. "Everything about what?"

"On Twoday, Quisenberry contacted one of my subordinates. He'd come across an alleged PR classified document, called Plan 827, and wanted to verify its authenticity. My subordinate saw some highly sensitive information in the document and brought it to me."

Tomas clamped down on a sudden jolt of betrayal. *Quisenberry, you vowed to keep it to yourself.*

"I redacted the highly sensitive information, then gave it to data forensics and our PR counterespionage expert to verify authenticity. It checked out. Quite the intelligence coup Quisenberry brought to us."

One more defense against a brain scan. Persuade the interrogator to believe your words instead of his own lying eyes. Tomas put on a questioning look. "I'm sure it is, but I still don't follow—"

"As soon as I saw the 'highly sensitive information,' I asked myself, how does a lieutenant colonel out at GFB West McAuliffe find a document like this? So last night we brought him in. A hell of a story he told us."

"Again, I don't follow—"

"Stop." MacAdams gave Tomas a flat stare. "You're trying one last time to throw me off the scent, I respect that, but it won't work. His scan showed you and Gen. Olafson are masterminding a coup attempt."

Tomas seemed to deflate. He wished he could melt and seep into the carpet.

"You recruited Quisenberry and other officers. Sokolov, Maj. Hamilton of the MP detachment, others, some lieutenant. You've met weekly for the last two months at the Daughters of Astarte temple at First and Nuova Toscana. I don't know how you got them to join you, the Daughters are usually shrewd enough to stay out of men's affairs."

MacAdams waved off the last sentence. "You shared the Plan 827 document with Quisenberry. Stop lying. Your scan confirms everything Quisenberry revealed, and more. Your body language from the moment we picked you up confirms it. You're plotting a coup against Forrester."

Tomas gulped a breath, like a drowning man breaking the surface one last time. "What do you want?"

MacAdams' eyes remained cold, but the corners of his mouth flexed upward. "In."

Tomas felt suspended in mid-air. Hope above, dread below, like charged plates in some physics experiment.

"I know Forrester is going to trigger a war against the PRs," MacAdams said. "Yes, the XM and the white mountain are trying to keep it secret, but it's my job to know these things. An attack on the PRs brings in the Unis on the PR's side, despite the wishes of the Aranjuez faction. We also know Olafson resigned because of Forrester's plan. Olafson wanted to avoid a two-front war we're going to lose."

"Yes."

"Even before he knew Forrester subconsciously dances to the PR's tune." MacAdams distended his mouth, as if he tongued at some piece of food stuck between his teeth. "You and your co-conspirators are true patriots, out to do what's right for the Confederated Worlds. I get that."

"You don't share it," Tomas said.

MacAdams replied with a flat stare.

Tomas went on. "Then why are you even thinking of joining us?"

"I want ConPol's directorship. And a twenty percent budget increase per year for the next five years. Give me that and you walk out of here a free man, plus I run counterespionage on your behalf. And if you don't give me that...." MacAdams shrugged. "There's a lot of rooms here you haven't seen. Yet."

Tomas squinted. "Why should I believe you can hold up your end of the deal? How many ConPol officials have the same information you do? Your subordinate. The scanner tech from last night. The scanner tech from tonight—"

MacAdams shook his head. "Both nights I did the same thing. When the scans got too 'highly sensitive,' I took over the control panel, routed the live data to a data stick, and sent spoof data to the main ConPol database. I'm the only one who knows. The choice remains the same. Give me what I want, or you don't leave our custody."

A second brain scan, conducted by another interrogator, would reveal MacAdams' offer to Tomas. *Don't leave our custody* meant a bullet to the brain. Tomas eased back in the chair. "Of course I'll say yes."

"I know." MacAdams waggled his finger. "And I know right now your yes is an airy promise. You might try reneging later, after you've got tanks in the street and Forrester's head on a pike. But you'd be wise to hold to that promise. I could cripple your new regime in ways you wouldn't even know. Are we clear?"

"We are."

MacAdams pushed back his chair. "It's a deal." He extended his hand above the desk.

Tomas stood. His knees wobbled but he shook with a firm grip.

"The lead agent will show you to the nearest subway station. I'll write up your interrogation as showing your innocence. You go and plan this and pull it off. And don't foul it up."

Dread burst in Tomas' gut. "What happened to Quisenberry?"

"We let him go. He didn't contact you? Good man, I guess. Trying to protect you by not contacting you."

Tomas grimaced. Quisenberry could put together the most plausible story, assuming MacAdams was loyal to the regime. ConPol discovered the truth from its scan of his brain, and would use it as a basis to round up the other conspirators. If Quisenberry avoided the other plotters, the odds went up that a ConPol dragnet might miss one of them. One person couldn't pull off the coup, but might be able to stop Forrester's rush to war with one desperate effort.

He had to tell Quisenberry the truth. But how? When? Knock on his door in the middle of the night? Call him, leaving a metadata trail of sender, recipient, locations, time, and duration?

Tomas had never socialized with Quisenberry. A call in the middle of the night would look suspicious, if some loyal drudge inside ConPol or some overzealous bluecoat found the call in a database. During business hours the next day would be safer. No one would question a call to a Ground Force senior officer originating inside the Executive Mansion.

After a night of choppy sleep, Tomas woke under a sheet damp and stinking with sweat. He made it to work early, 0815. In the basement, no one crossed his path to his office. He composed himself and made the call.

"Quisenberry." The man's voice carried a burred sound. He answered on audio only.

"Hello, I'm Captain Neumann. We met at the base jogging track a couple of months back. We also met—"

Quisenberry's words tumbled over themselves, like panicked soldiers of a routed army. "Who are you? Who are you trying to reach? I sometimes go to the base track, but months ago, who could I remember? Maybe you're trying to reach Maj. Quessenbury in civil affairs? People often confuse me for him. Good day, Captain—"

Silence ensued, followed by a dial tone.

The next Oneday night, Tomas arrived at the sacrament room around 2445. He paced across the circle of chairs, rehearsing what he would say to the others. *The good news, ConPol will help us. The bad news, we have to act within three days.*

Olafson arrived first from the adjoining door to the right. He headed toward a sideboard covered with bottles and glasses, then glanced at Tomas. "Late nights at the executive mansion?"

"I wish."

Olafson's left hand loomed over a shot glass. His right rested on the shoulder of an aquavit bottle. "What hap—?"

Hinges creaked. The left-side door slowly opened. Sokolov. His face haggard, he peered at Olafson, then Tomas. His eyes showed he craved from them a reassurance. Of what?

"You look like hell," Olafson said.

"Did you hear? Quisenberry. Killed himself."

A pit opened in Tomas's gut. His hands dropped to his sides, like all the ligaments of his arms had melted.

Olafson asked, "What happened?"

"He didn't report to brigade headquarters this morning. The MPs checked his usual places around base and town, no sign. This afternoon a hiker found his car on a side road in the Southcrest wilderness preserve, toward Finziburg. The MPs searched the woods and found his body about a hundred meters from the car."

Noises from both doors. Hamilton, a military police major, and Lt. Yeungling came in. Hamilton took in the faces of the men already in the room. "You be talking about Quisenberry?" he asked in his Zion-Against-Babylon accent.

Sokolov gave a ponderous nod. "Telling the general and Neumann everything. But just what I know, it isn't much. You know more?"

"MPs found him in the woods. Sidearm in his hand. Gunshot wound to his head." Hamilton grimaced. "His sidearm's data log and bullet telemetry showed the fatal round came from his weapon."

"Did he leave a note?" Olafson asked.

"No," Sokolov said. "I don't know why he did it. Hamilton, did you hear anything?"

"I and I be listening all day to chatter from the investigation teams. Heard nothing."

More new arrivals entered the room. A few moments of conversation made clear they too knew nothing more.

"Loki's *skith*," Olafson said. "We lost a good man. We're going to raise our glasses to him in a moment. But we have something more important to deal with first." Olafson shot a smoldering look around the room. "If the MPs or ConPol dig into his affairs and find a trail leading to the men in this room, they'll ace us."

"They won't," Tomas said.

All eyes turned to him.

"I know why he killed himself." Tomas stepped toward the center of the sitting area. "He wanted to verify the Plan 827 document. He promised me he would keep it secret." Tomas shook his head. "His need to verify the document must have outweighed his promise. Recently, he approached someone at ConPol to help with the verification. The document checked out, but Assistant Director MacAdams wondered how Quisenberry acquired it. So he brought him in for a brain scan."

All the faces around him froze. Hamilton broke first out of the shock. "How do you know this?"

"Because the next night, MacAdams did the same to me."

Sokolov's face twisted. "You're under surveillance and still you came here—"

"Wait." Olafson's voice commanded the room. "If ConPol brain scanned Neumann, they would have arrested us all by now. Unless...."

Hamilton's eyes danced in his dark face. "You talked MacAdams into joining us? Praise Jah."

Tomas scrunched up his mouth. "He talked me. From his brain scan of Quisenberry he knew what we're planning. He asked to join. Said he would provide counterespionage for us."

"He didn't do that for free," Olafson said. "What's his price?"

"The ConPol directorship. Hefty budget increases each of the next five years. I said yes, of course. He let me go. That was Fourday night and I've seen no sign he's double-crossing us."

Yeungling spoke up. "Why would Quisenberry—do what he did?"

Come on, son, it's obvious—a breath led Tomas to see things as they were. Yeungling didn't find it obvious.

Tomas said, "Presumably, the scan revealed to MacAdams that

Quisenberry lacked the authority to deal him into our plans. Likely, after MacAdams released him, Quisenberry assumed the brain scan revealed our plans and he was only released so ConPol could follow him to the rest of us. After MacAdams and I reached a deal, I called Quisenberry to get across the true story. He pretended I'd gotten a crossed connection and hung up, to protect me and the rest of our team."

Yeungling's face blanched. "You only called him once?"

"Of course," Olafson said. "Too many calls from Neumann to Quisenberry could have generated a fatal amount of sigint."

"He must have concluded he couldn't come here tonight without putting our plan at risk," Tomas said. "He likely decided he couldn't stay in our group but he couldn't drop out, so all he could do...."

Every expression turned inward for a long moment. "General," Sokolov said to Olafson. "Time to raise our glasses."

The word *wait* formed on Tomas' tongue. He held it back. First they honored Quisenberry's memory. Then they got to work.

Olafson's voice carried. "Fill your glasses."

Without speaking, the men approached the drinks table. Only the pour of liquids sounded. Tomas and the others wound their way into the oval of chairs and sofas. Yeungling craned his neck. Looking for cues how to act.

Tomas stood next to Yeungling. The gawky lieutenant bent at knees and waist as if to sit in a chair, but everyone else remained standing. Yeungling snapped his body fully upright and glanced around the room from downturned eyes.

Tomas gripped the lieutenant's shoulder with his free hand. Two pats, a nod. The boy—boy? What, all of five years Tomas' junior?—met his gaze and seemed to understand.

Olafson spoke first. "The Valkyries attend Quisenberry this night in Valhalla's feasting hall." He raised his shotglass of aquavit and held it high.

Sokolov spoke next. "God rest him." He crossed himself, two fingers touching four points on his body, then too lifted his glass.

The tradition jumped around the oval, descending the ladder of rank. Each officer said a few words from his spiritual tradition, if any, then raised his drink like a torch.

"It's irie, praise Jah...." said Hamilton.

"He has drunk the blood of the sacred bull...." a Mithraist said.

Tomas' turn. "He who walks in the Way is prepared for what life brings him, and for what death brings him." The glass of sparkling water fizzed near Tomas' ear.

Yeungling spoke last. "Ah, amen."

Olafson's voice sounded like a patriarch satisfied with the actions of his sons. "A moment of silence." Five heartbeats thudded in Tomas' chest. "*Prosit.*"

The men drank. They held their empty glasses for a few moments and looked solemnly at the carpet. After a ritual, like after a firefight, a man needed to slowly return to the mundane world, lest too many wonders and terrors come home with him.

A slow return, unless the next firefight came hot on the heels of the first. Olafson found a side table and set down his empty shotglass. "From the end of last week's meeting, our agenda items—"

"General," Tomas said. "We have a situation. The incumbent moved up his target date to next Fiveday."

All through the room, shoulders sagged. Breaths blew out. "Damn," Sokolov said.

Olafson moved his hands in a *calm down* gesture. "We have less time to finish our preparation tasks. Fine. We drive to the net when the opponent doesn't expect it, and he'll be too busy reacting to make a passing shot."

"General." Sokolov chewed at his lower lip. "We relied on Quisenberry to order the other battalions to remain on base during the operation. Now what do we do?"

"Contact the other battalion commanders." Olafson said. "Get them on board."

Tomas sucked in a breath through clenched teeth. The Daughters' dossier and his observations of Sokolov all agreed. Sokolov lacked the ability to sell the other battalion commanders on the plan.

"General," Sokolov said, "I don't know...."

Tomas spoke up. "There's a security risk in approaching multiple other battalion commanders. That's why we recruited someone in brigade headquarters."

A glum frown formed on Olafson's face. "You're right. Who else do we have at brigade headquarters?"

"No good candidates," Tomas said.

"Then we find a bad candidate."

A silence. Yeungling broke it. "Can we go up the ladder? The military district commander, Echevarria?"

Olafson scowled. Yeungling gulped and hunched his shoulders. "Someone else." Olafson's voice sliced across the room.

"General, if we get someone who can order the entire military district, there be no one better," Hamilton said. "Many other steps we would have to rush before Fourday, but with him, he could command them all away."

Olafson raised his voice. "Not Echevarria."

Tomas scrunched his mouth again. The general still smarted from Echevarria's knife in his back at the meeting leading to his resignation. But the Confederated Worlds' future mattered more than wounded ego.

Then the Daughters' dossier on Echevarria came to mind. *Extremely ambitious. Extremely self-serving.*

"Why be he bad?" Hamilton asked. "We can control every unit on the continent if we go through him."

Tomas spoke up. "We may be unable to control him."

"What do you mean?" Yeungling said.

"He'll do whatever offers him the most upside."

"That's joining us," Yeungling said.

Tomas shook his head. "Are you certain? The most visible part of our operation will be the fighting vehicles and soldiers securing travel routes into and key points within Confederal City. If the public sees ground units loyal to Echevarria, and the public hears an announcement that Echevarria, not General Olafson, will head the provisional government, he could stage a coup within a coup."

Olafson nodded. "In that case, everything we do here comes to nothing."

"We could fight him," Sokolov said.

"How many units could we pry out of his control?" Tomas said.

"Whether we win or lose, if we have to fight Echevarria, we give Forrester loyalists an opportunity to regroup."

"It's settled," Olafson said in a voice of command. "Not Echevarria. We look for the next best candidate at brigade headquarters and make the most persuasive pitch to him we can."

An intuition washed over Tomas. His skin prickled and his eyes grew wide. His thoughts poked at the intuition and it did not burst. "Let's not be hasty, sir."

Olafson scowled. "You just told us he's dangerous."

"We can mitigate the risk of a coup within a coup," Tomas said. "Here's how."

He talked for a few moments, outlining the contingency plan. He called it Case Red. He turned to particular people who would play extremely important roles. Hamilton. Yeungling. The faces around Tomas showed growing recognition the contingency plan could work. Not only could they prevent Echevarria from staging a coup within a coup. They could give their actions the maximum possible legitimacy.

A cold wave shivered down Tomas' arms. For Case Red to work, he would have to take the ultimate step. Could he?

Yes. Buoyed by certainty, he told them what that ultimate step entailed.

The room fell silent for five seconds. Olafson broke the silence, yet even his voice lacked its full authority. "Are you prepared to do that?"

The feeling remained. "Yes. The future of the Confederated Worlds depends on it. What do you think, sir?"

Olafson coldly smiled. "With the Case Red contingency plan in place, you and I can approach Echevarria."

They worked late into the night, setting plans and rehearsing their actions. Around 0030, Tomas made his way through the vestibule. A mix of confidence and fear churned in him.

Outside the temple, he descended the steps to the sidewalk. He turned for the subway station under a brightening sky. He had the sidewalk to himself. A few taxis, along with a delivery truck for the municipal fab utility, plied the street. The delivery truck reminded him to order high-powered magnets, strong enough to wipe the telemetry firmware of handgun ammunition. He placed the order on his phone, then looked up again at the nearly empty street. No pedestrians. One taxi at the curb near the subway station entrance.

He approached. The taxi door swung open.

Coldness flowed down his throat. Tomas slowed his steps. Someone monitored him? His head whipped around. His gaze roved the shadows for someone behind him.

The taxi door slammed. He turned back around.

Lissa stood on the sidewalk. Tendons visible in her neck, her eyes glistened in the fading glow of bioluminescent cypresses.

Tomas' throat tightened as if clamped. *She thought he—*

He gulped enough air to let impped skills take over. He widened his stance, bent his knees, then strode toward her.

"What are you doing?" she asked.

"Where are Stefan and Artur?"

She blinked, then a scowl returned to her face. "At home, asleep, with Capt. Krishnalingam's teenage daughter watching them. He's our neighbor? He has a teenage daughter? Did you know any of that? Or have you been so busy whoring you never noticed who lives next door to your family?"

"I work long hours at the executive offices—"

"Do you? How many nights—" Her breath caught. She cast a grim look toward the Daughters' temple. "How many nights have you come here? You were seen here at least once." The rigid mask of her face drooped. "We made vows to one another. Do you remember those?"

Longing formed a warm crimson pressure inside his chest. Despite all the challenges of children and careers, he did remember their vows. Sadness pressed behind his eyes. A few simple words would explain everything. She knew he'd never lied to her before. She would believe him if he told her used the Daughters' temple as cover for a conspiracy to topple Forrester.

And if he told her the truth, her life would be as much at risk as his. To leave their sons orphans? To go to his grave knowing she would soon be in hers? His heart seemed to crack inside his chest.

He could only lie. *I love you too much to tell you the truth....*

The crack in his heart widened. His voice turned steely.

"Part of those vows is that you meet my needs at home. You haven't. You scramble for work to make up for the soldiers and veterans the Restoration Party scared away, which leads you to give even less time for the boys, so you feel even more guilty when you are at home and devote all your attention to them, not me. Those rare days when you make time for me, over a year since Artur was born, you'll spend money on a babysitter, but you won't go to the gym to lose all your baby weight."

Her eyes bulged. Her mouth gaped.

Tomas tried to swallow. His next words would surely rasp his throat apart. He kept his face impassive. "I come here because only the priestesses satisfy my needs. And I will continue to do so."

Her lips trembled. A crinkle in her eyes showed the return of anger. "You, I, I could end our marriage for this."

"Divorce will not solve your problems. You're older, heavier, and have more children than when you married me. Divorce won't solve my problems either. We're tied each other for the rest of our lives." Behind her, the taxi lingered at the curb. "We're getting in that taxi and heading home."

Lissa stopped trembling. "Like hell."

"I said we're going home—"

"You even forgot I'm Catholic? Like hell an annulment won't solve my problems. I'd rather be alone the rest of my life than chained to a false man like you. I'm going to the bishop's office tomorrow to start the annulment process. They'll try to counsel me out of it and make me cool off until Fiveday. Nothing that can happen in three days will make me change my mind."

His stomach churned. Fiveday? Why this week, of all the times she could have made this threat?

He tamped down his emotions, then reached for her shoulder. "The bishop won't grant you an annulment."

She jerked her shoulder away from his hand. "Now you know what the Church will do? Go to hell."

The taxi waited along the curb. Spots swam in his peripheral vision. "We're going to go home and forget this ever happened."

Lissa reared back. "I'm going home," she said. "You can catch the subway and sleep on the couch. Or go back to your whores. I don't care." Her nostrils flared. She spun away and stalked to the taxi. Moments later, she sped away up Nuova Toscano Boulevard.

Tomas' heart pounded. Gooseflesh crawled over his jaw. The crack in his heart turned into a flood. He fumbled at it, like a man pressing a bandage against a wounded comrade's severed artery, as years of his love for Lissa poured out.

Footsteps scraped along the living pavement of the alley. From his seated position behind the loading dock of New Portland's Finest, Tomas stood up.

A broad-brimmed hat obscured the figure's face. His arms bulged at the sleeves of his rectangle-patterned shirt, and his blue trousers seemed a size too narrow at the waist.

Echevarria pushed up the hat's brim and turned his wide face to Tomas. Perhaps a trick of the dim light of 1100, his squinting eyes looked even narrower than usual. "You picked a hell of a place to meet, captain—"

Near Tomas, a grunt. Olafson stood.

Echevarria started. "General?" He recovered his aplomb. His gaze flicked between Tomas and Olafson. "Tell you me what this is about."

"In time," Olafson said, voice prickly.

"Were you followed?" Tomas asked.

Echevarria shook his head. "My driver took a roundabout route. He's waiting outside a tailor two blocks over. I saw not one single bluecoat on the walk." He peered at Tomas and Olafson. "I've got a hell-ton of action items on my calendar with Case White three days away. People around the white mountain will wonder if I'm too long getting there this morning. Tell you me what this is about."

"What's your opinion of Case White?" Tomas asked.

Narrow eyes studied Tomas, then Olafson. "It's a lawful order. It will give the president his wanted war."

"Will it win that war?"

Echevarria continued to peer at Tomas and Olafson. Abruptly, Echevarria laughed. "No be-damned way."

Olafson took a step forward. He forced out words through gritted teeth. "You let me twist in the wind when you knew I was right?"

"General." Tomas' voice bore a keen edge. Olafson shifted his weight backward. Their actions followed the game plan. Tomas' gut still tightened at taking that tone of voice with high brass, retired or not.

Echevarria turned up his palms. "The president wouldn't back down even if every one of us sided with you. I had to protect my career. You both would have done the same."

"Protect your career by presiding over a defeat?"

"General—"

"Forrester would yield before the Unis and PRs would land ground forces on Challenger. I'd be fine. Neumann too. Hell, general, you could have stayed chief of staff and still come out ahead. You could have spent the post-war years positioning yourself as the voice of reason against the president's mistake." Echevarria shrugged. "And who the hell knows, maybe we're wrong and Forrester will win his war."

Tomas gravely shook his head. "We're not wrong. I'll show you." He pulled out his phone and decrypted the Plan 827 document. He held out his phone and Echevarria snatched it.

Echevarria read. His eyebrows burrowed lower and lower with each page. Tomas said nothing and watched the alley mouths. Cars whirred by on the streets. No sign anyone noticed three men in the alley. They were alone with the stink of coffee grounds and curdling milk from the recycling bin.

Echevarria lowered his hand holding the phone, then looked at Tomas and Olafson. "Tell you me this is a hoax."

"It's been verified by multiple sources," Tomas said.

"Christ and the robbers. There's no salvaging our be-damned careers after the defeat he'll lead us into." Echevarria's eyes narrowed. "What are you going to do?"

Olafson rolled his eyes. "What do you think?"

Echevarria's face showed no offense. He slowly lifted the phone and handed it back to Tomas. His gaze remained on the phone's display until Tomas returned the phone to sleep mode and pocketed it.

"What do you need me to do?" Echevarria asked.

"When we send the signal," Tomas said, "order all GF formations in the military district to remain in their barracks."

"That's all?" Echevarria's face soon held a grin. "Who's with us?"

Olafson glanced at Tomas. Tomas minimally nodded. "Enough key personnel to make it work."

"Make it work? Tell you me a be-damned sight more. Who's shutting down access into and out of Confederal City?"

Tomas paused. "A battalion commander at GFB West McAuliffe."

"And the CC Telecom center in Finziburg?"

"The officer who installed the monitor and control system."

Echevarria's eyebrows rose. "Maj. Rolston?"

"Lt. Yeungling."

Echevarria's face showed thoughts churning behind it. "A lieutenant? The key to the whole operation and you'll send a lieutenant? Do you want to fail?"

Tomas raised an eyebrow at Olafson. The latter gave Echevarria a gruff look. "Yeungling is a competent young officer," Olafson said.

"Even his name—Youngling—choose you someone else." Echevarria gave them a solemn look. "Choose you someone else, or I stay out of this. I'm as serious as a Shirley Foxtrot hull breach. Choose you someone else."

Tomas crossed his arms. "Whom could we choose?"

Gears of calculation seemed to turn just beneath the skin of Echevarria's face. "I mentioned his name. Neumann, you and he were battalion staff officers together. Maj. Rolston."

Tomas winced at Olafson, then turned back to Echevarria. "We invite Rolston to join us, or you walk?"

"You're be-damned correct."

Olafson sniffed out a breath. "Deal."

For a moment, the corners of Echevarria's mouth lifted. His eye glinted. "Deal." He looked more solemn. "All you want me to do is keep Ground Force in its barracks? I could help in other ways. For example, assigning detachments to guard the prisoners you'll have to take."

With an offhand tone, Olafson said, "We have all the guards we need."

"You're certain?" Echevarria asked. "If the bluecoats catch a hint of—his—location, they'll descend on it."

"They won't catch any hint where we stash the incumbent," Olafson said.

Echevarria smiled. "The incumbent, that's a good thing to call him. But where could you hide him so they won't notice?"

Olafson cleared his throat. "We're settled on the location—"

"—the general's country clu—" Tomas' mouth hung open. Olafson glared at him. He snapped shut his mouth and ducked his head.

You're a terrible actor, Tomas. Surely Echevarria would see through the play he and Olafson put on? Surely Echevarria would guess the truck to be parked at the Confederal Heights Country Club, to be guarded by Hamilton's least dependable MP detachment, was empty?

Men see what they want to see.

His blood ran cold. The rare times men see reality can destroy you.

Echevarria's eyebrows lifted. He quickly looked away from Tomas. To Olafson, he said, "Doesn't matter where you stash the incumbent. More guards are better than too few."

"Unless more guards draw attention by their very presence," Olafson said. He set his fists on his hips. "Are you going to pick up your racket and leave the court if we don't give you this too?"

Calculation churned behind Echevarria's face. Finally, he put a contrite look across his broad features. "You make a good point. Forget you I brought it up."

"I will," Olafson said.

We won't.

"We don't need more of your time," Olafson said. "Captain?"

"The go signal will be an off-color joke, the kind men forward to a hundred of their friends," Tomas said. "It will come from me. When it arrives, tell all Ground Force units in the capital cities to remain on alert but in their barracks until further notice." Tomas drew a breath. "And thank you, sir, for helping us avert the greatest disaster in Confederated Worlds history."

"No, captain, don't you thank me. Of course I would do this, given the document you showed." Echevarria's face showed pure solemnity, except for a faint upturn at the corners of his mouth. He shook his head and extended his hand for Olafson's, for Tomas'. "For the Confederated Worlds."

"Indeed." Tomas gripped Echevarria's hand. Echevarria seemed sincere. All the more reason to think he wasn't.

Handshakes complete, Echevarria pulled his hat lower over his face. He headed for the end of the alley. Ten seconds later, he rounded the corner onto the street, out of sight.

Olafson sloughed out a breath. "We're going to have to use your Case Red."

Tomas slumped, suddenly weary. "I think you're right."

16

Zero Hour

The morning broke like any other around the capital cities, with Epsilon Eridani just past the zenith and the weather almost warm enough for shirtsleeves at 0900. Tomas kept his jacket on and waved his ID badge at the Executive Mansion gatehouse guards. They showed no sign of noticing a shape under his jacket, tucked inside his waistband.

Inside the gate, Tomas fell in with the crowd, mostly civilians, flowing toward the building. The civilians' chatter sounded the same as any other day, talk of restaurants and bars, entertainments seen or heard, the minutiae of work projects, reports, memos, meetings with agencies, meetings with Congressional staffers....

If not for Tomas and the others, within forty-eight hours, Forrester's confirming order would reach the trigger fleet.

Within seventy-two hours, essentially the entire human galaxy would be at war.

Inside the Executive Mansion, the civilians waited in line for the sniffers and metal detectors at the main employee entrance. Tomas stepped away from the mass of civilians toward the prescreened security entrance. Already his skin chafed along the insides of his lower legs, just above his ankles. He remembered Arden, Belmont, Constitution Square, and put on a placid smile.

Familiar faces among the guards at the prescreened entrance. Tomas lifted his ID badge. A bored nod in reply. Another guard pulled back the waist-high padded railing. Tomas gave the guards the rote greetings of two hundred mornings, received rote replies in return.

Within moments, he walked on toward the President's wing, with a shaped charge inside his waistband, a ring capable of delivering a dose of tranquilizer in his pocket, and two pistols strapped just above his ankles.

Tomas reached his basement office. He hid his contraband in a locked drawer already holding spare rubber gloves, hung his jacket, and double-checked Forrester's schedule. Domestic political meetings all morning, a lunch with governors from the Uni periphery, more domestic matters. The final readiness reports from Nuova Toscana should reach the white mountain by mid-afternoon, Forrester's desk an hour after that. A final planning session into the night, at least till 2700 if not till midnight or later, then the transmittal of the go order to the white mountain first thing in the morning.

Tomas's shoulders eased. No last minute wrinkles in the president's schedule. At 2200, Tomas would send one message through his phone's scheduler. An image of a buxom blonde in skimpy patriotic swimwear, with a link to what promised to be an even more risqué picture of the model, but instead was video of the rear end of a defecating donkey. The kind of crass joke men had sent one another electronically for a thousand years.

Embedded in the video, extractable by a steganographic deciphering application on every plotter's phone or tablet, was each recipient's objective and target arrival time.

The scheduler would stagger message deliveries so that all the teams would arrive at their objectives at the same time.

2500. Zero hour.

But a full day of waiting till then. Tomas remembered long hours in foxholes, tense minutes in a Badger's turret. Waiting for action was almost worse than being in the thick of it. He spent the morning at his desk, shuffling files in an effort to distract himself. Nervous energy circuited through his body. He and his fellow plotters knew their tasks. Even if some of their objectives couldn't be achieved—the bluecoats would have an opportunity to act—the advantage of surprise, coupled with visible control of key points throughout Confederal City, should be enough to carry the day.

Should? How did the old saw go? *No plan survives contact with the enemy?*

Tomas shuffled more files.

A few minutes after 1700, Forrester's assistant called. Her mousy expression, normally untroubled, bore traces of unease. "Captain, he's ready to see you."

"Thank you. Is all well?"

She started. After a moment, she drew a breath and looked more calm. "I appreciate you asking, captain. Yes, all is. 'Who knows the spirit of the sons of men, which goes upward, and the spirit of the animal, which goes down to the earth?'"

Tomas passed the hidden stairwell door leading up to the president's private office. He went up the visible route, past the assistant's station, through the Sutherland Office, to the private chamber. The room seemed smaller than usual, the video displays brighter, Forrester more potent behind the command desk. Sharma stood behind Forrester's shoulder. The two of them studied the central displays.

"Everything checks from Nuova Toscano," Forrester said. "The relief force is on schedule for departure to Arden via Navi Ambarsar. The strike force is circling the wormhole mouth, building velocity to go through the wormhole at high speed. The PRs won't know what hit them."

"We'll crush them with speed and surprise," Sharma said.

Tomas stood at parade rest. "Great news, sir."

"Superb news," Forrester said. "I might as well send the order now."

Sharma laughed. Tomas froze. A message could only travel at the speed of light. Wormholes only provided shortcuts through space, not a violation of the laws of physics. If Forrester sent the order, a recall would have to reach the armed relief force before it traversed the wormhole to Navi Ambarsar. Even if Tomas sent the message to the plotters now, that wouldn't be enough time—

Chest tight, he managed to say, "A great idea, Mr. President, but we don't want to hit the window too early. The strike force can build up more velocity if we wait till the scheduled time. More velocity increases our chances in battle against the PR fleet, doesn't it?" He looked at Sharma and Forrester.

"Superbly said." Forrester leaned back and interlaced his fingers behind his head. "I've waited over five years for us to avenge ourselves on the PRs. I can wait a few more hours."

"Later tonight, the proper time will come," Sharma said.

Forrester alternated between studying reports and talking about their content. Tomas had seen most of the reports, some dozens of times. Assessments of their forces, of PR forces, of the situation on Navi Ambarsar, and on worlds closer to Brotherhood of Humankind, the PR capital. Forrester ordered dinner with a tap on his smartglasses and a few words to his assistant. Pizzas with uncommon toppings, sunchokes, pickled ginger, sliced leg of lamb. Arrival time 2142.

Tomas gulped down two slices, then excused himself to go to the men's room.

In the tiled and mirrored space, he pulled out his phone. The clock showed 2159. He opened the message with trembling fingers and pressed *schedule delivery*. He splashed cold water on his face. The phone shook in his hand. *Scheduling complete.*

Three hours to go. He inhaled deeply and the jitters in his limbs eased. The smell of soap and cleaning solvents reminded him of the hospital on New Liberty. He exhaled and returned to Forrester's private office.

Forrester seemed even more at ease, as if his long limbs were vines twining around his command chair. With a languid motion he reached into a drawer under the desktop console. He pulled out a bottle and three squat glasses with thick bases. "I don't normally drink," he said, "but today is a day to raise a toast."

"Thank you, Mr. President," Sharma said.

"Mr. President," Tomas said, "I don't normally drink either."

"Make an exception." Forrester opened the bottle and poured into each glass three fingers of neat scotch. He set two glasses near Tomas and Sharma. He sipped, then set his own glass down next to an embedded display. "Neumann, I may need you to be my eyes on Navi Ambarsar."

Tomas sipped peaty liquid. His throat burned and he coughed.

Forrester chuckled. " 'Don't normally' is an understatement."

"You took me by surprise," Tomas said. "Eyes on Navi Ambarsar?"

A sip of scotch, then Forrester said, "The PRs sent a lot of commissars to remold Navi Ambarsar society. Even if we have to read between the lines, that's a truth we can all see." He set his glass down with a thud. "I don't trust Ground Force to drag them all into the light of day. I may need you to keep an eye on GF personnel, to make sure they do a thorough job." Forrester fixed his hazel eyes on Tomas. "I've read your file. You could uncover those PR commissars yourself."

Trapped on Navi Ambarsar when the PR fleet regained orbital supremacy, and pushed through the wormhole to Nuova Toscano? Tomas' lips compressed for a moment.

He relaxed and said, "I'll follow any lawful order, Mr. President." A need jabbed him. Keep Forrester occupied. "Could you walk me through the report on PR political officers on Navi Ambarsar? It would help me get up to speed."

Forrester nodded. Despite the late hour, his swept-back hair remained a rigid shell. "According to sigint from previous Arden relief forces...."

Forrester kept talking. His words massacred a thousand PR commissars on Navi Ambarsar, then grew more grandiose as the evening wore on. "Space Force can destroy every mol fab facility on Brotherhood of Humankind. We'll make brain scans a requirement for civilians to receive a ration card from our replacement mol fabs...."

Tomas stretched his arms toward the ceiling. His sleeve slid back to expose his wristwatch. 2450. Rolston and Yeungling should be near the CC Telecom facility in Finziburg. Sokolov's men were arriving at their blocking positions at the bridges into Confederal City.

Echevarria planned whatever his next move might be.

Tomas pulled down his hands and spread his fingers over his abdomen. Through a wince, he said, "Mr. President, sorry, I need a few minutes."

"Something you ate is looking at you cross-eyed?"

Tomas nodded. "Happened to me all the time before field action. I need a few minutes."

"Happens to a lot of men. Do what you have to, but keep your eye on the ball."

Tomas left Forrester's private office for the public one, then shut the door behind him. The Sutherland Office's lights glowed in the ceiling, like the set of a stage play. Beyond, dim lights and silence dominated the rest of the floor. Forrester's assistant and everyone else had left.

He passed the mens' room and entered the stairwell. First, a stop at his office, for his jacket and contraband. While he descended, he pulled out his phone and held it one-handed near his waist. A few swipes brought up a map. He looked for an unmapped part of the basement.

Here, an unmapped space, behind a plain door....

He reached for the door handle. Before he opened it, he paused and pulled off his wedding ring.

Lissa would go to her diocese's annulment office tomorrow.

He winced and drew a breath.* *He tucked his wedding ring into his hip pocket, then groped for the other ring. At first glance almost a twin to the first. Slightly thicker. He put on the second ring, carefully adjusted it with his right hand, then simultaneously pressed two spots on it. A snick echoed along the corridor. He held his left fingers straight and kept going.

A few moments later he approached the reactor room. The guard he'd met months ago would be there, as he had been every night for a week. A few muttered suggestions to the XM's security chief had done it. *He served in my unit during the war, he's too proud to mention it, but he needs the pay bump for the night shift....*

The guard's eyebrows crinkled. His expression emphasized

more than usual the pink splotch on his face. "Captain? But what brings you here?"

"Meetings till all hours. We took a break and I needed to stretch my legs. I realized I spend too little time with good honest machines. Or good honest men." He clapped his left hand down hard on the guard's shoulder. An extra flex of his fingers pressed the ring even harder through the guard's chameleonskin jacket. Unarmored fabric, standard for civilian security guards.

"Well, captain, I don't...." The guard's eyes rolled back in his head. His knees buckled.

Tomas caught him and dragged him into a corner. The guard would be unconscious for six hours, perhaps eight, and wake with his memories wiped going back to about 0600 that morning. More than enough time.

Tomas laid him on the floor in a back corner of the room. He cradled the guard's head with his hand and lowered his head the last centimeters to the mycocrete. Far from the reactor, and out of sight from the corridor.

Next step. Behind the reactor. Tomas untucked his shirt and pulled out thick plastic wrapping the green mass of moldable explosive, and its accessories. He put on rubber gloves and unwrapped the package. Rubber gloves not to prevent fingerprints, but to keep residues off his hands.

He tore off a chunk of explosive. A glance at the box connecting the output of the five polywells with the building's power lines, then he molded the explosive to fit. He remembered playing with Stefan and some modeling dough, far too long ago.

Shape correct, he applied it to the underside of the connection box. The amount and location should knock out electrical service for six to twelve hours, depending on how quickly facilities could get replacement parts from the city fab. From a pocket inside the plastic wrap, Tomas drew out a timed detonator. He jabbed it into the green explosive. He applied the rest of the charge, and another detonator, to the transformer box receiving city power.

He set each detonator's timer to go off simultaneously, in about four minutes, then stepped quietly to the hallway. From the corner of the room, the guard faintly snored. The generator hummed. No one knew.

Three and half minutes later, Tomas returned to the top floor, near Forrester's office. He rounded a corner and froze.

Sharma stood outside the men's room. "You all right? You took a long time and you weren't on the shitter here."

Tomas gingerly touched his belly. "I didn't want to stink it up too badly for you and the president."

Sharma chuckled. "Did I ever tell you about the time on *Mitchell* when somebody dumped dry ice in the forward lavatory—"

"Forrester's waiting." Tomas gestured at Sharma to get moving, then glanced at his wristwatch. The secondhand ticked down. 15, 14. Past the assistant's station. Through the brightly lit Sutherland Office. Tomas opened the door to the private office and waved Sharma in. He stepped in after, hung back.

"Goddam, Neumann, that must have been a bad shit," Forrester said. "Now whe—"

The hum of equipment cooling fans faded, and the video displays blinked off. Darkness filled Forrester's office. The president and Sharma melted into the darkness.

Wait, if it's too dark—

"What in the goddam hell?" Forrester said.

Under cover of the president's words, Tomas quietly deadbolted the door. The hidden stairwell from the basement was the only way out. Or in.

Gooseflesh stippled Tomas' jaw. How many people knew about the hidden stairwell? Yet another loose thread—

Forrester shouted. "I can't see a goddam thing! What in the hell is wrong with those shitbrained idiots in facilities?"

"I'll get you some more light, Mr. President," Sharma said.

Two seconds later, something rattled on the desk. A crescent of dim light came from Sharma's smartglasses, turned around to illuminate the room with their screen. Dim, but enough for Tomas to make out the other figures in the room.

Forrester jabbed an angry finger at his desk. "I don't need goddam light. I need the goddam command panel to work."

"We can use my smartglasses to get data," Sharma said. He picked up his smartglasses. "Which report would you like to review, Mr. President?"

"Get me XM facilities first."

Sharma spoke the command. The speakers in his smartglasses fed into the room a faint ringing. The ringing abruptly cut off, replaced by a woman's bland recorded voice. "Your call cannot be completed at this time. Please try again later. Your call cannot be completed—"

"What the shit is wrong with the voice lines?" Forrester asked. "Send a message instead."

Sharma spoke a message, then said, "Send."

Tomas came closer to the command desk. He flexed his face into an exaggerated frown. "You sent the message, but was it received?" He pulled out his phone. "I'll try making a call."

Tomas called Sharma. No ring, just a few seconds of silence. The same recorded voice followed. Tomas cut it off. "I'll send you a message. Let me know if it arrives."

With his fingers, Tomas tapped out a short message, to Olafson and Yeungling. *Obj 1 check.* He then wrote a brief test message to Sharma and hit *send*. "Message on its way."

They sat in silence for a time. Sharma muttered, "Reload. Reload." He dropped his smartglasses on the desktop. "It should be here by now."

A creak from behind the desk. Forrester stood, a looming shadow in the dim space. His voice wavered slightly. "For the power to be out this long, both the polywells and the reserve line to city power must be down. If communications are down too, there's only one explanation. PRs."

Tomas put a frown into his voice. "PRs?"

"They must have a spy who found out about our plan. They've sent in commandos to assassinate me and prevent us from starting the war of liberation."

Sharma said, "We should relocate, Mr. President."

Heart slamming, Tomas said, "A good idea."

Forrester's usual confidence returned to his voice. "If the PRs are sending commandos to assassinate me, their spy told them exactly where my office is. We're going elsewhere."

Indeed they were. Down the hidden stairwell, to where Hamilton would meet them.

Sharma took a step toward Tomas, toward the door. Tomas reached down to his right ankle and lifted up his pants cuff. The snub-nosed, the tougher pistol to reach, and not Ground Force standard issue.

With his left hand, he lifted his phone up and away from his body. The screen's glow provided a weak flashlight. He drew the snub-nosed pistol and released the safety.

He turned the muzzle back and forth between Sharma and Forrester. "Don't move. Either of you. Sharma, back away, and drop your smartglasses. Both of you, hands in plain sight."

Sharma raised his hands. His smartglasses thudded on the carpet.

"What in the shit?" Forrester's voice boomed. Still not loud enough to carry through the sound-dampening walls.

"Roderick Forrester, you are under arrest for treason."

A moment went by. "Treason? You have a shitload of gall—"

"I have evidence you are a PR agent under deep cover."

Sharma sucked in a breath.

Forrester glowered at Tomas. "That lie will fool nobody. I have hated the PRs with every fiber of my being since the day I was taken prisoner. Everyone in the Confederated Worlds knows that."

"What they don't know is, the PRs used psychological tests to gauge how useful you might be to them. Then they dosed you with lethe potion every time they took you to the skills amps to strengthen both your political skills and your blindness to disconfirming evidence."

"You lie."

Tomas went on. "They want you to launch this war."

"God damn you to hell. It was all a ploy from the start. You planted Walters in Firstlanding Square so you could capture him and worm your way into my good graces—"

Tomas' voice grew even more firm. "Your actions provide aid

and comfort to the enemy. That is treason."

Forrester stayed quiet for a moment. Then he chuckled. "Turn your pistol on yourself, Neumann, while you still can. Otherwise, look at the hideous fate you'll suffer. Put me on trial after this, and I will be acquitted, and when I return to power you'll be looking at your own treason trial and firing squad. Kill me tonight, and the Restoration Party will hunt you to the ends of the galaxy."

Hamilton's teams should have the Restoration Party's senior bluecoat in custody by now. "We'll see," Tomas said.

From his phone and Sharma's smartglasses, a siren blared. Again. Again. Adrenaline punched Tomas in the back. Yeungling, or? He kept his gaze on Forrester, yet focused his senses on the audio feed from the phone and smartglasses.

"What's this?" Sharma asked.

"The ancients in their banana republics would do this. Neumann's fellow traitors will broadcast their crime to the Confederated Worlds," Forrester said.

A male voice came out of the speakers and echoed around the room. "All citizens of the capital cities, of Challenger, and of all the Confederated Worlds, this is an hour of great need. Listen you to me."

Tomas' face turned cold and rigid. Rolston spoke.

"You did not know it, but the Confederated Worlds were on a path of great peril. Agents of the Progressive Republic infiltrated the highest levels of the civilian government and the military. President Forrester himself is one of these agents, and has systematically promoted his fellow agents into positions of prominence. The PR infiltration is so pervasive it cannot be combated according to our traditions of governance. Only extreme measures, undertaken with the utmost reluctance, will preserve the Confederated Worlds. Therefore, we declare a provisional government of national salvation led by Maj. Gen. Hector Echevarria, Confederated Worlds Ground Force."

"That fucker is behind this?" Forrester said. "You can't trust a goddam Endeavourite."

Rolston continued. "All citizens, assist you our efforts. Remain you at home, to allow the forces of national salvation to patrol the streets of the capital cities. Accept you a temporary suspension in non-essential electronic communications and delivery of orders by the molecular fabrication utilities. Conditions will return to normal after all known and suspected agents of the Progressive Republic have been taken into custody."

A pause, then Rolston said, "The following people are to surrender to the forces of national salvation at their earliest opportunity. Any citizen with knowledge of the location of any of the following people must do their patriotic duty and report that location to the provisional government. Use you this address." He enunciated a communications code. "For those watching, we will show that address on screen. Again, the following people are to surrender or be turned over to the forces of national salvation. President Roderick Forrester. Vice-President Fitzhugh O'Brien. Gen. Eric Olafson, CWGF, retired." Rolston continued down the list of plotters in descending order of rank. Name after name from the last meeting at the Daughters. "… and Capt. Tomas Neumann, CWGF. Again, any citizen with knowledge of any of these people's locations must contact the provisional government at—" He repeated the address.

Not Lt. Yeungling. The lieutenant had known his part in Case Red, should Echevarria attempt a coup within a coup. Profess to go along with Rolston and Echevarria's scheme while remaining true to Tomas' plan. Yeungling must have done so.

Unless Rolston killed him, rather than intimidate him into siding with Echevarria.

And even if Yeungling went along with Rolston as part of Case Red, would a gangly, pogey lieutenant have the capacity to follow through?

Tomas pocketed his phone, then balanced on his right leg. His left hand drifted below his knee and bunched up the inseam of his pants leg. Muffled by fabric, Rolston went on. "In this time of extreme need, the Confederated Worlds thank you for your loyalty. The provisional government shall communicate again during the night. Remain you calm, in your homes, and all will be well. May any god or gods you worship bless you, and may they bless the Confederated Worlds."

The silence echoed for a moment. Forrester and Sharma's figures remained shadowy in the pale light of Sharma's dropped smartglasses. Visible enough.

Sharma stood motionless near the president, gaping at him.
Craving guidance, a follower to the end.

Forrester remained behind his desk, but his head arched back
and laughter bubbled from his mouth. "You double-crossing cockbiter. You didn't see that coming, did you? Your name's on the proscription list with mine. What are you going to do next?"

Tomas set his left foot on the floor. His left hand held his pants
leg above the knee. He drew in one steadying breath. "What's best
for the Confederated Worlds."

He aimed the snub-nosed pistol at Forrester's chest and
squeezed off three rounds. Steel casings spun out of the chamber.
One stung Tomas' thigh and bounced off.

His ears rang louder than his pounding heart. He dropped the
snub-nosed and reached down to his left ankle for his standard issue
pistol.

The whites of Sharma's eyes showed starkly in the dark night.

Three more rounds from the standard issue pistol. Brass casings
jumped into the air.

Tomas went around the desk. His ears still rang with the gun-
shots. Forrester slumped in the chair. Three wounds in his chest.
Blood gushed in thick waves. Hazel eyes stirring, the last purposeful
gesture of his draining life.

Forrester gave Tomas a momentary glance of pure hatred. Then
shock glazed his eyes. His last breath rattled in his throat.

Fingers at Forrester's neck. No pulse. Hairs on the back of Tomas'
hand near Forrester's nostrils. No breath.

Tomas nodded to himself and went to Sharma. He too lay with
mutilated chest. His feet banged and his hands clawed at the blood-
soaked carpet, as if he could scrabble from it one more breath.

Ten seconds to bleed to death from a heart shot.

Sharma's limbs stopped their vain grasp for life. Lifeless eyes
stared at the ceiling. Just like enemy corpses, Uni and mike and Ar-

denite rebel and Papa. Every soldier's thought. *Bad luck, pal. Better you than me.*

Head shake. Back to work. Tomas reached into his inner pocket for two rubber gloves. Near the door, the dropped snub-nosed showed as an angular black shape on the pale carpet. Casings from both pistols, fat gray-white steel and longer, darker brass. He pulled on the gloves, then reached back into the pocket for a small cloth. He briskly wiped down the snub-nosed pistol. Wore gloves when loading it, so just grips, guard, trigger... done.

He toed one of the snub-nosed pistol's steel casings and kicked it toward Sharma's corpse. Then the next. Then—where was the third? His eyes bulged. His neck swiveled. Not on the floor—

Tomas dragged a gloved hand along the baseboard. The third steel casing glimmered half a meter along the carpet. He kicked it over and followed it to Sharma's corpse.

He set down the snub-nosed and picked up a steel casing. With his other hand, he squeezed Sharma's lifeless fingers against it. Dredged it in Sharma's blood. Dropped it into the red pool. Repeat.

The metallic stench turned his stomach. He clamped his facial muscles.

You can vomit after all this is over—

Repeat. Then the snub-nosed into Sharma's hand for finger and palm prints. Sharma's limbs were still soft. Tomas let go Sharma's hand. His hand slumped to the floor and the snub-nosed pistol slipped away from his dead fingers, to the blood.

Tomas drew a breath and stepped back. Not a perfect crime scene, but enough to tell the story he wanted. Especially after Assistant Director MacAdams' best ConPol forensics team came to gather evidence. Tomas pulled off his gloves and stuffed them, inside out, back into his pocket, followed them with the cleaning cloth. Out came his phone.

He winced. Blocked, of course. Echevarria would have ordered Rolston to shut down the other planners' communications when he seized control at CC Telecom's facility.

Everyone else knew what to do. But could they execute Case Red?

They had to.

Tomas went to the door. With a few steps ago, someone pounded on the other side. Dimly heard came the words, "Mr. President!"

Time to act. Tomas hyperventilated for a couple of seconds, then fumbled at the deadbolt. He swung open the door.

Flashlight beams bounced around the Sutherland Office, slashing across seven men. Three ConPol agents in dark suits. Four Restoration Party bluecoats watched Tomas through twelve eyes.

"I tried," Tomas said. "Too late. Couldn't stop him."

"What happened?" one ConPol agent asked.

The bluecoat with the most stripes around his cross barby armband asked, "Couldn't stop who?"

Tomas' head swam. He breathed deeper. "Sharma. He shot the president."

The ConPol agent hurried past Tomas. A flashlight beam bounced around the private office. "Jesus."

The other agents and Restoration Party security entered the private office. Tomas went in their midst. The lead ConPol agent aimed his flashlight at Forrester, then Sharma, then the snub-nosed pistol and the steel casings on the floor. "What happened?"

"We met with the President, as usual, when the lights went out and our phones stopped working. Sharma locked the door and held us at gunpoint. He shot the president."

The flashlight beam returned to Sharma's torn chest. The lead ConPol agent's voice took on a sharp edge. "And you shot Sharma?"

"I did."

The lead agent flooded Tomas' face with the flashlight. "You had a pistol today? Just a coincidence? How did you get it past security?"

Tomas squinted at Sharma's corpse. "The president gave me a security waiver. Sharma, for months now, I haven't trusted him—"

A Restoration Party security man studied something in his smartglasses. "Sharma? He's one of us. He joined the party months before the election."

"That's why I didn't trust him." Tomas raised a shaking hand, extended his index finger. "He acted too loyal. If I could have put my suspicions into words, I would have told the president." Tomas put on a mournful look. "He could still be alive. Or if I acted sooner. I had my service sidearm concealed, if only I could have drawn it faster—"

The lead ConPol agent swung his flashlight beam into Tomas' face. "Who are you?"

Tomas squinted against the harsh light. "Neumann. One of the president's aides."

"Neumann. Tomas Neumann? Ground Force captain?" The lead agent's eyes narrowed. He glanced at one of his peers and his eyebrow jumped upward. "Echevarria's communiqué mentioned your name."

Tomas' pulse quickened. The communiqué made him sound a loyalist. Which would help him. Unless the ConPol agents had switched sides.

"We'll need your sidearm," the lead agent added. "For evidence. And then we'll take you into protective custody until everything blows over."

Tomas' legs felt weak. He forced himself to speak boldly. "You're allied with Echevarria." The bluecoats looked up. "That's why you want to disarm me and hold me captive. Because I know the truth. Your ally killed Forrester!"

The bluecoats stood abreast of Tomas. They moved their hands closer to their batons. In close quarters, with agents who probably only fired their sidearms on the range once a year to remain qualified, the bluecoats would have a fighting chance.

The lead agent sized up the numbers standing against him and shrank a little. "Captain, I'm following Confederated Police standard contingency—"

"I'll believe you," Tomas said, "if I see Assistant Director MacAdams himself come in that door. Since the traitors want to arrest him, he must be loyal."

One of the bluecoats nodded. "You heard him. Assistant Director MacAdams."

The lead agent shifted his weight back, then forward. "Communications are down. I won't be able to get a hold of him."

"Send a runner," Tomas said.

The bluecoat team leader said, "Do what the captain said."

"Now, hold on, the assistant direct—"

From every pocket, sirens blared. The lead agent flinched. Screens lit up and speakers played the first brassy notes of *Challenger, Gem of the Spaceways*.

A voice spoke. Male, youthful, earnest and nervous as a new graduate. "Citizens, my name is Lt. Yeungling, Confederated Worlds Ground Force. I speak for all forces loyal to your proper government. We have reclaimed control of all communications in the capital cities. Communications will be restored, although military and police communications will be given priority until the rebellion is defeated."

He audibly inhaled. The nervousness evaporated from his voice, replaced with unexpected resolve. "For defeated it will be! The armed forces and police remain loyal to your proper government. Citizens, join us in defeating the rebellion! It consists only of a cabal of officers, led by Maj. Gen. Echevarria, who falsely ordered their soldiers out of their barracks. To all the soldiers manning the roadblocks, desert your posts! Join the thousands of volunteers taking to the streets against your treacherous officers! To those treacherous officers, surrender now, or pay the full price for treason!"

Yeungling signed off. In the following silence, Tomas leaned toward the lead agent. "Now you won't need a runner to bring Assistant Director MacAdams."

"Right, right." The lead agent pulled out his phone and stepped behind his two subordinates. He swiped and tapped. A dial sound came from the speaker. The screen lit up his scowl. "Come on, come on, get through," he muttered. Abruptly, someone on the other side picked up, and he moved the phone to his ear. He listened for a moment, then said, "In the Executive Mansion? I'm in Forrester's private office! Get me AD MacAdams. Do it already!"

Seconds ticked by. Tomas watched the ConPol agents and the bluecoats. His gaze kept sliding toward Forrester's corpse and he kept yanking it back.

The lead agent came to attention. Through his phone he said, "Yes sir. Terrible news. President Forrester is dead." Silence for a time. "I know, sir. Unbelievable. One of the President's aides. Assassinated him. Inside job. Who? Sharma. Another aide, Capt. Neumann, the one named in the rebel communiqué. Shot the assassin, but too late to save the President."

The lead agent listened for a few seconds. "Yes, sir. We'll seal the room till you come with a crime scene team. Yes, sir. And what about—?" More listening. "I see. Yes, sir." The call ended.

The lead agent returned his phone to his pocket, stepped back in line with his peers. "Captain, I don't know how much of that you heard, but AD MacAdams will come personally to examine the scene."

"I'll wait here, then. I'll tell him everything I know or suspect about Sharma."

"For now, wait outside the office for the assistant director."

They went to the Sutherland Office. The former presidents stared out of their portraits. Would they condemn him? Praise him? Tomas avoided their gazes and slumped into a chair. His fingers jittered. He slumped his head. The bluecoats formed a line between him and the ConPol agents.

Tomas fished his phone from his pocket. He tapped out an encrypted message to Olafson. *Case Red obj 1 check. MacA coming to XM.*

He hit *send*, let out a breath. Then unease nibbled at him. Rolston had pushed the communiqué through every phone, every communication display, and every pair of smartglasses in the capital cities. Lissa had heard Tomas' name on the proscription list. Regardless of her promise to seek an annulment, she deserved better than to worry about him.

"Call Lissa," he told the phone.

Ring. Ring. Ring. No answer.

Perhaps the phone system was overloaded. But Yeungling's tasks for Case Red involved more than killing Rolston. He would also give Tomas, Olafson, and the others priority for sending and receiving messages.

Tomas should be able to call Lissa.

He wrote a message to her. *I'm safe. We're regaining control from rebels. Stay safe.* He tapped *send*, then his upper teeth worried at his lower lip.

Had protecting her and the boys from Forrester exposed her to Echevarria?

His phone rang. His hands jostled it, like an athlete making a nervous catch. It showed the caller's name as Capt. A. Krishnalingam.

Who? Not one of the officers he and Olafson had recruited—

His next-door neighbor.

Tomas opened the call.

Krishnalingam's face appeared against a dark tableau, lit by bioluminescent cypresses and the glow of a phone screen. The tips of his mustache quivered. "Neumann, you are safe?"

"I am. Where are you?"

"In front of your house. It is dark inside and the front door was forced open." The image panned around to show ten centimeters of gap between the frame and the splintered alloy of the door and lock. Evidence of a small explosive charge. "Pardon me, I went in and called out for your wife and children. I looked in every room, upstairs and downstairs. No one is here."

Panic crawled up Tomas' throat. "Did you see anything? Hear anything?"

Krishnalingam winced. "About 2500, my wife and I heard a small explosion. To force the door, it must have been. We hurried to the windows. Two trucks, probably twenty soldiers with their rifles. They carried your wife and children from your house to the trucks and drove off."

Tomas shut his eyes and tried to breath.

"We could do nothing. We noticed too late, and it was only me, without even a pistol. The communication lines were dead, I could not call you, the MPs, the civilian police—then the rebels named you as a person to be arrested—"

"Did you see where they went?"

"Down the street," Krishnalingam said. "Toward the main gate."

Tomas' chest heaved. "They could be anywhere in the capital cities by now." He slumped his head against his free hand. He stared through Krishnalingam's image. *I did the right thing. I protected her and the boys as best I could....*

"I swear, if I could have done more, if I could tell you more now, I would." Krishnalingam's face was tight.

Echevarria had taken Lissa and the boys to further his power grab. They could be anywhere in the capital cities. An intuition clutched his heart. Unless he'd commandeered an ornithopter, to spirit them away to some hidden base—

No. He would keep them near him. He would not trust a subordinate to decide their fate. Echevarria would keep that power for himself.

Tomas noticed Krishnalingam's worried face. "You did all you could. Call the MPs. Call me if you see Lissa and the boys, or those soldiers. Stay safe."

Krishnalingam still grimaced. "What will you do?"

The ConPol agents and bluecoats stirred behind him, seemingly a million kilometers away. Tomas glanced up. He fixed Sutherland's portrait with a firm stare. Determination filled his chest.

"Find my wife and sons."

17

Countercoup

Tomas clutched the steering wheel of the sedan. Sweat from his palms slicked the wheel grips. He rarely drove, and the controls of the sedan, loaned him by ConPol agents at MacAdams' order, felt uncomfortable. Headlights off, he drove slowly and peered down the avenue. His head swiveled to take in the side streets. Bioluminescent cypresses lit the facades of low rise office buildings and the living pavement of empty streets. Oblivious traffic lights cycled. Tomas slowed for the reds, swiveled his head even more, then drove through.

Another red, a few blocks north of Challenger Boulevard. He slowed, looked both ways—

Motion startled him. He braked. The seat belt grabbed his chest and shoulder.

Five bluecoats walked in the street toward him. The bioluminescent cypresses left their faces in shadow. "That sedan looks ConPol," one of them muttered. Another swung a flashlight beam into Tomas' face.

The team leader yelled, "Who the hell are you?"

Tomas lifted his hands from the wheel. "Captain Tomas Neumann, Ground Force. I'm on your side! I used to be posted to the battalion blocking the bridge. I know those men. I'm going to talk them into turning against Echevarria!"

The bluecoats glanced and muttered among themselves. "Noymun?" the one who'd noticed the ConPol sedan said to his peers. "That's one of the names from the rebel communiqué."

"Because he saved President Forrester's life before the election," said the team leader. "Sarge told me all about it. Captain, you work for the president now, don't you?"

"I do."

"What's happening at the XM?" the team leader asked. His voice turned fearful. "Why hasn't the president broadcast a call to action?"

Tomas drew in an ominous breath. "President Forrester is dead."

Shoulders slumped. Faces fell. "What happened?" the team leader asked.

"Echevarria had an agent on the president's inner staff. I realized that man was a traitor, but a second too late to stop him." He rested his forehead against the palm of his hand. "I'm going to regret that second for the rest of my life."

Whispers circulated among the bluecoats. *The president. Dead. Traitor.*

The team leader stepped back and saluted. He dropped his hand in a measured movement. "We're on our way to join the freedom fighters at the roadblock. Please come with us, sir."

Tomas parked the sedan at the curb and climbed out. The team leader fell into position next to him and they walked toward Challenger Boulevard. The other bluecoats fell in behind.

They rounded the corner and came upon a crowd. Hundreds of people, about half of them bluecoats, the rest youthful men and women in civilian garb. A few poor people, in dull mol fab jackets, like a fellow with wide ears who looked vaguely familiar. Most of the civilians looked well-off. As bright as their clothes' colors seemed in the pale light of bioluminescent cypresses, they must look garish under sunlight. Easy targets.

Tomas glanced at the sky paling in the east, where Epsilon Eridani would soon rise, a few minutes before midnight. His fingers twitched. He tried to calm himself. Soldiers probably wouldn't shoot at civilians.

...Probably.

Tomas worked through the crowd. At the front, seven cars stood end-to-end across the street. On the ends of the line, tires rested on pavement and undercarriages scraped the curb. In the middle, an off-road vehicle sporting the Ecological Engineering Department's logo straddled the grassy median strip.

Two bluecoats with thick stripes around their cross barby arm-bands huddled near the rear of the off-road vehicle. Tomas strode to them. "Where do we stand?"

One of the bluecoats, a senior task force leader if Tomas correctly read his stripes, turned an arched eyebrow to Tomas. "Who the hell are you?"

"It's fine, sir," said the other. His small and narrow gray eyes looked enlivened. The old sergeant lifted his cap and ran his head over his scruffed blond hair. "Capt. Neumann's on our side."

The senior task force leader blinked at the name, then extended his hand. "Captain, truly sorry, I always pictured you as taller. Of course I'll fill you in. An element of GF First Brigade blocks the near end of Capital Cities Bridge. We came to deny them access down Challenger Boulevard toward the Capitol or the XM." The senior leader angled his head. "You came from there?"

"Yes."

The senior leader looked worried. "There's a rumor—I'm sure just a rumor—but you work for the president, you would know. There's a rumor...." Fear rimmed his eyes.

Tomas touched the senior leader's shoulder. He drilled his gaze into the senior leader's eyes to fight off the urge to blink. "President Forrester is dead. Echevarria had an agent in the president's inner circle. I couldn't stop him in time." The lie got easier with each telling. So much for seeing the universe as it was.

You can Observe your self after Echevarria is neutralized.

After Lissa and the boys are safe.

Around them, bluecoats shrank back as if the news scalded them. "What do we do now?" one murmured.

Tomas blinked heavily. "You resist." He stood taller. "For his sake."

"Remember our motto," the senior leader said. "Honor restored." The bluecoats around them lifted their chests and set their faces.

"You've done well to block the rebels," Tomas told the senior leader. "But we cannot remain here and wait for them to act." Every second gave Echevarria more time to harm Lissa and the boys. "We have to seize the initiative."

Tomas stepped away from the bluecoats. He held his breath as he stepped behind the partial cover of the off-road vehicle and looked over the hood of a small sedan at the rebel formation.

Less than a block away, two Badgers, the GF's primary infantry fighting vehicle, faced them. Both their main ordnance and their thirteen millimeter machine guns aimed straight toward the barricade of cars.

A thirteen's round would pierce a car's thin alloy body. The civilians wouldn't know that, nor the younger bluecoats.

Tomas swallowed thickly. His head swam but he forced himself to take a closer look.

The Badgers' cee-skin presented an urban camouflage pattern and revealed a unit designation. A squad from Unzai's company, part of Second Battalion, Tomas' former unit. Echevarria had kept Sokolov's orders the same.

Good. Tomas might have met some of these men during his duties on the battalion staff. If nothing else, this squad's old noncoms might know his name.

Both Badgers had their hatches up. The heads and shoulders of both Badgers' commanders showed in silhouette. One turned binoculars toward Tomas.

Tomas ignored the Badger commander. A few meters in front of the Badgers, a dozen infantrymen stood in a line stretching the width of the boulevard. Urban camouflage showed tense shoulders and heads swiveling to glance at their comrades. Rifles slung over shoulders, pointed at the sky.

Behind the Badgers, two Graywolf tanks also aimed their ordnance at the barricade. Even with that greater distance, the longer, wider main guns still looked more ominous than the Badgers'. At least the Graywolfs also sported open hatches, their commanders visible.

Further back, more Graywolfs and Badgers faced the other direction, toward the bridge. Dismounted infantry, their rifles impossible to see from this distance at night. The bridge's main lanes gleamed ghostly white with new mycocrete for a stretch, but the white cut off abruptly, replaced with a mass of blue mixed with dots of brighter color.

Civilians, apparently having crossed the bridge from downtown McAuliffe in dense formation, faced the soldiers.

Tomas sent Olafson and the others a message. One armored grenadier platoon, one armor platoon. Echevarria followed the plan Olafson devised for setting up the visible aspects of the roadblocks. Perhaps enough to intimidate civilians. To fend off a hypothetical relief force driving from GFB West McAuliffe, though, the hidden aspects of the roadblock mattered more.

The top decks of parking garages and the roofs of buildings along Challenger Boulevard toward the lake looked empty. Deceiving looks. RPG teams, two-man portable thirteens, anti-armor and anti-personnel missiles, the personnel in cee-skin set to full transparency—Sokolov stuck to the original plan and concealed some of his assets.

Tomas composed himself as he stepped back behind the off-road vehicle. To the senior bluecoats, he said, "We will win. Those soldiers don't want to fight."

"They're armed," a nearby bluecoat said.

"It's a bluff. They don't want to defy Maj. Gen. Echevarria, but they don't want to fire on civilians. When the time comes, we will cross our barricade—" He slapped the off-road vehicle's alloy. "—and ask those soldiers to join us."

"Is that wise?" the militia man said.

"You mean, will they fire on us? Not if we all march together." Tomas shook his wristwatch past his jacket cuff. 2814. Less than two minutes before midnight. Epsilon Eridani had just risen, out of sight behind the mycocrete towers to the east. "Vice-President O'Brien will broadcast a message at 0001. When he's done, we will move out. If you have a pistol, conceal it. If you have a rifle, leave it here. We will give the soldiers every reason to believe we're unarmed."

Down the block, the soldiers' demeanors remained uneasy, uncertain. Uncertain men were unpredictable. Beyond, in downtown McAuliffe, visible through the bridge's arches and suspension cables, the Freedom Tower's thirty-story high video displays, one pointing in each cardinal direction, remained dark.

Dark humor roiled in his chest. *You survived the raw terrain of New Liberty and Arden, but now you could die in the middle of the biggest city this side of Earth—*

No. He would will himself through, no matter what. For Lissa and the boys.

Will yourself to survive a battle? Don't feel bad for lying to others. You're also lying to yourself.

The time ticked to 0001. In people's pockets, phones blared, chimed, beeped. People wearing earbuds and wraparound smartglasses cupped their hands over their ears. Tomas peeked around the back of the off-road vehicle. Distant sounds chirped from the pockets of the soldiers. One pulled his phone out and held it close to his belly, then bent his neck to watch the display. Carrying personal communication devices on a mission. Sloppy work by Sokolov or Unzai.

Sloppy men would be uncertain.

Two klicks away, on the visible face of Founders Tower, Vice-President O'Brien appeared, larger than life, with the familiar backdrop of the Sutherland Office behind him. The lake's surface chopped up the reflected glow of his image. His voice boomed from every phone and earbud.

"Fellow citizens of the Confederated Worlds, this is Vice-President Fitzhugh O'Brien. The Confederated Worlds are under attack. Not from a foreign power, but from a tiny handful of Ground Force and Space Force officers who wish to turn our strong defense into an instrument of aggression. This tiny handful of officers has given illegal orders to their men. They have disrupted traffic at a few points into and out of Confederal City. They have killed President Forrester." O'Brien's craggy face hardened. "But despite the blows they landed against us, we remain unbowed. Fellow citizens, we know you too remain unbowed by militarism and armed rebellion. We know tens of thousands of you have turned against these rebel officers, and hundreds more take to the streets every minute."

O'Brien looked conciliatory. "I speak now to the soldiers manning the roadblocks around Confederal City. I know you are good citizens. I know your sole mistake lay in trusting your officers to give legal orders. I offer you this chance to lay down your arms and join the masses of citizens who stand with the Confederated Worlds against militarism and armed rebellion. Lay down your arms, good citizen soldiers, and your careers and your sacred honor shall remain intact."

Lowering eyebrows and a sterner voice transformed O'Brien into a patriarch of judgment. "But if you cleave to this rebellion, you shall be punished. Not only by the courts of military justice, but more importantly, by your own shame and guilt, for violating the oath of enlistment you took in full view of the officers and enlisted personnel in this room, any god or gods you may worship, and your own conscience."

Ignorant of Tomas' plan, how much had O'Brien been surprised, when woken and told Forrester was dead and Echevarria attempted a coup? His demeanor showed he'd adapted quickly to the situation.

O'Brien lifted his chin. His eyes glinted. "All citizens, the time has come to demand Maj. Gen. Echevarria and his cronies surrender. Your actions will ensure government of the people, by the people, and for the people shall not perish from the human settled galaxy. Good night, and may any god or gods you worship bless you and bless the Confederated Worlds."

His image on Founders Tower winked out.

Tomas turned to the bluecoats. The senior leader's cheeks tightened in a weak smile. The old sergeant cast a hooded gaze through the off-road vehicle—through the soldiers beyond it—as if he could pierce Echevarria with his eyes.

"You heard our lawful president," Tomas told them. "Follow me." He turned sideways and slipped through the gap between the off-road vehicle and the small sedan. On the other side, he squared his shoulders and started down the westbound lanes toward the nearest Badger.

The Badger's commander stood taller in the hatch. The lined infantrymen looked among themselves. One of them, by five centimeters the shortest, and narrow across the shoulders, unslung his rifle from his shoulder and held it across his body. He stared at Tomas.

Four meters to the rifleman's left, his nearest comrade turned to him. Two shuffling steps and the man said something too low to catch.

The rifleman kept his stare on Tomas.

Tomas adjusted his path to come face-to-face with the short, skinny rifleman.

Another soldier unslung his rifle, but held it loosely against his shoulder. The others kept their rifles slung, muzzles pointing up. Behind their line sounded the hydraulic whine of the Badger's turret. The thirteen traversed. Its barrel looked like a floating black dot.

Tomas gulped his next breath. Conversations from a bunkhouse on New Liberty came out of his memory. *How would you want to go?* someone asked.

Someone else replied, *You want a headshot from a thirteen. Splatter your brain before it has time to feel pain or think you're going to die.*

He licked his lips and kept walking.

Behind him, shoes scraped against the living pavement. Tomas kept his gaze locked on the short, skinny rifleman. More footsteps came from behind him, too many to count. Bluecoats, civilians, it didn't matter who followed him.

The muzzle of the thirteen lifted a fraction. Tactically sound. *Fire on the massed targets while leaving the advance picket for the dismounts to clean up—*

Tomas kept walking.

The rifleman squinted at the bars on Tomas' collar. The rifleman's jaws mashed his rolled-in lips. The rifle shook in his hands. "Stop right there, sir."

Tomas took another step. "Did Capt. Unzai know the Echevarria's plan?"

The rifleman's eyes boggled. "How, how do you know—?"

Tomas came closer. "I served on battalion staff. I know Lt. Col. Sokolov and Capt. Unzai are honorable soldiers. I see you're an honorable soldier too."

The rifleman swung the muzzle towards Tomas. Reflected bioluminescence jittered on the bayonet blade. "Stop or I'll shoot!"

Tomas' pulse hammered his chest. Another step. His chest came within a meter of the bayonet. "No. You're too good a soldier."

The whites of the rifleman's eyes gleamed like sun-bleached bone. The rifle shook in his hands—

One more step. Tomas lifted his left hand and pushed the rifle barrel aside. The rifleman did not resist.

Tomas gazed directly into his face. "Welcome back to the side of honor, soldier."

The rifleman buried his face on Tomas' shoulder. Tomas took the rifle from his grip.

"Sir, I'm sorry." Sobs choked the rifleman's words. "I'm sorry, I didn't know, I thought the order was in the right, I didn't know."

"I fault no man for ignorance," Tomas said. "But now you know the truth." With his free hand he gripped the rifleman's shoulder and guided him a step back. Tomas gave him a look of confident command. "Now we find your superior officers."

The rifleman nodded. His eyes blinked like a child's. "Yes sir."

Words and sounds around them came to Tomas' attention. Bluecoats and civilians surrounded each soldier. Kind words, shaken hands. A Daughter of Astarte craned her neck and kissed a soldier's cheek.

A dozen meters down the boulevard, the Badger raised the muzzles of its main gun and its thirteen toward the sky.

"Everyone, follow me!" Tomas called. Without waiting, he pushed ahead.

The Badger's fusion reactor, idling at a low hum, cut out. The vehicle sat like a thirty-ton boulder. Its commander, a lieutenant, climbed out of the top hatch, descended the side ladder. He jumped the last meter and held out his hand. "You're Captain Neumann, aren't you?"

"That's right. Are you arresting me?" Tomas grinned.

The lieutenant showed no sign of getting the joke. "Echevarria ordered us here under false pretenses. Screw him. I won't let him use me to make himself king."

In the absence of a protest, by civilians brave enough to march unarmed against riflemen and IFVs, the lieutenant probably would have done exactly that. Tomas kept his observation to himself. "Where's Capt. Unzai and company headquarters?"

"Nearby."

Tomas lowered his voice. "With the hidden platoon? On a roof or high in a parking garage? Don't look."

The lieutenant yanked his head toward the roof of a parking garage on the opposite side of the street. Tomas did the same. His gaze roved the parapet, looking for blurs in the lightening sky. Wait, there?

From this distance, it didn't matter. Tomas raised his hand and waved, then beckoned. *Come down and join us.* Around him, civilians crowded around the soldiers. Chat and laughter echoed off the facades. From the mouth of the bridge, near the western side of the roadblock, came the tramp of a thousand arrhythmic footsteps.

Still nothing to see on the parking garage roof. Easy to grasp the deployment. Every soldier up there remained nearly invisible inside cee-skin, and more cee-skin set to transparent shrouded their weapons.

Unease knotted Tomas' gut. The original roadblock plan called for two-man portable thirteens and anti-tank missiles to hide in support of the visible IFVs and dismounted infantry. In the crowded street, the thirteens could kill a hundred people in a minute. Even an anti-tank missile fired over the crowd's heads could start a panic. A single soldier or team could set off a bloodbath—

And only Capt. Unzai would have any inkling where Echevarria might be.

Tomas pushed down his unease. He beckoned again. He mugged an expression mixing annoyance and amusement, the same look he sometimes gave Stefan.

On the parking garage roof, two figures in mottled gray suddenly appeared. They crouched near one another, and an elongated orange shape came into view between them. A crew-portable thirteen. One dragged and the other pushed the thirteen's barrel away from the street below. The two men stood up to full height.

They needed backup. Tomas sprinted toward the parking garage's pedestrian entrance. He pounded up the mycocrete stairs. One flight below the roof, shouting voices echoed down.

He hesitated. Draw the standard issue pistol still holstered above his left ankle?

No. A confident air was the only weapon he would wield.

A few more steps and he reached the roof. Near the parapet, three machine gun and two missile teams, and their weapons, showed wrapped in mottled gray and bright orange. Some of the visible soldiers argued at vague shimmers in the air. One of the shimmers resolved into a thirteen gunner in urban camouflage. His assistant flickered into visibility a moment later, their weapon a moment after that.

A dozen meters from the parapet a broad, armor-plated jeep, cee-skinned to urban camouflage, squatted on run-flat tires. Shimmers of motion blurred the air in front of it. Exposed by a lifted helmet visor, a face floated amid the shimmers. From the profile, Tomas recognized Capt. Unzai. The shimmering figures, faceplates down, were likely the lieutenants and senior NCOs of his company staff.

A rifleman in mottled gray, standing near one of the visible missile teams, noticed Tomas. He turned his rifle on Tomas. "Sir, halt! Who are you?"

Tomas' knees wobbled. "Capt. Neumann. I need to talk to Capt. Unzai."

The rifleman frowned. "But whose side are you on?"

"They—" He extended his hand down and to the side, pointing through the parking garage to the civilian crowd on the street below. "—let me through."

The rifleman gestured with his bayonet. "Go on. Talk sense into him."

Tomas went past the rifleman. Capt. Unzai spoke sternly to the soldiers in urban camouflage. "Men, of course the vice president would say he represents the rightful government. He's on the brigadier's list—"

"So am I," Tomas said loudly.

Capt. Unzai snapped his head around. From the shimmers around him came blurs of black motion, resolving into officer's sidearms aimed at Tomas' chest. Red laser dots circled over his heart.

Tomas stopped. He held his hands down and away from his body. His chest tightened and his breath fought to enter his lungs.

"Who the hell..." Unzai said. "Neumann?"

"Unzai, the rest of you, you heard the vice president's offer. Go back to GFB West McAuliffe and your careers will survive this—"

Unzai peered at Tomas. "The vice president is a traitor. He's part of Forrester's conspiracy—"

"What conspiracy?"

"The brigadier showed all of us. Plan 827."

Tomas hesitated before frowning. "Plan what? Talk to me in Confed."

"Plan 827 was a PR plot creating deep cover agents to infiltrate the government and military after the first war. Echevarria showed us a copy."

Tomas injected disbelief into his voice. "Echevarria found a secret Papa document? Just lying on the sidewalk?"

The pistols held by the nearly invisible staff officers drooped a little.

"We had that same question for him," Unzai said. "He got the document from a reliable source."

Tomas arched his eyebrow. "One of our spies found a secret Papa document and handed it over to Echevarria? When the white mountain is full of higher ranked and more politically skillful officers? Think about it."

Unzai said, "I'm only telling you what he said."

"What's the name of this reliable source?" Echevarria would not have named Tomas or anyone else he would have to arrest to pull off his coup within a coup.

"He, he didn't say."

Tomas rotated his wrists to flash his palms. "Sounds like

Echevarria got played by someone. I know he loves the Confederated Worlds. Maybe he loves them too much. And maybe some Papa agent fed him false information and goaded him into—" He twirled his hand in the air to take in the rooftop and the roadblock below. "—this madness."

The staff officers holding the pistols on Tomas lowered the muzzles further. One pointed his pistol straight down to the parking deck.

Unzai looked pensive for a moment, but then his face hardened. "Or Plan 827 is true, and you're part of it, and you're trying to preserve a Papa conspiracy."

The staff officer holding his pistol straight down flickered into a mottled gray shape. He shook his head.

The other staff officer, though, raised the muzzle toward Tomas' thigh. Tomas' breath caught. A hospital could rebuild a penis and testicles, if a wounded man reached one in time, but a bullet through a femoral artery would bleed him out in a minute.

Tomas willed himself to stand taller. "You think I'm in league with the Progressive Republic? After all the times I talked about Arden and Papa's treaty violations to try winning the vote. After I told you I got a colonel court-martialed for trying to let Papa win. Do I sound like a Papa sympathizer?"

Unzai winced at the logic. "But you did that on Arden. More than five years ago."

"You were with me at that rally in Firstlanding Square. I had less of an opinion about Forrester than you did."

"True, but—"

"I happened to see the assassin and act in time. That's the only reason Forrester pulled strings to transfer me to his office. I earned his trust. And O'Brien? You think O'Brien received the vice presidency because he's part of some Papa conspiracy, and no one in this city would find out?"

The transparent staff officer flickered to urban camouflage. He lowered his pistol, then lifted his faceplate. Over his shoulder, he said to Unzai, "The captain is right, sir. Someone duped Echevarria."

"That's the only explanation that makes sense," Tomas said.

Unzai's floating face turned down to the parking deck. "Echevarria is a good officer. A loyal officer."

"I agree," Tomas said. A stray thought ran by his awareness, how many lies had he told that night? He blinked his gritty eyes. "I need to find him and get him to surrender."

A flash of mottled gray. Unzai revealed himself. He pulled off his helmet and the infantrymen around him cheered. "A great idea. He'll listen to you."

"Where is he?"

Unzai pointed across a jumble of midrise roofs to the northeast. "With brigade headquarters. Voyager Park."

About four kilometers north and east. "I have to go to him. Right now."

Unzai looked solemn. "I'll go with you."

"No!" Tomas softened his voice. "I don't have any responsibilities. We need you here to keep your men in order."

From the noise at street level resolved a song sung by many voices. *Challenger, Gem of the Spaceways.* "My men are under control," Unzai said. "I can leave my staff in charge here. Echevarria knows me—"

"He knows me, too," Tomas said. "Better just one of us goes. He'll be less embarrassed about being tricked by the Papa agents, and more willing to surrender."

Unzai tapped his fingers on his pointed chin. "You make sense, Neumann. Go to him."

Tomas gave Unzai a quick handshake, then hurried away. All the men and equipment on the parking garage roof were plainly visible in urban camouflage and blaze orange.

He pounded down the stairwell. His footsteps echoed off mycocrete. The singing voices, seemingly hundreds more, came to him indistinctly, distorted by mycocrete walls. They mangled the words in one of the later verses.

At the bottom of the stairwell, the pedestrian door slid open. The singing sounded even louder. Tomas hurried onto the sidewalk. People looked up. "Hey, you're the one who led the way!" a man shouted.

"Just doing my job." Tomas started eastward. People clumped around him. "Pardon me, need to get through."

The man cupped his hands around his mouth. "It's him!" he shouted across the crowd toward a tall man standing on the back deck of a Graywolf.

Confidence flowed from the tall man's posture. "Tomas!" shouted a long familiar voice. Lucien LaSalle.

Tomas grimaced. He briefly raised his hand, then turned away and pressed through the crowd.

"You're the man of the hour!" shouted Lucien. "Come here so everyone can congratulate you!"

Smiling faces thickened the crowd between Tomas and the jeep. He stopped and turned back to Lucien. "I can't! I have more work to do!"

Lucien paused a moment, then nodded. "Go get the traitor! Everyone, make room for Capt. New-maw!"

The crowd parted. He passed a Graywolf crew flirting with three Daughters, and a soldier napping in a Badger's open rear compartment. The street beyond the Badger held empty water bottles, snack wrappers, and a solitary magazine ejected from a soldier's rifle.

Tomas hurried toward the barricade of parked cars. He slowed and slipped sideways through a gap. Two or three scattered individuals walked on the sidewalks toward the roadblock. He ran, now, down the middle of the empty street. At his distance, the crowd's excited sounds still echoed, but quieter than his soles clacking against the living pavement. Quieter than his pounding heart.

Tomas rounded the corner onto Second Avenue. Cypresses dimmed their bioluminescence. The dim light of rising Epsilon Eridani refracted through the sky. The ConPol sedan remained at the curb. It turned itself on at the sound of his voice.

Confederal City seemed too quiet, like a site prepped for ambush and surrounded on three sides by waiting hostiles. Headlights off, he sped down dim, empty streets. In walk-up apartments, lights burned behind drawn curtains. Tomas craned his neck, looking for the glow of headlights as he approached intersections. None. He went through every red light at the same high speed.

Lissa, I'll never lie to you again.

A few blocks south of Voyager Park, he turned onto a side street. He would have posted guards at all the park entrances, and expected Echevarria to do the same. With luck, no one saw him make the turn. If he left the sedan and approached the park up a shadowed side street, he had a chance to infiltrate Echevarria's position and find Lissa and the boys before Echevarria could use them in some gambit.

Tomas checked the sedan's nav display. Three blocks east of Voyager Park. Far enough? It would have to be. Tomas turned left. Northbound on Eleventh Avenue, cross Heinlein's World Boulevard. Thin red of a traffic light bathed the intersection.

From the far side of the intersection, flashlights snapped into his face. Parked jeeps narrowed the street. Soldiers in urban camouflage filled the gap between the jeeps. The red light glimmered in the soldiers' bayonets.

Tomas slammed the brakes. He squinted. Soldiers on three sides held rifles in twitchy hands. Near the driver's door, a sergeant led a team closer.

Close enough to read his nameplate?

Face hot, he ducked his chest far enough to hide his nameplate behind the jeep's dashboard. With his right hand, he pinched the release button on the nameplate backing hardware through his jacket's thick fabric. Come on, open up—there—

His nameplate came loose. Tomas stuffed it into his pants pocket.

"Sir, hands where I can see them!" the sergeant yelled. "Who are you? What are you doing here?"

"I'm Capt. Walton. My duty post is the white mountain." A common name, and even personnel working at the Defense Ministry knew only a fraction of their coworkers. "I've got to get to Echevarria."

The sergeant peered through eyes older than his face. "Why?"

The nameplate backing hardware poked at his chest through his shirt. If the sergeant or one of his soldiers noticed the missing nameplate, and wondered....

"I've learned from our opponents news he needs to know," Tomas said. "I couldn't get through by voice, video, or text—"

"No one can," a soldier murmured.

"Shut it," the sergeant said over his shoulder. He turned back to Tomas and leaned closer. "What news, sir?"

"I can only tell him." Tomas injected a haunted tone into his voice.

The traffic light lit the sergeant's face sickly green. "We know O'Brien made a broadcast...."

Tomas checked to left and right, then lowered his voice. "Don't tell anyone this. The civilian protesters at Capital Cities Bridge got bold after O'Brien's broadcast. They marched on the roadblock from both sides. The dismounts and vehicle crews went over to O'Brien's side. I've got to tell Echevarria."

The soldiers shared glances. The sergeant gritted his teeth, then turned to Tomas. "Come on through, captain." The sergeant waved at the soldiers blocking the gap between the parked jeeps. They stepped aside. Open pavement beyond beckoned.

Tomas reached for the controls. "Where is he?"

"Last I heard, he set up shop near the east end of the park, on the service road between the duck pond and the ultimate flying disc fields."

"Thank you, sergeant. Keep your head down."

The sergeant gritted his teeth again. Tomas droved slowly past the men and between the parked jeeps. The backing hardware slid all the way down the inside of his jacket.

Tomas let out a breath and drove on.

A few blocks brought him to Navi Ambarsar Boulevard. A glance down the boulevard showed dozens of pole-mounted banners in a skipping pattern down both sides of the street. The banners glowed brightly, and all showed the same video loop. Grieving Sikhs and images of their fallen homeworld.

He turned left, toward Voyager Park. He left the ConPol sedan at the gate arm of a parking garage entrance. He went toward the park on foot. Blue tinted the eastern sky and followed Tomas' footsteps.

Guards at the park entrances, presumably. How to get in? Climb the fence between entrances? Or bluff his way past the guards just like the roadblock?

Bluff would work—unless the guards had seen photos of the men on Echevarria's hit list.

Tomas passed a stark wall of mycocrete. Movement ahead. From around a corner, two soldiers in urban camouflage, rifles slung over their shoulders, walked toward him. "Set it to transparent, will ya?" one of the soldiers told the other.

A featureless wall. No place to hide. Mouth suddenly dry, Tomas stopped in the middle of the sidewalk, stance wide.

"Transparent?" the other soldier said. "They'll think we're—"

The soldiers froze. The last one to speak narrowed his eyes at Tomas. He moved his left hand toward his rifle's barrel. "What do you want?"

Tomas stared back. Disrespecting an officer reeked of collapsing discipline. "I want you to follow the orders of our new commander-in-chief."

The first soldier to speak ducked his head. His cee-skin flickered, and his body vanished. A quick motion lowered his helmet visor to render his face nearly invisible. He trod away as a faint blur of moving limbs and refractions of streetlights.

The second soldier stared after his comrade. "Dammit, now you're making me do it too." The second soldier's body vanished from sight and he ran to catch up.

Tomas let out a breath. His intuition had correctly grasped the situation. Deserters.

Rumors must be spreading inside Echevarria's camp. If Echevarria's men decided his position was doomed, they would act accordingly, and doom it.

How would Echevarria respond?

Tomas hurried down the street. Across from the park, he looked both ways for guarded entrances. He saw only an iron fence and a dense stand of elms across the street.

He ran across the deserted street, climbed the iron fence. Even in the shadow of the elms, his wedding ring caught the dawning light. Difficult to move stealthily in the growing light. Yet he couldn't wait. Darkness would not return for almost four hours. By then, surrounded by O'Brien's forces and bold civilians, Echevarria would act.

Tomas pulled out his phone, called up a map of Voyager Park. He found his spot, the duck pond, the flying disc fields—Echevarria would be on that service road, *there*.

He picked a path and started out. He stayed under the elms until he came close to a pedestrian path. On the other side of the path, a flower garden ringed by a hedge would give him cover. If he could get across unseen.

He looked left for several seconds, watching for urban camouflage or glimmers of movement. Then right. Clear. Hopefully.

Tomas sprinted from the elms. One footstep crunched on the ground basalt of the path. He jumped the nearest hedge and landed on soft ground behind it.

A moment to catch his breath, then he started forward. *Plenty of time—*

His phone vibrated inside his jacket.

He pulled it out. A conference request. The callers, Olafson and—Echevarria?

Audio only. He dimmed the screen and turned up the microphone gain. "Neumann here," he murmured.

"I've got Echevarria on the line," Olafson said. His voice sounded dour. "He wants to surrender."

"What are his conditions?" Tomas asked. He walked at a crouch through the garden. A dozen meters ahead, ducks splashed. A faint hum came from the distance, where Badgers and armored jeeps idled without headlights. The vehicles showed gray mottled urban camouflage in the waxing light.

"Think you I have conditions?" Echevarria spoke quietly, with an echo of some enclosed space. He sounded in better spirits than a man expecting a court-martial should. "You're damn-all right. O'Brien doesn't know you two are behind this, nay?"

"Behind what?" Tomas said. "The coup was your idea. I'm a loyal officer whom you proscribed. Put on your hit list."

"Think you your lie will survive? Cut you me a fair deal, and perhaps it can."

"A fair deal for treason?" Olafson said.

"A fair deal for the captain's family."

Tomas reached the far side of the garden. He peered through the hedge. A family of ducks crossed the pond, seemingly skimming it. On the service road beyond, soldiers huddled together along the line of military vehicles.

"Loki's *skith*," Olafson said.

"You have my family?" Tomas said. "You're lying."

"Thought you you outplayed me, nay? Turn you on your video, and you'll see." Echevarria chuckled.

Tomas crouched deeper behind the hedge and tapped at his phone. Keep the camera off, turn video signal from Echevarria on—

The video showed the back seat of a jeep, with the camera between the front seats. Lissa lay on her side, asleep. Her arms clutched sleeping Artur. Stefan asleep too, cuddled against the backs of her knees, his head resting on her hip.

"Are they dead?"

The video swung around to show Echevarria's grizzled head of hair. His eyes looked puffy, with an air of desperate vigor. "Dead? Nay. They're no good to me dead. One of the medics sedated them. I don't want to hear babies cry. "

"Prove it," Tomas said. He checked the jeeps in the line. One figure in the driver's seat, no one visible in the rear.

The video panned again. A glimpse of the front passenger's seat, empty, and green beyond it. A blur of Lissa's and Artur's faces. The whispers of their breaths. Another pan. Stefan's face loomed into view. He exhaled and fogged the camera.

A squeak of a body against a seat, a rough pan, a steel-blue blur outside the jeep, and the camera showed Echevarria again. "The story will say, mental illness deluded me into thinking Forrester was a spy. You'll give me a medical discharge and a couple of years all-expenses-paid 'medical treatment' on a private island in the tropics. Then I'll retire at full pension."

A grin flashed across Echevarria's wide face. His grizzled eyebrows danced. "You have five minutes to agree, or Neumann's family dies." The video cut out.

"Neumann?" said Olafson's voice. "Are you there? Where are

you, anyway? Neu—"

Tomas hung up. He shoved his phone back into his pocket. His gaze remained on the line of military vehicles across the pond. There, third jeep from the back of the line. A solitary figure behind the controls. The only one that fit.

Unless Echevarria had already fled.

No, not if men remained on guard, as if they still followed him. Two guards at the back of the line. Two more further up the line.

Tomas had a straight line across the duck pond to Echevarria.

His phone vibrated. Tomas ignored it and drew his pistol. He found a gap between hedges and slipped through. He held the pistol just above the surface of the pond, gulped a breath, and slid in.

Arms stretched forward, not moving. Shod feet kicking below the surface. Eyes open to the murky water. A nugget of ache in his lungs, growing with panicked thoughts. If the guards noticed him crossing. If he blundered into the duck family and its squawks caught the guards' attentions. His lungs burned. A slow way to swim. Every second Epsilon Eridani rose higher, cast more light, made him more visible. One stray glance from a guard and his family would die. His lungs roared. He longed to take a breath—

His outstretched hands touched the mud and weeds of the pond's far bank.

Tomas lifted his head. He inhaled with a quiet gasp. He crouched amid the weeds and looked around.

Five meters to Echevarria's jeep. The glow of a phone lit Echevarria's grizzled face. He peered at something, then flexed his wrist to check his watch.

Adrenaline pushed Tomas out of the water. One foot slipped in the muddy bank but he kept his balance. He sprinted toward the jeep's driver's door. He pulled the handle. Distantly, someone shouted. A frown drawn across grizzled eyebrows transformed into alarm.

Door open. Two shots to the cheek. Blood gushed from Echevarria's nose and ear. Metallic and meaty and soapy stenches of blood and brain. Mad panic in the eyes, eyes already draining away life. He grabbed the front of Echevarria's shirt and yanked. Blood all over his hand and arm. He twisted his body and pulled Echevarria to the ground.

Somewhere far off, another shout. Dumbfounded guards ahead. A bang. Behind? Climb in. Right leg weak. What?

He pushed up with his left leg. Driver's seat slick with blood. Jabbed finger at *engine start* button. More bangs. Guards ahead fumbled with their rifles. Forward gear. Left foot jammed accelerator pedal. Hard right, turn around. Slewed left-side wheels through grass at top of drainage ditch. Steering wheel bucked in his hand. Arms rigid. Smells of blood and brain *Echevarria still in the jeep?* The seat underneath, his whole body, soaked *How much blood had Echevarria lost?* Passed last two jeeps in line. One guard ran to Echevarria. Other dumbstruck watched Tomas drive.

Empty service road. Right leg aches. Stink of blood and brain. Exit wound? His shaking hand groped front passenger seat. No bone, no brain. Stench in nose. The shakes crawled up right arm, rocked his torso. Stench in nose so deep. Cold gripped every limb. Nausea squeezed his gut.

One of the park's closed gates appeared in front of the jeep. He crashed through, turned left onto the avenue. Puzzled soldiers in the rear view mirrors.

His chest heaved. His leg ached, probably shot. He shivered, soaked with pond water and coming off the adrenaline peak. Stench of blood and brain in nose. So deep what could dispel it?

Tomas glanced in the mirror. Lissa and the boys remained asleep.

Epilogue
After Action

The thump of a car door roused Tomas from a restless sleep. Leather cushions, three men dead by his hand, *where am I?*

He jolted awake. His living room. Nearly vertical rays of Epsilon Eridani through the open blinds. His right leg ached from the bullet wound he'd suffered, how many hours ago? A hospital, home, Lissa took the boys to the base Montessori school. Now around 0900? He pushed himself to a fully seated position. A glance at his watch showed 0854. Fiveday.

Mind still foggy, he looked around the living room. Dark video screen on one wall. Litter of toy spaceships and tanks on the floor. Two portraits, Christ with his sacred heart and St. Benedict, His right-hand man, staring serenely from above the mantel. After the last fifteen hours, the tableau seemed unreal.

The front door squeaked. Sweat bloomed on Tomas' nape and his senses went on alert. He inhaled, steadied himself. Echevarria's followers had all surrendered. No one came to kill him. Lissa had taken the boys to school. She came home.

If an assassin came for revenge, Tomas could fight.

Eyes brooding, Lissa entered the living room. She started when she saw him. "You're awake. How's your leg?"

"I've suffered worse." He drew in a breath. His leg ached. Fog crept over his mind. Her eyes drooped too. They were both tired, but what he had to say couldn't wait. Tomas patted the vat-grown leather cushion. "Sit with me."

Her eyes narrowed. Still, her feet effortlessly navigated the litter of toys. She sat at the end of the couch furthest from him. Her skirt rose a few centimeters up her shins. She kept her knees together and pointed away from him.

"At least you came for me and the boys," she said.

The ache in his heart since their meeting outside the Daughters' temple burst open his shell of civility. "I love you too much. I couldn't have left you—"

"Or you love the boys so much you didn't want to leave them without a mother?" Her mouth scrunched. "I told you a year ago, working for Forrester would put you at risk. I was wrong. You put the boys and me in danger too!"

"I know. I didn't plan well enough."

She sobbed for breath. "You say you have some love for me, but it's not enough. Your whoring and your intrigues…." She shut her eyes and turned her head. A tear squeezed through the corner of her eye and trickled down her cheek.

He spoke gently. "You have your followup appointment at your bishop's office today?"

She inhaled. Her body tightened like a spring. She nodded.

"I can't prevent you from going. But before you go, I want to tell you as much as I can about what I did, and why."

"I don't want to hear anything about you and your whores."

Tomas took her hands. "About last night."

She tugged. Her hands remained wrapped in his. "You said everything you needed to a minute ago."

He shook his head. "At the hospital, after they reversed the sedative, you saw the broadcasts and news reports on what happened?"

"Gen. Echevarria attempted a coup." She shook her head. "Loathsome as Forrester was, what he tried was worse."

Actually, a major general—and what would correcting her gain either of them? "Many people share that view. You also learned one of his co-conspirators, an SF officer named Sharma, killed Forrester before I could kill Sharma?"

"You killed the man who shot Forrester? Do you want a medal?" Lissa angled her head his way. Her tongue dabbed her lips.

"No, I don't want a medal. I did what I did, but too late to save the president. Back to what you might have learned last night. Echevarria couldn't control the city's communication links, and those of us loyal to the Confederated Worlds turned against Echevarria and roused the people against him."

"One of the outer world politicians complimented you by name." She squinted. "LaSeur, was it?"

"Something like that." Tomas went on. "Then the subordinates Echevarria tricked into supporting him turned against him, and one of them shot him in Voyager Park. Around this time, amid all the confusion, I found you and the boys and took us all to the hospital." He fixed her with an insistent look. "That's our story."

Her eyebrows crinkled. "Our story?"

"If anyone ever asks you what happened last night, promise me that's what you'll tell them. Whether you seek an annulment or not. Promise me."

She turned her knees toward him. "What really happened?"

"Do you promise me that's what you'll tell anyone who ever asks about last night?" He leaned toward her. "In full view of the officers and enlisted personnel in this room, any god or gods you may worship, and your own conscience?"

Her eyes widened. Her service lay years in the past, but still she recognized the oath sworn before courts of military justice. Lissa's lips parted. "I promise."

He let out a breath. A wave welled up in him. His chest grew buoyant. His mouth stretched in a grin. Lissa's face filled his vision.

"Now I can tell you the truth…."

Afterword

Readers interested in the 'Peters-Stein Technique' presented in the novel may wish to explore the work of Ed Seykota and the Trading Tribe, http://www.tradingtribe.com, as well as Internal Family Systems, http://selfleadership.org. Neither Mr. Seykota nor The Center for Self Leadership endorses the author or the novel.

About the Author

Raymund Eich files patent applications, earned a Ph.D., won a national quiz bowl championship, writes science fiction and fantasy, and affirms Robert Heinlein's dictum that specialization is for insects. In a typical day, he may talk with biochemists, electrical engineers, patent attorneys, epileptologists, and rocket scientists. Hundreds of papers cite his graduate research on the reactions of nitric oxide with heme proteins.

Connect with the author at **www.raymundeich.com** or scan the QR code below.

Sign up for his mailing list to receive exclusive, pre-release content about his upcoming books. Your email address will never be shared and you can unsubscribe at any time. Go to **www.raymundeich.com/mailing-list** or scan the QR code below.

Other Books by the Author

Available wherever books are sold.

Learn more about these titles at our website, **www.cv2books.com**, or scan the QR code below.

Stone Chalmers

Earth barely survived the 21st Century. Biotechnological and nuclear terrorism, civil war, famine, and ethnic cleansing killed billions. Thousands fled on warpdrive ships to colonize planets around distant suns.

In the 22nd century, after the United Nations established control over Earth, it opened wormhole links to the distant colonies, to prevent a repeat of the previous century's chaos on a galactic scale.

Enter operative Stone Chalmers. Spy. Assassin. Instrument maintaining the UN's order on the settled galaxy.

Opposing him are hostile forces on colony worlds… and within the UN itself.

When Stone clashes with those forces, the UN—and every human world—will be transformed forever.

Learn more about the Stone Chalmers series at **www.cv2books.com/stone-chalmers**, or scan the QR code below.

The Progress of Mankind (#1)

To maintain order in the 22nd century, the UN relocates undesirables through artificial wormholes onto colony planets. Everyone benefits... except the planets' original colonists.

Now, the newly rediscovered colony of New Moravia learns the UN's plan and fights back.

The Greater Glory of God (#2)

Thousands fled the chaos of the 21st century on rogue warpdrive ships to settle colony planets. When Earth reunified in the 22nd, its fleets rediscovered the colonies and hunted down the warpdrive ships.

Every warpdrive ship but one.

To All High Emprise Consecrated (#3)

After unifying Earth, the UN has rediscovered the colony of Minerva. Prosperous and technologically advanced, Minerva quickly submits to UN supremacy.

Surprisingly quickly…

In Public Convocation Assembled (#4)

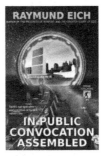

After unifying Earth, the UN controls all human colonies scattered through the galaxy by means of wormholes, warpdrive ships, and ruthless operatives. Operatives working to strengthen the UN.

Or destroy it.

Novels

The Blank Slate

Neuroscience entrepreneur Clay Shieffer must stop a tyrannical president... because he unwittingly gave the tyrant power over the human mind.

New California

After New California's founder committed suicide, two men vied to rule the colony.

Ashwin George, supported by the colony's elite and the Chinese company dominating half the settled galaxy.

Against him, Desmond Park, nanotechnology engineer, armed with the most formidable weapon of all.

A single idea.

Short Novels

The ALECS Quartet

He had a month to learn the planet's mysteries—and Juliette's.

His cover story: return to Elard to dismantle his sect's missionary work to the planet's natives.

His true mission: investigate decades-old mysteries of love and death.

His objective: return to Earth with his discovery.

If he can.

A Mighty Fortress

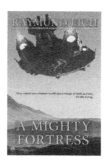

Theodore and his team from the Lutheran Interstellar Terraforming Society would transform a barren, rocky world into a refuge of faith and life.

Or die trying.

Collections

The First Voyages: The Complete Science Fiction Stories 1998-2012

From 21st century asteroid settlements to World War II Transylvania, from an Earth dominated by immortal aliens to Christ's empty tomb, a fresh, distinctive voice in science fiction will take you on journeys to the photosphere of the sun, the coding regions of DNA, and the complexities of the human psyche.

Stage Separations: The Complete Science Fiction Stories 2013-2018

In these pages, you can...

...race against time to solve mysteries hidden in a planet's vast desert—and in a woman's heart ...learn the true story of a president's assassination ...journey 14,000 miles to a high-tech fountain of youth ...win or go "home"—to an Earth you've never seen

and explore six other worlds created by a distinctive voice in twenty-first century science fiction.

Made in United States
Orlando, FL
29 April 2024

46321809R00408